"Fans will be enthralled, and the happy ending, all too rare in first volumes of series, will encourage new readers to seek out both future installments and past publications."
—*Publishers Weekly* (starred review)

"Marillier does her usual masterful job of storytelling here."
—*VOYA*

"A fascinating evocation of life in Pictish England and an emotional roller coaster of a story."
—*Interzone*

"Impossible to put down . . . the best book I have read for several years."
—*Vector*

"Well conceived and nicely crafted."
—*SFX*

"A wonderful sense of place and Marillier deftly evokes the wild landscape and harsh life in sixth century Scotland . . . An exciting and very enjoyable read."
—*Starburst*

BOOKS BY JULIET MARILLIER

The Dark Mirror

JULIET MARILLIER

TOR
fantasy

A TOM DOHERTY ASSOCIATES BOOK
NEW YORK

This is a work of fiction. All the characters and events portrayed in this book are either products of the author's imagination or are used fictitiously.

THE DARK MIRROR

Copyright © 2004 by Juliet Marillier

First published in Sydney, NSW Australia, in 2004 by Pan Macmillan Australia Pty Limited

Excerpt from *The Well of Shades* copyright © 2006 by Juliet Marillier

All rights reserved.

Edited by Claire Eddy

Map by Bronya Marillier

A Tor Book
Published by Tom Doherty Associates, LLC
175 Fifth Avenue
New York, NY 10010

www.tor-forge.com

Tor® is a registered trademark of Tom Doherty Associates, LLC.

ISBN-13: 978-0-7653-4875-3
ISBN-10: 0-7653-4875-6

First U.S. Edition: August 2005
First U.S. Mass Market Edition: March 2007

Printed in the United States of America

0 9 8 7 6 5 4 3 2

TO GOOD TEACHERS,
from whom we learn to think for ourselves

ACKNOWLEDGMENTS

The Katharine Susannah Prichard Foundation provided me
with the opportunity to work intensively on this book during
a period as Writer in Residence at Katharine's historic cottage in Greenmount, Western Australia. The cottage houses a
thriving Writers' Center, and I forged many new friendships
and learned a great deal during my time there.

Three editors have done sterling work on the book so that
we could produce a consistent English language version:
Brianne Tunnicliffe in Sydney, Stefanie Bierwerth in Lon-
don, and Claire Eddy in New York. I thank them all for their
professionalism and wise words.

My two daughters each played a significant part in the development of *The Dark Mirror*. I thank Bronya for a wonderful map that reflects the most important elements in the
life of the Priteni: the cycles of the Shining One and the symbols of ancient lineage. I thank Elly for her invaluable advice
on points of plotting and character development, and for her
heroic effort in reading the whole manuscript twice in draft
form during the final stages of her pregnancy.

I consulted a number of reference books in researching
Pictish culture. More information on the historical context
of the story can be found at the end of this book, and a complete list of references can be found on my Web site at
www.julietmarillier.com.

Kingdom

Lands of
the Caitt

Abertornie

To the
Western Isles

Pitnochie

Five
Sisters

Serpent Lake

Maiden Lake

Raven's Well

Mage Lake

Galany's
Reach

J. Marillier

King Lake

f Fortriu

Banmerren

Caer
Pridne

Northern Britain
550 A.D.

Light
Isles

Western
Isles

Caitt

Fortriu

Circinn

Dalriada

CAST OF CHARACTERS

PITNOCHIE

Broichan	chief druid to King Drust the Bull
Bridei*	his foster son, son of Maelchon King of Gwynedd and Lady Anfreda
Ferat	cook
Mara	housekeeper
Donal	a warrior; Bridei's tutor in sports and combat
Erip	an ancient scholar
Wid	an ancient scholar
Fidich	farmer
Uven	
Cinioch	
Elpin	} men-at-arms
Enfret	
Urguist	
Brenna	Cinioch's cousin
Tuala	a child of the forest
Pearl	a small pony
Blaze	a bigger pony
Snowfire	Bridei's horse
Lucky	Donal's horse
Sibel	Broichan's horse
Mist	a cat

*Pronunciation: brid (rhymes with bid)—ay (as in day). The accent is on the second syllable. This name is sometimes spelled Brude.

RAVEN'S WELL

Talorgen	chieftain
Dreseida	his wife, cousin to King Drust the Bull
Gartnait	their eldest son
Ferada	their daughter
Bedo	their second son
Uric	their youngest son
Cenal	interrogator

WARRIOR CHIEFTAINS

Fokel of Galany's Reach
Ged of Abertornie
Morleo of Longwater
Umbrig of the Caitt

CAER PRIDNE (COURT OF FORTRIU)

Drust son of Wdrost (Drust the Bull)	King of Fortriu
Rhian of Powys	his wife
Owain	Rhian's brother
Aniel	councillor
Tharan	councillor
Eogan	councillor
Ana of the Light Isles	a royal hostage
Faolan	Drust's spy and assassin
Garvan	Drust's chief stone carver
Carnach	Drust's cousin
Wredech	Drust's cousin
Breth	Aniel's first bodyguard
Garth	Aniel's second bodyguard
Imbeg	Tharan's bodyguard
Gwrad	Carnach's bodyguard

COURT OF CIRCINN

Drust son of Girom (Drust the Boar)	King of Circinn
Fergus	councillor
Bargoit	councillor
Brother Suibne	religious adviser to Drust the Boar
Cealtran	a chieftain

BANMERREN

Fola	senior wise woman
Kethra	her chief assistant
Luthana	tutor in herb lore
Derila	tutor in history
Morna	
Odha	
Reia	students
Deira	
Uist	a wild druid
Shade	Fiola's cat
Spindrift	Uist's mare

GAELS

Gabhran	King of Dalriada

THE GOOD FOLK

Gossamer
Woodbine

* * * *

DEITIES OF THE PRITENI

The Shining One	The moon; goddess of enlightenment, feminine energy, bringer of change; mother goddess
The Flamekeeper	The sun; god of warriors, life and growth, summer, masculine energy
All-Flowers	Young spring goddess of nature, fertility; maiden goddess
Bone Mother	Represents the dark time; sleep, dreams, death, winter; crone goddess; also represents the earth.
The Nameless One	Associated with the king's rite at Gateway; a god about whom as little as possible should be spoken aloud

RITUAL OBSERVANCES OF THE PRITENI

Gateway	Entry to the dark half of the year (October 31/November 1); sacred to Bone Mother and the Nameless One.
Midwinter	The Shining One is honored
Maiden Dance	Salute to new life, earliest signs of spring (February 1); All-Flowers is honored.
Balance	Spring Equinox
Rising	Fertility, seeding (May 1)
Midsummer	The Flamekeeper is honored along with the Shining One
Gathering	Harvest festival (August 1)
Measure	Autumn Equinox

The
Dark Mirror

1

THE DRUID STOOD in the doorway, as still as a figure carven in dark stone, watching the riders come up the hill under the oaks. Dusk had fallen. Beyond the screening trees, Serpent Lake was a dim shining, and rooks winged to their roosts in the last light, calling in their secret, harsh language. It was autumn: past the feast of Measure. The air was full of a crisp, blue cold that halted the breath in the chest.

The men at arms rode up to the level ground before the doorway, dismounting each in turn. At first it seemed they had not brought the boy. The druid swallowed disappointment, frustration, anger. Then Cinioch, riding in last, said, "Come, lad, stir yourself," and Broichan saw the small figure seated before the warrior, well wrapped in swathing woolen garments, a figure the others moved quickly to lift down from the horse and usher forward for the druid's inspection.

So small. Was this boy really in his fifth year, as Anfreda had said in the letter advising him of her choice? Surely he was too small to be sent here to Fortriu, so far away from home. Surely he was too small to learn. The druid felt anger rise again, and paced his breathing.

"I am Broichan," he said, looking down. "Welcome to Pitnochie."

The child looked up, his gaze moving over Broichan's face, his dark robe, the oaken staff with its intricate markings, the black hair in its many small plaits tied with colored threads. The boy's lids were drooping; he was half-asleep on his feet. It was a long journey from Gwynedd, two turnings of the moon on the road.

The druid watched in silence as the child squared his shoulders, lifted his chin, took a deep breath, and frowned in concentration. The boy spoke, his voice quavering but clear. "I am Bridei, son of Maelchon." Another breath; he was working hard to get this right. "May the—the Shining One light your pathway." The eyes gazed up at Broichan, blue as celandines; there was fear in them, that was plain, but this scrap of an infant would not let it unman him. And, thank the gods, Anfreda had taught her son the language of the Priteni. That would ease Broichan's task greatly. Perhaps, after all, four was not too young.

"May the Flamekeeper warm your hearth," Broichan said, this being the appropriate formal response. He scrutinized the small features more closely. The firm jaw was Maelchon's; so was the upright stance, the iron will that kept those eyes open for all the pull of sleep, and summoned the memorized words amid the strangeness of this sudden waking to a different world. The sweet blue eyes, the curling brown hair, the little frown, those were Anfreda's. The blood of the Priteni ran strong and true in this child. The mother had chosen well. The druid was satisfied.

"Come," Broichan said. "I'll show you where you'll be sleeping. Cinioch, Elpin, Urguist, well done. There's supper awaiting you indoors."

Inside the house, the boy followed silently as Broichan led the way past the frankly curious eyes of his serving people and into the hall, which was occupied by the two old men, Erip and Wid, and a tangle of large hounds before the fire. The dogs raised their heads, growling a warning. The boy flinched but made no sound.

The old men had a game board and bone playing pieces on the table between them. Bridei's eyes were caught by the carven priestesses, warriors, and druids, each no bigger than a man's little finger. He hesitated a moment beside them.

"Welcome, lad," Erip said with a gap-toothed grin. "You like games?"

A nod.

"You've come to the right place, then," said Wid, stroking his white beard. "We're the foremost players in all Fortriu. Crow-corners, breach-the-wall, advance and retreat, we're expert in the lot of them. You've a look of your mother, lad."

The blue eyes regarded the old man, a question in them.

"Enough," Broichan said. "Come, this way." He must remind Wid and Erip that the child's rearing was to be in his own exclusive control. Bridei's new life began from this moment; the child must tread the path unburdened by the knowledge of just who he was, and what he must become. Time enough for that when he was grown. They had ten years, fifteen if the gods smiled on them. In that time, Broichan must mold this infant into a young man fitted in every way for the great part he was destined to play in the future of Fortriu. Bridei's education must be flawless. Indeed, it was as well he had come so early. Fifteen years would scarcely be long enough.

"This chamber is yours," Broichan said, placing the candle he held on a shelf as Bridei looked around the little room with its shelf bed, its storage chest, its small, square window looking out on rustling birches and a patch of dark sky. "You seem weary. Sleep now, if you are ready for it. In the morning we will begin your education."

PEOPLE AT PITNOCHIE were always busy. Bridei became expert at avoiding the grim-faced housekeeper, Mara, and the ill-tempered cook, Ferat, as they barked orders at their hapless assistants or set their considerable energies to beating dust from wall hangings or turning a side of mutton on the spit. Even the two old men were always doing something. Often they were arguing, though they were never angry. They just seemed to like to disagree about things.

Bridei, too, was busy. Broichan's lessons were challenging, commencing with the lore of plants, trees, and creatures, and moving swiftly to include the practice of personal disciplines of silence and concentration. Bridei was a few years younger than the boys who went off to the nemetons for druidic training, Broichan said, but not too young to make a start on such work.

For a while, he fought back tears each night as he lay in his chamber waiting for sleep. But soon enough his mother and father and his big brothers began to fade from Bridei's memory. Little things stayed with him: his father's belt, broad, dark leather with a silver buckle in the shape of a horse. A sweet scent he associated with his mother, violets or some other hedgerow flower. When even these were becoming distant in his mind, he remembered his father's parting words: *Obey your foster father in all things. Obey, learn, and do not weep.*

The seasons passed, and Bridei followed this instruction precisely. He was pleased that, in a small way, he was meeting his father's expectations. Erip and Wid, who played their part in his education, had explained to him about fostering; how it helped families form alliances, and made young men stronger and more useful when they went back home. He did wonder why his family had chosen him to be sent away, and not his brothers, and he asked Broichan this.

"Because you were the most apt," the druid said.

"When will I go home?"

Broichan turned his dark, impassive eyes on the child. "That is a question only the gods can answer, Bridei," he said. "Are you dissatisfied here at Pitnochie?"

"No, my lord." And he was not, for he liked his lessons. He just wondered, sometimes, why he was here.

"Then do not ask such a question again."

BALD-HEADED ERIP AND hawk-nosed Wid welcomed questions, though not the ones Broichan would not answer. The old men knew lots of tricks. Over the first winter, Bridei learned the game with the little carven figures. Wid showed him how to make a corbie and a deer and a long-eared hare with the shadow of his fingers on the wall, while a candle burned behind. They were laughing over this when Broichan, poker-faced, made an image on the wall that had nothing at all to do with the shape his hands formed before the flame—what man with a mere ten fingers at his disposal can conjure a fire-breathing dragon, wings flapping, pursuing a whole host of terrified warriors?

In springtime, close to the feast of Balance, Broichan went away into the forest for solitary prayer and meditation. He was gone for three days, and in his absence the old men taught his foster son to swallow a whole beaker of ale in one gulp. The first time he tried this, Bridei spewed copiously on the flagstones, and the dogs had to lick up the spillage. The druid returned with a strange look in his eyes and a pallor about his face. He said nothing of his time away. But he discovered quickly what had occurred in his absence. The next night, when Bridei came to the hall for supper, the old men were gone.

Bridei was not aware that he was lonely. His father's parting words meant that he must accept what came; must deal with it and move on. He had once had a family, and they had sent him away. Erip and Wid had been kind to him, and now they were gone. There was a lesson to be learned in this. Broichan said there was learning in everything.

Broichan's lessons were generally about patterns: the ones that could be seen, such as the way the leaves on the birches went from cautious swelling to fresh green unfurling, from verdant midsummer strength to the crisp, dry brown of the frost time; the way they shriveled and clung, then fell to transform into fragile skeletons and to lose themselves in the rich litter of the forest floor, nourishing the parent tree. The way the new leaves waited, hidden, through the dark time, like a dream in the back of your mind that could not quite be put into words. There were other patterns that lay behind, chains and links so big and so intricate that Bridei thought he might be an old man himself before he truly understood them. But he grasped at them, and listened hard, and watched his foster father as closely as a young wild creature watches its elders, learning the great lessons: hunt or starve, hide or be taken, fly or fall.

Over the course of that first year, the child stood by the tall, stern druid through every one of the rituals that marked the turning of the seasons. First was Gateway, most secret of all, the entry to the dark time, the resting time, when Bone

Mother cast a long shadow over the earth, frosting the grass, icing the ponds, lengthening the nights until all longed for the sun. At the ritual of Gateway a creature shed its blood and gave its life right there before them on a slab of ancient stone. Broichan did not ask his foster son to wield the knife; that he did himself. But he did require Bridei to watch unflinching. The rooster's blood sprayed everywhere. Bridei did not like the sound it made as it died, even though the druid performed the act quickly and cleanly. It was necessary; Bone Mother required it. All over the land of Fortriu, she expected it. Afterward Broichan invited the spirits of the ancestors to the feast. Places were laid for them at table. If he half closed his eyes, Bridei thought he could see them, pale wispy shadows of grim warriors and slender women, and here or there a little silent child.

Next was Midwinter, a feast of the Shining One. At this ceremony Bone Mother's presence was still strong, but from now on her grip would relax day by day as the rising sun crept eastward. Sprigs of goldenwood were hung around the house, with glossy holly leaves and bloodred berries; there would be new life soon, and these were its first promises. It was a portent of a particularly good year to come, Broichan told his pupil, when the Shining One was at her perfect fullness on the night of the solstice. If that occurred, it was a sure sign of this bright goddess's blessing on the household and its labors. There would be lush crops and fat lambs, the trees would bow down under the weight of their fruit and new babes would thrive. It occurred to Bridei that, although Pitnochie did indeed have oats and sheep and pear trees, there were no babes at all here, nor any children save himself. But for the housekeeper, Mara, Broichan's was a household of men.

After the solstice came other festivals: Maiden Dance, sacred to All-Flowers, goddess of growing things; Balance, the feast of the equinox; Rising, of which Broichan did not divulge a great deal, save to say that in other places, among other folk, there was somewhat more to it, and that Bridei would learn the details when he was older. At Rising the days were warm, the scent of blossoms hung richly in the air, bees buzzed, birds sang, and Broichan allowed the men at arms to visit the settlement south of Pitnochie, a privilege granted but rarely. Bridei had never seen the settlement. Broichan said there was no reason for him to go beyond house and garden. There followed Midsummer, when the Flamekeeper was at his strongest; Gathering; and Measure, when dark and light fell once more into perfect balance before the year hastened on to its ending, and another Gateway.

Bridei watched and learned, going over the rituals in the quiet of his little chamber every night before he slept, practicing the steady, pacing moves Broichan employed, trying out the casting of the circle, the solemn greetings and farewells. At first, he worked hard because of his father's parting words; because he knew it was expected. Before long, he was learning because there was a thirst in him for it, a fascination for the mysterious and powerful things that Broichan could reveal to him. The more he discovered, the more he wanted to know. The rituals were a good example. It was not just a case of going through the motions. Broichan had made that clear from the beginning. One must know the gods, as far as gods could ever be known; one must love and respect them, and understand the true meaning of the festivals so well that the learning lay deep in the bone, and flowed in the blood, and existed in every breath one took. Such learning was a lifelong process; one never ceased striving for a purer bond between flesh and spirit, man and god, world and Otherworld. It was a mystery both wondrous and terrible, Broichan said, and they would indeed grow old before they touched its true heart.

In the spring of Bridei's sixth year, Donal came. Donal was a warrior with a fierce pattern in blue all across cheeks and chin and a fine design of interlocking rings around the bulging muscles of his upper arm. He had close-set eyes and an intimidating jaw, and a grin that made Bridei smile back without even thinking. They rode out together, Bridei on Pearl, the sweet-tempered pony Donal had brought for him, and the warrior on a bony horse of strangely mottled hue, whose name was Lucky. It was an unusual choice for a warhorse, but then again, Donal said, maybe not so odd; hadn't Lucky carried his rider through three battles with the Gaels, misbegotten carrot-haired wretches that they were, and neither man nor beast with a mark to show for it? Well, there was a broken tooth or two—Donal's—and a wee nick in the ear—Lucky's—but here they were, safe and sound and living a fine life riding around in the woods with a druid's son. If that wasn't lucky, what was it?

"Foster son," Bridei corrected.

"What's that?"

"Broichan is not my father. He's teaching me. When I'm bigger I will go home." Bridei was not sure this was so, but he could not think what else his foster father might have in store for him.

"Oh, aye?" That was what Donal always said. It meant maybe yes, maybe no: a safe response. It was the sort of response that would ensure Donal stayed in the druid's household longer than the old men had.

"I want to gallop," Bridei said, touching his heels to Pearl's flanks, and the two of them were off under the oaks, along the hillside above the lake. It was hard for Donal, tall on a big horse, to match the pony's pace in such terrain, and Bridei led him all the way to a place where the hillside dropped away steeply in a tangle of briars and brambles. The oaks grew on the lip of this sharp cleft, but within its shadowy confines were only smaller trees, their kind hard to discern, for all grew awry, in shapes wizened and strange. A mist hung above the rift even on this clearest of days; there was an eldritch stillness in the air that breathed fear.

"What's this place?" asked Donal, coming up beside Bridei and dismounting with a well-practiced roll from saddle to ground. "Got a bad feel to it, I reckon. We'd best not linger here."

"There's a path," said Bridei. "Look."

The way was not easy to see, for clutching fern tendrils and twiggy fingers of low bushes reached across to conceal it. The mist hung less than a man's height above the winding track, which was narrow and formed of hard-packed earth: not a natural gap, but a made one.

Donal was hesitant. "You been this way before, lad?" he queried.

Bridei shook his head.

"Don't like the look of it, myself," the warrior muttered,

making a little sign with his fingers. "We'd likely go down there and find ourselves in some wee clearing all surrounded by Good Folk making merry, and wake up in the morning in a strange realm we'd never come home from."

"Just a quick look?" Bridei asked, for this seemed an adventure. The pony shivered, twitching her ears.

"There's no quick looks in such a spot," said Donal tightly, mounting his horse again. "That's one of those doorways they speak of, I can see it clear; look at the stones there by the top of the path. A ward, they are, set there by folks like you and me to keep those others from coming where they're not wanted. Or a warning to our kind not to go down there. Come on, lad."

Bridei was not a willful child; to disobey did not occur to him. Besides, it was clear Pearl was as eager to go home as Donal was. As they rode back to the house, the hidden valley teased at Bridei's mind, a puzzle demanding to be solved.

THERE WAS A right and a wrong way to ask the druid questions. One did not raise them casually over supper. To do so was to receive the response of a lifted brow, an enigmatic smile, and silence. Some questions, Bridei was learning not to ask at all: inquiries about his mother, for instance, or about why he could not go down to the settlement where, the men had mentioned, there were other boys of about his own size. There would be no good answers to these. The place for questions was in the context of a lesson, and they must be presented as relevant to the day's topic.

Fortunately, at that point in Bridei's education Broichan was dealing with charms and wards of a domestic kind. Bridei had already learned that there were three types of magic. Deep magic, which was of the earth and the sky, the stream and the flame, the slow dream at the heart of things, that was the magic longest learned, hardest known. High magic was used by sorcerers of the most powerful kind, and sometimes by druids. High magic was perilous; it could change the course of wars and bring down kings. These days it was rarely seen. Lastly, there was hearth magic, and that was what they had been studying. Hearth magic could be employed by anyone, as long as people were careful. Small errors could make it go wrong; a man might end up with things upside down, so to speak, if he did not apply the charm in exactly the right way. Ordinary folk such as the cottagers up and down the lake made use of it to placate or fend off the mischievous presences that came out of the woods at full moon, or clung to fishing boats on the lake on misty days.

Take babies, for instance. Everyone knew a newborn was not safe until a key had been tucked into its cradle: that small charm ensured the Good Folk would not steal the infant out of the house and leave a wee figure woven of sticks and grasses in its place. The key secured the child to its home. Or there were doors, which had to be protected against the possible entry of meddlesome spirits. There were lots of different ways to do that, burying salt or particular herbs, for instance, or hammering iron nails into the wood.

They had been working on this kind of thing for several days, and Bridei knew now why juniper bushes grew by the entrances to cottages in the Glen and the reason for the chalk circles on front doors. These were the most basic of charms, easy to set yet powerful in their effect. The forest harbored many forms of life. Wolves stalked the lone traveler; a wild boar could turn on a hunter, gouging and raking with tusks and trotters. Common sense and skill could take care of those threats. Foxes came to steal from the henhouse and eagles to carry off early lambs. Vigilance and good husbandry could fend off such dangers, for the most part. A farmer would always carry some losses; that was the way of nature, so both man and the animals might survive. Creatures were one thing; not to be underestimated, certainly, but within the capacity of ordinary people to deal with. The Good Folk were another matter entirely. Good Folk. The name was misleading. People used it, Broichan told his pupil, so as not to give offense.

"There are other names for them, you understand, Bridei," he said gravely as they sat on a stone bench before the ashes of last night's fire. Early light was beginning to seep in, chill and pure, through the colored panes of the round window in the druid's hall. It made a pattern on the flagstones, red, violet, midnight blue. Bridei edged his cloak up around his neck, burying his hands in its folds. He would not let the druid see him shiver, though every part of him was cold. "Names I would not speak aloud out of doors, for to anger these folk is to invite their mischief. Their true names are such as . . ." Broichan's tone shrank to a whisper, "the Urisk, that dwells in the spray behind the waterfall and follows men at night crying his loneliness; or the Tarans, spirits of little children that died in the cradle; or the Host of the Dead. There are many such, all different, all perilous in their own ways. Many are fair-seeming. And we give them a fair name. That in itself is a ward against harm."

Bridei nodded, hoping the druid could not hear his teeth chattering.

"They are to be respected at all times," Broichan told him gravely. "Respected and feared; I cannot add *trusted* to the list, for such folk do not understand the word as we do. Our concepts of loyalty and trust are incomprehensible to them. Nonetheless, a wise man knows the importance of such beings in the scheme of things. We are all interdependent, plant and creature, stone and star, Good Folk and humankind alike. Now"—Broichan rose to his feet—"stand up, shut your eyes, and list for me what charms you have seen in place to protect my house against unwanted entry."

Bridei stood. There had been no study for this, no tour of inspection, no preparation: simply the ever-present expectation that he would watch and learn, every moment of every day. Eyes firmly closed, he saw in his mind the long, low house of gray stone, the thatch darkened with rain and frost, the roof-weights hanging on their heavy ropes. He pictured the margins of the house, the plants that grew there, the pattern of the encircling paths. Then the doors, the openings, each chamber, each corner. He listed them for the druid as fully as he could: juniper, ferns, and rosemary, a path of white pebbles in a circle, a box of holed stones under the front steps. Three nails in the back door, a triangle. Wreaths of leaves and thorns over doors, a plait of garlic.

"And?" Broichan asked.

For a moment Bridei's memory wavered; he took a deep

breath and went on. "The window, the special one—it's round like the full moon. That's the Shining One's blessing on all of us. The colored glass is so the—the Good Folk can't see where the entry is."

"And?"

"And—ordinary things, not magic. Mara leaves out bowls of milk. Ferat puts a loaf under the rowan trees. Then the Good Folk won't hurt the cows or the horses."

"Anything more?"

There was a pause.

"A man never finishes learning," Bridei said. This was a favorite statement of his foster father's. "But that's all I can think of now. And I have a question, my lord."

"You can open your eyes, son," the druid said. Bridei blinked, and saw to his relief that his foster father was setting wood on the hearth. Broichan was good at lighting fires; all he needed to get the flames going was a muttered word or two and a click of his long fingers. The pine logs flared, caught, and began to burn brightly. Warmth spread out into the chamber, touching Bridei's numb fingers, his freezing nose, his aching ears.

"Sit down, lad. Ask your question."

"What does it mean when there's a little pile of white stones set by a pathway? Does it mean pass or don't pass?"

His hands were thawing nicely now. Broichan snapped his fingers and one of the kitchen men brought oaten porridge, milk, and a jug of mead on a tray.

"Eat your breakfast, Bridei," said the druid, with a faraway look in his eyes and a little frown creasing his brow. "Tell me, has Donal been leading you on pathways you should not have been treading?"

A spoonful of porridge halfway to his lips, Bridei flushed.

"No, my lord. I led him. We did not go down that pathway, the one with the stones. Donal said it was better not. The horses were frightened. Donal said I should ask you about it."

"Before you go back to explore further, you mean?" Broichan did not sound angry.

"Not if you say no, my lord. Do you know that place?"

Broichan poured mead for himself, ignoring the porridge.

He took a mouthful, considered, set the beaker down. "I have another question for you first," he said.

Evidently the lesson was not yet over. Bridei put the porridge bowl back on the tray and sat still, waiting.

"You're not unobservant. You've an eye for what protects the house against intruders. I want you to consider your response again, and this time don't answer the question like a child reciting something learned, answer like a druid, with your wits."

Bridei thought fast and hard. He was not sure what response Broichan wanted. Perhaps the clue was in the question itself.

"It's not just the Good Folk," he said, considering the possibilities. "There's other kinds of danger. Kinds you can't use spells for."

"Go on," said Broichan.

"Donal teaches me riding," Bridei was thinking aloud now, "but he's a kind of guard, too. There are lots of armed men here. I know you call up mists, and set charms on the trees so they move around. Not many people come here. And you always carry a knife hidden in your robe. I think there's danger. You don't go away much, even though you're the king's druid. Erip said you're the most inf—infer— influential man in all of Fortriu."

"What does that mean? Influential?"

"You can make people do what you want," Bridei ventured.

"Hah!" The sound Broichan made was almost like laughing, but there wasn't anything glad about it. Bridei fell silent, concerned that his answer had displeased the druid.

"Would that it were true," Broichan added, picking up a spoon and prodding with evident distaste at the cooling porridge, on whose surface a gray skin was forming. "Would that wisdom might prevail in this confused and benighted land, Bridei. One druid, however influential he may be, cannot summon sufficient power to heal Fortriu's ills."

Bridei considered this, his breakfast forgotten. "But you can make fire, and change the weather, and you know lots of things, spells and charms, plants and animals," he said. "Aren't you more powerful than anyone? Even kings?"

Broichan looked at him, dark eyes watchful as a hawk's. "Your porridge is going cold," he said. "Best finish it. Even the boldest warrior does not choose to ride into battle on an empty stomach. That's what Donal would tell you."

Bridei was becoming used to Broichan's manner of speech by now. He swallowed the congealing mess and kept his thoughts to himself. He suspected it was not the Good Folk, with their trickery and strangeness, that were most to be feared. The danger came from elsewhere: from the world of men.

Bridei finished his breakfast and left the hall with his question still unanswered. When he went to the stables at the appointed time, the druid's black mare, Sibel, was waiting, saddled, beside neat, small Pearl and long-legged Lucky. Broichan and Donal were deep in conversation, but both fell silent as Bridei approached.

"Take us to the place you spoke of, boy," said the druid. "Show us the stones, the mist, the way in. Approach it with due caution. Apply your learning. We don't blunder about in the woods; you may be letting your pony do the work, but you must help her tread as you would go on your own feet, never losing the heartbeat of the earth beneath you, nor the awareness of what is above and about you. Always travel through the forest as a part of it, Bridei, not as an intruder. That way, you require no charms of protection. Shall we ride?"

It was a fair morning. The air held the crisp cold of autumn; the first frosts were not far off. The ways were thick with fallen leaves, brown, gold, russet, ocher, heaped here and there in great piles like a dragon's hoarded treasure. Still they fell as the breeze stirred the branches, here a whisper of yellow, here a fragile teardrop red as blood. The horses' feet made a soft crunching sound as they passed. Bridei could see the vaporous cloud of Pearl's breath and the smaller one of his own. He was glad he had worn his sheepskin hat.

Mindful of the druid's instructions, Bridei rode with care, looking around him. There were odd things in this forest, he knew that already from his walks: things you thought you saw out of the corner of your eye, and then couldn't see anymore when you tried to look straight at them. Flashes of red that weren't leaves; sudden ripples of movement that weren't passing birds. Bushes growing where there had been nothing the day before but moss-covered rocks; sounds like laughter or singing in places far from the nearest dwelling of men. Bridei shivered. Good Folk was a friendly name, a cozy name. What Broichan had told of them was a different matter.

The riders passed beneath great oaks and halted on the rim of the sudden cleft in the hillside. Bridei dismounted. The little pile of stones was still there. On the other side of the path, now, stood an identical miniature cairn. Between them the steep track, veiled in its vaporous shawl, plunged into the depths of the hidden vale.

The others had gotten down from their mounts. Donal held both bridles. Broichan, eyes hooded, features impassive, was watching Bridei.

"The choice is yours, lad," said the druid. "Interpret the signs and tell us what to do."

"We go on," Bridei answered straightaway, his heart thumping with a mixture of excitement and trepidation. "Pearl was scared to go this way last time. She's not afraid today, see?"

"All the same," Broichan said, "we will leave the horses here with Donal for safekeeping. The kinds of trouble he can protect us from will not pursue us into such an eldritch place. On the other hand, there are certain forces in these woods with a particularly keen eye for fine horseflesh, and this shrouded glen seems just the kind of place that would be to their taste. Your little Pearl will be a great deal safer up here with an iron-wielding warrior of Fortriu by her side than down there, however willing she may be to follow you."

Donal appeared more than happy to be left out of the expedition. He tethered the horses and pony loosely, then settled himself against the massive bole of an oak, long limbs splayed among the roots, apparently resting. It was a deceptive pose; the look in the half-shut eyes, the strategic position of knife and dagger within one quick snatch of the hands, were familiar to Bridei. Donal had already given him some lessons that were not to do with horses.

Walking down the steep track in the druid's wake, Bridei

had an uncanny sense that the creeping plants, the clutching bushes, the thorns and spines and prickles were drawing back upon themselves; that the smothering, tangled blanket of growth had made a choice to let intruders through on this particular day. He wondered if this was the result of a spell cast by Broichan, for he knew the druid had considerable mastery over forces of nature; he had seen how the trees around Broichan's house seemed to move about, tricking the eye and concealing what lay behind them. There was no sign of magic now. Broichan was simply walking down the hill, booted feet cautious on the precipitous slope, his staff in one hand while the other held the hem of his long robe clear of the ground. If he was casting a spell, it was not by means of the hands, nor by any words of incantation. The magic, Bridei thought, was here already.

He was not sure what he had expected to see: small people hiding under toadstools, perhaps, or grimacing, long-toothed faces protruding from the undergrowth, or the Urisk rising from the mist and shadow, all sad eyes and piteous, reaching hands. As it was, there was only the gray-blue shawl of vapor and the path leading deeper and deeper into its blinding thickness.

At last the ground leveled and, as if it were indeed at the mercy of a druid's enchantment, the curtain of mist re-treated, and they found themselves right on the brink of a dark, deep pool. One more step, and its waters would have swallowed man and boy alike. Bridei teetered a moment, then found his balance. Broichan had become suddenly very still. As the shreds of mist parted, other landmarks began to reveal themselves: squat, lichen-crusted stones set about the tarn like animals crouched to drink from the inky water; a creeper winding and binding all around, its spearhead leaves colored dark as jewels, its flowers tiny spots of purest white. Other than that the earth was bare; no ferns or bushes grew here, no bracken softened the pool's margins or fringed the rocks, save for that one luxuriant growth that wandered in profusion, following its own wayward path. The stillness was complete. Not a bird sang anywhere; not a creature stirred in the undergrowth by the track; not a fly disturbed the mirrored surface of the dark pool. It was like another world, a realm untouched by human hand, untrodden by human foot. It was so quiet that Bridei thought he could hear his own heart beating.

"This hollow is called the Vale of the Fallen." Broichan's voice was a whisper. In this still place the thread of sound was as intrusive as a shout. "I will tell you its story on the way home. Look in the water, Bridei. Come, stand here."

Bridei felt the druid's hands on his shoulders. Broichan's presence at his back, solid and strong, made him feel a great deal better. He gazed down into the dark waters of the pool and into his own eyes, staring back. He could see Broichan, too, black-cloaked, white-faced, grim and tall. And behind Broichan—Bridei squeezed his eyes shut, opened them again. Had he really seen that? An axe, whistling through the air, glinting, deadly, and the druid's hand going up to catch it by the blade, slicing, bloody, and—

"Careful, boy," Broichan said, gripping Bridei's shoulder hard. "Do not lose sight of what is vision and what is reality. Breathe as I taught you, slowly and steadily. There is much to be seen here, and not every eye discerns the same images. Indeed, there are many who see only water and light and a fish or two. What was it that alarmed you thus?"

Bridei did not answer. His gaze was on the water's surface, for now it was dancing with images. The pool flashed scarlet and silver and showed him a battle, not the whole of it, but the small and terrible parts that made the whole: men crying out, men afraid, men dauntless in courage, fighting on with smashed jaws and broken limbs and faces running red. Men with their wounded on their backs, with their dead over their shoulders, struggling to bear them to safety even as the enemy came on and on in relentless, vengeful pursuit. A little dog settled in faithful guard against the curled body of its dead master, its white coat stained with the fellow's lifeblood, its eyes desolate. A severed hand, a head without a body, young, fierce, somebody's son, somebody's brother. The enemy rolled forward like a great wave, shrieking their triumph, taking all that stood in their path. They passed, and Bridei saw the vale cleared of its human wreckage, empty of all save a sorrow so deep that none could well walk there again. It was a realm of mist and shadow, a habitation of unquiet spirits.

The images faded to gray, to black, and were gone. There was only the water. Bridei drew a deep breath; he wondered if he had been breathing at all while he looked into the pool.

"The Dark Mirror," Broichan said, releasing his foster son and squatting down by one of the weathered stones. Now that Bridei thought of it, they did look a little like ancient sages keeping vigil by this mist-guarded tarn. There were seven of them: the seven druids. "You will see me make use of such a tool from time to time, but not here; my practice is with my own artifact of bronze and obsidian, and I do not venture beyond the walls of my house to use it. As you saw, this place admits whom it chooses, and it chooses but rarely. You were meant to see something, and so you were summoned here. Can you tell me what you were shown?"

Bridei looked at him in surprise. "Didn't you see it, too?"

"I saw what I saw," said Broichan. "Weren't you listening? Maybe it was the same and maybe it wasn't. Now tell me."

"A battle," said Bridei, shivering. Suddenly he didn't want to talk about it at all. He wanted to be out riding with Donal, and the sun to be shining, and the thought of bread and cheese for dinner the most important thing on his mind. "It was horrible. Cutting; screaming; dying for nothing. Blood everywhere."

"It was a long time ago," Broichan said as they made their way back up the track. "The grandsons of those warriors are dead and in the grave; their granddaughters are old women. Their suffering was over long since."

"It was wrong," said Bridei.

"Wrong, that valor is rewarded by death? Maybe; but that is ever the nature of war. How do you know that those who were slain were our own kind, Bridei? Maybe those who were victorious were ours, and the courageous losers our enemies. What do you say to that?"

Bridei did not answer for a while. He had never seen anything as horrible, as sickening as those images of carnage and loss, and he hoped he never would again. "It shouldn't happen like that," he said at last. "It was wrong. The leader should have saved them. Got them out in time."

"That is how you would have done it?"

"I would have made a good plan. I would have saved them."

"A battle isn't about saving your men. It's about winning. A leader expects losses. Warriors expect to die when their time comes. It is the nature of man to war with himself. But you are right, son. It can be done better; a great deal better. And planning is indeed the key. Ah, we've reached the top at last. The walk has made me quite hungry; I wonder if Donal has any rations."

Donal, a seasoned campaigner, did not disappoint them. His saddlebag was packed with dark bread, salty cheese, and little apples, and they stopped to eat these on a rise over-looking Serpent Lake, where the horses could crop sweet grasses. Broichan ate sparingly for all his talk of hunger; in all things, he showed restraint.

"The Vale of the Fallen," he said at last, looking out over the silvery waters below them toward the dark hills on the other side, "was once a place of such ill-doing that folk have regarded it with both reverence and revulsion ever since. There was a battle; this you have learned already."

"And a lot of men were killed," Bridei said, abruptly losing his appetite for the crisp, tart apple he was eating.

"A whole community," Broichan said, "fathers, brothers, husbands, sons, the men of many settlements up and down the Great Glen. They had fought long and hard; this was the ending only, the last flickering of a conflict that had lasted from seeding to harvest. Our forces were already defeated; the enemy had taken the western isles and the land all along that coast, and was moving eastward like a plague. They seemed fit to rampage across the very heartland of Fortriu, not content until every one of our warriors was slain. You saw the result. Our men fell there, the last of them. When the enemy was gone another army crept out, the widows, the fatherless, the old folk, and gathered the broken remnants of their kin. They bore them away for burial. Then a watch was set on that place. Just who keeps it, nobody is quite sure. Folk speak of a dog that howls there at night."

"A sorry place," commented Donal.

"The Vale of the Fallen is not solely a scene of death and defeat," said Broichan. "It holds the essence of the men of Fortriu who fell there. Each of these doomed warriors held in his heart the love of his country, his kin, his faith. We must never forget that, for all our sorrow at their loss."

"My lord," queried Bridei, "what enemy was that? Their eyes were strange. They frightened me."

This time it was Donal who answered, his tone bitter. "The Gaels, curse them, that godforsaken breed from over the water. That invasion was under an old king. His grandson rules them now, Gabhran's his name. King of Dalriada. Huh!" He spat by the path. "Jumped-up incomer, that's all he is, meddling where he's not wanted. There's one king too many in these parts already; we don't need one of those bog-dwellers moving in and helping himself."

Broichan glanced at the warrior and Donal fell silent.

"Let us not speak of kings," the druid said smoothly. "There is time for Bridei to study these matters, and expert advisers to help him learn. But that's for the future. He has barely begun to scratch the surface of what he must know."

Bridei considered this as they completed their meal and made their way home through the forest. There was a question he wanted to ask Broichan, one that was often in his thoughts. His foster father talked about *later,* about *the future,* about all the things Bridei needed to learn. But Broichan never said what it was for; what was to become of Bridei when the learning was over. Would he go back to Gwynedd, home to the family he was starting to forget? Would he become a druid like Broichan, grim and tall, his mind all on learning? Or was it something else Broichan meant? Perhaps he was to be a warrior, like those men in the Dark Mirror. He shivered, remembering. It did not seem to be a question he could ask, not straight out.

"Tell me, Bridei," Broichan said, breaking into his thoughts, "can you swim?"

This was entirely unexpected. On the other hand, Broichan's method of conversation was ever full of surprises.

"No, my lord. I would like to learn."

"Good. We'll need to retain Donal's services over the winter, then, so he can teach you when the weather's warm enough. Rowing, too. It's just as well you didn't tumble into that pond. It's rather cold and extremely deep."

"Yes, my lord." There was nothing else to say. If you fell into the Dark Mirror, Bridei thought, drowning might be the least of your worries.

"Meanwhile," the druid said, preparing to mount his horse once more, "winter allows the study of numbers and codes, of games and music, and I think Donal can use the hall to start some rather specialized training that will equip you to be a little more self-sufficient. I may be away for a time. I will appoint other tutors as required."

"Yes, my lord." One thing was certain, thought Bridei. There'd be no time to get bored.

LOOKING BACK ON this period, years later, Bridei wondered if Broichan had forgotten that his foster son was still some time short of his sixth birthday. He was inclined to think not. The druid had simply assessed him to discover how quickly he could absorb information, what was his capacity for endurance, what was his inclination to obey, then instituted a program of learning that would ensure Bridei squeezed in as much as he possibly could. The days were full. He rode out with Donal. He spent time learning to fight with two knives or with one, or with his fists. He practiced rolling on and off his pony's back swiftly and easily, as he had seen the warrior doing. In the afternoons Broichan drilled him on druidic lore, starting with the sun, moon, and stars, their patterns and meanings, the alignment of the kin stones and the older markers that were dotted all across Fortriu, down into Circinn, which had its own king, and northward into the wild and mysterious land of the Caitt. They delved deeper into the study of deities and spirits, ritual and ceremony. As Broichan had said, so far they had barely scratched the surface. Bridei fell asleep at night with the lore tangling and twisting through his head and his body aching with weariness. He ate like a horse and grew apace.

Some time before Midwinter, Broichan went away to attend a king's council. The territories of the Priteni were divided into four parts: Fortriu, where Pitnochie was located, the southern realm of Circinn, and the more distant territories of the Caitt and the Light Isles. When Bridei asked where his father's kingdom of Gwynedd fit into this, Broichan smiled.

"Gwynedd is another land, Bridei," he said. "Your father's people are not of the Priteni. Cannot you remember how long it took you to ride here?"

Already, the memory was fading. Bridei said nothing.

"There will be representatives of two kings at the council," Broichan told him. "Our lands are divided; it was a black day when Drust, son of Girom, became a Christian, and his realm of Circinn split from Fortriu. Here in the north we are blessed with a king loyal to the ancient gods. Drust, son of Wdrost, known as Drust the Bull, holds power over all the territories of the Great Glen. When they call me king's druid, it is Drust the Bull they mean. He is a good man."

Bridei wished that Broichan would not go. His foster father did not smile much; he did not joke and play games as the old men had done. But Broichan knew so many interesting things, and was always ready to share them. He listened properly when Bridei wanted to explain something, not like Mara, who was always too busy, or Ferat, who often didn't seem to hear. Broichan always had time for Bridei, and although the druid rarely offered words of praise, Bridei had learned to recognize a certain expression in his foster father's dark eyes, the look that showed he was pleased. He wished Broichan would stay at home.

The day came. Sibel was saddled and ready in the yard; four men at arms were to ride with the druid as an escort. Donal would stay at Pitnochie.

"I will work very hard, my lord," Bridei said as Broichan stood waiting to mount his horse.

"Did I express any doubts as to that?" Broichan was almost smiling. "You will do well, son, I know it. Don't neglect the more intellectual pursuits in your desire to develop your skills in combat. Now I must go. Farewell, Bridei."

"Safe journey, my lord," Donal said from where he held Sibel's bridle. "I'll watch over the boy."

"Farewell," whispered Bridei, suddenly feeling quite odd. He would not cry; he had promised his father. He watched in silence as Broichan, surrounded by his guards, rode away under the leafless oaks and down the track to the lake's edge. They had a long journey northeast to Caer Pridne, great fortress of Drust the Bull.

"Right," said Donal cheerfully. "How about swords today? I've a little one somewhere that you might just about be able to lift up, at a pinch. What do you say?"

The lesson in swordsmanship kept Bridei occupied for some time, and while it lasted there was no place in his mind for anything beyond strength, balance, concentration. It was only in the afternoon, when the sky grew dark and rain began to fall in drizzling gray curtains, and his arms had begun to ache fiercely in belated protest at the morning's hard work, that Bridei felt sadness creep over him. Donal was out doing something with the men at arms. Mara was fussing over linen and the impossibility of getting it dry. Ferat, the cook, was in a foul temper that had something to do with wet firewood. There was nobody in the house to talk to.

Bridei's small chamber was next to the place where Donal lodged with the other men at arms, although in practice Donal usually slept in the hallway outside Bridei's door. He said the others snored and it kept him awake. Through Bridei's tiny window, hardly big enough to admit a squirrel, could be seen a silvery glimpse of the lake between the branches of a birch. Sometimes Bridei could see the moon from his window, and then he would leave an offering on the sill, a white stone, a feather, or a charm woven from grasses. Broichan had taught him the importance of the moon, how she governed the tides, not just in the oceans, but in the bodies of man, woman, and creature, linking her ebb and flow with the cycles of nature. The Shining One was powerful; she must be honored.

Today there was no moon to be seen, just the clouds and

the rain, like endless, sorry tears. Bridei lay on his bed and stared up at the window, a small, dim square in the stone wall, gray on gray. He knew what Broichan would say: *Self-pity is a waste of time, and time is precious. Use this for learning.* Then the druid would talk about the rain, and where it fit into the pattern of the seasons, and how the element of water was like the moon in its fluctuations. There was a lesson to be learned from every single thing that happened. Even when people went away and left you. But right now Bridei didn't feel like learning. Without his foster father, nothing seemed right at Pitnochie.

He sat cross-legged on the bed and recited the lore to himself until his lids were drooping over his eyes. Then he made himself stand up, and practiced balancing on one leg with one arm behind his back and one eye closed, which was what druids did for meditation. Then he folded his blankets perfectly, so that the edges were a precise match, and he took everything out of his storage chest and replaced it in a different, more orderly arrangement. He polished his boots. He sharpened his knife. It still wasn't time for supper.

Bridei stood by the window and looked out into the rain. He thought about the day, and about the expression in Broichan's eyes as he said farewell. He thought about the Vale of the Fallen, and all those men killed before their time, and their families with a whole life of sadness before them. He wondered which was the more difficult: having to go away, or being left behind.

DONAL WAS EXTENDING the scope of Bridei's combat training. It involved grips and holds and tricks, balance and strength and speed, and also the proper care and maintenance of weapons. Bridei learned to use a bow and to hit the center of the target nine times in ten. Donal began to move the target farther away and to add degrees of difficulty, such as a distraction at the moment of releasing the string or a sudden command to close his eyes. The lessons were never boring. With the careful instructions on cleaning and oiling his blades, on retrieving and refletching his arrows, on maintaining the bow in perfect condition, Bridei came to realize that long-limbed, wry Donal was, in his way, as self-disciplined a man as the tight-lipped druid.

In the afternoons, when he would once have spent time with Broichan in the recitation of lore or the study of the mysteries, he was now left to his own devices. They had been studying the elements. He did his best to remember everything Broichan had taught him, not just the words of the lore, which he sometimes only half understood, but the meanings behind them. The waxing and waning moon governed water, and was like the tides in the spirit, both strong and pliant. Water was storm, flood, rain for crops; the hot saltiness of tears. Water could roar in a great torrent, a mighty fall from precipice to gorge, or lie still and silent, waiting, as in the Dark Mirror. Then there was fire, powerful and consuming. The life-giving warmth of the hearth fire could keep a man alive; the unchecked raging of wildfire could kill him. The Flamekeeper's special gift to men was the fire in the heart: a courage that could burn on even in the face of death. Air was chill with the promise of snow, carrying the scent of pines. Air supported the eagle's flight, high above the dark folds of the Great Glen. Bridei could feel how it was for the eagle as he looked down over the land of Fortriu in all its grandeur. His land. His place. Earth was the deep heartbeat under his feet, the living, knowing body from whence all sprang, deer, eagle, squirrel, shining salmon, bright-eyed corbie, man and woman and child, and the other ones, the Good Folk. Earth held him up; earth was ready to take him back when his time was done. Earth could make a house or form a track; earth could blanket a warrior's long slumber. There was a whole world of meaning in the smallest things: a burned twig, a white pebble, a feather, a drop of rain.

There were certain rules that must be followed when Bridei went out alone. He could climb Eagle Scar, as long as he was careful. He could traverse the woods as far as the second stream to the south. He was not permitted to approach the settlement or to venture on foot to the wilder reaches of the forest, where he had stumbled on the Vale of the Fallen. When he asked Donal why not, the warrior simply said, "It's not safe." Because Donal invariably showed both common sense and kindness, Bridei accepted this rule. He suspected it had something to do with the Good Folk. Besides, there were his father's parting words, never to be forgotten: *Obey, learn.* He wandered the tracks, climbed rocks and trees, found a badger's lair and an eagle's abandoned nest and a frozen waterfall of fragile, knife-edged filigree. He met not a living soul.

That changed abruptly one afternoon as he was making his way home from a hunting expedition. Well, perhaps not really hunting; he had his bow over his shoulder and his little knife at his belt, but he did not really intend to use either. He'd killed a rabbit not so many days ago, but Donal had been with him then. Much to Bridei's relief, his shot had taken the quarry cleanly; there had been no need for the knife. Bridei, a child who had a great deal of time for thinking, knew it could have been different.

Today he had brought his weapons because it made sense to have them, that was all. Didn't Donal and the others always carry a wee knife in the boot? All Bridei had wanted to do was go up as far as the birch woods and sit on the stones by the big waterfall, the one they called the Lady's Veil, and watch for the eagles. The mountains wore caps of early snow, and the waters of the lake reflected the pale slate of the winter sky. The calls of birds were mournful, echoing across the distant reaches of the forest in lamenting question and answer. Perhaps it was the cold that made them cry so; how would they find food in winter, with the berries shriveled on the brown-leaved bushes, and the sweet grasses carpeted in snow? Perhaps they simply cried to make a music fit for this grand, empty place. Winter must come, after all; the wild creatures knew that as Bridei did. Winter was sleeping time for the earth, dreaming time, a preparation for what was to follow. That had been one of Broichan's earliest lessons. At such a time, a boy should be open to his imaginings, to voices that might be stifled by the clamor of busier seasons. There was learning to be gained from all things: especially from dreams.

The Lady's Veil was not frozen; its fall was too heavy, its face too open to allow the ice a grip. Pools at the base were fringed with tiny crystals and the ferns were frosted. Bridei scrambled up the rocks to the top. He stood awhile watching the sky, but the eagles did not pass over. He practiced his one-legged stance, wondering which of his eyes saw truer than the other. After a while his feet began to go numb and his ears to ache despite the sheepskin hat, and he gathered his bow and quiver and set off for home. Ferat could be relied upon to have hot oatcakes available on such a day, and Bridei was hungry.

Beside and below the waterfall a granite outcrop marked the hillside; around it clustered holly bushes, glossy-leaved and dark. Bridei was perhaps two paces along the track at the base of the rocks when he heard it: a snapping, small, insignificant. He froze. Something was there, not far off under the trees, something that had gone quiet as he had. Something following him; stalking him. A boar? A wildcat? Bridei's heart began to thud a warning. His feet wanted to run. He was a fast runner for his size; it wouldn't take him long to get down to the stone dike that bordered Broichan's outer field, where there was a guard. His whole body felt ready for flight. His mind said no. What if it was the Urisk? The Urisk didn't need to run. Once it saw you, once it wanted you, it stayed with you like a shadow, however quick you were. The only way to escape was to trick it: to stand so still it couldn't see you. Bridei was good at standing still.

Then the cracking twig became a footfall, not furtive at all now, and he turned his head to see a man clad all in brown and gray, a man not so easy to spot in the winter forest, and the man had a hood with eyeholes over his face and a bow in his hands with an arrow aimed straight at Bridei's heart.

No time to run; no place to hide. He would not scream. He would not beg for mercy, for he was Bridei son of Maelchon, and his father was a king. He reached for his bow, backing slowly against the rock wall as his assailant moved closer; he could see the fellow's finger on the string, and knew above the clamor of his heart, above the clenching tightness in his chest, that this warrior's purpose was death. The stone was rough behind him, full of chinks and crevices lined with soft, damp patches of moss. Part of the earth; part of the heartbeat ... As the man's finger tightened on the string,

Bridei slipped backward between the folds of stone and into the dim security of a tiny, narrow cave. He squeezed his body against the back, trying to get out of sight, out of reach.

Outside, the man cursed explosively and at length. Bridei waited, trying to remember to breathe. A sword came, angled through the narrow gap, slashing up and down, reaching, probing, seeking. Bridei pressed back, making himself small. The sword hacked, stabbed: it seemed the owner could not maneuver it into the position he needed, for the gap itself was too slight. Bridei wondered, now, how he had ever managed to get through.

"Godforsaken druid's get!" a voice muttered. "Smoke, that's what we need . . ."

Then there were other sounds, and Bridei knew the man was gathering twigs, leaves, bracken, things that would burn. Most of it would be damp; still, Bridei had seen Broichan's fires, started with no more than a snap of the fingers, and he moved cautiously in the narrow space so he could get a sliver of view. The man was indeed heaping material at the base of the rocks, his movements quick and purposeful. There was no point in calling for help. If this warrior was canny with a flint, thick smoke would fill this tiny chamber well before any guard could run up the hill from the fields. If he didn't want to die in this hole or walk out to certain slaughter, Bridei would just have to save himself.

In the tight confinement of the little chink in the rocks, he struggled to set an arrow to the string. His hands were shaking and there wasn't room to draw the bow fully. The man was kneeling now, perhaps already making fire. As a target, he was too low. The knife: Bridei could use that as he had seen Donal and the others do for sport, tossing it in a spinning arc. He'd never actually tried it, but that wasn't to say he couldn't. Bridei set the bow aside, reached for the knife's hilt. There would be one chance, one good shot at it, when the man had lit his wee fire and stepped back to admire it. One shot. Then he supposed he would have to leap out somehow, flames and all. Perhaps the leaves would not burn. Perhaps he would miss the target. No; he was a king's son.

A thread of smoke began to rise at the cave's entry and a

pungent smell wafted into the dim interior, making him want to cough. The thread became a ribbon, a plume, a small cloud, and all at once there was a crackling. The gray-clad assassin rose to his feet and turned, exposing his back for a long moment. Bridei sighted, balanced the weapon and threw even as the sound of running feet came to his ears, and a shout in a familiar voice. As the knife spun, satisfactorily, through the thickening pall of smoke, a form came hurtling across Bridei's vision, a furious, long-limbed form that crashed into the gray-clad man, removing them both from sight. The knife had disappeared. Bridei shrank back. Flames crackled before the gap, men shouted, metal clashed. There was a strange gurgling sound that ended in a rasping sigh. The flames began to die down; someone was stamping out the fire. Someone was saying, "You've killed him." The little cave was full of smoke; Bridei's eyes stung, his nose itched, his chest was heaving with the effort not to cough. He squeezed his eyes shut and pressed his lips tight. Wrong; he had got it wrong. Someone was dead. His knife had killed someone. Probably Donal. Donal had come to rescue him, and instead of waiting as he should have done, Bridei had thrown the knife without looking properly; without assessing the risks as Donal had taught him to do. He had done something truly bad and now he was shaking and crying like a baby, he could not seem to stop himself.

Voices, outside. "He's done for, all right. Snapped his neck. Worthless scum."

"Better to have kept him stewing; could've got the truth out of him, who sent him, who's paying him. Why'd you— Donal?"

Then a shuffling sound, like someone trying to get up and not making much of a job of it. It was getting harder and harder not to cough. Bridei needed to sniff; his nose was running like a stream in spate.

"What's this, man? You're bleeding like a stuck pig! Did the fellow wing you?"

"It's nothing. A scratch. Go after the others and be quick about it!"

Feet on the path, many of them now, and jingling metal,

and then silence. Or almost silence; Bridei could hear breathing, his own, snuffling with tears, and another's, somewhat labored. Donal was alive.

"Bridei?" It was little more than a whisper. "Are you somewhere near, lad? Answer me, curse it!"

Donal sounded strange. Perhaps he was angry. A warrior would not have hidden like a coward, and hit the wrong target, and then shed tears over it. Bridei found himself unable to move, unable to speak.

"Bridei!" Donal was attempting a shout. Bridei could see a little bit of him now, his shoulder in the familiar old leather jerkin, and the other hand clasped over it, and blood oozing between the fingers. "Bridei, you foolish wee boy, if you've gone and got yourself killed I'll—I'll—" The warrior's voice faded; Bridei had never heard him speak like that before, as if the life were draining out of him quicker than sand through a glass. Bridei edged forward, slipping out between the rocks, stepping over the smoldering heap of leaves and twigs to stand, small and still, by Donal's side. He tried not to see the form of that other man lying not far off with his head on a strange angle. Donal was sitting on the ground; his eyes were closed and his face was the color of last week's porridge. There was quite a lot of blood on his shoulder and upper arm, and he had Bridei's small knife held loosely in his right hand.

"I'm sorry," Bridei said solemnly, and gave a monumental sniff. "It was the other man I meant to hit, the one who was trying to shoot me."

Donal's eyes flew open. His mouth stretched in a grin and he half rose to his feet, then subsided again with a groan. "Blessed All-Flowers be praised! Where were you, you wee—in there? How can that be? Yon crack's not wide enough to admit a half-grown pup, let alone a great lad like you! I can't credit it!"

It was true. The opening looked hardly big enough for him to fit one shoulder through, let alone the rest of him. No wonder that man had failed to reach him with the sword . . . The thought of that slashing, rending blade made Bridei feel suddenly odd, and he sat down abruptly by Donal's side.

"Tell me." Donal's voice had changed again; now he really was angry, but Bridei sensed it was not for him. "Tell me what happened here, lad. All of it, every detail, everything you saw."

"You're bleeding," Bridei said. "I know how to tie a bandage, Broichan showed me. I'll do that now, and then I'll tell you while we go home. You should have a poultice of wormwood and rue, and drink mead, and go to bed early. That's what my foster father would say."

Donal regarded him in silence.

"I'm sorry I hurt you," Bridei said once more, and felt his lower lip tremble ominously.

"Oh, aye," said Donal, his voice oddly constrained again. "I think the usual thing is to rip up a shirt or two. It'll have to be yours; I can't get mine off over this shoulder. But make sure you put your jacket back on straight away, it's cold up here. And get on with it, will you? That mead's beginning to sound very good."

2

IT HAD BEEN a mistake, Donal said. It was Broichan whom the fellow and his companions were trying to harm, not Bridei. Bridei knew this was wrong. He had seen the expression in that man's narrowed eyes, had watched as his finger tightened on the bowstring. Broichan did have enemies. A man who is everybody's friend has no need of guards on the perimeters of his property, or doors with bolts. Perhaps those attackers were the druid's foes, but the one they wanted to kill was Bridei. Why, he could not tell. His father was a king, certainly, but Gwynedd was a distant place with its own councils, its own wars, far removed from the realms of the Priteni. Besides, his father had sent him away. If he'd been of any special importance, surely his family would have kept him. The attack just didn't make sense.

The man Donal had killed was buried in a corner of the

sheep yard. Others, sighted from Broichan's guardposts, had escaped into the forest despite energetic pursuit by the druid's men at arms. They remained unaccounted for, their mission and origins a mystery. Donal cursed that the fellow had obliged him to kill or be killed; he'd rather have bruised the other a little, trussed him up and got the truth out of him one way or another. Too late now; the gray-clad man could only tell his story to the worms.

Bridei was no longer permitted to wander on his own, but must go accompanied by at least two of the guards, and only when there was a real need for it. The daily rides were curtailed, for Donal was much occupied. Tense exchanges in lowered voices were frequent, and all the men had a guarded, edgy look about them. Mara muttered over the washtub. Ferat cursed as he plucked geese, and Bridei learned new words, which he did not repeat. He spent a lot of time in the stables grooming Pearl and talking to her, for her warm body and sweet, accepting eyes made her a good companion, as horses went. In the afternoons he studied. He tried not to notice how empty the house seemed, how quiet. He tried not to think of how small he was, how little he really knew of how to be strong, how to fight back. He tried not to worry about Broichan and what a long time it was taking him to come back home.

Without the druid, the household had not observed the ritual of Gateway, marking entry to the dark time. Mara said that farther along Serpent Lake there would be a big heap of logs, pine, ash, oak, set by the shore ready for burning. Bridei would have liked to go down and watch folk leap through the flames, as Mara had told him they did. But there had been no point in bothering Donal; why ask when you know already the answer will be no? So all Bridei had done was set out a little bowl of mead and a platter of oatcakes on the step outside the kitchen. This was a sign of respect; thus, he invited the dead to share the household's gifts, to be welcome there on this night when barriers opened and the worlds merged. In the morning, mead and cakes were gone; there was nothing left but a scattering of pale crumbs.

Gateway night was well past now, and it would soon be Midwinter. The king's council must be long over, but there had been no word from Broichan. The nights stretched out. Lamps burned in kitchen and hall throughout the day, illuminating an interior that was always smoky, for the fire was constantly burning save when all slept. Mara muttered about the soot and hoarded supplies of oil. In his small chamber Bridei huddled in a blanket, candlelight flickering on the stone walls, and tried to concentrate on the lore. It felt as if his foster father had been gone forever. When was Broichan coming home?

Three days short of Midwinter it snowed. The air had been hinting at it since early morning: there was no mistaking that stillness, that odd, deceptive sensation of warmth, as if the soft cloud blanket were easing winter's grip even as it blotted out the sun. Bridei was outside helping the men move sheep from one field to another. The guards kept their long watch on the upper margins of Broichan's land; their stalwart forms, their blue-patterned features were clearly visible up under the bare oaks on the forest's edge. They worked shorter shifts in winter; at any time, there would be men coming in for roast meat and ale with spices, and other men putting on layers of clothing, skin cloaks, leather helms, heavy boots, ready for another battle with the chill. Ferat was so busy he'd no time to grumble. There were two fellows to help him, both too terrified of the cook's temper to do anything but work at top speed and pray that they made no errors.

The snow began to fall as the last of the ewes were going through, herded by the overexcited dogs. Bridei's job was to sit on the drystone dike by the gap and make sure they separated out the right ones. The farming side of Broichan's affairs was handled by a man called Fidich. It was clear Fidich had once been a warrior of some note, for the patterns he wore on his face were almost as elaborate as Donal's, and he had markings on his hands, too, twists and spirals from wrist to fingertips. Fidich had strong shoulders and a grim expression, and a right leg that ended just below the knee. He walked with a crutch of ash wood, and could cover the difficult terrain of the farm with astonishing speed. He lived in a hut on the far side of the walled fields all by himself. Never a sheep dropped an early lamb, nor a pig ventured out into a forbidden plot of land, but Fidich knew of it. The leg did make some things difficult. That was why a boy for gate-work was useful.

"Right, lad, that's the last!" Fidich called over the voices of three large hounds clamoring in chorus, and Bridei hauled the gate shut and fastened the bolt. The sheep on the other side, the ones relegated to a winter of sheltering under scrubby bushes and gleaning a living from what little feed could be spared, showed momentary confusion, then wandered off as if nothing untoward had happened.

The snow made its presence felt first in isolated flakes, descending in a slow, graceful dance. As men, boy, and dogs headed downhill to the house, the flakes became soft flurries and swirling eddies, settling patchily on the frost-hardened mud of the track. Over the lake, the tree-clad hillside was disappearing behind a blanket of low cloud. The wind stirred, and the pines moaned in response. By the time Bridei and his companions reached the house, the dogs bore a wintry coating on their shaggy gray hair and the wind was howling in earnest. Looking back up the hill, Bridei could not see the field where they had been working, nor the sheep, nor the guards pacing beyond. There was only the white.

"Settling in for a good blow," Fidich commented. "I'll not stay; need to get home while I can still find the way. Hard night for the lads up on watch."

"Aye," said another man. "Be a foolish fellow would try to get in here in such a blizzard; he'd be wandering in circles, lying down for a rest and never getting up again, I reckon. Sure you won't stop in for a bite to eat?"

"Ah, no, I've my own fire to get lit and my own porridge oats," Fidich said, as he always did.

It was cold even in the hall before the fire. Bridei was in no rush to go off to bed, for he knew how icy his little chamber would be on such a night. Everyone was quiet. Mara was mending by lamplight; Ferat sat on a bench staring morosely into his ale cup. Most of the men had already gone off to their quarters. Donal was at the table working on some arrows. A variety of small knives and other implements, feathers and twines and lengths of wood, was set out before him.

He was whistling under his breath. Bridei sat beside him, too tired tonight to do more than watch.

The kitchen door crashed open, making them all start. A chill draft swirled through into the hall, setting the fire sparking. Donal grabbed his biggest knife and sprang to his feet, and the other men at arms leaped to block the doorway between kitchen and hall. Mara stationed her ample form in front of Bridei, effectively stopping him from seeing a thing.

"What the—?" was all Ferat had time to say before the door was heard slamming shut again, and the men at arms stepped back to let two figures through, one supporting the other. One was Cinioch, who had been on guard up in the snow by the dike, and the other, ashen-faced, blue-lipped, and covered with the scratches and bruises of a headlong flight across country in the dark, was Uven, one of the men at arms who had traveled with Broichan to the king's council.

There was work to do for Bridei then. He fetched one of the cloaks from the pegs by the kitchen hearth, brought a cup of ale, put it into Uven's trembling hands. Mara kicked the tangle of dogs away from the hall fire. Donal set the bench closer while the other men helped the half-frozen traveler to seat himself there. Uven was unable to speak for a while; spasms of shivering ran through his body and the cup shook so violently in his hands that the ale spilled down his tunic. Eventually he managed to drink, and a little later to start on the porridge Ferat had produced, piping hot and generously ladled.

"Good," Uven muttered, his blanched features assuming a healthier look. He looked up at Donal. "Message," he said. "Urgent. Private."

"Bridei," said Donal, "time for bed now; good lad, off you go."

"What's happened?" Bridei could hear how small his own voice sounded, high and uneven. A good child did not disobey an order, and he was always good. But he had to know the truth. "Is it Broichan?"

They all looked at him in silence, and then Uven muttered, "Time's short, Donal."

"Bridei," Donal said, squatting down and looking Bridei

straight in the eye, "this is men's business, and you are not yet a man, although you'll make a fine one some day. You can help Broichan best by doing as I ask. Take your candle, go to your chamber now. When I've heard Uven's news, I'll come and tell you about it. I promise."

HE LAY ON his bed waiting. Blankets could ease the cold of the little chamber. They could not help the chill inside him, harsher than winter, deeper than a well. Broichan was dead. What other explanation could there be for such urgency, such secrecy? Donal thought to protect him, to break the ill news gently. Well, Donal wouldn't need to break any news. This was just the next part of the same old pattern. You had something, you let yourself care about it, and then suddenly it was gone. Perhaps it was better not to care at all. Bridei wondered if the druid had looked into the eyes of his killer, had observed the finger tightening on the bowstring. Broichan would have faced death calmly, he thought. *There is learning in everything,* he would have said. The candle flickered in the draft; shadows crept across the walls, not deer and eagles and hares now but phantoms, visions, memories of the Otherworld, beyond the veil. Perhaps even now the druid journeyed among them. Bridei would not weep. They would send him away now, he supposed. Send him home to Gwynedd. Try as he might, he could not picture it.

After a while Donal tapped on the door and came in quietly to sit by Bridei on the narrow shelf-bed. In the candlelight the patterns on his face took on a strange life of their own, shifting and changing like still more manifestations of the spirit world. Bridei waited for the words he knew would come.

"Your foster father's in a bit of trouble," Donal said. "Sick, and far from home."

"Sick?" Bridei felt hope awaken inside him somewhere, a tiny flame doing its best not to go out again.

"Deathly sick, Bridei; I won't lie to you. It seems someone tried to harm him with a particular combination of herbs that Broichan took unawares in a dish of food or drink. He's recovering as well as he can; a druid is his own best physician. But he can't stay where he is; we need to fetch him home."

"We?"

Donal's grim expression softened. He gave Bridei a direct sort of look. "Myself, and a few of the lads. It's a long way, Bridei; all the way up to the coast, near the king's court at Caer Pridne, and back again. We'll need to set out before this place gets snowed in."

"I could help," Bridei said, squaring his shoulders in an effort to appear taller.

"I know that, lad. I also know that if I take you one step outside the borders of Pitnochie, he'll send me packing the moment he gets word of it. Of course, if you're so keen to be rid of me . . ."

"I just wish you weren't going away," Bridei said in a whisper.

"As a matter of fact," said Donal, "I've something I need you to do here. I can't take Lucky, and he misses me when I'm away. I need you to give him a bit of a brushing, tell him a joke or two, just to keep him happy. You'll be doing me a favor if you stay here and attend to that. I know it's hard."

Bridei nodded. There was a certain solace in what the warrior had said. "What if you don't come back?" he could not help asking.

"Don't come back?" Donal's brows shot up in astonishment. "Me, Donal, hero of more battles than you've got fingers and toes to count them on? Of course I'll come back! What are you telling me, that you think I'm not up to this?" There was the sound of a smile there somewhere, for all the challenge of the words.

Bridei looked up at the warrior and shook his head. A moment later he put his hand out and Donal grasped it firmly.

"We'll bring him home safe, Bridei, I give you my solemn word."

"Donal?"

"Yes, lad?"

"It would be hard to poison a druid." They had practiced identifying herbs by smell, he and Broichan, wearing thick blindfolds. His foster father never erred.

Donal nodded grimly. "Don't think I haven't thought about that."

"Who could do it?"

"That's what I intend to find out," Donal said. "But first things first. Broichan will mend better here in his own place, with you by his side and the rest of us to keep watch. I'm leaving the house in your hands, Bridei. You should pray for your foster father. Will you do that?"

"Yes," Bridei whispered, for this was one of those times when there is no choice at all. He managed not to cry as Donal took his leave, managed to watch dry-eyed and solemn as his friend set out on foot, at first light, with a party of four men all warmly clad and heavily armed. As for whether he wept when Donal was gone, and he was back in his chamber alone, that was between himself and the shadows.

WINTER SOLSTICE: THE lake ink-dark, the fells blue-white under a lowering sky, pine branches drooping heavily under their burdens until the weight became too great, the snow fell to the ground in powdery avalanche and the needled boughs sprang back up, resilient and strong. Sheep keeping close, pressed together for warmth. Smoke from the hearth fire rising sluggishly to hang in a pall above the house; dogs, for once, reluctant to stir themselves in the morning. The water trough hard-frozen, and Fidich breaking the ice with a staff so his stock could drink.

Bridei had helped to feed the ewes that were housed in the barn. He'd paid a visit to the pigs in their adjoining quarters. He'd spent some time in the stables grooming Pearl and telling jokes to Lucky. They were not very good jokes, but Lucky had seemed satisfied with them. Pearl was restless today: maybe she sensed it was a time of change. Tonight the year would turn to light once more, hard though this was to believe on such a day.

For all their anxiety about Broichan and the men who had gone to fetch him home, the folk of the household understood the importance of this night. The men had brought in a weighty oak log, which now stood ready by the hearth. Bridei, accompanied by two guards, had fetched a good supply of holly branches, ivy twists, sprigs of pine, and even a length or two of goldenwood resplendent with both berries and flowers, for this was a herb of as much mysterious oddity as any druid. With Mara's help he had made garlands, and now each doorway wore a crown of greenery. Ferat had splashed the great log with mead and sprinkled it with flour, and Bridei had festooned it with trails of glossy-leaved ivy.

In the evening they doused the fire, set the ceremonial log on the hearth and gathered before it in the cold. They put out the lamps; save for a single candle, all was dark. Frowning with concentration, Bridei did his best with the ritual, although he could not remember all of the words. He told the Midwinter story of how the goddess rocked a wounded ancient in her arms all night until he was changed into a little, golden-haired child who flew up into the sky, the sun rekindled out of darkness, hope reborn from death. The candle was smothered. Then Fidich struck a spark, blew on a handful of tinder, set one taper burning. From this they kindled a little piece of charred wood, sole remnant of last year's Midwinter log. This brand soon had the fire blazing brightly, the old giving life to the new, and warmth spread through the hall. Bridei walked the circle widdershins, making an end to the ritual, and it was time to relax and enjoy the rest of the night.

Ferat was smiling as he brought out the festive fare, the ale and mead, the spice cakes and carefully stored cheeses. Mara was packing a basket for the unlucky fellows out on watch. Uven, now fully recovered from his ordeal, was already on his third beaker of ale. The sound of chatter, the smell of Ferat's fine cooking, the grins and jokes brought the house to new life in perfect reflection of the ritual they had just enacted. But Bridei was suddenly tired; he sipped the watered mead they had given him, nibbled at his cake then fed it, surreptitiously, to the nearest dog.

"Good night," he said to nobody in particular, but one of the men was telling a story and everyone was laughing, and they did not hear him. Nor did any of them notice as he crept away to his chamber, rolled himself in the blankets and, to a background of hearty revelry from the hall, fell fast asleep.

That seemed a fitting conclusion to a long and testing day. But Bone Mother had not quite finished her season's work. Before she loosened her grip on the land she had one last change in store for Bridei, a change both wondrous and difficult. On this night of winter solstice his life was to be transformed more profoundly than anyone could have imagined.

BRIDEI AWOKE WITH a start, his heart thumping. He could not remember his dreams, only that it had seemed urgent to escape them. The house was still. Through the small square of the window the full moon looked in, her blue-white glow transforming his ordinary little chamber into a place of wonder, a realm of deceptive surfaces and secret shadows. Quiet, so quiet; even a mouse's footsteps would be heard in so profound a stillness. And yet, something called him, tugging at his mind, urgent, vital.

Shivering, Bridei set aside the blankets, threw his short cloak on over his nightrobe and, opening the door as quietly as he could, tiptoed barefoot down the passageway to the hall.

On the hearth the fire still burned cheerfully; the Midwinter log would last for seven days. Mara slept peacefully in a chair, mouth slightly open, shawl tucked neatly around her shoulders. Two of the men at arms, Elpin and Uven, were sprawled on benches near the fire, the dogs on the floor between them. The dogs lifted their heads as Bridei crept past, then went back to sleep.

The kitchen was empty: Ferat had retired to bed after setting his domain to rights, ready for the morning. The fire's glow followed Bridei into this chamber, outlining his small shadow on the stone floor in front of him. As he approached the outer door, the shadow went up the wall, bending into an improbable shape, tall and crooked. The heavy iron bolt had been fastened, a task Mara usually attended to after the late shift had gone on watch. During the day, the door stayed unbolted, for the nature of Broichan's household meant comings and goings were frequent.

A chill draft was whispering in; Bridei's toes could feel it. He shivered again. That something, whatever it was, the something that had woken him and brought him here into the dark of a winter night, was telling him now that he must step outside. With careful fingers, slowly for quiet, Bridei slid the great bolt across. He opened the heavy oaken door on the blanketing snow, the midwinter hush, the blue moonlight. The landscape was indeed wondrous under that shining. All was touched by it, touched to magic. The dark oak trunks were sage old druids, stoic and strong in the cold; the slender, graceful birches were forest spirits, dreaming of the fine cloaks of silver-green the springtime would give them to clothe their nakedness. In the distance, the pond gleamed like a mirror of polished silver, showing the moon an image of her own lovely face, remote and wise.

It was freezing cold. His toes were starting to go numb. They were probably turning blue. Bridei glanced down to check them.

And there it was: what he had been called here to find. On the step, right by his bare feet, was a small basket somewhat like the one Mara used for storing hanks of wool. But this was no sturdy affair of willow wattles. This was made of all sorts of things, feathers, grasses, fragile skeleton leaves, a little twiggy branch with red berries on it, bark and creepers and flowers that had no business being here in the middle of winter. The basket was lined with swansdown and had a pair of handles of plaited reeds, with holed stones threaded on them in threes and fives and sevens. The basket was not a thing of human make. The person who lay tucked up in it was . . . very small. Extremely small, and probably very cold. Bridei knelt down on the step, scarcely breathing as the moon gleamed on this gift as if to show him exactly what she had brought for him. The very small person seemed to be asleep. It wore a kind of bonnet with white fur all around, and had a wee blanket striped in many colors pulled up to its chin. Its face was pearly white, moon-white, as pale as the pelt of a winter hare. Weren't little babies supposed to be red-faced and ugly? This one had delicate dark lashes and a mouth that was pink and solemn-looking. Bridei stared, entranced. A brother. A little brother. He wouldn't be by himself anymore. Heart pounding, he rose to his feet, looking up at that great, silver orb in the dark sky. His hands moved in the sign of acknowledgment and reverence; it was clear to him that he would be in her debt forever.

"Thank you," he whispered, bowing in the way his foster father had taught him. "I'll look after him, I promise. I swear it on my life."

He reached down to pick up the basket, and halted. The small person was awake. Its eyes, gazing up at him gravely, were moon-bright, star-clear, of no color and every color. They were eyes like a dream, like a deep well, like a magical tale with no ending. Perhaps they were blue, but it was not like any other blue in the world. The small person stirred, and a hand no larger than an acorn came out from the striped blanket, reaching for something invisible.

"There," Bridei said, bending to tuck the little creature's arm back in, for if he was shivering from cold what must such a mite be feeling? The tiny hand fastened on his finger, holding tight. Bridei's heart was acting strangely, as if it were tumbling about in his breast. "You'll be safe here, I promise."

It was only after he had carried the basket and its occupant inside and bolted the door behind him that Bridei realized he would have to think fast. This was a place of order and discipline, a place where all moved to the tune of Broichan's life and Broichan's path. None of the people who lived here, Mara, Ferat, Donal and the others, ever spoke of families. Even Fidich, who lived in his own small dwelling, had no wife, no sons to learn the patterns of farming. Broichan's house was no place for children. This newborn would not be received with open arms. Indeed, it would be doubly unwelcome, for there was no doubt at all it was a gift from *them*, from the Good Folk. The moon had guided them to Bridei's door. And while an ordinary foundling would be kept warm, fed milk, and probably passed on to a childless couple in one of the settlements for rearing, a child of the forest would not be treated so kindly. Bridei had heard folk talking; such a gift was considered more curse than blessing.

It was useful, at such times, to have begun a druidic education. The basket stood on the kitchen floor, a dark oval. The face of the infant was a circle of white, translucent as if it bore some of the moonlight within. The eyes remained open, following Bridei calmly as he moved about, searching. A key, he needed a key. That charm was supposed to keep an infant safe; to keep it at home. If it stopped folk from stealing a baby away, wouldn't it also make those inside want to keep the child? He prayed that it was so. There had to be a key somewhere. He must be quick; if the baby began to cry, and someone woke up, they'd set the basket straight outside again and his little brother would freeze to death the way Uven nearly had. Quickly then, stop rummaging around and use his wits, as Broichan would have bid him do . . . Bridei stood still and concentrated. A key, he'd seen one, a tiny key with a curly bit on top . . . Yes, the spice box, Ferat's prized coffer of yew, that had such a key, and he knew where the cook hid it, it was right up there behind the oil jar. Bridei slipped it off its hook and, moving silently on his bare feet, put his hand down the side of the little basket, between the blanket and the soft, feathery lining. The key settled at the bottom, hidden, secret. Now nobody could send the baby away.

What Bridei really wanted to do was go back to his own chamber, where nobody could see, and keep his remarkable gift safe for as long as possible. He could not stop looking at those tiny, perfect features, the strange eyes that were both innocent and knowing, the little fingers like delicate petals. But it was cold in his room. Besides, Bridei understood that newborn creatures, such as early lambs, needed a lot of looking after. There'd need to be warm milk. How would they manage that in the middle of winter? There'd probably be all sorts of other things he knew nothing about. He carried the basket through into the hall and settled on the stone floor near the sleeping hounds. One of the dogs growled soft and low, and Bridei hushed it.

He reached into the basket, hands careful as if gathering eggs, and lifted the infant out. It felt warm and relaxed and weighed no more than a rabbit. It was clad in a kind of cloak, fur-lined, and a gown underneath so fine-woven, so lacy, the

thread might have been spun from cobweb or thistledown.
The child's lower parts were swathed in a bulky and practical piece of woolen cloth. Though this was undeniably
damp, Bridei didn't think he could do much about it, having
no handy substitute. So he held the baby in his arms, rocking
it a little, and the clear, strange eyes gazed up at him as if
working out just what to make of him. A lock of hair had escaped the confines of the bonnet and curled, black as soot,
over the pale brow.

"It's all right," Bridei said in an undertone, just for the two
of them. "I won't leave you on your own. I'll tell you a story
every night, and play with you every day, and keep you safe
from the Urisk. I promise."

PERHAPS THE GOOD Folk had made sure the infant's belly
was full of milk before they left the child for the moon to
dispose of. At any rate, it was not until the late winter sunrise began to send its low light through the chinks and cran-
nies around the door that the child became suddenly hungry
and began a shrill squalling that brought the whole household instantly awake. The dogs began to bark, the men
groaned and stretched cramped limbs, and Mara, one hand
to her head, got slowly to her feet and took two steps toward
the spot where Bridei, startled from sleep, sat by the hearth
with the red-faced, bawling infant in his arms. Mara's
shrewd eyes took in the strange, small basket, the swansdown lining, the tiny robe edged in white fur; they moved to
the child itself, now looking more like any other hungry
newborn, yet still notable for the pale, clear eyes, the delicate hands, the curl of coal-black hair. Then Mara looked
straight at Bridei. He held the child to him tightly and stared
back. They'd better not try to take his baby brother.

Mara moved her fingers in an age-old gesture, the sign to
ward off evil. Behind her, the men were doing the same.
"Black Crow save us," she said, squatting down, "what have
you been up to, Bridei? Here, give it to me."

Bridei held on grimly.

"Come on, lad. Use your head. Can't you see what that is?

Just think what your foster father would say. Give it to me, quick now. The longer it stays within these four walls the more ill it's likely to bring down on all of us. And with Broichan close to death and far from home, that's just what we don't need here."

Elpin reached down as if to take the child. The expression on his face was that of a person forced to touch something he finds repulsive or dangerous, such as an adder.

Bridei edged away. "He just wants milk," he said over the racket. Who would have thought such a scrap of a thing could make so much din? He could feel the cries vibrating right through the child's fragile body. "Shh, shh, you'll be all right," he whispered.

"Milk, is it?" inquired Mara. "And where do you think we'll find that in the middle of winter, with the cows and sheep all dry as a bone?" She stood with hands on hips, stolid as a big guard dog set on seeing an intruder off the premises.

"Best put it back out quick," Elpin said. "They say if you do that, the—the Others, they'll come and take such a child away again. If you don't leave it too long, that is."

"Pretty cold out there," observed Uven doubtfully. "The babe's very small."

"What's all this?" Ferat had been roused from his bed by the noise, and now wandered in with tousled hair and the look of a man whose head aches mightily. "Where did that come from, lad? Here, give us a hold—that's it—" And with a deft dip and lift, the cook scooped the infant from Bridei's arms and moved nearer to the hall fire so he could examine it more closely. He seemed to know what he was doing; after a scrutiny of the red, crumpled features he put the child against his shoulder, began a rhythmic patting of its back and, miraculously, the screaming died down to a thin, plaintive sobbing.

"It's hungry, all right," Ferat said. "And stinking like a midden—Mara, go and fetch some clean cloths, will you? Lad, stir up the kitchen fire for me, we need warm water."

The others stood mute, staring at him. This morning he was definitely not himself.

"Go on, get a move on," Ferat snapped in something

closer to his usual tone. "Wee creature's starving! What would Broichan say if he heard that fancies and superstitions made us treat a newborn babe worse than we would an orphan lamb? Shame on you!"

"That's all very well," said Mara, "but how are we to feed it? Besides, it's not what Broichan would want. It's not the right thing, and I can't believe you'd ever consider it—"

Bridei cleared his throat. "I was the one who brought him in. If my foster father is angry, he can be angry with me. But you can't put the baby out in the snow. He'd die."

"Looks more like a lassie than a wee lad to me," Ferat said, still patting. "And fey as they come, Mara's right about that part. See how pale she is now she's given up the shrieking for a bit? Long lashes like a fine heifer's, and a little rosebud mouth. She's like a thing from a tale; a fine gift, is how I see it. Mara'll tell you if it's a girl when she changes these wrappings."

"Me?" retorted Mara crossly, but she put the babe on the table and stripped off the dirty swaddling, and Ferat was right, it was a girl. Bridei was not at all sure how he felt about this. Duly washed and rewrapped in the cloth Mara had fetched, the baby stayed in the housekeeper's arms while Ferat did what he could with warm water and honey, and in a little, the tiny girl was being coaxed to suck the mixture from a rolled-up rag they dipped into the bowl, and was growing quieter. Uven and Elpin stood by watching; neither of them seemed in a hurry to be away. Ferat, in the kitchen, had summoned his assistants and was busy cooking breakfast and talking the while.

"That won't keep her happy long," he called over the clanking of pots and pans. "Didn't Cinioch say he'd a cousin that just lost a babe? You know the girl, went up to Black Isle to wed, but her man was killed while the child was still in her belly. She's in the settlement down the lake, came back to her sister's for the birthing. The infant didn't thrive; they buried him a day or two since. Can't recall the girl's name."

"Brenna," said Uven. "Shy little thing. Sad tale, that."

"Aye," said Mara, "sad indeed. But useful. That's if we're keeping this one." She frowned at the infant, now cradled in

Bridei's arms once more as Mara squeezed a few more drops of the honeyed water into the small, neat mouth. The eyes gazed up at her, pale and clear.

"Uven!" yelled Ferat. "Where's Cinioch this morning?"

"On night watch."

"Right. Get some breakfast into you then, and get up there as quick as you can. Tell him to come and talk to me before he does anything else. We need a wet-nurse; the longer we leave it, the more urgent it gets. Sounds like this Brenna might be just what we want."

"She'd have to be crazy," muttered Mara. "Who'd offer to nurse one of *them*?" But it seemed to Bridei her words were only half meant, otherwise why would she be trying so hard to get the baby to suck, and nodding encouragement at each successful swallow? The little basket stood empty by the hearth, the key well hidden in its network of tangled foliage. It was true, what Broichan had told him. Sometimes simple hearth magic is the strongest of all.

The day seemed very long. Cinioch snatched a quick breakfast and headed off down the lake. The baby was quiet at first, but later she cried and cried until she had no strength left for it. She would not take the honey water. Bridei took his turn at holding her and patting her. She seemed to get heavier as the day went on. Her little, hiccupping wails made him want to cry, too, but he did not.

In the early evening, Cinioch came home with a pale-faced young woman who was heavily shawled against the chill outside. Her features were pinched with cold, her nose and eyes were red and she was shivering under her layers of clothing. Nonetheless, as soon as she spotted the infant in Ferat's arms, it was off with cloak and shawl, and three steps across the floor to gather the child to her breast.

"Ah, poor mite, poor bairn," Brenna crooned, and the babe hiccupped weakly in response. "I'll take her off to a quiet corner, if you'll show me where," the young woman added. "Wee thing's starving, but we'll soon put that to rights." And she did; while Bridei was bid to stay in the kitchen when the women went through by the hall fire, he could hear the baby's voice subside through thin wails to a gasping, snuffling, desperate sort of sound to blissful silence. He let out his breath in a great sigh; Ferat, stirring up the soup, was nodding to himself in a satisfied way.

"We'd best get a joint of mutton on the spit," the cook said. "When a woman's in milk she eats like a horse. Your wee one'll do just fine now, lad, see if she doesn't."

IN THE WINTER woods outside Broichan's house, two presences hovered as the short day drew to its close.

"It's done," said the first. "He's taken her in, and nobody's put her back out again. And the crying's over. She's got a big voice for such a scrap of a thing."

"I won the wager," said the other. "I told you they'd keep her."

"Bridei's doing, no doubt. For one of the human kind, that child's canny beyond his years. A wee charm the druid taught him, no doubt . . . They'd never have held on to her otherwise. One look at her must have told them she's ours."

The other glanced across. "In a way she is. In a way she isn't. Now we've discharged our duty to the Shining One, and that's an end of it."

The first being gave a peal of tinkling laughter. "Hardly! This is just the beginning. The two of them have a long road ahead of them, long and hard. And we'll be there every step of the way. We all want the same ending for this, even the druid. Of course, the manner of it may come as a surprise to him."

"Come, let's for home. That was a long night. I tire of these human folk. They can be so foolish; so slow to comprehend."

"The longest night," the first being said gravely. "Night of the full moon; night of change; the start of a great journey."

"Bridei's journey."

"His, and hers, and all of ours. We walk forward to a new age, no less. The feet that make the pathway are small. Let us hope they do not falter. Let us hope they do not fail."

THE MAGIC SEEMED to be holding. Brenna settled into the household as if she belonged there. She was very quiet and always had a sad look in her eyes, not surprising for a widow only nineteen years of age who had just lost her firstborn. Mara refused to share her own sleeping quarters, declaring that she'd no mind to be up half the night when the child woke for feeding. So Ferat had his assistants clear out a little storeroom, and here Brenna unpacked her pitifully few possessions and settled with apparent gratitude. At night the babe slept by her side, not in its original strange bed woven from forest magic, but in a fine cradle of oak wood with sprays of leaves and acorns carved at head and foot. The farmer, Fidich, had surprised them all one morning by appearing with it and offering it rather shyly as his contribution to the small one's upkeep. That was useful for Bridei. When the new cradle came, Mara had muttered something about burning the old one to get the last of its influence out of the household before Broichan returned home. Bridei ensured the basket disappeared while Mara was busy elsewhere. Now it lay in his own chamber, safe within his storage chest, hidden key and all.

Ferat was not well pleased the day he needed spices and could not open his little coffer. He blamed the kitchen lads, at first, for the key's loss, cursing the two of them as he forced the box open with a knife, scratching the wood. The sight of the contents, arrayed in their neat packets and quite undisturbed, calmed his temper miraculously. As a cook, he considered the small collection of nutmeg, cinnamon, cardamom, and fine peppercorns infinitely more precious than the polished box that held it. Grudgingly he acknowledged that maybe the key's disappearance had been an accident of some kind; who would bother to steal it then leave the prize untouched? By the time he'd made his apple pie, he was humming again. Since the babe's arrival he seemed a new man.

"SHE NEEDS A name," Bridei had said on the second day, as they ate supper in the warmth of the hall. Brenna was managing to work through a generous serving of Ferat's special seethed mutton with dumplings, while cradling the infant with one arm. The baby herself was awake, her small features calm, her clear eyes watchful under what had been revealed as a generous thatch of soot-black curls. Even now that she was well fed, there was not a trace of rose in her cheeks; her complexion was milk-pale. Since yesterday she had cried very little; not so surprising, since her main need was for feeding, and Brenna had that well under control. In fact, now that Bridei's little sister was getting all the milk she wanted, she hardly seemed to need him anymore. Bridei knew that he must not be jealous. He sat beside Brenna now on the bench, and from time to time he looked down at the baby and she gazed up at him, and he knew she recognized him and understood the promise he had made by moonlight. Perhaps she did not really need him now, but when she did, he would be there.

"We should give her a name," he said again, and as he spoke there was a name in the back of his mind, one that suited the baby's pallor, her coal-black hair, her look of being very much herself.

"Huh," said Mara, "names, is it now? I know one thing. That's not the kind of child you name after your mother or your grandmother."

"Why not?" asked Bridei.

"Because she's not one of us," Mara said. "Probably she's not ours to name. Got one already, I expect, something outlandish like the folk that put her here. Black Crow protect us," she added hastily, making the sign of ward with her fingers.

Brenna spoke seldom, and mostly to say please and thank you. Her voice was soft, almost apologetic. "What name would you give her, Bridei?" she asked him.

Bridei put a finger to the baby's white cheek; she waved her small hands, and her mouth curved in what might possibly have been a smile.

"Tuala," he said firmly. "That's an old name, from a story. It means princess of the people. Broichan would like that."

"He won't like squalling infants in the house, and him some kind of invalid," Mara said drily. "Princess, is it? Poor little thing, she won't be much of a princess if she stays here with us. Princess of the pigsties, is about all."

"It's a pretty name," Brenna whispered.

"Aye," put in Uven. "It suits her. Leave off, Mara. You know you're as besotted with the mite as the rest of us."

So the foundling got her name, and Broichan's household expanded its number by two, and Bridei, reminded that his foster father had been near death, applied himself in earnest to his studies once again in an effort to ensure Broichan would not be disappointed in his progress, even if he was displeased with the new arrivals. It was hard to practice combat skills without Donal; instead, he helped Fidich around the farm. In the afternoons he perfected his story-telling. This was a time when the infant tended to be awake, and Brenna, who still tired easily after her recent confinement and the death of her own babe, was generally content to leave Tuala with Bridei while she retreated to her tiny chamber for a rest.

He knew quite a lot of tales already, for tales are the foundation of a druid's wisdom, containing as they do layer upon layer of understanding, symbol within symbol, code within code. Every time he told one it seemed to mean something different. For Tuala, Bridei did not choose tales full of battles and gore, nor tales of monsters and wraiths, losses and ancient griefs. He told her funny tales, silly tales, leavened with stories of heroic deeds and dreams come true. When he could remember no more, he made them up as he went along. Tuala was an excellent listener. She grew better and better at keeping quiet and watching with rapt attention as he spoke. Her bright eyes followed the movement of his hands as he illustrated a dramatic event; her small voice contributed here a gurgle, there a squeak. True, there were some tales that sent her to sleep. When that happened, Bridei simply turned his story into a song, which he sang quietly as he rocked the cradle. He was not sure where the song came from, only that it was not a thing Broichan had taught him.

> *Hee-o, wee-o*
> *Spinner come and spinner go*
> *Weave a cobweb fine and thin*
> *Fit to wrap my princess in*
>
> *Hee-o, wee-o*
> *Feather from the blackest crow*
> *Plume of swan all snowy white*
> *Fit to clothe my baby bright*
>
> *Hee-o, wee-o*
> *Frond of elder, birch and yew*
> *Garland woven fresh and fair*
> *Fit to crown my lassie's hair.*

And as she slept, she seemed to smile.

THEY BROUGHT THE druid home on a day when the air was clear and a cold wind whipped down the Glen from the northeast, harrying birds before it. It was at the travelers' backs as they came along the path that skirted the dark lake and wound up through the deceptive pattern of the oaks to Broichan's house. Bridei's stomach was churning with nervousness. He had longed for this day; had, indeed, counted each night with a mark scratched into the stone of his chamber wall, until Broichan and Donal should at last come home. But his anticipation was mixed with fear now. What if his foster father took one look at the baby and decreed she had to go? Nobody in the household ever disobeyed Broichan. They were not afraid, exactly. It was just that the druid was powerful and wise. It was just that he was always right.

Broichan was not looking so powerful today. He was leaning heavily on his staff as he made his way up the track with Donal on one side and a fellow called Enfret on the other. The druid seemed to have shrunk in on himself; he looked neither so tall nor so broad as Bridei had remembered him. And he was pale, almost as pale as Tuala, whose skin carried the gleam of moonbeams. One thing had not changed: Broichan's dark eyes still blazed with ferocious intelligence.

"Welcome home, my lord," Mara said as the travelers came up to the open door. She was smiling, a rare occurrence.

"Welcome, my lord," echoed Ferat, behind her. "It's good to see you on your feet. Donal, Enfret." He nodded at the two of them. Down the track, the other men at arms were walking by a pack horse laden with bundles. "You'll all be glad of a cup of mulled ale and a bite to eat, no doubt," the cook added. "A chill day."

If there was a touch of nervousness in Ferat's tone, it was nothing to the mouth-drying, paralyzing anxiety that was gripping Bridei where he stood by Mara's side. At this moment, the baby was in Brenna's chamber being fed. He prayed that Tuala would not make a noise, not yet; not while his foster father looked so grim and weary. Not until Bridei had managed to collect himself and think of the right things to say.

"Bridei!" A huge grin split Donal's face, and he strode forward to clap his young friend heartily on the shoulder. Bridei grinned back, his woes receding; he could count on one firm ally here, at least. "You've grown apace, lad. See how big and strong he looks, my lord!"

Broichan looked down, dark eyes, white face, long plaited hair. His features bore more lines than before, and were as ever governed by such discipline that there was no telling what was on his mind.

"Bridei," he said gravely. "I am glad to see you well. You have paid good attention to your studies, I am certain."

"Yes, my lord." Since Tuala had come, Bridei had got used to being one of the grown-ups, part of a household focused on the needs and demands of someone smaller. Now, abruptly, he was a child again. "I've done my best."

"I expected no less. Now I will retire to my own quarters awhile. Donal, assist me, will you? No, I don't need anything—" waving away both Ferat and Mara with a touch of irritation that was quite out of character. "Water, perhaps. I'm sure the men will welcome your offers of sustenance; it's been a long journey. Is there still an adequate guard around the perimeters? How many men do you have up by the northern dike?"

They were inside now, Broichan still questioning as he limped toward his private quarters, unable to conceal his need to lean on Donal's arm.

"I'll check all that, my lord," Donal said quietly. "Come, you're home now, and you must rest. Leave these matters to us."

"Rest, rest," the druid muttered bitterly, "I've been doing nothing but rest these two moons past. I can't afford the time. The days are over before there's a chance to put two thoughts together. Long enough, that's all I ask, just long enough . . . a pox on meddlers."

AS BABIES DO, Tuala made her presence known in her own time. There was a brief outburst in the shrill infant voice, a protest soon stilled by Brenna's soft voice saying, "Hush, hush, wee one, it's all right . . ." Not long after, Broichan walked out to the hall, purple shadows like bruises under his eyes, knuckles white where he gripped the staff, and stood there before them all, not saying a thing. From beyond, in the small room where babe and wet-nurse lay, there was now no sound. At the table, Donal and the men who had accompanied him wore their own masks of astonishment. Bridei had been working up to telling them the news, and both Ferat and Mara had been waiting for him to do it, seeing it as his job entirely.

It seemed Broichan was not going to ask the question, so Donal did it for him.

"Tell me that wasn't an infant I just heard," he managed. "Got a little secret you haven't told us about, Mara?" As a joke, it was pretty weak. Nobody so much as half smiled.

Mara was looking at Bridei, and so was Ferat. There was a silence. A moment later Brenna, the child in her arms, her hair in wisps around her flushed face, for she, too, had been sleeping, appeared from the passageway and stopped dead, her eyes widening at the sight of the druid standing tall and grim opposite.

Bridei rose to his feet. "My lord," he said with what confidence he could summon, "this is Brenna. And Tuala. I was going to tell you . . ."

"Bring the child here."

Such was Broichan's tone that Brenna, the charming rose suddenly gone from her cheeks, walked forward without question and proffered the small bundle for his examination. The druid's dark eyes narrowed. From the woolen shawl, Tuala waved a flowerlike hand in a kind of salute and gave a gurgle whose meaning could have been anything. Broichan's mouth tightened. He scrutinized the infant closely, without touching.

"Very well, Bridei," he said eventually, his tone level. "I'll hear this explanation of yours in private. Come." He turned without further ado and limped off. Bridei hastened after him. Behind them, nobody was saying a word.

Broichan's chamber was not the comfortably appointed domain of a wealthy landholder, although he was in fact a man of extensive resources. This room was in keeping with what he truly was: a scholar, a mystic, a philosopher. His discipline, his clarity of mind, his passion for learning, all could be seen in the orderly, uncluttered space that was his private sanctum. The only person who came in here when Broichan was away was Mara. The stone shelves held rows of jars, bottles, crucibles, and flasks, each in its place, each gleaming dully in the light of candles and the flicker of the fire on the small hearth—a concession to his illness, this, for it had ever been Broichan's habit to endure the cold. He constantly tested the mind's control of the body. The pallet was made up with fine woolen blankets and fresh linen, but it was narrow and hard: what meager comforts existed in this quiet space owed more to Mara than to Broichan himself, Bridei knew. There was an oak table and two benches. Scrolls were stored in a frame on the wall, and writing materials, goose quills, ink pots, were set out on their own shelf. A plait of garlic hung by the slitlike window. Dried herbs in bundles dangled here and there, lending a sweet fragrance to the air, and wizened berries in a brass bowl were evidence that Broichan had attempted, already, to begin some work.

Mara might eventually succeed in bullying him into resting, but it wouldn't be easy. The druid's cloak hung neatly on a peg; his boots were set by the hearth, side by side. The chamber was spotless; not a speck of dust could be seen on anything.

Broichan closed the door behind the two of them and went to stand by the table, leaning both hands on it. Bridei stood facing his foster father. He held himself very still; it was something he was good at, even when his heart was threatening to jump into his throat from anxiety, as now. He relaxed his hands. He made his features calm.

"Let me tell you what I see here." Illness had not muted the druid's voice: it rang deep and powerful as an ancient bell. "I see an infant that has no business inside the four walls of any human dwelling; an infant that holds danger in every blink of its fey eyes. I see several stalwarts of my household viewing this infant with expressions of doting indulgence. And I see a young woman who's most certainly not here by my invitation."

"I—"

Broichan raised his hand slightly, and Bridei's words dried up in his mouth. "I'm not finished," the druid said calmly. "I see one more thing: I see my foster son, a boy who promised to be good while I was away; to do as I would wish him to do." His midnight-dark eyes rested on Bridei in terrible question. It became much harder to keep still. It sounded as if Broichan had decided already. Tuala would be gone by dusk, cast out alone into the forest to freeze, to starve. She would cry and cry, and nobody would come. But no. Bridei clenched his hands so tight the nails cut his palms. Concentrate. Remember. *There is learning in everything.* He remained still, breathing slowly as he'd been taught, keeping his gaze steady. And realized, suddenly, that this inquisition was not, in fact, about Tuala or the Good Folk. It was about him. It was not about what he had done, but why he had done it. All he had to do was give the right explanations, the ones that complied with Broichan's way of seeing the world. He could do that. He just had to stay calm, as Broichan himself did, and talk, not like a child, but like a druid.

"My lord," he began, "Tuala—the baby—came here at midnight on the solstice. The moon woke me, shining in my window. I went out and there she was on the doorstep."

The druid frowned. "And where were the other members of my household while you were wandering about the place at night?"

"Asleep, my lord. It was after the ritual."

"I see. Go on."

"I—I thought she was a gift, my lord. A gift for—" not *for me,* however much he felt this to be true, "a gift for all of us. A trust. The Shining One wanted us to take Tuala in: to keep her safe."

"Bridei," Broichan's tone was stern, "don't tell me you are too foolish to recognize what that small creature is. No human infant ever had such eyes, such white skin, nor such a grave and knowing expression. She's not some local girl's by-blow; she's one of the Good Folk."

"Yes, my lord," said Bridei, realizing this was the first time anyone had actually put this into so many words. "She was cold. She would have died out there."

There was a pause. "A human child would certainly not have survived the night," Broichan acknowledged.

"Yes, my lord." Bridei was working hard to echo the druid's calm, detached tone. "I know Tuala came from the Good Folk. They brought her here on purpose. The Shining One woke me up so I would find her. It was meant. We're supposed to keep her." Bridei's voice wobbled a little, despite himself. "Tuala's a very good baby, my lord. She hardly ever cries. And she has nowhere else to go."

"I imagine there was a conveyance of some kind? A basket?"

"Yes, my lord."

"Where is it?" Broichan asked flatly.

Bridei felt a prickling behind his eyes; he clenched his teeth tight together.

"Answer me." The druid's voice was a death knell.

"In my chamber," Bridei whispered.

"Fetch it."

"Yes, my lord."

Bridei did not look at the others, could not look, as he made his way to his own domain and returned with the little forest cradle under his arm. All the same, he saw them, frozen as if carven in stone and all staring at him: Donal with his honest features full of amazement, Enfret and the other men at arms equally surprised, Ferat anxious, Mara grim, and sweet-faced Brenna with the baby in her arms: Tuala, who had become, so quickly, the still center about whom all else turned. She was so small . . .

His feet leaden, Bridei walked back to his foster father's chamber. It was hard to keep control of his thoughts, for his head churned with them. Tuala had nobody else, nobody but him. The others only loved her because of the charm, and as soon as Broichan undid it they would be all too ready to cast her out. Her own folk didn't want her any more than his family seemed to want him—he'd had not a word from them since they sent him here. But at least he had his foster father and Donal and the others. He had a home. Tuala had nothing.

Bridei was at the door now. He could beg, of course; he could weep and plead like the child he was. Weeping would be all too easy; he felt the tears in his eyes now as he looked down at the scrap of woven leaves and grasses in his hands, the strange winter flowers still bright and fresh, the stones of power threaded on the handles. Who could make enough magic to outplay a druid? The key lay hidden at the bottom, the key that was Tuala's only chance of survival. Bridei swallowed. Tears would be a waste of time; pleading was a weak man's strategy. A druid listens to reasoned arguments, to logic, to proof.

Broichan was standing by the small hearth. His expression gave away nothing. "Put it on the table," he said.

Bridei did as he was bid. The basket looked very small; already Tuala had outgrown it. "My lord, may I speak?" he asked.

Broichan's silence seemed to indicate consent.

"I hope you will not undo the charm," Bridei said, fighting to sound confident though his lip was trembling. "I know you think I did the wrong thing. I'm sorry I've made you angry. But I'm not sorry I took Tuala into the house. I'm not sorry I made the charm to keep her safe. I'm sure that was right. I'm really sure."

Broichan sighed. He reached out a hand toward the tiny cradle, tracing the curve of its side without quite touching it. "Bridei," he said after a little, "you are still very young, for all your manner of speech. You know nothing of the ways of men; nothing of the checks and balances we must maintain to keep our land from falling into chaos, strategies that are far more closely concerned with the misguided actions of our own kind than with the machinations of the Good Folk. Beyond the confines of the Glen there is a realm of which you have barely touched the farthest fringe. Your education has scarcely begun, lad. And it's important; it is so important we can afford to let nothing get in the way of it. I cannot spare the time to be ill; my household cannot spare the time for an infant, especially one who carries such a weight of uncertainty on her small shoulders. To harbor the Other is to invite danger, Bridei. It is to invite the unexpected."

Bridei swallowed. "A man must learn to deal with surprises, my lord," he managed. "That's what Donal says. It's important in a fight."

Broichan's lips twitched. "The Good Folk have powers that are a great deal more perilous than a sudden knee in the groin or a well-placed kick to the ankle," he observed. "This girl-child may seem sweet and harmless now. But you cannot know what she will grow into. Her influence could undermine everything I'm striving for—" He broke off, as if he had said more than he intended.

"My lord," Bridei said, "I'll work as hard as I can; I'll learn everything you want me to learn. I'll do whatever you want—"

"Stop right there." Broichan's eyes had a dangerous glint in them. "I don't make bargains with children. Beware your own words, lest they come back to burden you in a time when you have forgotten their solemnity. What if I said I wanted you to burn the cradle and give the key back to its owner? What price your promise then?"

Bridei's face went hot, not with shame but with anger, a helpless fury tangled up with something even worse, the sense that he had truly disappointed his foster father, whose good opinion meant everything to him. Almost everything.

"I will keep my promise," he said, and felt a tear rolling down his cheek, much to his horror. "I don't know what you want me to be, a druid, a warrior, a scholar. But I know I must learn. I'll work as hard as you want me to work; harder, if I can. My lord . . . I want Tuala to stay at Pitnochie. How can it be wrong? The Shining One brought her here."

There was a lengthy silence. Broichan had turned to stare into the fire, his hand resting on the wall beside the hearth. The chamber was quiet. The small basket remained on the table. A feather or two, a fragment of withered leaf had dropped to the polished surface of the oak.

"I could teach Tuala things," Bridei said. "Numbers, stories, songs. I could teach her to ride. In my spare time, of course."

"Of course," Broichan said grimly. He was still looking away. "I don't like this, Bridei. I was not expecting such a homecoming." He turned and moved to seat himself at the table, carefully, as if he were an old man. Bridei saw the gray pallor of his face, the way his hands were clenched as if to hold back pain.

"My lord?"

"Yes, Bridei, what is it? Pour me a little water, will you . . . Thank you, boy."

"You're not going to die, are you? They didn't—?"

A ghost of a smile passed the druid's lips and was gone. "We all die, Bridei. But no, my enemies have not made an end of me just yet. I, too, have made a promise; mine requires of me another fifteen years in this world, twenty perhaps, and I intend to get the best use out of every scrap of time I have. I cannot afford distractions. I do not go out of my way to invite trouble to my hearth, and I don't expect those who share my home to do it either."

"I was doing what the moon bid me," Bridei said. "Letting in a little bit of the wild. Don't you remember, you said it's all joined together, the Glen, the creatures, the growing things? If you hurt one part of it, it all gets weaker. Keeping Tuala safe is a good thing. Good for all of us."

"I've taught you all too well," Broichan muttered. "So, we

bring her up, like an orphaned fox, then set her loose again to wreak havoc?"

"No, my lord. We bring her up, and leave the door open."

Broichan sipped the water Bridei had given him. His brow was furrowed; there were deep grooves from his nose to the corners of his tight-lipped mouth. Unexpectedly, the lips stretched, and he chuckled.

"If I'd wanted to train you as a mystic, Bridei, I'd have sent you to be raised in one of the nemetons, where they'd have done a much better job of drumming the lore into you," he said. "All the same, already you talk like a druid."

Bridei waited. His heart was still thumping, but in a corner of it hope flickered.

"Give me the key," Broichan said abruptly.

There was no predicting what a druid would do. Heart plummeting again, Bridei stepped forward, reached inside the little basket, drew out the key, and dropped it onto Broichan's outstretched palm.

"Now pick up the basket."

Bridei stood by the hearth, cradling the fragile weaving as if it were Tuala herself in his arms. There seemed to be a lot of tears somewhere just behind his eyes, waiting to stream out, to flood his cheeks and demonstrate that he was indeed a child and helpless to prevent the actions of the powerful, even when they were terribly wrong.

"A man does not cry, Bridei," Broichan commented, as if he could read Bridei's mind. His hand was still open, the small key resting there. "At least, not without good reason."

"No, my lord," Bridei whispered. He could see it: not content with burning Tuala's cradle, her heritage, her only link with her kinfolk, Broichan was going to make *him* do it, as a punishment for getting things wrong.

"My joints ache today," Broichan said. "Climb up on the bench, lad. Put the cradle on the top shelf next to the rat skulls. Careful, now. Mara's going to have enough to do keeping me in passable health without any broken bones to attend to. That's it. Now get down."

Bridei obeyed. After all, there would be no burning. But there was still the key. As he watched, Broichan's long fingers curled around the little scrap of iron, and the druid slipped it into the pouch at his belt.

"Very well," said Broichan. "This stays with me from now on, and that means the responsibility is mine and the decisions are mine. If at some time in the future I see fit to send her away, I will do it, Bridei. You will not cross me on this. I have not lived as long as I have, and learned what I have learned, without acquiring a certain level of skill in anticipating the future and in making calculated decisions. My intuition tells me the child presents a threat to us. On the other hand, I suspect it is already too late to get rid of her. Key and basket may have parted company for now. Key might be returned whence it came; basket might be cast in flame. But I very much doubt that either of those actions would cause the folk out there a sudden reversal of their attitudes to the infant. No doubt they took her in, at first, because of the charm you made. But if she has indeed been in the house since Midwinter, I suspect your Tuala has had time to cast spells of her own. If I sent her away I would make a rod for my own back; create a place of discord where it is essential we have a sanctuary for learning. And for healing. My enemies were clever this time. They almost outwitted me. That won't happen again."

"Was it poison?" Bridei asked. For all his incredulous joy that the battle was won, he had not forgotten there was another struggle afoot, one that had nearly cost Broichan his life.

"It was something extremely subtle with nightshade in it. A combination barely perceptible by taste or smell. He thought he was clever. Perhaps he was a little too clever. There are few with the skills and knowledge to make such a draught."

"You know who it was?" Bridei breathed.

"I know enough. I will be watching from now on. Now, I believe I was attempting to meditate when the infant's voice shattered my calm. She has good lungs. The key stays with me, Bridei. Never forget that. Her future is not in your hands, but in mine."

"Yes, my lord. And . . ."

"What is it, lad?"

"Thank you for letting her stay. And—I'm happy you're home. You'll get better now you're back at Pitnochie." He did not attempt to embrace his foster father or offer any other gesture of affection. One simply did not do such things with Broichan. Bridei hoped his words, his face would tell the druid how glad he was that he had not, after all, had to defy his foster father openly. For Bridei knew he could never have cast the basket in the fire; he could never have let them put Tuala out in the snow. He would have fought for her tooth and claw, like a wild animal defending its young. In doing so, he would have gone against every scrap of teaching his foster father had instilled in him.

"Go on, then," was all Broichan said. "Something tells me both of us will have cause to regret this day's work. I hope very much that I'm wrong."

3

CAN'T CATCH ME!" called Tuala, as Pearl whisked away between the gray-white trunks of the birches like a dancing shadow.

All too true, Bridei thought, guiding his pony after her. Blaze had been a gift from Broichan, acquired on Bridei's eleventh birthday. Tuala had immediately claimed Pearl. It had hardly been necessary to teach her to ride. The small girl had a quicksilver lightness, a sense of not-quite-present that she carried with her everywhere. You'd glance away for an instant and look back to find her gone. They were used to it now, all the folk of Broichan's household. Nobody worried about Tuala getting lost or falling into trouble. It was as if she carried her own charms of protection, ones that were on the inside.

All the same, Tuala wore a moon disc around her neck, as

Bridei did. Broichan had insisted on that. These circles of bone, graven with signs that honored the Shining One and called down her blessing, were a solemn token of the household's adherence to the ancient pathways of the ancestors. To wear one was a privilege, a sharing of trust. Folk had been unsurprised when Broichan gave Bridei his own such talisman. The bestowing of a charm on Tuala, whose place in the household was less well defined, had been unexpected. Still, Broichan had his own games to play, subtle games beyond the understanding of ordinary folk, and no doubt he knew what he was doing. Bridei did not think Tuala needed a moon disc, really. It was plain to him that she carried the power and protection of the Shining One within her, had done so ever since that midwinter night when he had found her waiting for him, cradled in swansdown and bathed in moonlight. More than six years had passed since then, but her skin still glowed with that odd, translucent pallor; her eyes still held that grave, clear quietness. If ever the moon had a daughter, Bridei thought, that child would be just like Tuala.

"Come on!" she called from somewhere farther along the path, beneath the shadow of the spring-leaved birches. Bridei touched his heels to Blaze's flanks and set off in pursuit. It was late in the season, a cloudless day, and they were going up to Eagle Scar.

Tuala's natural ability for riding let her dispense with saddle and bridle and cling to her pony as if it were an extension of her own self. But Bridei had worked hard, obedient to his promises. He rode Blaze expertly, and the pony, a handsome bay with a flash of white on his brow, was quick and obedient. They followed the whisk of Pearl's long, silvery tail, the faint rustle of movement, the white face and black hair of the small rider, weaving in and out between the pale-barked trees, climbing the dappled pathways, skirting moss-covered stones and fording shallow streams until they came to the foot of the last steep climb to the top of the Scar. By the time they got there Pearl was nibbling at a tuft of grass by the massive rock wall and Tuala was nowhere to be seen.

It was not necessary to tether the ponies; both knew this

ride well and would not stray. Bridei dismounted and headed on upward. Tuala would be far ahead; she could climb like a squirrel. The top part of Eagle Scar was a vast granite out-crop, perhaps one monumental stone, perhaps many: its chinks and crevices, its secret places were home to a host of creatures. In all the years he'd been coming up here, Bridei had managed to explore only a small part of it. Every time he climbed up, the way seemed slightly different. Perhaps the rock itself played games just as those oaks did around the druid's house. Earth secrets, not to be shared with mortal man: the place was full of them.

He loved to stand at the top of Eagle Scar, where the past lay deep in the bone of the land. The ground was strong un-der him, the long sweep of the Great Glen was spread out be-low him, steep slopes swathed in the purple-green mantle of pines and the lighter scarf of birches, sheltering the long, glinting ribbon of Serpent Lake. In that place he would stand balanced between earth and sky, feeling the heart of the stone beneath his feet and the touch of the wind on his face. He would imagine he was an eagle.

Today, Tuala was there before him, arms outstretched and rotating on the spot, chanting to herself: *"Fortrenn, Fotlaid, Fidach, Fib, Circinn, Caitt, Ce . . . Fortrenn, Fotlaid . . ."* They were the names of the seven sons of Pridne, the an-cient ancestor from whom the Priteni were descended. The seven houses or tribes were named for them. It was not long since Bridei had taught her these; she was making sure she remembered them. She had chosen to stand right on the top-most rock, her feet balanced on a vantage point no bigger than a porridge bowl. Bridei saw her small figure against the pale spring sky, her black hair lifted by the breeze, her eyes full of light. Behind her, on the other side, was the long drop down the steep southerly face of the Scar. Dead Man's Dive, folk called it. It was just as well Tuala had no fear of heights. She turned and turned as if to make the world whirl before her eyes.

"Stop it, Tuala," Bridei said mildly. "You're making me dizzy." He hauled himself up onto the flat rocks just below her.

She halted instantly, as he had known she would; stood quite still, perfectly balanced, grave and steady. It was Bridei who felt the churning anxiety, the reeling loss of equilibrium.

"What are you doing, anyway?" he asked her with practiced calm. "Trying to fly?"

Tuala stepped down from her pinnacle and seated herself at his side, cross-legged. She wore a long tunic of plain woolen cloth and trousers beneath it for riding. The trousers had once been Bridei's; it was hard to imagine that he had ever been so small.

"I would like to fly," Tuala said. "Sometimes I think I could."

Bridei was unpacking the food he had brought: thick wedges of oaten bread and eggs boiled in the shell. He passed the water-skin to Tuala. "If you're planning to try," he said, "it might be better to stand on a bench or a barrel, not a mountaintop."

Tuala gazed at him solemnly. "I wouldn't just *fall*," she told him. "At least, I don't think so."

"You're a girl, not a bird," Bridei said.

"I am a bird sometimes." She moved a small, white hand to tuck her hair behind her ear.

"What do you mean?"

"In dreams. The moon comes up, and it wakes me, and I fly out through the forest. Everything silver; everything alive and waiting."

Bridei did not answer. It was a long time since Tuala had come to Pitnochie, so long that sometimes he came close to forgetting that she was—different. Then she would say something like this, and his memory would bring it all back.

"Swooping, snatching, feeding," Tuala said absently, taking a bite of the bread. "Gliding, hunting. Then the moon goes down, and the darkness comes again."

"Dreams are different." It wasn't much of an answer, and Bridei knew it. "You should be more careful. Just think if you fell down and—and broke your leg. You wouldn't be able to ride Pearl all summer." He would not tell her more than one man had died in a sudden descent from Eagle Scar.

She was still only a baby compared with himself. "Promise me you'll be sensible, Tuala."

"I promise."

The answer came readily; unfortunately, Bridei thought, Tuala's idea of what sensible meant was somewhat different from his own.

"What would you be?" Tuala asked him.

"What do you mean?"

"What bird would you be, if you could?"

"An eagle," Bridei said straight away. "I'd glide the length of the Great Glen, looking down over everything, watching it all, guarding it all. You'd have to be a crow, with hair that color."

Tuala shook her head. "An owl," she corrected gravely.

"You know they sick up pellets of all the bones and claws and beaks, don't you? All the tails and whiskers and—"

Tuala gave him a shove, not very hard. "I'm eating," she said. "Anyway, what about eagles stealing new lambs? They even took someone's baby once, Mara told me."

"It's all part of the balance," Bridei said. "Some give up their lives so others can survive. As long as you respect that, everything makes sense."

They ate awhile without talking, listening instead to the wild sounds of the Glen: the calling of birds high overhead, the cheeping and chirping of others in the woodland, the soughing of trees in the wind, the furtive rustle of something stirring in a rock crevice. Farther off there was a more domestic noise, Fidich calling the dogs, and a barking response. The farmer was checking ewes up on the fells.

"You know something, Tuala?" Bridei passed over the egg he had peeled for her and started on another. "Back when I was little like you, I wouldn't have been allowed to come up here by myself. Broichan wouldn't have let me."

"I'm not by myself," Tuala said. "I've got you."

"Yes, well, I didn't have you then, nor any big brothers to look after me."

Tuala opened her mouth. Bridei knew she was about to tell him she could look after herself, thank you very much.

"But it wasn't because of that," he went on quickly. "It

was dangerous in the woods back then. There were enemies. They tried to kill me once. And they tried to kill Broichan. Back then, I wasn't allowed out without two guards."

"How did they try to kill you?" Tuala's eyes were round now, her neat mouth very solemn.

Bridei began to regret starting this topic of conversation. "Oh, it was nothing much," he said, carefully offhand. "Maybe we should be going back—"

"With a sword? With a spell? Did they try to catch you in a trap?"

"With an arrow," Bridei said.

"Did you kill them?"

"No. But Donal did. I don't want to talk about it."

"Why did they try to kill you?"

"I don't know. Nobody would tell me. Anyway, it's all right now. That was a long time ago. Whatever the danger was, it's past. There used to be five guards just for the dike on the northern side and now there's only one. And we're allowed out. So count yourself lucky."

Tuala regarded him carefully. "You are lucky," she corrected. "Or you would be dead, and I wouldn't be here."

Bridei shivered. "It wasn't luck that saved me that day," he said, remembering. "It was something else."

"Donal?"

"He certainly helped. But there was more. It was as if the earth opened up and let me hide: gave me shelter. Even Donal said it was odd."

"She holds you safe," Tuala said in her small, clear voice. "Safe in her hand. Safe to go on."

Her words made the hair on the back of Bridei's neck prickle. He gathered the eggshells together in a neat pile, saying nothing.

"It's all right, Bridei," Tuala said, as if she were the big one and he the child.

Back at the house, Bridei led the two ponies around to the stables and tended to Blaze, while Tuala made a passable job of rubbing Pearl down. She had to stand on tiptoe to reach the top of the pony's mane; fortunately, Pearl seemed to understand this, and lowered her head obligingly while the child took a brush to the tangles.

"Pity she can't do the same for you," Bridei commented, eyeing Tuala's wind-blown locks. When they set out for the ride her dark hair had been plaited neatly down her back, but it seemed to have a life of its own. The number of ribbons she lost was a standing joke.

Tuala raised both hands to push the unruly mop back from her face.

"Want me to fix it?" Bridei asked.

Tuala came over to stand by him, her back turned. She fished in the pouch at her belt, brought out a small comb, put it in Bridei's hand. No words were necessary; this was a ritual of long standing.

"Keep still now." Bridei had a deft hand for this task, having practiced on ponies. He knew how to comb out Tuala's hair without pulling at all. As for the child, she stood completely still, almost as if she were frozen; it was a pose he himself had striven for through the control of breathing, through meditation, through sheer force of will, yet Tuala could manage it without even trying. His fingers worked systematically, weaving the long braid that hung down to her waist.

"Got a ribbon?" he asked, smiling.

Tuala shook her head, expression mournful. "I lost it."

"Just as well I've got one, then." He reached into his pocket and drew out a length of yellow braid, one of several he had put away for just such occasions. Tuala left them everywhere. He tied the ribbon in a neat, strong knot finished with a little bow like a butterfly. "There you are. Better try to stay tidy for a bit, in case Broichan sees you."

"Yes, Bridei."

SINCE THE TIME when Broichan went to a king's council and nearly died, there had been some changes at Pitnochie. A sizeable complement of men at arms still dwelt there, patrolling the borders and providing an escort for the druid whenever he traveled abroad. But there were fewer of them and more other folk now. Brenna had stayed; her sweet temper and natural quietness provided an excellent balance to volatile Ferat and dour Mara. Fidich became a frequent visitor to the house, standing awkwardly in the kitchen and chatting to whomever might be close at hand about shearing or milking or laying drystone walls. It was quite out of character, for the farmer had ever been one to retire to his small cottage when the day's work was done, apparently happiest in his own company. Donal noted, drily, that Fidich's visits generally included a brief talk with Brenna, a few words only, such as a hope that she was keeping well, and the exchange of the day's small news.

It had taken a long time for Brenna to lose the sad look in her eyes. Tuala had helped; the demands of a small infant had left the young widow little opportunity for dwelling on her own troubles. Of recent times it was increasingly evident that Fidich's visits had the effect of bringing out the rose in Brenna's cheeks. Both were awkward and shy. Perhaps, in time, it would come to something.

There was another new presence in the house. Not long after Broichan came home still sick from poisoning, Bridei had entered the hall one night at suppertime to find the two old men, Erip and Wid, ensconced in a corner ruminating over a game board, just as they had been the very first night he'd come to Pitnochie. He'd greeted them with astonishment.

"I thought you were never coming back!"

Erip, the plump, bald one, had given a chuckle even as he moved a small warrior subtly on the board, eliciting a hiss of annoyance from tall, white-bearded Wid.

"Who, us?" Erip had retorted. "It'd take more than a king's druid to keep us away, lad. Been traveling, that's all. Well, you've certainly grown apace. What's Ferat been feeding you, bull's—" The old man had broken off, perhaps catching Mara's eye from across the room. "Ah well, no matter. We're here to help with your education, Bridei."

"Oh." Bridei had wondered what aspects of his education they were equipped to deal with beyond board games and drinking.

Wid's fingers had hovered above a little priestess of soapstone. "Erip's expertise is geography," he'd said. "Territories, coastlines, tribes, and chieftains. My field is strategy:

seeing into men's minds; knowing what they want before they know it themselves. I hope you're prepared to work hard, Bridei." He'd plucked the priestess from the board, set her down in another spot, and raised his brows at Erip, expression carefully bland.

"A pox on retired battle-leaders," Erip had muttered, taking a long look at the board, then lifting his hands in helpless capitulation. "They're always three steps ahead."

Erip and Wid had settled in as if they'd never left. Now, six years later, the two of them were still lodged down at the end of the men's quarters and growing ever fatter on Ferat's cooking. And they had indeed proved they had a great deal more to teach than how to get into trouble.

There was, in truth, very little in the way of spare time. Lessons commenced just after breakfast and continued until the sun went down; that was not counting the nighttime vigils that were part of Broichan's teaching, nor the occasional dawn rituals, nor the study and preparation required in Bridei's own time. *Own time* was a joke, really. Some evenings after supper, all he could manage was Tuala's bedtime story before he himself fell asleep exhausted. But he never neglected it. The tales were part of the promise he had made her long ago. Bridei knew what it was to lie in bed in the dark, waiting for sleep to come, without a story to keep you company and follow you into your dreams. For him there had been many such nights, and he had grown used to it. But he swore to himself that Tuala should never have to endure that feeling of being utterly alone.

In the mornings he would work with Erip, then Wid. Increasingly, as Bridei's knowledge of the realm of Fortriu, its mountains and glens, its lakes and streams, its bays and islands developed, the two old men taught him together, their lectures growing into heated three-way discussions, for they encouraged Bridei's own contributions. From Erip he learned the history of the Priteni, the patterns of kingship, the nature of neighbor and enemy. The folk of the north were descended from the seven sons of the original ancestor, Pridne. It was from him that the name Priteni came, a name that embraced all the inhabitants of Fortriu, the folk of Circinn to the south, and in the untracked places of the far north, the wild tribe known as the Caitt. On the islands beyond that northern shore dwelt a people that called itself simply the Folk. The Folk, too, were of Priteni blood, and were powerful by virtue of isolation, with their own king and their own governance.

Fortriu and Circinn had once been a single kingdom, united in its adherence to the old gods, strong and secure. That had changed the last time a king was elected, for the voting chieftains had been unable to reach agreement on a candidate. Now the kingdom was split, with the Christian Drust son of Girom, known as the Boar, ruling the southern realm of Circinn and their own king, Drust the Bull, maintaining the old traditions in Fortriu, which extended the length of the Great Glen from the king's fortress of Caer Pridne in the northeast to the last line of defense against the Gaels in the southwest. Between these two realms and their kings there was a constant, simmering unrest.

Wid's lessons dealt with power games and councils, the reading of a man's expressions and gestures, the things that might or might not be said in certain company. They dealt with the passing on of secret messages and with learning to listen for what was carefully not being said. Those skills were hard to try out here at Pitnochie. It was all too easy to guess what Fidich, for instance, was thinking as he clutched a beaker of ale and pretended not to be looking at Brenna, or what Donal was dreaming of as he polished his sword and whistled an old marching song under his breath.

"I need to practice this," Bridei protested. "We talk all the time of assemblies and kings' councils, but all I ever get to see is the house and the farm. How am I ever going to learn properly if I'm shut away here all my life?" Such a complaint was unusual for him; he had ever been obedient to those he respected. It had been a long morning of theory.

"All your life?" Wid queried, brows raised. "An old man of—what, just twelve? I think you'll find there will be opportunities soon enough. If Broichan's not ready to let you travel, he may be prepared to bring a bit of the world to you. Perhaps not yet, but soon. Be patient. He has his reasons."

"Wid?" queried Bridei.

"Yes, lad?"

"I was just thinking. What will I become when all this is done? When my education is finished? A scholar? A councilor? Shouldn't I be learning about my own folk in Gwynedd? I suppose I will go back to my father's court some day."

"Maybe," Wid said with a little smile. He had been asked these questions before, but never so directly. "We'll touch further on Gwynedd and on Powys, its neighbor, and on other faraway lands. For you, Fortriu is more important. And a man's education is never finished. You should know that by now."

"But I am not one of the Priteni," Bridei pointed out. "I don't mean to be disrespectful. I love learning the lore and history of the north. But—"

"Your mother was from here," Wid said quietly.

"My mother!" Bridei was startled; he had not thought about her for a long time. "She was from Fortriu? Then I might have family here, aunts and uncles, cousins maybe. Why didn't Broichan tell me? What do you know about her?"

"Very little," Wid said, beginning to tidy up his scrolls. "Her name was Anfreda. That's about all I can tell you. Don't you remember?"

Bridei was silent a little. After a while, he said, "I was only four when I came here. I don't remember any of them really. Perhaps my father, a bit. Not the others."

"Mm. Broichan could tell you more."

"He won't talk about her. I don't think he knows."

"Ah, well," said Wid, "all things in good time. Shall we go in search of some dinner?"

❧

AFTER THE MORNING'S lessons it was time for Donal's tuition. Bridei had become competent with sword and staff, efficient with knives, adept at detecting covert pursuit and evading it effectively. He had honed his skills in archery until all that separated him from Donal himself was the need to use a smaller bow. He had learned, over the course of a summer's chilly ventures into the dark waters of Serpent Lake, to swim well enough to get himself to shore should he be out sailing and suffer some kind of mishap. He was able to row a small boat. Once he grew out of Pearl and moved up to Blaze, he learned how to take his pony over jumps, how to lean sideways from the saddle and snatch a bundle up from the ground and how to throw a spear into a target while galloping past. Donal's were good sorts of lessons; time went all too swiftly while he was doing them. He did wish that he could practice fighting with someone closer to his own size, but the settlement remained forbidden. Both Donal and Broichan said it was still unsafe.

Sometimes Donal finished the lesson early, and there was a little time before the final, most testing part of the day's learning: Bridei's session with his foster father. Those snatched times were precious. Tuala would be waiting for him, standing still and quiet under the oaks at the edge of the sward where Donal and Bridei practiced swordsmanship, or perched on a stone wall near the stables watching while they rehearsed maneuvers with knife or staff. She would take him to see some funny-looking mushrooms she had found, or tell him a bit of gossip she'd heard from Brenna, or demonstrate how she'd taught one of the dogs to chase after a ball. Or Bridei would tell her some of what he'd learned in the morning: kings and tribes, battles and journeys. Then, all too soon, it would be time for him to go to Broichan. Those were lessons Tuala could not watch. They took place in the druid's own quarters now, and she was forbidden entry there.

"Broichan doesn't like me," she said to Bridei one day as they sat under the oaks together, watching Fidich chop wood down by the stables. It was not a complaint so much as a simple statement of fact.

"He's just not used to children," Bridei told her. "He doesn't know how to talk to you, that's all. It'll get better as you grow up."

"What about you?"

"What do you mean?"

"He is used to children. You've been here since you were little. He talks to you, and teaches you, and lets you in his special room."

"He didn't let me in when I was your size. You just need to give him time."

Tuala shook her head. "He doesn't like me. Or he would let me have lessons, too. Brenna says all I need to learn is sewing and cooking. But I want to learn what you're learning: all about the world."

Bridei bit back the obvious riposte: *you're a girl.* Though plainly true, it did not seem at all the right response for Tuala. In his wildest imagination he could not see her sewing and cooking. "I'll teach you as much as I can," he told her.

Tuala twisted a stalk of grass between her small, white hands. "Can you teach me scrying?"

Bridei felt suddenly chill, though he was not sure why. "What do you know about scrying?" he asked her.

"I know Broichan does it with his bronze mirror. I know wise women and druids do it. You can see what's going to happen. And what happened before. I'd like to try that. I think I could do it." There was an odd note in her voice.

"Why, Tuala?" Bridei thought he could guess what the answer would be.

She bowed her head; the curtains of glossy dark hair fell forward, almost concealing her small face. "So I can see them," she whispered.

"Them?"

"The ones who left me here. My family. I think I might see them."

Bridei's heart twisted. "We are your family now," he said gently.

"*You* are," Tuala agreed, raising sorrowful eyes to meet his. "But Broichan isn't. He doesn't want me here."

"Did he say—?"

"He doesn't need to say. Bridei, will you teach me?"

"How can I? He keeps his special mirror locked away, and—well, I'm pretty sure he wouldn't want me to. It's a secret sort of study, you need lots and lots of preparation for it, and it can be dangerous if you get it wrong. *He* could teach you, but I don't think I could. I've only tried it a couple of times and I didn't do it very well. Broichan said it didn't matter. It's the other lessons that count more for me."

Tuala was silent for a little. Her fingers were weaving the grass into a minuscule basket. Then she said, "This one counts for me. I'll have to teach myself."

Bridei frowned. "Be careful. I told you, it's dangerous, like all the magical arts. Anyway, you don't have a mirror."

"I expect I can find one," she said, and tucked the tiny basket down between the roots of the great oak. "You'll be late for your lesson."

All the way back to the house he could feel her watching him, although she had remained where she was, under the trees. He worried about Tuala sometimes. One moment she was off through the woods like a little wild thing and the next she was sounding like someone's grandmother. Still, she was only six. With luck, by tomorrow she'd have seized on a new interest and forgotten all about being a seer.

Broichan was waiting for him. "You've been running," the druid observed.

Bridei worked hard at slowing his breathing. He would not apologize. Because he had run, he was not, in fact, late. He did not wish to be drawn into a discussion of how he should be spending his free time. "Yes, my lord," he said after a moment, his voice quite steady and not at all breathless.

"Sit down," Broichan said.

Bridei sat on the bench opposite his foster father with the breadth of the oak table between them. The table held a scattering of birch rods, each carved with its own particular marking. Bridei was careful not to disturb them. This was a pattern of augury.

"Tell me what you see here." Broichan's voice was deep and resonant, a sound full of both mystery and authority. The face was calm as always, the dark eyes hooded, the braided hair falling across his shoulders. There were gray threads in the plaited locks now.

Bridei studied the birch rods. He'd begun to learn these signs very early; by his first summer at Pitnochie he'd been familiar with their basic meanings, and now he understood there were as many ways of putting together their wisdom as there were stars in the sky. A skilled interpreter was not merely seeking to ascertain a meaning, but to select what was relevant amongst myriad meanings.

"Are you looking for an answer to a particular question?" he asked Broichan, examining the lie of the rods, the places where they intersected and which had fallen above or below the others. Of course, the person who had cast them down was the one best fitted to understand the pattern of their falling; no doubt Broichan had already completed his own interpretation.

The druid gave a nod. "The question I asked was complex. The answer, in its turn, is many-branched. Because you will see it in more simple terms, you may be able to provide a clearer resolution. It was a question about leaders and loyalties. A deep question about Fortriu itself."

Bridei thought awhile, letting the small sticks of birch go in and out of focus, making himself see what lay beyond the incised pattern of line and symbol that marked their pale surfaces. "I see two creatures here," he said, "bull and boar, each with its own kind behind it. Enemies are coming from the west and the south, attacking them both and trying to come between them. But there's one rod, here, that joins the two. The eagle. It holds them together, bridging the gap. And see here, a half-hidden one, underneath. The shadow."

"And?"

"One unexpected move, and many would fall: boar and bull and eagle all together."

"Leaving only the shadow," said Broichan gravely. "And alone, the shadow can achieve nothing. Thank you, Bridei; you may gather the rods back into their bag now, and while you do so, let's test the efficacy of your tutors' lessons in history. The symbolism here is obvious. Let us say it reflects the years to come, the next ten years, perhaps, or fifteen. How would you interpret this picture of bulls and boars?"

"The bull must be our own king, Drust son of Wdrost, for the bull is his kin-token; Erip tells me the stones that circle his great fortress are full of such images. The boar is Drust son of Girom, monarch of Circinn. That means the two tribes shown in the augury are the two kingdoms of the Priteni: we of Fortriu, who follow the true faith of our ancestors, and the southerners, the Christians."

"Beset by enemies, all of us," mused Broichan. "Yes, even a child could see that. Circinn's hard put to defend its borders against barbarian rabble from the south. As for us, we face wave upon wave of Gaels bent on seizing every last crag, glen, lake, and streamlet we have to call our own. And yet we are a strong people, Bridei. An enduring people. What meaning do you place on that one link, the eagle, bridging the gap so tenuously? The chieftains of the Priteni have minds of their own and their kings are equally stubborn. To unite bull and boar seems to me as unlikely as yoking a pair of wild stags and expecting them to work as a team."

The birch rods were packed away now, secure in their kidskin bag. Bridei fastened the leather cord around them and placed the bag on its shelf. Higher up, a tiny cradle, withered and faded, still lay in the shadows. He sat with chin in hand, thinking hard. Any answer given to Broichan must be well considered, or one might as well say nothing at all.

"I think," Bridei said, "that the eagle is the most important of all for Fortriu. It would be a good symbol for a king, better than bull or boar, although both of those are very strong in their ways. The eagle flies high above everything: he passes over the whole of the Great Glen, and beyond the Glen to the western isles, and northward to the lands of the Caitt, and southeast to Circinn. He can fly over the realms where both kings rule; his clear vision shows him that the land is not split tribe by tribe, but is one whole, strong and indivisible. Or should be. I don't wish to sound disloyal to King Drust, of course."

"No," said Broichan mildly, "and if you were in other company, I know you would choose not to express such ideas as these. No doubt Wid has cautioned you of the dangers of being misinterpreted. Here at Pitnochie, amongst trusted friends, you can speak your mind freely. And your sentiments are admirable, Bridei. We would all wish to see the Priteni united, as they were before the scourge of the new religion swept across the south and poisoned the mind of Drust the Boar. Now, of course, we have two kings, two realms, and two faiths. This has weakened us greatly. All your talk of eagles does not alter the fact that this schism has shattered our capacity to resist armed incursions. The Gaels have made themselves at home in the west; they breed a new generation in the settlements where our grandfathers dwelled, and their boots trample our hallowed ground. Each time they mount an attack they step a little farther in. Could we withstand another major offensive? I doubt it. You saw the shadow of their cruelty in the Vale of the Fallen, Bridei. We cannot allow them the freedom of the Glen; we cannot permit a repetition of that mindless slaughter of good men, that pollution of our heartland. Unfortunately our own kings show a marked reluctance to invite each other to the council table. How can they? One is loyal to the ancient tenets of Fortriu; the other is a traitor to his blood-deep faith."

"About the eagle," said Bridei, "it means more than what I said. Those men who died, the ones I saw in the Dark Mirror—that day, you said they never stopped believing in Fortriu even when they knew they were all going to die. I think that's what the eagle is, and that's what the link is in the augury: the spark inside each of us that makes us part of the land. It's what we get from our ancestors, what we give to our children. It makes us strong even when we're losing. It makes us kin whether we belong to north or south, whatever faith we adhere to. Maybe if everyone remembered that, we could stand firm against the invaders, if they come again. That day at the Vale of the Fallen, I didn't really understand. I was only a child."

"In years, yes," Broichan said, regarding Bridei with an odd expression. "As you are still. Most men would view you as a child, even now."

Bridei felt his cheeks flush. He said nothing.

"Your interpretation of the augury, however, is that of a man," his foster father said. "The sticking point, of course, lies in religion. If our land ever falls to an invader it will be because that weakling in Circinn opened his borders to missionaries preaching the doctrine of the cross. If we give way to that, Bridei, perhaps we deserve to fall. If we turn our backs on the wisdom of our ancestors, do we merit survival?"

"My lord, you do not believe our people would do that, surely?" Bridei protested. "Set aside Bone Mother and the Shining One, and the wisdom that governs every choice we make in our lives? Here in the north we are strong in our faith. Drust the Bull would never do as the other king did and let his people abandon the old ways. Erip even said he—" He broke off.

"Erip even said what?"

"That King Drust still observes the sacrifice at Gateway. In the Well of Shades. He said that while the wise women go down to the shore to keep Bone Mother's vigil, the king makes an offering to the Nameless One, the darkest power of all, that dwells beyond and beneath the Otherworld. A sacrifice made in living flesh."

"Erip said that, did he?"

"He hinted at it. And Wid told him such things were best not spoken aloud, even in the company of trusted friends."

"Both Erip and Wid were right. You should put this from your mind for now. You'll have other matters to occupy you soon enough. We're having visitors for Midsummer."

"AND SO," BRIDEI told Tuala some days later, "I have to put everything I've learned into practice." It was evening, and they were sitting in a shadowy corner of the hall, trying to be unobtrusive so nobody would order Tuala off to bed. "Every single thing," he went on. "These people who are coming are the sort of folk you meet at court: clever, subtle, tricky. Often what they really want from you isn't what they say they want at all. Often what they say isn't what they mean. Interesting people. People who know a lot about the world. Broichan says it's a chance for me to try out what he and Erip and Wid have taught me."

"A test," said Tuala, nodding her small head sagely. "A trial."

Bridei frowned. "I wouldn't say that. They're Broichan's friends, as far as I can tell. More of an opportunity."

"A test," Tuala repeated, not to be shaken.

"Well, maybe. It'll be good to have some new faces here."

Tuala did not reply. She had been increasingly quiet these last few days. There had been no solitary excursions into the woods to discover hidden wildflowers or a thrush's nest or a scattering of spotted toadstools. Now that Bridei thought

about it, since the news that there would be visitors to Pitnochie, Tuala had been spending most of her time close to
the house or yard, waiting for him like a small, silent
shadow.

"Is everything all right?" he asked her now, realizing how
caught up he had been in the excitement of anticipation.

Tuala nodded, saying nothing. She was hugging her arms
around herself, as if to keep out a chill. Her eyes took on the
faraway expression they sometimes had, as if they held secrets an ordinary boy could never hope to share.

"Are you sure?"

Another nod.

"You should tell me if something's troubling you," he
said, unconvinced.

"I will, Bridei." The voice was very small and rather remote.

"You're tired out. Look at those big bags under your eyes.
How about a story, and then you can go off to bed?" Tuala
slept now in the tiny chamber that had once been Brenna's,
and before that a storeroom. Mara had relented in time and
now shared her quarters with Brenna quite willingly, another
of the surprising changes that had occurred in the pattern of
things at Pitnochie since that midwinter night.

"Yes, please." Tuala snuggled closer, leaning against him,
resting her dark head against the sleeve of his tunic.

"All right, then," Bridei said. "Don't go to sleep before
I'm finished, mind."

"No, Bridei." The little voice was warmer now; nonetheless, there was something in the way her arm wrapped itself
around his, like a vine clinging for purchase to its tree, that
made him uneasy.

"What story do you want?"

"How you found me in the moonlight," she whispered.

"Again?" He had told this so many times over it had become a ritual.

"Mm."

"Once upon a time there was a boy . . ."

". . . called Bridei . . ."

". . . who thought he was all alone. His life was not so bad,
really; he had a place to sleep, and enough to eat, and he was

getting an education. But there was something missing. Bridei wasn't even sure what it was."

". . . a family . . ."

"Yes, but he didn't know that, not until later. Bridei was a good boy. He did his lessons, he worked hard, he tried to please everyone. Then, on the night of the winter solstice, everything changed."

"The moon came in his window."

"Yes, the Shining One woke him up, and he went outside, even though it was so cold . . ."

". . . so cold even the owl was hiding away . . ."

". . . so cold the Urisk's tears turned to ice the moment they fell from his eyes . . ."

". . . so cold the trees were shivering . . ."

". . . so cold that Bridei's ears and nose began to ache the moment he poked his head outside the door; cold enough to freeze your toes off, if you were silly enough to go out barefoot, which was what Bridei did. When he looked down to check if his toes were still there, he saw what the moon had brought him."

"A baby."

"That's right; a strange little baby, all wrinkled and ugly like an old apple . . ."

"I was not!"

Bridei grinned. "Just checking if you were listening properly. No, it was a nice baby, the sort of infant you'd expect the Shining One to leave you as a gift for Midwinter. She was in a funny little cradle made out of all the things of the forest: tufts of grass and skeleton leaves . . ."

". . . crow feathers, owl feathers . . ."

". . . a twist of ivy and a sprig of goldenwood . . ."

". . . green berries and cobwebs . . ."

". . . and stones with holes in them, threaded on rushes . . ."

"Bridei?"

"Mm?"

"Where is the cradle now?" She had never asked this before.

"It was stored away somewhere," he told her, not wanting to lie, but reluctant to give the full truth. He had never told her about the key, nor the spell he had made to win her a home. "It might have crumbled away by now; after all, that was more than six years ago."

Tuala nodded. "Go on," she said.

"So Bridei took the basket, and the baby in it, and brought them inside."

"Because it was too cold out on the doorstep."

"Much too cold. He kept the baby warm until the others woke up, and then Brenna came, and the baby had a home. And Bridei wasn't alone anymore."

"He had a family," Tuala said through a wide yawn.

"Yes," agreed Bridei, "and now it's bedtime. I'll see you in the morning. Sweet dreams, Tuala."

She detached herself from his arm and stood up, rubbing her eyes.

"Go on," he said. "You're asleep on your feet."

"What if it had been cloudy that night?" she asked suddenly. "You would never have found me."

"But it wasn't cloudy."

"Yes, but it might have been."

"Then whoever put you on the doorstep wouldn't have put you there."

"They didn't care. They would have let me freeze all up, like the birds that fall out of the trees in winter."

"They did care," he said, looking her straight in the eye. Her expression was alarmingly bleak; it was not a look that sat well on the face of a little child. "That's why they gave you to me to look after. Because they knew they could trust me to do a good job of it. And part of that's making sure you get enough sleep. Come on, I'll walk through with you."

MIDSUMMER WOULD BE a night of full moon. It was an auspicious conjunction. As the festival drew closer, Broichan's household began yet another metamorphosis. The anticipated guests were four: three men and a woman. As personal friends of the druid, they could not be asked to lodge communally with the men at arms. The earth-walled barn was cleaned as well as could be managed—there were still mice—and the men shifted their bedding out there, leaving their quarters for the male visitors. Erip and Wid pleaded creaky joints and troublesome backs and were granted dispensation from moving. And Bridei, to his delight, was allocated a spot in a corner of the barn next to Donal. His small chamber would be turned over to the visiting wise woman, whose name was Fola. Those who knew of her by reputation whispered of *Fola the Fierce,* but never in Broichan's hearing.

In the kitchen, ever a busy realm, the pace now quickened further. Ferat wished the offerings of his table to reflect Broichan's standing as a senior druid and landholder of considerable importance. Trout were brought up from the lake to be smoked, cheeses were retrieved from the storage caves, blood sausages were mixed and hung in bladders, and the carcass of a prime steer jointed and salted away. Puddings were planned; the spice box grew lighter.

In preparation for the visit all of Bridei's teachers were applying pressure. Where there had once been time, most days, for a walk, a game, an exchange of news, now there was no time for anything but study, meals, and sleep.

Tuala watched and listened. She was good at making herself unobtrusive, at blending into the shadows as if she were really somewhere else entirely. She stood under the oaks as Bridei and Donal battled with staves. Donal's tattooed features and leather cap gave him a ferocious look, but Bridei, his soft brown hair fastened back in a disciplined plait, his blue eyes narrow and intent, was giving his tutor a real challenge. He nearly managed to topple Donal with a clever sweep of the staff at knee level, but Donal sprang away at the last moment, blocking the blow with a counterswing. Bridei rocked in place, fighting for secure footing and, in a moment, finding it. Master and student clasped hands, grinning. The bout was over, but Tuala did not stir. Today there would be no time to talk to Bridei; tomorrow there would be no time. Nor the day after, nor the day after that. Broichan would call for his foster son straight away and keep him busy until suppertime. It was on purpose. It was to stop her from telling Bridei she was going away. It wasn't fair. Broichan should know that she would not tell; it was he who had made her promise. There was no need to rob her of these little gifts of time. There was no need to steal her one treasure.

Tuala was not afraid of very much. She loved all creatures, even the mice in the barn and the small, scuttling insects in the thatch. She had no fear of spiders or bats and only a natural wariness of more dangerous animals such as wolves, snakes, or wild boar. But Broichan filled her with a terror that was deep in the bone, a numbing, chill feeling that turned her mute and helpless whenever the druid looked at her. Tuala thought nothing of heading off alone for long excursions through the woods. She could climb the tallest tree, scramble up the steepest rock face; she was used to walking on small, confident feet across the walled field that housed the horned stud bull. The dogs were Tuala's devoted friends, and she was a favorite with the men at arms. Mara tolerated her; Brenna tended with firm kindness to her small needs. Ferat was a reliable source of honey cakes although, as the cook said, Tuala ate barely enough to keep a wren alive.

Broichan was different. It wasn't as if he spoke to her much. Most of the time he acted as if she were not there. But she could feel his dislike; she could sense that he did not trust her. She could feel his power, and that made her afraid as nothing else could.

He had called her in some time ago, when the talk of visitors first began. Brenna had brought her, after a hurried replaiting of the tousled hair and a whisking of a damp cloth over the small, pale face. It was the first time Tuala had been inside the druid's private quarters. The room was full of interesting things, but the hammering of her heart meant she could not look at them properly. Bridei had gone out riding with Donal and would be away all day. She wished Bridei were there.

Brenna was standing quietly, hands behind her back. Tuala edged closer to the young woman's skirts, pretending she was invisible. The druid was standing by the hearth, tall, so tall in his night-black robe. His eyes were dark as sloes and his mouth was pressed thin, as if he were angry or in pain. Tuala had seen Donal tighten up his lips like that, the time Lucky kicked him by accident and raised a lump like an egg on his shin. There were candles set about the chamber; they made the bottles on the shelves glow mysteriously, half revealing contents that might be pallid snakes, or a wrinkled little form with a goblin face, or layer on layer of fat, green slugs. There were stoppered stone pots and iron implements and beakers of baked clay. The place smelled of pungent herbs. Tuala began to count numbers in her head to keep the terror at bay. She could count up to fifty now: Bridei had taught her.

"... family farther down the Glen?" Broichan had been saying something, but Tuala had missed most of it.

"Yes, my lord," Brenna said, sounding a little flustered. "My mother and my aunt—Cinioch's mother, that is—live at Oak Ridge, where the track branches up to the Five Sisters."

"An isolated spot," Broichan commented. "So much the better."

Tuala was watching his hands; the fingers were long and bony, and there was a silver ring on one of them with a snake's head on it, with pale green eyes. She blinked at the snake, and thought it blinked back.

"How is the child progressing?" The druid's eyes were suddenly on Tuala, piercing, searching; she pressed herself back against Brenna, but there was no escaping that gaze, and she would not look away. That would be like giving up. She must be brave, as Bridei would be.

"She's a good child, my lord." Brenna seemed unworried by the question; she moved Tuala away from her a little, made her stand alone for inspection. "She's very quiet. Never a nuisance. Everyone likes her."

"Hmm," mused Broichan. "Nonetheless, she is what she is. Easily visible; visibly different. At such times as this, a distraction we cannot afford."

"With the visitors, my lord?" Brenna had reached out to take Tuala's hand now; her warm grasp was comforting. "I can keep her well out of the way while they're here. She can sleep in with us, Mara and me—"

Broichan silenced her with a raised hand. "It is not the disturbance of my guests that principally concerns me. It's the disruption to Bridei."

Outrage flooded Tuala's heart. Whatever a disruption was,

it sounded bad, and she would never do anything bad to Bridei. He was her family. "I wouldn't—" she began, and clamped her mouth shut at the look on Broichan's face.

The druid spoke to Brenna as if the two of them were alone in the chamber. "You will take leave from the household until the dark moon after Midsummer. You'll take the child on a visit to your mother. Ferat will arrange a basket of food from the household, a gift for your family—no need to thank me, you've earned it. I want the child confined to the environs of your mother's house and her presence there kept quiet. We don't want all sorts of tales up and down the Glen. I know I can rely on your discretion, Brenna. I understand there's some talk of a betrothal in the near future?"

Brenna's fair cheeks flushed scarlet. "Yes, my lord," she murmured. "Fidich was planning to speak to you after it's all over, the visit, I mean . . ."

"Then there's a certain amount riding on your compliance with my instructions. If all goes to plan, I can see you well settled, with some additions to the comforts of Fidich's cottage, which are somewhat slight at best. If not . . ." He left this unfinished. "I'm sure you understand the need for caution in this matter."

"I do, my lord," Brenna said. "For Tuala's own sake as much as anything. When did you want us to go?"

The druid frowned. "Unfortunately, Cinioch can't be freed to escort you until closer to the feast day, but as soon as I can manage without him you'll leave. Mara knows my intentions in this, as do Ferat and Donal. It's not to go any further as yet. Do you understand me?"

"Yes, my lord," Brenna said. "But—"

"But what? The instruction is clear enough, surely."

"My lord, the two of them are very close. Tuala and Bridei. You don't tell one of them a bit of news without the other knowing within a day."

Broichan's mouth settled in a grim line again. "There's one priority in this household," he said, "and that is Bridei's education. What occurs at Midsummer is critical to his future. There can be no distractions. You will go, and the child will go, and once you are on your way I will inform the boy of your absence. How he deals with the news will be a test in itself, a test of his maturity. Prior to your departure nothing's to be said. Do you understand?"

"Yes, my lord," Brenna said. "I won't breathe a word, I promise. But—"

"You may go now." Broichan turned his back abruptly to stand staring at the cold hearth.

"Yes, my lord." Tuala could hear the relief in Brenna's voice; hand in hand, they moved to the door. Her own heart had not quieted. What she had understood was wrong, all wrong. She was being sent away and she was not allowed to tell Bridei. How could that be? She always told him everything.

"Leave the child here."

Startled by the sudden command, Brenna dropped Tuala's hand and, after a moment, bent to tuck a wayward curl behind the child's ear and whisper, "Be good," before vanishing all too quickly out the door, closing it behind her.

The chamber seemed all at once much bigger and much darker. The tall form of the druid loomed over Tuala like a shadow, like a wraith, like a fell sorcerer from one of Bridei's tales. She could see the snake ring staring at her; its forked tongue was flickering in and out. She waited, hands behind her back so he would not see them shaking. After what seemed a very long time, Broichan turned toward her once more and came to seat himself on the bench nearby. She did not have to look up quite so far to meet his eyes. The druid's grim expression had not changed.

"Speak up," he said. "Do you understand any of what I've been talking about?"

Tuala's mouth went abruptly dry; her tongue felt swollen and strange. She could not summon a single word. And she badly needed to use the privy, but there was no way she could ask him for leave. She managed a nod.

"Tell me."

"I—I—" She just didn't seem to be able to speak. It was like a spell, a muteness charm come over her at the worst possible moment.

Broichan sighed. "Black Crow protect me from infants," he said. "Come now. I've heard you chattering often enough. I know you can speak sense and I know you can understand.

Let me set this out for you simply. You're going away, and if you are obedient to my wishes and do as Brenna tells you, then you may be, I stress may be, allowed to return to this house when the Midsummer visit is over. Ah, I see you do comprehend that; your eyes show it clearly. And it seems to matter to you. Of course, you view this as your home; there's no other household the length and breadth of Fortriu would have taken you in."

"Yes, my lord." Her voice came out as a whisper, the sound of a breeze in dry grasses.

"Do you understand about Bridei's education?"

A nod.

"I don't think you do, not fully. My foster son cannot afford the encumbrance of little girls taking up his time and distracting his mind from the very real and very taxing path of preparation that lies before him. Increasingly, Bridei will be with other folk, either here at Pitnochie or elsewhere. If I believe at any stage that you are likely to get in his way, I will ensure your removal from my household on a swift and permanent basis. Is that understood?"

She was quivering all over now, gripped by something so strong she could barely contain it: anger or terror, maybe both. "Yes," she said, for although she had not fully grasped the words, their meaning had lodged itself painfully in her heart.

"You are nothing to Bridei," Broichan said. "His kindness won you safety for a time. That's all it amounts to."

She took a huge breath, clenched her fists behind her back. "Bridei is my family." Her voice sounded very small in the big chamber. "I don't tell lies to my family."

Broichan shook his head gravely. "That is incorrect. If you have any family, they dwell out there, deep in the forest. Bridei is a good-hearted boy who took pity on you as he would on an orphaned lamb. He's no kin to you."

"He's no kin to *you*!" Tuala burst out, hurt robbing her of caution.

Broichan waited a moment before speaking. "He is my foster son," he said levelly. "Entrusted to me for reasons of which you can have no conception whatever."

This had to be answered. "And I was entrusted to him,"

Tuala whispered. He had better stop this soon and let her go or she would disgrace herself and leave a puddle on his floor, and then he really would believe she was an infant.

Broichan's eyes narrowed.

"The moon left me here," Tuala said. "Showed them the way, when they brought me. The moon woke Bridei up and helped him find me. The Shining One trusted him to look after me. I am his family. I *am*." She bit her lip, fighting tears.

"Listen to me, Tuala." It was the first time Broichan had used her name; she'd been starting to wonder if he had forgotten it. "Do you understand the word *destiny*?"

She nodded.

"Tell me what it means."

"It's in the tales," Tuala said. "The ones Bridei tells me at bedtime. Destiny is the big things that happen. Battles and voyages, marriages and kingdoms. Fighting dragons. Finding treasure. Uncovering secrets."

Broichan regarded her gravely; his eyes had lost some of their ferocity as she spoke. "I see Bridei has been assiduous in your education," he said. His long hands were clasped in his lap now; Tuala saw the little silver snake lift its flat head, looking at her.

"I would like more education," she ventured, encouraged by the fact that she had apparently managed to answer a question to his satisfaction. "About the stars and the tribes and all the things Bridei is learning. He can't teach me everything, he's too busy."

The druid's lips tightened. "For you, too much learning can only lead to unhappiness," he said. "Whatever life awaits you, there can be no place in it for knowledge such as this. You'd best apply yourself to the domestic arts and hope for a good marriage. That can be arranged, when the time comes."

Tuala was silent. Somewhere in his words was a terrible insult, but she could not untangle exactly what it was. The feeling of hurt, however, was unmistakable.

"Tuala," the druid said, "come closer. Sit by me, here. You wonder, I suppose, why I speak of destiny. Child, you see Bridei as your friend, your playmate, for all he is in so many ways a young man, even at twelve years old, and you a mere babe. It is not a bad thing for a boy to feel compassion for the weak. Up to a point. It is a fine thing for a lad to be obedient to the ancient ways, to comply willingly with what he sees as a request from the Shining One. However, don't think you've remained at Pitnochie because of Bridei's wish that the household should give you shelter. You are here solely because, for now, I have chosen not to send you away. You are not one of us, and you never can be. Your fate rests entirely in my hands, Tuala. Never forget that. In my plans for the future, the only one who counts is Bridei. If you think you owe him a debt, if you want him to live his life in the best way possible, then you will do exactly as I tell you. Bridei has a destiny. It is up to me to ensure he is raised correctly; that nothing, and nobody, gets in the way of the future laid down for him."

Tuala swallowed. "Then why am I still here?" she croaked, feeling bitterness lodge in her throat, making her speak when silence would surely be far safer. "If I'm so bad for him, why did you let me stay at all?"

"You're not listening," Broichan said. "There was a duty involved: the boy's duty to the gods, as he saw it. In all such decisions one weighs the arguments and reaches a balance. I do not dismiss my foster son's tale of how you came here; of the involvement of the Shining One. I accept his conviction that he carries some kind of obligation. Indeed, it would be dangerous to disregard that. All that you need to understand is that if you're fond of the boy and want him to achieve all that he can, you will comply with my instructions. And my instructions, this time, are that you go away with Brenna for a while, and that you do not speak to Bridei of this. You do not raise any of these issues with him. He'll come to a complete understanding of it all in due time."

The little snake was moving across Broichan's hand now; he did not seem to have noticed. The serpent was hissing, the miniature forked tongue extended from the tiny gaping mouth. Tuala placed her own open hand next to the druid's much larger one and the serpent flowed across to coil itself neatly on her palm, green eyes gazing up at her. It felt heavy for its size and carried the warmth of the druid's body in its own. Tuala would have smiled at its grace, its self-contained perfection of form, but for the feeling like a cold stone lodged in her heart.

Broichan was looking at the snake now. His expression showed no surprise, but he said, "This, alone, demonstrates with startling clarity your Otherness. You have grown up amongst us, have believed yourself accepted, no doubt. But this is a druid's household, child. What occurs here is no reflection of the conduct or attitudes of the world of men. As you grow older this will become ever clearer to you. It is very possible that Bridei, innocent as he was, did you no favors in taking you in that night. His act of compassion cut you off effectively from both worlds: the realm of your true kin, beyond the margin, and the world of mortal folk where you can never belong. In fact, his desire to provide you with shelter robbed you of any true home."

"Oh, no!" Tuala sprang to her feet, and the little snake, startled, twined itself around her wrist, clinging. "Bridei would never do anything to hurt me! He would never do anything bad, he couldn't!"

Broichan regarded her. He reached out a hand toward hers and the serpent moved again, gliding to his finger, circling around, forming itself back into a silver ring. The green enamel eyes stared, unwinking, at Tuala's small, quivering form. "And you would never do anything to hurt him," the druid said calmly. "You would not do anything to stand in his way, would you, Tuala? Do my bidding, then. Now and in the future. It is best for Bridei thus; best for all of us."

Tuala stared at him in silence. For a little he had seemed almost friendly, like someone she could talk to, someone who would have interesting things to tell her. Now, abruptly, he was his old self again, and she felt as if she had been somehow tricked. Her fear returned, robbing her of speech.

"I need your promise," Broichan said.

"Yes." The word felt as if it were squeezed out of her, despite her efforts to keep it in. "I will go if you want. And I won't tell Bridei."

"Good. You have no choice, in fact."

"But I won't lie to him," Tuala said, unable to help herself. "I don't tell lies. Not to Bridei."

Broichan smiled thinly. "Then you must be extremely

careful of your words," he said. "You know what will happen if you make an error, Tuala. Believe me, I do not possess my foster son's degree of compassion. If I see an enemy, in whatever fair guise, I strike immediately and effectively before my foe has time to inflict any damage. Bridei has yet to learn the necessity of that."

Tuala felt cold. He seemed to be saying she was bad; that she should not be Bridei's friend. That was wrong. It was so wrong she could not understand how anyone could think it. Bridei was her best person in all the world. Hadn't the Shining One herself sent Tuala here to be his family? She looked into Broichan's hooded eyes and a shiver ran through her. "I'm not an enemy," she whispered.

"Not yet," said Broichan.

4

ALTHOUGH HE KNEW it was unlikely, Bridei found himself anticipating an arrival such as occurred in the old tales, the guests riding up to Pitnochie in their rich clothes with men at arms and attendants and pack horses laden with belongings. He thought of banners, of gleaming weaponry, of silks and finery.

In the event, the four of them came severally, their arrivals days apart, and each with its own unique style. Donal had been testing Bridei's skills in tracking, and had kept him out in the forest four days in a row from sunup to dusk. By the time the two of them returned to the house, legs aching with weariness and stomachs growling, Tuala was nowhere to be seen; long asleep, no doubt, and the opportunity for a story lost. It was probably just as well. Bridei doubted he could find the energy for the least tale. He'd have been asleep himself before the princess so much as glanced at the frog. A quick bite to eat and straight to bed was all he could manage; he was asleep before his head hit the straw pallet set beside

Donal's in the barn. Next morning the guests began to arrive at Pitnochie.

There was no grand appearance. What Broichan did, he did discreetly, with an eye to the protection of his privacy and the preservation of his own interests. First to come was a spare, wiry-looking man of middle years, with cropped, graying hair and a face on which responsibility had set many lines. His eyes, nonetheless, were full of life, keen with intelligence. The eyes were gray like the hair, and so was the man's woolen robe: so much for silks and furs. He rode in with a pair of attendants, big, solid fellows, and all the baggage he brought was a couple of bundles tied behind his guards' saddles. All three men were well armed; expensively armed. Bridei knew enough by now to recognize a good sword when he saw one and to appreciate a finely honed axe blade. Since the two guards were housed in the barn with Broichan's men at arms, there was plenty of opportunity for comparison. The nobleman's name was Aniel, and he was a councillor in the king's household: Drust the Bull, that was, king of Fortriu. Bridei knew he should not ask too many questions, but it was hard to hold them back. There was so much he wanted to know.

At suppertime there was talk of the Gaels and the threat in the west. Bridei had studied this in considerable detail with his tutors; he had made maps in sand, with stones and twigs for markers, had imagined armies deployed up and down the Glen, had learned the nature of this enemy and the history of their destructive forays. The picture he bore in his mind, however, owed little to scholarship. Since he had seen their image in the Dark Mirror, Bridei had known them, not as a foe to be challenged and dealt with as one would any local raider, but as the force that sought to extinguish the spark in the heart of every loyal son of Fortriu. They were strong, cruel, and entirely without scruples. That long-ago day in the Vale of the Fallen they had killed wounded men, fleeing men, had mowed them down without mercy. The knowledge Bridei had been given in that place he would never forget.

Tuala was absent from supper and so was Brenna. Bridei observed this without surprise; Broichan considered Tuala too young to sit at table in such company, no doubt, and had sent her off to bed early with Brenna to keep her quiet. It was a pity, really. Tuala would have liked to listen, for Aniel was full of knowledge of the world and Tuala loved to learn about things. She would miss this, and she would miss her bedtime story yet again.

Broichan was at the head of the table. On his right hand was Aniel, and on his left Bridei, a challenging placement, since it meant every time Bridei glanced up from his meat he looked straight into those shrewd gray eyes. It was clear to him that he was being assessed, and he had the feeling this was going to happen four times over before the visit was concluded. Aniel's two guards stood behind him, and one of them took a mouthful of each dish before his master ate. It was as well Ferat was occupied in the kitchen; he would have been deeply offended. As for Broichan, he merely raised his brows at this sign of distrust. Bridei remembered that his foster father had nearly died of poisoning once, and at a friend's table. One had to accept that there were risks everywhere.

Next at the board were Erip and Wid, and below them Donal, Uven, and the rest of the men. Mara had taken pity on Ferat and, poker-faced, was helping carry platters in and out.

"I was fortunate to get here in time," Aniel was saying. "My mission to Circinn was long and arduous, and the challenges were not all in the woeful state of the tracks nor in the vagaries of the weather. Those I have learned to expect and to deal with. It was the manner of my reception and the pig-headedness of my hosts that dragged it out. I'm not looking forward to my return to Caer Pridne, I have to say. A brief sojourn at Pitnochie is most welcome. I'm hoping to replenish my strength before I convey the bad news to the king."

"So, Drust the Boar was immovable?" Wid asked through a mouthful of bread.

Aniel gave a wry smile. "Inflexible, yes, but not through any great strength of will. The man's councillors do him a great disservice; they poison his mind with their false reporting, and thus ensure he stands firmly in the way of any reconciliation among our people. He relies on the guidance of weasels. Perhaps, in his heart, there's still a spark of true kingship, but he lacks the strength to nurture it himself, and so his advisers are able to twist the making of decisions to suit their own ends. It is no wonder the Christian faith has taken strong root in Circinn. The court is corrupt, the king vacillates, what wise women he had are banished, his druids dismissed. If any observance of the rituals still exists in that realm, and I have reason to believe it has not been entirely suppressed, then its observances are covert, secret."

"Still, it does survive," Wid said, extricating a scrap of meat from his beard. "Where a single coal glows beneath the ash, the right breeze can fan it to a flame."

"One must ensure the fire does not go out completely," Erip put in.

"As to that," said Broichan, who had been silent for most of the meal, "there are certain strategies in place, as we know. A man watching here, another listening there. Folk who can traverse difficult terrain quickly and pass messages accurately. I'd like more. An ally in the Boar's own household would be useful."

"A spy in the stronghold of the Christian missionaries could be handy," ventured Donal. "Find out how they work, how they infiltrate and just who their friends are. Most of the clerics come from Erin, I've heard. I'd like to know if they have allies in Dalriada. We'd be squeezed on both sides, that way."

"Would the king in Circinn press for peace with the Gaels?" Bridei asked, unable to keep silent any longer.

Aniel regarded him. "Broichan assures me that we speak freely here in a way that would be unthinkable outside the home of an old and trusted friend," he said. "I wish very much that I could answer your question with an unequivocal no, Bridei. Drust the Boar has not governed Circinn as it deserves. A man who abandons the faith of his ancestors and lets his people turn their backs on all that is right is quite simply not to be trusted, whether he be a king or no."

"Yet, unfortunately, we need him," Broichan said. "At least, we need his fighting men. The chieftains of Circinn may have betrayed their oaths to the Flamekeeper, but they haven't forgotten the importance of maintaining their complements of well-trained warriors. They must do that; their own southern borders are far from secure. Britons here, Angles there, every man and his dog wants a bite of our land, so it seems. To mount a full offensive against Dalriada our own king needs not just the forces of the north, but those of Circinn as well."

"Indeed," said Aniel, folding his hands on the table before him. "I discussed that delicate issue with Drust the Boar, or attempted to. I see little possibility of winning him over at this stage. The atmosphere was less than cordial. He does need to deploy a considerable force on his southern border, I acknowledge that. All the same, I had hoped he might be prepared to begin planning for the future."

"One had hoped for an agreement to a joint council, at least," Broichan said.

"I did my best."

"Nobody doubts that, my friend," said the druid. "The king sent you because you were his strongest chance of influencing Circinn. That even your efforts could not secure their agreement is a sign of the desperate state of affairs."

"If the Gaels decide to make a move this season, next season, we'll be hard pressed to do more than hold a certain line," Donal said sourly, "and it may not be the line we want. I'd like to see a well-planned offensive, not merely a scrambled reaction to what they throw at us. It sticks in the craw to know our own kind won't lift a finger to help us."

"We all want the Gaels gone," observed Aniel. "To drive Gabhran and his forces back across the sea to Erin, that is a mighty challenge, a goal to aspire to. It will not be quickly achieved, not with our own land so bitterly divided. To drive out the Christian faith and win back the hearts of the folk of Circinn to the true way, that is perhaps still more of a challenge. Until the lands of the Priteni are united once again, I do not think that will be possible."

There was a pause. It seemed to Bridei that he could almost hear people thinking.

"My lord?" he ventured.

"Yes, lad?" Aniel's gray gaze was very sharp. Like Broichan, he was a man on whom one could ill afford to waste words.

"I just wondered—if the south won't help us in the struggle against Dalriada, perhaps we could seek other allies. That would enable us—enable the king—to begin planning for the future, at least."

"What allies did you have in mind? Reliable friends are few and far between these days, as no doubt your tutors have informed you."

"Yes, my lord." Bridei had debated this particular issue at length with Erip and Wid, and not got particularly far. "There's the tribe of the Light Isles, those that call themselves simply the Folk. They are strong in battle, so I'm told, and kin of our own people. They could be called in. I know we haven't always been allies, but their cooperation could be secured with hostages. And—" He hesitated.

"Go on, boy."

"And there's the Caitt," Bridei said, hoping the king's councillor would not snort with derision.

Aniel's brows lifted. "One might as well attempt to control an army of wildcats," he commented. "The ancient name they bear is an accurate reflection of their true nature. Who in his right mind would volunteer to cross that border as an emissary? He'd like as not be sent back in several pieces, and there'd be no message of thanks attached."

"All the same," Bridei said, glad that Aniel had not laughed at him, "they are of our own kind, steeped in the ancient ways of sun and moon, and they are fighters, we know that much. Fierce and dedicated fighters. Nobody seems to be threatening *their* borders. Perhaps, wildcats or not, they have something to teach us."

"That's an appealing argument," Aniel said. "But false. It's the nature of their territory that keeps the Caitt secure from invasion. Beside the crags and chasms of the northwest, the Great Glen looks like easy pasture land."

"Besides," put in Wid, "as I've already told Bridei, the Caitt are as divided as we are. Having no incursions to whet their teeth on, they war amongst themselves, princeling against princeling, chieftain against chieftain, tribe against tribe. It would take a phenomenal sort of leader to pull that into a coherent fighting force. A leader such as, unfortunately, we don't have."

"Could not King Drust the Bull do it?" queried Bridei. In the ensuing silence he realized he had asked one question too many.

"It's late," Broichan said to his visitor, "and you've had a long journey. We might speak privately over a jug of mead, perhaps, and then you'll want to retire."

Aniel ignored this completely. "Do you play games, Bridei?" he asked. "Crow-corners, maybe, or breach-the-wall?"

"Yes, my lord."

"Good. We have time for a game before bed, if my host here will allow it." The clever eyes met the druid's for a moment and Broichan inclined his head in consent. Under the rules of hospitality he could hardly do otherwise. "Nothing like a test of the wits to finish off the day," Aniel added, rising to his feet. "It will be good practice for you to meet a different opponent, one who will stretch you. If you wish, of course."

For a moment Bridei hesitated, imagining Tuala awake, alone and restless, missing her story. She'd not been herself lately; something was worrying her, something she would not tell. That bothered Bridei, for they did not keep secrets from each other. Broichan was watching him. Broichan, he thought, knew him all too well. And this was indeed a test. During this whole visit, every word he uttered would be weighed, every decision he made measured. Why, he did not know. He only knew it was important, so important he could not afford one false move.

"I'd be honored to give you a game, my lord." Bridei moved to fetch the inlaid board and set it on a small table while Erip produced the bone playing pieces and Donal and Uven moved stools into place. The meal over, the men at arms, in ones and twos, were retreating through the kitchen to their temporary haven in the barn. Donal remained, seated on the bench by the wall, and Broichan settled himself in the shadows near the hearth. A discreet distance behind Aniel, one of his guards remained watchful.

The game was long. As it progressed past early forays to more serious maneuvers involving the loss of flag-bearer, champion, and priest, it became clear to Bridei that however ably he might have defeated Erip or Wid in the past, and there was no doubt the two of them were expert strategists, he was going to need a great deal more subtlety and cunning to vanquish the king's councillor. Despite his clammy palms and, at times, thumping heart, Bridei was enjoying the struggle. But Tuala's pale face and shadowed eyes were still in his mind. He had promised that he would be there to tell her a story every night. She was almost certainly asleep. Of course she would not be lying awake waiting; it was past midnight. He had to concentrate . . .

"Ah," said Aniel softly. "If I move *thus,* and *thus*—I think your chieftain is trapped. And he no longer has his druid to conjure a way out."

By this stage Bridei had Erip at one shoulder and Wid at the other, whispering helpful suggestions. Broichan had neither moved nor spoken.

Concentrate. The position looked hopeless: his druid captured and most of his tiny men at arms knocked from the board. His chieftain stood proudly alone, the height of a man's little finger and near-surrounded by Aniel's bone warriors. In the far corners of the board the wise women, his and the enemy's, looked on. The wise women were embodiments of the goddess, the Shining One . . . the Shining One, maker of pathways, finder of futures . . .

"An untenable situation," Aniel said. "It's quite acceptable to concede defeat, Bridei. You play very ably, and you are, after all, barely into your thirteenth year, or so Broichan tells me. I expect it's well after your bedtime."

This was an insult, although kindly expressed. You had to let insults flow over you. That was one of Donal's lessons. When an opponent in battle shouted things like *son of a slack-bellied sow* and *blue-faced savage,* you couldn't let it put you off or there'd be a spear in your belly before you could snap your fingers. You had to let it pass you by and get on with things. Which meant, in Donal's case, yelling something in return such as *carrot-haired wife-beater,* and getting in first with the spear.

So, look at the board closely, and think about the wise women. There was his own, small and grave in her hooded robe of carven bone, moon-white. There, almost opposite her but not quite, stood Aniel's, identical save for the color, for one set of pieces had a mellow tinge, a touch of earthen gold-brown about the bone of their origin. Erip and Wid had fallen completely silent.

Bridei moved his wise woman forward into the path of the other. Erip sucked in his breath; Wid made a little hissing sound.

"A sacrificial move," observed Aniel. "Are you sure?"

The Shining One, opener of pathways. "I don't move unless I'm sure," Bridei said.

"It grieves me to do this." Aniel picked up his own playing piece and shifted her forward to knock Bridei's little priestess off the board. "At times this game appears quite disrespectful to the gods. Let us hope they take it in good humor. We are done, I think."

"Not quite," Bridei said, reaching to move an insignificant piece, a forgotten foot-soldier, one square to the left. "I think your chieftain is unable to escape now."

Aniel narrowed his eyes. Erip and Wid leaned closer. It was true. Whatever move the king's councillor made, there could be but one outcome: Bridei's chieftain would take his opponent's wise woman from the board and, in the next move, his lowly spear-holder would account for Aniel's chieftain, winning the game. Bridei hoped very much that Aniel would not be offended; that Broichan would not be annoyed. Judging by their grins, Erip and Wid were beside themselves with glee.

A frown appeared on Aniel's composed features, adding to the many weary lines his brow already bore. He stared at the board, as any true player does at the moment of defeat, searching to make sure that he has not somehow missed the one factor that may still allow him to triumph. Aniel looked back at Bridei and, a moment later, began to chuckle.

"Don't look so desperate, boy, I'm not about to bite your head off. I have been beaten in living memory, but not by a lad of your age, I must confess. You did well, very well. I must be wearier than I thought. Tell me, what made you see that? It was an unusual move; legal, of course, but well outside the conventional flow of the game."

"Erip and Wid taught me how to play. I learned all the

moves from them." Bridei gave his old tutors a glance of acknowledgment, as was only respectful and proper. "Sometimes I do think beyond that teaching. I mean, it's not just a game on a board, is it? It's like the real world only smaller: warriors, leaders, and goddesses, and the things that happen in the real world can give you strategies for play. Or the other way around. I just remembered the Shining One is the illuminator of pathways and the bearer of unexpected gifts, and then I saw the move in my mind, that was all. Thank you for the game, my lord."

"The pleasure was all mine," Aniel said smoothly. "I'll play you again when you're fifteen. If I practice every day I should be able to beat you by then. Come, my friend," rising and addressing the silent Broichan, "let's have that quiet word and then, most definitely, sleep. That's a promising lad you have there."

"Yes," said Broichan.

THE NEXT DAY Donal scheduled archery for first thing in the morning, and Bridei had no time to look for Tuala as he had intended, to apologize for missing her story again. The archery lesson turned into a contest, for one of Aniel's guards had quite a reputation with the bow and wanted to prove himself against whoever was willing. When he got word of what they were doing, Ferat sent breakfast down in covered baskets: fresh barley bread, honey in a crock, and cold slices of last night's roasted mutton. The kitchen servants made a second trip to bring ale. Nobody could complain about the hospitality.

Some of the men were absent, of course, for the guard must always be maintained on the perimeters of Pitnochie, but most were there and keen to join in. They set up targets and shot in pairs. One by one the losers were eliminated. As the competition progressed, the targets became smaller and more difficult. The crowd of onlookers grew larger as more men failed the test; it also grew louder as excitement built. Aniel's man, Breth, was exceptionally skillful. He was a tall, broad-shouldered fellow, a man in his prime, and watching him ready himself, draw his great yew bow, sight, and shoot was a beautiful thing, like seeing a wild creature take its prey or a sailing boat make a true course before the wind. Thus far, he had not missed a single mark. Nor had Donal, nor Enfret, nor Bridei.

Fidich, enticed away from his farm duties, was setting the targets. Erip and Wid had ventured out to watch; the men at arms had found them empty barrels to sit on, but the old scholars were leaping to their feet and yelling like everyone else each time a shot met the mark. Somewhat later both Aniel and Broichan, shadowed by the councillor's other bodyguard, came out to look from a distance. Bridei glanced up toward the oaks, to the place where Tuala should be sitting, the place where she always sat to watch when he and Donal were working here in the yard by the stables. She wasn't there, and it worried him.

"Your turn, Bridei," Enfret said.

This time the target was a pine cone set on the dike at the far end of the southern walled field, a distance of three hundred paces. It was just as well all the sheep were up on the fells for summer grazing.

Bridei set an arrow to the bow, drew, sighted, narrowing his eyes, and released the string. A whirr, a small whacking sound, and the cone was gone from the wall.

"Well done, lad," Breth said. "Wish I could claim to be your teacher. Of course, it's a smaller bow and easier to draw."

"It's a smaller bow and less powerful," observed Donal levelly. "Were you using a full-sized weapon at his age?"

"He can't remember." Enfret grinned. "Too long ago."

"Last stage of the contest should be men only," Breth said. "I didn't come here to be matched against children. Men only, same size of weapon, only fair."

"Scared the boy will beat you with his child's bow?" queried Uven. "Go on, give the lad a chance."

Fidich was fixing a new target, a glinting silver spoon hung by a string from the lower branches of a solitary oak. The sun caught the glittering metal, flashing its light into the eyes of the archer. A rising breeze made the thing dance like a will o' the wisp.

Breth shot first and severed the string, which was the desired result. The spoon fell to lodge itself between the oak roots. They all applauded, even Donal; it was an exceptionally clever shot. Fidich tied the spoon up again.

Enfret shot next and missed, his arrow lodging itself, shuddering, in the trunk of the great tree. The archer muttered under his breath; not a curse, Bridei could hear, but an apology. One did not lightly meddle with the powers of an oak.

Donal shot next. The arrow made the silver spoon spin on its cord, but did not release it. "Up to you, Bridei," he said.

Bridei was fairly sure he could do it. Then there would be another target, and another, and at some point either he would humiliate Breth by winning, or Breth would be the victor and himself a gallant loser, his youth canceling out any taint of failure. Actually, it wasn't very fair. He glanced up the hill to the place where Broichan, pale in his black robe, stood watching by Aniel's side. It was possible, Bridei thought, that in this particular contest winning was not the right thing to do. Breth was a visitor, a guest; he was a skilled man with a reputation to consider. To lose publicly, with his fellow guard and Aniel as witnesses, would cause him deep shame. Was that worth a momentary satisfaction for himself? Besides, Breth had been right. Bridei's bow was much easier to draw. On the other hand, telling lies was a bad thing, and losing on purpose was a bit like telling lies. Tuala would know what was right. Even at six, she had a gift for putting simple truth into a few well chosen words. But Tuala was not here. The place under her favorite tree was quite empty.

Bridei drew his bow. The breeze, obliging him, had died down; the target was almost stationary. Everyone had fallen silent. Bridei glanced at Donal, hoping for some kind of hint. Donal's lips twitched in a little smile. He shook his head so subtly nobody else would have seen it. It might have meant *better shoot wide*. It might equally well have been merely *this is your problem, don't ask me for advice*. That didn't matter. Bridei knew what was right. You didn't gain men's loyalty, you didn't influence them to do the right things themselves by making them look weak in front of their friends. It was good to win sometimes, but not good to win all the time. You had to learn which contests were vital and which could be sacrificed for a greater good. Bridei sighted, the hanging silver like a scrap of moonlight against the dark foliage of the oak, and released the string.

His arrow struck the spoon with a small metallic sound and fell to the earth beneath the tree. The wind got up again almost immediately, making the target near-invisible amidst the rustling leaves. It was just possible to discern that the string was intact.

"Oh, bad luck, Bridei!" That was Erip. "So close!"

Donal, who was well aware of the rules of hospitality, was first to congratulate Breth and to suggest some of them might follow up archery with swordplay or wrestling another day. Others clustered around, clapping the visitor on the back and offering their own words of praise. Breth was grinning now, pride salvaged, clasping a hand here, exchanging a joke there. It had been a good contest. And the boy had done remarkably well, considering. A real little archer in the making. Donal had done a fine job with him.

When the others were gone, Bridei and Donal began gathering arrows and dismantling the various targets.

"Bridei?" Donal asked.

"What?"

"Would you ever shoot less ably than your talents allowed you to do?"

Bridei had had time to work out his answer to this, knowing it would be asked of him sooner or later. Donal knew him too well to have misinterpreted that failed shot. "Would you ever encourage a student of yours to get something wrong?" he asked.

"It depends," Donal said.

"That's my answer, too."

"It could be the difference between life and death one day," the warrior observed. "Yours, not the other fellow's."

"If it was a matter of life and death, I would make certain I didn't miss," Bridei said. "But if it was just a matter of pride, I'd weigh everything in the balance. Then I'd choose what to do."

"Mm," Donal said, pulling an arrow out of the ground and

adding it to the ones he was carrying. "I couldn't have done what you did today. Don't have it in me."

"You didn't have to. You missed anyway," said Bridei, grinning.

Donal's smile was more of a grimace. "Wait till that fellow Breth sees what I can do with a staff. Won't know what hit him. Now go on; lessons don't stop just because there's a king's councillor in the house. I expect those two old rascals are lying in wait for you somewhere with a dose of obscure history. Off you go."

"Donal?"

"What?"

"Have you seen Tuala, these last couple of days? We've been busy, I know, but she wasn't there at dinner last night, nor the night before, and nor was Brenna. And she's not here this morning."

"As to that," Donal said after a moment, "the lassie's left Pitnochie. Gone away on a family visit. Brenna took her."

Bridei felt suddenly cold. Donal's tone was too casual, his answer too glib. "Gone?" he echoed, struggling for a way to make sense of this. "What visit? What family?" Tuala's family was here. What had Broichan done?

"Easy now, lad. Broichan gave Brenna a bit of time off, a few days to go and see her mother at Oak Ridge, that's all. Tuala's gone with her, and Cinioch as an escort. They'll be there by now."

"He sent her away." Bridei realized he had his fists clenched; he made himself relax them, but he could not stop the anger building inside him. No wonder Tuala had been sad and quiet. No wonder she had seemed to be guarding a secret. What had Broichan threatened her with, to keep her silent? "You should have told me," he added.

"And break an undertaking to your foster father? He asked us not to mention this to you, Bridei; not until Tuala was well away. He'd have told you himself, all in good time, if you'd waited."

"Why?" Bridei demanded. "Why would he send her there?"

"So you can make yourself known to Broichan's guests without any distractions. That's important, Bridei. Your foster father wants you to make a good impression. Don't clench your teeth like that, you're making me nervous."

"She was sad. She didn't want to go."

"Did Tuala say that?"

"She couldn't, could she? I suppose Broichan threatened her into silence. She's only six, Donal. Without a bedtime story, she can't get to sleep. The dark scares her."

"Brenna's there."

"And she'll miss Midsummer. She'll miss the ritual."

Donal's mouth twisted. "Perhaps that's what Broichan had in mind. Let it go, Bridei. This is a small thing. It's nothing in the pattern of your foster father's plans. Bridei?"

But Bridei was already heading for the house. He wanted an accounting; his foster father must give that, at least. Curse Broichan and his mysterious schemes! You didn't treat children as if they were no more than an inconvenience to be brushed out of the way when they didn't happen to suit you. You didn't send them away to be lonely and frightened. In particular, you didn't coerce them into keeping secrets from their friends. He would tell Broichan so, and if his foster father didn't care to hear the truth, too bad.

Righteous rage driving all from his mind save the words he would say, Bridei marched around a corner of the house and halted abruptly. There were riders before the door, a party of six men who must have come up from the east, shielded from view by the birches between house and lakeside way. Broichan was greeting them; Aniel stood nearby, a guard at his back. The new arrivals were warriors, their faces decorated with kin markings and battle counts. They were clad in gear serviceable and practical for fighting men in transit, leather caps and breast-pieces, felt cloaks and heavy tunics, leggings of a uniform deep blue, supple riding boots and protective gauntlets. All bore arms. There was a pack horse, lightly laden. The animals were stocky, bright-eyed, and strong looking.

One man, tall and curly-haired, had dismounted by the steps and was speaking to Broichan. He broke off the conversation as Bridei appeared.

"Ah, this is your foster son, I've no doubt. My greeting to you, Bridei! I'm Talorgen of Raven's Well. It's a great pleasure to meet you at last. I was a friend of your mother's before she took it into her head to wed Maelchon and go off south."

His mother again. Bridei clasped the man's extended hand. Talorgen had such a disarming grin that it was not possible to do anything but grin back and greet him with genuine good will.

"I've a son of your age," Talorgen went on. "His name's Gartnait. Shaping up well with bow and sword, but not as clever as yourself, from what I've heard."

"I'm sorry you didn't bring him with you, my lord," Bridei said.

"Ah, well, another time," Talorgen said easily. "His mother wanted him at home, and she can be hard to disagree with."

"Come," Broichan said. "I'll show you your lodgings. Your men will be quartered in the barn with mine. Bridei, will you take them down to the stables and ask Donal to settle them in?" The druid's dark eyes were scrutinizing his foster son's face closely. No doubt, Bridei thought, the rage still showed in his expression, although Talorgen's friendly manner had gone a long way to damping it down. He stared back for long enough to be quite sure Broichan understood he was angry, and why. Then he turned to Talorgen's men and motioned the way to stables and barn. What he had to say must wait.

At dusk that day the third of Broichan's guests arrived. When Bridei thought of druids, he generally pictured his foster father, the only one of that kind he had known: a man of incisive mind and daunting intelligence, a man whose worldly power was balanced by a deep reverence for the mysteries. There was another kind of druid he had heard of, the kind that appeared in the old tales. This was a wild inhabitant of oak groves in the deep heart of the forest, a man so steeped in lore, so attuned to magic, that he often seemed to the outer world quite crazed, as if he had stepped across the margin and existed with one foot in this world and one in the other. Such a druid was Uist, whom dusk brought to the threshold of Pitnochie. He came on a milk-pale mare that moved with a delicate, dancing gait, swishing her silken tail.

Uist had wild white hair, plaited as Broichan's was, but not as neatly; the braids were tangled with feathers and twigs and seeds, and wisps escaped them to stand out in an aureole around his head. There was a musky smell about him, like that of a forest creature. Uist's features were hard to describe, the eyes of changeable color, the face now one thing, now another, as if he were constantly making small adjustments so that nobody would remember how he looked. He seemed old, but stood straight and relaxed, one hand grasping a tall staff of birch wood with a polished stone set at the tip, palest gray speckled like an egg with a darker hue, and three white feathers tied below it with a silver thread. His garments were flowing; they stirred strangely as Uist moved, as if there were some life in the fabric beyond that the wearer's body imparted. Here and there the robes were rent, as if the druid had moved through briars or brambles. The mare, however, bore no scratches on her gleaming coat.

Uist made no attempt to engage anyone in conversation nor to greet any member of the household beyond his host. Offered a bed in the men's quarters with Talorgen and Aniel, he said it had been too long since he slept with any roof over his head but an oak canopy and the stars. He would spend his nights in the forest and tolerate the days in the confines of Broichan's house if that was strictly necessary. He needed the hands of Bone Mother under his back and the eyes of the Shining One looking down on him. If he had not those, he must walk out of Pitnochie within two days or run mad.

"You mean, madder than you are already," commented Talorgen with a smile, and the old druid's bushy brows creased in a frown.

The remark seemed to Bridei less than courteous, but Uist only said, "Ah, well, I was lost to your kind of society years ago, my friend, and I don't miss it a bit. The music, perhaps. Apart from that, kings' courts hold no attraction. Living wild suits me, and it suits those who whisper in my ears at night. I won't howl at the moon; you have my assurance of that."

Bridei was waiting for a moment when he could catch Broichan alone. But as soon as supper was over, his foster father and the three guests retreated to Broichan's own chamber and closed the door firmly behind them and, angry or not, there was no way he was going to interrupt their private council. Later, Talorgen came out and settled himself by the fire, and soon Donal, Uven, and two other men had him embroiled in a debate about the Gaels. This had all of them shifting knives and tankards and bowls around the table in enactment of a grand strategic push beyond the western end of the Great Glen and out across the isles, an advance that saw the invaders swept before it, back to the land of Erin where such miscreants belonged. Talorgen had fought some of Gabhran's forces quite recently; his territory of Raven's Well lay to the west of Pitnochie and a great deal closer to the enemy's settlements. He had information about the current positions of the Gaels that was new to Donal, and his account of his men's fierce skirmishes with their forward parties held everyone transfixed. By the time that was over, lamps were being doused and it was time for bed. It seemed Bridei had left it too late to see his foster father alone. But as he walked past Broichan's chamber to fetch his candle before he went out to the barn, the druid opened the door and stepped out.

"You had something to say to me," Broichan said. It was not a question.

Bridei's anger was not as fierce as it had been earlier. Talorgen had said he could come and stay at Raven's Well as soon as Broichan gave permission for it, and the exciting prospect of traveling outside Pitnochie and practicing his combat skills with this boy Gartnait had greatly improved his mood. But he had not lost sight of the injustice, nor the need for an accounting.

There was nobody else nearby, and Broichan had shut the door on his influential guests.

"You sent Tuala away," Bridei said, using the techniques his foster father had taught him to keep his voice calm and his body relaxed, though speaking of it brought the anger back. "She was unhappy, I could see it. And you forbade people to tell me. That wasn't fair."

Broichan waited in silence, regarding his foster son steadily.

"I think I deserve an explanation," Bridei said.

Broichan did not speak. His silences could be unnerving, but over the long years of his education Bridei had learned to deal with them. "Why are these people here?" he asked, deciding a direct question was required. "Why shouldn't they see Tuala? Are you ashamed of her?"

Broichan folded his arms. "You are angry," he observed. "Pace your breathing. School your eyes. You must learn to mask such feelings, for in the council chamber they do a man ill service."

Bridei thought he had been controlling his feelings quite well. At least he was not shouting and throwing things, the way Ferat sometimes did. "Will you answer my questions?" he asked.

"My guests are here to meet you. To observe you and to assess how well you have learned, thus far. It is of the utmost importance that you show them your best qualities. Tuala will return when they are gone. It is inappropriate that the girl be present at this time. She does not belong here."

"She is part of Pitnochie," Bridei said. "She belongs with me."

A ripple of something crossed Broichan's pale features. Bridei could not tell what it meant. "I had thought you almost a man, Bridei," the druid said. "You demonstrate tonight that you are still a child. Go to bed now. This is a trivial matter, and you will need all your energy for the days to come. We will not discuss this further." With that, he opened the door and stepped back into his chamber, and the conversation was over. It was deeply unsatisfactory, but Bridei knew he would get no more from his foster father.

As he dropped off to sleep surrounded by snoring men, Bridei told a story in his head, silently, thinking that thus he was in some way true to his promise, even if Tuala had no way of knowing it. *Once upon a time . . .*

BRENNA HAD SAID, "Don't go any farther than the holly bushes. I don't want to have to go searching for you in the woods. There are wolves up there."

But Tuala couldn't obey. It was different here; wrong. The

house was little and smoky, and Brenna's mother looked at her through narrowed, suspicious eyes. Brenna's aunt was even worse. She wouldn't meet Tuala's gaze at all and she kept making that sign with her fingers, a sign that meant she thought Tuala was a bad thing, a wicked thing. Brenna herself was unusually subdued. Her mother didn't approve of Fidich as a prospective son-in-law, what with his damaged leg and the fact that he farmed another man's land, not his own. The first night, Brenna had cried herself to sleep.

The only thing that was the same was the forest. Here at Oak Ridge, on the way up to the tall peaks called the Five Sisters, the trees hugged the cottage like an enveloping cloak. Brenna's father had made a living cutting wood and ferrying logs down the lake on a barge. He had died in the forest, killed when he miscalculated the fall of an ash. Tuala thought that was only fair, considering, but she did not say so.

Brenna's brothers had followed in their father's trade until both took opportunities to sell their services as fighters for King Drust the Bull. A good axe could be put to a variety of uses. Now it was a household of women and, at present, a place of angry words and bitterness. Each day, as soon as the meager breakfast was over, Tuala fled out of doors and up to the place where the dark, prickly leaves of the hollies made a screen, shielding the house from the wilder reaches of the woods. She'd sit there awhile, watching until it was clear Brenna had stopped checking on her, and then she would slip through, careful not to tear her skirt or tangle her hair on the prickles. A little farther up the hillside she had found a tiny hollow between the roots of an ancient oak, a tree similar in shape to her favorite one at Pitnochie. When she tucked her skirt in and squeezed up small, she was just the right size to sit there and feel as if she was part of the tree and the tree was part of her. If she listened hard, she thought she could hear a kind of heartbeat in it, strong and deep; she could catch a voice, a huge, slow, old sort of voice that was telling her something remarkable and wise. What had the tree seen, all the years it had held this hillside firm with its roots and shaded the smaller plants with its noble canopy?

How many creatures had it nurtured, how many wayfarers sheltered? There were so many tales in all the time it had watched over the Glen, tales of lovers, quests, and journeys, stories of great battles, glorious victories, bitter defeats: this oldest of trees held all of it in its monumental memory, humming the story to Tuala as she sat cradled by its feet. Sometimes, above and behind the deep narrative of the oak, she could discern other voices, high, ethereal, and mocking, or small, rustling, and furtive. She tried to shut those ones out.

At night she told herself the oak tree's tales again to a background of Brenna's smothered sobbing. It was not right. None of it was right. But Tuala knew she must be good, whatever happened. If she was not good, Broichan would not let her go home and she might have to stay here forever, here where everyone was unhappy and there was no Bridei.

Brenna had been very firm about the need to stay unseen. They'd traveled early in the morning, barely waiting for sunrise to set off, and Tuala had worn a hooded cloak to conceal her face. Visitors to the cottage at Oak Ridge were rare, for it was an out of the way place. All the same, Brenna had made herself quite clear. "Broichan doesn't want you noticed. I'm not going to make you stay in the house; that's asking too much of any six-year-old. But you mustn't talk to strangers. Not a word, understand? If you spot anyone walking up or down the track, come straight back inside. It's very important, Tuala. If you attract any attention, you and I will both be in trouble."

"It's all right, Brenna." Tuala had spoken with conviction, noting the shadows under the young woman's reddened eyes. "I'll be good."

ON THE THIRD day she was in her usual spot, crouched among the oak roots with one ear to the base of the trunk, listening with her eyes closed. Her mind was full of the dark, slow voice of the tree. Then, all of a sudden, she was aware that something had changed. Tuala opened her eyes.

There was someone else sitting there as she was, someone

not so much bigger than herself, gray-robed, hooded, a quiet, shadowy figure seated a little farther around the bole of the tree, leaning comfortably against a low arch of gnarled roots. Whoever it was had come there without making a sound. Tuala's scalp prickled. Was it one of the Good Folk, one of those who had left her on Bridei's doorstep in the middle of the night? Did such a one count as a stranger? As she stared, motionless, the figure turned its head to reveal the features of an old woman, not a furrowed, wrinkled kind of face like Wid's, but a small, strong sort of countenance with a prominent, beaky nose and dark eyes like polished beads of obsidian. Tuala could not tell if this was a human woman or something else. Mindful of her promise to Brenna, she held her tongue.

"Good morning," the stranger said.

It seemed rather impolite to respond only with silence. Tuala gave a nod.

"A fine place for listening: you've done well to discover it. And a good place for a wayfarer to rest her feet awhile. You don't object to my sharing it for a little?"

Tuala shook her head.

"You're cautious," the stranger said. "I understand that. Let me introduce myself. My name is Fola. I'm not of your kind; that much is obvious to you, I expect. Yet you don't run away."

Tuala's heart gave a lurch. *Not of your kind . . .* that meant this was, indeed, one of the forest folk, one of those tricky beings who showed you a glimpse of a white hand or a fluttering wing, a shadow of cobwebby cloak or a glint of silver hair then, when you tried to look properly, were gone as if they had never been. But no; that was wrong. *She* had come from the forest, *she* was the one who was Other. This woman, Fola, was from the human world, and thought she had stumbled on a child of the Good Folk. Words of explanation sprang to Tuala's lips, *I live with human folk, I live in a druid's house,* but she bit them back.

"Not talking today?" Fola inquired calmly. "I expect you do understand me, for all that. I have a lot of interesting things to tell; that's part of my work, teaching the young what wisdom I can. The world is changing fast. Things get forgotten if we don't work at them."

Tuala nodded again. She had heard much the same argument from Bridei. He had told her that, in the south, many folk no longer performed the rituals to honor the gods; that people were forgetting the wisdom of the ancestors.

"Here in the forest you know little of such matters, I suppose," Fola went on, hugging her knees with her neat, small hands. For a grown-up woman she really was remarkably little; little enough to be quite reassuring. Tuala was so much smaller than everyone else at Pitnochie, even Bridei. "History is precious; ritual is precious. Lose that and we lose the knowledge of our own being," Fola said. "Lose the thread of ancestry, lose the tales, and we are adrift without identity. How old are you, child? Perhaps that's a silly question; you do not keep time as we do."

Tuala held up one hand, five fingers, and the thumb of the other hand.

"Ah. Six years old. An excellent age. With one ear you can still hear the magic of earth, sky, and ocean in its true, pure form; with the other, you can begin to comprehend a more formal kind of knowledge: logic, judgment, numbers, language, and signs. Or would do, if you were a human child and given the right opportunities. The youngest of my own students are not so many years older than yourself. That interests you, I see; it makes your eyes sparkle. You are eager for learning?"

Tuala nodded vigorously. Her hands were clasped tightly together now. This was exciting; she could hardly wait to tell Bridei about it.

"If only . . ." Fola mused. "If only there were a place for one of your kind among us, how much we could learn, both you and I . . . I would never attempt such a thing, of course. Have no fear of that. There's nothing more cruel than taking a child away from all it's known and loved, merely because someone believes it's for the best. All of my students come to me willingly. You can't learn unless your heart's in it. Of course, some people do say education's wasted on a girl."

"It's not!" Tuala burst out, for Broichan's dismissal of her aspirations had left a wound unhealed within her. "I wanted to learn and I could have—Erip and Wid wouldn't have minded—but he wouldn't let me!" She clamped her mouth shut, but it was too late. She had broken her promise. She had spoken to a stranger.

Something in this speech had caused Fola's gaze to sharpen. "Who wouldn't let you?" she asked carefully. "Come, child, it's safe to tell me. I'm harmless."

"Broichan," whispered Tuala.

There was another pause, and then Fola asked, "And who is Broichan? Your father?"

Tuala shook her head. "No, he's Bridei's foster father. And Bridei's getting an education, he spends all day learning, but when I asked if I could, Broichan was angry with me. He said all I need to know is cooking and sewing. But I'm no good at those things. It isn't fair."

"What things are you good at?"

"Not fighting and sports. Bridei learns those: he's the best archer at Pitnochie. I'm a good rider. Bridei taught me. And I'm sure I could do what you said, rituals, history, numbers, and languages. All I want to do is sit there while Erip and Wid are teaching Bridei. I'd be quiet. I wouldn't interrupt at all. But Broichan won't let me. Bridei tries to teach me things, but he's so busy, there isn't enough time."

"Interesting," Fola said. "Was I wrong about you? About what you are?"

Reluctantly, Tuala shook her head.

"Yet it's clear you do not live here in the woods."

Tuala shook her head again, realizing she had already said far more than anyone would have wished, save the old woman herself. Maybe Fola was not what she said at all. Maybe she was an enemy trying to set a trap. Hadn't someone tried to kill Bridei once, long ago?

"What is your name, child?"

"Tuala." That could hardly make a difference now.

"A splendid name, fit for a princess. This Broichan of yours has misjudged you, I think. Men can be rather prone to that, even the more intelligent ones. Now tell me. If you live at Pitnochie, what are you doing all by yourself halfway up to the Five Sisters, in wolf territory?"

"You're all by yourself in wolf territory, too," Tuala pointed out.

"I'm grown up and responsible for myself. I answer only to the gods," Fola said calmly. "You, as you mentioned, are six years old, and not the wild sprite I thought you at first, but a member of a druid's household. Tell me, did he send you away?"

A nod.

"Ah, yes. I see it clearly. An embarrassment. He took you in, he was prepared to break the rules to that extent, but making it public is beyond him. That's men for you, ever bound by convention."

There was one point here that must be corrected. "Broichan didn't take me in. Bridei did. The Shining One showed him where to find me."

Fola was listening attentively. "Bridei," she mused. "The boy?"

Tuala nodded. "He's bigger than me," she said, "and very good at everything. Broichan said I would be in the way. That I would disrupt his education."

"Did he now? Well, perhaps there was a grain of truth in that. So, I suppose you are staying away until after Midsummer, is that it?"

"How do you know that?" Tuala challenged. "And how did you know Broichan was a druid?"

"I'm a wise woman, Tuala. It's my business to know things. And now," rising to her feet and shaking out her long gray cloak, "I must be on my way and hope the wolves decide they're not hungry. Oh, I have something here that you might like. Where is it, now?" Fola had a pack with her, a bulging cloth bundle fastened with cords. "Here we are," the wise woman said, reaching into a side pocket and bringing her hand out full of something furry, gray, and unmistakably alive. "I found her on the way," Fola said. "I already have a cat of my own, and Shade doesn't take kindly to usurpers. This one should suit you; she has a marked streak of independence."

Tuala took one look at the creature's soft coat, its neat pink nose and big, strange eyes, and fell instantly in love. She reached out her hands and brought the kitten, not strug-

gling at all despite its period of confinement, in to snuggle
against her breast. Its tail was like a brush, the hair long and
feathery.

"She's no farm cat, but a wild thing, a forest creature,"
Fola said. "I think she'll go with you, as she did with me.
Like knows like. Now I must be off; it's a fair walk to Pit-
nochie."

Tuala, absorbed in her wondrous, unexpected gift, took a
moment to react. "Pitnochie? Is that where you're going?"

Fola nodded, her lips curving in a little smile. "Indeed.
Your druid is well known to me, but I've yet to meet the lad,
his foster son. As for you, you're a complete surprise. Any
messages you want delivered?"

There were several. For Bridei, *I miss you. I miss the stories.* For Broichan, *I want to come home.* Neither could be
sent. Balancing the little cat with one hand, Tuala reached
into the pouch at her belt and brought out a scrap of ribbon
that had once been blue-dyed, but now was faded beyond
color. Her hair had already come quite unplaited and hung
wild about her shoulders.

"Could you give this to Bridei? Not when Broichan's
there, he wouldn't like me to send messages."

"Just give it to him?"

"And tell him I'm happy here."

"You would send this friend a message that is a lie?" Fola
asked. All at once she seemed taller, and her expression was
stern, almost as stern as Broichan's.

Tuala said nothing. Against her breast, the kitten felt
warm and comforting; its purring was vibrating through its
whole body and into hers.

"You're not happy at all; one look at you and your friend
could see that," Fola said. "You don't want to be here, you
want to be home. You don't want to cook and sew, you want
to be a scholar. Why say things are other than they are?"

"I don't want him to worry about me," Tuala said gravely.
"Just because I'm sad, there's no need for him to be sad too.
And . . ." No, this she would hold back at all costs. She must
not tell of her promise to Broichan, the promise on whose
keeping depended her whole future at Pitnochie.

"Very well," said the wise woman, slipping the ribbon away and hoisting her pack onto her back. "I'll tell him I've seen you, and that you said to say you're thinking of him and looking forward to coming home. A compromise, and honest. I don't convey messages that are untrue."

"Thank you," Tuala said as Fola bent to pick up a staff that had been lying unnoticed among the oak roots. She noticed the way the length of willow rose of itself to settle in the wise woman's hand. "Thank you for the cat and thank you for the message. I'm sorry I . . ." She trailed off, unsure how to put her thoughts into words.

"Sorry you mistrusted me? Sorry you thought me other than what I was? Don't apologize for that, Tuala. A little caution is always wise. Besides, I, too, was mistaken in my first impressions of you. Look after that creature well. It's a rare one, and may stand you in good stead one day. Farewell now. May the Shining One light your way, child."

"May Bone Mother hold you in her hands," Tuala replied. The pattern of the ancient farewells was one of the very first things Bridei had taught her.

Fola smiled. "I hope we'll meet again some day."

"Me too," Tuala whispered, knowing how unlikely that was while her future lay in Broichan's hands. The kitten wriggled; she glanced down, stroking its tiny head with her fingers, and when she looked back up, the wise woman had vanished as if she were no more than a dream.

FROM HIGH IN the branches of the oak, two pairs of eyes had looked down on this exchange with keen interest. One pair was luminous, liquid, the owner silver-haired, cobweb-gowned, and unmistakably female. The other eyes were round and nut-brown, those of a red-cheeked lad whose form was wreathed in leafy creepers and fronds of fern. Neither was of human kind.

"She grows apace," the girl remarked. "She is strong, clever, and wise, as we should expect."

"This meeting was fortuitous," commented the boy. "It

could be used, later. A time will come when the druid's fear of this child's influence will outweigh his loyalty to the Shining One. And the wise woman wants the girl. She sees her strength and recognizes her potential."

"You go too fast," the girl said with a toss of her shining hair. "Tuala is an infant yet, Bridei himself still a child. Each must be tested long and rigorously. The calling that awaits the boy demands the highest self-discipline, the deepest devotion to the gods and, more significant still, the ability to make his own decisions. To trust his own judgment."

"Tuala's part in it will be every bit as difficult," said the boy. "She's unhappy. Already she is set a test, and not by us."

"This?" the girl scoffed. "A little trip away from home in the company of a kindly nursemaid? Don't be so soft! Wait until this scrap of a thing reaches womanhood; then we will really test her. Bridei must prove worthy of the Shining One's trust; Tuala must equal him in strength. Each faces trials. They have been chosen, and the goddess expects no less."

The boy was silent awhile, swinging his legs as he perched on a high bough of the tree. Far below, Tuala sat cross-legged with the little cat on her knee, a tiny figure between the gnarled oak roots. "Mm," he murmured. "There will come a time when Broichan will send her away again, and there will be no coming back. When he is dying, the druid will weep hot tears for that."

The girl flashed her pale eyes at him. "You think him so blind?"

"He is blind in this one particular. His mind is all on Bridei; on the task of preparation."

"Just as well," the girl said. "There is not so very much time for that. Come! No need for us to linger here. Tuala will return to the woods; to the secret places. She cannot but do so. They are in her blood, as in ours. We can use that to our advantage. The call of kinship is our key to proving her strength."

"Maybe," said the boy, with a last look downward. The

small figure was making her way back toward the hollies, her new treasure cradled carefully in her arms.

"Come!" the girl cried again, and with a flash and a snap of silvery wings the messengers of the Shining One were gone.

5

So, WE ARE gathered at last," Broichan said. The five of them were in his chamber, with Aniel's man Breth on the other side of the door and the household quiet beyond. Outside, the moon shone on a summer night of murmuring birds and soft breezes; the Shining One was yet a day or two from her perfect fullness, but the solstice was almost upon them. Tonight the air of the druid's sanctum was heavy with conspiracy. They had waited long for such a council.

"Indeed." Aniel was seated at the oak table and had a parchment, goose quill, and ink pot before him. "And best make the most of this opportunity, for there's no doubt I, for one, am watched by my adversaries, and I know the same goes for Broichan. Should the least hint of our meeting reach the wrong ears, the entire venture could be in jeopardy and years of effort wasted. I still say this might better have been done openly from a far earlier stage, perhaps at court, with King Drust's public support."

"We know you're of that opinion, Aniel." Fola stood before the fire, her slight, upright figure outlined by flames. The withering look in her dark eyes was one she had often used to devastating effect on her more recalcitrant students. "If you believe your own words, you won't waste time going over the way things might have been, but focus on the present and the future. Nor do you and Broichan have a monopoly on risk, I assure you. I am, after all, a teacher of the daughters of the powerful. Now tell me. I haven't had a chance to meet the lad yet, being late come. Give me your verdict, if you've reached one. Is Broichan's smug look justified?"

"Fola the forthright." Talorgen chuckled. "Speaking for myself, I like what I've seen of young Bridei. Already he speaks like a grown man, fluently and with prudence. He's knowledgeable and not afraid to engage in debate, but he knows his limitations. And he's uncommonly skilled with a bow."

Aniel gave a wintry smile. "He knows when to win and when to lose," he said. "In time, I believe he will have the capacity to win the hearts of men. He's young yet; the maturity of his manner is deceptive. The lessons of the next few years must be harder. The decisions of his adulthood will tax him severely; he must develop the fortitude to make them without flinching."

Outside, a hunting bird gave a high, echoing call as it flew by over the forest. The fire sputtered, and Fola moved aside to let its heat reach the men, for even on this summer night the air in Broichan's chamber was chill.

"Uist?" Fola raised her brows in question.

The old druid stood by the window, staring out through the narrow slit as if he could only survive if some part of him, at least, were still free from the confines of human habitation, of stone and thatch. When he turned back toward them, his eyes were vague and unfocused.

"It's a hard journey for a good boy," he said quietly. "A road of many twists and turns, of knives in the back, of false friends and disloyal allies. Simple honesty, nobility of purpose, wit and compassion will carry him a certain distance. The lad knows the ancient powers, loves and respects them. Men will honor him for that. They'll flock to follow him. That should please you; it'll give us the result we've planned for all these years. But Bridei will pay a price. I see a choice ahead for him that would break the strongest man in all Fortriu. Remember that, for when it comes he'll need every friend he's ever had." Uist turned back to the window; a shower of small particles dislodged itself from his clothing, falling to the well-swept floor of the chamber.

"My foster son will be strong enough for any choice." Broichan's voice was deep and sure. Uist made no reply.

After a little, the chieftain Talorgen spoke once more. "Midsummer will be a test. The gods may show us whether the boy is worthy of the future we intend for him. There will be many claimants when the time comes. If we are certain Bridei is the one, we must plan for what comes next. His upbringing has been sound, that much is obvious in every word he speaks. But the lad needs further opportunities now—"

"His education is in my hands." Broichan's tone allowed no challenge. "We agreed to that when we made the decision to take this path. What opportunities are presented to Bridei, and when, are for me to determine."

"Talorgen has a point," Aniel said, fixing his gaze on Broichan. "You've kept the lad hidden here long enough, and you're beginning to sound as if this is a personal quest of your own. We are a council of five. None of us should lose sight of that. We share responsibility for this; we share the good or ill consequences of our scheme, and as a team we provide our own checks and balances. The boy must learn to think for himself. Donal tells me Bridei has never been down to the settlements, nor along the lake, nor to the homes of other lads of like age and breeding. He'll need that if he's to be a leader of men. It's not a druid you're educating here, my friend, but a king."

The word hung in the silence, full of hope and of danger.

"Besides," put in Fola briskly, "he'll need to be seen at court sometime. If not yet, then most certainly in the next few years. Before too long he must be made known to Drust. Winning the king's favor now can only strengthen Bridei's chances later. There are other young men with closer ties of royal kinship, Carnach of Thorn Bend for one. We'll get nowhere with a candidate who is unknown, however apt he may be."

"Come," Broichan said, "let us sit down and share this mead. And give me your honest opinion." It was the king's councillor he watched, Aniel of the cautious eyes and guarded expression. "How long do we have? Another five years? Seven?"

Aniel cleared his throat. "One must hope for that at least," he said, "or this boy, likely as he is, will simply be too young. The king's health is no better than reasonable; he's susceptible to winter chills and finds it hard to catch his breath. Still, barring anything untoward, he may see another seven years. More, if the gods smile on us."

"We must all pray for that," said Fola. She turned her shrewd gaze on Broichan, who met it with his own, dark and inscrutable. "Drust needs you at court, old friend," the wise woman went on. "He misses your wise judgment, your fault-less counsel."

"There are others to guide him," Broichan said crisply. "Aniel among them; who better qualified? Drust can manage without me."

"He'd have a better chance of keeping the factions under control and making some real progress on the western front if he had you by his side," Aniel observed. "He trusts you; he always did, for he knows your power to be god-given. Me, he merely tolerates."

"Then you must work to change his attitude." There was a touch of sharpness in Broichan's tone now, and Aniel's mouth tightened. "I swore fifteen years of my life to this task, and fifteen years I will give, more if I must, to see it through. Drust's anxieties are one thing. We speak tonight of the future of Fortriu; of the very survival of our people."

"Fine rhetoric," Talorgen commented, "but of no avail should the Gaels gather themselves to strike in two years, in four years, in five. How long can we wait for our new king while the old one slowly weakens and our enemies draw close? Your presence at court would give Drust new heart. Your influence might see Circinn coaxed or bullied to the council table. It would provide a visible check for those who seek subtly to destabilize the king's rule and grasp at opportunities for themselves. The boy could come to Caer Pridne with you. I understand the need for protectors; we'd arrange that."

"Protectors did not keep poison from my lips last time I ventured to the court of Drust the Bull. Protectors did not prevent assassins from entering my woods. I have more effective arrangements in place now, but these are momentous

matters, perilous times. The boy is young; young and innocent. He knows nothing of what we intend for him; I've kept
the knowledge of his mother's true identity from him. He
will apply himself more effectively to learning if he does not
bear the heavy weight of our expectations on his shoulders.
It's not appropriate to expose him to the dangers of court,
believe me."

Now they were all looking at him.

"What I *believe*," Aniel said rather pointedly, "is the hith-
erto unbelievable: that Broichan the superbly detached has
managed to grow fond of his foster son and simply wishes to
retain him at home a little longer. Such soft thoughts could
be dangerous, my dear druid; they could surely get in the
way of our shared purpose."

"Come now." Uist spoke without turning. "We cannot afford to squabble amongst ourselves. Fola, you suggest a
compromise. Let's all agree to it, then let the gods make the
choice for us once and for all."

Fola clasped her neat, small hands before her on the table.
"Very well," she said. "He stays here a few years more, for
you're right, the lad is still young. But from now on you allow visitors. Perhaps Talorgen's own children might spend a
summer here. That would be safe, surely. You let Bridei out
a bit, with suitable protection. A boy should be allowed to
see the village festivals, to enjoy some good music and good
company. Black Crow only knows what sort of a family life
you've managed to provide for the lad all alone in this
household of dour retainers. Bridei's mother would be horrified. It must have been hard enough for her to part with him;
to make a choice. Anfreda always understood the importance of faith, the power of the old ways in uniting the
Priteni and maintaining our people's strength. She gave us
the son best fitted to carry out the great task ahead: the wisest, the strongest, the one in whom her own blood ran most
purely. But she's a mother; it must have hurt her terribly to
send him away. I imagine she thought he'd be brought up in
company with other children, or she'd never have let us have
him."

Broichan said nothing.

"In a year or two you send him to stay with Talorgen at

Raven's Well," the wise woman went on. "He'll be a young man by then, and needing a period in the house of a war leader. Dreseida is his mother's kin; she'll welcome it, surely. By then, you'll have told him of his lineage and destiny. From there, Talorgen can introduce him to court along with his own sons. That way the boy's less likely to attract the wrong kind of attention. He'll still spend some time here, of course. You can't go past Erip and Wid for learning. I don't know how you coaxed those two old rascals out of their self-imposed exile, but you could hardly have done better."

Broichan was staring into the fire as if he had not heard her.

"You're worried," Talorgen said. "Arm him with knowledge and skills. And give him good guards as well. Donal's the best; he'll travel with the boy, of course. I'll provide others, discreetly. His presence at Caer Pridne will simply be as my son's friend. We can avoid undue notice, I think."

"If we knew which enemies are to be feared and which are simply to be watched, this would be managed a good deal more easily. There will be several likely candidates for kingship when the time comes. Each will have his supporters. Each will be vulnerable."

"This is far in the future," Fola said. "There's plenty of time for planning. Now, are we agreed?"

"Let us wait until the solstice." If Broichan had had a moment of uncertainty, it was past; his tone was commanding. "If the gods speak, if they confirm for us what we believe to be true, then this shall unfold as you suggest."

"And if not?" Aniel's brows arched in query.

"If not, I will return him to his father in Gwynedd," Broichan said smoothly. "Now let us retire; we'll talk again tomorrow. I understand Talorgen's made a commitment to an early morning ride. My foster son is keeping him busy. Good night, my friends; may the Shining One guard your dreams."

The men made their courteous farewells each in turn. Fola, however, remained seated at the oak table and, seeing the look in her eyes, Broichan closed the door behind the others and returned to sit opposite the wise woman.

"Well?" he demanded. "Have I displeased you in some way?"

Fola's expression suggested an inquisition was forthcoming. "Displeased? No, old friend. But you have added another surprise to the one I had on my way here through the Glen. There were references in tonight's conversation to Bridei's isolation, to the lack of company for him in a household of grown men and women."

"And?"

"Not true, is it?" the wise woman said, helping herself from the jug of mead and filling a goblet for the druid. "There's not just one child in the stronghold of the enigmatic and powerful Broichan, onetime royal mage and councillor. There are two."

A barely perceptible frown appeared on Broichan's brow. He did not speak.

"How did she come here?" Fola asked more gently. "I heard a little tale about the moon and the winter solstice."

"Who told you this?" His tone was icy.

"Never mind that. You owe me an answer. Bridei's rearing is not your privilege alone, however hard your need for control grips you, my friend. It is ours; it is a god-given task for the five of us. The members of our council do not lie to one another."

"I did not do so."

"You withheld the truth. It is the same. This is a matter that could affect the boy's future. You should have made this known before. She's been here six years, I gather. A child's attitudes can be fixed in a span far shorter than that. Why did you keep her? Sentimentality has never been part of your nature; compassion is not your outstanding quality."

The druid allowed himself a frosty smile. "You are forthright with your opinions, as ever, Fola."

"I see no need to withhold or temper them with you. You are strong enough to hear the truth."

"Tell me how you heard of the child, the girl. She's not here now. You cannot have seen her."

"You're surely not attempting a bargain? A tit for tat exchange of information?" Fola's brows rose in feigned shock.

"Would I dare such a thing, with Fola the Ferocious fixing her eyes on me in awful judgment? It was simply a request. My household is bound to secrecy on this, as on many other matters. I must know who breached that promise. There is no place for disobedience at Pitnochie."

"Does the same rule apply for children?" Fola asked lightly.

"All must obey. There are no breaches of discipline—" Broichan paused. "What are you saying? That you met the girl herself? That Tuala spoke to you?"

"The very same, six years old and fighting the longing for home with all her considerable strength," the wise woman said, folding her arms on the table before her. "I walked right by the place where it seems you sent her to be out of sight. She'd no wish to break any promises, Broichan. She held her silence grimly; it took quite a bit of work to get the story out."

"She will be punished," the druid said levelly. "Her place in my household is tenuous at best; the child may be young, but she understands the penalty for disobedience."

"Which is?" Fola's tone revealed nothing of her thoughts.

"This household cannot shelter her if she does not follow its rules."

"You would send her . . . where?"

Broichan frowned. "You saw what she is, no doubt. The tale is true: the infant was left on my doorstep at Midwinter, under a full moon. Bridei awoke and took her in; it is his belief that the Shining One entrusted this child to him, to us; that the goddess put her in our keeping. The boy won my household over by a simple trick of hearth magic. By the time I returned from Caer Pridne she was the beating heart of the place, and there was no sending her away."

"A problem," observed Fola quietly. "Come, drink your mead and stop being so stuffy about this. I understand your feelings and your difficulties. I haven't been a teacher of young women all these years for nothing. It's clear to me the girl has a deep attachment to Bridei; no doubt he feels the same, based on his conviction that the spirits have appointed him as her protector. The fact that you denied him the company of other children has no doubt strengthened the bond. They view themselves as sister and brother; they need one another, since both have been deprived of family."

"As foster father," Broichan's voice was tight, "I have done my best to guide and support the boy. He has the finest of tutors and a household in which all his daily needs are met."

"How sad," Fola observed, "that you seem to believe that is sufficient. Why did you send Tuala away? She seems a quiet and polite sort of child, one who would hardly be an embarrassment, even in the company of four daunting strangers."

"Come now, that's somewhat disingenuous. She is what she is. Therein lies the dilemma. I must respect the gods; I do not have it in me to disobey the Shining One, should Bridei's theory be correct. I have taught him to respect all forms of life and to view all beings as parts of the same interwoven whole. So, Tuala stayed. A simple matter, had Bridei been my true son and destined for a future as mage or warrior. But he is not my son. He's the son of a princess of the Priteni, and his destiny is to lead our people as a true king should. He is our chosen candidate. What do you think it cost Anfreda to promise us a son of hers for this purpose even before she left Fortriu to make her life in a far land? Every step of Bridei's path has been planned; every turn of his way must be controlled. If his future is not governed by our council of five, all will fall in ruins, and our sad homeland will never be reunited in the true practice of the ancient faith. I agree, this little girl seems harmless. But she is the one unpredictable element in this venture, the single, small factor that lies outside our power to control. You know the capricious nature of the Good Folk. We cannot well afford that such a one should insinuate herself into our plans, like a warped and twisted thread snaking across a great and perfect tapestry."

"However," said Fola flatly, "there is nowhere you can send her. Who would take her in? How could you banish her without betraying the trust of the Shining One? How could you cast her out without losing the love and respect of your foster son forever? No wonder you frown."

"I sense danger in the child. She's a scrap of a thing, but there's something there: a strength beyond the obvious. She fears and distrusts me, her manner makes that plain enough. It seems to me that, like a wild thing half tamed, she merely bides her time until she turns to bite the hand that feeds her. Such a creature could undermine our plans. If she exerts undue influence on Bridei, she has the capacity to divert him from his path."

"Maybe she's bored," Fola said.

"Bored?" There was utter astonishment in the druid's voice. "Impossible. Nobody has time for idleness here."

Fola looked at him. "My dear," she said, "I feel a certain sympathy for Bridei, and even more for Tuala, for your talk of creatures and biting tells me you have no understanding at all of what it is to be a child. Were you never young? Have you forgotten how it feels to be left out, to be lonely, to be denied what others are given by right? Or did you spring to life fully grown and able to deal competently with whatever fate tossed your way?"

Broichan did not reply.

"I don't like bargains and deals." The wise woman drank the last of her mead. "Nonetheless, I believe I may be able to offer you one that will go a long way to solving your dilemma, and also to allaying my concerns about these children's upbringing."

"Tell me."

Fola rose to her feet. "Not yet. I want to meet the lad first and see if my intuitions about him are correct. And I'll wait until the solstice ritual is past. That may give us the gods' answers. Then I'll speak with you again."

"You plan to discuss this with our fellows in the meantime? To seek their learned opinions on the subject of my deficiencies as a foster parent?"

Fola paused before she answered. "I've touched a raw nerve; forgive me, I never suspected you had such a thing, old friend. For now, let this be between us two. As for deficiencies, I'll not judge on those until I speak with Bridei."

IT HAD BEEN a satisfying morning. He'd ridden to Eagle Scar with Donal and Talorgen and Aniel's second guard, whose name was Garth, and they'd had a race on the way back in which Bridei and Blaze had acquitted themselves very respectably. Talorgen had won on his stocky, strong-legged mare. Then Erip and Wid had given a lesson on the use of kin signs, during which both the councillor Aniel and the wild druid Uist had come in and settled themselves to listen. Neither had been able to keep quiet; there had been theories and contradictions aplenty. It was one of the best lessons Bridei had ever had.

After that he excused himself and went up to the oaks to sit alone awhile. It seemed the right thing to do, even if Tuala was away and would not return until after the solstice. If he sat quietly in her favorite spot, Bridei reasoned, she might feel his presence close to her although she was at Oak Ridge, so far down the Glen. The magic of place was like that. Bone Mother held all of the land together; her body *was* the land, supporting and linking the life that dwelt on it. If he sat here among the oak roots, just as if he were Tuala herself, and thought of the way the tree stretched down, down into the core of the earth, perhaps his thoughts could travel from one part of Bone Mother's body to another, from Pitnochie to a small safe place in the forest where Tuala, too, sat thinking and dreaming. *It's all right,* he told her. *You'll be coming home soon.* With his eyes closed, he could see her small, anxious face, her big, strange eyes.

"I seem to keep finding young persons under trees," said a brisk voice. "What it means, I cannot say. Bridei, isn't it? I arrived too late to greet you last night."

Bridei leaped to his feet, brushing the earth from his clothing, and extended a hand in polite greeting to the old woman who stood before him. "I'm sorry," he said, "I didn't see you coming. Yes, I'm Bridei."

"And I am Fola; I'll save you the embarrassment of having to ask. I'm generally to be found at Banmerren, where I run an establishment in which young women learn the ways

of the goddess in all her forms. I have a message for you."
She pulled out a length of much-worn ribbon, which had
once been blue, and put it in his hand.

"Oh." He recognized it instantly; he'd refastened that plait
more times than he could count. "You came here by Oak
Ridge?"

"My business took me to that part of the Glen, yes."

"Is Tuala all right?"

"Of course. Why would she not be?"

There were several possible answers to this: *because she's
little, because she didn't want to go away, because she's
afraid of Broichan. Because she can't get to sleep without
her story.*

"It is a long way," Bridei said.

Fola smiled. "You've been trained by a man with a great
talent for not answering questions," she commented. "Your
sister seemed to be in good health. She was evidently missing you, although she did not say it in so many words. She
will be happy to return to Pitnochie, I think."

Bridei nodded and slipped the ribbon in his pocket.
"She's not actually my sister," he said.

"No?"

"Not exactly. We are both Broichan's foster children."

Fola smiled. "I doubt very much if that's the way
Broichan would see it," she observed.

Bridei said nothing. This was probably another test; it was
a harder one, for with this sharp-nosed, bright-eyed old
woman there was no telling which answers were the right
ones. One thing was certain; he would tolerate no criticism of
his foster father, even though Broichan had sent Tuala away.

"Perhaps not," he said cautiously. "But we are, all the
same. I was sent here by my father, to be educated. Tuala
was sent here by the Shining One herself."

"To be educated?"

"For a purpose," Bridei said. "And I am trying to teach
her. She can count up to fifty now and knows quite a bit of
the ritual and lots of stories. But there isn't much time for it."

"I'll speak to Broichan," Fola said crisply. "The situation's ridiculous. She must share your lessons. Much of it
she won't understand, but she'll soak up what she can."

Her confidence was impressive. Bridei doubted very much that Broichan could be persuaded to agree, but he did not say so. "Tuala would like that."

"I know. Now tell me, Bridei. I know the story of how you found her. I know you understand her background, what she is and where she came from. I'm not sure if you understand how difficult that could be for her later on. Think about it. Think about how it will be when you're grown up and Tuala's grown up. Consider the world the two of you will have to live in. What will she do? What can her life be?"

Bridei was not sure what the wise woman meant. "Here at Pitnochie, everyone loves her." That part was not quite true. One could not associate the word *love* with Broichan himself. "She's happy here. She belongs here."

"You will not live here forever, Bridei. One day you will be a man, following your own calling, making your own journeys. It seems to me you are the center of this small girl's world. Where will she be without you? People are wary of the Good Folk. Tuala will not always encounter kindness in the wider world of men."

"What do you mean?" Bridei asked, taken aback. "Are you, too, telling me I should have left her in the snow? I'm not going to listen to this—" He was suddenly angry.

"I'm not *telling* you anything," Fola said quietly. "Take my questions on face value. There are no lessons in them and no judgments. All I want is a considered answer."

Bridei made himself breathe in a pattern until the anger passed. He made himself look the wise woman straight in her dark, penetrating eyes. "Tuala's strong," he said. "She'll tread a path of her own choice. Her life can be anything she wants it to be."

"And you?"

"Me? I will help her and protect her, and make sure she isn't lonely. Like a brother, only not a brother."

"I see. What of your own life? What if your path takes you far away, and you cannot fulfill this responsibility to a small sister who is not a sister?"

Bridei frowned. "My foster father hasn't told me yet what he intends for me. Of course I might have to go away for a bit—Talorgen said I can stay at Raven's Well—but Tuala will be bigger by then. And when we're grown up we can have our own house. It would have to be near the forest; Tuala needs the trees close by."

"Mm," Fola said, lips twisting in a wry smile. "Most of the time one tends to forget how young you are, Bridei. Broichan's brought you up to speak like a scholar and to listen like one as well. Just occasionally I see the boy underneath, and I recognize that you are still just that: a boy. Tell me, what is it that *you* want? What future would you desire for yourself?"

The only way to answer this was with the truth. "To bring the kingdoms of the Priteni back together," Bridei said simply. "To make Circinn part of Fortriu again. To bring back the proper observance of the old faith, so all of us honor the ancestors as we should. To drive out the Gaels and bring peace. That's what I want to do."

"Anything else?"

It took a moment before he realized she was joking. He felt his cheeks flush. "It sounds too grand, I suppose; how could I even hope to begin? It is a task for a great leader. I understand why you would laugh at me. But you did ask, and I gave a truthful answer. Those aspirations should be in the mind and heart of every man and woman of Fortriu. We should all strive for them."

Fola nodded. "I wasn't laughing at you, son," she said. "I salute your courage and your ideals, and I pray that you live to achieve them. Now I have another question for you."

It had been a difficult conversation. Bridei was hard put to guess what might be coming next.

"Tell me," Fola said, "what if Broichan were to send you back home to Gwynedd?"

Sudden horror gripped Bridei. Did the wise woman know something Broichan had not told him?

"You are lost for words at last, after dealing so expertly with the rest of my interrogation. Now why is that, I wonder?"

"Did he say that?" Bridei blurted out, despite himself. "Is he going to send me back?"

She regarded him, solemn as an owl. "Don't you want to see your family?"

He bit back the first response, *my family is here, my family is Broichan and Donal and Tuala.* "Of course," he told her politely.

"I don't believe you," said Fola. "Your every utterance is hedged about by caution, save for when the conversation touches on something you truly care about. Then your face changes, your eyes light up, and you stop talking like a careful old man or an obfuscating druid and give me a little glimpse of yourself. What's important to you is Fortriu and the Glen; the Shining One; and, of course, the child the goddess placed in your care. You've forgotten Gwynedd. How long have you been at Pitnochie, seven, eight years? I doubt if you can even remember what your parents look like."

Bridei bowed his head.

"It must have been lonely," she said quietly.

"I was all right."

"Hmm. But you made sure it wasn't like that for her. Yes?"

"Broichan is a good foster father. The best."

"And you are a loyal son. Foster son. Very well, Bridei, you've acquitted yourself admirably; he's trained you expertly in this kind of combat. Your little sister's pretty good at it, too, for all she's not much bigger than a hedge mouse. You know the solstice ritual's a kind of test, do you?" She turned her sharp eyes suddenly on him.

"Yes," Bridei said. "Of what exactly, I'm not sure. I'll just have to do the best I can, and hope the gods will show me the way."

"I've no doubt at all that they will do just that," said the wise woman.

TUALA KNEW ABOUT the solstice. Bridei had shown her how to watch the sun, when Midsummer Day was drawing close, how to check its position against a point such as a tree or stone until the morning its rising moved back to give its journey a narrower arc. A sunrise vigil was kept for three days in a row, and each of these days had its particular ritual observance. Back home in Pitnochie, Broichan would enact the solemn ceremonies with Bridei to help him. Here at Oak Ridge the recognition of the year's turning was slight. There was a spring not far from the cottage, and they walked there when the morning's work was done, the two older women, the younger one, and Tuala herself, with the little cat, Mist, keeping pace in the undergrowth, here crouching still, here sprinting ahead, her tail a whisper of gray amongst the curling fronds of bracken and fern. The water welled up between stones and spilled into a small, round pool over which elder trees stretched long, spindly branches. Each of the women tied a scrap of colored cloth there—Tuala would have done the same, but she had lost her ribbon again, and had nothing else to use—and Brenna and Tuala together made a pattern of white stones by the water's edge. They spoke a simple prayer to the goddess; even this, Brenna's mother and aunt did with sour faces and grim eyes. Tuala had never seen such sad people, such angry people. There were lots of things to smile about, even when you were lonely: the sun coming out, the pattern the ferns made around the mossy rocks, the nice, damp smell of the little clearing, the whisper of the goddess's voice . . .

"Can I stay here a little bit longer?" she asked Brenna. "Just a bit? I can see the house from here; I'll come straight back, I promise."

Already, the older women were walking home along the path. Brenna hesitated.

"I promise," Tuala said again, trying to look like the most obedient child in the world.

"All right," Brenna said. Her face had a happier look now it was nearly time for Cinioch to come and fetch them home; her eyes were hardly red at all, and she summoned a wan smile. "You've been a good girl, Tuala. Be careful; don't get your clothes wet."

"Yes, Brenna."

In fact, Tuala had been here several times already, accompanied only by Mist. Since the morning she had discovered, accidentally, that scrying was in fact remarkably easy and that she hardly needed to practice at all, the pool had called her strongly, and she had spent as much time crouched here gazing into its shadowy waters as she had in the cradle of the oak's ancient roots. The first time, she'd been looking in the water for fish; before she had a chance to see if there were any, there'd been the image on the surface, a picture of trees and sky and forest paths, not a reflection, for what she saw was the hill above Pitnochie, and there in the middle of the little pool were Bridei and his pony Blaze, riding out to Eagle Scar. All that she had to do to keep the image was stay quite still and breathe in a pattern. It wasn't difficult at all.

As she visited the place more often and looked in the pool at different times and on different days, Tuala saw some images that worried her. They were things that could not be *now,* that must be *long ago* or *yet to come.* It was a pity Bridei was not here; she had so many questions she needed answers for. Why were people so cruel to each other, why did they have fights and arguments and get angry, when it never solved anything? Who were the red-haired warriors she kept seeing in the water, with calm, cold eyes bent on death? Was the young man there, the one with brown curls and a light in his face like a flame of courage, really a grown-up version of Bridei himself? And if so, why did she never see herself? Was it usual, when scrying, to have a strange, prickling sensation, as if all around the small glade where the spring emerged from the earth there were invisible, silent watchers?

They were here again today. Tuala could feel it: a ring of eyes fixed on her, a circle of beings centered on her. She could see nothing beyond a faint shimmering in the air, a slight disturbance of the way things were. Her eyes told her there was nobody there. Yet she knew she was not alone. When she knelt down by the pool, under the elder tree with its cargo of little scraps of wool, strips of leather, faded bits of ribbon, the offerings of season after season's wayfarers, she could feel them kneeling by her, opposite her, behind her, following her every movement, breathing her every breath, as if she and they were one and the same.

"Who are you?" Tuala whispered almost angrily. "Why don't you show yourselves?" But there was nothing save a little sound like the breeze in the leaves, and then silence.

The image in the water showed midday, midday at Pitnochie, for there was Broichan's house amidst the deceptive oaks, and there the waters of Serpent Lake glinting under the sun, sheltered by dark tree-clad hills. She saw Fidich limping up a steep track under pines to a bare hilltop where folk were assembling. Tuala knew this place. They called it Dawn Tree Hill, for a solitary oak stood there, a venerable ancient that caught the light of the sun's rising in its leafy canopy. Here, Broichan and Bridei would have kept vigil last night and for two nights before, marking the place where the Flamekeeper pierced the horizon.

On the flat stones at the summit a circle was forming; the household of Pitnochie was already gathered there. She saw Broichan, tall and solemn in his dark robe, with a ritual dagger in his hands, horn and silver. He wore a wreath of oak leaves on his plaited hair. His expression made Tuala shiver.

There were folk she knew and some she didn't know. There was Mara, and Donal and Ferat, and most of the men at arms. There were other warriors whom she had never seen before, their faces tattooed with kin signs and battle counts. There was a white-robed druid bearing a bundle of sticks. She could see that old woman, Fola, as well; Fola was carrying a bronze bowl of water which she set down now at the western quarter of the circle.

Tuala shifted a little, bending closer to the pool's surface. Mist crouched by her, tail curled, paws tucked neatly under her breast, narrow eyes intent on the water's stillness. Perhaps she saw a feline vision of her own.

The images unfolded like a solemn dance: Broichan pacing, his dagger's point casting the sacred space; at each quarter, his voice speaking the ritual words of acknowledgment and greeting. Water being sprinkled around the circle; smoke from burning sticks wafting across, an elemental cleansing. Then Tuala saw the wise woman step forward from the north, place of earth. Fola did not seem small and harmless now, but strong and powerful, the embodiment of Bone Mother herself. She raised her arms, calling a challenge: *Who are you? Why do you come here? Tell us!* Tuala could hear nothing; no sound disturbed the quiet of the little clearing. But she knew the words; Bridei's lessons had been as thorough as he could make them.

Three men stepped forward from the circle. One was the

white-clad druid, an old fellow with penetrating, pale eyes and a crazy mass of snowy hair tangled with seeds and twigs and leaves. He held between his gnarled fingers a feather as white as his own garments.

"The sun's light illuminates the mind," he said, "and makes the pathway clear. Keeper of Flame, let our eyes see only truth."

The man who spoke next was a warrior, tall, straight of carriage, his features marked with the blue tattoos of his calling. His eyes were keen, his bearing confident. He held before him an arrow fletched with the banded feathers of the great eagle. "The light of Midsummer is the light of courage." His ringing tone thrilled through the cool air of the hilltop. "Keeper of Flame, you give us the strength to be men. Your blazing glory inspires our deeds of valor. Through you, we are true sons of Fortriu."

The third man was bearing a bone; Tuala could not see what kind it was, but it was long and pale, like part of a leg. The man was gray-haired, gray-robed; his face was lined, his brow furrowed as with many cares. He spoke with quiet dignity. "Keeper of Flame, with your warmth you have nurtured the Priteni since the time before story, since the season before our grandfathers' grandfathers walked the Glen. In your life is our life. In your wisdom is our wisdom. We salute your splendor."

After that there was silence for a long time. Tuala understood that every man and woman there spoke the secret word of inspiration deep in the spirit, and felt it herself, humming its power through every single part of her. The unseen watchers remained, a circle of invisible presences right around the wellspring. Out of the corner of her eye Tuala thought she could see pale hands, shadowy faces, garments of green-gray willow leaves and soft feathers, silvery wings and strands of long hair in improbable shades of blue. Their eyes were a mirror of her own: colorless and clear, pale as ice. She would not turn her head to look; she must hold the image on the water. For now she saw Bridei; he was stepping forward from the base of the Dawn Tree and he held a lighted candle before him. Tuala's heart beat harder. He looked so serious, so worried, as if he thought the gods would be displeased if he took a wrong step or made a mistake in the words. And he looked tired; there were dark smudges under his eyes. That would be from last night's vigil. Broichan always made his foster son stay awake on Midsummer Eve. Bridei was biting his lip in nervousness. Silly boy; of course he wouldn't make a mistake. Of course the gods would not be angry. He was in the hand of Bone Mother; the Flamekeeper burned in him. The Shining One had singled him out. He was Bridei, who always got things right.

He moved forward again, stepping through the circle and beginning a spiral path from its edge inward; the candle burning strong and steady in his hands. His curling hair, brown as oak bark, was tied neatly back; his eyes reflected the sky's summer blue, warm and bright, and his steps were perfectly steady. He had a little scrap of faded ribbon tied around one wrist. Tuala found herself smiling; she had so longed to be there, to be a part of it. Now, in a way, she *was* there; he carried her with him. She hoped Broichan would not be angry about the ribbon.

Bridei's path wound in to the circle's midpoint, where his foster father now stood with the wise woman, Fola, by his side. Bridei raised his hands, holding the candle high. "This is the flame of hope and the promise of justice and peace throughout the land!" he proclaimed. There was no trace of nervousness in his tone. His voice rang out bell-clear; the sound of it made Tuala shiver, although she heard only with the ears of the seer, to which silence speaks. "I call down the power of the Flamekeeper, and I call forth the strength of our deep mother, the earth, and I invoke the bringer of tides, the Shining One! The sun has triumphed; today he reaches his peak. His life has awoken us and made fertile the land we walk upon. Now he begins his long retreat. Now we take his light within us, to illuminate our journey forward. Let each of us be as a lamp burning; let each of us step onward filled with the radiance of truth."

Broichan should have spoken next, but before he could open his mouth there was a rushing of wings and a stirring in the sky, and out of the east the eagles came. Gliding on the currents of air above the Great Glen, they made a perfect pair, now seeming to float, now beating strong wings in slow, powerful strokes to carry them on toward the place where the boy stood straight and proud with the flame of hope in his young hands. Broichan spoke not a word; as the birds circled the tor in their dance of ancient symmetry, their weaving of feather and bone and breath, Tuala saw with deep amazement that the druid had tears streaming down his cheeks. Three times the winged ones passed, and then alighted, each in the same instant, on the topmost branches of the Dawn Tree. They folded their great pinions and settled, a watchful presence. The sun touched Bridei's curling hair, lighting its brown to the deep red of autumn beeches; noon rays bathed the hilltop like the warmth of a blessing.

Then, without a word, Broichan took the candle from his foster son and with it lit a small fire from the sticks the old druid had borne with him. In that haphazard bundle, Tuala knew all the trees of the forest would be represented; oak and ash, pine and elder, holly and rowan, each gave a little of itself to strengthen the magic kindled today. The oak wreath Broichan had worn was passed around the circle, crowning for a brief space the head of each man and woman present. This was the moment for each of them, silently, to renew a personal vow to the gods.

At last the wreath came back to the druid. Broichan held it aloft a moment then cast it into the flames. Tuala gulped; she had known this came next, yet it still shocked her, seeming as brutal as the death of dreams. But it was not. All joined hands now to speak the ancient prayer of peace. The flames bore their dreams high into the air above the Great Glen, higher than the tallest tree, higher than the eagle's flight, beyond the clouds, up to the realms of the Shining One and, fire to fire, to the life-giving sun whose ascendancy this gathering celebrated.

Then bread and mead were blessed and shared, with Fola and Broichan offering the ritual foods first to each other, and Bridei then dividing loaf and pouring amber liquid for all there present. Donal clapped Bridei on the shoulder, making the flask of mead wobble. Erip and Wid were grinning as if they'd won a prize. Peering hard into the water of the reflective pool, Tuala observed that Broichan's impassive features bore no trace of tears now. Perhaps she had imagined that. Perhaps this had not been *is,* but *may be.* Scrying was a tricky business. All the same, she saw the pride in the druid's eyes as he watched his foster son's progress around the circle, and she thought she saw the same look on many other faces there, the wise woman's included.

"Tuala!"

Brenna was calling her. Tuala blocked out the sound, hunching closer over the water. Beside her, Mist was stone-still, gazing deep. Around the pool the invisible presences could still be discerned on the very edge of sight.

The feast was over, the circle unmade. Folk gathered their belongings and began the long walk down the hillside toward home. Atop the solitary oak, the pair of eagles had not moved since the moment of alighting there. But now, as Bridei stepped beyond the margin of the hilltop and onto the steep path downward, both birds arose once more into the air and, winging this way and that, crossing and passing with delicate precision, they shadowed the boy as he walked. The trees grew thickly on that hillside, clustering in ravines, blanketing slopes, swathing path and boundary with luxuriant summer growth of rich green foliage and dark piny needles, and beneath them flourished bracken, fern, and sharp-leaved holly. Still, eagles are keen-sighted birds, princes among hunters. It seemed to Tuala, as the picture before her changed and changed again, that these great creatures formed an escort, a guard for Bridei, proclaiming his journey as if he were an ancient mage of story or a new king coming into his power. They flew above as he came down through the high birch woods and into the heavy darkness of the pines; they danced their presence over him as he made his way under the venerable oaks and among the drooping elders that fringed beck and pool. Above the druid's house they circled him once as he walked out of the forest by the drystone wall where Broichan's guards kept their watch. Then, with a cry that made Tuala's spine tingle, the eagles flew off to the west and out of the image on the water. She saw Bridei turn to his foster father and say something, smiling, but she could not hear the words.

"Tuala!"

Time to go. She did not want to upset Brenna, who had enough to trouble her already. Tuala rose to her feet, reaching to gather up the little cat. Around the pool there was a rustling and a stirring, and a sound that was like hissing, only perhaps there were words in it: *usss . . . one of usss . . .* Then, abruptly, they were gone.

That night, lying awake while Brenna slumbered alongside her, Tuala whispered a story. Mist was a good listener; her small, warm presence in the half-dark of the summer night made loneliness easier to bear. "You know how the Priteni have two kings, Mist? They've each got a different kin sign, carved on the stones of their big grand houses, so everybody knows which is which. There's Drust the Bull and Drust the Boar." Tuala's fingers stroked the cat's soft fur; snuggled deep in the thin blankets, Mist was purring so hard her whole body throbbed. "But I'm not going to tell you about them. I'm going to tell you about a different king. It's a *might be* sort of story, like the pictures in the pool. This king was called Bridei, and his sign was the eagle . . ."

It was a good story, full of adventure and courage and hope. It was a story about destiny, and it seemed to Tuala to be deeply true in the way of the most ancient and best loved tales. The only thing that was wrong with it was that, try as she might, she could find no place in it for herself.

6

THEY WERE LUCKY, really. Tuala remembered to tell herself that, season by season, year by year, as she watched Bridei ride away for another visit to Raven's Well or another retreat to the nemetons with the wild druid, Uist, for this, too, was part of the education Broichan had determined for his foster son. It was more than six years since the time when she had been sent off to Oak Ridge, the time she thought of now as the summer of the eagles. She had watched Bridei grow from straight-backed, serious child to tall, keen-eyed young man, and she bid him farewell so many times she would have lost count, save for the talisman she kept hidden in her little chamber in the druid's house at Pitnochie. It was a double cord fashioned from very strong thread, the two parts of it twined together in a special way. Their story, hers and Bridei's, was captured in this object: the two strands had a small separation for every period of parting, a delicate knot for every wondrous reunion. The length of it bore the pattern of their lives, the two paths that diverged and came together once more and, for all their division, remained essentially one and the same. Although small, it was a powerful thing; Tuala made sure nobody saw it, not even Bridei himself. She had grown more cautious as the years passed, more watchful even as her privileges within Broichan's household expanded, for she felt, always, the druid's essential distrust of her. Broichan had never spoken of it, not since the first time he had sent her away. He did not need to. She could sense it in his closed expression, his cool tone, in the distance he kept between himself and this gift from the Shining One which he had never really wanted.

Yes, they were lucky. Broichan could have sent her away forever. He could have taken Bridei to court and stayed there. He could have denied her any learning save what little she could glean for herself. Instead, miraculously, the day she'd come back from Oak Ridge, she'd found that path suddenly open to her after all. Erip and Wid were to allow her to sit in on Bridei's lessons, to set her suitable tasks and ensure she completed them. Tuala had grasped this unexpected bounty eagerly, not asking the reason for Broichan's startling change of heart. It was enough that this door was no longer closed; she applied herself with the same intensity she gave to any new discovery.

As time passed, the balance of her life shifted. Brenna was married and moved into her new husband's cottage. Now she and Fidich were the proud parents of two small children, and Brenna was kept busy between farm and family. As for Erip and Wid, they became not simply Tuala's tutors in the disciplines of history and geography, kings and symbols, lore and tales, but also her firm friends. The lessons continued, informally, even when Bridei was away. Increasingly he moved in a wider circle and was gone from Rising to Midsummer, or from Gateway to Maiden Dance, the feast that heralded the arrival of early lambs. Had it not been for the patience and kindness of the two old men and the concessions Broichan made that allowed them and their small charge to establish themselves before the hall fire in the mornings with their scrolls and pens, life would have been bleak indeed. With Bridei gone, Tuala knew she was without an essential part of herself, a part as vital to her existence as eyes or ears or beating heart.

This winter would be particularly hard. Bridei was going to Raven's Well to stay with Talorgen and his family and Tuala knew, because she'd seen it on the water, that there might be fighting and deaths and grief. Her vision had shown Bridei with a look on his face that had never been there before, a look that meant he'd seen something he hoped never to see again, but knew he must confront over and over. She had seen shattered men and blood on the heather. She had heard, with the ears of the mind, a cry of unbearable pain, a sound that set the teeth on edge and made one beg the gods to end it, quickly, before one ran mad. But she did not tell him. Tuala understood that such visions could not be relied upon as a clear picture of what was to come. To use them as the basis for planning one's actions was to take considerable risk. Bridei was a man now: eighteen years old. Undoubtedly he would face battles and losses as all men did, whether or not she had foreseen it. There was nothing she could do to hold back the moment when that terrible shadow entered his eyes; only be there when he came home, to listen and to comfort him, for she was the holder of his inmost fears and the guardian of his dreams.

They said good-bye on Eagle Scar. It had become more difficult to snatch time alone together now that Broichan allowed more visitors to Pitnochie, more comings and goings. Talorgen was at the house now with his son Gartnait, a lanky, freckled youth who had quickly become Bridei's close friend, though never Tuala's. Gartnait regarded her as a child, and a rather odd one at that. He teased her for her silences, for her solemnity, for the strange pallor of her skin and her big owl eyes. It was good-humored, but Tuala did not know how to answer such banter. There seemed to her no point in it; what did it serve, save to reinforce what made her most uneasy in the druid's household: her difference? She did not wish to be singled out. She wanted to fit in. Erip and Wid never seemed bothered by what she was, and the things she did without thinking, such as moving the little kings and priestesses around the game board without touching them, or making the colored light that came in the round window into a dancing display of tiny, jewel-bright insects that dispersed in a shower of sparkling dust. Erip would clear his throat, *ha-rumph*, and Wid would stroke his white beard and nod sagely, and they'd just get on with the next part of the lesson, herb lore or astronomy or kings and queens. She remembered the kings and queens now, as she sat with Bridei on the flat stones at the top of the Scar. It was autumn. Today he was going away, and the year was turning to the dark.

"Bridei?"

"Mm?" He was gazing down the Glen to the west, perhaps looking for the eagles, perhaps searching out the track to Raven's Well, where he'd be riding soon.

"If you had stayed back in Gwynedd, you could have been a king one day," she said.

His attention was on her abruptly, the blue eyes piercingly bright. "It's not as simple as that," he said.

"Your father is king of Gwynedd," observed Tuala. "The way they choose their kings is quite different there, Erip told me. They don't elect them from the sons of the royal women the way the Priteni do, with candidates standing from each of the seven houses. In Gwynedd and Powys a man can be king after his father. So you could have, if you'd stayed. Could now if you went home."

Bridei was silent for a little. "Pitnochie is home," he said eventually. "It's home for both of us, you and me. I used to think that was what Broichan intended: to educate me, then send me back to Gwynedd. But even if that were so, I would never be king there. I can't remember my brothers, but I know I have two of them, both older. Their claim would be stronger; they have grown up at my father's side. Besides, Broichan didn't send me back."

"So what does he intend for you?" It was an artless question. Tuala knew the answer already; the signs were quite clear to her and had been since that long-ago day when Bridei had borne the flame of Midsummer and the eagles had come. But she was not sure Bridei knew, even now. Broichan's strategy was a deep and subtle one, spanning a period of many years. The druid was right, Tuala was forced to admit to herself, right to be covert, right to conceal his master plan from any who might seek to thwart him, right even to delay revealing the truth to the young man on whom his hopes rested. Ignorant of the weight of expectation he carried, Bridei had walked the path of his youth more lightly and learned more freely. Unburdened by the knowledge of his future, he had been better shielded against the machinations of those who sought power and position for themselves, those who had their own chosen pieces in play on the board.

"I could guess," Bridei said. "Broichan will not speak of my mother. But I did discover that she's kin to Talorgen's wife, Lady Dreseida. And Lady Dreseida is King Drust's cousin. Depending on the exact nature of the kinship, that could open certain possibilities; I'd be a poor scholar indeed if I did not recognize them after Wid's and Erip's lessons in genealogy. But I'm young and untried as a leader of men. I think it more likely Broichan wants me to play a part similar to what his own once was; to become an adviser to the king. Not as a druid, of course, but more in the way Aniel does, by traveling, negotiating, working to make truces and setting terms for agreements. A king's councillor. Perhaps a warrior, too; a man must be many things."

"You're a bit young to be a councillor to King Drust," Tuala said flatly. Bridei's cheeks flushed, and she regretted her words instantly, although they had been the truth.

"There will be other kings after him. I'm a man, Tuala, not a child. I will play my part."

Tuala held her tongue, though she sensed a silent message

that hurt her: *I am a man, and you are still a child. You cannot understand.* That was unfair; she did understand, and had done since she was a little girl who could not even keep her hair neatly tied. And she *was* a woman now, for all her slight build and short stature. At Midwinter she would be thirteen years old. She had seen her monthly courses three times already and observed with wonder the other changes in her body, signs that meant the tides of the Shining One flowed within her pale Midwinter child as in the ocean's deeps. But she could not tell Bridei this, of course. For all he was her dearest friend in the world, he was a boy, and there were some things you just did not discuss with a boy.

"Tuala?"

"Mm?"

"We may be gone all winter this time. There's to be a spring campaign against the Gaels; it's to win back the territory of Galany's Reach, where the Mage Stone stands. Talorgen may let Gartnait and me ride with his warriors." Bridei's eyes were shining; it was as if he saw it already, a vision of banners, weapons glinting in the sunlight, thundering hooves, glorious victory. Tuala shivered.

"Don't look like that," Bridei said. "I have to go to battle some time. It would have been years ago, but for Broichan."

"I'll miss you. Spring's a long way off."

"And I'll miss you, Tuala. I will come home as soon as I can, I promise. I'll have a lot to tell you."

Tuala nodded. This was undoubtedly true; Bridei could talk to her as she had never observed him doing with others, freely, from the heart, with no safeguards in place. And he would indeed have much to tell, news born of tears and fury, of grief and rage.

"What is it, Tuala? What's worrying you? I will come back, you know. I always come back to Pitnochie." Frowning with concern, he moved closer and put his arm around her shoulders. It felt strange to her; not the way it used to be, when she could lean against him and be comforted, when she could offer a ready hug of consolation in return. It felt awkward, different.

"Nothing." She disengaged herself and rose to her feet.

"How soon do you have to leave? I want to show you something."

"I have some time left. Not long. What is it?"

"Come on, then. It's a bit farther, up west. I need to show you."

But when they reached the place, the special, secret place she had discovered one day out wandering in the forest alone, Bridei halted his horse on the brink but would not dismount.

"Not there," he said, his face suddenly white. "That's not a good place for you to go, Tuala. Not suitable. We should head for home now."

Tuala was quite taken aback. "Not suitable? What do you mean? I've been here lots of times. I have to come here. It's where I can see . . ." Her voice trailed off as memories of treachery, of blood and death assailed her.

"Where you can see what?" Bridei got down from his horse. As was the pattern of things, Tuala now rode his old pony, Blaze, while he himself had Snowfire, long of mane and tail, stocky and sure, and palest gray, like shadow on winter hills. In fact Tuala was such a slight girl she could almost still have ridden the small, beloved Pearl, but Pearl was old and seemed content to dream away her days in stables or infield, watching the world go by.

"Where I can see you," Tuala whispered, not meeting his eye. "So I can know where you are and what you're doing when you're gone."

Bridei was silent a little. After a while he said, "There are terrible visions in that pool, Tuala. The Dark Mirror, Broichan calls it. I only went there once and that was more than enough. A girl your age shouldn't be subject to such influences. Broichan wouldn't want you to go down there, and I don't either."

"How old were you when you looked in the Dark Mirror?"

He did not answer.

"Anyway, it's not just that. Not just knowing where you are and if you're safe. There are . . . other things."

"What things?" Bridei was growing increasingly uneasy;

Tuala could see it in the grip of his hand on Snowfire's bridle.

"I can't tell you here. We have to go down there, into the little valley."

"The Vale of the Fallen." He supplied the name grimly. "There was a terrible massacre here, long ago. This place is full of the memory of death."

"And life. Come on, Bridei." Not waiting to see if he would follow, she plunged down the narrow pathway between the clinging fronds of undergrowth. The mists of the vale rose up to meet her. After a few moments she heard Bridei's footsteps behind her.

As they reached the rim of the pool the vapor cleared, revealing the bowed forms of the dark druid-stones and the weaving garlands of the star-flowered vine that swathed the banks with its luxuriant growth. The light was dim, green-hued, playing tricks on the stretch of water before them, for here it seemed dark and deep, here shallow and shining with tiny fish darting not far below the surface.

Tuala settled cross-legged by the water's edge.

"Don't look," Bridei said. "Why not stick to your bronze bowl? You can make this work wherever you want, so why come all the way here? This is—" He broke off. A moment later Tuala felt him settling beside her, not touching, but close enough for her to feel his warmth, the only human thing in the Vale of the Fallen.

This had always come easily to Tuala. She understood now that for others, for Bridei himself, even for Broichan who was steeped in the craft of magic, the art of the seer was hard won, hard learned; that the skills could not always be put readily into use nor the visions summoned on every occasion. For her it was entirely different, and she had come to realize, reluctantly, that this had to do with her origins, with what she was: different; one of *them*. That made her uncomfortable, yet the gift itself was one she cherished. It gave a window on the world beyond Pitnochie, beyond the Great Glen, beyond the here and now. She could conjure an image in a drop of rain, in a water barrel, in a jug of mead. But nowhere else could she find the wonder and terror that were revealed in the Dark Mirror. Bridei was right; the vale and its hidden pool held deep memories, a story of grievous loss and of courage beyond imagination. More than that, the Dark Mirror showed what was to come or what might come. It gave warnings and prophecies and guidance. And it was a place of the Good Folk. Here, at last she might see her own kind face to face, and ask them why they had abandoned her without a word. Perhaps it had been the will of the Shining One. Perhaps it had been simple mischief. If Bridei had been asleep that night, she would have frozen to death. The older she grew, the more that played on her mind.

Today the pool showed no battle. Instead, it was the ritual of Midsummer over again, with the household gathered on Dawn Tree Hill and a brown-haired child treading the spiral path to the light. But this was a time to come. The child was young, no more than six years old. The man who presided over the ceremony, who cast the circle and led the prayers, was not Broichan but Bridei; not a dark-robed druid but a man in his prime, broad-shouldered, tall and handsome, with bright blue eyes and a long plait of curling hair the color of ripe chestnuts. The wise woman who spoke with the voice of Bone Mother was not hawk-nosed Fola but a younger priest-ess, slight as a birch, white-faced, clear-eyed, her dark hair tumbling down the back of her austere gray robe. The eyes of these two met and met again; but when the ritual was over, the mead shared, the bread divided, it was another woman who stood at Bridei's side, a girl whose shapely fig-ure was clad in the fine gown and fur-edged cloak of a no-blewoman, a girl who wore a little circlet of flowers on her russet hair and a smile on her face that was just for the fine man who bent his head with familiar kindness to hear her words. The boy who had carried the candle now stood beside them, a miniature version of his father. Familiar faces could be seen: Ferat, Mara, Fidich and Brenna with their children. Donal was not there, nor Erip and Wid. Tuala could not see Broichan. But she saw herself, when the ritual was over, standing alone under the Dawn Tree, her face in shadow, her eyes bereft. She saw herself turn and slip silently back under the shelter of the birches, leaving the family of Pitnochie to their joyful celebration.

Tears were rolling down her cheeks. Those were not part

of the vision, but entirely real. Bridei sat close by her, his own gaze intent on the Dark Mirror. Tuala could not bring herself to look again. She closed her eyes, willing the images out of her mind. She had to remember that this might not signify *will be*. It could just as easily be only *could be*. Anything was possible. Any path might be trodden if you wanted it enough. After all, she was here, wasn't she? She had grown up in a druid's house. She had been given an education. She had been brought up just as if she were a human child.

She must will that future away; must think of *should be*. It was hard. They were here, she was surrounded by the rustle of their slight movements, the insidious whisper of their strange voices ... *Us ... one of us ... come back to us ...* They had never shown themselves fully, not in all these years. Perhaps they had cause not to trust her; perhaps there was nobody they trusted. But they were always here, clustered about the pool, ready to hiss in her ears, to brush against her arm, her cheek, to whisper their own interpretation of her visions. *Come back,* their soft voices were coaxing now, *come back to us. Here, you can be a queen ...*

"I'm not one of you," she muttered. "I'm an ordinary girl and I live among human folk. I am flesh and blood. I don't float about the forest whispering lies and playing tricks."

Ahhh ... The voices sighed. *He played a trick on you, when he took you in. He tricked you out of family and kin and home ... Come back to us ... We need you ... We will love you ...*

"How could I ever come back? I can't even see you!" Tuala responded in a furious whisper. "And you don't love me, that's just another lie. You left me out in the snow. Well, I've got my own life now. I don't need you!"

From a dozen places at once the voices made a whispering chorus. *You need ... oh, you need ... That is why you come to this place, and come again, and come again ... You need us ...*

Bridei stirred, stretching his arms; abruptly the forest presences were gone, as if in the space of a single breath they had folded themselves back into the land.

"You've been crying," Bridei said, surprised. "What's wrong? What did you see?"

"I'm fine," said Tuala, scrubbing her cheeks. "What did *you* see?"

Bridei's jaw was grim, his eyes very serious. "For me, there is only one image in the Dark Mirror," he said, rising to his feet. "I did not want to come here today. But I think it is timely, as I am to join battle against the Gaels in spring, that I have been shown this once more. I will use it to strengthen my resolve. We owe it to those brave souls who perished here to drive the enemy out of the Glen forever. It will be an act of vengeance pure and final. I'm glad you brought me here, Tuala. But I'm sorry that your vision made you weep. It troubles me to see you sad."

"I'm fine," she said again, although it was not true, and she knew he knew that. "Sometimes there are sorry things here, but we are shown them for a purpose."

"Was there something else you wanted to show me?" he asked her. The kindness in his voice, the courteous bending of the head toward her, were such sharp reminders of the vision she had seen that she felt them like a blow.

"No," she said. She had intended to tell him of the eldritch presences that increasingly followed her, somewhere between substance and shadow. She had needed to put into words the longing she had to find out about her true family, the reasons she'd been left on Broichan's doorstep and what those things might mean for her future. She had needed to tell him of the fear that went with such a quest for knowledge. What if she found her real identity and discovered in the knowing that she was truly outside the boundaries of the human realm? What if that knowledge cut her off forever from the one person in the world who mattered? Yet how could she live her life, not knowing?

"Sure?"

"I'm sure. It's getting late; I expect Donal will be wondering where you've got to. We should go."

"Tuala?"

"What?"

"If there was something wrong you would tell me, wouldn't you?"

"There's nothing wrong."

"I worry about you," Bridei said. "I don't like leaving you, especially when you look like that."

"Like what?"

"Sad. Anxious. Like the time Broichan sent you away when you were little." He reached out and brushed the tears from her cheeks with his fingers. At his touch, light as a butterfly, Tuala felt something stir deep inside her, something both wondrous and frightening, something she had not known was there. She closed her eyes a moment. She had to be strong about this, no matter how miserable she felt. He had no choice but to go; it was enough that he would think of her when he was away. And he still had a ribbon tied around his wrist. Always, when he left Pitnochie, he carried her token with him.

"I'm just sad that you have to go away again, that's all," she said. "With you gone, I have to answer all of Wid's and Erip's questions instead of only half."

SPREADING ALONG THE deep cleft in the earth that was the Great Glen were four long lakes, each linked to the next by a narrow waterway. It was possible to travel by boat all the way from the northern coast near the king's stronghold at Caer Pridne to the isles of the west, rowing or sailing the length of the lakes and carrying the vessels along the banks of the channels between, since these were swift-running and strewn with rocks. Each lake had its own particular name and its own unique character. Serpent Lake stretched from the northern firth all the way down past Broichan's residence under the oaks. Serpent Lake was deep and dark; shadows of ancient presences dwelt in its waters. Men who fished there wore amulets of iron about their necks and made sure they were back on shore before dusk.

Below Serpent Lake was the smallest in the chain, Maiden Lake, which marked the start of the way up toward Five Sisters. That was a steep climb but a fair one. The mist-shrouded glens and hidden waterways, the tree-cloaked slopes and high, bare crags made a fine sight for travelers.

There were wolves; folk did not journey there alone unless they cared nothing for their own lives. Some could pass; some were touched by the hand of the Shining One or trod their paths as chosen warriors of the Flamekeeper, and the wild beasts respected this, knowing it in their blood. A stag might offer himself to such a traveler as sustenance; a wolf pack might howl a greeting late at night while the wayfarer sat by a small fire in the immensity of the dark hills. That path led to the western ocean and the isles that lay there like resting sea creatures, swathed in a blanket of bright water in summer, scourged by winds and tides in the dark season.

The other way, southwestward by Maiden Lake, led to the broad expanse of Mage Lake. Mage Lake was an eerie place. Drumbeats could be heard in the hills; a distant braying of horns might ring out in ghostly reminder of what once was. These lonely shores were, no doubt, the scene of an ancient battle, a long-ago victory or rout whose noises of pain and challenge had become part of Mage Lake's deep memory. These waters had witnessed many lives of men; these stones, these trees held it all within their silence.

On the eastern slopes above Maiden Lake stood Raven's Well, home of the chieftain Talorgen, his wife, Dreseida, and their four children, three boys and a girl. The household was substantial. Talorgen had his own private fighting force equipped with armorers, blacksmiths, folk to tend to horses and to feed a small army of men. He had tenant farmers whose holdings provided the supplies of food he needed, the livestock, the leather and wood, and to whom, in return, he provided protection and a calling for their younger sons as fighting men or apprentice craftsmen. Talorgen was deeply respected. So was his wife. As a maternal cousin to King Drust, Dreseida could rightly claim to carry the royal blood of the Priteni.

Raven's Well held a commanding position high on the flank of Corbie's Rest, looking across Maiden Lake to a secret valley on the other side. Southwest, beyond the eerie expanse of Mage Lake, lay King Lake, great and broad, opening at last to the western sea. Perilous waters, a perilous shore: here were the strongholds of the Gaels. All along the western coast of Fortriu, from this point southward to the old borders and creeping north toward the wild lands of the Caitt, the interlopers had gained a foothold, and the best efforts of the Priteni, of Drust the Bull and other kings before him, had not been able to shake this parasite loose. In the south it was more than a foothold. The self-styled king of Dalriada had built a fortress at a place called Dunadd and had established settlements close by as well as communities on the isles themselves. The Gaels had made themselves right at home.

The position of Raven's Well was perfect for secret sorties into the territory of Dalriada. It also placed Talorgen at high risk of being spied upon, and his men were targets for attack each time they ventured out on their covert missions. Bridei recognized that Raven's Well held dangers of a kind far different from those of Pitnochie. This was the point from which the Priteni could strike forward and do some real damage. If things worked out the way Talorgen and his fellow chieftains hoped, by summer the Mage Stone would be won back for Fortriu. The Flamekeeper would sing then, and the Shining One dance for joy in the sky above the Glen. There would be great hope in such a victory.

Now that Bridei and Gartnait were young men of eighteen, they played their part in patrolling the boundaries of Raven's Well. Generally Donal went with them, or one of Talorgen's chosen men. A party of three made sense. Such a number could move covertly in the woods, maintaining contact by subtle signals, the hoot of an owl, the rustle of a squirrel in the undergrowth. If the worst happened and one were wounded, that left one to tend the fallen man and one to go for reinforcements.

It was a crisp autumn day, the air achingly chill in the lungs. Small clouds appeared before their mouths as Bridei and Gartnait moved silently along the upper margin of the pine forest, eyes and ears alert for danger. Today there were just the two of them, for the older men were in council with a chieftain newly arrived at Raven's Well, a man whose support Talorgen needed to win. Donal was required to attend, and so was the other man who usually shared their watch. In fact, Gartnait and Bridei preferred to patrol together with no third. They had formed both a fast friendship and an intense rivalry since the first summer the lanky, freckled Gartnait had spent in the ordered household at Pitnochie. It was hard to say who had been the more uncomfortable, Gartnait amid the world of scholarship, ritual, and magic or Bridei, the following summer, enduring the noise, the banter, the fierce family disputes of Raven's Well, where there were two younger brothers and a sister to contend with as well as Gartnait himself. Dreseida, their mother, was the most difficult of all with her sharply appraising looks and her volleys of unexpected questions. The first summer he spent there, Bridei had longed for Pitnochie, for Broichan's grave discipline, for the quiet order of the house, for the sharp wit and irreverent humor of the two old men. Most of all, he had needed Tuala, for if she was not there by his side, small and grave with her watching owl-eyes, he could not speak his deepest thoughts but must let them build and build within him. That summer, his dreams had troubled him.

He was quite used to Raven's Well now. He learned to laugh off jokes, although he never mastered the knack of making them himself. He knew he could not have acquired sufficient skill in battle craft to be considered for next spring's venture had he not had Gartnait as a sparring partner while the two of them grew from boys to men. Now Gartnait's little brothers looked up to both of them. Ferada was a different matter. Bridei sensed that Gartnait's sister did not trust him any more than her mother did. They were hard to read, the women of Talorgen's household, one moment smiling and courteous, the next showing sudden offense, posing questions he could not answer or lapsing into chilly silence. It was not surprising, Bridei thought as he crept along the remnant of an ancient stone wall, keeping low for cover, that he could never think of the right things to say to them, for he'd had no practice at all. The only women at Pitnochie were Mara, who was more like a big watchdog than anything else, and shy Brenna. Tuala didn't count; she was a child. If he ever got to stay at Caer Pridne when the king was in residence he might meet some court ladies and learn the right way to conduct himself among them. The prospect was less than appealing.

A tiny whistle: Gartnait up ahead, signaling danger.

Bridei froze. For a little there was nothing beyond the wind in the pines, the distant cry of a bird. He could not see his friend, but knew Gartnait was some hundred paces away under the first fringe of trees, standing as still as he was. Bridei felt his heart racing and willed it slower as he slipped the bow from his shoulder and fitted an arrow to the string, each movement a step in a ritual, balanced and careful. Under these pines the paths grew rapidly dim and shadowy, for between the massive trunks of the most ancient forest dwellers their descendants raised tall, slender forms skyward, reaching for their share of light. There was plenty of cover beneath them, rocky outcrops, fallen trees swathed in creeping growth, smaller plants nestling in sheltered crevice or sudden narrow ravine. To track a man through the upper reaches of these woods was quite a test; Talorgen's forces, Bridei among them, had trained night and day in such terrain.

Of course, it was possible what Gartnait had spotted was a deer or a wild pig. In these days leading up to war, men were all too ready to jump at shadows, to see antler as raised staff or tusk as sharpened blade.

The whistle came again, a single note, brief and urgent. With it came a flash of movement down the hill among the bracken, and a color that was not part of the natural brown and gray and green of the woods: the pale image of a man's face, here then gone as the fellow ducked down behind some natural cover, a bush, a fallen tree, a heap of stones. He'd been quick. A moment later Bridei saw Gartnait whisk by on his left to vanish behind a thicker stand of pines.

They had talked about this often enough; had rehearsed it, or something like it, with the older, more experienced men, Donal in particular. Today there were only the two of them, and neither with any real combat experience to his name. Bridei moved to the right, taking the opposite flank to Gartnait. Between them they would flush this interloper out. Of course, Bridei thought as he edged forward with bow in hand, moving silently on the forest's needled floor, this fellow could very well be leading them into a trap. There could be a group lying in wait to ambush them. He must go with caution, keep an escape route open and make sure he did not announce his presence until he saw what the enemy was up to. The aim was capture, not killing. Spies had information; they must take this one alive.

Bridei and Gartnait had settled, after several years of training together, into a recognition that each surpassed the other in certain disciplines. Gartnait would never quite have Bridei's skill with the bow. Bridei could not match his long-legged friend at running, nor did he possess Gartnait's natural flair for all activities to do with water. Folk had been heard to jest, to Dreseida's annoyance, that Talorgen's eldest son had one of the Seal Tribe somewhere in his ancestry. Gartnait lacked Bridei's affinity with animals, his ability to get the best from his riding horse, his gift for charming household cat or dog. And nobody at Raven's Well could walk as silently through the forest as Bridei did, a talent, Dreseida was heard to observe in the dry way she had, that could only be acquired through a druidic education. It was true. Broichan's earliest lessons were lodged deep in his student's memory: *Always travel through the forest as a part of it, Bridei, not as an intruder.*

His feet now made no sound, or at least none detectable by man. He went as a creature of the forest goes, wary but sure, feeling each ridge, each hollow, each root and leaf and stone as if his feet were an extension of what lay beneath them. His ears were tuned for the smallest sound, his eyes open for the least sign that might betray an alien presence, a sense of something that did not belong.

He knew where Gartnait was; the faint crunch of cautious boot on pine carpet, the whisper of breath revealed his friend's position. Besides, there was a pattern to what they were doing and each knew his part in it as they knew the old rhymes of childhood, almost instinctively, somewhere in the beating heart, the pulsing blood. Down the hill they crept on either side until they were close by the spot where the enemy had gone to ground. They could have done with a third man. Failing that, it was clear they must wait, for Bridei could see now that their quarry was hiding in a hollow between rocks where a fallen tree, its splintered limbs still thickly needled, provided a natural barrier and concealment. To attempt an assault into such a neat and secure position would be foolish, perhaps suicidal. Even a single man holed up in such a spot

could maintain an effective defense for some time, and do
some damage while he was about it. Two or more could last
as long as their weaponry allowed. If they had a stock of arrows or throwing knives they might pick off both attackers.
It had been a good choice of retreat. But not good enough;
the enemy was, in effect, trapped in a space with only one
point of exit, and if Bridei and Gartnait could maintain a
vigil long enough, eventually their adversary must show
himself. Then they would take him. Them. Bridei hoped
there were no more than two. Success in this venture was vital. This was not just the capture of a spy, a blow against the
wretched Gaels. It was an opportunity, if they got it right, to
be accepted as men among men; as warriors deserving of in-
clusion in Talorgen's elite.

Gartnait was in view and signaled that he was of the same
mind. They settled, on the alert with weapons ready, one on
each side and slightly above the hollow. From within there
would be no view of them. Now the only sounds in the forest
were the gurgling of a stream, the sigh of the breeze through
the trees, the rustlings of creatures in the undergrowth.

Standing still and staying silent came easily to Bridei, accustomed as he was to the disciplines of his upbringing. For
Gartnait it was more difficult. As their vigil wore on and the
man or men in hiding made neither move nor sound, Bridei
could see his friend shifting the weight from one leg to the
other, changing his grip on his knife, stifling a yawn.
Nonetheless, both young men held their silence. The longer
this took, the more likely it was that someone else would be
on the scene before any confrontation occurred. If any of the
men at arms came out, the whole pattern would change.
There would be less likelihood of getting wounded or killed.
On the other hand, they would lose the chance to do this
alone and to prove themselves at last. Bridei's own thoughts
troubled him, for he knew they were not worthy of a seasoned warrior, for whom overall strategy must play a greater
part than personal ambitions. *Let them not come until we've
finished the job.*

It was the enemy who broke the hush: there came a whispered word, indistinct but with a harsh edge to it that made
Bridei catch his breath. The fellow spoke in the tongue of

Dalriada; this was indeed their prime foe, and now it seemed he might be on the move.

Gartnait, knife poised, glanced across with raised brows. *Go in? Now?* Bridei shook his head: *Not yet.* Then, with the hands, a series of signs he hoped Gartnait would understand. Fingers across throat, then showing a negative: *not kill.* Pointing to Gartnait, to himself, then indicating where they would jump on their quarry. Wrists together as if tied: *We'll seize them, bind them.* There wasn't time for more, but Gartnait, freckles standing out against a sudden pallor, showed with a little nod that he understood.

This was going to be too close for the bow. It would be hand-to-hand combat with knives. Bridei's mouth went dry; his breathing became harder to keep in control. What if the enemy was not easily overcome? They had to avoid an extended struggle, for they must minimize damage to this foe so he could give them what information he had: with luck, Gabhran's positions, his armaments, his forces, his plans. A spy was like treasure, and treasure must be handled with care, even by a very young man who has never fought against a real enemy. Bridei's heart pumped; his blood surged. Every part of him was on edge. He used the techniques Broichan had taught him, slowing his breathing, calming his thoughts. When the moment came it must be controlled in every respect or all they would carry back to Talorgen, to Donal, to the rest of this influential household, would be a tale of opportunity squandered. Who, then, would want them tagging along on a major expedition, more liability than asset?

A little cough came from within the hideout, a sound almost as subtle as their own signals; an instant later two men erupted from cover, on their feet and bolting across the difficult terrain, so quick, too quick. Gartnait set off in pursuit. Bridei thrust knife in sheath, seized his bow, set arrow to string and loosed it in what seemed the space of a single breath. He had always excelled at this. His first shot caught one fellow in the shoulder, making him stagger before weaving away under the pines; his second took the other in the thigh. Then Bridei ran. Gartnait had downed one adversary and was grappling with him in the undergrowth. He was cursing as he sought to relieve the fellow of his weapons, and his opponent sounded to be returning the abuse in his own tongue. Bridei halted. His quarry, the man with a damaged shoulder, had disappeared as if by magic. He could not have outrun his pursuer, not with such a wound. Bridei had aimed with precision; the fellow would be weakened and in pain. But he'd still be able to use a knife, and it only takes a moment to step out from cover and slit your enemy's throat. Bridei held his breath, listening for a sound beyond the furious oaths of Gartnait's captive and the hissing epithets of Gartnait himself, who was now evidently trying to bind the fellow's arms. He shut those things out, using one of Broichan's tricks, tuning his ears to a single thread, a rasp of breath, a whistle of agony; he used his nose as a hunting creature would, to fix on the smell of fear. And there he was, the enemy, not far away under the bracken, crouched low, waiting. Waiting for Bridei to walk just a little closer . . . waiting to strike . . .

One step forward, decisive and bold. The bow held ready, the arrow perfectly aligned. "Get up!" Bridei barked. "Both hands on your head! Step out where I can see you or I put this through your heart!"

Silence. Nothing moved.

"Make no doubt of my aim." Bridei worked hard at an authoritative tone and thought he succeeded. "Want a taste of it?" And when there was no response, he loosed his shaft, praying that he had judged the shot correctly; there was probably less than two handspans leeway in it, judging by the sound of that breathing.

He heard his arrow lodge in wood—*thwack!*—and felt a surge of relief that he had not miscalculated and killed the man. A moment later the enemy rose to his feet, one hand on his head, the other arm loose and useless by his side. Red seeped across the shoulder of his tunic and down his shirt. His face was ash-white, his jaw set tight as if his teeth were clenched in pain. His eyes were coolly assessing.

"Move out here!" Bridei commanded, jerking his head, since there was little likelihood his captive understood the tongue of the Priteni. The Gael obeyed him, stepping to a point three paces from Bridei in the shadow of the pines. He

stared straight into his captor's eyes, then spat with calculated precision into his face.

Bridei took a slow breath. He did not raise a hand to wipe
the spittle from his cheek. "Turn around," he ordered, mim-
ing the action.

The other raised his brows as if to indicate incomprehen-
sion. His expression had become bland and calm; indeed,
the impression he gave now was that he thought the whole
thing a little ridiculous. He was young, Bridei judged, perhaps not so very much older than himself, although his eyes
had an old look about them.

"Turn!" Bridei showed him again, gesturing with the
knife and reaching for the rope he carried in his small pack.

The enemy turned his back. A moment later, as Bridei
made to fasten his wrists together with the cord, the man's
foot came around to deliver a crippling blow to Bridei's shin
and his good arm hammered back to catch his captor heavily
in the ribs. Off balance and winded, Bridei did the only
thing he could: lunged and grabbed the other by his injured
arm, letting his own weight drag his opponent down until,
after a painful, writhing tussle on the ground, he had him
pinned on his back, his breath wheezing in his chest and
Bridei's knife held firmly against his neck.

"Try that again and I'll break the other arm for you,"
Bridei gasped. "Gartnait!" Despite the disadvantage of his
injury, the Gael was ready for another trick, and another; he
would fight all the way. Bridei could see it in his eyes; they
held not the slightest trace of fear.

"Tie his hands, will you?" he muttered as Gartnait loped
up, his own opponent apparently trussed and compliant, for
there was no shouting now.

Gartnait busied himself with the rope. The captive
twisted, straining to free himself from Bridei's grip.

"Stop that, scum!" Gartnait delivered a sharp blow across
the ear, and jerked the cord tight so that it bit viciously into
the bound wrists. Bridei winced, imagining the surge of pain
up the arm to the damaged shoulder. The man's face showed
not a twitch.

"Can the other fellow walk?" Bridei asked his friend. "We'd
best move quickly. There could be more of them out there."

"I put a gag on," Gartnait said. "Best do the same here."

"You've already made enough noise to alert their reinforcements, if there are any," Bridei observed drily. "Go on, pick up your man; I'll handle this one. And thanks."

Gartnait grinned. "Don't mention it. No doubt you'll get the chance to return the favor before long."

There was a smear of blood on Gartnait's cheek and a look in his eyes that Bridei had never seen before. He could not quite place it, but it made him suddenly cold. Without turning to look, he sensed the captive's eyes on him. Bridei wound the end of the rope around one hand, leashing the fellow to him like a dog. He held the knife against the Gael's back. "Move," he directed, and they set off toward Raven's Well. Behind, Gartnait conveyed his own man more awkwardly, for the wound to the leg meant this one could not walk without support. Bridei slowed his pace, not to go too far ahead and seem to be claiming undue credit for himself. They'd done a good job; Talorgen must recognize that. Donal, too, would be impressed in his quiet way. Why, then, did Bridei feel uneasy still, his nerves on edge, his mind teased by something not quite right? Did more of the enemy lie concealed in pockets of the land beneath the pines, ready to strike? Surely not; the ideal moment for such an ambush was already past. Would their captives make a sudden break for freedom and this time make a better job of it? Hardly; Gartnait's prisoner was flagging, his features ghastly white, his leg buckling under him; there would be no more running for this one awhile. Bridei's captive had ceased his struggles, although the look on his face was not that of a defeated man. This fellow had not the red hair, the broad, fair-complexioned features that were most common to the men of Dalriada. Instead, the young warrior was long of face, dark of hair, a man of wiry, muscular build. He could almost have been one of their own save that his skin bore no evidence of the tattooist's needles and colors. Every seasoned fighter of the Priteni wore his battle marks with pride, alongside his signs of origin, the creatures and symbols that told his kinship. After the spring campaign both Bridei and Gartnait should have earned the first of the combat decorations for themselves. This man's skin bore no such patterns and that, as much as anything, marked him out as alien in this place.

For all his injury, which was bleeding steadily, the captive walked with purpose, eyes straight ahead, shoulders square. Bridei could not shake the sense that he himself was being assessed. If one grew up with a druid as a teacher, one learned to observe men subtly, to read the breath, to interpret the slightest change in the eye. It was the eyes of this man that were disconcerting above all. They were like the eyes of those killers in the Dark Mirror, the forces that had swept through the Vale of the Fallen, long ago, and taken all that lay in their path. Those eyes were devoid of both pity and hope; they saw only the task ahead of them and knew only the will to complete it. An army with such a look would be hard to withstand. It would, Bridei thought with a shiver, be near impossible to lead. Such men would fight without the awareness of their own mortality. They would kill without the knowledge of their enemy's humanity. A fell force indeed.

By the time they reached the stone walls circling the inner yards of Raven's Well, Gartnait's prisoner was leaning heavily on his captor's shoulder and appeared close to losing consciousness. The other walked with a back as straight as a king's and a supercilious twist to the mouth. It was not long before both Donal and Talorgen appeared, the council having been interrupted with news of this capture.

It was all Bridei had hoped for. Men gathered around offering congratulations, and as the prisoners were led away, several people commented that it was likely key information could be extracted from them. Talorgen's eyes showed surprised respect, Donal's a restrained pride. Yet all through the remainder of the day and into the evening that same uncertainty troubled Bridei. He could not identify its cause. It was a curse, in some ways, to have been brought up by a man like Broichan. Gartnait had been taught how to fight, how to conduct himself in company, how to ride, He was learning how to oversee a great holding such as his father's. Bridei, by contrast, had been trained in subtler skills: how to look and to listen, how to expect and prepare for surprises, how to read a man's moods and sometimes his thoughts from a tiny gesture, an infinitesimal flicker of the eye. He had been taught to learn from every single thing he encountered, the good, the bad, the triumphant, and the humiliating. Today, Gartnait's glowing eyes showed his delight at their success; his flushed cheeks revealed how he craved his father's approval. Bridei received Talorgen's congratulations as his friend did and acknowledged them with a courteous inclination of the head and the comment that without Gartnait's assistance he'd have lost his own man. But what Bridei noticed and Gartnait did not was a little note of hesitancy in Talorgen's voice, a small quirk of the lip, as if what they had done, courageous and resourceful as it was, had been in some way not quite what it seemed. And what Bridei observed later was that while Cenal, an apologetic shadow of a man whose unlikely job it was to supervise the interrogation of prisoners, did indeed disappear for some considerable time after their arrival, and while there were certain sounds suggesting the usual procedures were being employed, there was only one voice crying out from the isolated hut beyond the horse yard and he was sure it wasn't that of the fellow he had captured.

That could be easily explained, of course. There was a certain value in separating prisoners and playing them off one against another. But Bridei's unease lingered as the day wore on and the sounds from the hut subsided to faint sobs and groans and eventually silence. What was to be said? One did not march up to a powerful man like Talorgen and demand explanations, especially not when one's doubts were based on no more than a vague misgiving.

At supper time Talorgen mentioned that the prisoners had died under interrogation, and that some useful facts had been gleaned from both. Their deaths had been somewhat premature; from what Cenal had told him, the wounds inflicted by Bridei's arrows and the subsequent bleeding had weakened them greatly and reduced their resistance to pressure.

"You were not unduly heavy-handed, I trust?" Talorgen asked his interrogator, who sat at the next table.

"No, my lord. I'm a professional." A wounded look appeared on Cenal's unassuming features. Bridei set his knife down, his appetite for the fine cut of beef abruptly deserting him. He made no comment; it would have been out of place for him to offer an opinion on this. Maybe he should have taken the prisoners without inflicting such severe wounds. Yet now he almost wished he had killed them outright. It was common knowledge that any Gael foolish enough to be caught on Talorgen's land was subject to torture; it was expected Gabhran's chieftains would do the same to the spies of the Priteni, should the situation be reversed. But it was different when you'd caught the man yourself, had wrestled him to the ground, had led him on a rope, had looked into his eyes and seen blood flowing from a wound your own arrow had inflicted. It was different when you had yourself delivered him up to be tortured to death. Bridei recalled those features, implacable as a carving in stone. Not only would the dark-haired man have failed to impart any secrets, he would have died without a sound, Bridei was sure of it. And that meant that when Talorgen had said both prisoners had revealed useful information, he'd been lying.

There was only one person Bridei could talk to about this, and that was Donal. He had to wait awhile for the opportunity; supper was an extended meal, the family sitting at the upper board, the large household filling the long tables in the great hall, while the many men at arms who were quartered at Raven's Well in preparation for the spring campaign took the benches along the walls. Dogs roamed, torches smoked, ale flowed.

As Bridei's longtime mentor and bodyguard, Donal sat at the family table. Bridei tried to meet his eyes, to signal that he wanted to talk later, but Donal was debating a point of strategy with Talorgen, and it was Lady Dreseida who seemed keen to speak to Bridei tonight. Dark hair drawn back tightly into a headpiece with a fringe of pearls, beringed fingers resting with some elegance on the table before her, she leaned forward, fixing him with her searching gaze. Her interrogations were unpredictable and made him deeply uneasy; he had learned that whatever answers he gave, she always seemed dissatisfied.

"So, Bridei. You've been quite the hero today. I imagine Broichan would be very proud of you."

Bridei opened his mouth to reply, but Gartnait's sister, Ferada, was too quick for him.

"Broichan's a druid, Mother." Her voice dripped with scorn. It was very like Dreseida's, and so was Ferada's proudly upright bearing, her queenly lift of the head and her immaculate appearance, every hair in place, every fold of the gown just so. Ferada was younger than Gartnait; nonetheless, one could not look at her without seeing the formidable woman she would one day become. "Druids aren't concerned with feats of arms and deeds of bravery. If Broichan were here, he'd be asking Bridei whether he learned anything from spiking two men with his arrows then hauling them home to suffer a painful demise at the hands of Father's thugs. Isn't that right, Bridei?"

There was a hush, in which Ferada realized the talk and laughter around her had died down as she spoke, so that her final words were heard clearly by all at the upper table, her father included. A crimson flush of mortification rose to her cheeks.

"What Ferada says is true." Bridei spoke quickly, filling the awkward silence. "My foster father would be interested principally in what was to be learned from the experience, rather than in the occurrence itself. All the same, druids do care about feats of arms; it is not so many years since Broichan rode at King Drust's side in his great encounters with the forces of Dalriada. It is part of the role of a king's druid to advise him on matters of war: to cast auguries, to make predictions, to determine the best time for advance and retreat. To help the king in his decisions and to draw down the good will of the gods."

"Ferada may have spoken truth," Talorgen observed, frowning at his daughter, "but I am dismayed that she cannot control her tongue sufficiently to frame her comments with appropriate restraint."

Ferada's lips tightened and she blinked rapidly.

"Nonetheless," put in her mother, "your daughter deserves an answer to her question, however inelegantly she may have expressed it." Dreseida turned her piercing eyes on Bridei, arching her brows.

"What question?" queried Gartnait, perplexed. "She didn't ask any question."

Now Talorgen was watching Bridei, and so was Donal.

"True," Bridei said as evenly as he could, "but the question was there, unspoken. Broichan's question: what can be learned from today's events?"

"And?" Gartnait prompted. It was clear he did not intend to put forward any answers himself.

"One does not learn so quickly." There was a profound longing in Bridei to be home at Pitnochie, where the day held enough silences for the mind to contemplate questions like this, where there was the space to hear the voices of the gods, where there were folk who would sit silent and let him work his way through his thoughts in his own time. He needed Broichan; he missed Wid and Erip; he longed for Tuala and her deep quiet. "I would not wish to pronounce on this as if I held myself as wise as my foster father. This was our first encounter with the enemy, Gartnait's and mine."

"And well done," Talorgen said.

"Bravely acquitted," added Donal, but there was a question in his tone.

Bridei knew he must say more, although he would far rather have kept his thoughts to himself. For Gartnait's sake at least, he should continue to pretend that this had been an irrefutable triumph. Curse Ferada; she was a meddler and too sharp for her own good. "I was surprised to find this enemy had a human face," he said quietly. "That troubled me, for everything in our people's past binds me in enmity toward the Gaels until the day we drive them from our shores. Those things I must still learn to acquit. In time I will do so. On the field of war one cannot afford such scruples. I saw courage today. Cenal would tell us, I imagine, that the same courage was in evidence to the end."

Fortunately, Talorgen did not seem to take Bridei's speech amiss. "Maybe so," the chieftain said, "but we will not dwell on that, not with women and children present. War is a brutal business. You are young men yet; this is only a taste of what is to come. Believe me, all of us started with such sensitivities, but they cannot last long. If we did not suppress them they would cripple our will. Now let us speak of other matters. Change is upon us; spring's venture will be significant. Once the hostilities commence, Raven's Well will no longer be safe. Dreseida will travel up the Glen before Maiden Dance and take the family with her to the protection of Drust's court." He turned his gaze on Ferada, who had composed herself once more and who now met his stare with a distinctly challenging look. "That will provide, if nothing else, an opportunity for you to learn some restraint, daughter," Talorgen said, not unkindly. It was well known that he preferred his children to express their opinions, even if the results were occasionally an embarrassment. Indeed, he had been heard to comment that if Gartnait took as much interest in the affairs of Fortriu as his sister did, he might in time make something more of himself than merely a competent fighting man. "You will be lodged in the household of the wise women at Banmerren, where you can avail yourself of the excellent general tuition they provide for girls of noble birth. My wife will stay at court with her kinswomen; the boys, too." Talorgen could not have been unaware of the tense silence of both Gartnait and Bridei; their own places in this neat plan had yet to be clarified. Were they enumerated as boys still, to be sent off to safety as soon as anything interesting started to happen?

Donal cleared his throat. "I have Broichan's permission for you to be part of the venture against the Gaels, Bridei," he said. "He's not altogether happy about it, but he knows it's time; more than time, truth to tell. In fact he's contributing a small force from his own household, so we'll be seeing some old friends, Uven and Cinioch among them. I imagine Talorgen will let Gartnait here ride with you; you've proved your worth as a team today."

Talorgen smiled. "We'll make good use of the two of you. Be warned: it won't be like today's capture, a balanced man-to-man affair. War is dirty, cruel, and dangerous. A good man cannot fail to be sickened by it. But it's necessary as long as there are evil scum like the Gaels in this world. They've polluted our shores and devastated our lands long enough. Spring should see a turning of the tide: a new hope for the Priteni and for the king. Take Galany's Reach and we see hope restored, hope of bigger things to come. You'll be part of that."

"Don't grin any wider, Gartnait," Ferada remarked, "or your face might split in half."

Gartnait grimaced at her, entirely failing to conceal his shining-eyed delight. As for Bridei, his feelings were more mixed than he had expected. To be accepted, at last, as a man and a warrior, that was good, that warmed his heart. Still, after today, he wondered if he had the least understanding of what it really meant. The images from the Dark Mirror were close to the surface of his thoughts, full of sorrow and confusion, full of a terrible courage like that of the young man whose death he had caused today. Yet that man had been a spy. He had been the enemy, the same kind as those blank-eyed warriors of old who killed without thinking. How could one fight as one should when plagued by such misgivings?

"It's not fair." That was Gartnait's youngest brother, Uric, an explosive presence of seven years old, now leaping up and thumping the table so violently that platters and knives danced in their places. "We'll never be old enough to go to war! Who wants to visit court again? A lot of old men mumbling in corners, that's all it is, and people telling us to be quiet."

Talorgen's gaze moved to contemplate his youngest child, and under it Uric fell silent.

"It's true," put in Bedo, one year older and marginally wiser. "We're expected to be on our best behavior all the time at Caer Pridne. We'd much rather stay at home where the action is, Father. We could help. There are all sorts of things we could do. If Gartnait can stay, why can't we?"

"Fat lot of use you'd be," Gartnait said under his breath, digging his young brother in the ribs.

"You haven't the least idea what this is about, Bedo." Ferada's tone had returned to its customary note of calm superiority. "Gartnait and Bridei are men. You two are little children. Gartnait and Bridei could be dead by the end of spring. Did you think of that? Be glad you are too young to go. You'll get your turn soon enough. And if you think it's unfair, try being a girl for a while."

"Let us have no more talk of unfairness," said their mother, rising to her feet. "You'll do as your father and I bid you and that's an end of it. And now it's time for you lads to go to bed. Ferada, I have some tasks for you; let us leave these men to their war talk."

Much later, Bridei found Donal alone by the northern dike, gazing out over the dark hillside and down toward the dim, pale ribbon that was Maiden Lake. It was clear to him that Donal had been waiting; after so long as teacher and student, and then as something more like friends, they understood each other well. For a little they stood in companionable silence, listening to the small sounds of the night.

"About today," Bridei ventured.

"Mm?"

"Maybe I'm imagining things. I couldn't say it in front of Talorgen; it sounds foolish. On the face of it that was a good capture, the retrieval of useful prisoners. But something about it didn't add up."

"Oh, aye?"

"I don't know about the man Gartnait took. But the one I captured wasn't the kind to fold quickly under torture. And he may have been bleeding, but it wasn't enough to kill him. I aimed carefully; I always do. So why did they handle things the way they did? Was that necessary?"

"You tell me," said Donal.

"I've been over it and over it," Bridei mused. He kept his voice down; there were still other folk about. "That was a man who could have been useful, I sensed it. Maybe he wouldn't have talked, but he would have been of some value, perhaps as a hostage. It would have been better to patch him up and hold on to him, keep him in custody. What Cenal did was just . . ."

"Inhumane? It's the way things are, Bridei. There's no place for scruples when spies creep up to a man's very doorstep. These folk show no regard for niceties when they take our fellows prisoner. Their methods would disgust you."

"It was crude," Bridei said, undeterred. "Crude and, I suspect, entirely unsuccessful, whatever Talorgen chooses to say about it. Why take that course? Talorgen's neither stupid nor wantonly cruel. There's something here he's not telling us."

Donal nodded. "Maybe so. Still, unless you plan to ask him outright, I don't suppose you're going to find out what it is."

"You don't think," Bridei said, voicing his deepest concern, "that the whole thing could have been set up, do you?"

"What do you mean, set up?"

"I mean, somehow entirely faked so that Gartnait and I got the chance to prove ourselves without being in any real danger. A false ambush, men acting as enemy, a strangely convenient opportunity for the two of us to take them unaided. It bothers me that Broichan is so anxious about my safety. That was all very well when I was a child, back in the days when it seemed someone was out to get at him by injuring me. But I'm a man now. Doesn't it frustrate you that you must always be close to me, you or another of the chosen guards, that you must still sleep across my doorway and be my watchdog rather than my friend? It seems to me that, even as Talorgen tells me I am a man, the safeguards my foster father has set in place mean I am still a child to him, to be shielded from harm. Perhaps today's small triumph was a child's triumph, engineered for me by my elders and betters."

"I am your friend, Bridei." Donal's voice was very quiet.

"I know that; and a better one I could not hope for. But I must be allowed to stand on my own feet some time."

"I'll tell you one thing," Donal said. "The body I saw being taken from Cenal's house of pain this afternoon was no fake."

The chill returned to Bridei, fastening on his heart like the hand of a wraith. "Body? Which man was it?"

"Fellow with a bandage around the leg. Don't know about the other one; I didn't hang around to see him brought out. Their kind are rubbish, Bridei. They're not worthy to be under your boot sole. You shouldn't waste another thought on them."

Bridei was silent.

"As for boys and men," Donal said, setting a hand on Bridei's shoulder, "you'll play your part in the campaign as a warrior amongst warriors; it's something you have to face, you and Gartnait both. But Broichan's been right to set up protection for you. Maybe he could have explained the reasons better. That's something you'll have the right to demand of him, I reckon, after this campaign is over. It's time he told you more. As for me, I do as I'm bid. I know you think there's no need for such vigilance. But there's every need. You are a king's son, after all."

"We are a long way from Gwynedd," Bridei said.

"All the same. When spring's over, things might change. In the meantime you'll have to put up with me a little longer."

Bridei glanced at the tattooed warrior; Donal's expression was unreadable in the dim light. "I have no complaints," he said quietly. "Without you here I'd find it intolerable to stay. You're my bit of home when I'm away from Pitnochie. You help me make sense of things. But when I ride into battle, I want to be on the same footing as the other men, to have the same chances and take the same risks. You must not devote yourself to protecting me, but to pursuing the enemy. I don't know what instructions Broichan has given you, but I hope you will respect that."

"Oh, aye." It was not possible to tell what Donal meant by this.

"A man died today because of what I did."

"And more will die when you ride to war, your own as well as the enemy. You'll feel your knife twist in a man's heart. You'll see the expression in his eyes as he screams for his mother while you gut him with your spear. The first time's always the hardest. But it never gets easy; it never comes naturally. You have to remember what they've done, the filthy wretches. What has to be in your mind, every moment you're out there, is the evil they've inflicted on our land, the rape of our women, the slaughter of our children, the torching of our settlements, the destruction of our sacred places. Keep those thoughts alive and your hand won't hesitate to grip the sword and strike a blow for freedom."

"And today?"

"Put it behind you. Ask if you'd have such doubts if you'd seen Gartnait's throat cut this morning. You did the right thing. You did what a man has to do. That's all that matters."

SOMETHING FERADA HAD said gnawed at Bridei's thoughts, distracting him from the all-important tasks of preparation for war. *By spring, Gartnait and Bridei could be dead.* He had known this, of course. Protectors or no, he recognized that he would face the very real chance of falling foul of a Gaelic spear or stepping into the path of an accurately loosed arrow. It was not the prospect of death itself that troubled Bridei so much. It was the thought of dying without knowing the truth; of not being sure if the future for which Broichan was preparing him so assiduously was indeed the one he had increasingly come to suspect. He did not wish to wait, as Donal had suggested, and ask Broichan for answers in the spring. By spring it could be too late.

It was awkward. Talorgen, as Broichan's friend, could not be approached with such a question, not if Bridei had not first raised the matter with his foster father. Dreseida would be able to give him the piece of information he required, but he was reluctant to approach her. Her manner made Bridei uneasy, verging as it did on the inimical for no good reason he could see. She would tell him if he asked, but not without another volley of testing questions, the purpose of which was beyond his comprehension.

There was another avenue, and this he took when the opportunity offered itself. One morning before the day's work began he went to the kitchen garden at Raven's Well for a little solitude. It was a quiet spot, full of the pleasing scents of herbs, with a small pond in the center and low, clipped hedges neatly dividing the beds of culinary plants. There were not many places at Raven's Well where one could be quite alone; meditation was well nigh impossible. Even in this small sanctuary one was likely to be interrupted by Uric or Bedo chasing a dog, or someone with a knife and basket, seeking parsley for a pie.

Today, Bridei sat on a stone bench for a while, trying to set his thoughts in order. The capture; the Gael with his calm eyes and air of superiority; the battle to come. Broichan and his plans. Bridei thought of his family, far away in Gwynedd, the family he had all but forgotten. It had seemed for a long time that Broichan would bring him up, educate him, then send him back to Gwynedd to live his life among his own people. It was for this that most noble families sent sons out for fostering: to broaden their horizons early so that they might contribute more fully later as councillor, sage, warrior. As king's son. Bridei supposed his brothers were both seasoned fighters by now, riding out proudly at their father's side. It occurred to him that he might even have other siblings, younger ones of whom he knew nothing. A sister, perhaps. That was a strange thought. No sister could ever be closer to him than Tuala was, blood kin or no. Bridei smiled to himself. Although his little wild thing had grown now to a girl of nearly thirteen years old, he could not think of her without remembering that night: the moonlight, the snow, his frozen feet, and the moment when he first saw the Shining One's remarkable gift; the best moment of his life. He would never cease to be grateful for it. As for his own family, they seemed ever more distant as the years passed. All the same, it would be good to see them sometime, his father in particular. When the battle was over, perhaps Broichan would let him travel. Perhaps. Unless he was right about what the druid's plans really were.

"Good morning." Ferada was approaching across the garden, a tiny, bound book in one hand, her skirt held clear of the dewy grass by the other. She was clad in a perfectly pressed gown in a russet shade similar to that of her hair, which was gathered in a complicated knot of plaits at the nape of her neck. A single bright curl hung at her right temple, accentuating the pallor of her skin. Bridei rose to his feet.

"Don't get up," Ferada said, coming to sit beside him. "I'm after the same thing as you, peace and quiet. Uric committed some terrible crime, I think it was losing one of Bedo's lucky stones, and it's a battlefield in there. I wish to be out of everyone's way, particularly Mother's."

Bridei smiled. "I can understand that very well."

Ferada opened her book, but her gaze was not on the neat, hand-drawn script that filled its tiny vellum pages. She stared across the garden as the light of early morning set its golden touch on the ordered rows of winter vegetables, the fallow beds with their bare, dark soil in which a mob of tiny birds was already hunting for tasty morsels. "I wonder sometimes," she said, "if it's the royal blood that makes her like that. It's as if nothing can ever be good enough for her. None of us can ever match up to what she sees in her mind as the way we should be. I'm sorry," Ferada added hastily. "I shouldn't be speaking thus to you, Bridei, it isn't fair. Our difficulties are our own; we must find our own solutions."

"I am always willing to listen," Bridei said. "I make no judgments. I am hardly in a position to do so, having grown up without my own family."

"Thank you." It was evident Ferada did not wish to take the topic further.

"May I ask you a question?"

"Of course, Bridei."

"I'd like you to tell me exactly what the kinship is between your mother and my mother. Between my mother and King Drust."

Ferada stared at him. "All those years of education and you don't know that?"

Bridei felt his cheeks flush. Ferada could be relied on for honesty, but tact was not her strongest skill. "It seems to me that information was deliberately withheld from me. But I wish to know. I think it's important that I find out before we leave for the west."

"Mm," observed Ferada, regarding him closely. "So, when you lie dying in battle you'll know that, if you hadn't been in the way of some Gael's sword, you might one day have been king?"

There was a brief silence.

"Something like that," Bridei said.

"It's simple," said Ferada. "My mother's mother and King Drust's mother were sisters. That means my blood, and that of my brothers, is of the royal line; the female line. Horrendous as the prospect is, I'm forced to acknowledge that all three of my brothers will have a right to put themselves forward as claimants for the kingship one day, when Drust the Bull dies. I fervently hope that won't be for many years yet; the king's not an old man. I cannot for the life of me imagine Uric on the throne; Bedo, at least, is capable of putting two thoughts together when he tries. As for Gartnait," she shrugged, rolling her eyes skyward, "he's the least likely of all. He'd absolutely hate it. Of course, there are plenty of other possibilities. The sons of the royal blood are spread widely within the kingdoms of the Priteni."

Bridei waited.

"For me, what it means is a very particular kind of marriage, since any sons I have will be potential claimants in their turn. I can't wed just anyone. It has to be a chieftain or other man of high status, preferably from within the territories of the Priteni. Of course, if I receive a proposal from outside the borders, it's acceptable as long as he's a king. That's what happened with your mother."

"You do know her story, then?"

Ferada tossed her well-groomed head. "Of course. Such matters are of prime importance to my mother; she speaks of them often. Indeed, I'm surprised she hasn't seized the opportunity to explain it all to you herself."

"She thought, perhaps, that I already knew. Will you tell me, Ferada?"

"Your mother is kin at one further remove. The link goes back to Drust's grandmother. Anfreda is descended from that lady's sister."

He waited.

"Through the female line, Bridei. You, too, are a potential candidate for kingship. You guessed, of course."

Bridei could not reply. Suspecting was one thing; having the knowledge, suddenly, that those suspicions were true was making his head reel and his heart beat like a drum. He worked to steady his breathing.

"Anfreda was quite close to all of them once," Ferada told him. "That's what Mother said. She was a favorite with Drust and his wife; Father knew her, and so must Broichan have done, because he was at court in those days. Maelchon came to Caer Pridne to settle a matter of incursions in the north of his own domain; soldiers of the Priteni had been hired as mercenaries by his enemy, and he wanted to put a stop to it. He stayed somewhat longer than he'd intended, and when he went back to Gwynedd he took a new wife with him. It's quite acceptable, as I said. The royal women do wed outside the Priteni tribes sometimes. It's considered a good idea because it strengthens the bloodline. So here you are, and I'm obliged to say I consider you only marginally better as a potential monarch than I do Bedo."

"Oh." Bridei found himself a little put out by this. "And why is that?"

"You're too much of a scholar," Ferada said bluntly. "You think too much. And you're too kindly."

"I see," said Bridei.

"It seems to me," Ferada said, "that to be king you'd need a very thick skin and not too much imagination. And you'd need a lot of very clever advisers. Drust the Bull certainly has those."

"Ah, well," Bridei said, "the election may not be for years yet. And as you said, there could be many candidates."

"Seven, if each of the houses of Pridne has one to put forward. The king of Circinn, Drust the Boar, will be seeking to add Fortriu to his own domain. He wants the whole of the two kingdoms to become Christian, that's what Father says."

Bridei felt a shiver run through him, a premonition of dark change. "The chieftains of Fortriu would never allow that to happen," he said grimly. "The Flamekeeper would not permit it."

Ferada was regarding him curiously. "Mm-hm," she said. "It depends, doesn't it, on how divided we are among ourselves? That must be the key. One leader, one country, one faith. I expect that is what Circinn intends. Unless Fortriu can summon the same unity, we may not retain the kingship of our own realm, next time."

Bridei smiled. "I think you should be a royal councillor, Ferada."

She startled him by jumping to her feet and scowling at him. "Don't you dare patronize me!" she snapped.

"I didn't mean—"

"That's enough! Don't try to explain yourself, you're just like Father, let the conversation get to a certain point and then give that little look that says, oh well, you're only a girl after all, what do your opinions matter?"

"Really, I—"

"Don't even try, Bridei!"

He watched her walk away, her back very straight, her head held high. "You misjudge me," he said quietly, but whether Ferada heard him, there was no way of telling.

7

THE CHANGES WERE so slight at first that Tuala hardly noticed them. The winter of her thirteenth birthday was a particularly harsh season, and tempers were short in the isolated household of Pitnochie. When Ferat only grunted in response to her morning greeting, Tuala took it to mean his mind was on the difficulties of getting the fire going, what with the supply of dry wood at its lowest and the wind whistling down the chimney in a determined effort to thwart him. When Cinioch didn't seem to want to talk to her after supper she assumed he was worrying about the conflict to come, for Broichan had advised his men at arms that they'd be part of a challenge to Dalriada in the spring, and that would mean blood and loss. Mara's manner was brusque and distant, but that was nothing out of the usual. Broichan was the center of her world; others she'd little time for.

It was the day when Fidich barred Tuala from visiting the cottage where he lived with Brenna and the children that she realized the household's frostiness was more than the general bad humor of a hard winter. That day she felt the touch of something far colder, the glimmer of an awareness that she had been placed outside a barrier and would never be allowed to step back in. Why, she could not tell. She hadn't done anything to offend anyone. Yet all of them had changed.

"I'm sorry," Brenna whispered, catching Tuala on her way home after Fidich had announced she was no longer welcome in their small dwelling. "He's concerned for the children, that's all it is."

"The children? What do you mean?" Tuala was baffled.

"I'm sorry," Brenna said again, her features creased with helpless apology. Fidich was already limping back along the path, eldest boy clutching his hand, dogs at foot. "I know you mean no harm, it's just . . ."

"Just what?" A terrible calm descended on Tuala, a premonition of things to come.

"It's the tales. The men are mindful of the tales: the owl-wife, and Amna of the White Shawl, and others like those. They're afraid, and fear breeds fear. I've tried to tell Fidich, he's a good man, but he's got it into his head, they all have . . ."

"What? Got what into his head?"

But Brenna only muttered, "I'm sorry, Tuala," and was away off after her husband. When Tuala went back to the house it seemed to her that all of them were carefully avoiding her gaze, Ferat intently chopping herbs, his two assistants busy with the fire—the hands of one moved to sketch a charm, the sign to ward off evil, as she passed—Mara folding linen, lips pursed in disapproval, eyes distant. Broichan was in his own chamber as usual. He did venture out sometimes, but with Bridei gone, his interactions with his household were terse in character and restricted to what was essential for the smooth running of Pitnochie. Perhaps, Tuala thought, he was merely waiting for Bridei's return, as she was. It was rare for Broichan to speak to her, and she was glad of that, for her fear of him had not diminished as she grew older. One glance from those dark eyes had still the power to render her mute; one word of criticism could fill her heart, on an instant, with a paralyzing blend of fury and terror.

Fidich's decree forced Tuala to take stock, and she realized this had been creeping up on her for some time. It manifested itself in different ways: a subtle separation of her own place at the table; the removal of a certain fine wool coverlet from her chamber without explanation and its replacement with a coarse thing like a horse blanket; a refusal to let her take Blaze out for a ride, even on a fine crisp day that was entirely suitable, with the pony badly needing exercise. And there were the sudden silences as Tuala came into a room, as if others had been discussing her in her absence, not favorably.

She considered these things but could not make much sense of them. If Bridei were here, people would not dare to be so unkind. If Bridei were here, Broichan would wear a contented look, and Ferat would be smiling, and the men at arms would go back to exchanging tales of war and tales of wonder around the fire at night. Bridei made the household come alive. She longed for spring, for this battle to be over and Bridei home again.

There was one quarter to which she might still turn for reassurance. Her lessons continued. They were shorter now, for this winter Erip was ailing. He had a persistent cough that rattled his chest, and he was getting thin, a startling phenomenon in a man ever characterized by his smiling rotundity. Broichan had made him a curative potion in which the scents of nutmeg and honey did not quite conceal an underlying trace of something acrid and potent, a druidic herb specific to the illness. It was to be hoped this might see the old man well again before winter's end. Erip sat before the hall fire with a capacious shawl around his now-frail shoulders; he refused to take to his bed, saying that was as good as admitting defeat, and that if he must die he would die teaching. Wid said the truth was that he'd die arguing, and Erip responded, coughing explosively, that it amounted to the same thing, and they may as well get on with it.

The talk of dying distressed Tuala. The look in Wid's eyes worried her still further, for as the bearded ancient coaxed his old friend to drink, or wrapped him more warmly, or exchanged a gentler form of their usual banter, she could see the unmistakable shadow of impending loss on his furrowed features. They were close, the two of them. She had never found out their stories, their origins, why they had settled here in Broichan's house, why they seemed to possess no kin or homes of their own. What was the basis of their huge fund of knowledge? What kind of young lives had they lived, to build up such a diverse wealth of learning? Erip and Wid never spoke of these things; questioned, each was adept at turning the conversation along more general lines. Tuala began to wonder if she would ever know.

Today Mist was ensconced on Erip's knee, her claws kneading the layers of soft wool that swathed him, her purr resonating deep. Even as an adult cat she was quite a small creature, her bristling gray body perhaps half the size of a normal farm cat's. As a rat-hunter she had earned her place at Pitnochie many times over.

Tuala sat down by Wid on a bench. Winter lessons always took place by the fire; there was nowhere else warm enough.

"What's it to be today?" Wid stretched long, mottled hands toward the blaze; she could hear the creaking of his joints. It must be hard to be old in winter.

"Do you know a story about Amna of the White Shawl?" asked Tuala. "I heard it mentioned. And there's another about an owl-wife. Can you tell me those?" She tried to sound casual, as if all she felt was mild curiosity. The way both old men turned to stare at her, eyes suddenly sharp, told her they knew her too well to be so easily fooled.

"Harumph," Erip rasped, settling into storytelling mode. "Sometimes a child will ask for a certain story, and it'll be told, and she'll realize there's a truth in it she didn't want to hear. You understand that, I'm sure."

The chill came over Tuala again, the cold breath of an un-welcome future. "This is something I need to know," she said. Thank the gods for these two old men; with them, at least, there was never any need to pretend.

"I'll begin it, then," said Erip, "and my friend here will end it. Once there was a fellow called Conn, a brewer he was, maker of the best ale this side of Serpent Lake and very popular with the locals because of it. He didn't drink more than he should, just made sure other people got the best he could produce, and all in all he was known as a sensible, practical kind of man, one who could be relied on not to do anything foolish." Erip stopped to cough; it was becoming harder for him to catch his breath after these spasms, and his hand shook as he took the cup of water Tuala gave him.

"Are you sure you want to go on?" she asked. "Wid can tell it—"

"Rubbish," retorted Erip in a voice like the rustling of dry reeds in autumn. "Stop telling tales and I may as well stop breathing. Now where was I?"

"A practical sort of man."

"Yes, and being practical, he was all ready to wed and settle down; he'd found a sweetheart, the daughter of a farmer, and he had his own little house, and everything was looking rosy. The girl's father was well off. She would come to the marriage with a bag of silver and her own three fields to boot. Now it so happened that Conn was out late one night, visiting friends, and he walked back by a short cut, a wee track under hornbeams that passed by a pretty little stream fringed with ferns. It was full moon. He was a fool to go that way, any of the old folk could have told him. Conn was happy, and maybe that made him overconfident, for he must have known the warnings that hang over such a place. So he walked blithely down the path, and there on the water's edge he saw her."

"Amna?" asked Tuala.

"Aye, but he didn't know who she was. All he saw was the loveliest creature he could ever have imagined, a girl pale as pearl and shimmering in the moonlight, with long hair like a flow of soft shadow, and a white shawl the only thing she wore to clothe her nakedness. She had a hand lifted to her mouth as if in surprise that a man had ventured that way by night. One look at her, and his sweetheart vanished right out of Conn's mind."

"He followed the white-shawled woman up the stream and into the forest." Wid took up the story as Erip leaned back in his chair and closed his eyes. "What happened between them that night is not suitable for an old fellow like me to be telling an impressionable young woman like you, Tuala. Suffice it to say that it left Conn a different man. Next morning he wandered back home, and instead of settling in to his job of brewing, and getting ready for his wedding, all he could do was stand in his doorway gazing out into the forest and dreaming of finding Amna again. Day and night he stood there, and not a drop of ale did he brew from Maiden Dance to high summer. Each time the Shining One reached her fullness he'd slip away under the hornbeams, and when he came back in the morning his face would be wan and worn, and his eyes full of a wild delight that was close to madness, as if he'd tasted something whose rarity and wonder were such that he'd die from the craving of it."

"They all told him," Erip said, "his mother, his old grandfather, his sweetheart in tears, the elders of the settlement. It was plain to them he'd been enchanted by a woman of the Good Folk, and he must break the spell or die of it. But Conn wouldn't listen. Each full moon he'd have his night of ecstasy, and in between, those who loved him watched him fade away with yearning until he was no more than a madeyed puppet of skin and bones. What did Amna want of him? Nobody knew. Others had glimpsed her there by the pond, the whiteness of the shawl eclipsed by the pearly fineness of her skin, the deep shadows of night never as dark as her lovely hair. Others had had the sense to drop their gaze and walk on past. Not Conn."

"What happened?" asked Tuala, thinking how foolish men were to allow themselves to be trapped thus; surely Conn should have recognized how his life was being destroyed and simply have told Amna no.

"It's a sad tale," Wid said. "His family tried to intervene. One full moon, they tricked Conn and bound him, so he couldn't go to meet her. They thought that by interrupting the pattern they might break the spell and bring him to his senses. That night, folk said they heard Amna's cries out in the forest, cries that curdled the blood. That was not the calling of a young girl for her absent lover, but the baying of a wild animal for its prey."

"And was Conn saved?"

Erip shook his head. "You don't meddle lightly with the Good Folk. One such as Broichan could do it, perhaps, but not simple folk like these. Conn cursed them all through the night, wrestling against his bonds, and after that he barred his house to them. He waited until the Shining One was full again and he went out to meet his love. The next morning his folk found Conn facedown in the pool, stone dead. They thought he'd drowned himself until they turned him over. He was white as a sheet, drained of blood. The marks of her teeth were on him."

Tuala shuddered. "That's a horrible story." Horrible, and not useful at all; such a tale had nothing to do with her. "What about the other one, the owl-wife?"

Wid regarded her gravely. "Along much the same lines," he said. "A man drawn into the woods, this time by what seemed a white owl, a rare and beautiful creature. She became a woman by day, and consented to be his wife provided he respected her difference and did not pursue her when it was her time to change. A happier tale, for a while at least. She bore him daughters; he did not waste away from desire, only became dissatisfied with what he had, wanting the comfort of his wife's warmth in his arms at night while he slept. Surely, he began to think, that was not too much to ask. In time his wish to make her human, which she could never be, led him to follow her into the forest under a full moon. He saw the wondrous moment of her changing, and on that night he lost her forever. This man did not die as Conn did. He roams the dark paths under the oaks, eternally crying out to the wife who will never come back to him."

There was a silence. Tuala was in no doubt of what the connection was between these tales. Still, try as she might, she could not make the link between them and the household's sudden coolness toward her. After all, everyone knew she was a child of the forest, had known it from the moment she first came to Pitnochie. And yet they had welcomed her. They had smiled and told her stories and treated her as a friend.

"What is it, lass?" Erip's hoarse voice was full of kindness, and all at once Tuala was on the verge of weeping.

"Fidich," she whispered. "And Ferat and the men at arms . . . They're shutting me out. I'm not part of things at Pitnochie anymore. Fidich said I can't go and see Brenna and the children. And Brenna told me the men are worried because of those tales, Amna and the owl-wife. But that doesn't make sense. Why would they be scared of me now if they never were before? I'd never hurt the children, they should know that—" Now she really was crying.

Wid leaned forward, proffering a square of linen. "Do what we've taught you to do," he said calmly. "Think it through. The tales concern men seduced by women of the Good Folk, men sucked in by a power so strong they cannot resist it, not even when they are individuals known for great common sense, as Conn was."

Tuala thought as hard as she could. It didn't seem to help much.

"You ask yourself," Erip said, his fingers gently stroking the cat, "why everyone seems to have changed. I do feel bound to point out that Wid and I have not changed; we are, I think, beyond being afflicted by this particular phenomenon. But your mind must take another tack here, child. Perhaps it is something else that has changed."

Tuala looked at him for a long moment. "You mean me? This has to do with me changing, growing up? But—" She fell silent again, recognizing that this was indeed what he meant. Now that she thought about it, the cooling of the household's attitude to her did date from the time when her body had begun to alter, rounding here and hollowing there, giving her the form and rhythms of a woman. As a child, it seemed she had been acceptable to Pitnochie, for all her difference. She had been treated with kindness, even affection. Now those who had been friends were tiptoeing around her as if she were in some way dangerous. Surely they did not believe that, as a woman, she was the same kind of creature as Amna of the White Shawl? "You must be wrong," she said flatly. "Amna was of unearthly beauty, the sort of woman who drives men out of their minds. The sort of woman who exists only in stories. Nobody could think I would . . ." This was just silly. She could hardly believe they were having such a conversation.

"Try looking in your mirror, lass," said Wid. "What's there now will be there a hundredfold next winter, and a thousandfold the one after. The men have seen it and they're afraid. The women have more common sense, but they'll be wary all the same. It's sad but true; you're in your fourteenth year now, and your path from this point on will have this shadow over it, however hard you try to be one of us."

Tuala was lost for words. Surely this could not be true. She was no great beauty, she had no interest at all in men and the kinds of things men and women did in the privacy of the bedchamber. The whole idea of Ferat and Fidich and the others thinking of her in such a way made her feel sick. She did not want to entertain the least notion that this could be the truth. "What about you?" she challenged. "You're still my friends. You haven't changed. What about Broichan? He never changes. This can't be the explanation."

Erip began to cough; this time there was blood on the hand he clapped over his mouth. It took some time for the paroxysm to pass. At length the old man settled again. "As I said," his voice was a thread, "we are perhaps too old, beyond such foolishness. Or maybe it is the case that we fell in love with you when you were knee-high and bursting with questions, and that that is the way we still see you: Bridei's little treasure, a rare Midwinter gift. As for Broichan, his vision is a very particular one. No doubt he assessed you fully from the first, and continually weighs up the opportunities and the dangers you represent."

Tuala nodded. She could remember every word of what Broichan had told her, long ago, that time when he sent her away. There was no doubt he had seen her as a threat from the first. "What can I do?" she asked them.

The two old men regarded her in silence, their eyes full of kindness, their mouths grim. "Wait awhile and be patient," said Wid. "You've a difficult time ahead."

"Be ready for change," Erip added. "You'll need to be brave, Tuala."

"It would be all right if Bridei would come home." Her voice was very small; she had not planned to say this aloud, but it came out despite her.

Wid opened his mouth to speak; she saw Erip shake his head as if to silence his friend and then Mist, growing restless, jumped from the old man's lap and stalked off toward the kitchen. As if at a summons, the three dogs arose from their sleep beneath the table and suddenly the hall was no longer quiet.

"Loneliness can be hard to bear," Wid said, rising to his feet. "A good friend is the most precious gift in the world, Tuala. That's a lesson I've no need to teach either you or Bridei. Now, let's fetch this old man some soup, shall we? He's starting to resemble a scarecrow, and we can't have that. I thought I saw Ferat with ham bones before; the smell's definitely promising."

THE WINTER PASSED and the days grew appreciably longer, but Bone Mother did little to release her relentless grip on the land. Ice crusted the ponds; snow blanketed Broichan's house under the oaks. The men grumbled on their way to watch and an array of clothing steamed before the kitchen fire, filling the house with a pungent odor. The dogs were reluctant to venture out; Mist spent most of her time in Erip's lap before the fire or, later in the season, curled up on his bed in the crook of his bent knees. For a time came when the old scholar no longer had the strength to rise from his pallet, to venture forth into the household and make pretense that he would soon be better. They put him in Bridei's room; Wid kept vigil, feeding Erip sips of water or measured mouthfuls of Broichan's latest potion, wiping his brow, telling him tales as if he were an ailing child. Mara burned aromatic herbs near the doorway and bore away the stained linen. Tuala sought to help and found herself barred from the chamber. Mara had taken control; it was on her say-so that folk came and went now, and she had decreed that too many visitors would only weaken the old man. Wid, struggling with his own grief and exhaustion, had not the strength to argue, but he let Tuala in once or twice when the housekeeper was otherwise occupied. Erip's hands were so fragile now that the fingers felt like twigs, and his voice was a faint whisper. Tuala thought she saw a new kind of light in his eyes, a brightness that looked, already, beyond the mortal world and into another full of peace and possibility. It was as if his mind conjured a great new tale of which he only waited to begin the telling. She held his hand and swallowed her tears, and when Mara returned she slipped away like a shadow.

She made polite requests for admittance, pointing out that she was Erip's friend, that he had asked for her, that she could make herself useful.

"You're not required, Tuala," Mara would say.

"Off you go, lass," Ferat would tell her, the tone friendly enough, the look in his eye somewhere between impatience and unease. He, at least, seemed to feel a little guilt at the betrayal of someone who had been a loved child, a friend; all the same, his discomfort at her presence was clear enough.

Toward the end she was reduced to pleading with Mara. "Please. He's an old friend. Please don't shut me out."

"Erip's a friend to all of us," Mara said. "You're not needed here. Go on, and take your creature with you," and she made to push Mist off the bed, but Mist fastened tooth and claw into Mara's fingers, and was left where she crouched among Erip's mounded coverlets. Erip himself was too weak now to raise a protest, and Wid was dozing in a chair, worn out from the long watch he kept. In silence, Tuala retreated.

For a little she sat alone in her small chamber, staring at the wall. This was wrong; it was so wrong there didn't seem to be any learning at all to be gleaned from it. How could they not let her be there? How could they not let her say good-bye? She was one of them, reared among them, welcomed to their household and guided to knowledge by that same old man who now lay dying under the roof that had sheltered them both. A curse on Amna of the White Shawl. A pox on the owl-wife. That was just foolishness, and had nothing at all to do with her.

Suddenly Tuala was possessed with the need for action. Seizing her warm cloak, thrusting her feet into her heavy boots, she headed off outdoors. The chill clutched painfully at her lungs the moment she stepped from the kitchen; the air was like ice on her skin. But she had to get away, as far away as she could from Mara and Ferat and Fidich, from Uven and Cinioch, from the suspicious eyes of all those who had once seemed friends. She would not ask to take Blaze out; she did not want to hear another blank refusal. She would walk. She would walk all the way to the Vale of the Fallen, and there she would demand some answers.

As she grew up, it had become apparent to Tuala that there were certain talents she possessed that did not come readily to other people. From earliest days she had recognized that such skills should be kept concealed, since to demonstrate them would only underline the fact that she was different, and she did not want to be different, she wanted to belong at Pitnochie. Erip and Wid knew a little of what she could do, and so did Bridei. Her full range of abilities, and the ease with which she could use them, she kept to herself.

It might have been better, she told herself with some bitterness as she struggled up the track, boots sinking deep into the layer of damp and decaying leaves under the bare oaks, if she had never practiced those secret arts at all, if she had pretended even to herself that she had no such powers. Then she might have lost the knack. She might have forgotten how to use it, how to conjure images of queens and dragons and giants out of a ray of light through colored glass, how to coax a squirrel out of its hiding place and greet it in a way it understood in its small creature-mind, how to shape rushes and grasses and seed pods into a doll or a basket or a chain that held, not just the pattern of plaits and twists and knots, but a living power. She might have lost the ability to read the signs in the forest, signs left by the other kind, the Good Folk. Then she could not have found them, however much she felt the compulsion to seek. Their subtle scratches on bark or boulder, their small twistings of grass or bunchings of leaves were all messages and, without ever being taught their meanings, Tuala had long understood them. Their makers still eluded her. Those half-glimpsed shadows, those whispering voices were as close as they had ever come. Yet their messages were for her, she knew it. They called her; they wanted her as it seemed the human kind did not. With them there might be a home. It was one way; an impossible way. Step into that world and she must leave Bridei behind. To part from him was impossible. It would be like tearing herself in two.

Deeply enmeshed in her thoughts, Tuala covered the long

distance from Broichan's house to the hidden vale almost without noticing. The mist was thick today; she could barely see her own feet as she made her way down the steep path to the pool. The vapor seemed to close in above her, a suffocating, oppressive blanket. Somewhere in the woods a dog was howling, a sound of pure desolation.

On the rim of the Dark Mirror Tuala crouched down. At first she did not feel the cold, for the brisk walk had warmed her, but before long her nose, her ears, her fingers and toes began to tingle and to ache with a bone-gripping chill. Her teeth chattered. This had been foolish; she was a long way from home and nobody knew where she'd gone. Not that they would care, Tuala thought. If she never came back, Mara and Ferat and the others would probably welcome it. No irksome presence among them; no Otherworld temptress at hand to carry off their young men. That was so foolish she still could not come to terms with it. Herself some kind of unearthly beauty? Tuala casting spells to drive men mad from desire? She would simply laugh such a misguided theory off, were it not for the terrible reality of what it seemed to mean for her. She would scorn it entirely had not Erip and Wid, whose common sense was plain to her, told her that this was indeed how the household now perceived her. *Look in the mirror,* they'd said. So she did, leaning over the pool's still waters, seeking not visions or portents this time but simply her own true reflection.

She didn't seem much different from before. Her face was oval, the dark brows arched, the eyes large and light, perhaps blue if one had to give them a color. The eyes were questioning, and there were shadows around them; she had wept for Erip, and for Wid, and just a little for herself. The nose was straight, the mouth small and neat, pink as a rosebud. She was certainly pale. Tuala was forced to concede that in this respect, at least, she did somewhat resemble Amna in the story, for her skin had always been white and transparent, as if the Shining One lent her the gleam of moonbeams. Her hair was coal-black, long and glossy for all her neglect of brushing. That, too, made her like the girl in the tale. But she was young yet, not long come to her bleeding, and she shrank from the idea of what Amna had done with her lover under a full moon. Amna had been a seductress, a woman of sensual awareness and earthy passions. How could anyone think she, Tuala, had the same power as that dangerous creature of the night?

Tuala's practical outdoor clothes, cloak, shawl, tunic, and long skirt over sturdy winter boots, quite concealed her true form; the girl who looked back at her from the dark water could have been of any shape at all. Yet now, as she gazed, the image changed and she saw, shockingly, herself with not a scrap of clothing to cover her, standing there without the least shame, arms raised, neat, round breasts displayed like twin small moons, pink-tipped; curving contours of delicate waist, rounded hips, slender thighs all exposed for any eye to see. Even the small, new triangle of dark hair between her legs was visible. Horrified, Tuala clutched her hands across to shield her body, although here on the water's edge she was still well wrapped in her layers of wool. There in the Dark Mirror, her naked image turned and smiled and beckoned, and she recognized with sinking heart that a man might indeed find such a creature of pearl and ebony and rose enticing. She saw her own innocence in the vision, and the danger it carried in its very nature.

"Go away," Tuala muttered, angry tears welling in her eyes. "I don't want to see you! This isn't what I came for!" She squeezed her eyes shut, willing her own image into oblivion.

"Afraid to face truth?" said someone on her left. "That's not like you."

Tuala's eyes sprang open. This was not a subtle, hissing voice like those she had heard before in this secret fold of the land. This was confident and real-sounding, surely the voice of a flesh and blood woman. She had time only to blink and take in a glimpse of a cloaked figure standing beside her, close enough to touch, when a second voice spoke. Tuala jumped to her feet, turning the other way.

"Besides," observed the second personage, "this sight is pleasing. You cannot deny that. A fair image. Take one look at it, and a man would be eager to discover if the reality were fairer still."

It was a young man who spoke. Tuala's skin broke out into

goose bumps at his words; she could imagine what Donal or Bridei or even Broichan would have to say about her foolishness in coming all the way up here alone in winter without telling anyone. She held herself very still and tried to breathe slowly. She made herself observe, as Bridei had taught her to do. This was not a man, not exactly. He was not so very much taller than herself, and his wild, straggling hair had a mossy, greenish hue. Here and there his locks seemed to wander into the shape of tendrils and leaves, ivylike. The eyes were bog-brown and round as an owl's. Definitely not a man, although the mischievous grin he turned on her as she assessed him reminded her painfully of Erip in his better days.

"You're shivering." The other spoke and Tuala felt, as she turned back, the soft weight of a cloak settling around her shoulders. It seemed a thing of thistledown, fragile and insubstantial, yet it rendered her instantly as warm as a cat curled up before a hearth fire. The girl met her gaze calmly. She was somewhat taller than the young man, if man he could be called, and her hair was long and silvery fair, plaited and knotted elaborately with glinting threads and skeleton leaves, cobwebs and tiny white berries threaded through the strands. Her hooded cape was of a blue-gray cloth that moved about her like wood smoke. She, too, seemed young; her skin was winter-white, as pale as Tuala's, her figure slender, her bearing graceful. "You feel the cold; that is not so surprising. You have been raised among human folk; their tides are shorter and move with more violence. Already your body tunes to their patterns. You have come to us just in time."

The words Tuala had prepared for such an occasion were abruptly gone. She had wanted this so badly, had rehearsed the questions: *Who am I? Who was it abandoned me, and why?* Now, afraid of the answers, she could not bring herself to ask. At length she said, "Why now? Why show yourselves now? I've been here over and over; I've seen visions in the Dark Mirror, I've been teased by others of your kind who would never quite reveal themselves. What has changed?" The answer was in her head even as she spoke, the same answer others had already given: *You have changed.*

"Those whom you encountered were not of our kind," the leaf man said. "They are a lesser breed; many share our forest. Those others, they would not let you see their true form. Not while you still have one foot in a world of druids and heroes, kings and councillors."

"*One* foot?" Tuala could not help asking. She did not think what she felt was fear, despite the utter strangeness of this appearance, only astonishment that at last they had decided to reveal themselves to her, and a wariness that was bred of her knowledge of tales. "I live at Pitnochie; I belong in Broichan's house. Nobody really knows where I came from. I could be some poor lass's by-blow. I could be an ordinary human girl." She should ask them straight out. She wished she could make herself do so. *Do you know who I am?* The laughter that rang out now stopped these words before she spoke them aloud. The sound of their mirth echoed around the little glen like seeds rattling in a pod, making Tuala's neck prickle with its strangeness.

"Ordinary?" the girl mocked. "You believe that no more than we do. You are ours, a child of the forest. You have magic in every hair of your head, in every touch of your fingertips. Tell us why you have come here today, Tuala. Tell us why you sought us out."

The young man squatted down; his garments, like his hair, seemed an extension of the woodland foliage, mats of verdant, tangling growth. He smelled faintly of leaf mold. With long, knobbly fingers he patted the ground invitingly; the gray-cloaked girl was kneeling now on Tuala's other side. Tuala sat down, cross-legged, every sense alert. If she needed to run, she wanted to be ready to do it instantly. Her heart was pounding; there were many possibilities here, and she must be ready for any of them.

"I came for answers," she said. "And the questions are not the same I might once have asked you, had I had the chance. Folk have changed; those who were friends are suddenly afraid of me, wary and strange. My teachers said it's because . . . because, as a woman, they see me as dangerous." She swallowed. "Like Amna of the White Shawl," she added reluctantly. "And now my old friend is dying and they won't let me in to hold his hand and say good-bye." She would not give way to tears; it was important to remain in control of the situation. There would be plenty of time for weeping before long.

"Amna, hmm," the leaf man said. "Human women invent such tales to keep their men from straying, you know."

Tuala stared at him. His cheeks were as brown and shiny as ripe chestnuts. "Invent?" she echoed. "You mean it's just a made-up story? What about the owl-wife, is that the same?"

"Maybe yes," the man said. "Maybe no."

"That's not very useful," Tuala retorted. "I need some answers. I need to be able to show people that I'm no threat to them. I need to convince them that . . ." Her voice trailed off; this was just too embarrassing to put into words.

"That you've no desire for a man?" The girl slipped back her hood and folded her hands in her lap; there were many rings on her long fingers, intricate silver constructions in branching shapes studded with pale stones. "That's of no import, Tuala. The danger, as they see it, is that a man should desire you. They avoid you because they believe it perilous, from now on, to look or to touch. They think that to allow you too close may become a death sentence. We know your story. Bridei took you in. He was a child then and quite innocent of what it meant. The druid saw how it would be, but he saw it too late. He cannot allow you to stay at Pitnochie. To do so would indeed bring death: the death of his vision. So he believes."

Tuala's heart was cold. "But you said Amna was a made-up story. Anyway, I'm not like that. I've been brought up like a human girl, I will just live my life as an ordinary girl does. I won't harm anyone." The future she wanted contained herself and Bridei and Pitnochie all together; how could she bear anything else?

Neither of her companions spoke. In the lengthy silence, Tuala heard the echo of her speech and recognized how childish it sounded, how simple. It was too late for such easy solutions. She could never be a child again. "How do you know all this, anyway?" she challenged eventually, although the answer to this was here before her, in the still water of the Dark Mirror. "What is it to you?"

The forest girl smiled. It was an odd smile, in which sorrow and resignation were tempered by a kindness that seemed almost reluctant. "You surprise me, Tuala," she said. "You do not ask the one question that most troubles you. Is not that question the answer to this one?"

Tuala did not respond. These people were Other; they were as unlike her as wild creatures were. If they were her kin, she would almost rather not know.

"Ah, well," the girl said on a sigh, "you have not yet earned the right to such an answer, so I could not give it even if I knew it. That truth is for later, when you have shown that we can trust you. The time will come when you need us so badly you will do anything to know. As for the source of our knowledge, we watch you and we watch Bridei. Our patterns are longer than those of humankind, but that does not mean we have no interest in kings and druids, in battles and struggles and the governing of Fortriu. There's great change coming. Your friend is at the center of it, or will be. You are aware of that, we suspect."

Tuala nodded, though she would not put an answer into words. Even as a small child she had understood the kind of future Broichan had mapped out for his foster son.

"What part do you expect to play in such grand and momentous events?" the leaf man asked with brutal bluntness. "That is the question you must ask yourself, for it may not be long before Pitnochie is closed to you forever."

"Stop it," Tuala muttered, putting her fingers in her ears, but she went on listening; after all, she had come for answers, and that was what these were, for all they were not those she wanted.

"Broichan faces a dilemma," the forest girl said. "He can't simply abandon you. Bridei's good opinion means a lot more to him than he'd ever let anyone know. The king's druid has one weak spot, and that's his affection for the boy. Besides, Broichan is nothing if not loyal to the gods; he would not wish to fall foul of the Shining One by casting out her daughter. Fortunately for him, there's a solution. If I were Broichan, and my mind worked in the way of a mortal man's, I would be glad you have reached childbearing years.

Now he has only to find you a husband and he can be rid of you quite respectably, without offending anyone."

"Don't look so horrified," the leaf man said, licking his lips with a long, greenish tongue. The sight of it made Tuala's flesh crawl. "It's the usual thing for human girls once they've begun their bleeding. Haven't you been trying to convince us you are just like a human girl? Of course, a suitor for such as yourself could be tricky to find. Any man who knew the story of Amna of the White Shawl would be a fool to take you. But a lonely widower, an older fellow perhaps, might well be persuaded by a glimpse of that delicate flesh, that fresh little figure. And Broichan's a man of means; he can offer a solid sort of dowry. I'll wager you'll be off his hands by Midsummer. That's if you don't take the other option, the one we can offer you."

Tuala felt she might be sick. "Bridei wouldn't let him do it," she whispered. "He would stop it."

The man smiled again. "Bridei is much occupied with other matters," he said, and gestured toward the pool, where images sprang up in an instant shimmer of movement. "Life and death matters whose course will influence not just his own future, but the future of Fortriu. Should all unfold in accordance with Broichan's plan, Bridei's destiny will take him far from you. See for yourself."

"I won't look," Tuala said, and heard the tremor in her voice. "You can manipulate these images, you'll only show what you want me to see. You can't make me look."

"Why do you come here, if not to see him?" the girl asked softly. "Why linger in this lonely place, if not to be close to him when he is far away? When these waters show you his face, you cannot but look."

Tuala bowed her head. They were right: to come here in the cold, all this way, and not to see Bridei when she knew his image waited there on the surface of the Dark Mirror was indeed beyond her. Yet she felt awkward as she bent over the pool once more. It was not so long since her own naked form had gleamed pale and strange there in the water, and it unsettled her to be searching that same still surface for a picture of the dear friend of her childhood. There was something not right about it. She did not believe for a moment that her Otherworld companions would not change and distort the message of the Dark Mirror to their own ends. Still, she must look.

They were little glimpses, each gone almost before she had time to absorb it: Bridei riding with Gartnait beside him, the two of them pushing their horses fast in unspoken rivalry. That did not surprise Tuala. There had been plenty of opportunity to observe Talorgen's laughing, red-haired son during the summers Gartnait had spent at Pitnochie. Behind his clownish facade Tuala had seen something else: a passionate striving to be Bridei's match in feats of strength and skill, since he knew he could never come close in matters of learning. She had recognized the desperation with which Gartnait sought to prove himself before his father, and understood what Bridei did not: that his easy-going, jocular companion had fierce ambition in his heart. To a boy such as Gartnait, perhaps it might seem that things came too easily for Bridei. Gartnait knew nothing of the long times of loneliness, the patient hours of self-discipline. He did not understand what it meant to be sent away when you were too small to understand why.

The image changed, and Tuala saw Bridei wrestling with another man, a life or death struggle with knives. It was only a moment. Then Bridei alone at night, staring into the dark, a solitary candle showing his shadowed eyes, the little crease between his brows, the tight set of his mouth.

"He needs me," Tuala whispered.

Then it was not night but day, and he was sitting on a bench beside a fish pond, and there was a girl. The girl had red hair like Gartnait's and freckles sprinkled becomingly across her delicate nose. She was dressed in a way that marked her as a lady, the hair held back by an embroidered band with a single artful wisp allowed to escape over one ear, the gown a soft red-brown embroidered in the same green and blue as the headband. Her feet were shod in soft kidskin. The girl was seated beside Bridei; she seemed as solemn as he was, and she was listening attentively as he talked. Bridei bent his head courteously and she said a few words, raising her face to him. In a sharp-featured way she was very pretty, a little like a vixen. Tuala could see in Bridei's eyes that he admired her.

"Highly suitable," the leaf man observed drily as this image fractured and dispersed. "The daughter of a family friend, of royal connections, healthy and presentable in every way and but a year or two his junior. He must go to battle first, of course; this spring he must prove himself in the field. But it can be seen how this will unfold. Already he confides in her."

"He needs me." Tuala was shivering, for all the warmth of the strange cloak they had wrapped her in. "He needs to come home." No elegant girl of royal connections knew how to listen as she did, how to coax a smile to that solemn face, how to be there beside him as he wrestled with the great questions that beset him, and would do more and more. No dazzling vision could convince her otherwise. All that it meant was that nobody understood the bond between them; nobody but herself and Bridei.

"No, Tuala," the forest girl said. "Already he flies far from your grasp; would you seek to clip an eagle's wings?"

"Even the eagle cannot fly without his times of stillness." Tuala worked to keep her voice confident. "He needs rest, so he can go on with courage. For that, he needs me."

"How can you be certain of that?" asked the leaf man. "Would you not be better to make your own path and use your own talents? You have barely begun to discover what you are."

"Bridei no longer needs you." The girl's voice was soothing as honey mead, gentle as a mother's. "This was a friendship of children and it did you both some service. Those times are over now. He moves ahead on his own journey. It is time you gave thought to yours."

"You seem to fear Broichan's plan for you," the man said. "You need not do as he wishes. Choose the other way. That is why you came here to us. Don't try to deny it. You know there is a path for you here in the forest. We will show you how to find it. We will open the gateway so you can step across."

"We will bring you home." Now the girl's voice was like

the chime of a sweet, unearthly instrument, ringing across the dark waters. Tuala's scalp prickled. A charm, that was what this was, a spell, a trap; she had been wary of the leaf man with his sly smiles and his salacious looks, but it was the other, the seeming fair and sounding kindly, who was the more dangerous. She had been foolish to let this go so far, to let that soft voice, those taunting visions influence her. Her hands scrabbled to push the cobweb garment from her shoulders. Her body tensed itself, ready for flight. All she needed to do was get up and run, she knew the way, up the path, along the rim of the vale, down under birch and oak and holly, back to the borders of Broichan's land and safety. They would not follow, not once she passed the white stones at the entry to the Vale of the Fallen. At least, she hoped they would not follow.

But if she fled, they would know their barbs had hit their mark. They would know they had managed, at last, to frighten her. She would not allow them that small victory, not after they had hurt her with their cruel comments. They were not the only ones who could twist and turn the images of the seer to illustrate a particular point. Tuala took a deep breath and looked again into the waters of the Dark Mirror. She fixed her mind on the Shining One; she imagined the silver orb of the Lady's fullness, conjured a picture of a woman tall and lovely, bearing a tiny fur-swathed infant in her arms. The water shimmered, rippled, grew still again. There on its reflective surface was the child Bridei, small bare feet blue with cold below the hem of his nightrobe, standing on the doorstep at midnight. He looked down. The mirror did not show what he saw, only the wondrous change in his face, a face too solemn, too wary for such a child, whose mind should surely have been all on sunny days and games and family. In the water, he knelt and looked and his eyes were suddenly filled with light, his somber, small countenance suffused with joy. He rose to his feet and gazed up, and the Shining One looked down at him, touching his face with unearthly silver. Tuala could not hear what he said, but she recognized its meaning in her heart; it was a promise deep and binding, an affirmation of responsibility. He bent to gather up what lay at his feet; he smiled. Now there was a different look in his eyes, a look that was just for her. The image faded and was gone.

It was suddenly very quiet in the Vale of the Fallen, so quiet it was as if time had stopped while this image inhabited the Dark Mirror. Tuala blinked and rubbed her eyes, looking to right and to left. She was alone. As subtly and silently as they had arrived, her Otherworld companions were gone. Her chosen vision had displeased them, that much was certain. She did not entirely understand that; were not they themselves loyal to the Shining One? Perhaps it was her own stubbornness that had driven them away. Perhaps they had expected that she would take their hands and walk off into the forest this very day, never to return to the mortal realm. She had not even asked them for their names.

Rain began to fall, increasing with alarming swiftness to a drenching downpour that soaked her through cloak and shawl and tunic. She put up her hood and kept on going. Her boots were soon thick with mud. She had long wished the Good Folk might manifest themselves and begin to give her answers. Now at last they had done so, but she had learned little. Perhaps there was a kind of home for her among such folk. *We will open the gateway so you can step across,* they had said. She would like to find out what that meant, but only if she had a guarantee she could step back again. And Tuala had heard too many old tales to believe such a course would be possible. Cross into that other realm and you'd be trapped there forever, or you'd stay for a day's feasting and dancing, then come home to discover your family had been dead for a hundred years. Besides, she would not step across to anywhere without Bridei, and Bridei's path most certainly lay in the world of human affairs, of druids, kings, and battles. And she would not believe, however many charming fox girls she was shown, that anyone could fill her own place in his life. The two of them belonged together; it was as simple as that.

She arrived home after dark, cold, wet, and exhausted. As she emerged from the path under the bare oaks, her boots squelching, her saturated cloak hugged around her, she saw the pale faces of the men on watch, gathered by their little fire, turn toward her and turn quickly away.

The kitchen door was bolted; Tuala did her best to knock with frozen, aching hands. She thought of the image in the pool, a child standing in this very spot, gazing down at a babe abandoned in the snow of a solstice midnight. She waited, her body wracked with waves of shivering. This time there was no Bridei to let her in. She lifted her hand to knock again, but before she could do so the bolt was slid across and the heavy door opened on lantern light, the warmth of the fire, and Mara's dour countenance. Tuala stumbled inside.

"Erip's taken very bad," Mara said, ramming the bolt home again. "Get out of those wet things and bring them back to me, then you're to go in."

"How bad?" Tuala asked through chattering teeth. The sudden shock of the fire's warmth was making her faint and dizzy.

Mara tightened her lips. "It could be a long night," she said. "Go on, get into your dry things. Give me those boots right now. You're leaving a trail on Ferat's clean floor."

Tuala eased numb feet from the sodden boots, grasped the lighted candle Mara proffered, then fled to her own small chamber. She stripped, trembling with cold, rubbed herself tolerably dry on a cloth, and scrambled into clean small-clothes, a woolen gown, and an old shawl of Brenna's that still hung on a peg by the door. She bundled her soggy garments and returned to the kitchen. She felt a certain gratitude to Mara; one could not call the big woman kind, but at least she was consistent. But Erip: how could Tuala have stayed out so long, when her old friend was on the threshold of death?

Mara took the dripping clothes without comment and began to hang them up by the fire. A pot of soup was steaming on the hearth, and a bowl of it had been set on the stone shelf Ferat used for his preparations, with a hunk of dark bread beside it.

"Eat up," Mara said. "I can't be troubling myself with you sick as well, and for nothing more than a mad notion to run off into the forest on your own. Get it into you, it'll warm you."

"You said I was to go in," Tuala managed after most of the soup was gone. "Does that mean the rules have changed again?"

"Rules? The only rule I follow is common sense: an old man, a small chamber, no need for a gaggle of folk in there exhausting him. It's no thanks to me that you're bid go in to-night, it's thanks to him. He asked for it."

"He would have asked before, he would have wanted me there," Tuala felt bound to say. "He was too weak, that's all. I told you."

Mara gave her a look, but had nothing to say.

In Bridei's little chamber with its square, high window, Erip was resting on several pillows; it eased him to be propped thus. Tonight, for all that, his breath was rattling and rasping in his chest like a stick playing on bones, a ghastly music of death. Wid sat by his side, long, knotty hands folded in his lap, expression calm as the light from lamps set about the chamber played on his beak of a nose, his snowy beard, his hooded eyes. At the foot of the pallet, tall and still in his long robe, stood Broichan.

Tuala froze in the doorway. The druid's eyes met hers, impassive as always.

"Oh . . ." she began, not at all sure whether she intended to frame an excuse, an apology, or a plea to be allowed to stay, since her old friend had said he wanted her here.

"Come in." Broichan's tone was grave. He gestured to a stool set next to Wid's, by the pallet. Tuala bit back her words, realizing suddenly that it must be the druid who had asked for her; he was the only one who could command Mara's instant compliance. Tuala moved forward and sat by Erip's side, taking the old man's hand in hers. She did not look at Broichan. Perhaps, if she kept her eyes away, he would not know what a coward she was. It seemed she could not be in his presence, even now, without becoming five years old again and beside herself with terror.

Erip was saying something, his voice a rough thread of sound. "Out . . . rain," he managed. "Silly girl . . ."

Tuala nodded, swallowing sudden tears. One did not weep at such a time; one sent one's friend on his journey with hope, with gladness, and with love. "Yes," she said quietly, "I went for a walk and got caught in a downpour. I should have dried my hair properly, but I wanted to see you straightaway. Mara said I could come in." Still she did not turn, although her senses told her Broichan watched her intently.

"We've been telling a few tales," Wid said. "Singing a few songs; remembering old times."

Tuala glanced at him. It seemed to her the grief that had marked his features in recent days had eased a little, for all the impending loss. Perhaps the sharing of tales had helped both of these old friends. As for Broichan and how he fitted in, that she could not imagine. He seemed the kind of man who would never have had any friends.

"Where did you go?" he asked abruptly, the question as sudden as a cat's spring to pin a mouse with its claws.

Tuala made herself breathe slowly, as Bridei had taught her. "To a place in the forest where I can . . . where I can see images of what may come."

"Look at me, Tuala."

She turned to face the druid; his dark eyes fixed themselves on hers. Broichan was pale tonight; the lines from nose to mouth seemed deeper.

"What kind of images? Whose path do you seek to know? Your own?"

She did not want to tell him this. She did not want to tell him anything. The Dark Mirror and the truths it told were secret, private. To tell would be like sharing a confidence, and Broichan was the last person she would ever confide in. He was the person she distrusted most of anyone. Besides, if she spoke of what had happened today she might let slip that she had not been alone there at the pool.

"I don't look for anything in particular," she said, hearing the tight, prim tone of her voice and the way it revealed how she was lying. "I just look for whatever comes." She could no longer hold his gaze; she stared down at her hands, which were clutching Erip's like a lifeline.

"Tell the truth," Broichan said. "That is the least I expect of any child brought up in my household. You learned this skill from Bridei, did you not? I cannot believe he did not impart to you some little sophistication in its use."

Then Erip began to cough and to fight for breath, and for a while all of them could do nothing but try to aid him in what seemed a losing battle. His body had grown too frail for this choking, thrashing, desperate struggle. At length the spasm subsided; the old man breathed again, but shallowly, each inward gasp a wheeze of pain. There was blood on the sheets. Wid held out a cup of water; feebly, Erip shook his head. He was trying to say something; he had turned his rheumy, pain-filled eyes toward Tuala.

". . . Bridei . . ." he whispered.

"Indeed," Wid said, glancing up at the druid. "What Broichan meant to ask you, Tuala, what he would eventually have asked you in his circuitous, druidic way, was whether your journey into the forest today provided you with any news of our boy. Erip is sad that his prize pupil is not at home; Bridei, too, will grieve that he could not be at Pitnochie at this time. If you have seen aught of him in your scrying place, and if you will tell it, that could ease Erip's mind considerably. It is hard for you; we know that."

It would not be hard, Tuala thought, *if I did not have that man looking at me with his eyes full of power and hate. To my old friends, I could speak gladly.* For all her unease, she knew she must tell what she had seen, some of it at least. "I saw him." It came out in a whisper; Tuala cleared her throat and tried for a more confident tone. "Fighting hand to hand; riding with Gartnait; talking to a girl, I think it must have been Gartnait's sister. They seemed to be images of now; the season was winter, and Bridei looked much as he did last time we said our good-byes."

"Did he seem well? Content?" It was Broichan who spoke, an edge in his voice that had not been there before. It came to Tuala that it was more for himself that he wanted this news than for Erip.

"He seemed well enough." She recalled the image she had not spoken of, Bridei in the night, beset by some weighty problem. Despite herself, she blurted out, "He wants to come home."

There was a little silence. Then Broichan said, "How can you know this?"

"I saw it in his face. He has . . . misgivings." Now she had said too much and, whatever pressure Broichan chose to apply, she would not say one word more.

Erip sighed. His fingers moved to pat hers, their touch like a dry leaf, a frond of grass, soft and insubstantial as if he had already begun to quit his clay self and journey to a realm of pure spirit. "Thank you," he said, and closed his eyes.

"He cannot come home until Talorgen's foray is over." Broichan's tone allowed no room for challenge. "And it will not be over until well into the summer, even if all goes to plan. The lad must find what resources he needs within himself. What else did you see? A fight, you said. A battle? A major undertaking?"

Tuala looked up at him. "I saw nothing of that," she told him. "Only a struggle between Bridei and another man. They had knives. I know that he is safe."

"How do you know?"

"I would know if he were harmed. I need not look in the Dark Mirror for that."

"The Dark Mirror," echoed Broichan quietly. "So you do go all the way up there to the Vale of the Fallen. Why there? What do you see there that cannot be found closer to home? What secrets? What presences?"

"Nothing that you cannot see, my lord, I am certain. Your own abilities in this art must far surpass mine, untutored as I am." Indeed, she wondered greatly that he would interrogate her thus. He was a king's druid, after all; he could surely summon infinitely more powerful visions than her own. "I have told Erip that Bridei seems well and is missing home and his old friends. He is happy with that news; it is the truth. More, I will not tell."

There was silence after this, a silence in which Tuala waited for Broichan to order her from the room. Standing up to him had made her break out in a cold sweat. But Broichan said nothing, and when at length she ventured a glance at him, he was simply standing there at the foot of the pallet, watching Erip, his distant expression showing his mind was on other things entirely. In that moment, Tuala recalled something the forest girl had said. *The king's druid has one weak spot, and that's his affection for the boy.* It was just possible Broichan's fierce questions had less to do with his strategies and plans, or with his disapproval of her, and a lot more to do with something a great deal simpler: the love and anxiety of a father for an absent son. This was a revelation. The more she considered it, the truer it seemed. The truer it seemed, the more it became possible to view Broichan as a man and not a presence of terrible, overwhelming power.

"Did we ever tell you," Wid asked, "about the time we taught Bridei to drink ale like a man?"

Tuala grinned. She had heard this account many times.

"It was like this . . ."

After it was told there was another tale, and another. Tuala contributed some of her own, children's stories Brenna had told her, tales of wondrous beasts and valiant heroes that Bridei had passed on night after night before she went to sleep, tales he had probably learned from these same two scholarly ancients. Toward dawn, when Erip had moved beyond tales and both Tuala and Wid were hoarse from talking and gray-faced with exhaustion, Broichan began to recite prayers. He kept his voice low; it was, nonetheless, resonant and strong as he called down the blessings of the Shining One and the Flamekeeper, and finally made a solemn request of Bone Mother, guardian of the great gateway through which this weary old scholar must now pass. Tuala wept then, but Wid did not, although the predawn light through the small window caught the brightness of unshed tears in his deep-set eyes. Erip's breathing had shallowed to the least rise and fall of the chest, the slightest trembling of the open lips. His eyes were closed. Tuala held one hand, Wid the other.

"A giving spirit, strong in generosity," Broichan was saying. "A man whose journey has been long; he has trodden many paths and has found learning in all that has befallen him, the fortunate and the adverse. Strong in the teachings of the ancestors, for all he tried to hide it when it suited him. Faithful to the tasks he undertook in the name of the gods. A good teacher. Receive him now in recognition of that, above all, for such a tutor is rare: he knows not simply how to make a scholar, but how to make a man. Ease his passing, for he has been well loved and has loved well in return, but his first love was always for truth. Take his hand; guide him forth, Mother of All, into the shelter of sleep. Let him rest awhile in your care and dream good dreams of his new journey. In your name, Dark Mother, we ask this for our dear friend. And in the telling of his tales we will honor him, and we will remember him."

Whether it was the solemn prayer of a king's druid, or whether it was simple kindness to a good old man, Bone Mother let Erip slip through as gently as she does any mortal soul. There was no final paroxysm, no ghastly struggle for air; he breathed one long outward breath and was still. Tuala touched her lips to his frail hand and laid it on his breast; Wid placed the other across it. They sat in silence as the birds began to sing and chatter and chorus outside; as the light of dawn came pale and clear through Bridei's little window, where the talismans he had placed there before he set out for Raven's Well rested on the sill: three white stones and the tawny feather of an eagle. Tuala became aware that others stood just outside the doorway, had perhaps been standing there for some time: Mara, Ferat, one of the kitchen lads, Uven, and a second man at arms.

"He's away, then," Mara said eventually. "You'd best come through to breakfast, all of you; Erip wouldn't want you to go hungry because of him. He always was fond of his meals. After that, I'll wash him and get him ready. Brenna can come up to help me. There's some here need sleep; the old man will wait for that."

THEY LAID ERIP to rest in a cairn of shaped stones up on the hill not far from the place of the Dawn Tree. The rain eased off just long enough for the ritual to be concluded. Afterward they drank ale, ate a pudding with dried fruits and spices from Ferat's special store, and exchanged tales of Erip's time at Pitnochie. In recognition of the occasion Broichan remained in the hall for the evening, but he contributed little, and it seemed to Tuala that his watchful, silent presence made everyone uneasy.

She had sat by Wid all evening, keeping as quiet as she could. Her one attempt to contribute, the recounting of a trick Bridei had once played on Erip and how the old scholar had got his own back, had been greeted with blank-faced silence, as if she had no right to speak, no right to pretend herself one of Erip's friends. Wid had chuckled quietly and patted her shoulder. From the others, she could almost feel the chill of disapproval.

The day after Erip's funeral rites, a visitor did arrive: that same old disheveled druid, Uist, who had come to Pitnochie the summer Tuala was sent away, and who occasionally passed through the Glen on mysterious errands of his own. He greeted Broichan in his usual way, which showed a total disregard for the niceties of custom, but was undoubtedly honest. He visited the cairn and spoke prayers that nobody quite understood. Then it became apparent to Tuala that Uist was not going to be staying at Pitnochie, and neither was Wid. Wid appeared in the hall with his warm cloak on and a small satchel on his back and Uist, who had just returned from his brisk walk up to the cairn, said, "Are you ready?"

It was freezing outside; a heavy mist hung over the slopes above Pitnochie and blanketed the waters of Serpent Lake from sight. Here and there the bole of a great oak, moss-crusted, loomed eerily green out of the gray-white vapor. It was not a day, or a season, for old men to go out walking in the forest.

"Time to be off," Wid announced calmly and took up his staff, which was resting in its customary spot by the hearth. He looked at Tuala where she stood by the fire. Through her shock and dismay, she read in his expression the truth about what seemed a terrible, sudden betrayal. She saw that if he stayed here, his grief would overwhelm him. To survive it, there was a need to begin a journey, as Erip had done.

"I'm so sorry you are going," she said softly. Others were close at hand and she could not say all she felt. She could not say how cruel it was to lose the last friend she had left. "I wish you had told me. But I understand." She even managed a smile as she rose on tiptoe to kiss her old friend on one cheek and the other. "May the Shining One light your pathway."

"Be brave, little one," Wid said. "May the Flamekeeper warm your hearth and your heart. We'll meet again, I've no doubt of it. I'll expect you to be able to demonstrate that you've built on the excellent education we gave you, the old man and I." His lips were trembling.

"I'll do you both proud, I promise," Tuala said, making her expression as confident and strong as she could. But as she watched them go, the white-robed, mysterious Uist in front, the tall, bearded figure of her old tutor walking steadily behind until the mist swallowed the two of them, she felt the chill weight of utter bereavement in her chest. Everyone was gone. Now she was truly on her own.

8

THE MAGE STONE was considered the most impressive of all the Kin Stones that marked the ancient territories of the Priteni. Greater than a tall man's height, it was carven on either side with patterns of subtlety and grace. The north face bore the tale of a great conflict: at the top, a king and his warriors advancing into battle, the monarch astride a stocky horse, his men marching behind, spears at the ready, curling hair bold and fine across their shoulders, eyes set straight ahead. In the center was depicted a melee as the Priteni clashed with their foe; here, the king drove his spear through the breast of his adversary. At the bottom could be seen the heads of the enemy displayed on pikes and the corpses of the slain set in neat rows. Beside them a hound devoured a goose. Perhaps each king had one of these creatures as his kin token.

The south face of the great stone had a less formal pattern—it was a wild and joyous tribute to the gods, the entire surface filled with small carvings of every kind of animal that was to be found in the kingdoms of the Priteni: wolf, stag, fox and badger, marten and vole, eel and salmon, bull, boar and ram, all rioted across the face of the stone in wondrous celebration of life. On the eastern and western sides of the Mage Stone were great swirls of interwoven snakes, with here and there small, grinning faces of man, woman, or creature.

Bridei had never seen it. The Mage Stone stood far to the west, where King Lake opened to the sea, and in an ill season the Gaels had moved in and seized control of the hillside from which it had looked down for generation on generation. It was Broichan who had first described the stone to him: "It is a true wonder, Bridei; not merely a marvel of the carver's craft, but heavy with the lore of our people and full of the mystery of the ancestors." Erip had told Bridei, later, that the strange little faces on the sides were the sculptor's own touch, his personal contribution to the overall design; in all great works of art, he'd said, one would find such evidence of a need to break free of established patterns, if one looked hard enough. That had provoked a heated argument with Wid; Bridei remembered it fondly. He imagined the two old scholars, back home at Pitnochie, still devoting their days to endless debates on philosophy. It was good that they had Tuala to teach now that he was gone; she was clever and would keep the old rascals well occupied. Thinking of that, imagining the three of them before the hall fire, telling tales or playing games or arguing a point of history, made Bridei feel better. Knowing that world remained at Pitnochie awaiting his return was like knowing he had an anchor to keep him safe, or being assured his spirit would remain strong even when he must see unthinkable things, face unknowable risks.

It was not that Bridei was afraid. He had been taught to assess any situation, weigh up opportunities and dangers, make a decision and act on it. Years of Broichan's tuition had ensured he responded thus no matter what the event; Talorgen had commented, when Bridei began his seasons of battle training among the warriors of Raven's Well, that in strategic grasp, in decisiveness, and in making sound judgments, Broichan's foster son had little to learn. On the other hand, no young man, however promising, knows just how capable he is until his first real taste of war. The small skirmish in which Bridei and Gartnait had taken a prisoner apiece was one thing. A genuine battle was quite another. Talorgen had trained them hard. They'd had long expeditions across country in weather fit to freeze the stoutest man; they'd been hungry, exhausted, angry, bored. It seemed to Bridei that they must by now be ready for the real thing. He knew, all the same, that perhaps one could never really be ready.

It helped having Donal around. Donal did his best to tell it straight; to prepare Bridei for both best and worst.

"Remember what I told you once," Donal said when the two of them were alone together, snatching a moment's peace between the endless training sessions. They were riding out soon and the pace was relentless. "The first time's always the worst. That's the time you think about the fellow you're killing, what's his name, does he have a wife and children, is he scared and so on. You stick your knife into him anyway, because if you don't, he'll have you. After that, you learn to snuff out that part of yourself, the part that asks questions like, should I really be doing this? You don't think of them as men like yourself, you think of them as the enemy, stinking Gaels with your countrymen's blood on their hands and pure darkness in their souls. Then you don't strike to kill a son, a husband, a father; you strike to destroy the bane of Fortriu. There's no other way to do it, Bridei. It seems odd to say this, but the best way to fight isn't with your heart or even with your belly, it's with your head. Cold, clean, detached. Not a killing, a just execution."

Bridei greeted this with silence.

"Believe me," Donal said, "you can't afford any scruples. That's why we practice the forms of it over and over, swords, spears, knives, bare hands—so when it comes to the point, we just do it. Helps hold back fear, too, if you know the moves so well you could do them in your sleep. Don't look like that, Bridei. You will be afraid. We all are. Even Talorgen."

Bridei glanced at him. "I didn't think you would be," he observed. "Donal, victor of more battles than I've got fingers and toes to count them on, isn't that what you once told me?"

Donal grinned. "I doubt if you'd notice when I'm on the field," he said. "Fear's good, if you use it right. Keeps you sharp; keeps you on your toes."

"I don't think I'll be afraid," Bridei said. "I think I'll be able to do it."

"Aye," said Donal. "I've no doubt of that. But you'll see things you won't like, things it can be hard to come to terms with. There's no way to prepare a man for the death of his friends, nor for the acts of savagery that are the daily bread of these Gaels. That can stay with you a long time."

Bridei did not ask a question, simply looked at his companion.

"I've learned to put it away," Donal said quietly. "Lock it away inside where it's best kept. Sometimes it comes back. Sometimes I dream. Not often. A man can't well afford that if he's to be any use as a fighter."

Bridei considered, not for the first time, the fact that Donal, a man of middle years, had neither wife nor children to his name. He said nothing.

"I'll be with you, lad," Donal said. "Don't expect it to be easy, that's all."

"I'm not a fool," retorted Bridei, feeling a flush rise to his cheeks.

"No," said the warrior, "and I did not say so. All I'm saying is, a druid's wisdom may teach you a lot, things far beyond the comprehension of a simple man like me. But it can't prepare you for this, and nor can all the combat training Talorgen and I can give you. Just so you know."

"I do know," Bridei said, thinking of the Dark Mirror. "The gods have shown me."

"They show glimpses, images, shadows," said Donal. "This is blood, gore, hacked limbs, severed heads, women lying sprawled where the vermin have left them, infants smashed, houses torched. It's the smells and the sounds that go with that. Worse, it's your comrades turned suddenly into strangers. That's the hardest part."

Donal's voice had changed; Bridei looked at him sharply. "What do you mean?"

Donal folded his arms. His close-set eyes took on a distant look. "Maybe it won't happen," he said. "Maybe you'll walk through it shielded by the breath of the gods. Would that it might be so. Now, I think I can hear Elpin calling us; must be our turn for spear throwing. You coming?"

⁂

THEY MOVED DOWN the Glen in groups of ten, setting out from Raven's Well as soon as the leaf buds began to swell on the birches. A small force was left behind to guard Talorgen's property from raids; his family had traveled up toward Serpent Lake, heading for the safety of court.

Talorgen's army numbered close to a hundred men when it set out. It was, by its leader's choice, principally a force of foot soldiers, although there were horses with them, pack ponies to bear supplies and a few riding mounts which allowed the quick relay of messages when the terrain was suited to it. There had been a debate over this: whether the problem of fodder outweighed the creatures' usefulness in the field, where a mounted man had increased visibility, range, and speed. There was a further dispute concerning the use of the lakes; forces and goods could be quickly conveyed by sailing vessel or barge, saving long, weary marches that sapped the men's energy and dampened their spirits. The reverse argument was that boats were clearly visible to spies on the open hillsides above Mage and King Lakes; there'd be no element of surprise if they used the water paths. Besides, carrying the vessels overland beside the linking streams was just as wearying as tramping the whole way on foot.

It was, in the end, the long, slow way, the more covert route that was chosen. The small groups went severally, camping close but keeping each to itself, covering their tracks as best they could and keeping to the natural concealment of rocks and trees by the water's edge. Cold and wet it certainly was; clothing never quite dried after the first drenching rainstorm, and Bridei became used to the smell of ill-dried boots, sweat-soaked wool, and unwashed bodies huddled close. They caught their food on the way, when they could, to conserve the supplies the ponies carried.

They had set out not long after the festival of Balance, and the journey stretched out until some of the men were heard to utter dour jokes about not getting there until time for Rising. When it was possible, the daily marches were long, but the season did not always smile on their endeavors, and there were times when mist or rain slowed their progress to a painful, creeping advance. An ailment that caused retching and purging stopped them in their tracks for many days on the southern shore of Mage Lake. They lost two men to that, burying them with a brief ceremony before they moved on again. Day merged into night and night into day; suppers were taken for the most part in silence, the men like dark, despondent shadows around their little fires.

Bridei kept a count of the season's passing, neat lines incised on a birch twig he carried in his pack. It had been many days' walking, many nights' restless sleep. They sent scouts ahead, but saw nothing of the enemy. Gartnait grumbled that he wished they could hurry up; his hands were itching for a Gael's throat, and he wouldn't be so careful of the fellow's safety as he'd been last time. Donal told him to shut up, and he did. There had been no meat to share that night beyond a couple of rabbits among the whole team, and their bellies were complaining.

At a point where Bridei judged they must be nearing the bridge that marked the northern tip of King Lake, Talorgen called the groups in for a council. What had set out as a force of near a hundred had become somewhat larger as it passed down the Great Glen. There were two other chieftains here now, Morleo of Longwater, tall, lean, dark-bearded, and Ged of Abertornie, a flamboyant, cheerful man given to garments woven in bright colors and elaborate patterns of stripes and squares. Each of these leaders brought his own substantial force; Ged's had adopted their chieftain's mode of dress and Donal commented, behind his hand, that the Gaels would see them coming from halfway down King Lake, for they shone bright as beacons in their red and yellow and green.

The council was businesslike. Several leaders there might be, but all understood this was Talorgen's undertaking, done in the name of King Drust and of all Fortriu, and that when it came to it, decisions must be reached quickly and effectively, with a single voice. After conferring with Ged and

Morleo and the most trusted of his own men, Donal among them, Talorgen addressed the assembled forces. The men were gathered in a place where a stony outcrop hung above a natural clearing. A stream ran there, and the mossy ground was like a soaked sponge, but it was the only open space big enough to let all of them see their leader as he spoke. Bridei stood at the back with Gartnait; he wondered how he would feel if Talorgen were his own father. He supposed that, as his father Maelchon was a king, there would indeed have been times when he had stood thus before his troops and exhorted them to courage. Bridei thought he might have liked to see that. He could not tell if Gartnait was proud of his father; Gartnait seemed to have nothing on his mind these days beyond an anticipation of killing Gaels.

"We are a strong army," Talorgen was saying, "bold of heart and steadfast of spirit. But this is not the kind of battle in which we can charge forward in numbers, assailing the enemy and overpowering him with the sheer force of our initial assault. Gabhran of Dalriada knows this country now." At the mention of this name there was a general hiss of disapproval. "His folk are settled far and wide across what was once our own territory."

"And will be ours again!" someone was bold enough to shout, and other voices arose in support.

"At Galany's Reach, where the Mage Stone stands, there is now a fortified settlement. Our spies tell us it's not heavily manned. A garrison of thirty, perhaps; more if they've had word of our coming. There are also ordinary folk there, wives and children, craftspeople, slaves."

"Scum," someone muttered.

"A force the size of ours could take it easily. But as I'm sure you realize, holding it would be a different matter. That hill and the lonely vale below it were once the lands of Duchil of Galany, one of the bravest of our chieftains. Duchil was slain in the last great struggle against the Gaels," Talorgen bowed his head briefly. 'Those of his folk who survived were driven out; they live their lives in exile. Fokel, son of Duchil, will ride with us at the end, he and his warriors."

A couple of the men greeted this with a half-hearted

cheer; most were silent. Perhaps, thought Bridei, they had heard what he had about Fokel, a man whose name was seldom mentioned without the words *mad, wild,* or *unpredictable* alongside it.

"We know," Talorgen said, "that we can take the settlement and the hill. We know also that the moment our force emerges from the woods to cross the bridge at Fox Falls, the enemy's forward sentries will carry word to their leaders of our approach. That word will go to all their fortresses, all their strongholds; it will reach their king at Dunadd soon enough. The speed of their response depends on where their fighting men are currently deployed; the information we have on that is now somewhat stale, I think. We might hold Galany's Reach for one turning of the moon at most. Likely we'd be surrounded by Gabhran's forces long before then, and find ourselves besieged on the hilltop. I'll put it to you plainly, men. This is a symbolic mission; a taste of what is to come for the forces of Dalriada. We go in, attack, withdraw. We destroy their garrison and we take hostages: the leader, the women and children. We retreat."

To Bridei this made good sense. It was precisely the way he would have conducted the mission himself, had he been leader. Erip and Wid had taught him the long history of this struggle. The three of them had analyzed exhaustively the great and bloody battles between Fortriu and Dalriada, the heroic advances down the Glen, the harried retreats, the patterns of victory and defeat. It was plain to Bridei that a force the size of Talorgen's could not hold a territory so far to the west for long. Without the backing of the armies of Circinn, Fortriu would never drive the Gaels back to their homeland. These men, however, had not had the benefit of his education. Their blood ran hot with the desire for vengeance; their every energy was fixed on the killing of Gaels. A chorus of protest rang out.

"Retreat? We're not in it to retreat!"

"What, let the scum keep the lands they've stolen? Not likely!"

"Kill 'em all, I say!"

Morleo of Longwater, who stood beside Talorgen, raised his hand and the shouting subsided to angry muttering.

"This venture," he said gravely, "is a sign to them that we are bold, quick, and clever; that our numbers are growing, our alliances strong. That we have not forgotten the ills they have inflicted on our people. We raise there the banner of Drust the Bull, and beside it those of Raven's Well, of Longwater, and of Abertornie." He nodded acknowledgment at Ged. "We raise also the stars and serpent that are the ancient symbols of Galany's Reach itself."

"And then," said the brightly clad Ged, "we hold a ceremony. Perhaps the feast of Rising, perhaps another ritual. We stand on that hilltop around the Mage Stone and we consecrate it once again to our own gods: to the Flamekeeper and the Shining One, to Bone Mother and the fair maiden All-Flowers. We ensure our captives are present to witness it. We release one or two of them to convey the tale of it to Gabhran and his henchmen. Then we retreat. In time we will return. We will return with a greater army than these Gaels have ever dreamed of."

The warriors roared approval; Ged had an amiable manner about him and a rousing tone of voice, and the simplicity of his speech touched something in the spirits of the men. Bridei did not cheer. His mind was on that army, the force that would be big enough to scour the land forever of the menace of Dalriada; the army that could never be assembled until Circinn came to Fortriu's aid. Not until the divided kingdom of the Priteni was united and working for a single purpose might this be achieved. He observed the men's shining eyes, their looks of pride and purpose, and knew they were thinking they would do this next summer or perhaps the one after. They did not think beyond the bright words of hope. They did not know true victory would be a very long time coming. Perhaps, on the eve of battle, that was as it should be.

They moved on in the morning, now in bigger groups. They stayed with their own leaders, Talorgen's men together, and Ged's and Morleo's, though one or two of the fellows had friends in the other teams, and campfires were shared at night along with the occasional prize such as a whole roasted sheep—the farmer must be compensated later—or a lucky catch of fat trout. Tales were told and songs sung, always quietly. The weather improved; Talorgen ordered two days of rest, and the lower branches of alder and willow were festooned with garments steaming in the spring sun's faint warmth.

They were now not far from the bridge at Fox Falls. There would be no further advance of the main party until Fokel joined them with his men. This band of exiled warriors dwelled in the mountains near Five Sisters. It was a grim and marginal area, and from what Bridei had heard, this war leader and his small group of dedicated followers had developed temperaments to match it. Bridei wondered if Fokel would be content with a token raid on the ancestral territory for which his own father had fought and died. He commented on this to Donal as they squatted by the stream, attempting to rinse the accumulated grime from their smallclothes.

"You wouldn't want to say that too loudly," Donal murmured, "true as it undoubtedly is. Talorgen would have been better to leave Fokel right out of it, if you ask me. But he couldn't. It's Fokel's own land; his own place. How could Talorgen not tell him what was planned? Calculated risk. Caused him a few sleepless nights. Still, it's more men, and they're good fighters."

"Mm," said Bridei. "The question is, whose orders do they obey?" He was becoming increasingly uneasy about the venture. He agreed with Talorgen's plan; it was the only one that made sense, given their numbers and the position of their target. He approved of the idea of a ritual on Galany's Reach, for in any great venture the role of the gods must be recognized and honored. Yet he felt in his heart that it fell short of what was required. What price this symbolic victory if the banners of Fortriu were torn down the instant Talorgen's forces were out of sight? What price the joyous celebration of Rising when the Mage Stone still stood in enemy territory to be ignored, reviled, perhaps even defaced? Did that show due respect for the ancient powers that were bone and breath of the land? Deep inside him, Bridei knew it was not enough.

"Of course," Donal observed, wringing out a sodden garment of indeterminate hue, "Drust will use the hostages to win concessions from Gabhran, if he can. Capture a chieftain of high birth, or the kin of such a man, and you gain quite a bit of leeway. Talorgen does think ahead. You're looking very doubtful, Bridei. What's eating you? Having scruples again?"

"Just thinking." Bridei hung his own undergarments on a supple willow branch, suspecting that by nightfall they'd have dried only to a clammy dampness. He settled on a mossy rock, watching the men as they enjoyed the unexpected time of respite: some were fishing, some heading off up the hill with bows and quivers, some tending to their small domestic tasks. A good many were rolled in their blankets, fast asleep.

"Thinking about what?" Donal asked casually.

But Bridei did not answer. In the back of his mind a plan was forming, a plan so wild he could not believe it had come from his own head. It was a crazy idea, the kind that sprang from emotion and not from a balanced consideration of risks and opportunities. All the same, it was there, grand, implausible, utterly mad: a symbolic act that would ring out in the tales of Fortriu like a great bell of hope.

"No," he muttered to himself. "No, I don't think so."

"What?" said Donal.

"You've been to Galany's Reach, haven't you?" Bridei asked him. "How close is the hill to the lake shore? Can you draw me a plan, here on the earth?"

❧

TUALA VOWED TO herself and to the Shining One that from now on she would be strong. She recalled that Bridei had come to this house when he was very small, that he too had been quite without friends or family, and that he had managed it all remarkably well. He had even made friends with Broichan. True, if Bridei's upbringing had been different, perhaps it would not be so hard for him to smile now. But there was no doubt Bridei had made the best of his opportunities, and she owed it to him to attempt the same.

With Erip laid to rest and Wid gone, there were no more lessons. Mara made it clear she did not want Tuala's help around the house. Brenna's cottage was forbidden, and the men were not talking to her. What was she to do? It was folly to attempt the trip to the Vale of the Fallen with winter's grip still hard on the land, and all her movements furtively watched by one or another member of the household as if she might suddenly turn into some kind of evil sorceress and cast a spell on them.

There were moments when she wished to do just that, and wondered what would happen if she tried; but Tuala did not try. It was one thing to give those powers a little exercise in the presence of trusted friends like Erip and Wid. To employ them before those who already feared her would be touching a match to dry tinder.

She practiced scrying in the relative privacy of her own chamber, using a little bowl of bronze that she had found in a store room. It was a strange vessel with clawed feet and dragon handles. Remembering the precepts of her teachers, Bridei among them, she tried to extend her skills and find new ways of using them. What was the purpose of such activities if not learning? Thus, she practiced the summoning of images related to a theme or strand, such as kingship, or the ancient lore of symbols, or Pitnochie itself: the secrets and memories that resided deep in the thick stone walls, the heavy woolen hangings, the dark, smoky chambers. The place had seen many inhabitants, chieftains, families, other druids such as Broichan, although there were fewer of those. His had been an unusual path. He had dwelled long years at court, fulfilling the role of king's adviser and moving among men of affairs. Later, he had returned to reside here as if he were more wealthy landholder than spiritual leader. Appearances were deceptive; Tuala did not need the images of the water to tell her that Broichan was both of these things and a great deal more.

Sitting too long over the scrying bowl made her neck sore and her eyes weary. Sometimes the visions made her sad; sometimes they made her stomach turn. She could not always work out what lesson was to be learned from them. A child's body broken and maimed; men dying in their blood, others helpless to save them; a little dog crouched by its fallen master: what did those images tell but that the world held cruelty and loss, and that humankind brought its own tragedies on itself? She understood this already; there was no need for the water to show her this lesson over and over. Sometimes she dreamed the same signs and portents at night, with the bowl emptied and shut in a box. When that happened, she made herself stop awhile. It was something Bridei had once warned her of, that the overuse of certain skills of magic could lead one to obsession and thence to madness. A great part of the craft lay in knowing when to stop.

She was aware that she was getting tired. Sleep did not come easily, and the dreams were a tangle of staring eyes and clutching fingers, of knives in the heart and cords around the neck, of people going away and never coming back. Often she did not feel like eating. At the table it was as if she did not exist, folks' eyes sliding over her, their comments excluding her. The only one who looked her in the eye was Broichan, and his stern features seemed to hold either remote disapproval or a kind of appraisal that unsettled her still more, for there was a calculation in it that told her the druid was making plans.

As the season passed there came more and more clear days, and Tuala fled the house to make her way up into the forest once more. It seemed to take much longer now to reach the Vale of the Fallen, and her legs ached from the walk. The cold of early spring made her chest hurt, and each breath was an effort. How everything had changed, she thought as she rested, leaning against the moss-covered trunk of a birch. How had she become so tangled up in misery that she could not even summon the strength to look around her and see what she and Bridei had marveled at back in the days of their childhood? There was so much of beauty here: the neat, small tracks of a foraging creature, a stoat or marten; the intricate tracery of a skeleton leaf, still clinging vainly to its parent tree as, little by little, time stripped it of its substance, leaving only the delicate remembrance of what it had been. The many pale shades of willow bark; the first brave green of bluebell shoots in sheltered hollows; the cry of a hunting bird high overhead and the sudden rustling retreat for cover of a small animal in the leaf litter: had she forgotten the magic in these everyday things? What was wrong with her?

The Vale was dim today. The spring sunlight could not penetrate its depths; the foliage dripped with moisture and the vapor hung low over the blackness of the pool. The shapes of the seven druids hunched under their cloaks of lichen; Tuala could almost see them shivering. Somewhere in the back of her mind a little dog was howling, a mournful sound that clutched at her heart, awakening her own sorrow with its forlorn note of loss.

Tuala sat on the flat stones. She had told herself she would not look today; that she would simply see if her two strange visitors reappeared, ask them some questions if they did, and then go home. She was too tired to deal with the visions of the Dark Mirror. Common sense told her their power would overwhelm her today.

She waited a long time. She waited until her back ached from sitting still and her mind had gone over the reasons for their nonappearance fifty times over. Of course they would not come to her summons, being creatures of the Other-world: who did she think she was? Perhaps she had offended them last time when she caused the Dark Mirror to show only images of her own choosing. Maybe they had given up on her because she had not come back for so long. Perhaps they were punishing her; after all, she had scarcely wel-comed what they offered.

"Come on, come on," she whispered. "I don't want much; just an answer or two." But time passed, and above this rift in the earth the sun moved close to day's end, and Tuala knew they would not come this time. She had already stayed too long; she must set off now or she would be out in the forest after dusk.

Just a quick look, she told herself; just one look, so this would not have been for nothing. She would keep control and make herself stop after a little. If she saw him, a glimpse, a single image, today's venture would have been worthwhile.

Bridei at table, among men; Donal at his left, instantly recognizable by the big jaw, the close-set eyes, the flowering of blue symbols across the skin of his face. In this image

Bridei, too, wore the warrior's markings, the signs of manhood freshly graven on the fair skin of the right cheek, showing he had fought and survived on the field of war. Gartnait, who sat on the other side, bore a similar pattern, but Gartnait wore also his kin signs, which were generally given to a young man of high birth at the same time as the others. On the left cheek, balancing the warrior's blazon, Talorgen's son bore the hound and shield of his father's clan, and above it the crescent and broken rod of his mother's lineage: the royal blood of the Priteni.

They were happy, relaxed, Donal joking, Gartnait tossing back his ale and laughing, even Bridei almost smiling as he listened to them, although his eyes bore a shadow. Others were at the board, men Tuala did not recognize, some in warriors' garb of leather and felt and coarse woolen weave, others more richly dressed with here and there a coat of red-dyed fabric, a belt with a silver buckle, a braided headband. There was meat on the table, a haunch of venison of which not much was left. There was a fire. This was a victory celebration.

Someone called for a toast. Tuala could not hear the voices, but the mood and purpose of the gathering were plain. All rose to their feet. A tall man spoke formal words. They raised their goblets and drank.

She felt the pain an instant before she saw it; her throat tightened, her heart lurched. Then, on the water, Bridei dropped his goblet and put both hands to his throat, his face suddenly gray, his eyes staring horribly, grotesquely, his mouth gaping open. For a little nobody noticed; they were shouting, drinking, carried away on the tide of revelry. Tuala could not breathe; her fists were clenched so tightly the nails cut into her palms. *Do something, quick, quick . . .*

Donal saw, moved like the wind, clearing the way with brawny arms, easing the stricken man to a bench, calling for room, for help. Gartnait seemed frozen in shock, staring uselessly. Tuala could not bear to look; she could not drag her eyes away. Somewhere, in the distance, she heard her own voice whimpering like a beaten child's, *no, no, no . . .*

It is not a pretty sight when a man dies from poison. At least this was quick. She saw what Donal tried, his honest features contorted by desperation: the struggle to make Bridei vomit out whatever it was, the fingers down the throat, the salt draught poured into the foaming mouth to wash, futile, down the stricken man's clothing to the ground. The attempt to get him to his feet and walking, defeated when convulsions seized him, making his fine young body into that of a jerking, hideous puppet. At last, nothing to be done but hold him as he died, and weep. To close his eyes, touch his cheek with a roughened, gentle hand, fight for words and find there were none.

Even as the images faded and dispersed, Tuala threw herself facedown on the cold ground, her hands clawing at the earth. A wailing came from her like the cry of a wounded animal, a sound she would not have believed she could make. The power of this rent her gut and shredded her heart; it was too much to be borne. She sobbed and screamed in furious abandonment. Above the voice of her own grief she could still hear that lonely howling that was almost constant in this place: a little dog's lament. It was as if the creature sat right beside her; as if they grieved the selfsame loss.

She wished the earth would swallow her; how could she go on after such a vision? All the same, after a time she picked herself up, shaking with sobs, brushed the worst of the mud from her clothes, and sat with head in hands, forcing herself to apply common sense as Erip and Wid would have bid her do. The battle over, both Bridei and Gartnait with their warrior signs already complete: this was not a vision of now, it could not come to pass until well into the spring, for such a party of warriors could not readily travel down the Glen to the territory of the Gaels until Balance at least, Wid had said so. Set off too early and there could be snowdrifts, flooded streams, blinding mists, rock falls. Bridei was not dead. She would know if he was dead, know it in her heart, instantly. This horrible thing had not yet come to pass. There was still time to stop it.

Tuala got to her feet, dizzy and faint. Broichan; she must take this news to Broichan. She had already wasted enough time with her weeping and wailing, time she could not afford to squander. She tied her cloak tighter, gritted her teeth, and ran.

FROM THEIR PERCH on a tree branch high above the Vale of the Fallen, the two of them watched her go.

"She's young yet," the ivy-clad boy observed. "A difficult test, this, and a distressing one."

"There's another trial waiting when she gets home," the girl said, "and that one's all of Broichan's making. With this druid as a player, our work will be too easy."

"Not easy for Tuala."

The girl turned her light-filled eyes on him. "It is necessary." Her tone was cool. "They must be fully tested, the two of them. Each must prove as strong as the other. Each must balance duty with loyalty, love with purpose. Would you go into battle with a weapon not properly tempered? Would you build a house with green timbers?"

"I understand," the boy said. "I find it difficult to stand by and observe, nonetheless. This is a good child. And when all's said and done, she's ours."

"Good?" the girl scoffed. "Of what worth is that, if she flees her responsibilities at the first touch of unkindness? Tuala has a hard road ahead. We must ensure she develops sufficient endurance to walk it as the Shining One requires."

"And the young man?"

"Bridei's path is mapped. All that we need do is continue to watch him. There will come a time when the gods set him one final trial; we may play a part in that. Not yet. This season he faces the tests of men."

THE TERRIBLE IMAGES stayed with Tuala all the way home, giving wings to her feet. She arrived just as the sun was setting. In the kitchen, Ferat and his assistants were busy with a heavy joint on the spit, but they turned to stare as she flew past, her hair in her eyes, her breath coming hard. Mara was setting platters and knives on the table in the hall. When Tuala whisked past her to rap loudly on the door of Broichan's private room, the housekeeper began to say something, her voice sharp with disapproval, but Tuala took no heed. There was room for nothing in her mind but the one picture, the terrible dark future she must change at all costs. When Broichan did not answer, Tuala thrust the door open and almost fell into the room.

"I must tell you—Bridei—" she gasped. "You have to—" She looked across the chamber and fell abruptly silent, chest heaving from her long flight in the cold.

Broichan was not alone. He had been standing by the small hearth, ale cup in hand, and beside him was another man, a stranger, solidly built and plain of appearance, perhaps one of the local landholders or a minor chieftain. The fellow was looking at her with undisguised curiosity and not a little surprise. Belatedly, Tuala became aware of the trail of mud her boots had left on the clean floor, the strands of wild hair in her eyes, the way both hands were clutched into her shawl like desperate claws. Her eyes were probably staring and crazy. Broichan's only response had been to raise his eyebrows a trifle. His self-control had always been remarkable.

"I . . . I'm sorry," she managed, inclining her head briefly to the stranger; no matter what the circumstances, one must always greet such folk correctly. "The light of the Shining One attend you in this house. I am sorry to intrude, but I must speak with you, my lord," now turning her gaze on Broichan again, "please, I must tell you . . . it's Bridei, he's in terrible danger . . ."

"That's enough, Tuala." The druid's voice was deep and calm.

"But I—"

"That's enough." Broichan turned to his guest. "I regret the intrusion, Garvan. Will you allow me a few moments to deal with this?"

"Surely," the visitor said equably and, setting his cup on the table, he went from the room, not without giving Tuala an appraising look up and down on the way. The door closed behind him.

"Make this good," Broichan said. "Brief, coherent, and worth the interruption. I had hoped you might make a better impression on Garvan. After this, he will no doubt think you no more tame than a young she-wolf. Now account for yourself."

Tuala was beyond being afraid of him, beyond even any real comprehension of his words. "I saw—in the water—I saw Bridei, not now, but soon, after the battle. They were feasting, and someone had poisoned his drink, and—" No, she could not say this. How could she make the worst news in the world brief and coherent? She thought her heart would burst with anguish. The room seemed to reel around her, the candles swirling in mad dances, the strange and wondrous objects on the shelves mixing and blending in a grotesque realignment; the world was awry, nothing was as it should be.

"Sit. Here," and Broichan was steering her to a bench, easing her onto it, giving her ale. Now he knelt by her, and the dark eyes met hers, intent, questioning. He had gone very pale; his look, perhaps, mirrored her own. "Tell me," he said.

"They killed him," she whispered, the cup in her hand shaking so the ale spilled over onto her cloak. "I watched him die. Donal, Gartnait, the others, they could not save him. He—he—it was horrible . . ."

"Drink." He watched as she took a mouthful. "Now, once more. This was not an image of the present time? Are you quite sure?"

Tuala nodded. "I told you. It was later, after the battle. Gartnait wore both kin and warrior tattoos, Bridei only the battle counts. There's time to stop this. We have to stop it."

"Drink again. Now catch your breath. You have run far to bring me this news."

Tuala felt tears coming. She sniffed, rubbing her eyes like a child.

"So, it begins once more," Broichan said. He rose to seat himself opposite her. "Now, Tuala, I'm aware your talent in this field owes little to tuition; it is a natural thing, and as such perhaps less than perfectly reliable. On the other hand, what it lacks in control it seems to make up for in strength. You realize, I suppose, that the visions of the Dark Mirror do not always show an accurate picture of what is to come. They do not represent simple truth."

She stared at him. "Of course I know. If this were truth, we could not change it. Bridei would die thus no matter what action we took. This is only one possible future, and we can't let it happen."

"Indeed not. Fortunately, a few simple precautions will be sufficient to prevent this particular course of events. I will arrange to have them put in place, although there will be some delay; I must send a message to Raven's Well, and the track is likely to be snowed under above Maiden Lake. It is the general threat to Bridei's safety that concerns me more. If an assassin will try poison once, he will try it twice. If poison proves ineffective, he will investigate other means."

"You mean Bridei will be killed anyway?" Tuala's voice was no more than a thread.

"No," Broichan said. "I cannot allow that to happen. Bridei is needed. The future of the Priteni depends on him."

"I know," she said, although she could see from the look in the druid's eyes that it was not really to her that he spoke. "Does this mean he will not go to battle? Can he come home? He'd be safe here, surely."

"Home?" Broichan seemed startled at the suggestion; it was as if he had forgotten her while some great scheme unfurled in his mind. "You mean here to Pitnochie? He cannot do so, not before summer's end. And he must fight in the spring; it is necessary that he prove himself in the field. As for afterward, I think, at last, it is time for me to resume my place in the world of affairs. It's been a long exile. Drust will have his druid back, for a little."

"For a little?" Tuala queried, trying to make sense of it while swallowing the bitter disappointment contained in his words.

"For as long as it takes." Broichan regarded her again, this time with a critical look in his eye. "That means changes for you, as well. You cannot remain here at Pitnochie when I am gone. The household could not well sustain that; there have been enough mutterings already. Go now, tidy yourself, change your clothing, and let us see if you can make a better impression at suppertime."

Comprehension dawned, and with it horror.

"There's no need to look like that," Broichan said levelly. "Garvan is a good man, wealthy, steady. He would be kind to you. And he's prepared to take you, or was before you burst in here like a demented wood-sprite. There are few choices for you, Tuala. This is very probably the best of them."

She was lost for words once more. The old terror, forgotten in the overwhelming need to share her desperate news, now claimed her anew.

"Don't concern yourself," he said, misunderstanding. "I will ensure Bridei comes to no harm. Go now; I expect you to show my guest you can be a lady when required. You may join in the discussion at supper and demonstrate your education. I think Garvan would find that interesting. And get Mara to do something with your hair."

She was almost at the door when he spoke again.

"Tuala?"

She waited, not turning.

"You did well to bring this news straight to me."

Tuala heard in his tone how difficult it was for the druid to speak these words. She nodded and fled.

SUPPERTIME WAS A trial. It was evident to Tuala that she was on display, set out for inspection as if she were a prize heifer at a farmers' market. For all the visitor's evident attempts to conceal this by making polite conversation on safe, general topics, she could see his interest in his eyes, and a reflection of it in the attitudes of all those who sat at table. Tonight this was a much smaller group than usual: Broichan and Garvan, herself, Mara, and a mere four of the men at arms, all long-serving and of relatively mature years. The others had been sent off to eat in the kitchen, from where no doubt they were listening in on every word. They were probably counting the days until the squarely built, thick-necked Garvan loaded her onto his cart and took her off home, a good investment for the future, young, healthy, and educated into the bargain. The more Tuala thought about it, the more her fear was replaced by anger. How dare they seal her entire future thus? How dare Broichan make such a decision without even asking how she felt? Most painfully of all, how could they do this while Bridei was far away down the Glen, not knowing? Didn't anyone understand?

Garvan was trying his best, she could see that. It was not his fault he was a big lump of a man with a face like something carved out of a turnip. He asked her about her tutors, talked of the passing of the season, even raised the topic of kin symbols in passing and seemed surprisingly knowledgeable about it. He was trying hard not to stare at her. She had put on a clean skirt and tunic. She had combed and plaited her own hair; Broichan had been stupid to think she would ever seek Mara's aid for so intimate a task. Pulling the comb through the tangles, it had been impossible not to remember Bridei doing this for her when she was little and asking her with a smile in his voice what she'd done with the ribbon this time. His absence was a constant ache in her heart.

There was wine on the table tonight, imported all the way from Armorica, Broichan said; he allowed her a small cupful. It was a heady brew, reminding her of summer, of days past, herself and Bridei climbing Eagle Scar, galloping their ponies through the forest, trying to tease trout out of the lake. Gone, all gone; if Broichan had his way she might be married before Bridei came home again. Her hands balled themselves into fists. Something dangerous began to awaken inside her, like a little licking flame. There seemed to be a whispering in her head, *Show them. Stand up to them.* Tuala blinked, startled. This voice had not spoken aloud, that was evident; around her the talk continued to flow. Strange; she could have sworn it was a voice she knew, an Otherworld voice. That odd young man who seemed made of all the twiggy and leafy things of the woods, just so had been his manner of speaking. But the words had sounded inside her, as if they sprang from her own thoughts.

"We might finish the evening with a tale or two," Broichan suggested. This was most uncharacteristic; he really was putting himself out to play the good host. "Would you care to offer one, Garvan? The work you do cannot come without a great fund of lore, I recognize that. Will you share some of it with us?"

Garvan looked disconcerted. "My hands tell the tales for me," he said, flushing a little. "I haven't the gift to recount them in fair and powerful words, as your kind do. But I'm sure Tuala has learned many stories worth sharing. Her upbringing sounds remarkable. Perhaps she will favor us with something." He glanced at her almost shyly. Perhaps, she thought, he'd suddenly been infected by the same malady as the other men, a fear she might entrap him with her eldritch wiles. A pox on the man. A pox on them all. *Show them. Tell your tale and show them.*

Broichan was about to speak, perhaps to offer a polite refusal on her behalf.

"Of course," Tuala found herself saying smoothly. It almost felt like someone else speaking. She was icy calm, and a new tale came to her complete and perfect in form, a tale that would reveal her strength and provide a test for the listener, both at the same time. "But first, tell me what craft you ply, my lord. You said your hands tell the tales for you. What does that mean?"

"I am a stone carver."

"A little more than that, my friend," Broichan said quietly. "He is a craftsman and artist of the highest order, Tuala; the ancestors speak through him."

"You do me too much honor," Garvan said, looking down at his big, scarred hands, which were loosely clasped on the table before him.

"Hardly," Broichan said. "Does not your work stand in the court of the king of Fortriu himself? I can scarcely think of a calling more closely linked to all that is sacred in our land than yours."

"Save that of wise woman or druid," said Garvan, smiling. "I hope that is what you need, Tuala."

"Let us say this tale concerns a stone carver." Tuala had been expertly trained in the recounting of stories of heroes and magic, monsters and quests. Tonight's offering would be different: well outside the repertory of her dear old tutors. "I'll call him Nechtan. Now this Nechtan was a lonely man and a proud one. He had his craft, and in that he excelled. He'd had a wife once, but she was dead, and his sons had gone off to fight for the king: neither one of them had shown interest in learning the father's trade. All day long Nechtan labored with mallet and chisel and with his bare hands, coaxing the fair secrets from the heart of the stone, mysterious owls and proud bulls and strange water beasts, spears and shields and men on horses, riding to battle. By day the stone carver was caught in his dreams, fashioning them into wondrous, eternal form. By night he lay open-eyed and wakeful, feeling in his heart's core the depth of his loneliness. By night the dreams were fled, replaced by a shadowy gulf of despair. In that bleak time a yearning came on Nechtan, fierce and dark, but for what he did not know.

"Now it happened in springtime that Nechtan traveled up the Glen, for he had a commission for the king and he needed to visit court to discuss the details of it. The weather was kind; the days were crisp and bright, small birds busy in alder and hazel, leaves starting a tentative unfurling on the bare branches and a carpet of snowdrops beneath. When it was growing too dark to travel on, Nechtan camped by a little stream and made a wee fire between stones, and he settled to sleep, his blanket rolled around him. He was used to the cold; being in the forest at night didn't bother him. If he could have slept, he would have. But sleep never came easily to the stone carver. He lay awake under a gibbous moon, curled up on himself for warmth as the little fire collapsed into glowing coals and then into powdery ash that stirred in the chill whispers of the night breeze. He lay and wished, hoped, longed for something whose name he did not know. Whatever it was, he needed it with body, heart, and soul; without it he would surely shrivel away like the last berries of the rowan left wrinkled on the branch.

"'Man?' came a little voice in his ear. There before him, just beyond the remnants of the fire, was a hunched figure in a cloak of ash gray, perhaps an old woman, though it was hard to tell.

"'Who are you?' Nechtan asked, mindful of the hour and the place and the only kind of folk one might expect to find by moonlight in such a spot. 'What do you want?'

" 'Proper hearth, proper home, better there than on your own,' the person said, and Nechtan, getting up, saw that it was indeed an ancient, hook-nosed crone, and that her bony finger was beckoning him to follow her.

" 'I'm quite comfortable here, thank you,' he said as politely as he could, though this was far from the truth. But he remembered from the tales of his childhood the perils of obeying a summons such as this. On the other hand, it was growing very cold and a proper hearth and a roof over his head did sound quite appealing.

" 'Warm fire, warm bed, dreamless sleep for weary head,' the crone muttered, beginning to shuffle off under the trees. Still Nechtan hesitated; what if he followed her and she led him all the way to the perilous realm beyond the margins? From there, he might never return; and he had a commission for the king.

" 'Soft hands, sweet embrace,' came the voice of the old woman. He could hardly see her now as she moved away. 'Spirit's solace, resting place.'

" 'Wait!' Nechtan cried and, snatching up his bundle of possessions, he stumbled after her along a path dimly illuminated by the moon."

Tuala paused in her tale. Her listeners had been quite silent, Broichan watching her gravely, Garvan leaning forward, intent. Mara pursed her lips now and said, "He was a fool, then. Doubtless he never came back again to his own time and place."

The men at arms were looking anywhere but at the story-teller. However, it was clear they were absorbed in the tale; not one of them had stirred since Tuala began it.

"She took him to a small cottage all hedged about with briars," she went on. "Inside, it was indeed snug and warm, with soup heating on the fire and a jug of ale ready on a little crooked table, almost as if someone had been expecting him. Seated by the hearth was another cloaked figure. Indeed, this one was swathed and wrapped about with layer on layer of woolen cloth, so Nechtan could not see the shape of the person at all. What he did see was a pair of lovely white hands, soft and graceful; and the face that was turned toward him was a woman's, and pleasing in form. Its most remarkable feature was the mouth. This was the prettiest, most be-guiling mouth Nechtan had ever seen and, being a stone carver by trade, he'd an eye for beauty. The lips were not too thin and not too full; they were red and sweet as a ripe cherry and curved in what seemed to him the perfect shape for kiss-ing. Looking at that mouth he almost forgot where he was and what had led him there. But not quite.

" 'The blessings of the Shining One on your hearth,' he said with only a slight tremor in his voice. 'The old woman said I might come in to get warm. It is very kind of you.'

"The woman smiled. Her mouth developed a charming dimple at one corner, her eyes grew brighter and her hands reached for jug and goblet to pour him ale, but she could not quite stretch far enough. The crone, mumbling to herself, came over and did it for her.

" 'I'm sorry,' the younger woman said. 'I cannot walk; my friend Anet, who brought you here, must perform many tasks for me. Please sit, drink and warm yourself. Then I have a proposition for you, or a challenge, if you will. You are a man of judgment, I read that in your eyes. You know, then, what margin you have crossed to visit me tonight.'

"Nechtan's hand halted, the goblet halfway to his lips.

" 'It is safe to drink,' she said. 'You are already in our realm, but I will not seek to hold you here against your will, nor will Anet. What choices a man makes in my house are his own choices.' She sighed, and Nechtan heard in that sigh an uncanny reflection of his own secret sorrow, the empti-ness of the heart he would give much to banish. He lifted the cup to his lips and drank, watching her over the rim.

" 'Nechtan,' the woman mused, 'that is your name. A maker of fine things, strong, lovely things. Why has such a man, a man with a craft and a position in life, a man with his own house and the king's favor, such sorrow in his eyes?'

" 'I don't know,' Nechtan whispered, looking at her and thinking those white hands, that delicious mouth might drive him to a despair still greater, if he was not careful. 'Tell me, since you seem to know my name already, what is yours, lady?'

"She smiled, but it was a smile whose sadness seemed

all too familiar to him. 'They call me many names,' she said, 'such as Crookshanks, Twistabout, or Half-Maid. It is not for nothing that I go clad thus; nobody may see me as I am beneath my wrappings, save Anet there who tends to me.'

" 'I would give you a new name, if you would allow,' Nechtan found himself saying. His cheeks grew hot as he realized his temerity; what would the lady think of such boldness?

" 'And what would that be?' she asked him softly.

" 'Ela,' said Nechtan. 'That name is for a swan; and it is of such a creature that you remind me, pale and remote, of a beauty beyond the understanding of human folk. Forgive me; I do not know you, I should not have spoken thus . . .'

" 'Ela.' She echoed it, and the name hung in the air of the little smoky cottage, sweet as a promise. 'That is . . . acceptable . . .'

"She waited while he drank a bowl of soup and warmed himself by the fire. Then she gave him her proposition. She had, Ela said, the power to take away his loneliness and to assuage his secret sorrow. If he wanted to stay with her, to live in her cottage and to share her bed at night, she would grant him dreamless sleep and days that were free, so that he could cross back into his own world and continue to ply his craft. 'For I see,' she said, 'that to give up this calling would cause you to wither away before your time. Stay with me a year and a day, and you shall have honest work while the sun is up, and under the moon, nights of such sweet content that there will be no room left in you for sorrow.'

" 'But, lady—Ela—' Nechtan could feel the heat rise to his cheeks, the warring of his body's desire with his mind's caution, 'you said—forgive me—you said none but your elderly companion could ever see your form as it truly is. How can you welcome a man to your arms and to your bed if that restriction holds?'

" 'You need not see me unclothed,' Ela told him gravely, 'nor hold me against you, flesh to flesh, for this magic to work. Believe me, you would not wish to see what lies beneath these bindings I wear.'

" 'Then how . . . ?'

" 'Trust me, stone carver, and accept what I offer you. You will sleep the better for it.'

"Nechtan was silent. His mind was full of questions that could not be asked.

" 'You don't believe me,' Ela said, her long lashes drooping over her clear, light eyes, her lovely mouth sad. 'Or you do not trust me. Stay tonight, only tonight, and I will show you this is true.' "

Tuala paused; around the table, the silence was absolute. "Tell me," she said. "What would you have Nechtan do?"

Broichan offered nothing. She thought perhaps she had achieved the impossible and rendered him mute with surprise.

"He should never have got himself into that situation," Mara said bluntly. "A craftsman, a person of substance, he knew what was what; he was a fool to follow the crone, a fool to drink from the woman's cup, and he'd be even more of a fool to accept the offer. He should at least ask what the terms are; what she wants of him in return. I think he says no, thanks her politely, and gets on with his journey as quick as he can. There's no time for secret sorrows and suchlike in a man's life. He should just do what has to be done and be glad of what he has."

"Can't do that, though, can he?" ventured one of the men at arms.

"That's right," said another. "It's not how the tales go. Take one look at such as her, and a fellow's lost forever. He probably gets in her bed, and undoes the wrappings even though she told him not to, and finds she's a monster waiting to gobble him up."

There was another silence. Tuala waited.

"As an artist," Garvan said, "he knows the paths of the gods are never straight and obvious. As a man who works with stone, he understands that beauty exists with the release of dreams from the forms that restrain them. He has no choice but to agree to what this woman offers him; it seems to him this might be what he has long searched for but never found." He glanced sideways at Tuala, a question in his eyes.

"That's good," Tuala said, surprised that such a man would offer such a response. "He stayed, and it was exactly as Ela had promised. She shared her bed with him, but it was understood he might not hold her close, nor take off the many swathing garments with which she concealed her body. And she did indeed work magic; her skills and her sweetness awoke a fire in Nechtan that he had never known he possessed, not in all the years of his marriage nor in his casual encounters with women through the time of his widowhood. Ela's soft voice, her listening ear, her gentleness and kindness soothed his spirit wondrously; he felt he could tell her anything and she would understand. By day he returned to the mortal world and continued to ply his trade. At night he hastened back to his Ela, his hunger for what she could offer undiminished by familiarity, for her presence seemed always fresh, always new, a wondrous world with ever more treasures to discover. There were no more nights plagued by shadows and desperation; now it was all sweet fulfillment and the profound sleep that follows it.

"A year and a day passed, and not a night of that time but Nechtan spent it in his new sweetheart's bed, which proved difficult for his trade at times; a stone carver needs to be free to travel, to go where his commissions take him. But he had assistants, and he managed, for he could no longer bear to sleep without her.

"Then, when the time she had set him had passed, Ela asked Nechtan what he would do now. 'For I see,' she said, 'that although we are happy together, and you are no longer troubled by loneliness, there is a new sadness in your eyes. What is it that troubles you, dear one?' "

Tuala glanced around her audience again. "What does he tell her?" she asked them.

"He wants to see what she looks like," a man at arms offered, eyes averted. "It bothers him that she still has a secret from him. That's in many tales; curiosity gets the better of folk, and then everything goes wrong for them."

"That's right," said another. "If one of the—the Good Folk—sets a rule like that, you dare not go against it. That can only end in sorrow. But in the tales, that's what people do, every time."

"He probably unwraps her binding when she's sleeping and takes a peep," Mara said, "and after that Ela vanishes, her and the crone and the cozy little house, and he's left just as he was before, beset by foolish longings for what can never be."

Tuala waited.

"No," Garvan said. He seemed to be considering his reply. "No, I don't think that's it. Of course he would have liked her to show him her body; if she could not do so, it meant she didn't yet trust him. But that was not the cause of his unease. He told her that what he wanted above all was to be able to give her the same pleasure she had afforded him so generously, night after night, without seeking anything in return save his company. He longed to be able to heal her wounds as she had his. He wished she would tell him how he could do this; he wished she would say what she herself needed for true content." He looked at Tuala, suddenly hesitant. "At least, that is the way I would tell it, had I your gift for words."

"A carefully crafted answer, friend," Broichan commented with a twist of the lips.

"It seems an honest answer," Tuala found herself saying. "Have you a better one, my lord?" Something had made her bold tonight, perhaps the inner voice that had conjured so unlikely a tale from nowhere.

"No," said Broichan. "I simply wonder how this fellow found the time and the energy to maintain his trade when his head was so full of feelings and anxieties and sensitivities. I am inclined to concur with Mara, and say he should have left well alone when he had the chance. I suppose the tale works to a conclusion in which we discover this Ela was under some kind of enchantment, and her stone carver found out the secret for undoing it and made her straight and beautiful again. Simple tales for simple folk; the patterns are always the same."

It seemed to Tuala there was a challenge in those eyes and in the cynical words. "The Shining One is not predictable," she said. "Her cycles may be constant, but the tides she awakens in the minds and bodies of her creatures, she governs at her own will. When Ela heard Nechtan's answer, tears spilled from her eyes. He longed to take her in his arms and comfort her, but he respected the limits she had set him.

Far better, he had thought from the beginning, to accept this strange shadow of a marriage than to lose altogether the one who had become his best friend, his solace, his heart's joy. So he only reached his hand to curve it around her cheek, and touched his lips to her face, kissing away the marks of her weeping.

"That night, at dark of the moon, she let him undress her. Whatever it was she revealed to him, it did not make the house disappear in a puff of smoke, nor Ela and old Anet vanish. It did not drive the stone carver away. Indeed, those who saw Nechtan in the years afterward commented that he was becoming dreamy with contentment. As for the images of his carvings, they grew stranger season by season, bull and boar and goose replaced by curious animals that were neither one thing nor another, and patterns so intricate they seemed to change even as you looked at them: spirals and mazes without beginning or ending. This story is a bit like those patterns. Nechtan took Ela to see the swans on Maiden Lake. She shared with him her deepest secrets. They had great and lifelong joy, each of the other. That is all I know, or all I choose to tell."

Silence again. It was broken by the one of the men at arms protesting, "You mean that's the end?" In his outrage at the tale's abrupt conclusion, he seemed to have forgotten to be wary of the teller. "But what was her secret? What did she look like under the wrappings?"

"Maybe fair, maybe foul," Tuala told him. "That's not the point."

"Without that, it's not properly finished," Mara said. "Such a tale, a tricky sort of tale, needs a conclusion. It needs to explain the secret of the thing."

Tuala did not comment. Probably not a single one of them understood the meaning of the story. It made them uncomfortable that it did not conform to the accepted way of such tales.

"This is not a story about spells or about beauty." Broichan's comment surprised Tuala; she had not expected his support in any form at all. "It concerns choices," the druid added.

"True," Garvan said. "We need not learn if Ela was a god-

dess or a monster; the point is that Nechtan showed he valued her needs as equal to his own. With that, he won her trust
at last. And, of course, that was what he needed and wanted
most of all."

"It's very possible," Tuala said, "that under the wrappings
her body was as fair and unblemished as her hands and her
face, and always had been. She set him a test and he passed
it."

"What learning is to be derived from this?" Broichan
never forgot what he was.

Tuala drew a deep breath. "The learning is that the Shining One expects her daughters to have freedom in their
choices. Remarkably, Nechtan came to an understanding of
that, and was rewarded. I am her daughter as Ela was, and I
need the same freedom in my own choices. I sit here tonight
and tell my story because it is expected of me; thus I show
my gratitude for the hearth and home I have been given here.
The weaving of tales is one thing; being sent away, being
sold off once I become inconvenient is quite another." Her
voice shook; whether it was with anger or with sudden terror
at what she had ventured, she herself could not tell. "I'll bid
you good night now; I would not wish to disrupt your gathering further. May the Shining One light your dreams." She
turned to Garvan. "You gave good answers," she said. This
was only fair; he had surprised her with the depth of his understanding. A pity she had not the slightest wish to marry
him.

"Good night, Tuala," said Broichan. What he thought of it
all, there was no telling.

SHE FOUGHT SLEEP that night, knowing her dreams would
bring again that dark vision, Bridei falling, dying, his dear
features racked with unspeakable pain. She must trust
Broichan to prevent it. He had seemed sure he could send
warning in time. She must believe this was so. The images
of the Dark Mirror could be changed when what they
showed was still to come; a man or woman could act to fore-
stall them. It must be so, for they had been contradictory al-

ready, showing her one future in which Bridei wed a red-haired woman and sired a son, another in which his life of promise was cut cruelly short. Perhaps these visions spoke of a choice. Her choice. If he were to live, she must accept that he would move away from her. Was the goddess telling her she must let him go?

There were tears waiting to fall, heavy behind her eyes. There was something else as well, the same something that had stirred within her the day she bid Bridei farewell. When he had touched her that day, his fingers gentle against her flesh, she had known, without really understanding, that what was between them had changed forever. Tuala sat up in bed, hugging her arms tight around her knees in the darkness. Garvan was a good man. He seemed kind, courteous, thoughtful. And she could not marry him. She had loved Bridei from the first, as a brother, a best friend, a wise companion, so familiar he had always seemed a part of herself. And now she loved him as a girl loves her sweetheart, as Nechtan loved Ela, with beating heart, with quickening of the blood, with anguish and tears and deepest joy in the knowing of it. It was right, after all. She really had changed, and when she did so, her world had changed with her.

9

BROICHAN SENT FOR her next morning. Garvan was already gone; Tuala heard Mara telling Ferat that the stone carver's precipitate departure was, without doubt, a response to the tale he had heard last night and the look on the face of the teller, "for you could see," Mara said in a whisper, "that Otherworld glamour, the danger of it. I'd never have dreamed the lass had such a tale in her. You should've seen the look in the men's eyes. And here's me thinking she's as innocent as any maid of her years should be."

However, when Tuala came to Broichan's chamber and

stood before him, hands clasped behind her back, heart thumping, it was not to receive a reprimand for driving her suitor away, nor a punishment for attempting to seduce the men at arms with her tale.

"Garvan asked to speak with you privately." Broichan stood in his customary spot, his back to the hearth. There was no fire today and the chamber was full of little eddying drafts. The druid's tall frame was black-robed, his eyes fixed on Tuala, intent as a hawk's. "I refused his request; it did not seem to me appropriate. Is it that you do not wish to marry him, or that you do not wish to wed at all?"

Tuala swallowed. "It is too soon," she managed. "I am not ready for marriage."

"You are of marriageable years, Tuala," Broichan said. "Other girls are most certainly handfasted at your age, and are often mothers within the year. Perhaps all that is required is more explanation, more reassurance . . . You could speak to Mara about this. On the other hand, the remarkable tale you chose to tell my guest last night does suggest . . ." The druid's manner was diffident now. His eyes had gone distant, as if the topic were somehow beneath him.

"I know what it means to share a man's bed," Tuala said bluntly. "One does not grow up on a farm without learning certain basic facts. My lord, I have no wish to wed Garvan or any other man. If that displeases you I regret it. You have given me a home here and I understand I am in your debt. I know you didn't want to take me in. I haven't forgotten what you said, long ago, about my place here at Pitnochie depending entirely upon you. But I want to stay. I need to stay." *I need to be here when Bridei comes home.*

"You cannot stay," Broichan said. "You are no longer welcome among my people. This change has occurred despite me. Now I myself am moving on, indeed I must do so as soon as I can, for Bridei's sake. And you must go."

"Go where?" Tuala clenched her fists behind her back, trying to keep her voice calm. "Have you found another likely suitor?"

"I don't need to. Garvan was concerned that you might misunderstand his reasons for leaving so soon. He explained to me before he rode off that his offer for you still stands, and that it is up to you to make the decision in your own time: a year, two if you need them. He's a remarkably generous man; generous to the point of folly, some might say. He asked me to tell you that he wants no dowry, nor has he promised anything in return for your hand; your talk of 'selling off' was unfounded. He wished you to know this."

"I see."

"That choice, therefore, remains open to you. It seemed to me, last night, that there was a bond of sorts between you and Garvan, if only in your approach to the interpretation of tales." Broichan regarded her, brows lifted; it seemed a comment was required.

"I don't want to marry." Tuala felt cold all over. "I don't want to be sent away."

"In that, there is no choice. Whether or not you wish to consider the prospect of this marriage for some time in the future, I will not leave you at Pitnochie. However, there is another option, one that has become more possible with the advent of a messenger from Raven's Well this morning."

"From Raven's Well? What is the message? Is Bridei safe?"

"It did not concern Bridei," Broichan said, "but we can assume from the lack of news in that regard that all is well with him. The messenger brought a request that Pitnochie provide shelter for the lady Dreseida and her family for a night or two; they travel to Drust's court, where they will remain until the time of conflict is past. The lady will be here as soon as the weather makes her journey practicable. I'll be gone by the time her party arrives, but Mara will see to things."

The lady Dreseida and her family. Fox Girl. And Broichan leaving for court in such a hurry after so long away . . . He must really be worried about Bridei's safety, not just in the battle and the aftermath her vision had shown, but afterward as well. Tuala waited for more.

"This would provide a highly suitable escort for you," Broichan said. "It means we can, if necessary, follow the other path that is open to you. It was not my preferred way, and the tale you chose to tell last night only strengthened my doubt as to whether it is a desirable course for you."

"What path?"

"Long ago the wise woman, Fola, offered a place in her establishment at Banmerren for you when you reached a certain age. She wanted you to receive your early education here; what Erip and Wid could provide was far superior to the training offered to most girls of high family. You do not realize, perhaps, how privileged you have been in that respect."

"I know the debt I owe them."

"Banmerren is on the north coast, around the bay from Caer Pridne," Broichan said. "It's a secluded establishment in keeping with the nature of the tuition. Whether a young woman of your origins can ever fulfill the sacred duties of a servant of the Shining One is for Fola and her fellow tutors to discover. Once accepted there, you need not return to Pitnochie. And you need not marry, of course. That should please you."

A confusion of feelings gripped Tuala. She had no words at all.

"I have not mentioned this before," the druid said, "because I have doubts, serious doubts, as to the desirability of it. Fola is a friend whose wisdom I value. I fear, nonetheless, that you may be at risk of . . . exploitation. Your skills and talents, coupled with your unusual education, will not win you friends in such an environment. And there's a danger you carry with you: if your abilities are not guided wisely and strictly you could wreak havoc."

Beneath the cold sense of impending loss, Tuala felt outrage. Words came to her lips, *Then why didn't you teach me? Who better to train me in the mysteries than a king's druid?* She bit them back. It was too late for this.

"Perhaps you were not aware of the impact of your tale last night," Broichan said. "I think you lack awareness of many things, Tuala. To bring you into the mortal realm was less than wise."

"Must I go away? Couldn't I stay here and . . . ?" And what? Stay and get under Mara's feet, stay and terrify every man at Pitnochie merely by existing? A memory came to Tuala: a small, lonely girl confiding in a crone not much taller than herself, a child with a desperate hope in her voice. *I want an education, but he won't let me.* It seemed Fola had made a very long bargain.

"In my judgment you would do better to wed Garvan," Broichan told her. "His protection would ensure you of a home in which you were always welcome. His influence would buy you respect and security. Elsewhere, I think it likely the same distrust and suspicion that now dog you at Pitnochie will continue to be present, wherever you go."

"How soon will they come?" Tuala's voice cracked. "Lady Dreseida and the others? When must I go?"

Broichan sighed. "When the weather clears they will set out," he said. "It will be by boat, up the lakes, with men to bear the craft where the waterways are not navigable. If this is your choice, you'd best see to getting your things organized without delay. Mara will know what's required."

"It does not seem very much like a choice," Tuala said, the bitterness of it making her chest ache. "May I not even wait until summer?"

"It would be foolish not to avail yourself of Dreseida's guards as escort. Her own daughter travels to Fola's establishment; as well as the training of priestesses, the women there also provide learning for the daughters of noble families. This is highly convenient. None of my own men can be spared to ride with you, nor would any of them be content to take on such a task. For myself, I will leave without delay, for my need to see Drust is now urgent. And I do not go by the paths of ordinary men."

IT CAME MUCH sooner than she expected, a long spell of dry weather and the arrival up the lake of four boats, bearing the lady Dreseida, her red-headed daughter and two very loud small boys, along with a miniature mountain of luggage and a cohort of grim-faced guards. Lady Dreseida's presence seemed to fill the household; even Mara wilted under her searching stare. It might have been easier had Broichan still been at Pitnochie. As it was, an already miserable Tuala retreated into herself. She answered questions in a whisper, and soon took to losing herself out in the woods when she thought a new inquisition might be forthcoming. Young Uric and Bedo, for all their shouting and running about, were much easier to tolerate than the women of Talorgen's family. When the boys asked questions, it was with straight-out, innocent curiosity.

"Is it true you were found under a hawthorn bush?" Bedo asked.

"No. I was left on the doorstep. A foundling."

"You're very white. Whiter than anyone I've ever seen."

"That's just the way I am."

"Ferada says," Uric's voice was lowered a few notches from the customary shout, "you're not really human. She says you're a daughter of the you-know-who."

"I'm just ordinary," Tuala told him. "I do all the same things ordinary girls do."

A pause.

"Bridei never told us he had a sister." Bedo's tone was slightly accusatory.

"I'm not his sister. We were brought up together. We're friends." A little word like *friends* was woefully inadequate to explain it, but the child seemed to accept her answer.

"Mother said you're going to Caer Pridne with us."

"That's right. Not to Caer Pridne, just to the school for wise women."

"Is that what you're going to be, a wise woman?"

A breath of cold passed over Tuala; she recalled a vision that had troubled her greatly, herself in gray robes, an outsider, as Bridei smiled at his wife and held his small son's hand. "I don't know," she said.

"Can you do magic? Charms and things?"

The safe answer to this was a flat negative. Tuala found she could not give them an outright lie. "It depends what you mean by magic," she said.

"If you wanted, could you turn me into something else, a newt or a toad?"

"I'm not sure," Tuala said, offhand. "Want me to give it a try?"

A look of utter terror appeared on Bedo's small face; he had turned as pale as linen.

"She's joking, silly." Uric's tone suggested he was not entirely convinced by his own words.

"Another time, maybe," Tuala said.

"Is that your cat?" Uric had spied Mist where she sat washing herself by the wood pile; it was a good opportunity to change the subject. "Does it bite?"

Bedo hissed something in his brother's ear.

"Is that true?" Uric demanded. "Is it a familiar?"

Bedo, suddenly red-faced, looked away.

"Like me," Tuala said, "Mist is perfectly ordinary. She doesn't mind being stroked, as long as you're gentle." Oh, Mist; another friend to be left behind. Tuala's memory was good. She had not forgotten something Fola had told her when she was so kind and gave her the kitten, about having a cat of her own that didn't tolerate interlopers. It might well still be at Banmerren, ancient and ill-tempered. Mist would be better off here in her familiar territory with a regular supply of mice to be caught. But to sleep at night without that comforting warmth beside her, a reassurance that she was not quite alone, that would be hard indeed.

She had a task planned for her last night at Pitnochie: a night of full moon. It was something she needed to do if she must be gone when Bridei came home. Unfortunately, the little boys had been housed in Bridei's old chamber, top to toe on the narrow pallet, and that made her task difficult. She'd no wish to draw attention to herself in any way at all. Dreseida intimidated her; Ferada alarmed and annoyed her. Their eyes, the haughty tilt of their heads, their immaculate gowns and perfectly dressed hair seemed to mock her own plain clothing and general air of dishevelment. Somehow, however tightly she plaited her hair, strands of it always escaped to curl around her ears or down over her eyes. She carried spare ribbons with her just in case. Perhaps the little boys were right; perhaps she would always look wild, however hard she tried to tame herself. Perhaps she would always look Other.

There was a charm that must be worked tonight under the gaze of the Shining One. She had planned to slip into Bridei's room when all were asleep and perform her ritual as part of a night-long vigil. This, now, was impossible. Still, Tuala reasoned, children slept soundly after a day's activity. The most vital part of it could still be done if she was careful.

She waited in her own chamber, listening as the household went through its evening sequence of sounds. Voices filtered through from the hall, Lady Dreseida's guards exchanging tales around the fire with those of Broichan's men who had been left behind to protect Pitnochie while the others rode to join Talorgen's battle force. The lady herself and her daughter Ferada would be in the hall as well, but the little boys were already abed. Tuala had heard their high voices from Bridei's chamber some time ago. Now they were quiet; almost certainly asleep. There was clattering from the kitchen: Ferat's assistants scouring the suppertime cook pots and rinsing platters. Ferat's grumbling voice accompanied the din. It was getting harder all the time to remember the cook as the man who had once helped a small girl form bread dough into rabbits and frogs and tiny men, and had whirled her around and around with his strong arms until she squealed with excitement; the man who had listened with pride as she recited the first poem learned by heart, and had laughed at her childish jokes.

Now, the creak of the door to the men's quarters; booted feet passing. Soon, snoring. They worked a long day. The visitors were very quiet, walking like the ladies they were on graceful soft-shoed feet. The two of them were in their chamber now, Mara's chamber; while they were here, the housekeeper was sleeping in Broichan's room. That had impressed Tuala; such a prospect seemed to her alarming beyond belief. Might not the druid manifest as a midnight shade of himself, all piercing eyes and dark, accusatory words? And what if those things in the jars started to move about in the night? The fact that Broichan was far away in Caer Pridne made no difference at all.

The kitchen was quiet now. Ferat and his helpers were done, and had retreated to their own sleeping quarters behind. Mara's slow, heavy footsteps moved across the hall. There was a creaking sound: she was damping down the fire and setting the screen before the hearth. More steps. She was going into the kitchen, checking that fire as well. She'd be casting her eagle eye over all for signs of disorder, dust on the flagstones, a ladle left out, a cloak fallen from its peg. Then there was the grinding metallic sound of the massive bolt being slid into place, barring the door until the night watch came in for their early breakfast. Mara's steps came back, paused a moment in the hall—what was she thinking about? Was she imagining Broichan, now far off at the king's court?—then made their steady way to the druid's chamber. The door opened and closed. Silence, save for Mist's purring as she kneaded the coarse blanket by Tuala's knees.

After that, more waiting. There was no danger of falling asleep; the importance of what must be done was too great. Tuala rehearsed it in her mind until sufficient time had passed for all of them to be fast asleep, ensnared by their dreams. Then she put on her favorite skirt and tunic, soft garments of fine pale wool with narrow borders of blue braid. These had once been Brenna's and were a little large, but they were the first grown-up clothing Tuala had possessed, a gift made before Fidich had barred her from the cottage, and she knew Brenna had spent precious time mending the skirt and altering the tunic for a better fit. The clothing smelled faintly of lavender; long ago, Brenna had shown her small charge how to layer garments with dried herbs to keep them fresh, and while Tuala was ever less than orderly in such matters as folding, she did not forget her supplies of aromatic leaves. To carry such a scent with her made her feel nearer to the forest, closer to the wild world of plants and creatures, a safer world by far than that of men. She left her hair unbound, brushing it and letting it fall down her back, a dark cascade that reached below her waist. She took off her slippers. Bare feet were quieter. Around her neck hung the moon disc she always wore, the pale bone warm against her skin. She slipped from her chamber without a sound and tiptoed to the doorway of Bridei's small room.

The door was ajar; perhaps these little boys feared the dark and needed the light from lamps kept burning in the passageway to watch over their dreams. Tuala slid through the gap and inside the chamber. They slept, the two of them. Uric was a snuggler, wrapped fast in his blanket, knees up, arms hugged across his chest, face buried in the pillow. Bedo was a sprawler. He took up his own share of the bed and half his brother's as well. His blanket was on the floor; Tuala picked it up and laid it lightly over him. The boy did not stir.

Through the tiny square window, the Shining One sent a beam of cool light; she was moving now into the patch of dark sky that could be glimpsed through this opening, and by the time her full, perfect form was framed there, Tuala must have everything ready. On the sill, Bridei's own offerings still lay; she could see they had been moved. Boys are curious creatures and these two, no doubt, had examined the eagle feather and played games with the white stones. No matter; the innocent's touch cannot harm the sacred. Tuala replaced the talismans the way Bridei had laid them and, reaching into the little bag she had brought, began to add her own, each with its particular words of power. A charred twig, pale at one end, charcoal dark at the other:

> *Rising flame, rising sun*
> *Blade of Fortriu, chosen one . . .*

A feather, not the barred pennant of the eagle this time but a soft, downy scrap of white, perhaps from the breast of a snowy owl, a winter creature:

> *Breath of promise, wings of life*
> *Ancient wisdom, banish strife . . .*

Tuala drew a little stoppered flask from her bag, uncorked it, sprinkled droplets of water on the sill, once, twice, three times.

> *Flowing, giving, subtle, free*
> *Clear and honest ever be . . .*

Lastly a handful of earth, rich and dark, scooped earlier from the forest floor. She laid it gently beside the other tokens.

Ancients hold you safe and strong
Past and future be your song
Clothed in spirit pure and bright
Lead your people forth to light . . .

The Shining One moved slowly, her careful dance bringing her into the window, framed for a little by its old stone
edges, letting her light fall on the offerings and, beyond
them, on Tuala's pale face gazing up at her, whispering her
charm. Now was the most important part, the part she must
say before she was taken away from Pitnochie forever. The
goddess must understand how crucial this was. If Tuala herself were not here for Bridei, someone else must take up the
task, the listening, watching task; the task of loving him for
what he was, and not for what he must become. Without
such a watcher, his burdens would in time become too heavy
for any man to bear. This Tuala knew in her heart; there was
no need for visions on the water.

Her hand reached again into the little bag, drawing out the
last item left: the talisman that was the unfinished tale of
herself and Bridei, the times together, the times apart, the
glad reunions and terrible farewells. If she had the power of
a goddess, Tuala thought bitterly, she would simply weave
the two strands of cord together, clinging, twining, cleaving
one to the other, and she would keep them thus indivisible
forever. But she was no supernatural being. Forest child she
might be, but what power she had in her was surely no more
than an ability with hearth magic, the kind anyone could do
if they put their mind to it, little spells of limited efficacy and
limited danger. She'd never have been able to turn a child
into a newt, even in the unlikely event that she'd wanted to.
And she could not protect Bridei from a future of loneliness
and perplexity and terrible choices, not if she was to be separated from him forever. But the Shining One could, and if
Tuala was anyone's daughter, she was the child of the moon,
born of winter shadows and snow under the oaks, of frost
twinkling in cold light and of bare-branched birches stark
under a midnight sky. Now, therefore, the most solemn
prayer must be spoken while the goddess had her eyes on her
small, pale daughter; while the Shining One turned her im-

partial gaze in through this little window. Winding the twisted cord about her hands, Tuala began to whisper the words.

"Hear me, Bright Mother, hear your daughter. I call upon your power, your love, your shining purity. Through you I call the Flamekeeper, embodiment of true courage, and I call the fair All-Flowers, who casts her gentle gaze on everything that lives and breathes on the earth. Through you I call Bone Mother, keeper of ancient tales, holder of the songs of the Priteni since time before time."

The moon looked down, silent. The only sound in the little chamber was the faint whispering breath of the two sleeping children.

"I seek nothing for myself. If it is your desire that I leave this place and serve you as a wise woman, I must accept it. Your will is beyond question. It is for Bridei I need help. You know the path that awaits him. I see in his journey choices that would drive the sanest man out of his wits, betrayals that will wound him to the core, peril at every turn and a loneliness to freeze the warmest heart. Without me, who will know his need for counsel? Without me, how can he let his tears flow? Alone, he will bear a load too heavy for the strongest man. No leader can carry such a burden and go on. But he must go on. And I must go away. What was once home to me is home no longer."

The Shining One was beginning to edge out of the window, seeking to move on in her journey.

"I ask, then," Tuala said through brimming tears, "that I may pass this care into your hands, Great Goddess, Bright Mother, illuminator of us all. You know he will be king; you know the strength he has in him. You know also that he has what some would call a weakness; a readiness to understand the mind and heart of his adversary, an open spirit that will give him pause even in the moment his arm wields the sword of justice. Take him in your hands, Bright Lady; comfort him in the dark of night when his heart is filled with unease. When his mind is shadowed by doubt, cradle him in your arms and give him rest. I ask this in the name of all the gods, and in the name of all that is sacred . . ."

There was a little knife in Tuala's belt; setting the cord down, she took the weapon in her hand and raised it to sever a long, thick lock of her dark hair, leaving a ragged end at her brow. There was only one more part of this to be done and then, if she had performed it perfectly, the Shining One would give her a sign and she would know that, however much her own sorrow lay in her breast like a cold stone, Bridei would walk forward under the goddess's protection. She raised her hands and drew breath for the final charm.

"What are you doing?"

Tuala's heart thumped; she spun around, arms still outstretched before her. The girl who had been standing behind her flinched back, eyes widening. The knife was pointed straight at her chest. Tuala sucked in an unsteady breath and lowered her arms.

Ferada crossed the room to the bed in two strides, a vengeful spirit clad in soft slippers and embroidered nightrobe, red hair plaited neatly down her back. "Tell me!" she hissed. "What are you doing in my brothers' bedroom? Why have you got a knife?"

Tuala did not seem to be able to get her heart under control, nor her breathing. The Shining One had almost left the window and the rite was not yet complete. She tried willing Fox Girl away, *Go, go now, quickly, so I can finish this and keep him safe,* but the red-haired girl stood her ground, lips tight, eyes glaring and suspicious.

"Well?" demanded Ferada. "Speak up!"

"I mean your brothers no harm." Tuala's voice was less steady than she'd tried for. "And it's not their room, it's Bridei's. This is my house, not yours. I can go anywhere I like."

Ferada's lips curved in a little smile that was entirely without humor. "My mother's unlikely to be impressed by such childish arguments when I tell her I found you in here in the middle of the night with a sharp knife in your hand," she said. "If you want her to include you in our entourage for the trip to Caer Pridne, and I have to say she's far from enthusiastic about the idea, you'll need to do rather better than that."

The moon was creeping out of view; there was barely enough time left. "Please," Tuala made herself say through gritted teeth. "Please let me finish. You can watch; you can make sure I do nothing wrong. This has to be done now, while the moon still shines in the window. It must be done before they send me away."

Something in her tone made Ferada's expression change, though the eyes were still wary. The red-haired girl moved closer to the pallet where her young brothers lay. "Go on, then," she said crisply.

It was hard to pick the ritual up again; hard to slow the pounding heart, swallow the tears, pace the breath. This must be done properly or there was no chance of it working. Bridei had impressed on Tuala from earliest times the significance of ceremony; the immense privilege it was to be granted the ears and eyes of the gods at such solemn times.

"I offer this token of myself," Tuala said, laying the long, glossy lock of hair on the sill beside the other objects. "The rest I will relinquish to fire, that the Flamekeeper, guardian of warriors, may also know my lifelong loyalty. And I offer this." A slash of the knife across her right palm, quickly, before she could think too hard—she heard Ferada's gasp— and she was holding up her hand so blood could run from the deep cut scored there onto the talismans of power set under the window. "Thus I show my reverence to the ancient ones, which lasts as long as blood flows in my veins; as long as breath passes through my body; as long as my feet walk the paths of womankind; as long as my heart knows truth."

The Shining One was almost fled; a mere sliver of her lovely shape was all that remained in the window space, although her light could be seen on the frail forms of the birches beyond the house. "You know that he is wise and strong and good," Tuala whispered. "But he is also human, beset by fears, plagued by doubts, open to deep sorrows. I ask only this, that if I cannot be by his side to help him, you will ensure he does not face his times of darkness without a true friend to light his way. This I ask in recognition of the bond you made between us, Bright Mother . . ." There was more she would have said, but Ferada's presence made it impossible. Indeed, to have any of this overheard was not only unsettling but felt in some way dangerous. Tuala put the knife back in her belt and clutched the bag against her wounded hand in an attempt to stanch the bleeding. She managed a formal bow as the moon slipped beyond the window frame and out of sight; then things began to blur before her eyes, and she sat down suddenly on the end of the bed. The children slept on, undisturbed.

"Ancients preserve us!" Ferada exclaimed in an undertone, crouching down by her side. "That, I most certainly didn't expect. Here, show me your hand—that needs salve and a bandage—"

"It's nothing." Ferada's sharp features were coming and going; Tuala heard a buzzing in her head. "I'm fine. And this is finished. You can go now."

Ferada lifted her well-shaped brows. "You don't look fine. Besides, I can hardly leave you here with Uric and Bedo. Come on. I'll fetch some clean linen, Mother has some—"

"No! Don't wake anyone. There's nothing wrong with me, I'll just go off to bed now . . ." As Tuala rose to her feet a new wave of dizziness came over her, and the walls reeled around her. She swayed.

"Stupid girl," Ferada said. "Where's your own chamber?"

They got there easily enough and paused in the doorway. Letting Fox Girl into the only part of Broichan's house that was all her own was not something Tuala planned to do, now or ever. "Thank you," she said as firmly as she could. "Good night."

"Not so fast." Ferada had pulled aside the rough curtain that was all the door this little space possessed, and was peering into the darkness within. "You can't dress that wound properly yourself. Besides, I have some questions."

"I don't need you. I don't want you." The pain in her hand and the fogginess in her head made Tuala blunter than courtesy required. Under that lay the realization that the Shining One had given no sign, no recognition that she had heard the prayers and accepted the offering. Fox Girl's interruption had probably ruined any chance of that. The goddess was displeased, and would cast both Bridei and Tuala adrift, apart and without friends to help them.

"Too bad," said Ferada, helping herself to a lantern that

burned on a stone shelf near the doorway and carrying it into Tuala's little chamber. "By all the ancestors! I thought Bridei's room was small enough, but this must be like sleeping in a closet. How quaint. Don't glower like that. You know very well that if I choose to tell my mother what I saw you doing she'll refuse to take you to Banmerren. But maybe that's what you want. Maybe you don't want to go." The brows rose again; the eyes were very shrewd in the lamplight.

"That's not your concern," Tuala said, knowing even as she spoke that there would be no winning a war of words with this confident young woman. How old could Fox Girl be, fifteen, sixteen? Not so very much older than herself and yet, worlds away.

"That's it, isn't it?" Ferada challenged. "Where do you keep cloths, linen—in here?" She rummaged in the storage chest. "You really don't want to go to Fola's school, even though you'll get the best chance any girl could have of escaping the marriage bed and making something of herself. You'd rather molder away here in Broichan's odd domain, hoping your brother will come home at last. I can't believe it." While she talked, Ferada found linen, relieved a mute Tuala of the knife, tore a serviceable strip and began to tend to the wounded hand with quick, deft fingers. "You have some salve? Good, here—just a little, then I'll bind it. You know, I suppose, that there are hundreds of girls who'd kill for a place in Banmerren? Fola doesn't accept just anyone."

Tuala was sorely tempted to respond, *She took you, didn't she?* But there was no point in such cheap barbs. Besides, Ferada's mother was the king's cousin. Reared on Erip's lessons in genealogy, Tuala understood the privileges and responsibilities such a connection must carry. "If I don't go I have to marry," she said quietly. "Being at Banmerren will be better than tying myself to a man I don't love."

"Love?" Ferada mocked. "Love's got nothing to do with marriage. If I were you, I'd count myself lucky if my proposed spouse had ten fingers and toes and all the required bits in between. Mother says men can be molded. Love is for tales. It has nothing to do with you or me or the lives of most young women of Fortriu. The best we can hope for is some control over the paths we follow. Some slight element of choice." For a brief moment she sounded different, as if the dauntingly competent exterior housed another girl entirely.

"I wanted to choose for myself," Tuala said. "But in the end, all the choices were Broichan's." This was not quite true; there was one choice she could not speak of.

"Who was it you were praying for?" Ferada asked. "Your brother, I suppose?"

Tuala did not reply.

"I shouldn't think he needs such a degree of devotion," Ferada said drily. "He's always appeared pretty capable to me. Lacking in humor, a little dull maybe, but very much in control of his own affairs. If I were you I'd stop fussing over him and get on with my own life. Be realistic about it, Tuala. A place at Banmerren is a great opportunity for such as you. I mean, where else would you go?"

That this part was plain truth did not make it any less hurtful.

"Funny," Ferada went on. "Bridei never talks about you. I only knew you existed because Gartnait told me. Really, I think you may be wasting your time."

Tuala waited a little, making herself breathe before she spoke. "I'd like to go to sleep now," she said politely. "If you don't mind. Thank you for bandaging my hand. I would be grateful if you didn't mention this to the lady Dreseida." *He didn't mention me because what is between us is special; precious; not to be shared.*

Ferada regarded her closely, eyes narrowed as if trying to work out a puzzle. "Hmm," she said. "She'll know soon enough when the boys are asked to explain the mess of hair and blood on the windowsill."

"I'm not asking you to tell a lie," Tuala said.

"We'll see," said Ferada. "You know, this could be quite interesting. I'm beginning to think sending you to Banmerren is a bit like putting a stray kitten into a cage of wild dogs."

"Kittens have claws."

"Indeed. It should make for lively entertainment if nothing else. I think it's best if Mother knows as little as possible. For now, at least."

Tuala put her hand up to mask a yawn.

"No need to overdo it," said Ferada. "There are still questions needing answers. But they can wait. Good night, Tuala."

"May the Shining One guard your dreams." Even at such a moment, the right farewells must be spoken.

The curtain lifted and fell. Soft footsteps faded. Tuala was alone once more. Clutching a shawl around her shoulders, she felt the deep throbbing in her hand become a fiery aching up and down her arm; she felt the tears as they built up behind her eyes, then began to fall, hot and bitter, down her cheeks. Mist slept on. What was in her feline mind, there was no telling. Her paws twitched from time to time; maybe she was dreaming of rats. As for Tuala, her thoughts were on certain things Fox Girl had said, things that were lies, wounding, horrible lies. *He's not dull. He's the best person in the world, he tells wonderful stories, he always listens properly. The gods love him. And I'm not fussing. I'm taking care of the future. Someone has to do it for him, and he's only got me.*

These thoughts did not seem to make it better; the tears only flowed more quickly, too fast to wipe away. She worked hard to stay silent; there was no way she would let Fox Girl, or anyone else, hear that she had been reduced to weeping. What if the Shining One did not accept her offering? What if Bridei had to go on his pathway all alone? *He won't be alone,* a small internal voice reminded her. *What about the vision, Midsummer at Dawn Tree Hill? He wasn't alone then, was he? Who do you think that was with the russet hair and the elegant gown? A wife fit for a king, that's who.*

Tuala lay down, closing her eyes tightly, putting her hands over her ears. But the voice could not be silenced thus, the insidious, intimate voice of the leaf man, one of her own kind, determined to open her mind to her own folly. *It was her, wasn't it? Highly suitable. And if she cares nothing for love, what matter if she thinks him a bore? He'll be a king. That's all that counts.*

At length Mist awoke, or half woke, crept up the bed, circled three times, and settled again close to Tuala's neck.

Much later, worn out by sadness, her bandaged hand curled into the cat's soft fur, Tuala surrendered to sleep.

THERE MUST HAVE been a strong wind that night, a capricious wind that eddied in circles. When Bedo looked out of the window to see what sort of day it was, he noticed the eagle feather was gone. This was a disappointment; he had planned, secretly, to slip it into his baggage before they traveled on. He looked about; it wasn't on the floor, nor on the bed amidst the crumpled blankets. After breakfast he went to check outside, but there was no sign of it. All that the wind had left on the bare sill was the three white stones.

The next morning they rode on toward Caer Pridne, taking the witch girl with them. Her hair was looking odd; it had been roughly hacked off level with her ears, and now somewhat resembled Bedo's own, although it was a lot less tidy. The girl was very quiet. Her mouth was set in a thin line, as if she was trying not to cry. As the druid's house vanished into the oaks behind them, she didn't look back, not even once.

BROICHAN'S MAN HAD set out before his master left Pitnochie, equipped with a small pack of rations, adequate means to defend himself, and a message to Talorgen in his head. The message was not complex: there were only two parts to it. First, the old man, Erip, was dead and the news should be passed on quietly to the boy. Second, the boy must have a taster from now on. It was easy enough to remember.

The messenger was accustomed to covering ground swiftly, even in the most inclement of conditions. It was expected he would catch up with the advancing army within the space of twelve days or so, less if the rain held off. He knew how to avoid wolves and cramps and spies from Dalriada. He knew how to keep going on scant rations and little sleep.

He was no match for the rock slide above Maiden Lake. It had been wet; he was traversing a narrow path high above the water when he heard the unmistakable grumbling sound above him, growing rapidly to a splitting, roaring cacophony of tumbling boulders. Grimly he clung on, pressing himself against the incline, gritting his teeth and praying to Bone Mother that it might not yet be time for her to gather him to her breast. The tumult abated; small stones dribbled down the hillside to bounce and settle on the massive pile of rubble far below. And, after all, it was not time; not quite yet. The messenger blinked the dust from his eyes. He took a deep breath, full of joy that he had been spared. His leg was hurting; he looked down to assess the injury and felt the blood drain from his face. A massive stone had lodged itself hard against the rock wall where he had sheltered. Between boulder and cliff face, his leg was trapped to the thigh. Cold sweat broke out all over him. That single glance had told him the leg was crushed almost beyond recognition; he would never walk again.

For some time he tried to free himself by straining against the rock with his hands and by chipping at it with a smaller stone. His pack was still on his back; he blunted his knife scraping at the hard surface, leaving a network of desperate scratches. He had food for many days, water for three. At first he rationed the supply, a sip at a time, thinking of rescue. But nobody came. When the water ran out, he thought of taking the knife to his leg while he still had the strength, of severing the limb somehow, and then . . . and then what? He would bleed to death, crawling along paths known only to badger and squirrel, marten and beetle. It would be quicker, at least. But the knife was blunt, and he could not bring himself to try.

Rain fell the day after he emptied his water skin. He licked it from the rock that pinned him, wondering through a haze of fever at his own will to cling to life, despite all. He had forgotten the message. He had forgotten all but the pain and the cold and the creeping darkness of despair. That night, moving in around him like death's own messengers, the wolves came.

WHEN IT CAME to the point, it was not possible to think
very much at all. Paused in their march, gazing across the
lonely glen toward the hill of Galany's Reach, they saw
smoke rising, a banner flying above the settlement, and they
saw that the Gaels were ready for them; the walkways behind and below that rampart of sharpened stakes were lined
with archers. On the hilltop beyond, even at such a distance,
the tall form of the Mage Stone stood out against the skyline,
guarded by rowan trees. It drew the eye and set purpose in
the heart.

"They are not so many," Talorgen said, eyes narrowed.
"That is why they have chosen to go within, to defend rather
than come out and face us. We proceed to plan. Are you
ready? Morleo? Ged? Fokel?"

Grunts of assent. Ged's troop, resplendent in its rainbow
colors, was to take the right flank, Morleo's the left, with the
main force to approach the gates directly. Close behind
Talorgen's men rode Fokel's small band. Bridei had seen
this leader's dangerous eyes, his air of barely contained energy, as if he were in imminent danger of exploding. The
bristling armament borne by each of Fokel's grim followers
did nothing to lessen his unease. These men resembled some
Otherworld dispensers of arbitrary justice. Perhaps they
would not trouble to look where they struck until it was all
over. Their close proximity was scarcely reassuring.

The king's councillor, Aniel, had sent his two personal
guards to join this venture in the name of Drust the Bull.
Now his man Garth came forth, bearing the staff with the
king's banner, and others lifted high the symbols of every
chieftain here present, Longwater, Abertornie, Raven's
Well, and the ancient flag of Galany. Talorgen raised a
clenched fist into the air and gave a great ringing shout,
"Fortriu!" A hot, rushing pride coursed in Bridei's blood,
like the touch of the Flamekeeper himself. He raised his own
voice along with the rest of them in response, "*Fortriu!,*"
and the men of the Priteni marched forward into battle.

The approach to the settlement was across a wide vale, where a stream flowed down to empty itself into the vast waters of King Lake. The ground was boggy and their boots sank deep. There was little cover beyond a few bushes and meager trees hugging the banks farther upstream. As they approached the water, the gates of the settlement swung open and the enemy came out to meet them. It was not, after all, a desperate defense of an undermanned outpost, but a well planned counterattack, army against army; someone had given the Gaels good intelligence and they had used it well.

"How many?" Bridei managed to shout to Donal, who was shadowing him grimly, spear in hand.

"Enough," said Donal. "We'll do it. They'll try to draw us within reach of their archers. Talorgen will hold the fellows back, that's if that madman Fokel doesn't charge in first. Stay close if you can, Bridei. I need you in sight."

Still, thought Bridei, *still, on the brink of battle, Broichan's hand reaches out over me, as if I were a child to be sheltered. When will it be time for me to be a man?*

Then, beside him, before him, behind him the men began to run, and to shout, and the day turned to madness. The cries rang like trumpet calls in his ears; his heart, already racing, now took on the rhythm of a fierce drum, his own legs carried him forward in the surge, the press, the hot wave of bodies and then, abruptly, arrows began to rain down, men fell pierced in eye or throat or shoulder, there were bodies underfoot, blood bright on cloak or helm, on clutching hand or staring eye or shattered limb. He could not stop to help them; it was on, on, his feet carrying him forward with the tide, the ranks thinner now, his own throat hoarse with screaming above the din, *"Fortriu! Fortriu!"*

Past the arrows and into the melee, thrusting-spears used to skewer and pierce, Donal with a fellow spiked like a fine trout, wriggling on the shaft; Gartnait, glimpsed between straining, gasping figures, piercing a downed man's heart with one savage thrust of his dagger. Gartnait's eyes strange, exalting, almost as if he were in the presence of a god. A big man, Breth, seeking the space allowed by a hillock crowned in low bushes, using his bow steadily, coolly, to pick off one then another from among the chaotic tangle of men.

Stay close? thought Bridei. *That's a joke.* He scrambled up the rise to Breth's side, readied his own bow, began to loose his shafts with care; the slightest miscalculation and the arrow intended for a hulking warrior of the Gaels might instead pierce the breast of one of their own comrades.

"Over to the south," muttered Breth. "See, beyond the main mass of Ged's men? Give Fokel cover."

From here it was just possible to see what Fokel was doing, though in the press of the battle all had seemed random, the pattern of the day's conflict reduced to a single man with a big knife who was trying to kill you, another with a spear who had just killed your comrade. Down there all was moment to moment, strike, breathe, survive, press on. From the little rise, Bridei saw that Talorgen's forces were making slower progress now; they were barely past the stream bed, facing a sizeable number of Gaels, and many men from both sides lay prone or writhed on the ground, their moans drowned by the shouting of exhortation or insult, the clash of blades, the whistling of arrows.

Ged and Morleo were doing little better. Their forces, somewhat farther from the settlement walls, were bearing the brunt of the archers' work. From down there none of them could see Fokel and his small band of fighters. Fokel had taken his men far upstream, and now they snaked their way back on the other side, making use of the bushes that grew on the banks for cover, edging ever closer to the chaos before the gates.

Following Breth's lead, Bridei sighted and loosed an arrow and another, trying for the Gaels at the back of the throng, those most likely to be in the way when Fokel's men broke cover and surged up the hill toward the walls. It was crazy; it was just the sort of thing Fokel could be expected to do. Likely his entire squad would be picked off before they reached the enemy positions. Still, that man whose chest Bridei's arrow had just pierced would not see them coming. Nor would the fellow Breth got in the eye, nor that one, nor that . . .

"Always said you were a good archer in the making," muttered Breth, sighting and loosing again.

"How many arrows have you got left?" Bridei asked him.

"Two. Here."

They shot together; a pair of Gaels fell. Then it was down the hill again, into the nightmare. Donal was nowhere in sight; Gartnait, too, had disappeared in the melee. Talorgen, shadowed by Garth, was using his sword to devastating effect; this was a leader ready to put his life on the line with his men's. Ged's forces, bright tunics now spattered with blood, their own, the enemy's, were across the stream and making progress up the hill. And now, beyond the seething mass of men, something new could be seen. From within the neat palisade of sharpened staves came a brilliant glow of light, a harsh crackling and the voices of women raised in screams of alarm. Fokel's men had set fire to the settlement. Their creeping approach had brought them within range; flaming arrows had done the rest.

The archers on the upper walkways ran, deserting their posts; quenching the blaze was more urgent. Grimly, the Gaels on the ground held their positions. Perhaps it was their wives, their children in there where flames caught hungrily at grain store and tannery and sleeping quarters, where folk scurried desperately for buckets, where lads too small to fight set their puny arms to pumps, where women used sacks and blankets to beat at the engulfing flames. The men fought on, hard-faced, as the smoke blew over the battlefield, bathing sword and spear, splintering shield and blood-drenched banner in an eerie half-light, rose and gold and shadow gray.

Bridei had not carried a thrusting-spear; he had a short sword, a knife, and his bow, now useless unless he could scavenge a new supply of arrows. It became impossible to see what was happening; to know what the leaders wanted them to do. It became purely moving forward in a general direction of uphill and managing not to be killed. It was one small desperate battle, then another and another. Bridei made use of both sword and dagger. There was a young warrior, a Gael, with a hideous wound to the stomach, his entrails dangling, his face whey-pale with terror. Bridei had not thought he could reach down and slit a man's throat in pity but, when it came to it, he did so without hesitation, muttering a prayer to whatever gods this fellow believed in, *Take his hand.*

After a long time, a very long time in which his body simply moved on, wielding weapons in the well-drilled patterns, thrusting, dodging, stabbing, and his eyes stung with smoke and sweat and tears, and his throat grew painful with shouting, it became evident the tide had turned. Up ahead through the curtain of gray could be seen a bright flowering of fire, and silhouetted against it were, not the Gaels of Galany's Reach in implacable defensive array, but Fokel's wild warriors, all bared teeth and long serrated knives, moving down on the enemy from behind like vengeful furies. It was a terrible sight; that they were on Bridei's own side made it no less so. Fokel's band cut down all in their path. They fought with a savage efficiency that brought to mind the fiercest of forest predators, perhaps a great wildcat, blank-eyed at the moment its jaws close on the neck of the quarry, knowing nothing but the smell of blood.

Bridei found himself right on the edge of this grim onslaught, exchanging sword thrusts with a broad-shouldered warrior of Dalriada while beside him Fokel held a prisoner in a ferocious lock, twisting the fellow's arm behind his back and forcing the Gael to his knees before him. Fokel poised his knife before the captive's eyes. Bridei's own attacker was a solid man, leather helmed, his hair as red and wild as the fire that now devoured home and family behind him. Bridei read on his weary face that he no longer cared if he lived or died. Still he fought grimly on; both taller and broader than Bridei, the only advantage he did not have was youthful agility.

In the back of Bridei's mind was the fire; the need to get the women and children out now, before it was too late. Talorgen should give the order. He should send men up there. If he did not do so soon, all would perish, and the Priteni would prove themselves no less barbarous than their enemy . . .

"Ah!" Bridei gasped as pain lanced through his thigh; his opponent's sword had slashed him, drawing blood, and he staggered. The Gael raised his weapon anew, aiming for the neck this time. Bridei did not stop to think. He threw himself to one side, ducked, turned, and thrust hard. It was over before the fellow had time to blink. The warrior fell forward, a surprised look on his face and Bridei's sword lodged hilt-deep in his chest.

Bridei knelt, breathing hard; rolled the dead man over and extracted the weapon glistening with blood. He reached to wipe it on grass already besmeared with any manner of unspeakable things. In the instant that he moved, he saw a man rising from the ground behind the bending Fokel, a man in whose hands was a spiked club poised to descend with crushing impact on the chieftain's head.

Bridei leaped. His body slammed into Fokel's, sending them both crashing to the ground and out of range. The club fell, delivering a stunning blow to the Gael who had been Fokel's prisoner, the one who, a moment earlier, had been facing the point of a sharp knife. That weapon would no longer be necessary; the club had smashed the fellow's skull. Bridei was sprawled across Fokel, face down in the blood and mud of the battlefield. He drew a deep breath; felt his heart racing and bade it slow. He rose to his feet, every joint aching, and reached out a hand to Fokel. Behind him, the Gael who had wielded the club and killed one of his own now lay on the ground, his body pierced by no less than three Priteni spears.

"Black Crow save us!" spluttered Fokel as he got to his feet and retrieved the dagger he had dropped. "You young fool! Are you completely out of your mind?"

Bridei looked at him. He could think of nothing to say. The battle seemed to be moving away from them; through the thick smoke, he could see small groups of men still locked in their own particular nightmares, but there seemed now to be a general movement up the hill toward the burning settlement. He could hear Morleo's deep voice shouting orders, and could see the banner of Fortriu, white with the royal symbols in blue, held high amid a crowd of cheering men.

"Didn't you see the knife in my hand? You came within a whisker of getting that right through the neck!" Fokel said, sticking the weapon in his belt and giving the fallen Gael a token kick. "Who taught you to fight, a lunatic?"

Bridei smiled. "A man called Donal. He's about as far from a lunatic as you could get."

"What's your name, lad?" Fokel was not a man who could ever appear friendly; his face was like a wild creature's, wary and dangerous even in moments of repose. Still, it seemed to Bridei that the chieftain was not displeased, for all the manner of his words.

"Bridei, son of Maelchon. I am the foster son of Broichan, the king's druid."

"Broichan, eh?" Fokel's eyes narrowed. "Maybe that explains it. Not a lucky chance, but a calculated risk. I see I'll have to watch you, young Bridei."

"My lord." Bridei bowed his head courteously.

Fokel startled him by bursting into laughter. "Such lovely manners, and such rash acts on the field! You are a rare one! Sure you don't want to join the wild men of Five Sisters, lad? No, no, don't bother to find a courteous reply, no doubt your druid has other things in mind for you. Now, let's be moving. It looks like this is over, and I want to be inside those walls before too many of the men are; there's a fire to be put out and order to be restored."

He began to walk up the hill, glancing over his shoulder as he did. After a moment Bridei followed him. It did seem to be over. Now that it was, he was beginning to feel very odd indeed.

"I owe you a favor, druid's foster son," Fokel said. "Let me know when it's time. The chieftain of Galany always pays his debts."

Bridei was inclined to a polite demurral such as, "It was nothing," or "There's no need," but he merely nodded and walked on. This was a pact between men; not to accept would be an insult.

It came to Bridei, after that, that it was not the battle itself that was so hard to come to terms with; it had passed in a haze of frenzied, chaotic action, of choices made so fast there had scarcely been time to think what they meant, a whirlwind of time, of pounding heart and panting breath, of bodies torn between the cold sweat of utter terror and the rushing exhilaration that is the other side of fear. Its gruesome sights were still in his mind somewhere and would no doubt return redoubled in his dreams. In the midst of it all, he had seen them and simply moved on to what was next.

The harder part came when the fighting was over; when the heart slowed and the breath steadied. Then the mind came back to itself and the eyes began to see with balance and consideration. It was then, walking through what remained of the settlement at Galany's Reach, that Bridei began to recognize the true meaning of war.

Morleo's men were putting out the fire. They had brought down a long section of burning staves and demolished the huts that had been crowded in behind; water was conveyed in buckets, men standing in line to pass them, while others beat at the flames or shoveled earth to smother them. Here and there, blankets covered still forms on the grass; at the end of one such bundle a small bare foot protruded. There were men of Talorgen's here now; Bridei saw a young fellow he had trained with sitting bent over with his head in his hands, wracked by violent spasms as if with an ague. Beside him squatted the big warrior Breth, his quiet voice a counterpoint to the youth's helpless sobbing. A light rain began to fall; soon the blaze would be quenched. Morleo's men worked on, orderly, disciplined.

Ged's warriors were outside the gates, finishing off the last of the opposition. A party of Talorgen's men could be seen beginning to scour the field for their own wounded. Some, surely, must already have been sent up here to evacuate women, children, and old men, to take prisoners and to flush out any pockets of resistance.

Bridei followed Fokel through the splintered gates and into a settlement eerily darkened by the haze of smoke, the air dense with particles of drifting ash and glowing cinders. The chance of spot fires flaring seemed high, despite the rain; while some of the houses were built of stone, many were mere hovels of mud and wattles, and it had already been demonstrated how fiercely that outer wall could burn. The pathways between were narrow, of beaten earth; here and there hens squawked hysterically and pigs added their own resonant complaints. There was no sound of women's voices now, nor children's, only the shouts of Morleo's men working on the fire and the more distant, deadlier sounds from beyond the wall, where even now the husbands, fathers, sons, and brothers of Galany's Reach lay dying. No; that was wrong. What had Donal said? You couldn't let yourself think that way. Start seeing your enemy as a real man, a man like yourself, and you could never bring yourself to stick the knife in his guts. And if you couldn't do that in the heat of battle, you would lose. It would be you who would die, and in time all that you cared about would die as well. So, forget sons, brothers, fathers. Think only, the enemy. Remind yourself that they had stolen the Mage Stone, and that they deserved to die.

Bridei managed to hold that in his mind just as long as it took to reach a fork in the path.

"You go right, I'll go left," Fokel said. "Check for survivors. The whole place might go up, Morleo or no Morleo. Anyone you find, get them out that gate while there's still time. If their chieftain's still alive, he's mine." Just in case there was any doubt about his meaning, he bared his teeth in a ferocious grin and made a sharp gesture, fingers across throat. Then he headed off up the left path, vanishing into the smoke.

The way seemed deserted. Bridei moved forward cautiously, sword in hand, knowing such a patrol should be carried out by two men at least and better four: one to batter doors down, one to cover him as he did so, two to wait, weapons in hand, for whatever might emerge. On his own, he wouldn't be breaking down any doors. Instead he hammered on them one after another, shouting, "Out! Quick! Fire!" and silently thanking his old tutor Wid for the few words he'd imparted in the tongue of the Gaels.

No sign of life. Where only threadbare curtains hung across the meager entries, he made himself draw them aside, look in, scan the gloomy interiors for crouching children or huddled women. He found none. He walked on, heart gripped by a mounting unease that had little to do with the fact that he was alone in a place where well-armed Gaels could be waiting, concealed, until he moved closer, and a lot more to do with the instincts of a mind and body druid-trained. Something was wrong here; he felt it.

He rounded a corner and found himself in an open space,

a meeting place around which the modest buildings clustered. A haze from the fire hung over all, but Bridei could see a plum tree in early blossom and by it a cross made of stone, with snakelike patterns carved on it. Beyond, he heard men's voices laughing, speaking in his own tongue, and saw movement half shrouded by the pall of smoke. Bridei moved forward, passing the cross, and halted abruptly.

The women and children who had been hiding in those wretched small dwellings were all gathered here now, crowded up against a wall, pressing back on one another to escape a semicircle of Priteni weapons aimed toward them. A young mother clutched a squalling babe in her arms, her face contorted by terror and rage. An old woman crouched, enfolding two wailing children. Others stood silent, ashen-faced. Bridei stared, disbelieving. The men who had herded them here and now held them at spear point were not Fokel's wild warriors, those commonly thought capable of almost anything. They were not Ged's brightly clad followers, nor the forces of Morleo of Longwater, all of whom were busy with the fire. These warriors were Talorgen's. And although their weapons were pointed at their pitiful clutch of prisoners, it was not at these the men were looking. Not far off, two Priteni warriors held a young woman pinned against the wall, and a third, bare-buttocked, was fumbling with her long skirt. More stood behind him, watching with grins on their faces.

Outrage seized Bridei's heart; his fingers tightened on his sword and he opened his mouth to roar he knew not what, a string of curses, an order, something they would not heed, since he was young, unknown, untried. An instant later, Broichan's teaching asserted itself along with Donal's, and he found himself possessed by a cold calm. He walked forward, weapon in hand.

"By all that is sacred," he said, and felt in his voice some little echo of the power Broichan summoned at the great rituals, a depth that came from realms beyond the merely human. "In the name of the Shining One and the vows you have made to serve your king in courage and truth, let this woman go at once!" He strode toward the half-naked soldier, raising the sword. "Leave off! Is this the act of a true warrior of the Flamekeeper? You two, release her!"

The fellow stepped back, cheeks flaming with what might have been either shame or merely frustration. The men who had been holding the woman released her arms and she subsided to a crouch, hands over her face as if this might make her invisible.

"Who do you think you are?" challenged one of the men who had stood behind. "Some sort of self-appointed chieftain?"

"They're scum," said another. "What else are they good for?"

"That's right," said the first. "It's been a long time, druid's boy. You wouldn't know, I suppose. Scarcely out of swaddling yourself. You should watch and learn—"

"Enough!" Bridei's voice was quieter now, but there was something in it that silenced them. "You know this is wrong. It mocks your comrades' bravery on the field of battle; it shames those of our men who have fallen. The Shining One would look down on this with horror; you cannot say you fight in her name when you commit such deeds." He held out a hand to the crouching woman, thinking to help her to her feet. She raised her head and spat at him, her red-rimmed eyes bright with hate. He wondered how many would have abused her, here with her friends looking on, perhaps her mother, her children, if he had not arrived in time.

"You will not touch these people further; Talorgen's orders were to take captives, not assault them," he said. "There are many of you here, more than enough to escort these folk safely out to open ground. Now do it without further harm, and be sure I will convey a full account of this to your leader. If further ill befalls these women, he will know whom to blame."

There was a disturbance now from behind one of the huts. As Bridei turned, he saw a pair of men emerging, dragging another Gael between them. The two were laughing, exchanging ribald quips. The captive was a girl of eleven or twelve, a skinny child in a shapeless, faded garment. One man held her thin arm in a bone-breaking grip; the other had his fingers in her long dark hair and hauled her along that way. The swirling smoke concealed his features; all the same, the look of him, his stance, his walk, sent a shiver of

something indefinable through Bridei. Without quite catching the words, he knew just what they were joking about.
The girl's face was as pale as her worn shift, her eyes blank
with terror. A sudden piercing memory of Tuala clutched at
Bridei's heart, threatening to unman him entirely; what was
this world he had suddenly stepped into?

"Release her!" he snapped and, striding across, he used
the hilt of his sword in a crippling blow to one man's fore-
arm. The fellow howled, his grip on the girl's hair lost. As
the other began a protest, Bridei's left fist caught him hard
on the jaw; it was a punch perfected over many mornings
with Donal. The man reeled back and the captive was
abruptly released. She whirled, all skinny legs and flying
hair, and fled back the way they had come. Bridei made himself look again, and saw that the man whose arm he had just
come close to breaking, one of the wretches who had manhandled this child, was Gartnait, son of Talorgen; Gartnait,
his own friend.

There was no need to speak; perhaps he could not have
done so anyway at such a moment. Fokel's men were coming into the square. At the sight of them the women paled
still further, shielding their children with their own bodies.
There was a fell look about these warriors; their every move
breathed danger. Fokel rapped out orders; all the men, his
own and Talorgen's alike, obeyed them. The captives were
led forward, the guarding weapons now at a discreet distance, but still unsheathed; it was rumored that the women of
Dalriada could fight as fiercely as their men. Who knew
which might choose at any moment to make a run for it, or to
snatch a knife and inflict some damage? In the swirling haze
of smoke, the warriors moved and mingled and were joined
by others. Talorgen himself was here now, telling them the
fire was nearly out, that the chieftain of the Gaels had been
taken, reminding them that there was to be no looting, no
harm done to those who were not warriors. The men nodded
assent, all of them; their faces gave no indication that here
was an innocent man, here an abuser of women, here a
courageous fighter, here a fellow who thought to molest a
child. On the surface they all looked the same. Only the gods
knew the workings of their hearts.

That night, as Talorgen's victorious forces sat about their small fires, their joy at victory muted by exhaustion, injury, and the loss of so many of their comrades on the battlefield, a powerful longing came over Bridei to be home again, to be sitting at the top of Eagle Scar looking down across the Great Glen, with sunlight on his face and the wind in his hair and no sound but the high, pure cries of birds. Tuala would be there, small and quiet by his side. He would drink in the beauty of the place, its wild freedom, its stark loveliness. And then he would be able to tell his tale, and to weep. She would listen, her big eyes grave and wise; she would have the right words. Then perhaps he might begin to see a way through this.

"All right, Bridei?" Donal had come up quietly and settled by him, cross-legged, chewing on a bone. There had been ample stock for slaughter, pigs, geese; after the long march down the Glen on scant rations, it was a feast. They had broached what ale barrels were to be found in the settlement, but there was little merriment. The bodies of their fallen comrades lay each under a blanket, awaiting burial. The enemy were heaped high, with branches and bracken piled around their sprawled limbs. In the morning a new fire would be lit.

Bridei nodded, not trusting himself to speak.

"No, you're not," Donal said. "It'll take a while. As I said, the first time's the worst. The men are talking about you."

Bridei tightened his lips. He had already been approached by Gartnait, a Gartnait full of tales of misunderstanding, of the straightforward capture of a prisoner which Bridei had most unfairly chosen to interpret as something else. This had been followed, with some inconsistency, by something between a plea and a threat, that Talorgen should not be told Bridei's own version of events, or things would never be the same between them. Bridei had turned his back. What could he say? Things could never be the same anyway. The sound of his friend's voice sickened him. He could imagine, now, what the other men would be saying about him: young upstart, throwing his weight around, who does he think he is, personal emissary of the Flamekeeper? As for those earlier comments, the ones about women and

how much he had or hadn't done, he would not allow them
to affect him. His attitude to matters of the bedchamber was
impossible to explain even to his friends; such men as these
would think him a fool. Only Donal knew the truth of it,
since explanations had been necessary in order to avoid
awkwardness. Donal had many willing female acquain-
tances, one for every settlement up and down the lake, and
some of them had friends. Rather than keep on declining in-
vitations, Bridei had explained himself early, at around his
fourteenth birthday. He remembered it clearly. They'd just
returned from a ride in the forest above Pitnochie, the two
of them, and they'd been in the stables attending to Lucky
and Snowfire, with nobody else about. Donal had made another of his offers, to do with a trip to the nearest settlement
and a certain sweet-tempered, generous young woman who
would be only too willing to teach Bridei certain skills that
it was perhaps time he began to learn. This had been delivered somewhat diffidently; it had been clear Donal did not
want to force the issue.

"Thank you," Bridei recalled saying in somewhat formal
tones. "But I can't. Not yet."

"Can't?" Donal had echoed. "What are you trying to tell
me, lad?"

Bridei had struggled not to flush with embarrassment,
even though this was his trusted friend. "Not what you think.
Not that I am too young to be . . . capable. Or that I am not
disposed toward such activities."

"But?"

"I made a vow. A promise. To the Flamekeeper. It had to
do with . . ." It had not been possible to be precise; this was
tied up with conjecture, with guesswork, with the thing that
nobody in the household was quite prepared to tell him. "It
has to do with preparing for the future in the best way I can,"
he'd said, for this was the truth, if not quite all of the truth.
"It seems to me I must practice both the deepest loyalty to
the gods and a perfect self-discipline. As perfect as I can get
it, that is. I made a solemn vow that I would not lie with a
woman until the day I am handfasted. That I will do so only
in the marriage bed. That seemed to me to show respect for
the Shining One, since all women are reflections of her pu-

rity, and also to the Flamekeeper, who values strength and self-control in men. So, you see, I cannot go with you to the settlement."

"Oh, aye," Donal had said, apparently unsurprised. "And who heard you make such a vow?"

"Only the gods."

"Oh, aye." Donal had returned to rubbing Lucky down, and that had been an end of it.

"They're saying you saved at least one man's life today." Donal's voice brought Bridei back to the present. "They're saying that if it hadn't been for you, Fokel of Galany's Reach wouldn't be here tonight to reclaim the land his father died for. You did a good thing, Bridei. You did bravely, son. How's that leg?"

Bridei glanced down. The wound was bandaged with linen now, cleaned and tended to by Talorgen's own physician. He could hardly remember how he had come by the injury. "He won't reclaim it," he said. "Only for a day or two; then we have to go back. That will be hard for him: to come all this way and have to leave his lands behind again."

Donal glanced at him. "We will hold a ritual," he said. "That was decided. A symbolic victory; a rededication to the gods."

"I don't think we should," Bridei said. "Not now. Not after what has unfolded here. The Shining One can only look down on this in shame and grief."

If this surprised him, Donal gave no sign of it, nor did he ask any questions. "All the same," he said, "there should be something. A token of victory; a sign of hope. Whatever you may have seen, whatever you may think of it, our men fought bravely here today, Bridei, fought and died, many of them, in the name of Fortriu and of Drust the Bull. And Fokel's father fought and died, and countless others with him when the Gaels first came to Galany's Reach. No matter what you feel, we should not walk away as if our comrades' sacrifice is cause for shame."

There was a silence.

"And after all," said Donal, "you do have a solution. A crazy solution, but then Fokel's a crazy sort of fellow. You going to put it forward?"

Bridei did not answer. In the altered world of today, there no longer seemed a place for heroic schemes, for gestures designed to make the heart soar. In this world darkness walked and had a human face.

"Bridei," Donal said. "Tell me, come on. It's not that, is it, not what I thought? It's not the battle, it's something else. Tell me, son."

"I'm not a child!" Bridei snapped. "If there's a problem, leave me to solve it myself, will you? What are you, my nursemaid?" He buried his head in his hands, hearing the sound of his own voice, its petulance making a lie of his words.

"I'm your friend." Donal's voice was quiet; there was no judgment in it.

"The men, some of them," Bridei said, "they were—I came upon them in the settlement, before Fokel's men got there. They were—they were frightening the prisoners, threatening them, and . . ."

"You'd better tell me all of it now you've started."

"They were going to rape a woman. I saw it. If I hadn't stopped them, they would have done it. And . . ." No, that was enough. It was more than enough.

"Who?" Donal hissed. "Did you recognize them? What were their names?"

Bridei swallowed. There had been several whose faces he had recognized, but it was Gartnait's that filled his memory, the eyes not shamed or sorry at all, but angry, resentful, challenging. Gartnait's voice, torn between lying excuses and pleas not to shame him before his father.

"Talorgen's men," he said. "I won't name them. It's too late to undo the harm to those who were hurt, and the captives are safe now." Ged's men had taken custody of the women and children, holding them under guard within the settlement until the question of hostages was resolved. The enemy chieftain was with Fokel's troop, manacled and collared. His men were slain; those who had not fallen in battle had been subject to summary execution. To attempt to convey such a band of captive warriors all the way up the Glen was deemed too risky, and setting them free had never been under consideration.

"You should," Donal said grimly. "Talorgen would expect the names. You know how he frowns on breaches of discipline. No matter if these are wretched Gaels, no better than their godforsaken menfolk."

Bridei was silent a little. There seemed to be an unspoken question hanging in the air. "Talorgen, I think, might not want these particular names," he said eventually. "I made it clear to them that I would tell him the full tale if any harm came to the prisoners. And if it comes to that, I will."

"Oh, aye?"

"Yes. I said it and I meant it. But I hope I won't have to. Donal?"

"Mm?"

"I made new enemies today. Those men resented what I did. Our own men."

"They'd have resented it even if it had been Ged who did it, or Morleo, or Talorgen himself. Those fellows have been a long time without a woman, Bridei. I suppose they see helping themselves to the prisoners as somehow their due."

"It is a strange attitude, to view a woman merely as an object to be taken; to be so overwhelmed by the body's cravings that a man must satisfy them even at such a cost. Such actions are surely the bitterest insult to the Shining One, who embodies womankind at its purest and most wise."

Donal glanced at him quizzically. "We don't all have your druidic discipline," he observed, "nor your degree of self-control. These are simple fellows, Bridei. They see things in black and white. It's a lot easier."

"In battle, maybe," Bridei said, remembering the cold calm that had carried him up the hill of Galany's Reach, the automatic sequence of offensive and defensive moves that had made him, for a little, an effective and passionless tool of war. "But that's no way to live your life. Men who act thus act in spite of the gods. Were I a leader, I would not want such men to follow me."

"They obeyed you today," Donal said. "If they stopped what they were doing when you stepped in, they obeyed you despite themselves."

"They obeyed me with eyes full of bitterness and words of scorn spoken under the breath."

"You're young, that makes it worse. Some men don't like to hear the truth from a youngster, no matter who he is."

They sat a while longer as the small fires died down and men settled to sleep close by, exhaustion and full bellies doing their work. Today's undertaking had been a victory for the Priteni; news of it would indeed spread across the lands of Dalriada, striking fear into the hearts of the enemy. It occurred to Bridei that perhaps war was always like this. Perhaps even the most triumphal, the purest, the noblest victory still felt, in some ways, like a defeat.

Somewhat later, when Donal had fallen asleep by his side, Bridei saw a man walking up the hill beyond the settlement, a lighted torch in his hand. He rose, wrapping his cloak around him, and followed. The other climbed steadily, using the spiral path that led to the summit where the great stone stood flanked by its guardian trees. It was a brisk climb, but the slope of the hill was even, the sward free of large rocks or bushes. When Bridei reached the top of the path, he saw the other standing by the Mage Stone, the light from the burning brand revealing its intricate patterns of conflict, triumph, and death in all their wondrous interweaving. It could almost be a depiction of today's events.

He called out softly to Fokel, announcing his presence; to approach such a man from behind in silence was to invite a knife between the ribs. Bridei walked across, boots quiet on the grass. They stood side by side as the torchlight played over the tale of Fokel's ancestors, the true custodians of Galany's Reach.

"I feared I would never see this as a grown man," Fokel said, his voice oddly constrained. "That the gods would not grant me an opportunity to witness it: the sacred trust for which my father fell, and my uncles, and so many others of my kin. I was a child of three years old when the Gaels took our lands; too young to understand what it was we had lost. Here, take the torch. Show me the other side."

In silence they circled the monolith; it was indeed imposing, a massive thing taller than the tallest man and nearly two handspans thick. It must be lodged deep in the earth, close to Bone Mother's heart, to have held so strongly to the land. They regarded the riotous pattern on the south side, creatures of earth and ocean, stream and hillside and wood-land, crag and cave and the vast reaches of the open sky. In that wild creation was captured Bridei's own imagining, in which he stood on a hilltop and saw the Glen with the clear vision of the soaring eagle, and felt the heartbeat of Fortriu under his feet. And although he had not planned to say it, al-though the day's events still weighed so heavily in him that there was scant room for anything else, he spoke the words. "We should take it with us."

"What?" It was clear from Fokel's tone that he had only half heard; had not understood.

"We can't leave the stone here; that's admitting defeat. We know we can't hold Galany's Reach with the forces we have; we know the time's not ripe for that. But we can take the stone back. Back where the Gaels cannot touch it."

"You really are mad." Fokel stood next to the stone, his brow resting against its tall, cool form, his hands spread flat on its face, as if by this closeness he might absorb some of its ancient power. "That's the craziest thing I ever heard. What are you, a mythical hero with the strength of fifty gi-ants? You can see the size of this, the weight of it. Or are we going to use druid magic?" For all these words, the torch-light revealed a change in Fokel's eyes; somewhere in their darkness was a spark of excitement, an answering madness.

"That, and more practical means," Bridei said calmly. "It will be a lot of work and we don't have much time. But we do have a considerable number of men, that's if we can con-vince Talorgen and the others. Here's how we'll do it . . ."

10

WELL," SAID FOLA, "you're here at last. You're such a small thing, it's hard to believe you're in your fourteenth year, but Broichan tells me it's so. Welcome to Banmerren, child."

"Thank you, my lady." Tuala was trying very hard to sound calm. It had been difficult coming into this strange, stone-walled compound, with girls everywhere looking at her in amazement, and even more difficult hearing her presence announced by the intimidating Dreseida, who had entered Fola's sanctum first: "We've brought that strange child from Pitnochie." Now Ferada and her mother were both gone, escorted away to see the section of Banmerren where the daughters of noble blood were lodged, those who did not require the more esoteric parts of the education offered here. Tuala stood before the wise woman with only one other in attendance, a brusque person of middle years who had given her name as Kethra. For all her misery, Tuala was struck by the quiet of the place, the mellow stone of the buildings, the little figures set in niches here and there, each different, each surprising, the hanging garlands of herbs and the curiously wrought lamps.

"You may call me Fola. We don't stand on ceremony here; all are equal under the gaze of the Shining One. Are you happy to be here, Tuala?"

This difficult question had come out of nowhere. "I'm grateful for the opportunity, my la—Fola." It felt odd to be addressing the wise woman thus as if she were a familiar friend. Small as she was, Fola looked grander and more imposing than Tuala had remembered her: her hair, unhooded, revealed itself as silver-gray and long, coiled up in a heavy bundle at the back of her head, and around her neck, over the soft gray robe, she wore a moon disc clasped by a clawlike silver setting and suspended on a fine chain. Fola's eyes were as before, of a darkly assessing intensity. Her smile was warm. Behind her, on a stone shelf, was curled a pitch-black cat of enormous size; its tattered ears and scarred visage seemed the equivalent of a warrior's tattooed features. It watched Tuala through half-closed yellow eyes.

"But?" Fola queried.

Tuala looked straight at her. "I'll work very hard," she said, "and learn all I can. I owe that to you for being prepared to have me here. I owe it to those who have taught me before."

"You're not being quite honest with me, child," Fola said.

"I know you'll work hard. Those who are not prepared to do so find their stay at Banmerren short. Kethra can vouch for that." She glanced at the other woman, who stood to the side, hands folded before her, and Kethra's lips twitched in something that did not seem much like a smile. "Tell me, Tuala. If there's a reservation of some sort in your mind, I need to know it now. Here at Banmerren we are all servants of the Shining One. She commands our whole selves: body, heart, mind, and spirit."

Tuala bowed her head. "I am her daughter," she said. "I serve her in all things. If it is her will that I become her priestess, then I will apply myself to that calling as well as I can. But it was not my choice to come here. Not my true choice." Images came flooding into her mind: Pearl in the stables, nuzzling at Tuala's neck, unaware that it was the last time; Mist yowling in complaint behind a closed door, as if she knew Tuala was leaving her; the moon through a small window and an eagle feather on the sill. She glanced at the silent Kethra, who stared back, impassive.

"You may leave us, Kethra," Fola said. "Ask Odha for a small pot of her peppermint infusion, will you, and some honey? Thank you."

Kethra swept out, straight-backed, disapproval in every corner of her body.

Fola sighed. "Kethra is in charge of the younger students," she said. "My principal assistant. Now sit down, Tuala. You've had a long journey; the lady Dreseida has told me something of it. And since her own daughter Ferada is to stay with us a while, there will be at least one familiar face here for you among us."

Tuala managed a tight nod.

"However," Fola went on, "I think it is more than weary days on the lake and in the saddle that gives your eyes that desperate look. I know you've told the truth so far. But there's more to it than that, surely."

"It was supposed to be a choice," Tuala blurted out. "But it was his choice, not mine."

Fola waited a moment, and then said, "His choice? Broichan's?"

Tuala nodded miserably. "To come here, or marry a man

with a face like a turnip. I'm sorry, that's not fair. He seemed a good man. But I didn't want to get married and I didn't want . . ."

"You didn't want to come to Banmerren?" Fola asked gently.

"To go away," Tuala said in a whisper. "To be sent away from Pitnochie. He doesn't understand. I need to be there."

There was a tap at the door; a girl came in with a little tray. She wore the blue robe Tuala had seen on most of the young women at Banmerren. There had been many of them walking across the garden, hurrying along pathways or busy with scrolls or basins or bunches of herbs. A few were in green; only the older ones, like Kethra and Fola herself, wore the wise woman's gray. The girl put the tray down and departed in silence. The cat stirred itself, stretched expansively, and jumped down, strolling over to investigate what the visitor had brought.

"I see." Fola took up a little pot from the tray, poured a steaming, aromatic beverage into two tiny cups, spooned honey, handed a cup to Tuala. Finding no food available, the cat had lost interest and was washing itself.

"I am obedient to the Shining One," Tuala said. "I love her; why would I go against her will? But I never believed she wanted me to leave Pitnochie. If this was what she intended, for me to serve her as a wise woman, why did she make sure it was Bridei who found me, all those years ago?" She heard her own words, too many words, and clamped her mouth shut.

Fola sipped her drink calmly. "Let us say Broichan acted in error," she said. "We must bear in mind that Broichan is not known for lapses in judgment; his purposes can seem obscure at times, but that is generally because his schemes are more far-reaching than we ordinary mortals can grasp." It was hard to tell if she was joking or not. "But let us say the Shining One does not wish you to be her priestess. What, then, does she intend for you, do you think?"

Tuala remained grimly silent.

"I wonder," said Fola, setting her cup back on the tray. "Drink it, child; it will give you heart. Broichan has ever been fond of reminding folk that there is learning to be had even in the most trying experience; even in the most desperate disappointment. You will learn something here at Banmerren, and I expect the rest of us will, too; we've never had a child of the forest among us before. It won't be easy for you. A challenge; no doubt you enjoy those. Drink up. Then I'll call Kethra back to show you where you'll be sleeping. You can rest before supper. After that it'll be all hard work. In time, no doubt the Shining One will make her purpose known."

In Kethra's wake, Tuala walked through passageway and eating place and hall of study, through a storeroom where a frankly staring girl handed her a pile of folded garments, a blue robe at the bottom, other things on top; she passed through the gardens again, noting more girls tending a vegetable patch, forking straw, tying up straggling vines; she heard singing coming from inside somewhere, a pure, clear sound of young voices lifted in a hymn to the maiden All-Flowers. From an open doorway wafted a wholesome aroma of new-baked bread.

The whole of the Banmerren compound lay within a wall; stone set its boundaries and effectively blocked off the world outside. The only entry Tuala could see was the way she had come in, a heavy iron gate with bolts across it. There had been a place outside she'd have liked to explore, a place as different from the craggy hills and blanketing forest of Pitnochie as a gull was from an owl: she'd glimpsed wide, empty sands and beyond them a whispering sea. From within these walls, nothing of that could be seen.

Several girls, not uniformly robed but clad in fine skirts and tunics of varied hue, were sitting on a bench in the garden talking among themselves. As one, they turned to stare as Tuala went past, her feet moving swiftly to keep up with the brisk strides of her impatient guide. She heard the whispers, the suppressed laughter. She could not catch the words. A girl who was sitting alone smiled at her, a warm smile in a face notable for its fine gray eyes and natural serenity. This girl had hair that gleamed like spun gold in the sunlight, falling in a ripple down her back. She was clad in palest cream with a touch of blue at neck and wrists. Tuala nodded courteously. To summon a smile in return was more than she could manage right now.

"Up here," Kethra said. She had made it abundantly clear she had no time to spare and did not appreciate the requirement to play nursemaid to this particular new arrival. It felt depressingly like those last days at Pitnochie. "Fola says you're to sleep in the tower. It's been empty a while. Maybe it's best. The others will be wary of you. I suppose you know that." She led the way up a steep flight of stone steps on the outside of the building, along a perilously narrow walkway and into a small chamber whose doorway was almost level with the top of Banmerren's outer wall. It was quite dark. A scurrying sound in the corner ceased abruptly as they went in.

"You'll need a candle," Kethra said. "Ask in the kitchen when you come down for supper."

"When—?"

"Next bell. Wear the blue. It'll be a long time before you need the green. If ever. Anything else?"

Tuala cleared her throat. There was a wooden bed frame in the chamber with a straw mattress on it; she could not see any other bedding. There was no fire.

"Could I—?"

"Speak up!" Kethra said. "I've work to do. I expect you're used to folk running around after you, picking up for you. There's none of that here. We all do our share, no matter what we are."

"A blanket," Tuala said firmly, deciding she would not be intimidated. "Two, if that's allowed; I see there's no hearth up here. I'll come down and fetch them myself, there's no need to—"

"Anything else?"

"Not just yet," Tuala said politely.

"You'll have to wait; the storeroom is locked now and everyone's busy. After supper, ask again. Now, if you'll excuse me, I have a class to teach." Kethra turned on her heel and was gone.

Tuala dropped her bag onto the pallet and pulled her cloak tighter around her. Resting was certainly not going to be possible; it was so cold in here that her breath made a little cloud before her mouth. It seemed an odd place to have been allocated for her own. There were many girls here, and among the chambers glimpsed during her hurried tour had been several long rooms for sleeping, housing pallets in rows. She was pretty sure she had seen hearths there with turf laid ready for burning. She had expected to be lodged with other girls, living communally as the men at arms did at Pitnochie. Perhaps this isolation was meant to underline still further her difference. In truth, bleak as the small chamber was, Tuala was much relieved to be alone.

Her eyes grew gradually accustomed to the dimness. The room did have a window of sorts, a mere slit between the shaped stones, unshuttered. A chill draft swept in, carrying a salt smell: that must be the sea. Birds were calling, their voices harsh and strange, telling a different tale from those of the wren and thrush, the owl and raven. These were travelers, singing of long journeys over perilous waters. In time she would learn to understand them.

There was rustling again and a faint scratching sound. It was clear she would be sharing her quarters with mice. Mist would have liked it here. Tears prickled Tuala's eyes; she would not let them spill. Mist had a good home, plenty to eat, folk who would be kind to her now Tuala herself was gone. Mist would do perfectly well; it would be Tuala who would suffer the parting more, lacking the cat's comforting presence in this chilly bed. In winter, sleeping in the tower would be very hard. Perhaps that was part of the training. Maybe she was meant to accept the cold and not to ask for blankets. Druids did it, after all, trials by earth and fire, by deep water and empty air. They hung themselves up in ox hides and waited for prophetic dreams. What were a few uncomfortable nights compared with that?

Clean water would have been good, to wash the travel stains from her face and hands. Never mind that. Trembling with cold, Tuala unfastened her bag and began to unpack her meager belongings. There was a storage chest here, an ancient, heavy thing festooned with cobwebs. Spiders still dwelt in its cracks and corners; she did her best not to disturb them, since they had prior claim. Mara had made sure she had a change of smallclothes, two shifts, warm stockings, a nightrobe. There was the skirt and tunic she had worn to tell the tale of Nechtan the stone carver and his mysterious lover, Ela. There were two more such outfits, similar in style but plainer in fabric and trim. Shivering, Tuala stripped off the gown she had worn for riding and slipped the blue robe over her head, tying it around the waist with the matching girdle she found in the small pile of supplies she had been allocated. There was no way to check how it looked, but the fit seemed reasonable. She suspected it was the smallest they had. Most of the other girls had looked alarmingly tall and shapely, close to her own age, perhaps, but in appearance very much young women. It was all very well for the men of Pitnochie to view her as some kind of mysterious seductress; that was all in the mind. Beside those others, she was indeed still a child.

When all the clothing was laid away, Tuala took out the smaller items she had packed beneath, where they would be less visible to prying eyes such as those of Ferada's little brothers. Her special knife; her collection of feathers gleaned from the forest floor; her hair ribbons, those of them she could find before she left Pitnochie. There was no need for them now. She had chopped her hair off level with her chin, roughly, with the knife, and consigned the long dark locks to Broichan's hall fire. The Shining One already knew the depth of her daughter's commitment to the gods and to the future of Fortriu; with this small sacrifice, Tuala made it known also to the Flamekeeper, guardian and inspiration of warriors. Whether either of them accepted her gifts remained to be seen. She was here, after all, and that felt wrong.

The ribbons: grass green, sky blue, blood red, sun yellow. When she was little, people had brought them home for her. Men at arms went off on an expedition and happened to pass a market. Ferat got a couple every summer from a fellow with a pack of goods to sell. Brenna found old ones of her own or made new ones with needle and thread and strips of cloth left over from other projects. These ribbons were home; they were Bridei plaiting her hair with careful hands and a little joke; they were Ferat's oatcakes and Mara's clean linen; they were Uven and Cinioch telling stories and Mist purring, curled up on Brenna's knee. These ribbons were a household that no longer existed; they were a love that had never been real. Tuala put them away in the chest.

The blue robe was warmer than her own clothes, but not enough to keep out the draft. Outside, clouds had covered the sun and the breeze blew fresh and strong from the sea. Who knew when the supper bell would sound? She could go back down the steps, of course, and try to disregard the frankly curious stares of the other girls, their ill-suppressed laughter and whispered comments. She could sit on the grass, perhaps spend time in meditation. It would be more sheltered there. If the girls bothered her she could simply ignore them. Tuala grimaced. She was fooling herself if she thought that would be possible. Judging by Kethra's inadequate instructions, survival here at Banmerren depended on learning the rules as quickly as possible and making sure one abided by them. Odd, that; of course such an establishment must have its codes of behavior, but a lack of flexibility, a falling short in care, those were failings Tuala would not have expected in a school run by Fola. Her memory of Fola, from the forest, was of someone who not only understood rules, but knew when it was time to break them.

Tuala's hands lingered on the last item in her bag: the twisted cord that told the tale of herself and Bridei, the meetings and partings, the smiles and tears. It seemed the two strands were destined, from now on, to remain forever apart. She had been foolish to think it might be otherwise; to believe in her heart that it must be otherwise. Tuala rolled the little thing into a ball and hid it under her folded nightrobe. She closed the chest and went outside. It was just as cold, but at least she could see the sky. The same clouds that blocked the sun over Banmerren would in time pass above the forest at Pitnochie and set their moving shadows on the deep waters of Serpent Lake. Perhaps, before they dispersed, they might even look down on Talorgen's army, marching along the Glen to confront the fierce warriors of Dalriada. They might cross the sun again, and a young man with curling brown hair and eyes of brilliant blue might look up, thinking suddenly of home. Perhaps.

The narrow walkway continued past her door. Turn right, and it was back down the steps and along the path to the garden, following the base of the moss-coated stone wall. Turn the other way, and the ledge went on to reach a sloping, shingled rooftop, and thence to another stretch of wall which met Banmerren's main boundary at right angles. Close by this barrier an ancient oak grew, its upper branches towering high above the stonework, its trunk gnarled and knotted, its roots forming a great network of arch and twist and cranny, spreading themselves across a wide expanse of ground before their descent deep into the earth's heart. Spring was not far advanced; the dark boughs bore only the smallest swelling of new leaf buds at their tips. Last year's nests still hung here and there in the branches, signs that this giant nurtured new growth of many kinds year by year.

The oak's canopy did not stretch all the way back to the shingled roof. There was a section of wall, three strides long and perhaps a handspan wide, that must be traversed in order to reach it. The height was considerable; a fall would, at the very least, result in broken bones. Tuala tucked the skirt of her robe into her girdle, spread out her arms, and walked across, small feet steady on the narrow stone. She had never been afraid of heights.

This was better. A little scrambling took her to a fork in the tree and a branch broad enough to accommodate her comfortably, her back to the mossy trunk, her feet together on a limb and a view of the world beyond Banmerren clearly visible above the outer wall. It would, indeed, be possible to climb across to the top of that wall if she had the inclination to do so, since the tree spread its branches with generous expansion in all directions. The supper bell would probably ring when she was halfway over, and she would be late on her very first day. No need to venture farther; this tree held her secure, supported her small body with its own, ancient and strong. If she was quiet and opened the ears of the spirit, in time it would begin to whisper its stories.

She could see right along a wide, pale bay to an eastern headland. She could see a fortress. Banners flew above its stone ramparts, blue devices on white. From its topmost level it would be possible to look far out to sea; to know the approach of raiders early and to set guards on what lay within. There were earthen defenses, too, mounds and ditches; if she squinted her eyes she could see small figures moving there. Caer Pridne: stronghold of Drust the Bull, monarch of Fortriu. It was so close. Dreseida might be there by now, settling at court with her small sons, catching up with friends, happy, no doubt, that the long journey was over. Dreseida would not have stayed at Banmerren beyond the time required to see her daughter settled, for no men might enter here save druids, and Tuala could not imagine Uric and Bedo waiting with great patience for their mother outside the stone walls.

Caer Pridne. They told strange tales about that place. Or rather, Erip and Wid had hinted at tales too strange to be told, and had then gone quiet. There was a well, its entry deep under the earth, a place of dark ceremonial. That was as much as her old tutors had been prepared to say.

If the flags were flying that meant King Drust was in residence, while far down the Great Glen his warriors battled the Gaels. Broichan, too, would be at Caer Pridne, restored to his place as royal druid, a place he had relinquished for long years while Bridei grew from child to man. It seemed that wherever Bridei went, Broichan attended him like a dark shadow. He might not be by his foster son's side on the field of war, but he would be ready and waiting when Bridei came to court, as in time he surely must if Tuala was right about what was intended for him. She pictured, fleetingly, Bridei as a man of mature years, brown curls threaded with gray, and an ancient Broichan hovering nearby, still in control, still manipulating every player in his own long, private game. Fola had said something about his schemes being beyond most people's grasp. Tuala shut her mind to that vision of the future, lest a certain red-haired woman decide to make an appearance in it. Druids didn't know everything. Even the most exacting self-discipline, the deepest knowledge, did not enable a man to outwit the gods.

IT BECAME A routine of meals, study, domestic work, sleep. She discovered, after summoning the courage to ask, that every girl got a pillow and two blankets, and that because she was in the tower and had no hearth, she could have three. She learned what the bells meant and obeyed them when she remembered. In the tree, sometimes, or in trance before a rain puddle or a basin of washing water, she lost track of time, moving beyond the world of ordinary hearing. For these lapses, Kethra never neglected to reprimand her.

"What do you mean, you didn't know the bell had sounded? Where were you, in some other realm entirely?" Kethra's words stung; despite Tuala's best efforts to be like everyone else at Banmerren, there was no escaping her origins. However unobtrusive she sought to make herself, she would always look different, and such comments did not help. "The bell can be heard from every corner of house and garden, Tuala. You will be prompt next time."

"Yes, Kethra." Once, she had thought Mara unduly bossy. Compared with this irascible tutor, Broichan's housekeeper seemed both kind and reasonable.

The day's pattern was easy to follow. They rose early. The students took turns with all domestic tasks, from drawing water to the preparation and serving of meals, from cleaning floors to chopping wood, from tending fires to sewing and mending garments. These duties were scheduled around the times of study; those who had no chores to do on a particular day were expected to practice the skills Kethra or others had taught them: making herbal balms and tinctures, rehearsing the words and movements of ritual, interpreting the stars, and for those who had the aptitude, languages, scribing, and reading. Banmerren had a small library of its own. In addition, the arts of augury, divination, and prophecy were introduced to the blue-robed junior students. The serious study of these aspects of the craft was principally a matter for the seniors, those who had reached a certain level of both competence and understanding. Tuala liked the seniors. There were only seven of them, and they had a universal calmness of gaze and kindness of manner that made her wish she were one of them, not a mere beginner stuck with a gaggle of chattering girls who hardly seemed to know geography from genealogy, astrology from arithmetic. Used to the intense, sometimes fiery tuition of the erudite old scholars, she shrank now into silence during classes. Her very presence among them drew attention; she did not want the raised brows, the wry smiles she knew her questions would provoke.

Two turnings of the moon passed thus, and it was summer. Tuala discovered the best class of the day was history, for which the daughters of noble blood were present along with those students seeking places as servants of the Shining One. Tuala had never thought she might be glad of Fox Girl's presence, but Ferada, at least, was honest in her approach; she was not a giggly, whispering kind of girl. From her first days at Banmerren, Tuala had seen Ferada watching her at suppertime, when the noble daughters sat at their own table to eat and the others at three long boards under their elders' scrutiny. At mealtimes Tuala always sat alone. The others left a space on either side of her as if she bore a contagion. This tended to mean the bread would not be passed her way until only the merest scrap was left; it sometimes meant very little to eat at all. Tuala, ever a girl of birdlike appetite, refused to let it worry her. At least it removed the need to think of the right things to say. Evidently it worried Ferada; she watched with a small frown creasing her elegant brows and she exchanged comments with the girl beside her, the one with hair like a golden waterfall and friendly eyes. This girl was interesting. Tuala had discovered her name was Ana, and she was a royal hostage from the islands to the north, required to remain in the custody of King Drust as an assurance that her kin would mount no attack on the coast of Fortriu. Ana had left homeland and family behind, through no fault of her own. She had lived her life between Banmerren and Caer Pridne for four years now, cut off from all she loved. And she was young; less than a year older than Tuala herself. Every time she traveled outside the encircling walls of Banmerren, the talk went, Ana was accompanied by a team of four very large guards, in case her kinsmen might decide her freedom outweighed the risks attached to defying Drust the Bull. At court she was shadowed by armed men. Ana's cousin was king of the Light Isles, and of lesser status than the monarch of Fortriu. In the four years she had been a hostage, there had been no attempt to win her release. How the fair-haired girl managed that serenity, that air of deepest calm, Tuala could not imagine.

When it came time for history, a shared class, Ferada seated herself on one side of Tuala and Ana came to settle on the other, and after that the three of them sat together every morning. For this hour, at least, Tuala could pretend she was not alone here. One of the green-clad seniors, Derila, conducted this class, a welcome relief from Kethra's sharp questions and scathing comments. Derila was both clever and fair; she expected every student to participate and dealt kindly with errors. There was no keeping silent in Derila's classes.

Ferada was clever, too. Her hand shot up in response to every question; if she disagreed with a position she would argue with wit and cogency. Tuala began to reassess her.

Ana, too, was talented in this subject. Less ready to dispute, she nonetheless held her ground in debate and learned quickly, being the kind of student who rises early in the morning to study while others are still abed. Ana was capable of doing fine needlework and reciting the ancestry of the kings of the Folk both at the same time, with no error in either. She could make maps in a tray of sand, and identify which stars meant a fortunate time for a child to be born and which presaged a life of struggle. She could sing and play the harp.

As for Tuala herself, this became the lesson in which she was not afraid to speak. She responded cautiously to a question, then answered another, and was asked to tell what she knew about kin signs and the different ways they were used on the carven stones, depending on whether one were in Circinn or Fortriu. The explanation took some time, for it was a complex issue, often debated with Wid and Erip. The class sat mute, listening, and so did Derila. From then on, the tutor asked Tuala often for elucidation, and sometimes engaged her in discussion after class. It was not quite like the old times at Pitnochie, but it was good.

Scrying was quite the opposite. This discipline, the noble daughters did not study; during these sessions they were allowed to go riding, their own mounts being stabled at the farm outside the walls. Ana's guards were never far away; they, too, were quartered at the farm while their charge was at Banmerren. In inclement weather the noble daughters sat together sewing and chatting; what Tuala overheard of this generally involved a detailed comparison of various young men of their acquaintance.

Tuala and her fellow juniors gathered in a cold room under Kethra's gaze, a bronze bowl on the table before them. Kethra was explaining the rudiments. "You'll probably see nothing more than your own reflection . . . quite usual . . . need to focus the mind . . ."

Tuala stared at a stain on the wall that was somewhat in the shape of a little dog; she looked at the scratch marks on the benches, the rushes on the floor, the clasped hands of the girl beside her.

"Concentrate the will . . . shut out distractions . . . make the breathing slow and steady as I showed you . . ."

Odha, white-faced with tension, was leaning over the bowl, which another girl had filled from the heavy jug set on the table. Tuala gazed at Odha's felt slippers; at the door frame; at Fola's cat, Shade, which sat in a corner glowering. Anything, anything to keep her eyes away from that shimmering surface, bursting with secrets. Anything, not to reveal what she would be able to see there.

"Breathe, Odha. Clear your mind . . ."

A long wait in silence. At length Odha straightened up, small features anxious. "I couldn't see anything at all," she said, crestfallen.

"This skill is in the gift of the Shining One," Kethra told her, not unkindly. "In your prayers, speak to her and seek her wisdom; it will come in time, when she deems you ready for it. Such aspects of our craft are not learned in a day, or a season, or a year, but with exacting discipline and rigorous practice over all the time of our service. This is not a test, child, merely a beginning. Tuala!" Her tone had changed sharply; ice had entered it.

Tuala started. "Yes, Kethra?"

"No doubt you find those rushes on the floor deeply fascinating; perhaps they don't bother with such niceties where you come from. This is a time for learning, not dreaming. Or maybe you feel I have nothing to teach you, is that it? That you are already expert in all the skills I have to impart?"

There was a ripple of giggles, quickly suppressed as Kethra's quelling gaze swept around the circle. Tuala looked down at her hands. She did not want to tell a lie; it seemed to her the Shining One would expect the speaking of complete truth here in the house of her wise women. "I don't think I should be in this class," she said quietly.

No laughter now, but a general, horrified intake of breath. Kethra's tongue was universally feared; nobody ever challenged her. Besides, as Fola's principal assistant, Kethra was known to be a font of wisdom. That her classes were to be endured rather than enjoyed made no difference to that.

"You may be correct in that," Kethra said drily. "There are some students who never manage to master the art of divination; from whom the images of the scrying bowl are forever veiled. We do, at least, expect everyone to try. It is for your elders to determine whether you have aptitude or not. Other tasks can be found for those without talent."

"Scrubbing floors," someone muttered.

"That's not what I meant," Tuala said in desperation, willing herself to stay quiet but unable to hold her tongue under the wise woman's gaze, which seemed to place her at the level of something one would squash beneath a boot sole. "I would prefer not to do this here, in a class—it's best performed alone, with prayers and due ritual—"

Kethra's look changed again; now there was something in her eyes that was truly alarming. "Do I have this correct?" Her tone did not match her look; it was silken. "You, a new student, a child of the forest taken in only through the kindness of our senior priestess, are trying to tell me how to conduct my class?"

Tuala shook her head; misery fought with anger in her breast. She met Kethra's gaze, still doing her best not to let the shining water cross her vision. "No," she said in the politest tone she could summon. "I am neither wise woman nor teacher. But I have been brought up in the love of the gods and in the strict observance of ritual. I have studied these matters since I was a little child. I am sure you know what is right for your students. All I can say is that, for me and for others of my household, this practice was always a thing of solitude, a rite shared only between seer and spirits." It was not quite true; she had looked in the Dark Mirror side by side with Bridei, each seeking their own visions. But Bridei was part of herself, and she of him; it was different. "I ask to be excused from this class; I will spend the time practicing alone. Or scrubbing floors, if that is deemed appropriate."

Kethra regarded her for a long moment. Then she stepped aside, and the bronze bowl was suddenly in full sight, the still water catching the light of two tall candles set on the table close by. The surface danced with images, drawing Tuala closer despite herself. The room went very quiet.

"Your turn," Kethra said softly. "Tell us what you see, little wild girl."

By then it had gone beyond choice. The water called her; the vision beguiled her and she must look. Tuala moved closer, and the world of tutor and students, of flickering candles and quiet chamber and stone walls dissolved around her as the eye of the spirit drew her into trance.

A tall woman walked across the mirror, the embodiment of the Shining One herself, clad in robes of silver, her face so radiant Tuala could not look at it, could not see features or expression, but knew they were lovely beyond compare and full of a sweet compassion. On her shoulder was perched an owl, its eyes round and lustrous, its plumage purest white. In the goddess's arms lay an infant robed in snowy fur; she held the babe tenderly, as if it were a precious thing. She faded away, and in her place a scene appeared so strange that for a little Tuala could not put its pieces together and make sense of them. It was all frenzied activity, men cutting trees, shaping their trunks into smooth logs; men working with ropes, fashioning a net or harness; men digging deep in the earth. Men by the water's edge building a great raft. Men on guard as if expecting an attack. Some of them she knew: Donal with the rope workers, Enfret on guard, Ferada's brother Gartnait standing by a wall, not doing anything, just watching with a twist to the lips. Then, a terrible sight: a great mound of bodies, burning. Tuala bit her lip, hearing with the ears of the seer an outcry of women, a desperate keening farewell. It seemed the battle was over; Fortriu had triumphed. But what were they doing?

Then, at last, came Bridei: she felt the tears well in her eyes to see him. Alive; still safe. He stood on a hilltop, the wind in his hair. He was giving orders and men were scurrying to obey them. He looked so tall; so solemn. So much a man.

More digging; astoundingly, it seemed they were loosening a huge standing stone from its bed deep in the earth, lowering it with ropes, many men on these to control the weight until the monolith lay on tree trunks set as rollers. As she stared dumbfounded at the images, the massive thing was conveyed down the hill, men running to move the lengths of wood from back to front, others leaning their whole weight on the ropes to slow the descent, and all the time Bridei beside them, exhorting, encouraging, altering the angle of the precious burden that it might not have to be lifted again, a task surely beyond even such a great force of men. A dark, wild-looking fellow beside Bridei, his mad grin at odds with the tears in his eyes. A long and grueling march, men straining on ropes, hauling forward now on flat terrain, and the runners maintaining their endless lifting and replacing of the heavy rollers. At last the water's edge, and a complicated transfer with wedged timbers, long levers, and thick ropes, the stone maneuvered from elevated bank to a kind of net cradle within a barge. Tuala wondered if the whole thing would sink without trace; if the gods would punish these men of Fortriu for what seemed an act of outrageous mischief, although the thing they stole was indubitably their own. But, to a chorus of wild cheers—it was a wonder these men had breath left for more than a whisper—the Mage Stone floated, nestled in its rope hammock, its vessel borne up by the choppy waters of what must be King Lake, at the western end of the Great Glen. Talorgen clapped Bridei on the shoulder in hearty congratulation. Donal was close by, his tattooed features transformed with pride. Gartnait was not to be seen.

Bridei was smiling. Tuala knew that little smile, and she knew by the shadow in his eyes, the pallor of his skin, the way his hands showed white at the knuckles that for him this double victory held also some kind of defeat, some perceived failure. Now it was over and they would come home. They would come home, and Bridei would need to talk, he would need to tell someone what burdened him, what it was that set a darkness in his spirit, that confused his thoughts and tugged at his heart. Such secrets as these he could not speak to Donal, not fully. He would not let Broichan see his tears. Bridei would need her, and she would not be there.

She was not sure, afterward, if she had willed the image away or if it had faded of itself. For a long time she stood in a daze, departed from the world of the seer, not quite returned to the other. Then a voice said, "She's crying."

Kethra spoke then, her tone quiet, wary. "Hush, Reia. One of the first things you must learn is not to disturb a person in trance. They must be given time to emerge; time to come back to themselves." Then, after a carefully judged wait, "Tuala?"

Tuala blinked; the candles flickered, the circle of faces came into view, young, staring faces, their eyes uniformly big with amazement. She felt weak, sick; it was so long since she had seen him, too long, and now this . . .

"Sit down," Kethra said. "Odha, fetch her water. You others, give her some space. Breathe slowly, Tuala."

The big cat, Shade, chose that moment to stroll over and jump up beside Tuala on the bench; he pushed his head against her, purring, and she reached a hand to scratch behind his tattered ears. That touch was reassuring; it brought the everyday world back in a way human speech had not.

"Drink this," Kethra said, putting a cup of water in Tuala's hands. "Girls, there is much to be learned from this. If nothing else, it shows you the dangers of experimenting on your own, unsupervised. Don't do it. Such an experience taxes both body and mind. Until you have attained a certain level of control you must always have a watcher." She turned her attention back to Tuala. "So," she observed, "you were telling the truth. What did you see? Share it with us."

Protesting was pointless; a refusal would only draw more attention. Kethra was not going to leave off before she got an answer. "I think these were images of now, or of recent times," Tuala said. "Of course, sometimes these visions are only of what may be, or what might have been. It's not always possible to see what you think you need to see. Sometimes there are no answers. Other times the answers are there, but hidden. I saw glimpses of King Drust's men on their campaign. You know they have traveled under the chieftain Talorgen's command far down the Glen in the hope of reclaiming the territory of Galany's Reach, where the Mage Stone stands."

Her audience was completely silent, waiting for more.

"This seemed to show that they had won their battle. And . . . they were moving the stone. Lifting it from the earth with ropes and timbers, bringing it down to a barge, so it could be floated back up to our own lands." She would not speak of the Shining One; she would not mention Bridei.

Kethra wore a little frown. "Why would a child like you be sent such a vision?" she asked. "What could you know of such matters?"

"*Moving* the Mage Stone?" queried Reia in amazement. "Isn't it supposed to be taller than a giant and as thick as the neck of a bull? How could they move it?"

Tuala saw again Bridei's young features, full of purpose; his bright eyes in which awareness of the gods was never far below the surface. *With the right leader, men can achieve the impossible.* "They did it with druid magic, and with cleverness," she said.

"Hmm," said Kethra. "It is a strange tale, indeed. An unlikely one; why would they do this, when the stones are set in place as symbols of the ancient descent of our people from the seven sons of Pridne? They are markers of both territory and blood; to move them seems almost an insult to the gods, an act of ill omen. Who would choose to do this at a time of victory in battle?"

"I can understand the reasons," Tuala said. "It does seem a strange act; an act that might cause an imbalance in the fabric of our land. But that place, Galany's Reach, is within the boundaries of Dalriada now. It was lost to Fortriu years ago. Talorgen's forces could take the settlement, but not hold it; it is too isolated from our own strongholds. This campaign was never intended for the purpose of seizing back the territory of Galany's Reach. It was a symbolic strike; a warning of more to come, should Dalriada seek to expand its grasp further into the Glen. The bringing back of the stone is an act of courage, of bold inventiveness. Difficult; back-breaking; inspirational. It must have put great heart into our men and further unsettled the enemy. At least," realizing she had said a great deal more than she intended, "that is how I see it."

"How do you know all this, anyway?" challenged one of the girls. "Battles and territories and everything?"

"She's making it up," someone muttered behind a hand.

"I've had excellent teachers," Tuala said. "I was lucky."

"Luck is part of it," said Kethra crisply. "Making astute use of your own good fortune is also an advantage. Then there's natural talent. Girls, I hear the bell. There will be food and drink for you in the dining hall. Don't run, Odha, you're not starving."

The room emptied; only Kethra was left, and Tuala sitting on the bench, knowing this was not finished yet.

"I'm sorry," Tuala said, and meant it. "I did try not to look, but it happens like that sometimes. The visions are there, waiting for me."

Kethra sucked in her breath and let it out again. "You have learned this skill before you came to Banmerren, obviously. Who taught you? Broichan?"

Tuala would have laughed if she were not so nervous. "I was taught many things by my two old tutors, but never this; never the arts of druid or wise woman. And Broichan didn't teach me anything at all." *Except how to be afraid.* "He didn't think I needed any education."

"It would seem," Kethra observed as she tilted the basin, emptying its contents back into the jug, "that in respect of scrying, he was absolutely right. You are telling me this is self-taught? That you can summon these visions without technique, purely through an effort of will?"

"Oh, no," Tuala said, shocked. "Such images are sent by the gods; they cannot be called up by man or woman alone. It is possible, sometimes, to bend or shape them with the mind. To shut out some parts and strengthen others." That was what she had done when the Good Folk had sought to fill her mirror with images she did not want. Then, she had called on the Shining One and the goddess had shown herself in the clear water. "I think that if the seer has a particular need to know something, perhaps to interpret an augury for the future, the gods shape the visions in a way that will help. At least, that has been my experience."

"I see." Kethra looked stunned, baffled. Her deft hands wiped out the basin with a cloth, covered the ewer, clasped themselves before her as she came to stand by Tuala. Tuala got to her feet respectfully.

"Tuala," said Kethra.

"Yes?"

"I think it best if today's lesson is not discussed openly among the girls. If they question you about what happened, give them a brief, truthful answer and leave it at that. Don't allow yourself to be drawn into discussions of technique, nor tempted to demonstrate. These are beginners, and vulnerable. Do you understand?"

"Of course. They won't ask me, anyway. They don't talk to me."

There was a brief silence.

"Did we make an error, housing you on your own?" Kethra asked.

"Oh, no!" Tuala was filled with horror at the prospect of being moved into those communal chambers, to be surrounded by whispering girls at all hours of day and night. The tower was hers, her place, safe, silent; the oak was her refuge, her piece of Pitnochie here in an alien realm. Whoever had made the decision to put her in the tower had shown wisdom and kindness. "I am happy where I am. It suits me very well."

"Perhaps," Kethra said. "You may go now. Tomorrow, instead of attending this class, you will go to see Fola. She wanted a progress report, and it's time. I will tell her to expect you. Now hurry up or you'll miss the food."

Tuala was almost out the door when Kethra spoke again, behind her.

"Do you think it's true? Have they really brought the Mage Stone up the lake?"

"I suppose we will find out when Talorgen's men come home," said Tuala, seeing Bridei's face in her mind and knowing in her heart that every scrap of her vision was a true and exact record of the way things had happened. Another image crept across that bright memory: a man clutching at his throat and dying in agony. In today's image, Bridei had not yet worn his battle marks. Still, Broichan had promised action: there would be a taster now, and extra guards. All the same, she longed to know Bridei was back at Pitnochie and safe again.

"I suppose we will," said Kethra. "If true, this could be a powerful portent of good times to come for the Priteni. Most powerful." Her tone changed. "Off you go, then," she said. "I've things to do if you haven't."

NEXT MORNING AS the others made their way to class, Tuala waited at the entry to Fola's private chamber. Shade, too, was outside the door; she had seen him earlier in the garden, stalking birds. He sat now, ears pricked, tail twitching irritably, impatient for admission. The cat had his routines like the rest of them at Banmerren and did not appreciate their disruption. But Fola's door was closed; from within, her voice could be heard, measured and calm. Tuala bent to stroke Shade's coat; layers of ancient scars had left it rough and threadbare. Eyeing her with an old cat's skeptical gaze, he purred despite himself.

The door opened abruptly and the girl who emerged had to put out both arms to avoid falling over the two of them and sprawling flat on the rush-strewn floor.

"Oh—I'm sorry—here—" Tuala reached out a hand to steady her.

The girl flinched away, eyes wide and blank. Tuala vaguely remembered her from the very first days at Banmerren; a thin, solemn-faced thing, very quiet. What was her name: Morna? Morva? She had not been in any of the classes recently; now that Tuala thought about it, she hadn't seen the girl walking on the grass with the others or seated at table for a long time. Perhaps she had been ill. Her eyes were very strange. Now she turned and vanished like a shadow, not out to the communal area but back toward the place where the senior women had their sleeping quarters. It was only after she was gone that Tuala realized Morna had not been wearing the blue robe of the junior girls, but garments of pure white.

"Come in, Tuala." Fola's tone gave no suggestion of her mood. Shade had already made his way in and was up on the bench beside the wise woman, circling on a cushion. Tuala wondered if the cat ever had the temerity to sit on his mistress's knee. Maybe that would be too undignified for both of them.

"Kethra has spoken to me of what occurred yesterday," Fola went on, "and of your own request not to practice scrying with the other juniors. You surprised her."

"I'm sorry—I did try to tell her—"

"I was, perhaps, unfair, both to you and to Kethra. This comes as no surprise to me; my intuition seldom fails me, and I detected something in you when we first met, something that would in time come to fruition and be both powerful and perilous. I have waited a long time for you to join us at Banmerren; waited while your tutors at Pitnochie provided a grounding far beyond what can be offered in this house of women. I could have warned Kethra and the others what to expect. It seemed to me better to let matters run their course for a while; to see what you made of Banmerren and what Banmerren made of you."

Tuala said nothing. This felt uncomfortably close to Broichan's games of strategy, games with human pieces. She remembered that Fola and the king's druid were old friends.

"Do you think your vision was an image of the present time? A reflection of truth?" There was an eagerness in the wise woman's tone now, the same Tuala had heard in Kethra's, asking this. Neither had missed the true import of Tuala's vision.

"I know it was," Tuala told her.

"You *know?*" asked Fola sharply. "That is arrogance, child; we cannot know the gods' intentions until these portents become reality."

"I do know. I know because Bridei was in it, and I always see true for him. Except when it is the future, which can be changed." She shivered; but for Broichan's swift action in sending that warning message down the Glen, the future might have been bleak indeed.

Fola's eyes had narrowed. "Bridei. You did not mention Bridei to Kethra, not by the account she gave me. What was his part in this?"

Tuala bit her lip, suddenly reluctant to tell more, even to someone who had always seemed a friend.

"I mean no harm to him, Tuala," Fola said. "Quite the opposite. Like Broichan, I am committed to Bridei's future. You can trust me; this is the truth."

"He was leading the endeavor when they brought the Mage Stone down to King Lake," Tuala said. "It was his idea, his vision, his undertaking. They all followed him, warrior and chieftain alike. He awoke the light of inspiration in their eyes, the touch of the Flamekeeper. I think men will long remember this."

Fola nodded. "Broichan will rejoice to hear it," she said. "And so will the king. These are indeed interesting times. Momentous times."

"Fola?"

"Yes, child?"

"I have tried to work hard since I came here. I've tried to do as I promised. I'm sorry I made Kethra angry."

Fola regarded her in silence for a moment. "Kethra's not angry," she said. "Perhaps a little annoyed with herself for not seeing this earlier, but not in any way aggrieved with you. Like me, she appreciates talented students; we get them seldom enough. I asked all your tutors for a progress report. Kethra has recommended you have private tuition in most of the branches of the craft that she teaches, either with her or with me. Derila tells me your background in history, geography, and politics is exceptional; she would prefer to keep you in her class, as I gather some of the noble daughters are quite apt and that all of you can benefit from robust debate."

Tuala nodded.

"Derila's enjoying herself," Fola said, smiling. "The best crop of students she's ever had, she tells me. Have you made any friends, Tuala?"

"Friends." Tuala could hardly think what that might mean, here among these girls who seemed so different they might be from another world. "Not really. Fox—Ferada sits by me; Ana has been kind to me. They are the daughters of chieftains; I am—what I am. I don't think we could ever be friends. The others—well, they look at me and whisper and laugh behind their hands. It doesn't matter. It was already like that at Pitnochie before I came away."

Something in her voice or her face made Fola lean forward, scrutinizing her closely. "What do you mean, Tuala?"

Tuala's voice came out unevenly, despite her efforts at control. "I became unwelcome. Broichan never wanted me there. But the rest of them did. Until I started to grow up. Then they were afraid of me. It was stupid, but I couldn't change it. That was when Broichan said I had to go."

"What about your friend? Bridei? Is he afraid of you, now that you are a woman?"

Tuala stared at her, outrage robbing her of speech.

"It's a reasonable question," Fola said calmly. "A very apt one, indeed, since the young man is of exactly the age to be most vulnerable in such a respect, one might think."

"He's been away," Tuala said, blinking back sudden tears. "And of course he isn't afraid of me. Of course he isn't. It's not like that between us . . ."

"Not like what?"

Tuala pressed her lips tightly together. This was unfair; cruel. Nobody understood the way it was; nobody but herself and Bridei. Nobody but the Shining One, who had brought them together at Midwinter, long ago.

"Let us leave that for now, since it distresses you," Fola said. "Perhaps you came here just in time. As for the other matter, we'll alter your day's work to fit in private tuition with me in the mornings, in place of Kethra's lessons. You'll continue in Derila's classes. I sense you do gain something from those, as a natural scholar. The noble daughters will be returning to court once Talorgen comes to Caer Pridne; if your visions are as accurate as you believe, that may be quite soon. After that, Derila may make use of you to help teach some of the other girls, if you agree to it."

Tuala stared at her. "I don't think they would welcome me as a tutor—it would make them resent me still more—"

Fola's brows rose. "If it is in the service of the Shining

One you would do it regardless, would you not?" she asked.

"Yes, Fola." *There is learning in everything,* Broichan always said. Even in being set somehow above those who see you as an inferior form of life, forever different, forever beyond acceptance.

"Also," Fola said, "I want you to talk to Ferada and Ana about alliances through marriage, about what awaits them as chieftains' daughters and what rules govern the choices that are made for them."

"But—"

Fola silenced her with a look. "I know you know all about it already. In theory. The royal descent, the importance of cross-links between the seven houses and so on. That, believe me, is far removed from a discussion with girls of your own age, whose personal futures are entirely governed by such rules."

"If you wish. But I don't understand why."

The wise woman regarded Tuala closely for a little. "It is reasonable, I suppose, that you seek an explanation," she said. "I would be somewhat reassured if I thought you accepted that Banmerren is good for you; that we can indeed teach you something of worth."

"I didn't mean—"

Fola raised a hand. "Nor did you say so; but you give me sufficient clues to your state of mind, Tuala. I think there is another future you envisage for yourself that is not as priestess of the Shining One, nor as scholar and teacher, admirably suited as you appear to be for either of those roles. You speak often of Pitnochie, with a tone of voice and a form of words that go beyond the natural homesickness that affects all of my new students. You do not speak a great deal of Bridei. But when you do, it is clear to me that he is much in your thoughts."

Tuala said nothing. She did not know where Fola was heading with this, nor how it related to what she had asked before.

"It's very important that you realize what an opportunity you have been offered here, Tuala," Fola went on gravely. "Talk to Ana and Ferada. Consider your other options, which are perhaps fewer than you realize. Think about the life we lead here and what it means for us. We may dwell within high walls, but the protection they offer provides us with a particular kind of freedom; a freedom of the mind and spirit that is precious indeed. I do not doubt your love of the Shining One, my dear. I just want you to get things in perspective."

"Yes, Fola. I will speak with the noble daughters."

"Good. You may go now. Kethra tells me you like the tower. You do not think you should be housed with the others? That perhaps you might be more readily accepted by them if that were so?"

"Maybe I would. But I do not think I could endure it long. I like to see the sky. I am accustomed to silence; to being alone."

Fola nodded. "And you like trees," she said. "I do seem to remember finding children under trees, long ago. Very well, off you go now. I look forward to working with you; I expect we'll both learn something."

❧

WHAT MAY HAVE seemed a simple matter to the wise woman did in fact require a certain courage. Being on the outside, excluded, could be seen as carrying its own strange sort of pride. Approaching the noble daughters outside the accepted conduct of a history class was to seek admission to a circle where she did not belong. It was inviting humiliation.

Ana and Ferada had taken their bread and cheese out into the garden. They sat in their usual place, on a stone bench under a pear tree, with several other girls around them. It was a pretty sight: they might almost have been two manifestations of the maiden All-Flowers, Ferada representing autumn in her russet gown, her fiery hair pinned up high, her sharp features softened by a dusting of freckles across the bridge of the nose. Ana was all springtime, with her ashen-fair locks spilling across her shoulders, her clothing the traditional tunic and straight skirt of her island people, woven in palest cream with borders the hue of forget-me-nots. She wore a silver brooch at the shoulder, pinning her shawl; it was wrought in the shape of a sea-beast, part horse, part seal, part something else: one of the ancient signs of lineage in the Light Isles. It seemed to Tuala, watching these two and wondering what she might say to them, that something set them apart. Whether it was their noble blood, or the advantages of education and upbringing, or the touch of the goddess herself, both looked lovely, powerful, and—for all her own reservations about Fox Girl—somehow good. Tuala became aware that she was staring.

"Come and sit by us, Tuala," Ana said in her soft, melodious voice. "The sun is so warm today; I think the Flamekeeper must be smiling on Fortriu." She shifted across to make room on the bench; Ferada stayed where she was, expression mildly amused. As Tuala walked over, all the other girls got up without a word and moved away out of earshot.

"I'm sorry," Tuala found herself saying, "I didn't mean to—"

"Shh," Ana said. "Sit down; don't mind them, they're just silly girls. Ah!" she added triumphantly as Tuala seated herself between them. "You owe me, Ferada!"

Tuala looked from one to the other and Ana's cheeks reddened slightly.

"A wager," Ferada said. "How long it would take you to pluck up the courage and come over to sit with us. Unfortunately, here at Banmerren we have nothing much to wager with. I have to wash Ana's hair tonight, something we do for each other anyway while we're here."

Fox Girl was sounding almost human. It was surprising; she had maintained her distance up till now, save in the history class.

"I heard you were going to court," Tuala ventured. "When your father returns."

Ferada grimaced. "Inevitable," she said. "We're here for a while, shut in behind high walls, and there for a while, being polite to men our families think suitable. I don't know which is worse, really."

"But you'll be wanting to see your family," Tuala said, surprised. "Your mother and little brothers."

Ferada raised her brows. "Would you be in a hurry to see

Uric and Bedo if they were your brothers? Frogs in the bed, shouts and shrieks when you're trying to study, weak jokes about which of the men you like best?"

Tuala smiled despite herself. "I thought they were fine little boys," she said. "They made me laugh."

"Didn't you threaten to turn Bedo into a newt? I'm sure that's what he told me."

"I may have said something like that," Tuala replied. "He knew it was a joke. Eventually."

Ana laughed. "Little brothers would be nice," she said. "I have only much older ones. And a sister." Abruptly, she was solemn. "She'll be nearly eleven now. She probably doesn't even remember me."

"Hmm," said Ferada, breaking off a piece of bread and tossing it to a thrush that waited on the grass. "Big brothers can be a worry; wouldn't you agree, Tuala?"

"I don't know," Tuala said. "I have neither brothers nor sisters." There was a picture of the forest people in her mind, girl with cobweb hair and pale jewels on her fingers, boy all of nuts and berries and creepers. If folk like those were her family, it was no wonder the other girls looked at her askance.

"You do really," Ferada said. "You have Bridei. A foster brother."

There was a little silence.

"I need to ask you something," Tuala said.

"Go on, then." Ferada's interest was caught; there was a speculative glint in her eye.

"Fola wanted me to find out about—about what's expected for young women such as yourselves. With marriages and alliances."

"Why would you need to ask us?" Ana was amazed. "Fola should hear you in history class. You already know more than the rest of us put together."

"That's not what she means," said Ferada. "She's talking about the bits that elderly male tutors don't tell."

"You can't mean—" Ana flushed again, her cheeks turning rose pink.

Ferada gave a crooked smile, glancing sideways at her

friend. "I doubt very much if Fola intends us to provide expert tuition in matters of the bedchamber," she said drily. "It's more about what's expected of us, and others like us. Do you think?"

Tuala nodded. "That's what she said. I know both of you are daughters of the royal line; that Lady Dreseida is a cousin of King Drust, the child of his mother's sister, and that Ana is descended from a more distant branch of the royal line, the one that rules in the Light Isles. That means your sons would have a claim to kingship one day; it restricts who you can marry."

"And it limits our other choices," Ferada said glumly. "Be glad you have the option of staying at Banmerren, Tuala. You may be shut off from the outside world here, but it's a whole lot better than being a royal brood mare. That may seem like having power, when so much depends on us, but there's no real power in it. When it comes to it, the men make the decisions; all we are is breeders."

"We don't do so badly," Ana put in. "It is a life of privilege compared with the hard work of a farmer's wife or the lot of a servant."

"How can you say that?" Ferada was outraged. "You're captive here, stuck at Drust's court for years and years, and you can't go anywhere unless you're surrounded by big men with knives. How long is it since you saw your family?"

Ana looked down at her hands. "A long time," she said. "They do not come here. I imagine my cousin is afraid any who visit may become hostages in their turn. My presence here has kept my kinsmen compliant. It has done what it was meant to do."

"You always seem so calm," Tuala ventured, choosing her words carefully. "As if you didn't mind being a prisoner."

"There is no point in complaining," Ana said. "I was sad at first, sad and frightened. I missed my little sister terribly. But they have been kind, the king and queen. And it helps to be able to spend time here at Banmerren. I like learning. I like the other girls' company, Ferada's in particular."

"And you need not have those large guards always lurking somewhere close by when you're in here," Ferada said drily.

"Indeed, cannot," agreed Ana. "There are times when the rule banning all men save druids from this sanctuary is most welcome."

"Ana?" Tuala asked.

"Mm?"

"What if your cousin . . . what if he . . . ?" It was too terrible to say this in full; the whole situation seemed, indeed, quite unbelievable.

"Difficult question." It was Ferada who replied; Ana had folded her hands together in her lap, her gray eyes suddenly shadowed. "What if her cousin decides to stop being so obedient? Decides to attack Drust the Bull or ally himself with an enemy such as the Gaels, maybe? I wouldn't like to venture a response, save to say that if I were a hostage I'd be a great deal less sanguine about it than Ana is."

"I don't think they'd kill me," Ana said in a small voice. "But I suppose it is possible; if they are not prepared to make good that threat, then there's little point in holding me here in Fortriu. It is hard to believe that they would do it. Queen Rhian has been very good to me."

"You're safe as long as your cousin believes they'd carry it out," Ferada said. "That makes it fortunate he doesn't visit. One look at the way you're treated at Caer Pridne, for all the guards, and he'd realize the king couldn't bring himself to lay a finger on you."

Tuala could not tell if Ferada believed her own words, or had made this speech to reassure her friend. "I'm sorry," she said. "It is very difficult for you. I shouldn't have asked."

"I've accepted it," said Ana. "Our ancestry makes us significant, not only as what my friend here calls royal brood mares, but also as pieces to be deployed to advantage in the game of political strategy. I learned this early. For me, the time as a hostage may not last much longer. I'm deemed to be of marriageable years now, and it's likely to be more useful to King Drust to wed me to a dangerous chieftain or petty king whom he wishes to placate. Then I suppose he will take new hostages."

"How can you be so calm about it?" Ferada exclaimed. "This makes me so angry sometimes I could scream, if ladies were permitted to do something so uncouth. We have so much to offer, so much we could give—and because of the accident of our birth, we have no free choices at all."

"Shh," warned Ana. "Don't let Kethra hear you talking about accidents of birth. It sounds dangerously like an insult to the gods. We must accept the lives they give us, Ferada. We must work within the pathway they allot us."

"Hmm," said Ferada, her lips twisting in a humorless smile. "To get back to your query, Tuala, we're about to return to court for another round of introductions to men our families deem suitable future prospects for us. There aren't many to choose from. They must be high born, healthy, of good character, and steadfast practitioners of the ancient faith of Fortriu. In other words, they must be in all ways fit to father a future monarch. I've yet to meet a single one I could bear to have touch me, let alone do what a husband does to his wife. Most of them look me up and down like a choice cut of meat. They can't help themselves."

"That's a little unfair," Ana said, frowning. "There are worthy men among them."

"Worthy!" Ferada gave a snort of derisive laughter. "Who wants worthy? Never mind. I know there's no choice in the matter. If there were, I would tell my parents I want nobody. I would make my own life as Fola has done."

"It could be lonely," Tuala ventured.

Ferada regarded her curiously. "That's odd, coming from you. Don't you like being alone? You're always scuttling off to your hidey-hole up in the tower. Maybe Fola's like you. Maybe she enjoys being by herself, with only her own thoughts for company."

"A wise woman has the company of the gods," Ana said. "That means she is never lonely."

"Sometimes we speak to the gods and they do not answer," Tuala said. "That is the loneliest of all." She thought of Bridei with a shadow in his eyes, his face ash-pale with tension. The answers he needed, neither man nor god had been able to provide.

"What is it, Tuala?" There was concern in Ana's tone. "What's the matter?"

"Nothing." She must guard her thoughts with more care if they showed thus in her face. "When must you marry? How soon? Broichan wanted me to—I only came here because—"

"He had a suitor for you already?" Ferada asked. "Who? Tell us!"

"A man called Garvan. A stone carver. I did not want to marry him. I don't want to marry anyone."

"You're in the right place, then," Ferada said.

"Garvan," mused Ana. "You mean the famous Garvan, the one who carved the bull stones at Caer Pridne? He must be quite old, surely."

"I don't know if he's famous. He might be; Broichan did mention commissions for the king. He seemed old. Maybe thirty."

"A stone carver wouldn't do for either of us," Ferada said, "however famous. It's chieftains or their sons; sometimes kings from other lands. The royal women do go away. I suppose that's a kind of escape. Look at Bridei."

"What about Bridei?" Tuala tried to sound nonchalant.

"That's what his mother did. Married the king of Gwynedd, went off and had her children there. The royal descent goes from father to son in those parts. Bridei has elder brothers, of course. One of them would most likely follow the father. Bridei's a bit like Ana; parted from his family for other people's reasons. He, of course, is entirely suitable for me or for Ana. He meets all the qualifications. The only drawback is the possibility that he could be a candidate for kingship; it's preferred that the king wed outside the royal line, to avoid his sons becoming contenders in future years. To wed a woman of the blood, even a distant cousin, would concentrate too much power in one family; it would make the line of descent too narrow. Still, chances are Bridei won't even put his name forward when the time comes. There are several older, more experienced men who are eligible, one or two of them widely respected. Your foster brother is unlikely to be a candidate, and so can be considered as marriage material for us. I'm forced to admit that it's not such a bad prospect. Life with him might be rather too solemn, but at least he's not an oaf, as so many of them are. Broichan's brought him up to love the gods and to demonstrate impeccably good manners."

"You think him too solemn?" asked Ana. "Some men find it hard to laugh; that is not such a bad thing. Better than a man who laughs too much, and foolishly."

"Ana likes him," Ferada whispered to Tuala, brows raised. "She saw your brother from a distance two summers ago, when Talorgen took the boys to court. She said he was handsome."

"I said no such thing." Ana was blushing again. "I never even met him."

Tuala was seized with a desperate need to turn the conversation to safer ground. "Your brothers could be candidates for kingship, too," she said to Ferada.

"Well, yes," Ferada said with a grimace. "Technically, they can, as my mother's sons. But Uric and Bedo have a lot of growing up to do yet, and Gartnait's entirely unsuitable. I love my big brother, but he simply doesn't have it in him to take on such a weighty mantle. He's lacking in so many of the essentials of a true leader, qualities which, I'm obliged to acknowledge, the worthy and rather dull Bridei demonstrates more and more as he grows older. Father would never consider putting Gartnait forward as a candidate. In fact, they are saying such a decision will face Fortriu within two summers. Drust is ailing. I heard Kethra say that. So, no chance for my little brothers; by the time Uric and Bedo reach manhood there'll be a new young king on the throne."

"Perhaps not young," said Ana. "Bearing in mind that each of the seven houses of the Priteni may put a candidate forward, there could be several men of middle years in contention. Some of my own kinsmen would qualify by blood, although I doubt they'd declare candidacy if the election comes soon. My own situation is likely to prevent that."

"True," Ferada said. "The voting chieftains will surely choose someone who's tried and tested as a leader of men; someone like Drust's first cousin Carnach, who's youngish but well respected and powerful in his own territories. And loyal. I think we can safely forget about both Bridei and my brothers in such a contest; put their names up and folk would only laugh. The biggest threat is from Circinn. From Drust the Boar. This will be his chance to claim the crown of Fortriu to add to that of Circinn, in order to unite the two kingdoms in the observance of the Christian faith."

"The Shining One protect us from such a horror," Ana muttered.

"Do you think it likely Drust the Boar can gather the numbers for that?" asked Tuala, shocked. "Would sufficient of the voting chieftains support him?"

"It'll be close," Ferada said. "They'll be interesting times. Dangerous times. Hold out the prospect of such power before a group of men and anything can happen. We should go, Ana. It's fine enough for riding today. Why don't you come with us, Tuala? I'm sure we could smuggle you out somehow." She rose to her feet with a mischievous glint in her eyes.

"Thank you, no," Tuala said. "I must—I need to—"

"It's all right, Tuala," said Ana kindly. "You must not break rules. Ferada gets a little carried away sometimes, especially when she's been shut in too long. Like a caged cat. I hope we gave you the answers you wanted."

"Yes, I—"

"The thing is," Ferada said, "it's just as bad for the boys as it is for us, in a way. The young men of royal blood, those who could be candidates for kingship, have their own set of rules to follow. Their wives are chosen as carefully as our husbands, not because of breeding, but because a royal wife must be perfect, beyond reproach. Just imagine having that kind of pressure on you. You'd be nothing but your husband's shadow, your only purpose to reflect the glory of his role as human embodiment of the Flamekeeper and symbol of Fortriu's aspirations. Every single thing you did would be scrutinized. You'd have no life of your own at all."

"If you loved your husband," said Ana, "that wouldn't matter, surely?"

"Listen to her," Ferada scoffed, "and her talk of love! How you manage to keep such foolish dreams alive in the face of so much evidence to the contrary I can't understand. Now, we really are going to be late—enjoy whatever it is you'll be doing, Tuala." With a quirk of the lip, she turned and walked away, and Ana followed.

THE TREE CRADLED Tuala, its limbs secure and strong, anchoring her to earth's heart. Its canopy spread fresh and green under the warmth of the sun. Ana had said the Flamekeeper smiled on Fortriu. Well he might; the Mage Stone had been brought home, and soon the land would have a new young king. For all Ferada's dismissive words, Tuala knew how it would be. There was a deep certainty in it that allowed for no doubt.

She would not practice scrying. She knew what would appear on the water to taunt and torment her. It would not be Fox Girl this time, Ferada as a grown woman in an elegant gown, smiling up at her husband as he inclined his head with impeccably good manners to hear her words. No; this time it would be Ana. Tuala's heart was cold. A young man who might one day be king needed the right bride. That could not be challenged; he could not walk a path of such terrible responsibility unless his wife could support him with all her own strength. He could not be fully accepted among the influential men surrounding him, both allies and possible adversaries, unless he had made a marriage entirely acceptable in the eyes of both his people and the gods. Tuala knew that. She had known Ferada was a possible choice, but she had been able to discount that, almost, because quite plainly Ferada would never be chosen. The Shining One would intervene before Bridei allied himself to a girl who thought him dull, for such a girl could never love him as he needed to be loved. But Ana; Ana was a different matter. Ana was young, beautiful, clever, of royal blood, and both sweet and kind as well. It hurt to think about it. Ana liked Bridei. No doubt he would like her in return; how could he fail to do so? She was absolutely perfect, and utterly suitable. It was all too easy to imagine Bridei confiding in Ana as he had once done in Tuala herself, telling her his troubles, working through his quandaries, sharing with her every part of his struggle to know what choices were right. It fit perfectly; it was as if the gods had intended it.

She would not weep. She would swallow these tears. If this would help Bridei, if it was right for the future of For- triu, then it was a good thing. And if her own heart broke over it, that was a small enough matter in the great unfolding of it all.

Tuala drew her knees up, wrapping her arms around them. There was a chill inside her at odds with the sunny bright- ness of the day. She would probably never see him again. Never. She might spend her whole life within the walls of Banmerren or another of the houses of wise women that were dotted across Fortriu. If she truly loved the Shining One as she had always thought she did, that should be a blessed life, a life of dedicated service, of purity and strength. She could teach. Already, the opportunity was there.

The tears began to spill despite her. A powerful wave of feeling swept over her, a raw longing for home, for the woods above Pitnochie, for those other oaks, for the hall fire and the shrewd, kindly faces of Erip and Wid as they cajoled her out of her mood. For Brenna's friendship and Ferat's grumbling and Donal's plain, honest strength; for Mara's dour pronouncements and the smell of clean linen and oat- cakes baking. She wanted that world back; she wanted to be riding Blaze through the forest, with Bridei beside her on Snowfire and the whole day ahead of them, full of wondrous new things to discover. And yet she knew that it would not be enough, not now. She no longer wanted Bridei to love her like a sister. She wanted . . . she wanted the impossible.

You cannot go back, said a little voice inside her, the same that had whispered the tale of Nechtan and Ela in her ear. There was nobody here in the tree but Tuala herself and a small bird or two. But they were with her all the same, cob- web girl and leaf man, a part of her that could not be ig- nored, not even here at Banmerren, so far from home. *There's no going back.*

Not to that world. It was the other voice, the girl's, and Tuala thought she could almost see her graceful, airy form among the branches, silver rings and gossamer robes, translucent skin and shimmering hair. *But our world is waiting for you; your world, Tuala. That is where you belong. You must come home to your own kind. There is no place for you here. Neither king's court nor house of ritual can hold you long. Like the wild creatures of the forest, you chafe at confinement. Sooner or later you must fly away.*

So many tears. The leaf man spoke, and Tuala felt a touch, as if a twiggy finger reached to wipe the torrent from her cheek. It was both tender and deeply unsettling. *Among us, you will have no cause to weep, little one. You will be surrounded by love. Owl and badger, otter and wild deer will be your friends. You will drink of the honeysuckle and dance in slippers of moonlight. You will live your days without fear or sorrow, and your sleep will be visited only by good dreams. Leave all this behind; you are not meant for such a world. Come home; come back to the forest. We will show you the way . . .*

They were coaxing her back. Coaxing so tenderly . . . and yet, these same folk had abandoned her as a babe without a second thought. Were they obeying the will of the Shining One? Or was it just a cruel game, another piece of trickery? For all her doubts, there was such kindness in the leaf man's tone that Tuala knew if she had been there, now, in the Vale of the Fallen, she would have reached for his hand and let him lead her away under the trees to the land he spoke of, the realm where her true family awaited her and all her questions would be answered. But she was not there; she was here at Banmerren, perched high in an oak tree all by herself, and these voices were not real. They were a thing that came from inside her, a manifestation that had little to do with Ana or Bridei or the fact that tomorrow she had a private lesson with Fola that she should be preparing for. Scrubbing her cheeks with her hands, Tuala climbed over to the inner wall, balanced her way across to the roof, sure-footed on the narrow stones, and returned to her cold chamber. She knelt on the floor and closed her eyes. Breathing in a slow pattern, she bent her thoughts on the Shining One, powerful, compassionate, and wise. If the truth could not be found in prayer, then she was indeed all alone.

11

HIS HEAD ACHED fit to split asunder. He walked on, keeping pace, each step a hammer blow to the skull. Tree and rock and hillside swam around him, their forms distorted by the haze of pain. This was nothing; he must go on despite it, for by nightfall they would be home. They would reach Pitnochie, and he could let it go at last. He could share the anguish, the guilt, the wrongness, and then perhaps this vice that gripped his head, this chill that clutched at his heart might ease a little.

Donal was dead. Donal was dead, not as he would have wished to go, with valor in battle, but in a cruel act of cold-blooded murder. He had drunk from another man's cup, and he had died in Bridei's arms, his body wracked and twisted by convulsions. Bridei had not thought himself capable of hate, but whoever had done that deed, he hated them with a white-hot fury. If ever he discovered their identity, he would punish them as they had punished his loyal friend. He would put his own hands around their necks and watch them struggle as Donal had struggled to the end, gasping, retching, fighting death like the warrior he was. Donal was a good man, a fine, brave, straightforward sort of man. It was not Donal who had been meant to die. It was Bridei.

It had happened on the very day he and Gartnait received their warrior marks, at Raven's Well on the journey home. There was a man in Talorgen's household with the skill to incise the delicate patterns on the flesh of cheek and chin, employing fine needles and colored pigments; it hurt, but it was a good pain, and they sat together, Bridei and Gartnait, while the markings were etched into their skin, symbol of their participation in a major battle for their king. Afterward, they talked quietly of times past, mending the friendship they had almost lost in the smoke-darkened settlement of Galany's Reach. Gartnait made his explanation again, with an apology; Bridei accepted it and kept his doubts to himself.

When the tattooing was over, there was a feast. Although the lady of Raven's Well was still away, Talorgen's household mustered a fine spread of roast meats, a good flow of ale, even puddings. After the march up the Great Glen to Maiden Lake, the men were hungry and fell to with gusto. Fokel of Galany had left them now; his was the responsibility of conveying the Mage Stone to a place where it might be set in earth once more, within the lands of Fortriu and beyond the grasping hands of the Gaels. The stone lay now near the head of King Lake; Fokel's men must devise a method to move it overland, a challenge that would exercise their strength and their wits to the utmost. Rolling the thing down a hill had been all very well, but the steep slopes and narrow ways of the Glen would require something beyond ingenuity. There was talk of summoning druids.

Ale flowed freely at the feast. There were toasts, tales, laughter, and jokes; the jugs passed from hand to hand, cups were set here and there on the board, spilled, drained, shared, refilled. Nobody knew who it was that poured the ale into Bridei's goblet. Whoever did it was unlucky. Bridei had, in fact, drunk very little all evening, and had eaten only sufficient for courtesy. The fresh tattoo stung, his head was aching, and thoughts of the battle and its aftermath were never far from his mind. He had enjoyed little sleep on the nights they had camped under the trees, journeying up from King Lake. Donal's cup was empty. Instead of fetching a jug to fill it anew, Bridei had slid his own untouched ale across, knowing he would take no more himself.

"Here."

And then . . . oh, then . . . Bridei closed his eyes, the image searing across his mind in all its brutal reality. He remembered every detail, every single moment . . . It had not taken long. Whatever it was, it was powerful stuff. They tried, desperately, to make Donal vomit up the poison. They tried to get him walking, but spasms soon seized his body, arching his back, causing his limbs to thrash and his eyes to roll crazily. He made noises, hideous, animal noises. No, it had not taken long; it was one terrible, vile moment after another, a hundred, a thousand moments of horror until, at last, Donal lay in Bridei's arms, with blood and vomit and ordure staining their clothes, the floor, the benches and rushes all around them. Donal had not managed to speak again, after his first clutch at the throat, his hoarse whisper of anguish, "Bridei!" He had gone without saying good-bye.

Pitnochie. Think of Pitnochie; think of home. Those things, at least, were strong and sure: the ancient oaks, the whispering birches, the farm with its walled fields and Fidich's little cottage. The house, low and secretive amidst the screening trees. Broichan, stern and wise, able to find the learning in any tale, however grim and cruel. Erip and Wid, full of the laughter and wisdom of long lives lived well. And Tuala . . . gods, how he needed Tuala to hold his hand and listen and tell him it would be all right again . . .

THEY REACHED BROICHAN'S house before sunset, making their way up the hill under the oaks, a smaller body of men than had fought in the battle for Galany's Reach. Most had returned to their homes, but Talorgen and his son were heading for court with Ged of Abertornie and a sizable contingent of men at arms, including Aniel's two bodyguards, Breth and Garth. Beside them came the men of Broichan's own household who had joined the fight for Galany's Reach: Elpin, Enfret, and Cinioch. Urguist had not returned; they had left him sleeping, blanketed in earth, on the shores of King Lake.

On Talorgen's orders, Breth and Garth were now attached to Bridei, shadowing him as Donal had done, though Bridei refused to let them taste his food. It seemed an outrageous thing to expect another man to die in your place, as if you were somehow of greater value than he was. To see one man die for you was enough for a lifetime.

The welcome was warm, but the house seemed quiet. They discovered straight away that Broichan was not there. To Bridei's surprise and dismay, he had gone to resume his duties at Caer Pridne, leaving instructions for Bridei to ride on to court with Talorgen, for it was time for him to meet King Drust the Bull at last. Ferat grinned broadly, admiring Bridei's warrior marks: "Ah, look at you now; what a man!" Mara was less voluble, but could not suppress a smile to see him home safe and sound.

Then, quickly, the travelers imparted the bad news, before there were too many questions asked. The battle was won, but there had been losses. Urguist had fallen bravely. And another old friend would not be coming home. Bridei told these tidings himself, knowing how they would hurt. Donal had been part of this household nearly as long as Bridei had; such a loss would be keenly felt.

"Ah, poor lad," Mara muttered. "That's a sad death for a fighting man. They're terrible times, terrible. As well the old fellows are gone from us; it would have distressed them."

"Erip and Wid? They're not home? I had hoped to see them—" Something in Mara's eyes stopped Bridei short.

"Broichan sent a messenger," Mara said, looking at Talorgen. "To you, my lord. A long while ago."

"No such messenger reached me," Talorgen said. "What news did he bear?"

"Another death. The old man, Erip, was carried off in the winter; a terrible chill. His chest hadn't been sound, even before. We buried him up on the hill. And Wid's gone. Gone off with the druids."

"You'll want to get the men settled in," Ferat said. "Stay a night or two, rest your horses. Let me show you—"

"Where's Tuala?" asked Bridei. An uncanny feeling had crept over him as he learned of each absence, each loss; it was like being four years old again and having everything taken away.

There was a brief silence.

"Gone," Mara said flatly. "Long gone."

Bridei turned his eyes on her and the housekeeper flinched visibly.

"She's at that place up north, the school for wise women. Banmerren," Mara said. "There was an opportunity to become a servant of the Shining One, a great chance for such as her. She traveled up there with my lord's family." She glanced at Talorgen. "Very suitable. Broichan was much relieved."

Bridei did not trust himself to speak. Indeed, he was not sure he could form words at all. His heart seemed to have forgotten how to beat.

"Thank you for the offer of hospitality." Talorgen spoke into the awkward silence. "We are somewhat travel weary; the men would welcome what supper you can provide, and a warm corner for sleep. We will not trouble you long. Ged and I must both be at Caer Pridne as soon as possible."

"No trouble," Ferat said. "Give us a bit of time and we'll cook you a supper fit for a king." And, seeing familiar faces, "Enfret! Cinioch! Welcome home! Elpin, lad! Give me the news!"

*

ALONE IN HIS old chamber, Bridei fought to exercise control over himself. He was a man: eighteen years old, a warrior proven, and the foster son of the king's druid. He was no longer the child who had lain awake here, looking up at the moon and longing for stories to banish the shadows. He was no longer the small boy who had hidden once in a mere chink in the rocks while an assassin's blade swept in savage strokes before his body. He was Bridei, son of Maelchon; he had brought the Mage Stone down from Galany's Reach and had won the friendship of warrior and chieftain alike. Fokel of Galany had sworn lifelong loyalty; Ged of Abertornie had presented him with a cloak woven in alarming squares and stripes of vivid green, orange, and scarlet. Morleo had invited him to spend a summer at his home by Longwater, where the trout were as big as young seals. He was a man.

He was a man, and his head ached, and his eyes were full of unshed tears. He was a man, and his best friend had died before his eyes because he had offered him a drink. Bridei laid a clenched fist against the wall by the small, square window, where three white stones still lay in offering to the goddess. He rested his brow on his hand and closed his eyes. Why couldn't he weep, even here behind a closed door where nobody could see? Why couldn't he talk, even to Gartnait, even to Talorgen? Why did he need her so much it was like an ache in every part of his body, a yawning emptiness that pleaded to be filled? What was wrong with him? And why had she gone? How could she do that? Tuala loved the Shining One, and the Shining One had always smiled on her; that had been clear from the moment the goddess had shown him where to find her, a tiny, precious gift of life in the snowy chill of Midwinter. But a priestess, a wise woman: that, he had not expected. Logic said it was reasonable, even desirable. His heart screamed no.

People went away, he knew that. They went away and never came back. That was the way things were, and you learned to deal with it. But not Tuala. Tuala could not go away; she could not leave Pitnochie. She could not leave him all by himself. It was not right. If she were not by his side, how could he ever be what it seemed they wanted him to be; what the gods expected him to be?

He laid his brow against the cool stone by the window. It didn't help much. The throbbing was a harsh drumbeat; it was like the memory of war. A woman treated as an object of vengeance. A young warrior curled on himself like an infant, quivering with shock. A terrified child. Corpses burning, a dreadful wailing, a lament from the very bowels of despair. Donal . . . and Erip gone, his dear old friend, his grinning, mischievous, bald-headed sage . . . By the sword of the Flamekeeper, his head must break asunder, surely, if this pain lasted much longer. Why couldn't he let go? What was it that held back these tears?

There was a single hair on the windowsill, caught in place under one of the little white stones. The breeze lifted it; Bridei took it between his fingers, the long dark strand curling around his hand as if it bore its own life. Hers; Tuala's. She had stood here before she went away; had kept vigil here, perhaps, saying her good-byes. Had Broichan played a part in it? Had he sent her away again, this time forever? Bridei touched the token he still wore around his wrist, a scrap of faded ribbon worn so thin it was close to fraying apart. *Why would you let this happen?* he asked the Shining One, although her face was not yet visible beyond his window; it was barely dusk, and on the long summer nights her image was but a pale shadow in the half-dark of the sky. *Why would you take her away from me?* And the image of Donal's twisted body and distorted features came back, Donal who had died because of him. Bridei lay down on the pallet and closed his eyes. It was necessary to go on. He had been trained to endure, to cope, to be strong. He must ride to Caer Pridne, and there, at last, Broichan must give him answers: answers about Tuala, and answers about himself.

"YOU HAVE NOT told him yet?" Aniel asked, gray eyes intent on Broichan, elegant hands held palms together on the table before him. They sat in a chamber at Caer Pridne, the hall of one of the lesser dwellings that were clustered within the fortress walls of Drust's stronghold, overlooking the sea path from Fortriu to the Light Isles and beyond. Their meeting would be brief; this council had evaded notice for many long years by coming together rarely, unobtrusively, and in a different location each time. Its business was secret and perilous. That business was becoming increasingly urgent, and they had come together as soon as Talorgen arrived back at court; he was still in his riding boots. Drust the Bull was ailing. The whispers said the next observance of Gateway would be this king's last. They had less than a year, perhaps only a season, to set their pieces in place and make their last, vital play. And there had been the attempt to kill; not the first, but surely the most audacious.

"I wished Bridei to take part in this endeavor without the weight of such high expectations on his shoulders." Broichan's tone was calm as always, but there was a wariness in his eyes. "It is time for the truth now, I agree. But he has only just arrived here; he'll be weary after the ride from

Pitnochie. I will speak to him tomorrow. He'll still be griev-
ing the loss of his friend; I imagine he thinks himself responsible, illogical as that is. He knows, of course. Bridei is
too clever, too astute to have let this obvious truth evade him
for so long, careful as I and his other tutors have been not to
become specific on the subject of his own parentage and
what that could mean."

"You should have discussed it with him long ago," said
Talorgen. "Or allowed me to do so. Bridei could then have
begun to prepare himself for what now seems alarmingly
imminent. We don't have long. The boy must be presented to
Drust within days."

"Tomorrow night, in fact," said Aniel. "A celebratory supper; the king wishes to congratulate you, friend, and those of
your warriors who have accompanied you here to court. Already he hears tales of the young man whose bold ingenuity
saw the Mage Stone snatched from the enemy's grasp. He's
eager to meet the lad; the story put life back in his eyes."

"Then Broichan must indeed speak to Bridei without delay." Talorgen drummed his fingers on the table, frowning.
"The king knows the boy's origins; he recognizes this is a
potential claimant. We need Bridei to have his wits about
him. And his eyes open; if murder can be committed at my
own table in Raven's Well, then it can surely follow us right
into the security of Caer Pridne. Breth and Garth must be
vigilant."

"But not too obvious." Fola had been silent up till now. "I
believe we need something more here; not merely the capacity to guard our candidate from a knife in the back before we
get so much as a chance to put him forward, but the ability to
nip that threat in the bud. By my count, there are at least
seven men who could be proposed for kingship when the
time comes. I'll wager there's no more than one among them
with so little sense of his own worth that he must stoop to assassination attempts. Talorgen has failed completely in his
efforts to uncover the assailant's identity, let alone the name
of the man who hired him. What's to stop this fellow trying
his hand day and night from now until spring, or however
long Drust holds on? Bridei needs the bodyguards, nobody

could deny that. He also needs special protection. An investigator with particular talents. A man who is not squeamish; who can seek out the truth, and who will use his own knife without hesitation, should it come to that."

Aniel gave a wintry smile. "You're utterly wasted at Banmerren, Fola," he said.

"There is such a man, of course," Broichan said. "Drust would have to agree to his release for this purpose. Were I to ask such a favor of the king, I would need to tell him the truth."

Aniel raised his brows. "Do not you always tell your king the truth?" he asked in mock surprise.

From a corner, Uist gave an explosive bark of laughter. The others started; they had almost forgotten the wild druid's presence among them. "There is a particular kind of truth reserved for kings," Uist said, peering at them from the shadows with his bright, changeable eyes. "It consists of whatever their advisers think they should know. My belief is, you'll have no need to do any telling at all. One look at this boy and Drust will recognize what's plain in the lad's bearing, his eye, his speech; what's manifest in the way men respect him. He's a king in the making; the only choice for Fortriu. After that, Drust will lend you as many dangerous men with knives as you want."

"We only need one," Broichan said. "A particular one."

"It must be handled carefully," said Talorgen. "You know what occurred when they last happened upon one another, Bridei and the man we speak of."

"They are men. They will deal with it. As for Drust and this feast you mention, we must have a word in the king's ear, I think. We don't want every person at court gossiping about Bridei and taking wagers on his chances. Why do you think I've kept him out of the public eye for so long? That's his advantage; the lack of foolish distractions has allowed him to become strong in the love of the gods and pure of courage and purpose."

"The world he must live in is this one," Aniel said. "The world of power plays, of machinations, of lies and half-truths, of implications and uncertainties. A world of shadows. The moment you tell him formally, he must step into that realm and still remain strong."

"He will be strong enough," Broichan said. "Since first he came to me at Pitnochie, every moment of his life has been bent toward this end. The raw material was good; fourteen years of rigorous preparation have made it perfect. He will not fail us."

Fola gave a little cough; the four men turned as one to look at her where she sat, tranquil and still in her soft gray robes.

"You wish to express a reservation?" Broichan's voice held a slight edge now.

"To make a comment, merely. It is a heavy weight of expectation to lie on such young shoulders. I, too, hold high hopes for Bridei. It seems to me he walks with the breath of the gods at his back. I remind you simply that we should not forget the cost of this in our haste to congratulate ourselves."

"Cost?" echoed Broichan. "What do you mean?"

"That perhaps this might not have been his choice, had choice been open to him. That the life of a king is anything but easy. It is a lonely path, as Uist once told us; a path of impossible choices, of constant pressure. Bridei will accept it; there is no doubt in my mind that the gods whisper in his ear. We should not expect that this will fill him with gladness."

"Give me your honest opinion, Broichan," Talorgen said. "Yours too, Aniel. You've both been close to the king in recent times; you've had a good opportunity to assess the situation. To put it bluntly, how long does he have? They're speaking of Gateway, more than a full season ahead. Gods willing, Drust will be with us to enact that dark ritual once more; it will indeed seem strange when we see another man kneel by the Well of Shades. Now tell me. Will Drust survive another winter?"

Aniel glanced at Broichan; Broichan gazed steadily back, dark eyes unreadable.

"It would be almost a mercy," Aniel said quietly, "if he did not. To hear him straining for breath in the cold winter air is to hear purest pain made sound. If Bone Mother is merciful she will gather him to her breast by solstice time."

"I see," Talorgen said. "Then we must busy ourselves, my friends. When birds of prey sense a weakening of their quarry, they ready themselves to swoop, talons extended. We must protect both the old king and the new. We must see the mantle passed on, in spirit at least; the flame kept alight through times of darkness."

"Very poetic," Uist observed, "if somewhat muddled. Fola, I will walk back with you to Banmerren. It's a long path for a woman on her own. Not that I constitute much of a protector; still, one look at me and folk tend to run off quite quickly lest I take it into my head to transform them into geese or swine. Once I return you safely to your women's fortress, I'm thinking of wandering off in the direction of Circinn. We need a little intelligence from those parts. If what you say is true, and the gods do indeed intend to take Drust from us in the space of a season or two, I doubt very much that his namesake in the south will allow the succession to go our way unchallenged. With luck a wandering druid who seems somewhat addled in his wits can pass unsuspected. I'll report back in due course."

"Be careful," Aniel warned. "You may believe the robe of your calling protects you, but they've no love for the old faith in the lands of Drust the Boar. No love and no respect. You'd best visit only the more isolated settlements; stay well away from his court. The king of Circinn may treat you with some civility, but his advisers are weasels, ruthless and cunning."

"Come, Fola," Uist said, ignoring the warning. "A walk by the sea will do our old bones good. Let us leave these devious men to their own devices and enjoy the song of the waves and the gulls awhile. Unless you are too dignified to be seen in the company of a crazy old man like me?"

"I can bear it, I think," said Fola, rising to her feet. "Broichan, you haven't asked after your other foster child."

Broichan stared at her blankly; it was clear she had achieved the unlikely feat of catching him off guard. "You mean Tuala," he said after a moment. "How is she?" The tone was devoid of inflection.

"Doing very well. She's cooperative, demonstrates remarkable skill, and applies herself diligently."

"I'm pleased to hear it." Broichan spoke as if this bored him; it was plain that he responded at all only out of basic courtesy, and because others were present.

"She's also deeply unhappy, profoundly lonely, and desperately homesick."

There was a pause.

"Not uncommon, I suppose, in your new arrivals," Broichan said. "I'm sure you deal with it as capably as you do with everything else. Tuala had the opportunity of a good marriage. Very foolishly, she chose to let that go. Considering what she is, she should be on her knees thanking you for your kindness."

"Marriage," Fola mused. "She would have been—what—twelve, thirteen at the time?"

There was an undercurrent in the chamber now; Aniel and Talorgen, gathering cloaks in readiness to depart, were making pretense that this was of no interest to them. Uist listened unabashed, eyes bright and curious as a raven's.

"Old enough," Broichan said. "Girls are commonly wed at such an age, are they not? Why are we talking about this, Fola? We have an agreement. The girl's happiness, or lack of it, was never a part of that. This is unimportant. Irrelevant. And I must go; if I linger here my absence may be noted." He swept past her, dark robe flying out behind him, pushed open the oak door and was gone.

"Hmm," Aniel said. "You have an art possessed by no one else in all of Fortriu, Fola. The only times I ever see that man let his control slip, it's in your presence. Who is this girl? Broichan never mentioned a second foster child. Is this of any import, or do you speak merely to vex him?"

"You heard what he said. He is the master of this plan and, in his mind, the girl is of no consequence at all. Are you ready, Uist? Come then, let us slip out the back way; with your abilities and mine, I expect we may go entirely unnoticed. Farewell, Aniel, Talorgen. I will not return here until Gateway. Send a message if there's an urgent need for me before that time. Otherwise, I expect I will occupy myself well enough with my unimportant students."

"I HAVE A misgiving," Aniel said to the chieftain of Raven's Well as they strolled along the upper wall-walk at Caer

Pridne, stopping here and there to gaze northward over the sea as if they had merely taken it into their heads to go out for some fresh air. "I want you to tell me if you share it."

Talorgen waited, eyes fixed on the horizon beyond which lay the Light Isles, home to puffins, seals, and a king whose kinsmen might well have a claim to Fortriu themselves, should they be so bold as to declare it. There were plenty of sons of the royal blood to choose from: almost too many, this time. There was only one on whom the gods smiled.

"It concerns this poisoning. A man died in your own hall. But for a lucky chance, it would have been Bridei. The way you tell it, the only folk there present were your own, Ged's, Morleo's—men we trust, men their chieftains have vouched for personally. Your own household, all carefully checked. My bodyguards. A handful of Broichan's fellows, who have proven loyal since Bridei was not much more than an infant. Nobody could have breached your security; that's what you told me, and I've no cause to disbelieve you. So, this attack was carried out by one or more of our own; within the ranks of our trusted men, there is a traitor."

"My own thoughts exactly."

"Now that Bridei has distinguished himself on the field of battle, we must expect that there will be gossip and conjecture. Folk know that he is Maelchon's son. It is a long time since Anfreda wed the king of Gwynedd and rode off to make her new life far away from Fortriu. But there will be those who remember; before long, everyone at court will realize Bridei has a right to stand as a candidate for kingship."

"You are saying this attempt on his life will almost certainly be followed by another?"

"I think it very likely," Talorgen said, "and so, I imagine, does Broichan. We walk a narrow path, my friend. On the one hand, this young man must be seen to shine. He must work to impress and convince the powerful men at Caer Pridne that he is the best candidate for Fortriu. On the other, the more his strengths become apparent, the harder our enemies will be working to remove him from contention. We must be vigilant."

"You still have no idea who perpetrated this attack that claimed Donal's life?"

"None at all. I've interrogated every man who was present, checked the arrangements five times over, had a herbalist try to identify the substance that was used, all to no avail. One further thing we know about our adversary: he's clever."

"Talorgen?" The king's councillor spoke now in a whisper.

"Mm?"

"I do not wish to believe it; I shrink from the possibility. But I will ask you. Is it possible that, even within our very small circle, one is not what he seems? After so long, can I have been mistaken in trusting those I judged to be entirely true to our cause?"

Talorgen was silent for a little. "That would be a risky game indeed," he said, jaw tight. "Such a traitor, uncovered, would do well to shake in his boots. There are powers among us, the five of us, that could bring the strongest man down. Who would choose to make an enemy of Broichan? I will not entertain this notion, friend. We must pray; we must entreat the Flamekeeper to protect the lad for long enough."

"And we must enlist what earthly help is available to back him up. Engaging the services of the king's assassin should be a good start."

"THERE'S A CHILD," Fola said to her old friend Uist. They were traversing the flat, pale beach that curved around the bay between the fortress promontory of Caer Pridne and the wooded headland of Banmerren. The tide was low; Uist had taken off his sandals and was digging bare feet with pleasure into the fine wet sand. Beside them, the druid's white mare walked quietly, making her own way without need for halter or bridle. Fola bent to pick up a shell; its delicate rosy exterior had broken to reveal chamber on chamber in perfect spiral. A tiny, mysterious creature of the deep had once made its secret lodging here. "Not a child, a young woman. Coming up to fourteen years old, by my count. She concerns me."

"This is the girl you mentioned, who made our friend's eyes go distant and his mouth tighten? I do recall the old scholar, Wid, mentioning a second student; he was deliberately vague about the matter. Who is she?"

"I suppose it is no longer a secret. She's a child of the Good Folk; Broichan has had her in his house from infancy, since Bridei was very young. They grew up together."

Uist gave a low whistle. He halted in his tracks, looking down as his feet sank into the sand, water welling up around them to soak the hem of his ragged white robe. "Broichan's kept that very quiet," he said.

"I think he hoped it would just go away."

"Hasn't it? Hasn't she? I gather you have the girl now; that removes her conveniently both from Pitnochie and from Caer Pridne. I'm assuming the problem was an attachment between these two children, one of whom was deemed unsuitable as a friend for the other? Why did Broichan keep her at all? A man with his foresight must have realized how dangerous that choice was."

"He kept her because he respects the gods," Fola said. "He must always put their will before his own, even though his commitment to the plan consumes his whole life. And he kept her because Bridei wanted it thus. Broichan loves the boy like a son. Love . . . it complicates our games, old friend, it insinuates itself, disrupting the most carefully laid plans and unmanning the most disciplined heart. I'd like you to meet this girl and give me your opinion, not as a man, but as a servant of the Shining One. I never thought I would say this, but I'm beginning to wonder if our council is in danger of losing its way, thanks to Broichan's fierce dedication to our cause. I don't want to believe his zeal has made him blind to the goddess's will. This child—this young woman is desperate to go home to Pitnochie, even though she realizes she is no longer welcome there. Something calls her, something bigger than herself. I see what is in her heart and it looks to me disturbingly like truth. She turns her strange eyes on me and I see the Shining One looking out."

"You intrigue me," Uist said. "And you alarm me. As I am coming to visit Banmerren anyway, I will engage this young person in conversation, I think. It will be a welcome diversion from my major purpose in your establishment. How is the other girl progressing?"

Fola's expression darkened. "The preparation has been thorough; Morna will be ready by Gateway. It is difficult, as always; difficult for all of us."

"There are preparations you can use," Uist said gravely. "I suppose you know them. Herbs that can deepen her trance. Infusions that will purify the body and enable her to detach herself more effectively from this world and enter the other more easily."

"We know of some; we try to delay their use until closer to the time of the ritual. It depends on each girl. Some are strong in themselves and will go ahead without the need for such aids. Some hear the voice of the gods and walk the path willingly. To alter the mind or the body with herbs and potions too early may lessen the effectiveness of such aids at the end; that would be cruel indeed. I have not yet seen a candidate who took that final step without at least some fear."

"Ah, well, I will spend some time with your chosen one," Uist said. "I will give her what counsel I can. But it's the other girl who really intrigues me. I've never met a child of the Good Folk in the flesh. Is she of unearthly beauty, like the women in the tales?"

Fola grinned. "You're too old to be asking such a question," she said. "Tuala is herself. No more need be said."

IT HAD BEEN Bridei's intention to confront his foster father as soon as he reached Caer Pridne and to demand a full explanation of a number of matters: Donal's death, Tuala's betrayal of their childhood friendship, Broichan's own choice to wait so long, withholding the truth about his plans until far past the time when Bridei had recognized their nature. Then there was the need to be guarded and protected like a vulnerable child even now, when he bore his warrior marks. Staying close to him had killed Donal. Who would be next, Breth of the strong shoulders and keen eye? Garth with his deceptively sweet smile and powerful sword arm? It was time Broichan began to treat Bridei like the man he was, and to trust him with the truth.

In the event the king's druid pre-empted his foster son's demands. They met in Broichan's own quarters within the fortress walls, where Bridei, too, would be lodged with his two bodyguards while he remained at court. He was weary after the ride up from Pitnochie; he had seen Snowfire settled in the king's stables, snatched a bite to eat with his guards, then sought out his foster father. Breth and Garth were unpacking their gear in the sleeping chamber. Bridei found Broichan in a customary pose, standing before a cold hearth, apparently deep in thought. The chamber had been set out much like the druid's private quarters at Pitnochie; the tools of his trade lay on shelves or hung from rafters, his scrolls and writing materials were neatly stowed. A shelf at the far end with a folded blanket laid across it appeared to be Broichan's own somewhat unforgiving sleeping arrangement. Bridei found himself hoping there would be straw mattresses, at least, in the other chamber; his nights had been much troubled by dreams, and the headache never quite went away now.

"My lord?"

"Bridei. Welcome home, son."

It became possible, then, to stride forward and offer a quick, firm embrace; to feel how thin his foster father had become under the concealment of the black robe. Bridei stepped back, observing new lines on the druid's face, new threads of gray in the dark plaited hair. "You are well, I trust?"

"Well enough, Bridei. I find life at court pleases me less than it once did. I would not speak thus before King Drust, of course. He needs me; I serve him. The gods require no less. You're looking tired. There have been losses; I am sorry. Talorgen told me the messenger I sent never reached you with the news about Erip. I also . . . never mind that. The old man passed peacefully; it was a good death in the end. He was surrounded by friends."

"Donal did not die peacefully. He perished in my place. I

put the cup in his hand myself." By effort of will, Bridei kept his voice from shaking.

"Sit down, son. We have some talking to do. You know this is not the first attempt on your life, or on mine. A new enemy now, I think, but the motive is the same. You've no need to ask me why someone's trying to remove you, I imagine."

Bridei was silent.

"Tell me."

"Is it not for you to tell me, my lord?"

Broichan sighed and came to seat himself opposite Bridei, the work table between them. "I think we can dispense with 'my lord' now that we are two men together," he said quietly. "Call me by my name, if you will. Now tell me. You are a hero, they say: the man who devised and executed the bold and ingenious plan to snatch the Mage Stone from under the enemy's nose. Talorgen also tells me you acquitted yourself extremely well in the battle and behaved with coolness and maturity in the aftermath. I suspect, from his tone, that he wishes you were his own son. So, you do better than anyone would have expected, you win allies and friends, you offend nobody. Your tale sweeps up the Glen before you, a legend in the making. The Flamekeeper smiles on you. And still someone tries to kill you. Why?"

"You know why. Because I am my mother's son."

"Ah!" Broichan leaned back, hands behind his head. "How long since you worked this out for yourself?"

"A long time since I first suspected. Wid and Erip avoided it carefully in all those long lessons in genealogy. The way they skirted around the question of my own ancestry alerted me to its possible significance. I could not remember her name; to a small child his mother is simply that, Mother. In the end I asked Ferada, and learned that my mother is indeed related to the king through the female line. Others have a closer relationship, that of direct cousins. Carnach of Thorn Bend is one such, the lady Dreseida another. I hope Drust the Bull is not lost to us too soon. But if that should occur, this means I am one of those who could be put forward as a claimant for kingship. I imagine it is for this that I have been prepared."

"Why didn't you challenge me sooner with this, Bridei?"

"If I'd been wrong, to suggest it would have been arrogant in the extreme. Presumptuous. I have no particular qualities that make me an obvious claimant."

Broichan smiled. "Save that you are both Maelchon's son and a son of the royal blood of the Priteni," he said. "Combine that with the preparation we have given you and the result is a man every bit a king in the making. Your mother would be proud of you."

Something in his tone caught Bridei's attention. "You knew her, didn't you?" he asked. "My mother?"

"Oh, yes."

He had not mistaken it, that softening of the voice, that little change in the impenetrable dark eyes. "Tell me. I have no memory of her at all."

"Anfreda was—exceptional. Wise, merry, a slip of a thing with hair glossy as a ripe chestnut and a smile to stop a man's heart. She did, indeed, break many hearts when she chose to wed Maelchon and make her life away from Fortriu. He was a sound man, but driven; it seemed to me . . . never mind that. There is much of your mother in you, Bridei. Possibly of Maelchon as well; he was a leader."

Bridei would not ask, *Was your heart one of those she broke when she went away?* Broichan was surely above such human weakness. "It will be soon, won't it?" he asked quietly. "They say the king is quite sick; that he may not last the winter."

"Indeed. We've a great deal to do and little time to achieve it. You'll meet Drust tomorrow; your claim cannot be made until he is gone and the formal process begins, but the candidates will begin to show their hands from now on. We expect a delegation from Circinn, and that is probably our most serious threat. The others, we'll work on. Some can be bought with silver or incentives; some can be persuaded by other means to throw their lot in with yours rather than become rival claimants. Apart from you, there are two other possibilities from the house of Fortrenn, the more likely of whom is Carnach. It's far better if the north puts up only one strong candidate. If the chieftains of Fortriu are divided amongst themselves, there's no hope of defeating Drust the Boar, who is likely to have the support of all the voting chieftains of the southern regions."

"What of the Light Isles?"

"They have two or three men of the blood, but I suspect the Folk will stay out of the contest this time. We have a royal hostage here; they'll have her safety in mind. Drust showed excellent foresight in retaining the girl when she accompanied her kinsmen here on a visit a few years ago. You'll meet her; she's back at court."

"Do you believe this assassin was in the employ of Circinn? That Drust the Boar seeks to extend his reach over both Circinn and Fortriu?"

Broichan shook his head. "The latter, most certainly; no king worth his salt would pass up the opportunity, and the Boar is surrounded by ambitious advisers. But assassination? I think not. He has a strong enough claim without resorting to that, and he does not know you. I doubt that he would see you as a serious rival. Yet."

"Then who—?"

"We don't know. That means you must comply with my wishes where your personal freedom is concerned, Bridei. I know you don't like it; that even Donal's presence sometimes irked you, friend as he was. You must have Breth or Garth close by at all times. You must use a taster. And there'll be another man as well. I've summoned him to meet you; he'll be here shortly."

"I don't need another bodyguard."

"It is agreed among those with your best interests at heart that you do."

Bridei opened his mouth to argue, then thought better of it. There was a pressing question that he must ask now, before this other guard, whoever he was, came to disturb their privacy. 'Tuala was gone when I reached Pitnochie," he said, finding it difficult suddenly to meet Broichan's eye for fear of what he might read there. "They told me she had gone to the house of the wise women at Banmerren. Gone away to become a servant of the Shining One."

Broichan folded his long hands before him. "That is correct," he said. "She was appropriately supplied and safely escorted."

"Once before you sent her away," Bridei said, working to keep his voice under control. "Once before you didn't want her at Pitnochie because she'd be an embarrassment to you. Did you send her away this time? Did you make her go?"

Broichan regarded him in silence, pale features calm, dark eyes devoid of emotion. "No, Bridei," he said eventually. "It was Tuala's choice to go to Banmerren. Fola offered her a place; Tuala accepted the opportunity. The situation is highly suitable for her."

Cold crept through Bridei's body. In his foster father's words was the unmistakable ring of truth. Tuala had done what he would never have believed possible. She had severed the bond between them as suddenly and completely as if she had died. "I see," he said unevenly.

"It is a high calling to become a servant of the Shining One," Broichan observed. "The old men were effusive in their praise of the child's talents as a scholar. For all her difference, I expect she will be quite at home in Fola's establishment."

Home, thought Bridei. How could home be anywhere but Pitnochie? "I expect so," he made himself say, and at that moment there was a little sound from the doorway. Broichan was looking past him to someone who stood there. Bridei rose to his feet, turned, froze for an instant. Then Donal's training asserted itself. Seizing his knife, he hurled himself across the chamber. In the moment it took, a dagger appeared in the other man's hand and a little smile on his face, a face Bridei had seen before and had not forgotten.

"Stop!"

Bridei halted in his tracks, knife two handspans from the other's raised blade. The fellow's look of amusement turned to irritation, then alarm. Broichan did not often make use of magic; when he did employ it, one was reminded just why he had become the king's druid, held in both fear and respect across both Fortriu and Circinn. All he had done was lift his own hand a little and point his finger, the one that bore a silver ring in the form of a snake, at the two of them. Bridei waited, unable to move save for the rapid beating of his heart. He glared at the other man, who was held equally immobile by the druid's charm, and whose eyes stared back at him with inimical intensity.

"My apologies," Broichan said, sounding not a bit sorry. "Before you set upon one another, I need a little time to explain. You're early, Faolan. My foster son responds as a warrior must, seeing an enemy in a place where he does not belong. Bridei, contrary to appearances, this man is one of ours. Now I'm releasing this charm, and the two of you will put your weapons away and sit down while I explain this. Opposite sides of the table, and keep your mouths shut until I'm finished."

He clicked his fingers; the two men could move again. It took all Bridei's self-control not to leap forward in attack. "This man is a spy!" he protested. "He's a Gael! I know it, I captured him myself! But . . ." He fell silent. The man called Faolan had sheathed his knife, walked calmly across, and seated himself at the table. "He's supposed to be dead," Bridei said, hearing how foolish it sounded and wondering if he'd been right in his first misgivings about that day at Raven's Well. Perhaps the whole thing had been set up purely to allow him and Gartnait to achieve their little victory without any real risk. But no; one thing was clear enough. "He's a Gael," he said again. "I heard him speaking the tongue. Like a native. What is he doing here? I thought—"

"Didn't you hear me, Bridei?"

"I'm sorry, my lord. Broichan."

"Faolan is indeed a Gael by birth and upbringing. He is in King Drust's employ and has been for several years. What happened between you at Raven's Well was unfortunate. It must be forgotten, put behind you. Faolan works for us now. He will shadow you, protect you, seek out your enemies where Breth and Garth cannot go. He has an ear at every door, a foot in every camp. With him by your side there's a passable chance you will remain safe. If you do as he tells you."

Bridei found himself glaring across at the Gael, who was now examining his fingernails with a supercilious expression. "Why was he in the woods with a man whom Talorgen later had tortured to death? Why were they trying to escape us and speaking in that language? Why was I told he was dead?"

"I've a passable grasp of the tongue of the Priteni, and am not lacking in my wits," Faolan said, lifting his brows. "I think I might manage to speak for myself."

"Then account for yourself!" Bridei demanded.

"I was returning from a mission; I had a man to bring back, a man with information. He believed we were gathering facts about Talorgen's forces. It was my intention to lead him to a point where we would be taken. You happened to be on guard that day; it could have been anyone."

"You mean you were working for Talorgen even then?"

"For Drust. Talorgen knows me."

"I could have killed you!" Bridei was astounded, insulted, mortified.

"You overestimate your own skills if you believe that," Faolan said, sounding more than a little bored. "You did draw me to the public eye rather more than suited either myself or Talorgen. That reduced my effectiveness in the region of Raven's Well. Gabhran's advisers believe me to be their creature, or did; that made travel across Dalriada and access to the councils of the Gaels possible. Unfortunately the more men who know my face, even our own men, the less my effectiveness as a spy. Hence Drust's decision to bring me back to court to cool my heels awhile. I've you to thank for that, and for this." He rolled up the sleeve of his tunic to reveal an ugly scar across his upper arm. "It's as well I can still wield my weapons or you would have earned yourself a dangerous enemy."

"Forgive me," Bridei said politely, "but it seems to me I already have one."

"I bear no grudges," said Faolan. "As long as I'm regularly paid. But you're right. I'm told you do have an enemy. That's why I'm here."

Bridei turned to the druid. "Why did Talorgen lie to me?" he asked. "Why did he let me believe this man was dead?"

"You must ask him that yourself," Broichan said. "I imagine it suited him, and Faolan here, that as few people knew the truth as possible."

"But that meant—" Bridei bit back his words.

"If you felt any guilt for it, you were a fool," Faolan said bluntly. "Start sympathizing with your enemy and you've lost the battle before you begin to fight. It's as well you hired me, my lord."

"Yes," Broichan said. "Your lack of scruples is as well known as your skills and your discretion. We need you. Bridei, you must accept this."

"What's he to do?"

"Faolan is his own man. One hires him on the understanding that he will carry out the required work according to his own rules. It's been explained to him why you must be protected and the probable nature of those who seek to harm you. He will explain to you what is required."

"So he's to stay in these quarters? To follow me about everywhere, despite Garth and Breth doing a perfectly good job? Despite the fact that I am no longer a little child who needs a watchdog to keep away the shadows?"

Broichan twisted the silver ring around on his finger. "Would you dismiss Donal as a mere watchdog?" he asked quietly.

Alarmingly, Bridei felt sudden tears well in his eyes; it seemed the little child was not so far below the surface, for all the warrior marks. "Donal was my friend."

Neither Broichan nor the Gael responded. It must be plain to both of them, Bridei thought, that Faolan could never in a lifetime become anyone's friend.

"I have skills," Faolan said. "I can protect you. It's not a requirement that we like each other."

"Forgive me," said Bridei, "but I wonder what credibility you can have here at court, a man of Dalriada in the very heartland of Fortriu. True, your appearance does not immediately suggest your origins, but folk must surely question why a man who goes armed as a warrior bears no battle counts on his face. And as soon as you open your mouth, the accent must give you away." He glanced at Broichan. "You say this man can go where Breth and Garth cannot; that he has a foot in every camp. How can that be so, when it must soon become plain that he is a Gael?"

Faolan gave a thin smile. "What?" he said in mocking

tones. "The king of Fortriu trusts me and you will not? I've plied my trade for a long time, Bridei. I'm expert in all facets of it. One of those is the ability to make oneself invis-ible; to blend into any setting, be it here among the Priteni or in the halls of King Gabhran of Dalriada. In every place I have a different name, a different guise. Each is instantly forgettable. The accent varies; today, I saw no need to change it. As for Caer Pridne, the king has made it clear I am here under his protection, Gael or no. I'm known to his inner circle. If awkward visitors arrive at any time, I simply make sure they do not see me. Oh, and a small correction. I am not a man of Dalriada. I work for a fee. My allegiance lasts as long as the mission."

"I see." Bridei found that less than reassuring. It was tan-tamount to saying one was prepared to change sides for a heavier bag of silver.

"Now," said Faolan, "will you take me to have a word with these two guards of yours? I'll need to start by checking your quarters and making some general arrangements."

"Follow me," Bridei said, struggling for courtesy. It was evident there was going to be no choice in this.

"Bridei." Broichan spoke behind him. "This is what it means, the path we have taken. This is what it is for Drust, and what it will be for you. Walk the path and you accept what comes with it: protectors, advisers, men who greet you with slavish adulation, others who will not hesitate to plunge a knife in your back. Believe me, a man such as Faolan is a good companion on such a journey. He has proven himself a hundred times over."

Tuala, Bridei thought. Tuala gone forever; Tuala shut away behind high walls. Tuala in a place where men were forbidden to tread. Tuala choosing to leave him behind. If not for that news, he might have dealt with things in a con-trolled manner and not given this Gael the impression that he was a petulant child. As Faolan strode into the sleeping quarters, and as it became evident that Breth and Garth ac-cepted without any qualms that he would be in charge from now on, Bridei stood silent in the doorway, his fingers on the narrow band of ribbon he wore around his wrist. As he touched its familiar softness, the fraying ends finally gave way and the short length of braid fell into his hand. Perhaps it was a sign. Even if she had not chosen to leave him, even if she had stayed by his side, what sort of life would this be for her, for a child whose whole being was attuned to oak and birch and rowan, to owl and otter and deer, to the glimmering waters of Serpent Lake and the high, lonely peak of Eagle Scar? What joys could life at court hold for a girl who loved tales and dreams and silences? Surrounded by guards and courtiers, by assassins and plotters, how long would his forest flower survive? To expect her to stand by him, knowing, as he suspected she had long done, where his future would lead him, was to ask her to wither and die in the name of a promise made between children. He must let her go. He must walk on alone. That was what the gods demanded.

12

"WEAR THE GREEN," Dreseida said. "And dress your hair more softly; you can't afford to look too regal, none of the men will dare come near you."

"Why would that bother me?" snapped her daughter, who was rummaging through a little chest, discarding one item of jewelry after another.

"Don't be foolish, Ferada. You know why you're at Caer Pridne. You understand the importance of tonight's gathering, and indeed of every such occasion at court. You're sixteen now; leave it much longer and the likely prospects will start overlooking you in favor of something younger and fresher. I want you to talk to Bridei tonight."

"I expect I will, given that he's Gartnait's friend."

"Don't be obtuse. You know what I mean. Talk to him; charm him; encourage him to confide in you. Broichan's up to something, and I want to know what it is."

"Bridei's not stupid, Mother. He'll see through that the moment I start. When I talked to him at Raven's Well, it was always about history or politics or other scholarly matters. That, I'll gladly do. It will make a welcome change from the others' roaming eyes and stumbling efforts to make intelligent conversation."

"Ferada."

Ferada became still, a pair of silver earrings shaped like dolphins held halfway to her ears. There was a certain tone her mother used on occasion, a tone that required instant obedience. "Yes, Mother?" Her heart was thumping.

"You will do as I instruct you. I need this information. Do you comprehend what I am saying to you?"

"Yes, Mother."

"Talk to him. Sweetly. Exert a little charm. Mention Broichan. I want to know what the two of them will be doing between now and the winter: where they'll be traveling, who they'll be seeing. Watch Bridei's eyes when you ask him."

"Mother, I—"

"It's not like you to be inattentive, Ferada. You must know that failure to comply with my wishes is a failure to obey the will of the gods. That can only limit your own choices sorely in the future. There's an election for kingship coming. It's a chance to exert some influence; to play a part in the way the future unfolds. As women, we are rarely presented with such opportunities. I seek to exploit this to the full, and for that I need knowledge. I can hardly accost either Broichan or his foster son myself. I require you to act for me. I'll be watching you closely, and I'll expect to see progress."

"This is like—it is like being a commodity for hire," Ferada said bitterly, unable to contain her words. "As if I have no value of my own. I am your daughter, not a tool."

"You're a woman," Dreseida said drily. "Play the game well from the beginning, and your time will come to wield some power. This is only the first step."

"It's not my game." Ferada's voice was shaking. "It is all your own, and hardly to my taste. I wish I had stayed at Banmerren."

"But you'll do as I say. To attempt defiance would not be at all wise. Don't forget that the choice of a husband for you lies entirely in my hands. Your father will comply with my wishes. Be an obedient daughter and I may allow you some freedom in that."

"I assume it is not Bridei you have in mind. You've never liked him much."

Dreseida gave a mirthless laugh. "Didn't you once say you found him humorless? Let us bide our time awhile. Caer Pridne will be full of chieftains by Midwinter. You'll be spoiled for choice, if you're good."

TUALA COULD SEE the torches from all the way around the bay, a double line of them flaring in the half-dark of the summer night, marking the road along the promontory to the gates of the king's fortress. More were set on the triple rampart of Caer Pridne itself. Drust's stronghold danced with light like a palace in an ancient tale. A celebration; the old druid, Uist, had spoken of it, and Fola had confirmed it. This would be a victory feast, a recognition of bravery and triumph. Bridei would be there. Tuala knew he had returned and was safe, for Uist had volunteered this information without being asked. She had thanked him for the news with what she hoped was perfect calm. It was becoming ever clearer that she was to play no part in Bridei's future; that her friendship would only hold him back. Better, then, to make pretense that this did not matter to her. Perhaps, if she kept reminding herself how lucky she was to be at Banmerren, how suited she was to a life of scholarship and dedication to the gods, she would end up actually believing it.

Uist had brought both good news and bad news. Wid was well and had retreated to the nemetons to spend time in prayer and contemplation. Tuala hoped he was not missing Ferat's cooking too much. When Uist delivered the bad news her control almost snapped. Donal was dead; Bridei's stalwart companion, a friend to all at Pitnochie, herself included, poisoned at what should have been a time of joyful celebration. Her belly knotted with the thought of it. This was her own vision made reality, yet turned upside down: the awful thing that had made her run through the forest like a frightened deer and beg Broichan to help her. So slight a change in the fabric of events, the casual passing of a cup of ale from one man to another, and Bridei's life had been spared, but his closest friend had paid the price of it with his own. She knew how Bridei would be feeling: guilty, sad, weighed down by the burden of it all. If only she could be with him . . . He was at Caer Pridne now, just along the bay, so close, and yet it might be another land. It was forbidden for Bridei, or any other man save a druid, to visit her here. She'd thanked Uist politely for the news, and kept her expression calm.

That was last night. Tonight was different. She had made herself as busy as she could all day. With the noble daughters gone to court, Derila had divided her class in two and Tuala herself now acted as tutor to the younger ones, girls close to her own age. It was a trial; they resented her elevation to teacher, her youth, her pale skin and strange eyes. Her difference. At the same time that difference fascinated them. They liked the things she could do. With some reluctance she had shown them the tricks of movement, the plays with light, the small transformations she had been performing, almost without thinking, out in the forest since she was a little child. They liked being told how to listen to the thoughts of a squirrel or an owl or a wren; they liked the tales that could be heard in the heart of an ancient oak. Tuala showed them just enough to keep them interested. The history part of the lesson was done eagerly as they awaited the reward of those secrets she chose to share. They did not sit by her at supper; that had not changed. But they no longer laughed at her.

The long day over, now she sat in the tree and gazed along the shore to Caer Pridne. Some of the torches were moving; perhaps a procession wound its way up that long road to progress in stately formation into the grand hall of Drust the Bull. They said the entry was imposing in design. There were carven stones there, sixteen of them in pairs; it was some of the finest work in Fortriu, Erip had told her. Any man or woman approaching Drust's court would be greeted by this monumental statement of control. Tuala could not hear anything; the fortress was too far away for that. Perhaps there would be horns sounding, maybe drums and singing.

For certain there would be tales. The lifting of the Mage Stone was a story to rival any for heroism and ingenuity. That, too, had truly come to pass; Fola had told them so. At last Bridei had begun to come into his own.

Tuala shivered. Even summer nights could be cold at Banmerren when the wind blew from the sea. She must go in; it was foolish to be up here on her own after dark. The moon was waning, and it would be easy to slip and fall from her high perch. But maybe she wouldn't fall. Maybe she would fly. As a child, she had always dreamed that she could fly.

She took a long last look toward the fortress; observed the flat expanse of wet sand, its surface shining with reflected torchlight at the other end. It was not so very far. For a child who had grown up running wild in the hills above Pitnochie, it would be an easy walk. On a good day, a person could be there and back almost before anyone noticed. The only thing was, there was no going out, not for her or for any of those who wore the blue. The noble daughters had freedom to move between school and court at certain times and to go out for their rides; the others ventured forth only when they must. There was an occasional walk to gather herbs under the strict supervision of Luthana, who oversaw the work of garden and stillroom. At Gateway the wise women would travel to Caer Pridne for a solemn ceremony; asked just what this entailed, Kethra had been less than forthcoming. One ritual for the men, conducted by the king's druid; another for the women, held at the same time and led by Fola. The seniors would attend along with those who wore the gray robe. The rest of them must wait until they had earned the green.

Tuala would have liked to test her theory tonight; to launch herself from atop the outer wall and see if she fell to the earth below, broken, shattered, or soared through the darkness like an owl until she alighted on the ramparts at Caer Pridne, ready to look in on a king's feast. Instead, she climbed back across the wall and returned to her tower room. She must be strong. She must think of Bridei and not of herself. It was perfectly true: she *was* lucky. She could be what Fola wanted her to be, it would simply take time. Others would be there to listen to Bridei's fears, share his dreams, stand by his side in a way she never could, because of what she was. In time he would learn to trust those others. Ana, for instance. He would see Ana at the feast tonight, and Ferada. He would talk to them, his blue eyes bright and intense as he gave an explanation, his hands moving in illustration; Ana would answer in her sweet, grave way and Bridei would bend his head courteously to hear her . . . Tuala buried her face in the pillow, squeezed her eyes tight shut and pulled the blanket up over her head. She had abandoned the scrying bowl lest it torment her with such images. But they had a life of their own. They made their cruel way even into her dreams.

"SHE HAS BEGUN to doubt what was once crystal clear in her mind," observed the silver-haired presence that remained in the tree, perched on a high branch, invisible to humankind. "There is a lost look in her eyes."

"She does not doubt the love of the Shining One," said her companion. "That, surely, must sustain her in this time of loneliness."

"It may be all too strong. Stronger than her attachment to Bridei; stronger than the voice of her heart and the call toward the long task she must undertake."

"It is the Shining One who calls her to that task; it was the goddess herself who brought this child into being," said the vine-clad young man, "and who sent us to lay her on Broichan's doorstep. If Tuala chooses to stay at Banmerren, she defies the intentions of our Great Mother."

"To become a priestess is an act of obedience to the goddess's will. Thus it must seem to all who know Tuala in the human realm, Bridei included. How is the girl to know the Shining One has decreed another path for her?"

"She has little choice, indeed. She can hardly climb over the wall and make her way to Caer Pridne. She will always act in the way she believes is best for Bridei. Even if that means cutting herself off from him."

"Ah, well," said the girl, running a careless hand through her glittering locks, "she is still a child in many ways, a child who has been banished from home. I think we must make the test more difficult."

"Difficult for whom?" the boy asked.

"For Bridei. Tuala is despondent; downcast. She is surely more ready now to consider that other choice, the choice that lies not merely outside the house of wise women, but entirely beyond the world of humankind. We'll tempt her away. We'll coax her to the very brink. We'll call her in a way she cannot but answer: through the blood we share."

"What if she follows all the way? What if she crosses the margin and finds there is no returning?"

"She will not."

The vine-clad boy shivered. "You are all confidence," he said. "There is much to be lost here."

The girl nodded, luminous eyes suddenly grave. "Fortriu must have its true leader," she said, "the only one who can unite the realms of the Priteni in loyalty to the ancient gods and in due acknowledgment of the elder races of the land, our own especially. The new order in the south runs rampant, walking with heavy feet on the sacred places, dislodging druid and wise woman, burning and breaking the homes of the wild folk of the forest. The goddess needs Bridei."

"And Bridei needs Tuala."

"What I plan will ensure both are ready for what awaits them."

"You sound very certain. There are the vagaries of the human kind yet to consider; their ill-considered scheming and petty power games have the capacity to play havoc with the best laid plans."

"True, Bridei has more trials to endure, both those of the human world and those the gods prepare for him to ensure he is worthy of their trust. I have confidence in him. The true light of the Flamekeeper burns in his spirit. But he has a long path to walk still before anything is sure. There are shadows on his way, and not all of them are of our making."

CAER PRIDNE WAS ablaze with light. Torches flared along the wall-walks, illuminating the fine work on the bull stones, the creature on each incised with delicacy yet captured in all its muscular strength and virility. Drust's great hall stood high on the promontory, encircled by Caer Pridne's upper rampart. The fortress had three levels, each with its own protective wall of stone laced with timber. Triple mounds and ditches provided additional barriers to attack. Within the walls worked and lived a whole community dedicated to the upkeep of the king's court and the support of his household. On the westward side, between stone breakwaters, there was sheltered mooring for boats. Steps led up to an iron gate. To landward was the road, a broad way of hard-packed earth, tonight edged in flame from brands set on tall poles to either side. Men marched or rode in to be greeted by a formidable presence of guards before the double gates that barred entry to the walled fortress itself. Drust was both powerful and careful. He had been elected king at a time when feeling ran high among the chieftains of the Priteni, and the assembly of nobles had been divided over the succession. The south, increasingly influenced by Christian teaching, had wanted Drust son of Girom, known as the Boar, a man who himself followed this new faith and could be relied upon to encourage the missionaries desirous of spreading it. The north had fallen in behind the much older Drust son of Wdrost, steeped in the ancient ways and dedicated to the protection of Fortriu's borders. Broichan had supported Drust the Bull; how could he not? Drust the Boar, in his turn, had had strong and outspoken adherents. So the assembly had been split. A casting vote, that of the wise woman Fola, had been disallowed by the chieftains of Circinn as invalid, since such a participant might seek the use of pagan magic to bend men's minds to her will. After a time of uproar and chaos, a bitter compromise had been reached. Always, before, a single king had ruled the lands of the Priteni from the Great Glen south to the Roman wall. A lesser king in the Light Isles had been subject to this monarch's rule. The Caitt, of course, were a law unto themselves. Nonetheless, the territories had belonged together; when it counted, they had worked in unity. After that divisive assembly, the land of the Priteni had been split into two kingdoms, Fortriu to be ruled by Drust the Bull and the southern realm of Circinn by Drust the Boar. It was an open secret that each of them had agreed to this with the full intention of claiming the whole territory the moment the other died. No wonder there were so many guards at Caer Pridne now.

Bridei walked into the hall, Breth and Garth a discreet step behind him. He had begun to notice, now that he was obliged to be shadowed thus whenever he ventured forth, that there were more than a few other men who carried a similar protective presence. Not Broichan; he had always walked alone. But Aniel, the king's councillor, had acquired a new bodyguard who could be seen standing close by the elegant, gray-haired nobleman now and trying to look as if he were not there. Others about the hall bore that same expression, the look of men constantly on high alert, yet working at being unobtrusive. They were generally big men who wore rather plain garments and hovered on the margins of rooms. There were other kinds of protection, of course; King Drust had Broichan. The very presence of the king's druid should, one might suppose, be sufficient to deter most attackers. It was common knowledge that such men possessed immense power; that they could summon what forces they required to aid them. A druid might call on the Flamekeeper to make a man sweat and burn until he was consumed by fever; he might invoke the Shining One with a request for floods or freakish waves. None but another mage might dare to challenge such a man.

And yet, whatever people might choose to believe, Broichan was a mortal man and he was vulnerable. Bridei had never forgotten that night, long ago, when the news came that his foster father lay gravely ill from poison. He recalled his own desolation and Donal's kindness. Someone had been clever enough to get under the guard of the king's druid. Was that assailant the same who had pursued small Bridei through the forest with bow and sword? Nobody had ever said. Perhaps, even now, nobody knew, nobody but those who wished them ill, king's druid and foster son. It was becoming clear that Broichan had spoken truly: from this point on it would always be thus, each step to be guarded, each day to be lived in the awareness that enemies were ready to strike. If one such adversary were detected and removed, another would simply step up to take his place.

Drust the Bull . . . Bridei had long wondered how he

would seem. Perhaps the king would appear massive, strong and solid like the creature he had chosen as his token; perhaps he would be majestic and bright, as if he carried the light of the Flamekeeper within him. The king of Fortriu was, after all, in many ways the embodiment of this god; his special role in the rituals underlined it. Perhaps it would be disappointing. Maybe Drust would be an ailing slip of a man, a poor thing clinging to the last shreds of life and power. They did say he would be lucky to last the winter.

The hall was packed with men and women, some seated at the three long tables, others clustered in the spaces between. The air was alive with laughter and talk. From somewhere farther down, music could be heard above the din: a pipe, a drum, perhaps a harp. There was a smell of roast meat and spices and the place was very warm. Logs burned on a great hearth set at one side of the chamber; this vented cunningly through a structure of stone, keeping the hall relatively clear of smoke. The movement of folk there seemed to Bridei like a dance, or maybe a game, a very complicated game of strategy with several different sets of rules. Prepared well in advance by Broichan, he tried to identify certain men, influential men about whom warnings had been provided. The exceptionally tall fellow with copper-colored hair to his shoulders must be Carnach, a cousin of the king and a potential claimant. To be watched. The broad-shouldered man speaking to Talorgen was probably another claimant, Wredech of the house of Fidach. Talorgen possessed information about Wredech that might prove useful; he was to be cultivated, cautiously. Where were the king's councillors?

Bridei glanced to the far end of the hall, and there was King Drust, seated at a smaller table set crosswise to the others and raised on a dais. There were gray streaks in his dark hair and neat beard; his features were distinguished by a prow of a nose and heavy brows that overshadowed his eyes, eyes that were scanning the chamber even as he leaned sideways to listen to Broichan, who was seated by him. One could not assess a man so quickly, of course. But it seemed to Bridei that there was power in this king's little finger, authority in every blink of his eye. It was in the way he held himself, upright, regal, relaxed yet aware; it was in the steely intelligence of the dark eyes, the strong set of the jaw, the economy of the gestures. It was in the way Broichan listened to him, and in the tilt of the druid's head. If the king was indeed gravely ill, he showed it little. There was a line between the brows, a tightness to the mouth that might indicate the presence of pain suppressed by will: no more than that.

The crowd moved, passed, grouped, and regrouped. There were women in the hall; after the long time of preparation for war and the march to Galany's Reach and back, it seemed almost odd to see them. Lady Dreseida, clad in silver and black, was talking to a group of elegantly attired women, their hair caught up in elaborate structures of plaits and coils. Gartnait was with his sister, Ferada. She caught Bridei's eye and gave a nod, unsmiling; he returned the sober greeting. She was an odd girl, clever and prickly, with an anger in her that made her always combative. Interchanges with Ferada were generally interesting, but seldom relaxing. Gartnait, good company as he was for sport or combat practice, had a narrow scope of conversation. Ferada could hold her own on most topics; talking to her at Raven's Well had made a welcome change from the endless days of preparation for war. However, her company was not something he would seek out here. Ferada generally gave the impression that she was somehow mocking him; that, indeed, she held much of the world about her in contempt. That troubled Bridei, for it seemed to him there was only one world to live in, and that if it had flaws, one should not complain but take steps to change it.

"Talorgen's daughter." Aniel, the king's councillor, had come up beside Bridei, his bodyguard pausing to speak to Breth. "You'll know her, I suppose. The girl beside her is Ana, Drust's hostage from the Light Isles, a fine young woman. It's been arranged that the two of them spend time at Banmerren with some others, and the girl appreciates that, being a quiet, ladylike kind of creature. Remarkably pretty, too, don't you think?"

Coming from the reserved, cautious Aniel, this speech was somewhat of a surprise. Bridei took in Ana's grave look, her cream and rose complexion, her fall of shimmering golden hair. Sadness overtook him again; he could not put the image of Tuala from his mind, turning and turning on the top of Eagle Scar, her dark curls tossed like a banner in the wind. He had no words for a reply.

"Be sure to speak to these young women later," Aniel said, unperturbed. "It's appropriate that you do so. Another step you must take. See the thin, dark fellow to the right of the king? A dangerous man: Tharan, one of my fellow councillors. Extremely influential, and a fierce supporter of the candidate from the House of Fortrenn, who has a strong claim. It's a waste of time trying to change Tharan's mind. On his other side, Eogan, also a councillor, close to the king and possessing some flexibility of thought. An approach from you might have better luck than one from myself or Broichan; we are not universally admired. The small woman is Drust's wife, Rhian of Powys. She has been an excellent support to him, but is unlikely to seek a role once he is gone. Her brother, Owain; insignificant. Now, it seems we are to be seated; after the meal, the king will call certain men forward to receive his personal thanks. You will be one of them. Are you ready for that?"

"I think so, my lord."

"Good. I see someone's dressed you well; that's important, too. Rich but not too ostentatious. You'll develop your own style in time."

This could hardly be answered without giving offense. It was Faolan who had procured these garments, on Broichan's orders, and wearing them felt decidedly odd after so many days and nights of marching, climbing, eating, and sleeping in the same tunic, trousers, smallclothes, boots. The soft, fine wool, the silver-buckled belt and carefully draped cloak seemed alien to Bridei. He had washed both body and hair; warm water had been brought to their quarters for the purpose, with soap that smelled of rosemary. After that, his brown curls had dried to a wild, untameable frizz, and he had had to endure the humiliation of allowing Garth to work the strands into a neat plait at the back.

"It's a new world for you," Aniel murmured. "Learn quickly; you don't have long." Then he was gone; a place awaited him at the high table, near the king.

Bridei sat with Talorgen's family, Gartnait on his right, Ferada on his left, the alarming Lady Dreseida opposite. Garth was taster tonight; it had been impossible for Bridei to refuse this. Garth stood behind, by the wall; Breth was strategically placed a little farther down the board, apparently enjoying himself with his friends. However, he took no ale, and ate with his attention on his fellow guests, the entrances to the hall, the shadowy corners and what they might conceal. Faolan's technique was different. Earlier, Bridei had noticed him several times, always on the fringes, always listening. He had moved from one group to another so unobtrusively folk would scarcely have noticed him; likely he had had an ear to every significant conversation, every little plot, every tossed-away comment in the hall. Now he was seated among a group of men Bridei did not know and appeared to be eating and drinking quietly, keeping himself to himself. The girl with the golden hair was seated at the high table. She was of royal blood, kin to the vassal king in the Light Isles; it was appropriate.

"My friend Ana," Ferada said drily, following Bridei's gaze. "Pretty, isn't she?"

"I hear she is a hostage. So young; she must be younger than yourself, I think. It must be very hard for her."

"She's about the same age as your sister, Tuala. Yes, Ana is homesick. It's a common affliction at Banmerren. But Ana's one of those good creatures who makes the best of everything. She never complains."

Bridei's hand rested on the pouch at his belt; he would not reach inside to touch the little item it held. He had intended to cast the ribbon into the fire: an act of sacrifice to the Flamekeeper, a promise of adherence to the path before him, whatever losses it held. Instead, he had put the scrap of cloth away; had kept it close.

"She is a sweet-looking girl," Bridei said, noticing Ana's little smile as she listened to something the councillor Eogan was saying, and the flush of delicate rose in her cheeks. "You look fine yourself tonight, Ferada. The earrings suit you." Courtesy demanded no less. Besides, even if she were most likely to scoff at his comment, he spoke only the truth. A new scattering of freckles across Ferada's nose softened her sharp features; the styling of her hair was somehow different, making her less formidable.

"Ah, well," Ferada said, looking down at her platter, "we all make an effort here; it's part of the grand performance our lives become at court." She cut a sliver of beef and stared at it. "I see you have a taster," she said.

Bridei grimaced. "Broichan's orders."

"That seems a bit odd. Aren't tasters only for men of power and influence? Even Father doesn't have one."

"Bridei's friend died." Gartnait spoke through a mouthful of meat. "You know that, Ferada."

"If it were I," Ferada said, "I would not be wanting another friend to die for me."

Bridei set down his knife, appetite suddenly gone.

"Stupid," said Gartnait, glaring at his sister across Bridei.

"Oh, dear. I'm sorry, Bridei," Ferada said, crumbling bread with her fingers. "What else shall we talk about?"

Bridei said nothing. This was a game for which he had neither the skills nor the inclination, especially not with the hawk-eyed Dreseida listening to every interchange from the other side of the table. Besides, he realized that there was indeed something he wanted to talk about. There were questions he needed to ask Ferada, who was newly returned from Banmerren. They could not be broached now, not with Dreseida listening and others close by. The hurt inflicted by Tuala's desertion was too new, too raw. He recognized this as an area in which he was vulnerable; in which he must take his own steps to avoid attack.

"After a season or more on the march," he said, "we are happy to turn our attentions to this fine food and ale. You will find us somewhat lacking in conversational skills, I'm afraid."

Ferada gave a brief laugh. "That would be nothing new for my brother," she said, and Gartnait made a face at her. "You, on the other hand, cannot use such an excuse, as you don't seem to be eating, taster or no taster. I think maybe court life suits you no better than Banmerren suits Tuala."

Bridei drew a deep breath and let it out in stages. He fixed his mind on the Shining One, perfect, calm, serene. His druidic education, with its techniques for maintaining balance and focus, stood him in good stead at such moments. "The transition can be difficult, I imagine, even for a seasoned warrior such as your father," he said quietly. "The world of blood and conflict, of nights in the open and supper caught on the run makes this seem . . . artificial."

"But it's the same world," Ferada said, setting down her cup. "They fight different sorts of battles at court, that's all. Given the choice, I think I might prefer nights in the open and supper caught on the run."

Gartnait scowled at her. It was uncomfortable to be seated between them. Bridei did not remember such antipathy from the summer at Raven's Well. "You wouldn't last two days," Gartnait said. "You've got no understanding at all of what it means."

"I—" Ferada half rose, cheeks scarlet.

"Your sister has an excellent grasp of strategy," Bridei put in quickly. "We've spoken of such matters often at Raven's Well. It is not Ferada's fault that, as a woman, she cannot experience at first hand the blood and cruelty that exist, the courage and sacrifice men exhibit in times of war. I'm sure she has as thorough an understanding of what it means as any young woman can. But you are right, Gartnait; one cannot know the true nature of war without being part of it. Such events bring out both the best and the worst in men."

There was a little silence where they sat, while all around them folk still laughed and chattered, knives scraped on platters and jugs clinked against goblets.

"Wisely spoken, Bridei," said Dreseida, unsmiling. "You, I hear, are now considered something of a hero. Amazing; your very first battle, too." She had a way of making even complimentary words sound like an insult.

"Many men showed courage, my lady," Bridei said levelly. "Some died; some suffered grievous wounds. My part in the battle was small."

"It is not to the battle I refer; one would hope all of you played a part in that. It is what came afterward that has earned you a reputation: the man who stole the Mage Stone from right under the Gaels' noses. Remarkable. One could hardly calculate a sequence of events more cleverly to enhance one's prestige and to win men's trust. Even their adulation, if what Gartnait reports is true."

Bridei could feel the flush in his cheeks. "If Gartnait said that he's exaggerating. It seemed the right thing to do at the time; an opportunity worth seizing, an act the gods might welcome. Many men contributed: Fokel of Galany; Ged of Abertornie; Talorgen, too. I merely offered what expertise I had. My education made it possible for me to direct the removal of the stone, its passage to the water, and its conveyance up the lake. That was all."

"It was, in fact, a substantial *all*," Ferada said, her tone for once quite lacking in malice. "A fine thing to do. And the idea was yours; without you it wouldn't have happened. That's what Father said." She glanced across at her mother and fell silent.

"Thank you," said Bridei. "I did learn from it. I learned that sometimes risks are to be taken. And I learned to value the fellowship of men. For those gifts I am grateful to the gods. I hope Fokel succeeded in conveying the stone safely to the point where it will stand proudly once more. When next we travel to Galany's Reach, it will not be for a symbolic victory, but to set our banner there for ever. That land is ours; it will be restored."

Dreseida was staring at him, eyes slightly narrowed. It was clear she was framing one of her challenging questions.

"My lords! My ladies!"

The chatter died down. The music wavered and faded. It was one of Drust's guards who had called out, a man evidently chosen for his barrel chest and trumpet of a voice. "Silence for the king!" he brayed.

Drust rose to his feet. Bridei could see how he rested a hand on the table for support. His voice, nonetheless, was strong and steady. "Welcome, all," he said. "I extend my hand especially to those just returned from the west, bearing glad news of a victory against the Gaels of Dalriada. For the men who were lost in this noble cause, we offer a prayer for a swift and peaceful journey to the realm beyond the veil. May they sleep soundly in Bone Mother's arms, and wake to a new dawn of promise. At the feast of Measure we will honor them." He bowed his head briefly; every man and woman in the chamber did the same. Everyone, that was, except Faolan; Bridei caught a glimpse of the Gael sitting with folded arms and the customary expression of mild amusement on his face. This man was in Drust's employ? By all the gods, he must have rare skills indeed to be allowed to show such contempt in the king's own hall.

"The wives and children of the slain will be provided for," the king went on, "and the wounded receive the attentions of my own physicians, where that is possible. It does this hall honor to receive two of the leaders of this great expedition tonight: Talorgen of Raven's Well and Ged of Abertornie are with us, and will receive my personal thanks, with gifts. In due course I hope that Morleo of Longwater and Fokel, son of Duchil of Galany and true chieftain of those lands in the west, may also travel here to receive my gratitude. To the warriors who ventured forth to do battle under the leadership of these fine chieftains, I salute your deeds of valor. The Flamekeeper smiles on you; he delights in the acts of brave men and honors courageous hearts. The Shining One looks down on you with love. I bid each of you attend the high ritual here at Caer Pridne; may each of you in turn wear the crown of dreams, and continue to tread your path with the fire of the gods' inspiration to light your way."

The men cheered fit to raise the roof; feet drummed on the floor and fists on the table. Bridei found that he had tears in his eyes. Aware of Ferada's close scrutiny and, worse still, that of her mother, he paced his breathing and did not let them fall.

"Come forward, Talorgen, my friend. Ged, come up beside him. Black Crow save us, man, who weaves your cloth? There are more hues in that than any rainbow ever held." General laughter greeted this. Ged, grinning with good nature, slung his multicolored cloak over his shoulder and came to kneel beside Talorgen. One did not stand upright so close to the king until permission was given.

Drust moved out from the table. He stood facing the assembled folk, the tall, dark figure of Broichan a little behind him, like a shadow, and Aniel by his side with a coffer in his hands. Two bodyguards hovered close, flanking the kneeling men; a third was behind the table, others at either end of the dais. Drust was taking no chances. If such precautions were needed now, Bridei thought, what would happen when the delegation from Circinn arrived to stake a claim? What about the other contenders? The place would be swarming with large, heavily armed men pretending they were not doing anything in particular. If it were not so serious it would be almost comical. He wished he could tell Tuala about it.

"Get up, Talorgen, Ged. We are old friends. I thank you from the bottom of my heart. You've won a powerful victory for Fortriu, an achievement that will live long in song and story. In token of the Flamekeeper's love and gratitude and of his pride in the war you waged for him, I give you this, Talorgen," Aniel drew from the little box an arm ring of twisted gold, thick as a heavy rope, "and for you, Ged, this to clasp those outrageous cloaks of yours." The gift was an ornate gold brooch of penannular design; Bridei could not see the details, but it appeared to be inset with ovals of enamel in a number of startlingly bright colors. Ged grinned widely, pinning it immediately on his cloak. It seemed this powerful king had a good and amiable sense of humor.

"Thank you, my lord king," Talorgen said, bowing.

"You honor us," Ged added.

"You must sit at my table," said the king. "We shall have music and tales yet. I understand there is a new song; it concerns a certain young man and the moving of an impossibly large object over improbably difficult terrain. My bard has been sweating over it these last two days and nights. That deed brought inspiration to my spirit and delight to my heart. The man who devised it and who led you in its execution is dear to me even before I meet him. Step forward, Bridei, foster son to my own druid."

Bridei's heart lurched. He had known something like this was coming, but not so soon; for him to be next to receive the king's praise after Talorgen and Ged seemed so inappropriate as to be almost ridiculous. He did have words prepared; he hoped he would remember them.

He knelt before the king, and felt Drust's presence as a power, a warmth near tangible; the Flamekeeper's purpose did indeed burn brightly in his earthly representation. When the king laid a hand on his head in blessing, the touch thrilled through every part of Bridei's body.

"You may stand up, Bridei," Drust said. "We are kinsmen. You have a look of your mother; a little of your father as well. Maelchon I remember as a strong-willed man, a leader of iron purpose who did not suffer fools gladly. He, however, lacked the advantage of a druidic education. He was not raised in the love of our ancient gods, nor in reverence for the fair lands of Fortriu. I have a gift for you, young man. I hear Ged presented you with a cloak. You're not wearing it tonight."

Out of the corner of his eye Bridei caught the flash of Ged's grin and saw Talorgen's wry smile. "No, my lord." If he had walked into this hall with that many-hued garment over his shoulder, he would indeed have been the center of attention.

"Never mind," Drust said. "This brooch will do just as well on a plain cloak; let me pin it for you." As the assembled court looked on in complete silence, the king took a silver clasp from the coffer Aniel held for him, and reached to fasten it to Bridei's cloak with his own hands. It was a lovely thing wrought like a bird, wings spread wide, with a blue stone for the eye. The eagle in flight: the flame of Fortriu. "Well done, son," Drust said quietly. "We're proud of you. I hear you lost a close friend not so long ago. Come, sit by me; you can tell me that sorry tale and then the account of your exploits. Broichan assures me the Mage Stone could not have been moved without the use of druid charms. He and Aniel have a wager on your answer. I have no part in that; my wife frowns on such things." Drust smiled at the queen, who sat farther along the table, and a becoming dimple appeared at the corner of her mouth. "Come, join us." He lifted his voice once more, addressing the throng. "Eat, drink, enjoy the music, my friends! And let my bard ready himself for the singing of songs."

After that it became much easier, even though the king had, in effect, announced Bridei's identity to every man and woman there present. The fact that he was related to Drust had to be made public some time, and of course this did not necessarily equate to a valid claim for kingship. That depended on a particular kind of relationship; a contender must be the son of a royal princess of the blood. And Drust had chosen his words carefully. At no point had he spoken Anfreda's name. It was possible that, between those too far gone in drink to pay attention and those without the wit or interest to put the pieces together, Bridei's status as a potential claimant might remain unknown to most of the court. For now. After this, he was going to be in the public eye whether he liked it or not.

Drust was friendly, intelligent, keen to listen. All the same, it was not possible to recount the tale of Donal's death in any detail. There was only one with whom Bridei might ever share that, since to tell it all would mean letting the listener see his tears. He kept to the bare facts, and the king, his eyes shrewd, moved on quickly to questions about pulleys and levers, barges and rollers. And to queries about how such a large and disparate group of men, weary from a long march and eager to depart for home before the arrival of Dalriadan reinforcements, could yet be mustered to a backbreaking task whose grandeur was matched only by its apparent craziness.

Explaining it properly required the use of knives, bowls, and goblets in illustration. The king followed each step with lively interest; when Bridei was finished, both Broichan and Aniel claimed to have won the wager. Aniel said all could be explained by force and leverage and balance. Broichan declared that without the intervention of the Flamekeeper, for the stone to be lifted at the start, and the goodwill of the Shining One, which allowed such a massive thing to float at all, the removal would have been impossible. Prayers had most certainly been spoken, invocations chanted as the men labored at the ropes. The gods had smiled on this son and his wild plan; they wanted the Mage Stone in the hands of the Priteni, who had been steadfast in their faith. And so it was restored.

"And Fokel is left to wrestle the thing up to Mage Lake," Drust mused, bearded chin resting on his hand. "That, too, was well considered, young Bridei."

"It did seem wise to leave it in his hands, my lord king. His folk lost almost everything when the Gaels took their land. Fokel found it hard to walk away from Galany's Reach after treading his ancestral soil at long last. He is a leader; he may have a reputation as impetuous, but he was wise enough to recognize it was not yet time for him to remain there, so isolated, so far from our nearest outpost. His men, however, are not all so wise. Without a strong purpose, a quest, it might have been difficult for Fokel to force them away. If they had stayed, they'd have been massacred when Gabhran's reinforcements came. Taking custody of the stone allowed them to retreat and keep their pride." Bridei became aware that not only Drust but all the other men at the high table were staring at him intently.

"You discussed this theory with Talorgen and the other chieftains, I take it?" Drust asked.

Bridei felt a telltale flush rise to his cheeks, as if he were a child caught out in a lie. "Not exactly, my lord king. I'm sure they were aware of it. To put such a thing in the open, at the time, might have appeared an insult to Fokel of Galany. It would have seemed as if I thought I knew what was best for him. Fokel is a fine man; I respect him."

"Mm," Drust said, sitting back in his chair. The tabletop was a jumble of knives and cups, with here and there a crust or bone representing some item in the story. "Broichan, you've raised an unusual young man here."

"Thank you, my lord king." If Broichan had been surprised for a moment, before, he now wore his customary expression, one that was entirely unreadable. He could have been feeling pride. He could equally have been feeling nothing much at all.

"I see you've put Faolan to good use already," the king said more quietly, looking at Bridei. The Gael had moved to sit in the place Bridei had vacated, and appeared to be trying to engage Lady Dreseida in conversation. Her expression was glacial.

"Yes, my lord."

Something in Bridei's tone caught the king's attention. "Don't misjudge him, Bridei," Drust said. "He is the best man you could ever hope for in such a job. Why do you imagine I've survived so long?"

Aniel cleared his throat.

"Of course, I have excellent advisers," Drust added, "and a druid of exceptional qualities, although he did choose to desert me for long years. Don't be deceived by Faolan's manner, Bridei. He's an expert."

"It troubles me," Bridei ventured with some hesitation, "that he works against his own people. Why would a Gael make the choice to spy for Fortriu? Why make a life among folk he appears to despise? I'm sorry, my lord king," catching Broichan's eye. "I speak too bluntly. I know the man has served you well."

"As he will you, while you need him. You should not undervalue his services; they are worth twice fifty silver brooches. Don't ponder his motives too deeply. And don't ask him about his past. Whatever lies there is best left where it is: buried. The man is a weapon, a tool, efficient and deadly. Be glad of him, and ask him no question."

"Yes, my lord king."

At that point mulled ale was served, and little cakes with honey and spices, and the music struck up again. The talk became general; Broichan moved away to engage Talorgen and Tharan in conversation, the king called Ged to sit beside him awhile, and Bridei found himself next to the fair-haired girl, Ana, who had remained completely silent since he had joined the king's table.

"My apologies," he said to her a little awkwardly. If she was anything like the women of Gartnait's family, she would proceed to put him in his place with a few well-chosen words. "That was somewhat lacking in courtesy. Men have a habit of assuming ladies are not interested in such topics. Your friend Ferada has already taught me that is often incorrect. I am Bridei, son of Maelchon."

"My name's Ana, from the Light Isles. My cousin is king there."

Bridei nodded. "Ferada told me. It must be difficult for you."

"I've become used to it," she said, toying with the fringed edging of her girdle. "It's hard at times. King Drust does allow me certain freedoms."

"You spend time at Banmerren, I'm told. An education?"

Ana smiled. It transformed a face already pretty into one of dazzling charm. "A very fine one," she said. "Of course, Ferada and I and the other daughters of noble blood do not study the more esoteric pursuits, such as scrying or prophecy. We touch on herb lore, which can be useful. We do not learn the full conduct of rituals, only the role a chieftain's wife may be called upon to play in them. We have a very good tutor in history and politics. Your sister excels in that class." Ana was studying his face; her wide eyes looked deeply into his and their expression changed. "You miss her," she said softly.

Bridei looked down at his hands. He must be tired; he should not have let his guard down thus. He had learned the concealment of his feelings from a master in that art. Perhaps it was the headache, which had eased at the king's touch and now returned, throbbing like a deep drumbeat behind his eyes. He said nothing.

"I will take her a message, if you wish to send one," Ana said. "We will be going back to Banmerren before long. I think Tuala would like to hear from you. Although she does so well at her studies and pleases our tutors with her cleverness, I believe she is quite lonely."

It became impossible not to ask. "You speak to her often? She is a friend?"

Ana twisted the girdle in her fingers. "Tuala doesn't make friends, not really. She speaks to me and to Ferada, whom she knew already when she came to Banmerren. They gave her a little room of her own, up in a tower. That seemed odd to me; as if they were trying to show how different she was. But I think Tuala prefers it. There's an oak tree growing outside her door; she likes to sit there. I think maybe she's dreaming of home. She's an unusual girl. Like a little wild creature."

"Are they kind to her there?" He could not trouble this girl with the question he really wanted answered. Only Tuala herself could give him the reasons for her decision to enter Banmerren and turn her back on him.

Ana began to answer, then fell silent. The king's bard had come to seat himself, small harp on knee, in the space before the high table. It was time for the heroic tale of the Mage Stone to be told in all its splendor. Bridei found himself hoping fervently that his own name would be mentioned as little as possible. At the time, it had been a fine thing, uniting the men and keeping his own mind occupied; it had held the dark dreams at bay for a little. He saw no reason for his actions to be in any way immortalized. One did what one had to; if it worked well, it was the gods who deserved thanks.

Much to his relief, while Bridei's name was certainly in the account, the emphasis was on King Drust, under whose banner the entire venture against the Gaels had been undertaken: Drust who was the earthly embodiment of that most heroic of warrior gods, the Flamekeeper. Talorgen was in the tale, and Ged with his rainbow warriors. Morleo of Longwater and Fokel of Galany received their dues. There was a lengthy and poetic description of the stone itself, with an interpretation of its carvings.

The king's bard had a powerful and smooth-toned voice for the declamation; his long fingers flew over the harp strings, evoking here wonder, there terror, here mystery, there pathos, with the expertise of a seasoned professional and the heart of a true poet. When it was over the assembled crowd shouted acclaim then called for more music. Pipes shrilled, drums commenced to thump out a rousing rhythm, and folk began to move the tables aside in readiness for dancing.

Ferada was approaching, her mother close behind. It was clear they were coming for Ana, who rose to her feet. A decision must be made now; who knew when the opportunity would arise again?

"Here," Bridei said, glancing around to make sure Broichan was not watching and fishing the frayed ribbon out of his pouch. "Please give her this."

Ana took it and tucked it under her girdle, out of sight. She glanced at him once more, a question in her eyes.

"If you could keep this to yourself . . . I imagine such communications are forbidden," Bridei said quietly.

"No message?" Ana asked.

Ferada had stopped to speak to her father. Dreseida was

looking out over the crowd, her attention on the flurry of activity as couples arranged themselves in a double line down the hall.

"Only that I respect her decision." It sounded cold, formal; in no way a truthful representation of what was in his heart. "And that I hope she will be happy. I did not expect that the Shining One would call her thus." He made himself stop; already it was too much.

Ana gave a little nod, then all at once Ferada was there to whisk her friend away for dancing, and the moment was over.

MUCH LATER, WHEN all were abed and a white-gold, waxing moon hung low in the sky over Caer Pridne, Bridei stood on the wall-walk near Broichan's quarters. The throbbing in his head had made it impossible to lie still, feigning sleep; he might be forced to ask Broichan for some kind of potion in the morning, although he suspected even the most potent brew of druid herbs would be ineffective against this.

There was a tiny sound behind him. He whirled, knife suddenly in hand, every sense alert.

"Good," said Faolan, stepping from shadow to torchlight. "I thought I'd caught you dreaming. Do you make a habit of wandering alone at night? Where are your guards?"

"Sleeping. I told them to rest. Breth is by the doorway, a matter of four strides or less. He could be here in a moment."

"A moment is all it takes to stick a knife in a man's heart," Faolan said. "You are incautious. I had not taken you for a fool."

"It irks me to spend my life jumping at shadows. I will learn to do what I must, despite that. Drust's example is a fine one."

"He's had expert protectors." Faolan moved to stand by Bridei at the stone rampart wall. There were few torches lit now; all was quiet, save for the hushed sound of the sea as it broke gently over the rock walls sheltering the anchorage below. The moon illuminated, dimly, the pale beach and ink-dark water of the bay. "And so will you. You must learn to take their advice, if you would live as long as he has."

Bridei could not let such smugness go unchallenged. "You are young," he said. "You must have some understanding of how it feels to be restricted thus; to be fettered always by those who seek to keep me safe. I was raised by a druid. I am accustomed to times of quiet, of solitude. I'm used to walking the forest undisturbed. How can I know the gods' will if I cannot hear their voices? How can I hear them if I cannot stand in their great wild places alone? How can I be what I must be without that?"

"On such matters, I'm entirely unqualified to comment," said Faolan, "save to point out that others seem to have managed it before. A number of people express a high degree of confidence in you. Should you become king, you will find it easier to make your own rules. You may dispense with my services; I am contracted only to keep you safe until that point. I care nothing for your need to hear whatever deities you believe may be whispering in your ear. I care only that my job is done well. I don't expect you to thwart that possibility by taking stupid risks."

Bridei did not respond, indeed could not, as a new wave of pain washed over him. He felt his head might split open; with sheer effort of will, he managed not to vomit by Faolan's feet.

"What is it?" The Gael had moved closer and was scrutinizing Bridei's face. "Are you hurt? Too much ale? No, you hardly touched a drop. In pain? A headache?"

Bridei felt a deep shiver run through his body. "It is customary," he said in a whisper. "I don't sleep much. It will pass."

"Drugs. Distraction. Hard labor. Or a woman," Faolan said, counting off the options on his fingers. "How long since you had a woman? That can be arranged."

"No." Bridei hoped very much that he would not have to explain his reasons for this. Faolan was the last man to whom he would choose to confide such a personal matter as his vow of celibacy, the vow he had sworn to adhere to until the day he took a wife.

"Then I suppose we will stand here in awkward conversation until morning," Faolan said. "Or sit, perhaps. The steps might be more comfortable. That's it; sit there. How long have these headaches plagued you?"

The Gael sounded almost friendly. Of course, it was part of his job to win trust.

"Since the battle at Galany's Reach. Maybe earlier."

"And why is that, do you think? Is it possible this, too, is the aftermath of poison? Something subtle and slow-working?"

"I doubt it. I suppose we will find out soon enough; Breth or Garth will come down with the same affliction."

"You dislike showing weakness."

There was a silence.

"I've been trained to reveal as little as possible," Bridei said. "You'd understand how that can be useful, I imagine."

"I read you with no difficulty," said Faolan quietly. "You have no one you can trust. Even your druid is not privy to your secrets. In that, you have learned already what it is to be a king."

"Shh," hissed Bridei.

"Would I speak thus if we could be overheard? In this, at least, you can trust me. I have no desire to hear your inmost thoughts, believe me. I am interested in banishing this malady. I bear the responsibility of keeping you alive and capable at least until Midwinter; as long as it takes."

"Then leave me alone," Bridei said, unable to keep the weariness from his voice.

"Alone with the stars," mused Faolan. "Will that cure the headache? I will retreat into the shadows where I belong, Bridei. Don't leave this part of the wall-walk; I need you to remain in sight."

"You intend to stay awake all night?"

"The last thing that needs concern you is my sleep or lack of it. Pray, meditate, dream, do what you will. Just stay where I can protect you. As for the great wild places and the voices of the gods, perhaps those, too, will come in time. If not, I suppose it's all been for nothing."

13

THEY HAD TAKEN up residence in her tree. As summer turned to the cool, crisp sharpness of early autumn their forms could be spotted sometimes amidst its canopy of sheltering green, elusive as squirrels, a whisk of cobweb gray, a whirl of berry red and nut brown. Nobody else could see them. They came only for Tuala.

At night when she sat there under the moon, dreaming of home, they settled one on either side, the girl spreading skirts of smoky silver, the young man merging into the shadows and textures of the tree, such was the form of his own body, the nature of his raiment, all bark and leaf and curling fern frond.

"Do you have names?" Tuala asked them one night, tired of calling them, in her mind, merely *she* and *he*, forest girl and leaf man.

"Not such names as human folk use," the girl said with a tinkling laugh. "Tuala, they called you. What kind of choice is that? It ill befits your beauty; they should have named you for the white owl, or the little flowers that cling tenaciously in cracks on the high tors. Tuala: that is a name for a woman of status, the wife of a king."

Tuala did not say that perhaps that was why Bridei had chosen it. In the little songs of their childhood, often he had called her princess. "I ask only to make things easier, so I can address you by name as you do me."

"Human folk would likely choose names for us in keeping with what they see," said the young man. "For my companion, Gossamer, Willow, Vapor. For myself, Woodbine, perhaps."

"Gossamer. Woodbine. Those are fair names."

"They'll do," the girl said. "Now tell us: what have you learned today?"

"Kethra comes to my private lessons now. I showed her and Fola how I make things move without touching them.

Kethra wanted me to do more; I have only ever used that for small objects, the pieces on a game board, perhaps a knife or comb I needed to reach. She asked if I could do it with objects I couldn't see; if I could manipulate the pace at which things move. If it mattered how big they were, or how heavy. She wanted me to try it outside, with barrels or lengths of iron."

"And did you?"

"Fola said no."

The young man, Woodbine, was frowning. "You didn't learn a thing. You gave away your secrets."

"This is no good for you," said Gossamer. "You see why these folk are keeping you here. They are merely using you. One day you move barrels onto a cart, the next you send an iron bar through the air to crush a man's skull, or a woman's. One day you create pretty images of butterflies and flowers from a beam of light, the next you send that light to dazzle a man while another man drives a spear through his heart. You're foolish if you think they brought you here to learn."

"There is learning in everything."

"Ah. You repeat your druid's favorite dictum. And there is, I suppose; you should learn from today that our kind are easily exploited by the human folk, if we allow them to gain control."

"I don't think—"

"No," said Woodbine. "You don't; not as you should. This is no place for you. Your eyes have dark circles around them and you're as skinny as a half-starved chicken."

"You're wasting away for Pitnochie," Gossamer said softly. "Let us take you home."

Tuala would not allow herself to cry. "There is no home at Pitnochie any more," she said. "At least Fola and Kethra want me here. I can make a contribution. I can serve the Shining One. My teaching is going well; the girls are starting to trust me. I can make a life at Banmerren."

"Rubbish," Woodbine said. "You hate it here. Besides, we don't mean home to the druid's house. Nobody wants you there. Come home with us. We are not visited by sorrow or loneliness. We do not feel the touch of death."

Tuala shivered, drawing her shawl closer around her. Not

374 § JULIET MARILLIER

long ago, Ana had passed her a message. Bridei had given back the ribbon, the token he had worn next to his skin every moment of every day he was parted from her. The words that came with it were cool and courteous, the kind of words one would expect from a young man who might soon be monarch of Fortriu. He respected her decision. He hoped she would be happy. It was meaningless, save to convey that he was prepared to let her go without protest. That must be taken as confirmation that her choice was right. Bridei did not need her; he would find another to take her place by his side.

The last part of the message was different. *I did not expect the Shining One to call you thus.* Perhaps she was deluding herself, but this seemed to her to speak of unhappiness. If only she could see him, talk to him, look in his eyes and know what he really thought. Tuala longed for that as a starving woman longs for fresh bread or a thirsty one for clear water: the plain, simple truth seen in the eyes of a friend who cannot lie. One chance to know his heart, and perhaps she could walk on more easily.

"I can't come with you," she whispered. "That would be to leave too many things behind. I can't believe there is nothing at all for me in this world, a human world. Even if I cannot have . . . even if the life I'm granted is not what I thought it would be, to go with you, to cross over into a realm so different, a place from which I cannot return . . . It would be too final. Like severing the last thread that ties me to the things I love."

Gossamer laughed again, a high pealing. It was extraordinary that nobody else at Banmerren ever seemed to hear it. "Love," the girl echoed. "You are overfond of that word, Tuala. There is much to enjoy in our own world, fine things, beautiful things. You would be loved by all there; you'd be in every way the princess that you were named, so many years ago. The Shining One looks down on both our kingdoms with equal light, my sister. Step across, and you will continue to rejoice in her sweet benevolence eternally, living a life entirely free from cares such as those that beset you now. No more worrying about folk who want you to exhibit your tricks and give them your secrets. No more watching the one you think you love getting close to a certain other girl, one with hair like a cascade of sunlight. That won't bother you a jot once you cross over; you'll wonder why you ever cared. Did you know that when one of our kind weds a human she forfeits her immortality? Who would choose death over eternal life?"

"I don't want to hear this. I've told you, over and over. I will stay here at Banmerren. The goddess wants me as a wise woman. This must be the right choice." With sinking heart Tuala realized that the more often she repeated these words, the less she was inclined to believe them.

"Why don't you put it to the test?" Woodbine's voice was sly; he reached a knotty hand to touch Tuala's knee and she edged along the branch away from him.

"Don't do that! What do you mean, put it to the test?"

"He sent you a message." Gossamer was standing now, her slender form outlined in moonlight, graceful arms stretched above her head to rest on an upper branch, gown of cobweb-fine fabric floating about her body, small, white feet confident on the high perch. "Send him one in return. If you are unhappy, tell him so. Test him. If he fails it, you will know your doubts were right. Then accept the truth, and we will take you home to the forest. Don't you miss it, the soft green and the silence?"

"It is forbidden," Tuala said. "He took a risk, giving Ana the ribbon to bring to me; those of us being trained as priestesses are not supposed to have any contact with the world beyond these walls, unless Fola or Kethra sanctions it. I mustn't get him in trouble. And he can't take me home. He has to be at Caer Pridne."

"If he thinks you not worth the risk," Gossamer said carelessly, "then he will not respond. Make it subtle. He knows you very well. Send something others cannot interpret. That should be safe enough."

"Why would you suggest this?" These two were certainly not to be trusted; they followed their own impenetrable rules.

"Because we know you will not come with us until your mind is satisfied," said Woodbine, rising to his feet on the branch beside Tuala. "You must have it in black and white, in cruel, unadorned truth: that you are not first in his life;

that he will go on without you. That, indeed, burdened with you, he would be unable to fulfill his destiny. When has a king of Fortriu ever taken one of the Good Folk as a bride? And what else could you be? What wife would possibly tolerate your presence in her house, sapping her husband's energy, distracting him at every turn? You're surely not expecting Bridei to sacrifice his opportunity to seek the kingship just because of you? Of course, being a kindly young man, Bridei will not express it so baldly. But you know him. You will comprehend his message. Better do it and put us all out of our misery. Act boldly. King Drust has another chill; he won't last long."

They tended not to linger for farewells, these two. It would be one final remark, generally calculated to wound, and they would be off, dissipating among the moonlit leaves like wisps of smoke, leaving Tuala alone with her thoughts. So it was tonight; between one blink and another they were gone. And in her mind, complete in an instant as if she had already planned for it, was the message, telling Bridei when and where to find her with perfect clarity, yet, she thought, in terms quite obscure to anyone else. She hoped so. Ana, for one, must be trusted. As for those cruel words of brides and kings, she would pretend she had not heard them. Heart thumping, Tuala plucked a single withered leaf from the oak and returned to her tower.

BEFORE THE SEASON began to darken toward Gateway, Drust sickened. The nights were chill; the men on watch shivered in their sheepskin jackets, their fur-lined cloaks and felt hats, and fires were kept burning in the drafty stone chambers of Caer Pridne. The king's cough rattled through the hallways like a hoarse cry of death, some emanation of Black Crow herself. Drust's cheeks bore a rosy flush in a face drained of color; Queen Rhian, a permanent frown of worry on her amiable features, haunted the stillroom, setting her own hands to the making of draughts to ease her husband's chest. It was whispered that only Broichan's magic was keeping the king alive.

But Drust was no weakling. He had not held on to power for so long by giving up in times of challenge. He moved his center of operations to a small chamber that could be effectively warmed, and had them set pots of steaming water by the fire, water in which floated the bruised leaves of curative plants, fennel and calamint. He took a drink made from crushed hazelnuts and honey, but he could not conceal his flagging appetite. About the chamber were protective charms aplenty: white stones for the Shining One, set in threes and fives and sevens; a hanging chain of little men woven from straw, each wearing a garland of autumn leaves on his tiny head and a belt of bright thread in scarlet and gold: sons of the Flamekeeper, whose warmth generated bountiful crops. There was a wreath of greenery above the door and a plait of garlic by the hearth. It reminded Bridei sharply of a time long ago, when Broichan had catechised him on the protective devices at Pitnochie. *Do not answer like a child, but like a druid.*

He could answer like a druid now. The king was dying, and he knew it. Bone Mother danced toward him, arms outstretched; these charms could not hold back her advance. They might perhaps delay it for one, maybe two turnings of the moon, no more. The truth was in Drust's eyes and he faced it unafraid. He sought only to be sure his kingdom would not descend into a chaos of rivals and challenges and power plays the instant he was gone.

Like flies hovering about a dying creature even as it still breathes and walks the earth, the nobles of the south had descended on Caer Pridne. Drust the Boar had not come, not yet. In his place were his two chief councillors and a Christian priest. It was a gesture of outrageous insolence. Caer Pridne had never yet given house room to a Christian and had no desire to do so now; who would be foolish enough to offend the gods so, with their good king on the brink of death? Unfortunately, the fact that Brother Suibne—a Gael by origin, therefore doubly unwelcome—was part of a royal delegation made it essential that he be not only housed, but housed well and with an appearance of genuine courtesy. Faces wore forced smiles; voices were edged with ill-concealed resentment. The three were given a fine chamber with a private anteroom where the fellow could practice his outlandish rituals out of sight of god-fearing folk. The one to watch, Broichan told his foster son, was the chief councillor from Circinn, a man named Bargoit. He had a smooth tongue and few scruples, and over the years had learned to bend Drust the Boar entirely to his will. The other, Fergus, was under Bargoit's thumb. What one decreed, the other supported. They had come early. One must hope they did not whisper in too many ears and do too much damage. As for the priest, if priest he could be called, his presence was an insult. In this, Broichan suspected Drust of Circinn had done his own claim for kingship of the north a disservice. One look at Brother Suibne and every voting nobleman of Fortriu would be put in mind of what could occur if the two parts of the kingdom fell in behind Drust the Boar. Those loyal to the gods could never make such a choice.

The time passed quickly. Bridei found his days filled with cryptic conversations, whispered exchanges in hallways, delicate maneuvering with one influential man or another. At first, on Broichan's advice, he played the young innocent, quiet and courteous in his manner, sparing and simple in his comments. They knew, of course. If they had not recognized on the night Drust gave him the eagle brooch and his royal blessing that the druid's foster son from Pitnochie was a genuine contender for kingship, they discovered it soon enough. All assessed him. In turn, Bridei began to work his way through them, dealing with each according to the degree of threat he represented and the probability that existed of changing his mind for him.

It was customary for each of the seven houses to offer one candidate only, and this time there might be less than seven in all; the southern tribes, in particular, were not likely to put up contenders of their own when Drust the Boar was in effect overlord of all those territories. The royal line was of the house of Fidach, whose heartland was in the Great Glen, but because the descent came through the female side and the princesses of Fidach wed chieftains from all across the realm of the Priteni, and indeed beyond its borders, there were generally valid claimants to be found in each of the seven houses.

It seemed the Light Isles would not be in the contest this time. The presence of Ana at Drust's court, and the possibility that others of that family might be similarly taken at any time, was likely to stay their hand. It was whispered, also, that an assurance had been made to the chieftain of those isles, whose status was as vassal king to Drust the Bull. It had been pointed out that the royal hostage would be ideally placed to wed the new king, should he not already have a wife. That would immeasurably enhance the status of her family, elevating her cousin to something close to the level of Fortriu's own monarch. Trading agreements and other advantages might well flow as a result. Someone had been clever.

The house of Caitt was unpredictable. Bridei had once believed an alliance might be struck with those savage northerners; Broichan had dismissed that. Generations had passed since the Caitt had last attempted to claim the kingship of Fortriu. Nobody expected any surprises from that quarter. As for the future, Bridei had his own plans. The Caitt were of Priteni blood, and they were strong. Should he become king, there was a possibility there that he must at least begin to explore.

Of Drust's two closest kinsmen, red-headed Carnach was the stronger contender. He was well spoken and capable, and he was gathering the backing of a number of influential men, the king's councillor Tharan among them. Aniel had said Tharan was dangerous. There was some work to be done in that camp.

Wredech was left to the mercies of Talorgen. A little gentle pressure was apparently required, no more, to persuade this kinsman of Drust the Bull that it would be wiser to drop his claim, in view of a certain matter of some cattle that had mysteriously wandered, and a purse of silver pieces that had changed hands right under Drust's nose. Should Wredech's role in this become public, as it surely would if he declared his interest in the kingship, he would be utterly discredited before his peers. And he would lose the cattle, including a fine stud bull already hard at work among his cows. On the other hand, if he took it into his head to declare support for the candidate Talorgen himself favored, nothing would be said at all. And there could be a small incentive in it, by way of some further additions to Wredech's growing herd.

Talorgen was working on this; such propositions were not made openly, all at once, but by subtle degrees, working on a man's fears and his weaknesses. There was nothing for Bridei to do but be friendly and respectful to Wredech when they met, and to avoid the topics of kingship and cattle.

He could not avoid the councillors from Circinn, Bargoit and Fergus, and their Christian priest. Bargoit played challenging games; he was a master of innuendo, trick questions, skillful evasions, and unexpected attacks. Retaining control of himself and the situation taxed Bridei hard; the headache was more or less constant, and it did nothing to improve his concentration. He did not ask Broichan for a potion. The druid was much occupied, spending days and nights at King Drust's side, brewing cures, burning powerful herbs, saying prayers, perhaps also simply acting as friend and companion, for they had been together long, in the days before Bridei came to Pitnochie.

Bridei had thought, at first, that he would never get used to his three guards. Remarkably soon, in the charged atmosphere of the overcrowded fortress, he began to find the constant presence of one or other of these large men reassuring. If Garth or Breth was at his shoulder, watching for trouble, Bridei could concentrate on other things, such as a debate with Brother Suibne about the nature of men and gods, or a game of crow-corners with the sharp-eyed councillor Tharan, before a tense audience made up of Aniel and the two councillors from Circinn. He knew he was on show; his guards ensured he need not also be watchful, every moment, for a knife in the back.

Faolan left Breth and Garth to share responsibility for the waking hours between them. He was far from idle; he gathered information, looked into men's pasts, spoke to servants and slaves and performed solitary examinations of the visitors' allocated quarters while the occupants were busy elsewhere. By night, he watched as Bridei failed to sleep. Whether he himself ever rested, and when, was not possible to discern. He exhibited no signs of weariness.

The young women had gone back to Banmerren some time ago, and were due to return to court any day. Tuala was much in Bridei's mind. At night he stood on the wall-walk gazing at the moon and imagining her in the gray robes of a priestess, bearing a bowl of water for the rite of Midsummer or scattering white petals at Balance. He thought of her looking into the water of a scrying bowl, her strange eyes open to a whole world that was beyond his understanding. He pictured her laughing, her hair tangled by the wind; his hands knew that head of hair intimately, for his fingers had braided and tied it more times than he could count. He thought of a promise he had made long ago, and how he had done his best to keep it. She was not a child now, in need of his tales to quell her fear of the unknown. She was as old as Ana; a young woman. And she had moved away from him. The Shining One had touched her as an infant, and now reached out to her again, calling her home. What purer form of service to the gods than that of druid or wise woman? How could he grudge her that? And yet . . . and yet . . .

"Bridei?"

"Mm?"

"We're having a day off tomorrow," Faolan announced from his dark corner by the steps.

"What?"

"The weather seems set dry. I don't know about you, but I've had a bellyful of all this. We'll take a couple of horses, ride along the beach, find some of those great wild places you mentioned and tire ourselves out. No kings, no councillors, no priests, no druids. A whole day. What do you think?"

"No Breth, no Garth?"

Faolan did not smile. "They're due a break. You have me; you don't need them."

"So you'll be on duty."

"I'm always on duty, Bridei. It'll be a change, at least."

It did sound good; remarkably good. To escape from court for a whole day would be a wondrous reprieve.

"I've told Broichan," Faolan said. "I'll procure some rations. Be prepared to leave early."

"You know," said Bridei, "I'm finding it impossible to believe this is what it seems, coming from you. You are not the kind of man who goes out for a day's enjoyment when there are other, pressing matters to attend to. If there's more to this than meets the eye, I'd prefer that you tell me."

Faolan said nothing for a little. "We may do this more than once," he offered eventually. "Establish a pattern. It could be useful."

"For what purpose?"

"To draw an attack," the Gael said coolly. "Not tomorrow; once we've given an indication of where we might be found on certain days at certain times."

"Wonderful. I'm to enjoy myself riding through the hills waiting for an arrow in the heart."

"I thought you were supposed to be the best archer in Fortriu," Faolan said lightly. "Don't let it bother you, Bridei. I know what I'm doing. Caer Pridne is so full of noblemen's personal guards right now that nobody dares try anything. They'll be looking for an opportunity. We're going to give them one."

"I see."

"Tomorrow will be safe. Tomorrow you can listen for the voices of the gods to your heart's content."

"I'll welcome the ride. Thank you." Indeed, assassins or no assassins, Bridei recognized how much he craved the freedom of that, the chance to traverse woodland and moorland, strath and glenside with his eyes and ears open to the wonder of the wild. In Caer Pridne the eyes were full of rich apparel and lying faces, the ears assaulted by chatter, by sly whispers and hissed asides. He had not ridden out with just one companion since Donal . . .

"What is it?"

Curse Faolan; he was too quick. "Nothing. I'll try to sleep now. Good night. May the Shining One guard your dreams."

"Good night, Bridei."

IT SEEMED FAOLAN was determined to tire him out. Perhaps the Gael hoped the day's activity would allow them both a good night's sleep. But Bridei had grown up on long expeditions through the forest above Pitnochie. He was at home in the wild, attuned to its rhythms since childhood, and to be thus released back into it awoke him in a way the most tense maneuverings, the subtlest games of Drust's court could not. While the headache did not vanish, it retreated. While doubt still plagued him, to be here under a great stand of pines, looking out across a wide salt marsh where birds moved in endless, flowing masses of gray and dun and white, now rising as one to wheel above the tidal flats, now descending to settle and forage, was to recapture something of that inner wonder that had ever warmed his spirit as he traversed the crags and glens of Pitnochie, alone or with one trusted companion.

Faolan did not seek to fill the great silence with idle talk; his presence was unobtrusive, efficient, accepting. They had warmed up the horses, then galloped them along the wet sand from Caer Pridne to Banmerrèn. It was not a true contest, but they had challenged each other, all the same; Snowfire had relished the opportunity to stretch himself, underused as he was these days.

At the western end of the bay, the walls of Fola's establishment rose high among the softening shawl of undergrowth, the groups of wind-shaped pines that made this headland not fortress, but haven. The gates were of heavy iron and were shut fast. It was not possible to see what lay behind them, for the place was set out with a screening wall not far within, probably to deter such curious eyes as his own. The rule forbidding any man save a druid from entering this realm sacred to the Shining One was well known. Even to think of breaking it was to offend the goddess. For a man who might be a contender for kingship to entertain such a notion was both sacrilegious and foolish. A king must be flawless in his loyalty to the gods. With his intellect, Bridei understood this only too well. His heart, however, beat fast with a longing to breach the wall, to find her, to know the truth.

He could not see the oak tree Ana had mentioned. He did not know on what side of this enclosed place there might be a small tower chamber suitable for one young woman on her own. Close by the school compound was a sprawling assemblage of farm buildings, stables, a barn, a long, low dwelling house. Sheep grazed in walled fields; there was a track down to the tidal flats beyond. Bridei could imagine Tuala there, stooping for shells, her dark hair wild, her skirts tucked up, her small bare feet imprinting the pale sand with tracks as delicate as a tern's . . .

They rode by, passing to the west across dunes and flats, traversing swamp and heath, stopping to look out over a sandbar that curved across the mouth of a limpid bay where, this morning, a vast flock of geese was flung across water and shore like a living shawl. The voices of the birds filled the remote place with their strange, honking music. It was a reminder that the year was almost come to its end; winter visitors, these, whose sojourns in Fortriu came from Gateway to Maiden Dance, before they flew off to summer in other climes.

"It is less than one turning of the moon until the ritual," Bridei said, his eyes on the movement of the geese, a wondrous, ever-changing pattern.

"Mm," said Faolan. "Will Broichan keep the king alive long enough?"

Bridei shivered. "I pray daily that he does."

"They say Drust is holding on for that purpose," the Gael said. "His lungs fail him; it is a constant battle for breath. He wishes to perform the ceremony one last time; to pay his dues to the Nameless One before he must step beyond the veil."

"One does not speak of such matters aloud."

"Ah. But I am not one of you."

"All the same. If you live among us and accept our silver for your services, you should heed such prohibitions. This is a god whose rituals are dark and secret. There is peril even in the mention of them."

Faolan looked at him curiously. "You realize, I presume, whose responsibility this particular observance will be next year, and for many years to come?"

"Yes. It is not something I dwell on. The gods make certain calls upon us, according to our position in society. If we love them, as any true son or daughter of Fortriu must, we obey. No more need be said. Besides, I am not king yet. At this stage I am only one among several possible candidates."

"You know what the ritual entails?"

"Didn't you hear me, Faolan?"

There was a silence. Then Faolan rose to his feet, heading to the tethered horses. "We cannot ride all the way to your beloved mountains; not today," he said. "But there is fine moorland, gentle hillocks, secret folds of the land, a river to ford if we ride inland from here. Shall we go on?"

"Places for ambush? Boltholes for hired killers?"

"Maybe. As I said, today is for leisure, and to assess the lay of the land. We must hope this dry weather continues so we can do it again."

THEY RODE UNTIL the sun was at its peak, giving the horses their heads over the moor, leading them cautiously across the stony ford; when this river was in spate, the passage would be perilous indeed. At length they came to a place of gentle grass-clad hills and narrow, treed valleys. They traversed a moss-coated plank bridge over a gurgling stream, and rode along one such glen to find it broadened to fields. Farther down stood a grove of tall trees, dark, bare elms and spreading oaks in the last of their russet autumn raiment. Bridei touched Snowfire's neck, halting him, and Faolan reined his horse to a stop. Beneath these guardian trees, sheltered and secret, three round cairns lay, each encircled by a ring of standing stones.

"It is a place of the goddess," whispered Bridei, dismounting. He could feel the breath of the Shining One in every corner of this sanctuary; there was a stillness here beyond the ordinary quiet of wild places, a sense of both profound serenity and powerful warning. "As men, we can go no closer," he said.

Faolan got down from his horse. "You may wish to stay a while, all the same," he said. "Where we cannot go, others can. Move back a little, here, up the rise where there is more cover."

"What do you mean, others can?"

Faolan was already leading their two mounts back behind the bushes; now he took a packet from his saddlebag and proceeded to settle himself on a flat stone. He was, of

course, a Gael, and deaf to the voices of the old gods of Fortriu. Possessed by a powerful need to be gone from that
place, a women's place, Bridei was nonetheless aware that
the day was half over, that they still had to ride all the way
back and that he was extremely hungry.

"I mean what I say," he said, sitting beside the Gael and
accepting a wedge of cheese, a slab of oaten bread. "No
closer; and we should leave here when we've eaten. I am
glad that I have seen this. I've heard tell of this place. Those
chambers are very old, a construction of the ancient ancestors. Generations of women have conducted their deep rituals here and offered prayers of reverence to the goddess in
her triple form. A man should not set foot among the cairns;
even if I did not already know this, I can feel it in every bone
of my body."

"Ah, well," said Faolan, munching steadily, "a man must
still have his dinner; your goddess would surely not grudge
us that. Plenty of time. I have mead in this flask; here."

Autumn was well advanced, but here on the hillside above
that secret place of circle within circle the sun had a warmth
in it that belied the season. The horses were content to crop
the grasses. Faolan sat quiet, eyes tranquil, pose relaxed. The
food was excellent, the mead of fine quality; Bridei suspected it was from the king's personal supply. His headache
was almost imperceptible now. A kind of peace crept over
him that he had almost forgotten, that sense of deep contentment that came only in the quiet of the outdoors, and then
but rarely. He was, after all, the smallest of creatures before
the immense, the wondrous tapestry of living things; his own
concerns were dwarfed by it. It existed in eternity, strong
and sure. The heart of the gods beat in every darting
meadow bird, in each gold-brown leaf that spiraled earth-
ward from the oak's dark branches, in every drop of dew and
grain of sand, in pebble and waterfall, broad lake and high
tor. The same heart beat in him; here in this place of sanctuary he could feel its steady rhythm, linking him intimately to
the life of the Glen and of the land of Fortriu, the land whose
leader he might all too soon become. His back resting
against the trunk of an elm, Bridei closed his eyes. The retreat of the headache was a blessing, a gift. He had not real-

ized how much it weakened him until now, when it was almost fled.

"BRIDEI?"

The tone alerted him instantly; it was a warning, making silence imperative. His eyes sprang open. The shadows had moved; the sun had edged toward the west. He had been asleep, and for some time. His limbs were seized by cramp; wincing, he struggled to a crouch. Faolan was peering down the hillside between the bushes. He had a finger to his lips. Following his gaze, Bridei saw that they were no longer alone. A number of cloaked and hooded women moved now between the ancient stones, stooping here and there, while others walked farther afield on the banks of the little stream close by. He shut his eyes tightly and turned away.

"The ritual is finished," Faolan murmured. "It's safe to look. I waited to wake you until it was done. Now they're just walking about chatting and gathering herbs."

"This is wrong; disrespectful," whispered Bridei. "Spying on women . . . I will not do it. Why did you bring me here? I don't want to see this." Yet within him something clamored to be heard, something he fought to suppress: *perhaps she's here, so close . . . If I don't look now, she'll be gone, and it will be too late . . . .*

"Would you lie to me? I think you do want to see. I don't know which of these girls is the friend whose absence caused you to look at Banmerren's walls as if they were a defensive barrier to be stormed, but I think I could hazard a guess. Is she a rare, small creature with skin like snow and tresses dark as a crow's wing?"

It became, then, impossible for Bridei to keep his eyes closed, his head turned. He looked, and on an instant found her, down by the water where several girls were picking stalks of an autumn-flowering plant and laying them in rush baskets. Tuala was at a little distance from the others and had taken off her enveloping cloak and laid it on the bank nearby. She held a frond of foliage in her small hand and was staring at it as if she hardly knew what it was; as if she had lost track of the task entirely. The coal-black curls had escaped their binding and sprang in wild confusion about her delicate features . . . Her hair, her lovely long hair, it had been chopped short, falling scarcely to her shoulders. Who would do such a thing? It made her look different, older. Older . . . She wore a plain skirt and tunic, blue like her cloak and belted in gray. Was it really only a year since he had seen her? The stark simplicity of the garments served only to reveal that she was no longer the slight child of their last meeting. She remained slender and small, but her figure had acquired subtle curves and sweet contours; it was a delicate poem of young womanhood. And yet, Tuala was herself, from the rosebud lips to the winged brows and cascade of untameable, silky hair. She stood out among these other girls like a young owl in a flock of pigeons.

He must have made some small sound. Black Crow only knew what Faolan could read upon his face. Bridei put both hands up to mask it; in that moment, all of Broichan's training had deserted him. Self-control? He felt as if his heart were splitting apart. It was all he could do not to break from cover, to run down the hill and . . . and what? Terrify all of them? Commit an act of utter sacrilege, offending the gods most bitterly? Ask Tuala to throw away the life of peace and purpose the Shining One had offered her and follow him instead to an existence of whispered conspiracy and constant guards and knives in the dark?

"We must wait now." Faolan pushed him back to sit on the stone, himself remaining crouched. "To be seen here would be disastrous for your future. We must wait until they are gone. Then we will ride and talk. You shed tears. She is a beguiling creature, that much I see plainly. In the tales of my homeland many such women appear. They are both beauteous and perilous."

Bridei made a graphic gesture indicating an intention to slit the Gael's throat for him if he did not stop talking, and Faolan, who was smiling, obliged with silence. Below them, half glimpsed through the bushes, the women gathered their tools, their cloaks, and set off in orderly file for the long walk home. Despite himself, Bridei moved to look again, just for a moment more. Tuala was at the end of the line, by

herself, although the others walked in pairs. She kept turning
to look back; one slender white hand came up to brush the
curls from her face, and they fell in a defiant tangle back
across her brow. Her eyes were shadowed as if she, too, had
been troubled by her dreams.

"Don't move," Faolan said quietly. "Let her go. I see how
you long for this; it explains much. Let her follow them. To
act now would spell ruin."

He was right. That did nothing to quell the aching of
Bridei's heart, a pain that seemed to spread into every part
of him, urging him forward, now, now, before she vanished
from his sight forever, for how could he bear to be so close
and not to speak, not to touch . . . He stayed quite still and
silent as Tuala moved down the stream and away. He waited
longer, as the ache in his heart was joined once more by a
deep throbbing somewhere behind his temples. What he had
suspected was true; this was a malady for which Broichan
had no cure. Eventually Faolan got up and went to untether
the horses. It was safe to begin the ride back to court.

They went awhile without a word. It was Bridei who
broke the silence. "Was that another part of your calculated
strategy? To make me weep before you, so you can report
my weakness back to the masters who pay you? Did you
know these women would be here?"

"Yes and no," Faolan said. "Certain information came to
me suggesting Fola might bring her charges out on the first
fine, dry day; there are rites that must be performed here in
preparation for Gateway. And I'm told the students need to
gather herbs in the wild as part of their training. I did not
know exactly the day and the time; in that, your gods inter-
vened. They play a complex game with you, Bridei."

"Why? What interest can you have in this? It is my own
particular misery; it need not be drawn into what we do at
Caer Pridne."

"No? I seek to discover the source of your malady. That
is most certainly part of my job. A man who is beset by
crippling headaches, a man who cannot sleep more than a
snatch at a time, and that plagued by nightmares, will eventually become incapable of fulfilling the role that awaits
him. You told me you did not need a woman; that such re-

lease would not help. What I see today suggests that you were wrong."

Fury made Bridei's teeth clench tight. His head was pounding like a war drum. "Do not speak of her thus," he said. "You cheapen this. She is my oldest and dearest friend; closer to me than any other could be. Last time I saw her, she was a child. You see what she is now: a wise woman, a daughter of the Shining One, called by the goddess herself. Tuala is no forest enchantress sent to lure me to my doom like the sprites in the tales. Nor is she some common creature for easy taking. She is . . ." He made himself stop. The more he said, the fiercer the pain.

"Brought up in Broichan's house. Your sister."

"No. Not my sister; we were ever closer than sister and brother. More like the two parts of one whole: kernel and shell; petal and stalk; pipe and reed; harp and string." Bridei anticipated a withering response, but none was forthcoming. They rode on in silence until, in the distance, the walls of Banmerren could be seen once more and along the bay beyond them the looming shape of the king's fortress. They had gone by ways which, Faolan had said, did not cross any likely walking tracks; they might be wishing to establish a pattern, but it was the spies of influential men they wanted to attract, not a gaggle of women.

"Very well," Faolan said abruptly, reining his mount to a halt. "What do you want to do?"

"I don't understand you."

"I'm sure you do. Here's the dilemma: a man who needs to be at his best, and soon, for the fate of a kingdom depends on it. A man with a problem to resolve before he can be well again. A problem that cannot be resolved unless he breaks the rules. But he cannot break these rules for fear of offending someone: his foster father, the monarch, the gods. So I ask again, what do you want to do?"

"Are you presenting me with a choice? You, the man paid to stop me from walking into danger? The man who dogs my every step?"

"Give me a plan," Faolan said. "A strategy. If it meets with my approval, we'll do it."

"A plan. A plan for you to take straight back to Broichan. He's the one with the silver pieces." Bridei heard the edge in his own voice and felt shame, but right now this seemed to be the best he could manage.

Faolan sighed. "I am my own man, for all the silver pieces. A fellow has to eat; that need not render him mindlessly obedient. Broichan's particularly busy right now. The king requires his full attention. Besides, from what I've learned of druids, they're not your best experts in matters of the heart. I don't think we need reveal anything to Broichan just yet. It's plain to me you must see this young woman alone, speak to her, bed her if you have to—on second thoughts, that could cause all manner of complications, so perhaps better not—and sort this out once and for all. You have certain challenges to overcome. She's behind high walls. She may not wish to see you; who knows a woman's mind? You have enemies. Nobody must know, save for myself. Work it out; make it foolproof. Then tell me. It must be soon. We don't have long."

Bridei cleared his throat. He was momentarily lost for words. This was probably just part of another convoluted scheme. "It is not a case of bedding, as you so crudely put it," he said. "Tuala is—was—a child; it is not appropriate . . ."

"You're deluding yourself," Faolan said. "Look at me and tell me you watched her down there with her pearly skin and her dreaming eyes and didn't feel desire. What is it you want? Isn't it, at heart, as simple as that?"

There was no answer to this. It was and it wasn't. He needed her as fledgling trees need rain, as opening flowers need sun. He yearned for her as the salmon yearns for the home pool high in the hills. He craved her as a lonely child craves a friend of the heart. And he wanted her as a man wants a woman. That much, after today, was starkly clear to him. Not as occasional lover nor as convenient mistress; not as temptress from beyond the margin. As his wife. There was no other way it could be. And it was impossible. Apart from the objections Broichan would raise, and Aniel and the others, Tuala herself had made it so. The Shining One had taken her from him.

"I love her," he said simply.

"Mm. You mean purely, honorably, nobly, that kind of thing?"

"It is, I imagine, beyond your understanding."

"No doubt. Let us ride; best if we appear at Caer Pridne while it still lacks some time until dusk. I want us to be seen. You work on your plan and I will devote tomorrow to mine. If your gods visit you tonight, ask them for more fine weather. I've no desire to be riding out in a tempest."

IT WAS THE morning of Gateway. The moon was a few days from her perfect fullness, but the weather was wet and windy; the face of the Shining One would not be seen over Caer Pridne tonight as the darkest of rituals took place deep under the earth by the Well of Shades. Bridei had slept little. He felt like a stretched wire, every part of him jangling, every sensation magnified. His head swarmed with thoughts, ideas, unresolved questions. Foremost among these dilemmas was tonight's ritual. He had an idea of how it would be enacted here at the Well, based on court whispers and on the details Wid and Erip had half explained. The thought of it chilled him to the marrow. There were gods and gods. The Flamekeeper he loved wholeheartedly, a deity of light, courage, and strength, who rewarded men for their valor and expected nothing more complicated in return than loyalty and purpose. He revered the Shining One in her beauty and wisdom; he respected Bone Mother as a child respects an ancient elder, with both love and fear. But the god whom the men must honor tonight was a different matter. What he demanded was terrifying, repellent, a test of utmost obedience that must stretch the will almost beyond sanity. Bridei did not know, in truth, whether he would be able to look on as it happened and maintain his composure. He must do so; it was another test. A man who would be king could not afford to fail it.

Those others, Carnach, Wredech, they would have experienced this before, as the king's close kinsmen. Drust the Boar would have enacted it himself in the days before he turned to the Christian God; his advisers, having turned their backs on the old ways, were unlikely to attend tonight. For Bridei, this would be the first time. Passing Broichan's door, he saw the druid kneeling alone, facing the wall, deep eyes distant, arms outstretched in pose of supplication. The chamber was almost dark; a single candle burned, throwing Broichan's shadow across the stones in a looming, distorted shape. Bridei was reminded, sharply, of the day he himself first came to Pitnochie; of his sense of his foster father as immensely tall, shadowy, a presence alive with harnessed power. He stood in the doorway watching for quite some time. Broichan never moved from that pose of total concentration and utmost discipline. Eventually Bridei walked on, a silent Garth at his shoulder. He sought out Gartnait, thinking what was needed today was a simple activity to tax the body hard and drive away dark thoughts: wrestling, perhaps, or a bout with staves. But Gartnait was unexpectedly busy. He sat with the king's scribe, laboring over his letters.

"Sorry," Gartnait said. His rueful grin sat askew with the look in his eyes; they were uncharacteristically bleak. "My mother has taken it into her head that certain gaps in my learning must be filled; she has set an exacting schedule for me. I may have some free time later."

"I'll look out for you," said Bridei, retreating. This was odd; surely Lady Dreseida knew her son well enough to realize the scribe was wasting his time with Gartnait. Some men were simply not made to be scholars. The heir to Raven's Well was able enough in other spheres; he was a powerful swimmer and adept with sword and staff. He rode capably. He would never grasp reading and writing, history and philosophy. Bridei had only to compare his own attempts to share some of what he knew with Gartnait and his efforts with Tuala. Tuala soaked up learning as if born to it; Gartnait simply wasn't interested. When you were bored, you didn't learn. It seemed both Gartnait and the scribe were in for some long, fruitless days.

Faolan was nowhere to be found. It was too wet to go out riding, too cold for any but designated guards to be out on the wall-walks. There was nowhere tolerably quiet save their own quarters, and to spend the day there was to leave his mind open to thoughts of the ritual to come. The silent, still figure of Broichan in the adjoining chamber would do nothing to keep them at bay.

They went to the hall. Breth was there already with a group of men throwing knives into a wooden target, an effigy that was all staring eyes and hair done in scarlet paint: clearly a Gael. Others gathered close to the hearth. Men were sitting over game boards, women listened to the king's bard as he coaxed a mournful tune from the harp, others were deep in conversation. Bridei had become expert at scanning such groups and identifying those he must engage in talk and those better avoided. Talorgen was watching the knife throwers, and so were the king's cousin Carnach with several of his men, and the councillor Tharan. Aniel was absent; the king was ailing and would be in need of support to strengthen him for the night's ordeal. There was no sign of the queen, nor of her brother. But among the men who stood near the hearth, talking in low voices, were the two emissaries from Circinn. The cold-eyed Bargoit was doing most of the talking, while elderly Fergus listened and nodded. The Christian, Suibne, was smiling amiably and tapping his foot in time to the harp, as if there were not a good king dying in this place. Bridei did not allow himself to become angry. This must be treated as an opportunity; he must force his mind from the other matter that sought to drive even the ritual from his thoughts. The little packet lay safe in the pouch at his belt. There had been no other message, nothing save what Ana had slipped into his hand as they passed in the hallway, the day the girls came back once more from Banmerren. Only this: a scrap of cloth bound with a green ribbon, and within, a shriveled oak leaf and a round white pebble. Tuala was clever. Who could interpret that save druid or wise woman? Who could recognize its meaning save a child raised in such a household as Broichan's? It gave, instantly, the *when* and *where* he needed for Faolan.

Bridei had been through all the arguments. He had sworn to himself, after that day at the ancient cairns, that he would not seek her out; could not. She did not wish it; she had chosen Banmerren. She would send no reply. He must not doubt the wisdom of the Shining One. Should he become king, should Tuala then agree to become his wife, he would be condemning her to a life of unhappiness. At court she would be subject to gossip, whispers, perhaps outright hatred. Nobody trusted the Good Folk. How could one of them ever be accepted as queen of Fortriu? Over and over Bridei had told himself these truths, while every day he had waited with beating heart for Ana's return. She had watched his face with some curiosity as she slipped the packet into his hand. Bridei had turned away quickly with a murmured thank you; his heart had been behaving unreliably, and he'd felt the flush in his cheeks. He had acknowledged, then, what he had known all along since he had seen Tuala by the stream that afternoon, so grave and sweet, so wonderfully changed yet so remarkably still herself. He must see her, despite the risk. To be discovered within the walls of Banmerren was to throw away the prospect of kingship; to venture there was to insult the goddess. He must do as Faolan had suggested, then; make a plan and ensure it was foolproof. Tuala had given him half the plan with her stone and leaf, a message clear as any words: *the oak tree at full moon.* Only four days away, so soon, so soon he would see her again, and this time touch her, tell her . . . no, that was getting too far ahead. He had to smuggle himself and Faolan out of Caer Pridne and along the sand to Banmerren unseen, by moonlight. He must take a rope. He must trust that Tuala would be waiting for him, no matter when he got there. And he could not be there long. But he would go . . .

He could not think of that now. Bargoit had ceased his narrative and was eyeing Bridei, arms folded, expression challenging. Beside him, his fellow councillor Fergus had taken up a similar stance. If they wanted some kind of debate, he would give them one. Every meeting must be used, and used well, if he was to have the numbers when it counted.

"Play knives if you want," he murmured to Garth.

"Best if I just keep an eye on them; too easy for someone's hand to wobble, in here, and something sharp travel beyond the target at an unfortunate moment. You planning to talk to that long-faced misery from Circinn?"

"That's the plan. Better be quiet if you're coming over with me. We must at least make pretense of being civil."

"To a fellow who throws the wise women out of their houses and installs wretched foreigners like that Suibne instead?"

"To just such a fellow, Garth. He's one of our own, whether or not we like his approach."

"Silent as the grave, that's me."

"Good man."

A conversation ensued that covered a wide range of topics without ever quite mentioning the sad fact that Drust the Bull was dying, or the undeniable truth that Fortriu would soon be needing a new king. They began on neutral territory, speaking of fishing and hunting and what opportunities existed in the Great Glen as opposed to the gentler lands near the southern court of Drust the Boar. Circinn was not without hills, although nothing there could rival the high, bare peaks of the Five Sisters or the snow-capped mountains of the west. Drust the Boar's own fortress was set atop an ancient mount, close by the sacred hill that had been a place of pilgrimage since time before time: the Mother, it was called. Wise women no longer made their climb up the Mother's bony flanks, nor kept their vigil on her peak at Gateway or at Measure. Christian missionaries had put a stop to that. The houses of the goddess in Circinn had been closed down one by one, the wise women displaced. Bridei wondered if folk still made the journey secretly, alone or in little furtive groups. He turned his thoughts back to the topic under discussion: what game might be found on the wooded slopes of that region.

"You hunt deer yourself?" Bargoit inquired. "A good pastime for a young man."

"I was raised by a druid," Bridei said quietly. "I have participated in the hunt at Raven's Well. But my knowledge of wild creatures is based on the understanding of the world we share, not on a need to pursue and kill. At Pitnochie our table was furnished chiefly from the farm. And with fish, of course. The hidden glens north of Serpent Lake are home to some of the finest trout that ever graced a man's table."

"Mm," said Bargoit. "They tell me Morleo's lands at Longwater are rich with lakes and streams. You fought with him at Galany's Reach, did you not? What opinion did you form of the man?"

"I think Morleo an admirable leader," Bridei said cautiously; this topic was more complicated. "Forthright, flexible, respected by his men."

"And Ged?"

"Well loved. Valiant."

"You describe Morleo as flexible. No man who adheres unswervingly to the old ways can be called that. You're living in the past, all of you. No wonder . . ." Bargoit appeared to think better of what was to follow. His sudden reticence was more than a little artful.

"No wonder what?" Bridei could not let it go. Others were listening, Bargoit's fellow councillor Fergus and, from farther away, the Christian priest, Drust the Bull's adviser Tharan, and the red-headed Carnach, a contender for kingship.

"No wonder your victory at Galany's Reach was a short-lived thing," Bargoit said bluntly. "Who but a man who looks ever backward would seek to make such an expensive gesture? A whole season wasted, grievous losses sustained, homes and farms neglected, and for what? The momentary seizing of a trifling objective? The symbolic removal of a lump of stone with a few cryptic signs carved on it, an animal or two, a depiction of headless corpses arrayed in rows? No territory gained and precious few useful prisoners taken. One petty chieftain, that was about all, from what they tell me. That's no way to conduct a war. With that approach, Fortriu will never drive out the invaders. Before you know it the Great Glen will be overrun by Gaels. They'll be burning your homes, laying waste your farms, slaughtering your children, and helping themselves to your wives."

It was necessary to remain calm. Not far off stood Talorgen, suddenly very white, with a grim set to the jaw. Bridei used one of Broichan's patterns for breathing, unclenched his hands, willed the headache into the background. "Such comments intrigue me," he said smoothly, moving to seat himself in what he hoped was a relaxed pose on a bench near Bargoit. "May I? Do sit down; let us continue our discussion. Breth, will you ask someone to bring ale? Now," lean-

ing forward to address the other, "the way I've heard it told,
Circinn has its own border problems. A different enemy, Angles and others from the south, a multitude of fierce tribes
whose incursions inside your lands require great numbers of
armed men to be stationed more or less permanently in those
parts. A heavy toll on the court, or on whichever chieftains
must maintain those outposts. I would not provoke a childish
contest here by asking if you, in your turn, have ventured
forth into the south and attempted to reclaim the territories
lost to your people. I will not ask if your own victories are
symbolic or real. I will say that a wise man does not look at
his realm piece by piece, as if he believed he could comprehend a whole shore by examining a single grain of sand, or
an entire forest in a solitary leaf. I adhere to the ancient
gods; I am loyal to them in every way, for they are the very
foundation, the beating heart of Fortriu. That does not mean
I look backward, Bargoit. My view is backward and forward
and on every side. My eyes are open to every opportunity, to
every challenge and every threat. That does not render me
blind to manifestations of spirit. The two go hand in hand; a
man cannot live his life well and fully without the breath of
the gods at his back, their whisper in his ear. You accuse us
of living in the past. That is incorrect. We carry the past
within us; it hums in our veins, it beats in our hearts. It
strengthens us on our journey forward; it carries us bravely
into the future."

There was a little silence. The priest, Brother Suibne,
cleared his throat apologetically. "You speak well," the
Christian said. "It is no wonder men follow you. All the
same, these gods you talk of are no more than shadows. If
they call you to such dark acts as that which must take place
tonight, then those voices you hear are manifestations of the
Devil; whispers of pure evil. You must turn from them and
walk toward the light. There is but one true way, and it is not
this, with its harvest of cruelty and death. How can you—"

"Shh," hissed a circle of horrified voices, and Suibne fell
silent, but not for long.

"Your gods rule you through fear," he said. "The way of
the one true God is a path of love, of forgiveness, of joy.

Trust in him, and you need no longer appease your dark deities with acts of violence that fill you with unease."

"You are a guest here." It was the king's councillor, Tharan, who spoke now. He and a number of the others had moved closer during Bridei's speech and now the sharp-eyed elder addressed Brother Suibne in a tone calculated to silence the boldest of men. "The king has offered you the hospitality of his hall, as he is obliged to do, since you travel with emissaries from Drust the Boar. We accept your presence among us. But none of us will permit your flagrant violations of ancient custom. They place us all in peril. When you speak aloud of this ritual and of the one it honors you offend the god, and you offend every one of his loyal adherents. This is law. We imbibe it with our mothers' milk. I will not speak of this again, save to say that in breaking silence on the matter you risk bringing down the god's punishment not just upon yourself, but on every man here present, be he of Circinn or of Fortriu. I hope I need say no more."

Suibne had not even the grace to blush or to mutter an apology. He gave a little shake of the head and touched his hand to the cross he wore on a cord around his neck.

"Fortriu is full of men, and they are full of words," Bargoit observed with a lift of the brows. "Young men, older men, men in their dotage. They all sing the same song. This is a time of change, my friends. We of the south have embraced it; our folk turn increasingly to the new faith."

"That is not the whole truth," said the king's cousin, Carnach. "My own lands border northern Circinn. The tales I hear are of people displaced, wise women harried from the settlements, men of faith dispossessed and turned from their homes, ancient places of worship laid waste to make way for Christian temples. These accounts have not suggested to me a peaceful transition to the new faith under the leadership of Drust the Boar. I would not seek such a man for my own king."

This was dangerously close to a clear statement of what it was they were really discussing; too close for comfort. Drust the Bull still lived. Tonight he would perform the ritual of Gateway, a ceremony in which the shades of those departed hung close, and Bone Mother's outstretched hand was but a hair's-breadth away.

"It is an error," Bridei said quietly, "to assume that because something is old, it is no longer of use. We learn from our elders. We learn from the past; how else can we gain wisdom? I owe a great debt to the tutors who were present for the years of my childhood, venerable ancients, the two of them, and living exemplars of all that is good in a man: wisdom, courage, humor, faith. The old ways are the heart and spirit of Fortriu. Toss them aside and you are left with an empty shell. Discard them and you make of a living, breathing land a dead husk, devoid of meaning."

"As the young man said," the councillor Fergus remarked to Bargoit, "he was raised by a druid, none other than Broichan. We should not be surprised that Bridei expresses himself thus. Such a man thinks in riddles and answers with questions. His mind follows paths far removed from those of ordinary folk such as ourselves."

"Bridei expresses only the truths that reside in all of us." This from an unexpected quarter: it was the gaunt-featured Tharan, the man Aniel had once called dangerous, who spoke. "Whatever our differences, true men of Fortriu share the same loyalties and the same aspirations. We love the gods and we love this land entrusted to our people since time before time. We do not always love one another; it's in man's nature to dispute, to jostle for power. For all that, here in the north, at least, our goal is a common one: to adhere to the will of the gods and to clear the invader from our shores."

"There was little sign of that in your recent venture, so I hear," said Fergus. "A few Gaels slain, a momentary presence in the settlement at Galany's Reach, a circumspect retreat; that can hardly be construed as sweeping the invader away. As for the old gods, they must have wept in shame, surely, to see the great stone wrenched from the earth and manhandled across half the countryside. Was not that an insult to your ancient lore? Besides, your own actions hardly match your claims, Tharan. Where were you when all this was unfolding? Warming your hands at Caer Pridne's house fires, I imagine."

The group of men by the hearth was much larger now; this dialogue had attracted the attention of many. Bridei saw a look of deep offense and mounting anger on Talorgen's honest features; he observed the twitch in Tharan's cheek, sign that the most dangerous councillor in Fortriu was not impervious to insults. The king's cousin, Carnach, was glaring openly; Bargoit maintained his supercilious expression. The Christian priest had wandered off to listen to the music.

"That is unjust, and you know it," Bridei said bluntly. He had not expected to be springing to the defense of Tharan, of all men. But he felt compelled to speak. Fergus's words had been outrageous and could not be allowed to go unchallenged. "Do you and your fellow councillor here ride out to do battle against the Angles, leaving your king without advisers by his side? I doubt it very much. Tharan remains at Drust's right hand; the Bull's councillors have served him long and wisely. A good monarch understands the value of such support, indeed, friendship. It is true that Tharan, Aniel, and Eogan are not always of one mind, but that serves only to strengthen the role they play, allowing the king to sift possibilities and be open to ideas. Our councillors do not go to war; we have chieftains such as Talorgen here to control those endeavors, men expert in sorties and defenses and in the daily leadership of warriors. A king does not throw his entire strength out to the farthest reaches of his realm with no thought to the maintenance of what is closer to home. As for our own venture, it was worthy. Talorgen led us with honor and purpose. It was never our intention to reclaim that territory, for the time is not ripe for such an undertaking. We sought to test the water for the future; to put fear into the enemy's heart. We killed twice fifty and more of the men of Dalriada. We took a hostage of significance, held now in confinement at Fokel's stronghold. As for the Mage Stone, no man questions the gods. It remains to be seen whether their wrath will descend on us for an act of sacrilege, as you suggest. All I can tell you is that when we performed that feat, it seemed to all of us that the Flamekeeper smiled on us. We felt his love even as we feel the warmth of the sun; his goodwill sustained us and saw us safely home. The power of the gods is beyond measure; it raises us above the cheap taunts of those who would mock our endeavors and scorn our comrades who shed their blood on that field of war."

"That's all very well," Bargoit said, spreading his hands in a placatory gesture. He was now encircled by angry men. "But your arguments lack something in logic, young man. You spoke in poetic mode before: grains of sand, single leaves and so on. If it is so important for a man to view our land as a single entity, whole and undivided, then surely we need one rule, one court, one king? One faith? If this is truly your belief, young Bridei, then I find myself in perfect agreement. We of Circinn and Fortriu are one people, even if we forget that from time to time."

"The Caitt, also," Bridei said quietly. "You would include them in this unified realm, of course."

"The Caitt?" hissed Fergus. "Those barbarians?"

"Of Priteni blood," said Talorgen, who now stood at Bridei's shoulder. "You mention logic. Let us take this to its inevitable conclusion. All would be one: Fortriu and Circinn, the Light Isles and the territory of the Caitt. Disparate realms, but united under one king and one faith. It is not such a leap of the imagination. In my father's time, Bargoit, and in your father's time, it was indeed thus. The territories of the Priteni were a single kingdom. It was the decision of Drust son of Girom to admit the missionaries of the Christian faith to the south that split our homeland apart. You advocate now its return to its former state? You'd find no argument against that among the men of Fortriu."

Bargoit smiled thinly. "I advocate no such thing, as you are well aware. The old practices are gone from Circinn and will never return. There is another way, one that is open to us now, should Fortriu make the choice to move forward instead of backward."

"Fortriu will never turn against its ancient gods." Bridei felt a shiver through his body, like a cold touch of winter in the bones. "Our good king lives yet, and we pray the gods preserve him to lead us for the seasons to come. I, too, would wish to see our land united under a single leader. Indeed, I believe that is the only way we can secure our borders, both to the west against the Gaels and to the south against the Angles. I believe it is the only course for us if we would remain strong in a time of such change. Such a leader would not be a man who trusted his councillors more than he should. He would not be a man who displaced druids and banished wise women. A true king could never spit in the faces of the gods so. That is what I believe. Such a leader would be strong and good, steadfast in his faith and ready to sacrifice much to carry his people forward with hope and purpose. Drust son of Wdrost is such a man. We love and honor him. And he still lives. To draw the talk, as you have done here, to a future beyond that offends every one of us. But you are his guest. So, I offer you ale, and suggest we move the conversation to other matters. We did begin this, I recall, with a discussion about fishing. That was not only respectful to our host, but a good deal safer. Caught any big ones lately?"

The men of Fortriu laughed despite themselves. It was adept, and they began, quickly, a lively exchange about the size and quality of trout to be found in the different lakes and what kind of bait was best. Bargoit, lips compressed, did not contribute.

"Well done," Talorgen murmured in Bridei's ear a little later, after they had extricated themselves from the crowd. "You achieved a number of objectives rather quickly, including at least one that surprised me. You got Tharan to agree with you publicly. We might work on that."

Bridei nodded, as a sudden weariness came over him. In one sense, Talorgen was right; one should not lose sight of how much was to be gained here, how much lost if one got it wrong. These were powerful men. In the choice of candidates for kingship, theirs were the voices that counted. And yet, as he had spoken today, Bridei had forgotten what was riding on his finding the right words, the right tone. He had not been thinking of his own future, only of the need to tell these men what was in his mind and his heart. Talorgen misjudged him if he thought this had been a calculated bid for support. "Tharan spoke from a love of Fortriu," he said. "Carnach also. In that, at least, the men of the north are in agreement."

"But the south has solid numbers," said Talorgen. "Circinn will send twelve chieftains to the voting when it's time. The process allows them an entire turning of the moon to get here. Unless we pray for particularly foul weather, there's likely to be a full complement. We'll need to put in some solid work or Fortriu cannot present a united front against that. A single candidate only, that's what we want. There's a lot further to go. You look tired, Bridei."

"When I'm out there among those men, it almost seems easy," Bridei said, "as if the gods tell me the right things to say. Afterward, when I'm alone, I remember that I am only one man. That there are other worthy contenders ready to stand against me. That, in the eyes of these chieftains, I am young and untried, a nobody. You have invested a great deal of faith in me: you, your friends, Broichan particularly. I do not wish to fail you. I do not wish to fail the gods."

Talorgen looked at him curiously. "Had we believed you might do so, Bridei, we would not have pursued this to the end. It seems that end may be closer than we imagined."

"Yes; I've heard the king's health continues to fail."

"Drust will not be with us much longer. Aniel is by his side today, with the queen. The gods are merciful; they will see our king perform the ritual one last time and then, I believe, he will be called away. This will be a cold winter."

Bridei said nothing. He thought of the deep well, colder than any winter, and the voice of the dark god, calling.

"He will endure the ceremony," Talorgen said. "Drust's will is very strong. It will tax him sorely. Are you prepared for this, Bridei?"

"I must be."

Talorgen nodded. "Even Broichan dreads it. It must be done. It is part of what we are; a darkness within us that must be recognized. You should rest. The night will be long."

14

THE SUN HAD not shown his face all day. Lowering clouds spread from north to south, from east to west, their bellies heavy with rain. From time to time they released themselves, sending a drumming deluge over the roofs of Banmerren, a thunderous downpour that streamed from the thatch and lost itself in a hundred rivulets snaking across the waterlogged gardens, where even the ducks had retreated under a bush for shelter. Within the walled compound day seemed like dusk, and when at last the sun sank somewhere behind the clouds, night fell abruptly, as if the secret god were impatient to receive his dues.

The oak was almost bare; rain pooled in the hollows between its exposed roots. The light of Kethra's oil lamp touched the mounds of leaves, yellow-gold, russet red, nut brown, all turning now in the wet to a common hue of rich decay as the earth reclaimed them to nourish next season's new growth. The voice of the rain drowned all else. Tuala followed the older woman along the covered walkway and inside the main building, where a hearth fire burned fitfully in the large central chamber, as if all too aware of the power of this deluge. The fire would be quenched before the time of the ritual; such presences as attended this ceremony were known to shun the light.

It was quiet in the house. The din of the rain had faded from an ear-assaulting roar to a distant rumble as they closed the door behind them. The girls, who generally welcomed the opportunity to gather together and speak of home and friends, to share fifty little secrets they'd been saving up, were unusually solemn tonight.

Before dusk, they had watched as Fola walked out from Banmerren, hooded head bowed against the rain, and after her a procession of cloaked women making a solemn progress along the path to Caer Pridne. It was whispered that

Fola didn't like Gateway. They said the wise woman preferred to enact the rituals in places of the goddess: here
within the sheltering walls, or on the wide strand just beyond, or in the secret hollow of the triple cairns. Not at Caer
Pridne, a realm of men and power and ancient darkness. Not
this form of the ceremony, in which women's part was both
rarest privilege and deepest shame. But Fola obeyed the
gods. She obeyed all of them, even the one that could not be
named. So she led her women out, all of the priestesses save
Kethra, who would remain behind to watch over the younger
girls; all of the green-clad seniors, the historian Derila and
her peers. None of the juniors; those who wore the blue robe
might not yet learn the conduct of this ritual, and could most
certainly not attend its enactment.

Odha had challenged Kethra on the subject earlier. "Why
can't we go, too? We're here to learn, after all. And we want
to see Caer Pridne, the bull stones and the king's court and
everything."

Kethra's face had changed; every part of it had seemed to
tighten. "That is beyond foolishness, Odha. You should
kneel to the Shining One and thank her from the bottom of
your heart that you need not be there tonight. Your time will
come. That's if we don't send you home for sheer stupidity
before you get anywhere near earning the green robe."

"But—"

"Not another word."

Now they gathered before the hearth. Nobody said a
thing. They listened to the rain, avoided one another's eyes
and thought their own thoughts. Tuala had wanted to spend
the night of Gateway in her tower alone, holding Bridei
safely with her mind as he witnessed the ritual, willing him
strong in spirit and steadfast of purpose in this darkest of
tests. But Kethra had made her come into the house. It was
cold in the tower and the roof leaked. Tuala must join the
others; they would keep vigil all together.

The girls were familiar with Gateway itself, of course.
Every household in Fortriu, every settlement, every community observed it. Bone Mother was honored, lights
quenched, the spirits of the departed welcomed; chill, eddying drafts signaled the spiral dance of these shades among

the living, before, behind, around, between, touching a cheek or hand with icy fingers, a trembling mouth with frosty lips. Broichan had always sacrificed a creature to the god, generally an autumn lamb or a chicken. The first time she was allowed to stay up for the rite, Bridei had told Tuala to put her fingers in her ears and shut her eyes when they came to that part, but she had peeked, and then wished she hadn't. After the offering came prayers, a sharing of the ritual foods, and the lighting of a single candle: hope restored, the way forward still miraculously illuminated even in a time of darkness and death. Tuala understood that; she had even as a little child. The oak tree slept; no sign of green, no hint of life save in the deep, slow tales at its heart, the strange and wondrous changing of withered leaf to rich soil, nurturing its hidden growth. Thus did men and women rest as the pathway ahead formed itself anew somewhere in the secret maze of their dreams.

That was Gateway at Pitnochie, at Raven's Well, and in every part of the land of Fortriu. It was different at Caer Pridne. The promontory on which the king's fortress was built housed a deep place in the earth, a dark cleft sacred to the most ancient of gods, him whose name could not be spoken, so feared was he among the Priteni. Over countless ages, the kings of Fortriu had made their way to the Well of Shades at Gateway to enact the particular ritual this deity demanded. It was necessary; history had proven this most cruelly. Wid and Erip had spoken of a certain monarch who could not bring himself to see it through; under his command the well had been sealed off, the pathway closed. All seemed unchanged at first. Then came the seasons of darkness: three years without a summer. A haze masked the sky day in, day out; the Flamekeeper shrank to no more than a slight paling, giving scant light and less warmth. The Shining One retreated behind her veil and would not look down upon this disobedient land. Crops failed before they rose a handspan from the earth; hunger and sickness ravaged Fortriu. Folk perished in their thousands and the survivors became half crazed, starving for both food and light. They prostrated themselves in their despair, begging the gods to be merciful to them. In the fourth year of darkness, Bone

Mother bore the king himself beyond the veil and the chieftains of Fortriu chose a new monarch. That Gateway, the
men of Caer Pridne gathered once more by the Well of
Shades and the ceremony unfolded in its ancient form. The
summers returned. It took the Priteni a long time to recover
from the seasons of darkness; how can a man encompass the
terror of living in perpetual shadow? This had taken place
within the memory of men still living. In the south, beyond
the Roman wall, it was said the scourge had lasted even
longer, for the dark season had been followed by plagues,
and the few who survived the years of famine and sickness
had neither strength nor will remaining to begin the long
task of turning wasteland back to fertile farm and healthy
pasture.

Tuala knew the general form of the observance would
have much in common with the version Broichan had performed at home. But it would be different: the king's ritual
was attended only by men, and the exact manner of it was
secret. The wise women of Banmerren did not go down to
the well. They had a certain duty to perform, and when that
was done they kept vigil on the shore below the fortress until sunrise. That would be especially hard tonight; the Shining One had shrouded her brightness, perhaps in shame at
what must be done to placate the oldest of gods. The women
would be cold and wet when they came home. And sad. How
could they not be sad?

Tuala stared into the fire. She wondered if the others really didn't know what would happen tonight, or if they were
just pretending because the truth was too hard to accept. Between them, Erip and Wid had given sufficient hints over the
years. What Tuala did not know, she could guess. That pale-
faced, strange-eyed girl, Morna, had walked out behind Fola,
hooded and caped in gray as if she were already a priestess
fully fledged; impossible, Morna was much too young and
had been at Banmerren only a year or so. Morna had walked
oddly today, as if in her mind she were not making her way
along a muddy track under threatening skies, but treading
some other path entirely, one shared only with gods and
spirits.

The night wore on; the fire struggled to remain alight.

None of the girls asked to be excused, to retire to the comfort of her bed. Tonight there were too many dark corners in the sleeping quarters, too many odd-shaped shadows. But, one by one, the young women leaned against walls or laid their heads down on tables or stretched out on benches and were claimed by sleep. When the time for the ritual drew close, only Kethra and Tuala knew it, seated as they were one on either side of the hearth.

"Tuala?"

"Yes?"

"I've watched you scrying; I've seen the power of the images you can summon. Why aren't you using this skill anymore? I had thought, in excusing you from my class, to see you blossom on your own. I had hoped Fola and I might teach you how to harness your talent to best use. But I haven't seen you with a scrying bowl since that first time."

"I think it might be . . . dangerous. Often, what I see disturbs me."

"The eye of the spirit does not open so the seer can be comforted, but so she can learn," Kethra said. "One expects to be disturbed; one accepts a draining of body and spirit after such visions. To shy away from using this talent, especially when you are so strong in it, seems disobedient; a flouting of the goddess's will. And you are here in Banmerren as her servant. Does not a good daughter of Fortriu obey the Shining One in all things?"

Tuala said nothing.

"Tell me." Kethra leaned forward, elbows on knees; the firelight showed her questioning eyes, the little lines around her mouth, the tightly disciplined hair. "Can you summon whatever you wish to find in the water? Can you control your gift to that extent? If you desired it, could you look now and see what unfolds in the dark, secret place at Caer Pridne?"

Suddenly Tuala was extremely cold; it was as if she stood on the brink of the Well of Shades, teetering above a square of inky water. "Sometimes I can command it," she whispered. "Sometimes the goddess sends other images. I think, if I looked tonight, that is what I would see. The king. The well. But it is forbidden for women to attend that ritual."

"We would not be attending," said Kethra softly. "Merely

being granted a reflection that somewhat resembled the reality. Are you able to draw another into your vision? To share it?"

"I don't know." Tuala was shivering. Kethra's suggestion had alarmed her; still more alarming was the realization that this was exactly what she herself wanted to do, needed to do, so she could share the dark time with Bridei, step by step, breath by breath.

"If we linked hands," Kethra said, "and both of us turned our will on this, perhaps the goddess would grant us the self-same vision. You possess a strong natural talent. I am practiced in this craft and have tools to keep it in check. Together we might do well."

Tuala stared at her. Kethra was a wise woman. She must know this was forbidden. It was surely little different from attending the secret ritual themselves, something no woman might do. To spy on this rite was to anger the gods; to risk a terrible retribution. Yet she wanted to do it. Her desire for it grew stronger the more she thought about it. Bridei was there. Do this, and she could see him now, right away. She could hold him safe in her thoughts as he endured what must unfold. "Fola wouldn't approve," she said.

"Fola would have come to this in time." Kethra's voice, held quiet not to wake her slumbering students, nonetheless possessed complete confidence. "Your abilities fascinate her. She brought you here, I suspect, less for what we could teach you than for what skills you could impart to us. Believe me, if Fola were not required to spend tonight shivering on the seashore, she would be here beside us looking into the bowl. Will you do it? It must be almost time."

Tuala said nothing, simply rose when Kethra did and went to fetch a ewer of water while the tutor readied the bronze bowl. The water swirled and settled. She took Kethra's hands across the table so they stood face to face with the scrying bowl between them, and together they bowed their heads over the surface. The fire was almost dead, the chamber near dark. One candle burned; the faces of the sleeping girls were pale ovals in the shadows. Tuala felt her heart slow, her breathing grow quiet. Then the goddess claimed her and drew her down into the darkness.

A procession; the wise women approaching Caer Pridne, the rain now retreated, Fola with her silvery hair loose down her back. Another woman walking beside her. No, not a woman, a girl, an ashen-faced, empty-eyed girl with brown curls to her waist and a pristine gown of whitest linen beneath the gray cloak of a wise woman. Morna: the one who had suddenly disappeared from classes to be glimpsed again only as a shadow, there then gone, the one whose eyes seemed to see nothing but dreams. On her other side was Luthana, expert in herb lore, she of the long days spent digging and pruning and slaving over steaming kettles. They came up to the iron gates of Caer Pridne; Tuala could see the bull stones on either side of the path, formidable slabs on which the creature's image showed dimly in the light from torches. Perhaps that man, Garvan, had carved these things of beauty, Garvan, whom she had failed to surprise with a story of desire and self-control. Garvan, whose wife she would be now if she had not chosen the path of the Shining One.

They waited in silence, Morna standing still and pale between the two older women and the priestesses of Banmerren behind them in pairs, hoods back, hands crossed on their breasts. Fola and Luthana did not adopt this pose; each grasped one of Morna's frail wrists, as if the girl might drift away if not thus anchored. Morna was staring straight in front of her through the gates. Just thus, Tuala thought, would a blind woman gaze, not knowing if what lay before her were beautiful or piteous, thing of wonder or object of terror. Kethra's grip tightened on Tuala's hands. Tuala was accustomed to seeking her visions alone; to do so in any company save for Bridei's had always seemed utterly wrong. When the Good Folk had looked over her shoulder into the Dark Mirror she had felt anger and resentment. Tonight she welcomed the reassurance of Kethra's presence, the warm reality of her touch.

In the water, time seemed to pass; the clouds swirled and roiled in the dark sky. Rain came, but the women left their hoods back, their heads bare. At length men appeared within the gates, a file of warriors, two and two, and at their head were three in robes of black: Broichan in the center, his dark hair in the many small plaits of the druidic calling, his eyes shadowy hollows in a face rendered skull-like by the uncertain light of veiled moon and guttering torches. On his right stood a spare, gray-haired man with tight lips and shrewd eyes. On Broichan's left was a taller man, hard-eyed and grim in appearance. A pair of guards slid back the iron bolts and hauled the great gates open.

There was an exchange of words: Broichan spoke, Fola replied. A formal sequence of question and answer. With the ear of the spirit and her knowledge of ritual, Tuala sensed its meaning.

Why come you here?

To mend what is broken. To return what was taken. To pledge ourselves anew.

What do you offer?

Purity. Obedience. Sacrifice. The relinquishment of self in the essence of the god.

Is this a perfect offering?

It is perfect. Fola bowed her head.

It is whole. Luthana spoke, then released Morna's hand and moved away, walking to the back of the line. In turn, each of the women of Banmerren stepped forward and made her statement to the druid; to the dark god whose representative Broichan must be tonight.

It is pure.

It is full of light.

It is complete.

It is willing.

It is fresh with youth.

It is obedient.

It is wise.

Each woman spoke and retreated, until only Morna stood there, silent, immobile, with Fola small and straight-backed by her side. Then Fola moved to slip the cape from the girl's narrow shoulders, and Morna stood before the men in her gown of purest white, a slight, fragile figure in the torchlight. For all the rain and the bite of the winter cold, she remained utterly still.

It is perfect, Fola said again, and moved to stand before Morna. Fola was a little woman; she had to stand on tiptoe to bring the girl's face down to hers. The wise woman kissed Morna on the brow, a formal farewell, then released her and stepped away. Morna's features remained impassive; she was walking in a different world.

It is good, Broichan said and, moving forward, he touched the girl on the shoulder. There was no flicker in her eyes, no recognition of change. Then Morna walked in through the gates of Caer Pridne, following in the druid's footsteps, and the gates closed behind her, leaving Fola and her wise women outside.

Tuala drew a shaking breath; felt, rather than saw, Kethra do the same. The water rippled and was once more still.

The wise women were by the shore, their cloaks lifted by the rising wind to swirl around them, giving their forms the look of birds or bats or creatures from some hidden part of the forest, manifestations of Black Crow that were neither quite one thing nor another. Fola was leading them into a circle. No ritual; no greetings, prayers, or elemental weavings. They stood in silence, not touching, like standing stones on a shadowy plain; like a grove of small trees in a secret glen. The wind blew stinging sand around them; it tangled their long hair, gray, white, russet, fair; it tugged at their clothing and chilled their bodies. Salt spray followed the sand; rain fell on them, mingling with their tears. Even Fola was weeping, Tuala could see it. They did not move. They would keep vigil thus until morning.

The image shifted, dissipated; the water in the scrying bowl grew dark and remained thus for some time. The only point of light was the candle's reflection, struggling in the little drafts that eddied through the chamber. Faintly, the sound of sleeping girls' steady, soft breathing could be heard, a comforting thing.

A pale glimmer on the water: Morna's white dress, her whiter face. The trance still held, whatever had caused it, prayer, fasting, herbs, long solitude, hard preparation. A procession wound its way around Caer Pridne, inside the king's fortress, no mere line of warriors now but a grander assembly, although there were few torches. This god loved darkness; these men bore only sufficient light to keep their steps on the path. Morna walked among them like a wraith, shadowed by the dark form of the king's druid. They trod a spiral path, following the wall-walks and climbing the steep steps from level to level. When they reached an upper court, the warriors formed a great circle around the space, with the white-robed girl and the druid in the center. A deep horn sounded; Tuala could not tell if its note was only in her mind, or if it was borne on the harsh wind all the way around the bay from the king's fortress to the sheltered house of Banmerren. It was a call like that of a huge wounded animal crying in distress. Doors opened; a party of men emerged from inside the fortress. All wore dark clothes; all bore somber faces. One could be singled out immediately: the king, no doubt, although he had neither silver circlet nor golden torc, jewels nor other finery, but the same dark robe that shrouded his fellows. His identity was in his face, a gaunt, gray-hued face, the eyes bright with pain, the mouth stern with discipline, the features blazing authority through a mask of death. Drust's will was formidable. He stared across the courtyard at the waiting Broichan and the druid sank to his knees. Every man present followed; every head bowed in acknowledgment. It was a moment of utter courage; a demonstration of true kingship.

For a time, then, the water showed only glimpses. A snatch of Fola, Derila, Luthana, grimly still, standing strong under the scourging of the wind and the gnawing chill of the night. Men walking again, along the hilltop and down a little secret way. The warriors standing back, the torches slotted into holders. Only a few going on as the path grew narrow and deep, descending into the heart of the hill. Tuala could see their faces, illuminated each in its turn as they walked past the torch that stood at the head of an impossibly steep flight of steps plunging down into the very bowels of the earth. There was the king, stoic and strong-willed, with pain written stark across his countenance. His councillors followed. Then came Broichan, his face a mask, and Morna with her white gown and unseeing eyes. Perhaps she knew nothing, comprehended nothing; perhaps she knew it all, understood and accepted, traveling now through a realm in which the Shining One saluted her goodness and Bone

Mother held out her arms in promise of peace. It was to be hoped, wished, prayed that this was so.

Other men came behind, a tall one with red hair, several more, Talorgen and his son among them. And Bridei; Bridei was there, clad in a long dark robe, his hair loose on his shoulders and a narrow green ribbon tied around his wrist. Tuala could look, then, at nothing else. She willed her thoughts to reach him, her love to encircle him. He had a headache; she recognized it in the set of the mouth, his hands reaching to brush the high banks as he passed down the sunken way, the line between his brows. He hadn't been sleeping; purple shadows lay under his eyes, and he was thinner. He held himself straight and strong for all that, and did not let his mind wander, but watched the others: the king, the councillors, Broichan. Especially Broichan.

The water in the bowl was changing. As Tuala stared down, tiny crystals of ice began to form at its edges, frosting the surface, and a chill arose that set her shivering and made her nose and ears ache. Yet the chamber still held the fire's last warmth; the cat, Shade, dozed on the hearth, curled tight on himself; the girls slept peacefully, covered only by their cloaks. It was the vision that held the chill. The icy breath came straight from the secret place of the god: the Well of Shades.

They made their way down the steps, the path illuminated dimly by candles lit from that last torch. The fitful light barely revealed slick surfaces of stone, a vaulted roof. At the foot of the steps a chamber opened out, whose floor was not earth nor rock nor rushes, but sudden dark water. Cold; colder than the touch of frost on the hawthorn, colder than the sharp wind that shivers across the fells, colder than the kiss of a dead man's lips. Around the rim of the well there was a ledge just broad enough for a man to stand on; one by one the king, the warriors, the councillors moved to take their places here, framing the water. At the far side, opposite the steps, stood the king and the druid, and between them Morna. Among the dark-clad men, the girl shone dimly in the candlelight, as if she were a lesser manifestation of the Shining One herself. The water was ink-dark; neither white-gowned young woman nor small flickering flame showed its reflection on that forbidding surface.

Tuala's heart began a drumbeat, for all her efforts at calm. Her hands were damp with sweat; Kethra was clutching them so tightly it hurt. Where was Bridei? Ah, there, not far from King Drust. Broichan had taught his foster son well. For all the headache, Bridei was masking his expression, giving little away. Others were less adept. The tall, red-headed man looked as if he was about to faint; many showed signs of cold, hugging cloaks or robes close about them, and there was one hard-eyed fellow whose features wore revulsion quite undisguised.

It was a simple rite, and brief. Tuala understood the reasons for that. The chamber of the dark god was not a place where a sane man would choose to linger, nor was this an observance that would be aided by lengthy prayers, by delays, by chances to question too fully its nature and meaning. By opportunities to begin to doubt.

Broichan spoke: ritual words accompanied by gestures, a sequence of signs quite unfamiliar to Tuala. Perhaps it was a druid charm; at the end he spread his arms wide and gave a great cry, and darkness seemed to gather about him, rising from the water, from the chill air, from the ancient stones, rendering him immensely tall, ancient beyond count of years and full of an implacable, hungry power. Tuala could hardly breathe; the faces of the men were startled, fearful, like those of trapped creatures awaiting a hunter's blow. Broichan called again, an incantation in a tongue Tuala could not understand. Then he took Morna by the shoulder, and on the other side King Drust did the same, and the two men sank to their knees, bringing the girl down between them.

"Pray that she does not come to herself before it is done." Kethra's whisper was tremulous, the voice of a terrified child. "Pray that the goddess does not avert her gaze at the end."

Tuala saw Bridei's face, young, frozen, with too much in his eyes; the king's, where duty warred with pain. In Broichan's stern features was something too terrible to look upon, for in this moment the nameless god inhabited him, and power was in every corner of his being: not the vibrant, living power of the Flamekeeper, nor the eternal ebb and flow of the Shining One, nor yet the deep wisdom of Bone Mother, but a dark energy that flowed beneath and beyond all of these, a secret, terrible thing that caused men's eyes to slide away, yet drew them, despite themselves, for this deity's awful hunger had its small reflection in each of them, hidden deep.

Morna's back was rounded, her face bent over the water as she knelt between them, king and druid. Her long hair fell forward, a finger's-breadth from the inky surface. She was still; acquiescent. Tuala held her breath.

From outside the chamber, above on the hillside, the horn sounded again, a wailing, wrenching note of suffering. It summoned the god; the offering was ready. Then, quick as an arrow in the heart, Broichan put his hand up to the back of Morna's neck and pushed her face down into the water. On the other side, Drust did the same, but more weakly; the sick man had not the druid's strength, which tonight was the strength of a god. Tuala's heart leaped to her throat; sudden tears of fright filled her eyes. There was no struggle; Morna knelt immobile on the narrow shelf, white skirts flowing around her, dark hair spreading in dark water, face invisible beneath the surface. The druid's long-fingered hand was strong on her small neck; he and the king gripped her arms, holding her balanced there, drowning, dying. It was an act of perfect obedience.

Tuala had forgotten to breathe; spots danced before her eyes, she would lose the vision, she wanted it gone, she wanted . . .

"Ah!" Kethra sucked in her breath. Broichan's pose had become awkward, strained. His hand was white-knuckled in Morna's hair. Her body was rigid now; the two men were struggling to hold her there. A paroxysm of coughing seized the king; he covered his mouth with his hand, struggling to maintain his purchase on the narrow ledge. Now Broichan alone held the girl in place, her face beneath the water. Drust drew his fingers away from his lips. They were stained with blood. Beside him, Broichan made a little sound as his foot slid across the slick stones of the well rim. There was a splashing; Morna had felt Bone Mother's chill touch at last and was fighting with all the strength she had. Half-crouched on the very rim of the well, Broichan muttered something under his breath, and Drust's gaze went in urgent plea to those who, by kinship, could be called upon to assist him. Tuala saw the tall, red-headed man bow his head, not moving. A second pretended not to understand. "Help me," Drust said aloud, and looked straight at Bridei. Ice gripped Tuala's heart; almost, she closed her eyes, released Kethra's hands, but she could not. This must be shared in all its horror and grandeur; the gods required it. Bridei edged around the pool, feet careful as a cat's; other men pressed back against the stone walls to let him by. At Drust's side, Bridei knelt and, supporting the king with his arm, held him balanced and safe as Drust stretched his hand down once more. It did not take long; the water was very cold. It was no more than the time it takes to count a man's fingers and toes twice over; no longer than the time it takes to cut a sheaf of rosemary or tie a ribbon neatly. Perhaps a little more; it was necessary to be certain the thing was really done, the sacrifice complete and perfect, the god satisfied. Then they raised Morna from the water, limp and white, and the king, rising to his feet with Bridei's aid, made a sign of blessing over her blanched face and laid her hands on her breast. One of the men, a big fellow who had stood by Broichan on the ledge, took Morna up in his arms, ready to carry her forth from the deep chamber. The druid raised his arms once more, his sleeves falling back to reveal row upon row of small marks tattooed there, not a warrior's signs but the deep and subtle symbols of the druidic calling, creature and herb, standing stone and distant star, spiraling across the pale skin with here and there words written in the secret script of the brotherhood, like rows of tiny, mysterious trees. He called once more, a sound deep and harsh, and it seemed to Tuala that his cry made the chamber brighten, and that on the walls and high roof above the Well of Shades carvings showed themselves, signs of the god incised there by the ancient ancestors, a reflection of the patterns that flowed across the druid's skin, linking him intimately with the power that dwelled here in the heart of the earth, as in the darkest recesses of the hearts of men. His call made Tuala's skull ring painfully and set her teeth on edge. She felt the trembling of Kethra's hands.

The sound died down. The procession began once more as the men made their slow, careful way around the ledge to the steps leading up to light and air. The big man bore Morna easily; she was a slight girl, a slip of a thing, who had come to Banmerren from the west, her parents killed in a Dalriadan raid, and nobody else to take her in. A quiet girl who sought only to please; that was what Tuala remembered them saying. Bridei walked close to the king, steadying him with a firm grip on the elbow. Drust looked weary to death; his eyes glittered as if with fever and his skin was stretched tight over the bone. Still he walked like a king, back straight, head held high. As for Bridei himself, he seemed impassive, calm. He was strong; Tuala had not thought he could sustain this. Men looked at him and she saw respect on their faces, grudging perhaps, but real. They looked at him as if he were the man they might wish to be themselves, had they the courage. His expression revealed nothing; he appeared the very model of control. Nothing, save to Tuala. She knew him as she knew herself. She read his eyes and the pain in them. She felt the harsh throbbing as if it were her own head it inhabited. She knew his pounding heart, his guilt, his revulsion. She recognized the touch of the dark god and was helpless to banish it.

"It's gone," said Kethra in a strange voice, and released Tuala's hands. And it was; the bronze bowl held nothing but a dim pool of clear water. The chamber was cold and very quiet. Tuala blinked, rubbing the tears from her eyes; saw Kethra, opposite, wipe a hand across her own cheeks, heard her draw her breath in sharply. Standing in silent circle around them, drawn, helpless, by the power of their dark vision, the junior students stood, white-faced and big-eyed in their blue robes. Like children woken suddenly from a nightmare too terrible to recount, they stared, mute, at those who had given it form. In that moment, Tuala saw the import of her disobedience. She had looked where she should not; she had intruded where no woman belonged. Like a stone cast into a peaceful pond, such an act might have ripples that were far-reaching. Who knew what punishment this dark god might choose to deliver? And yet, she could not find it in herself to be sorry.

Kethra found her voice first. "Odha, stir up the fire. Deira, bring wood from the basket. You others, light some more candles. The ritual is over, for us at least. We'll sleep here tonight, all together before the fire. Move that cat, he's soaking up what little heat there is. Now, we need bread and honey and an herbal infusion to help you rest. Then, questions if you must, but not too many. I don't know what you saw here, but I do have one thing to say to you. The visions of the scrying bowl appear and form themselves at the goddess's will. If you see images that disquiet you, it may be that you looked when you should have known better." Kethra's hands were tightly clenched. It seemed to Tuala the tutor spoke without the awareness that the two of them were the guilty ones here, and nobody else. Then she saw the look in Kethra's eyes, and knew this for a demonstration of extraordinary presence of mind. The eyes were shadowed with knowledge, and with fear. "Focus your minds on obedience," Kethra went on. "It is a lesson we all learn at Banmerren; even the oldest and wisest among us must bow to the will of the gods."

"I want to go home." This tremulous voice might have come from any of them; its message was plain in every eye.

"What are you," Kethra challenged in a tone made strong and brisk by sheer force of will, "a servant of the Shining One or a sniveling baby? Tuala, take the younger ones to the kitchen to fetch soporific herbs; if you don't know which to choose by now, then Luthana hasn't been doing her job. You others, don't you understand a simple instruction? The fire, Odha. The wood, Deira. Fola and the others will be cold when they return, and weary. Since it seems we are all awake at an hour when only owls and hedgehogs stir, let us make them a fitting welcome."

BREATHING: DEEP, STEADY, measured. A count of numbers, an old rhyme, a little song to pace it by. *Hee-o, wee-o, feather of the blackest crow* . . . Now they had reached the king's chamber, where Queen Rhian, dry-eyed and somber, stood ready to receive her exhausted husband. Her brother, Owain, had not attended the rite, being a man of Powys and loyal to the observances of his own people, but was here now to take Drust's arm and convey him within. The king's breathing was like the scraping of ice from a railing, the susurration of dry leaves lifted by an autumn wind. He turned, at the last, and saluted them all with a little nod of the head. His eyes, fierce as a fighting bull's, forbade expressions of concern, offers of support.

"It is over once more," the king said in a wisp of a voice. "I thank you." He looked at Bridei. "It is a lonely way. All that I am, I give to the gods and to Fortriu." His eyes moved again; his gaze lighted on his wife's plump form, her sweet features in which desperate concern was but thinly masked. "I've been fortunate," Drust said in a different tone. "Fortunate in my friends and fortunate in my family. The trust of the gods is a wondrous gift and a terrible burden. A man cannot well bear it alone. I bid you all good night, although sleep does not come easily on such a night as this. May the Shining One guard your dreams."

"May the Flamekeeper light your waking," came the response, many voices speaking as one: Aniel's and Tharan's, Broichan's and Bridei's, and those of the king's close kinsmen, red-haired Carnach and sturdy Wredech of the fine cattle. The door closed; Drust the Bull was gone.

BRIDEI HAD EATEN little, the headache robbing him of appetite. Nonetheless, he retched and retched, bent double in the small space behind the steps on the upper wall-walk, his belly twisting, clenching, heaving until every drop of bile and water was emptied from it. At a certain point, he recognized that Faolan was there, a wet cloth in his hand, holding Bridei's head, offering sips of water that stayed in his stomach no longer than it took to swallow them. At length it seemed to be over and he sat on the steps, shivering convulsively under the thick blanket the Gael had wrapped around his shoulders. Somewhat later, Garth came out with a steaming infusion of some kind, and Breth with dry bread, which the others ate, since Bridei would not. The three of them stood or sat by him through the dark hours, saying little. Here and there on the wall-walks or down in the courtyards within the earthen ramparts, other small groups of men could be seen clustered in silence or talking in undertones. Lanterns were dotted about the fortress; a kind of vigil was being kept, a watch to ward off shadows. There was not a man here present tonight with the courage to face his dreams. Light blazed from within the king's chamber, bright through the cracks around the shutters. The sound of Drust's coughing made its way to every ear; the memory of his courage was felt in every heart. Somewhere in a quiet corner, a big man would be digging a grave. The chosen ones did not go home to Banmerren.

Some time before sunrise it became possible to move, although Bridei's legs felt strangely weak, his head dizzy. He rose to his feet, looking at the three of them: keen-eyed Breth, stifling a yawn; amiable Garth, gray-faced with weariness; wiry, dark Faolan whose customary look of mild amusement had been replaced by something else, an expression Bridei was too tired and sick and sad to interpret.

"Thank you," he said simply. "I'm going to bed now," and made his way inside, hoping his back was as straight as Drust's had been, his steps as steady on the way. But he did not seek the chamber he shared with Breth and Garth; a flicker of candlelight from Broichan's private quarters caught his eye, and he walked soft-footed to pause in that open doorway.

It seemed, at first, that nobody was there. Where, on Gateway morning, the druid had knelt in pose of strength and obedience, the stone floor was bare of all but shadows. A candle burned in a niche. The narrow, hard bed with its neatly folded blanket was untenanted. The shelves held their complement of jar and bottle, sack and bowl and crucible; garlic hung from the roof and a scattering of wooden rods lay on the stone table, sign of an earlier augury. Bridei made to turn away, to seek his own bed until morning. He would not sleep; still, if he made pretense, at least the others might get some rest.

A small sound held him there in the doorway; the ragged,

whispering breath of a man who fights a desperate battle with himself. Bridei took a step into the room. Broichan was standing by the place where a narrow slit of a window pierced the stone wall. His hands, clenched into white-knuckled fists, were by his sides; he had not removed the dark robe of the ceremony. He was leaning against the wall, quite still, his forehead resting against the cold stone, his eyes shut. There was a look on his face that Bridei had never seen before. The mask had slipped entirely; guilt, confusion, grief, long endurance were all starkly evident, and on the austere planes of the druid's cheeks, the candlelight revealed the glistening tracks of his tears.

Others had tended to Bridei tonight with courtesy, with restraint, with true friendship. He could do no less for Broichan. Like all of them, he had believed his foster father a creature of powerful certainty, beyond the frailties of ordinary men, his mind filled only with plots and plans, with learning and druid magic; he had thought Broichan's heart had room for nothing but the love of the gods. He recognized, in this moment, how wrong he had been. All these long years, from that first, confusing arrival at Pitnochie, that first glimpse of the tall, remote figure who was to mold his own future, he had never once thought of Broichan as a man. He had never thought how lonely such an existence might be.

"I'm here," he said quietly, walking into the chamber, taking up the candle to light a lamp on the table, pouring water from jug to cup. "Come, sit down, drink. It is over." And did not say, *for now. For this time.*

"IT IS AS well," said Fola, "that these young women are only novices in the art. Had they seen all, as it appears the two of you have done, I would have a full-scale revolt on my hands, Banmerren empty, the Shining One bitterly offended. What were you thinking of? Such secrets are forbidden even to the wisest among us; the Well of Shades is not a place where women tread. To expose these children thus . . . I'm almost without words, Kethra. As a servant of the goddess, a priestess of experience and dedication, it is unthinkable that you could make such an error of judgment, even if Tuala led you into it."

Kethra's lips were tight, her eyes red. "It wasn't Tuala's fault," she said. "It was my idea. I pressed her to use her gift to this end."

"The responsibility and the guilt must be shared equally between you," Fola said, her dark gaze traveling from her chastened assistant to Tuala herself. The two of them stood before the wise woman in her small private sanctum, wilting under her disapproval. If Fola felt burdened by the role she had played in last night's ritual, she gave little sign of it. Her back was straight, her features calm. The eyes, however, were chill. "It matters not at all which of you was the instigator and which the follower. It is of no account which is teacher and which student. You are both skilled and clever. Each of you possesses her own unique talents in this art. Each of you knows the ways of the Shining One and is open to her voice. Each of you is culpable. Each must live with the aftermath of her error."

"You wish me to leave Banmerren." Kethra's voice was toneless. "I am no longer fit to teach; to spend my days in the goddess's service."

Fola sighed. Watching her through a haze of sorrow and confusion, Tuala noted the web of lines on the wise woman's face, the discoloration of the skin about the eyes, and realized Fola was indeed old, perhaps almost as old as that druid, Uist, and beset by her own doubts. To deliver Morna thus to the gates of the fortress, to hand her over, to wait out the time of darkness on the shore in full awareness of what was unfolding there in the belly of the earth was a terrible thing indeed; only a woman faultlessly loyal to the gods' will might carry it out, surely, and return to the normal pattern of her days with wits intact. They were strong, these holy ones, dauntingly strong. Tuala doubted she herself could ever be so obedient. Her every sense shrank from what had been done last night, even as she accepted its necessity.

"Tuala!"

Fola's voice broke sharply into her thoughts.

"Yes, my lady?"

"I have not become a different person today merely because you have transgressed so foolishly. Call me by my name. You are one of us now. Or have I been wrong on that score? Perhaps I should take the events of last night as proof that I made a grievous error in admitting you to Banmerren. Your gift is dangerous. It tempts folk to seek knowledge beyond what is permitted. It is a tool for the ambitious; for those who crave power." Kethra flinched before the wise woman's glance. "You should not have agreed to this, Tuala, knowing what was in your command to summon to the scrying bowl."

For part of what had occurred, at least, Tuala was truly sorry. Still, she could not summon the groveling apology that seemed to be expected.

"Speak up," Fola said. "Kethra has named a suitable penalty for herself, and expressed regret. What have you to say?"

Tuala drew a deep breath. "We erred in trying this there, in the chamber where the girls were sleeping," she said. "Although we never dreamed they would wake, that is no excuse, I know. You should not send Kethra away. She is a fine teacher. Her abilities would be best used here, in mending the harm that was done by ensuring the girls understand what they saw and how it links into the lore of the gods."

There was a brief silence.

"I did not ask you to comment on Kethra's situation," Fola said.

"No, my—no, Fola."

"There was something yet to come in your speech, I believe. You are sorry the girls were involved; I'm relieved to hear that, it is the least I would have expected from you. Is there a *but* to follow this expression of regret?"

Tuala gritted her teeth. The truth must be told here, even if it meant being sent away; even if it meant Bridei would come to Banmerren at full moon, and she would be gone. Gone. Where was there to go to?

"I cannot regret the act itself," she said, and heard Kethra draw her breath in sharply. "It has always been my belief that the visions the Shining One reveals to me are those she wishes me to see for her own reasons. She grants them so I can find my way; so I can guide others. Sometimes it does seem that certain images come because I ask for them, because I want them, but I do not believe a human girl to be capable of drawing down sights the Shining One forbids. The goddess is too powerful to be thus deceived. What I see in the water sets out the pathway she determines for me, and for . . . others of my acquaintance. Even last night. She showed me that dark ritual because I needed to know it."

"You horrify me, child. What of Kethra?"

Tuala hesitated. "I suppose it is the same for her; it was the Shining One who sent the vision, not myself, not Kethra. You spoke of power; of the misuse of gifts. This may have been some kind of lesson."

Fola gave a grim smile. "Indeed. If that is so, it seems to me Kethra has learned from it and you have not, Tuala."

"We are different, Kethra and I. The lesson to be learned is also different."

"I see. I might point out to you that, although a human girl may not have the power to summon forbidden images to the seer's eye, you are not, in fact, a human girl. Is it possible we are dealing here with matters darker still than we imagined?"

A strange feeling crept over Tuala, a separation, as if she stood there within the lamplit chamber and yet was set apart, behind an invisible margin. It was a chilling sensation of Otherness; of being entirely alone. "This *was* a vision of the Shining One," she said in a whisper. "I know it. She has guided my steps since the day she brought me to Pitnochie as an infant. It is not she who brings darkness, but the one who demands of men such acts as we were shown in the vision; such acts as would break the stoutest heart and tear the strongest will in pieces."

"Hush, child." Fola's voice shook; at last, the aftermath of Gateway could be seen in her eyes. "We do not give voice to these matters. Those images were not for women's eyes, especially not an innocent young woman such as yourself. Why would the goddess choose to reveal such grim secrets to you? For what purpose?"

Tuala was mute. The truth was plain to her; it concerned Bridei, and she would not say it. The Shining One was playing a difficult game: giving Tuala the tools she needed to help the one she loved, then setting a high wall between them, a wall that was not merely the barrier of stone and earth that sheltered Banmerren, but a rampart of custom and expectation, history and protocol, far harder to breach. Perhaps what Fola said was true. Was last night's vision a warped and twisted thing, conjured from that dark place that lay beyond and beneath the realm of the gods?

"This requires some thought," Fola said. "Kethra, I will give consideration to your future. What has occurred must alter the path for you, one way or another. For now you will remain here. These children need guidance; they need explanations from those they can trust. This is your opportunity to prove to me that you are indeed trustworthy. Do not abuse it again, or you will walk from the gates of Banmerren and will not return. Go now."

Kethra bowed stiffly. Her face was white; it was common knowledge that she had aspired, indeed expected, to govern Banmerren after Fola. Now she would be lucky to keep a place here at all. Tuala stood stock still while the tutor passed her, features rigid, and left the room.

"As for you," Fola said in a slightly different tone, "you have shown a certain understanding, a certain compassion, as indeed did Kethra herself, and I thank the goddess each of you still possesses a little of her inner wisdom. You know I was not present at the Well of Shades; indeed, I had no desire at all to be there, nor have I wished for that in all the long years Drust has enacted this ritual. The part I must play in it taxes me sorely. I envy Broichan's strength and his certainty. Tuala, I don't want an account of what you saw. I know what you were seeking. Did you find it?"

Tuala nodded, saying nothing.

"Tell me, then," said the wise woman, sharp eyed for all her lack of sleep, "what part did Bridei play in this? Don't look like that, child. Your expression is transparent; I know your mind. Did the young man look on in horror? Did he squeeze his eyes shut, not to see? Or was he a model of control, like his foster father? Tell me."

"King Drust needed help, when it came to the . . . when they . . . Broichan couldn't do it by himself, and the king was coughing and fighting for breath. Drust turned to certain men, his close kinsmen, I suppose they were, for that is the rule, as Wid told me . . . No other may touch the . . . no other may . . . The only one who would help was Bridei." Tuala heard the softening of her own voice as she spoke his name, the perilous revelation of her secret feelings.

"I see," Fola said, and there was a weight in her tone that made this a statement of great import; a recognition of momentous change.

"Bridei did it calmly and without hesitation. His face revealed nothing of what he felt."

"Broichan was ever an apt teacher." Fola sighed, and rested her chin on her hands. "I'm weary, Tuala; I should take Luthana's good advice and rest awhile. You may go."

"I—am I not to be punished, too?"

"Perhaps it is I who deserve chastisement, for thinking to cage you here," Fola said quietly. "But yes, there must be a penalty of sorts; it was beyond folly to risk the girls so. You will no longer be housed in the tower. It's unsuitable for winter anyway. Move your things downstairs; you'll sleep with the other juniors in the communal room."

Tuala felt the blood drain from her face. Not now, not yet; not before the full moon . . . "Oh no, please—" she began.

"You may go, Tuala." The voice was very soft and utterly implacable. "Move your belongings today. And let Kethra mend what harm has been done; the students will accept her explanations more readily than any of yours, I daresay."

"I—"

"Did you not hear me?"

At the look on Fola's strong features, a look that showed, at last, all the anguish and exhaustion of yesterday and today, the guilt and responsibility of a lifetime of tomorrows, Tuala swallowed her protest and fled. Never mind rules. Never mind doors and locks and watchful tutors. At full moon he would come, and she would be waiting.

"ACCOUNT FOR YOURSELF," Dreseida snapped. "And make it quick; I need to see Gartnait as soon as we're done here.

He's not progressing as he should."

"He can't, Mother." Ferada stood in the women's quarters at Caer Pridne, looking into her mother's fierce eyes, eyes that reminded her of a stalking creature of the wild, with herself the quarry fixed in its sights. "You know Gartnait's not a scholar. He simply can't remember that kind of information. I don't understand why you're making him—"

"Then you'd better try harder, Ferada. I need your assistance with this. I need your complete loyalty. Have I mentioned that the chieftain of Fib approached your father on the question of an alliance? An alliance through marriage? What's his name, Coltran, Celtane?"

"Cealtran." Ferada supplied it grimly, a picture in her mind of the portly, red-nosed chieftain newly arrived at court. Cealtran's belly wobbled when he walked, and his little eyes were sunk deep in folds of slick pale flesh. He was fifty if he was a day; Dreseida must be joking. "He's old, Mother. He's from the south. And he's a Christian. Father would never—"

"As I've made abundantly clear to you, any such decision will be mine. Your father has assured me of that. There are other possibilities, of course, provided we don't wait too long. Ana has uncles, not all wed. The queen has young kinsmen in Powys. And what about the chieftains of the Caitt? Plenty of possibilities, if all somewhat far from home. Now give me your accounting. You know how this works, Ferada. Do as I ask, don't talk about it elsewhere, not to your father, not to your brothers, not to your friends, that's if you've managed to unbend enough to make any, and you will indeed be granted choice in the matter of a husband. I don't ask much, Daughter. Just a little information. Just a little play-acting. For a clever girl like you, it should be easy."

"Mother . . . Gartnait, and all of this . . . what is it for? What is your purpose?"

"If you think I'll answer that aloud you're more of a fool than any daughter of mine should be," Dreseida said. "This place is bristling with spies. One's not safe even in one's private quarters. There's an election coming. Not quite yet, since Drust has surprised us all by clinging to life longer than anyone would have believed possible, but soon, very soon. I seek to use what little power I have, as a woman, to ensure a satisfactory result. No matter that I cannot vote. Men are remarkably malleable, Ferada. One simply needs to learn the techniques to mold them. Now tell me, what have you learned?"

"Not much. As I told you, there was little opportunity to speak to Bridei before I went back to Banmerren."

"What about the girl, his sister? Any signs, messages? Does she talk about Bridei? About Broichan and his plans?"

"No, Mother. Tuala's very quiet; she keeps her thoughts locked away."

"I need more, Ferada. Think of Cealtran, just itching to set his hand in yours and bear you home to warm his bed. The fellow wants heirs. Lots of them."

Ferada shuddered. "Tuala did send a message," she said grimly. "Ana took it."

"Ana told you? What message?"

Ferada shook her head. "Ana didn't speak of it, but I saw. You did ask me to spy, after all. Tuala sent Bridei a little packet with a leaf and a stone in it. That was all."

"And a ribbon."

"I suppose it was tied up with a ribbon," Ferada said, surprised. "How could you know that?"

Dreseida's smile was thin-lipped, her eyes hard. "I've learned to observe. The young man wears a ribbon around his wrist, like a lady's favor, yet it's common knowledge among the men that Bridei never goes near the houses of pleasure, never grants a girl his attentions; some folk whisper that he prefers boys, but Gartnait tells me there's no sign of that either. Bridei appears to be as chaste as a Christian monk. You'd think that in itself would be sufficient to make men doubt his suitability to act as the Flamekeeper's worldly embodiment. One expects one's king to be virile. I cannot imagine why anyone is taking him seriously as a candidate, but the word is that he has his followers. Of course, the boy was raised by Broichan, and that goes some way to explaining his oddity. He does wear the ribbon. It used to be an old scrap of a thing, but now it's a new one, green-dyed silk. I've seen such a ribbon tying up a long plait belonging to a certain little wild creature of our acquaintance. It's clear what it means. He regards the witch girl not as his sister, but as his sweetheart. You must learn to be alert for detail, Ferada, if you're to be any use as an informant."

Ferada pressed her lips together.

"The message," her mother said. "What does it mean? A leaf, a stone? What sort of leaf?"

"How can that make any difference? An oak, I suppose; there's a big oak tree outside Tuala's tower room. It stretches all the way across to the outer wall."

"Ah."

"Mother, I—"

"What kind of stone? Small, I imagine. Black, white, gray? Smooth, rough, round, long?"

"I think it was white. Mother, I don't like this. Why do you—"

"This is what you'll do. Seek out Bridei. He talks to you, I've seen it; he likes your quickness. Be a woman for a change. Wear your blue gown and the silver clasp. He'll be troubled after Gateway. If your father's account of what occurred is accurate, the king set a heavy burden on his close kinsmen that night, and it appears to have been Bridei who acquitted himself best of the three. You heard what happened."

Ferada shivered. "Officially, no; but it is not possible to be deaf to the whispers. Ana and I knew that girl, Morna. We had spoken to her, broken bread with her. It changed the way I felt about Banmerren, and about Fola. It filled my mind with questions that have no answers."

"That should make you a good companion for Bridei. As Broichan's protege, he seems to think in questions. Find him; be a listening ear for him. Let him talk it out. Win his confidence. Get as close as you can; use all you have, Ferada. I'm seeking an opportunity here, and you can provide it for me."

"What opportunity?"

"Later. All in due time."

"Mother?"

"What is it? Make it quick; I told you, I've other matters to attend to."

"It seems to me," Ferada ventured, "that what happened at Gateway shows Bridei's strength, his courage, his self-discipline. It shows he can be put forward as a strong candidate when the time comes. Some folk are saying this singled him out as the only possible choice; that Carnach may now throw in his lot with Bridei rather than stand himself."

"What folk? Who is saying this?" Dreseida's tone was a hiss.

"Perhaps it is not I who must learn to listen," Ferada said, and an instant later her mother's ringed hand struck her a sharp blow across the cheek, leaving a bloody welt. Dreseida regarded her daughter through narrowed eyes. Ferada, breathing fast, did not lift her hand to touch her face, to wipe away the blood.

"You think your brother a fool," Dreseida said. "He could teach you much about loyalty. Don't ever speak to me thus again. If you imagine I will let such insolence pass without retaliation, you're clearly unable to envisage your own future. Make Bridei your friend. Be his confidante. In particular, I wish to know his movements; any ventures planned beyond the environs of Caer Pridne. Act soon, for time's running out. And you'd better do something about your face or you'll frighten the young man away. That would be most unfortunate for all of us."

BROICHAN HAD TAUGHT him better than any of them guessed: masks and mirrors, tricks, charms and concealments. Every day he demonstrated the worldly skills he had learned, not just from his foster father but from Erip with his fund of lore and from Wid, who could read a stranger in a single glance. The court recognized Bridei now as a man of subtlety and depth, clever, ingenious, well able to hold his own in their dangerous games. They knew a great deal less about his other skills, those learned in the earlier years at Pitnochie; the things only a druid can teach.

Faolan was uncomfortable with Bridei's plan for getting to Banmerren. A cloak of concealment, achieved by the use of magic, did not constitute, for him, an infallible protection.

In short, he did not believe Bridei could do it, and said so bluntly. "We'll be seen the moment we step out the door. What are you trying to do, lose me my employment here?"

"We won't be seen. This deceives the watcher's eye; only a druid could detect us. Of course, we'll exercise due caution as well, keep to the cover of dunes and bushes, maintain careful watch as we go. Trust me."

"They said you were mad when you took it on yourself to move the Mage Stone," Faolan observed. "Folk did what you bid them, despite that. All right, we'll try this. How do you plan to get over the wall?"

"A rope. I'll carry it."

"How do you—"

"Trust me, Faolan."

"Hmm. It'll need to be quick. Don't allow yourself to get distracted. In, out, home before we're spotted. I may have expressed a wish to draw attention on our ride to the west, but you must not be seen at Banmerren. Men are strictly forbidden inside those walls, as you well know. Be caught breaking that particular rule and your candidacy won't be worth a scrap of straw. A king must be pure, perfect, and obedient. He doesn't go off chasing women at midnight in a place he's no business being anywhere near."

"I won't be chasing women, as you somewhat crudely put it," Bridei said. "I'll be visiting a friend. And I'm bound to point out that this was your idea in the first place."

Faolan's lips twisted in what might have been a smile. "Don't try to pretend you don't want it," he said. "The look in your eyes is truly painful to behold. Just don't forget, in the young lady's embraces, why it is you're there: to work this out of your system once and for all."

Embraces, thought Bridei; that was hardly the way it would be, even though the thought of touching, holding, kissing had begun to possess him for a great deal more of his time than he could well afford. Not only would he be unable so much as to put a hand in hers, likely he would not even be able to summon the right words when at last he saw her face to face. Tuala was a priestess now. That was her choice. He had nothing to offer her but a life of unhappiness, a life of confinement within fortress walls. It would be like shutting a butterfly in a little box and expecting it to be satisfied. He could not ask it of her; to do so would be utter selfishness. And yet, she had sent the message. She had sent the ribbon.

FULL MOON: THE sands of Banmerren bay palely shining under the gaze of the goddess, the sea washing in and out, obedient to her call. The air was clear and chill. Two men made a silent way under the partial cover of low bushes. Their movement was scarcely visible, such was the spell Bridei had cast: a charm that worked, not by making them vanish, for he lacked the power to accomplish that, but by causing their forms to blend with whatever surrounded them, stone wall or pale sand or twigs and stems of green-brown. Nobody had seen them slip out through the water-gate; it seemed no guards had been alerted, although they had most certainly left tracks on the shore before they sidled into the cover of the dunes. Faolan had two knives in his belt; Bridei carried a coil of rope. His heart was beating strangely, as if he had run a race; no amount of druidic discipline could force it to a less violent rhythm. His mind was forming words to say and discarding each possibility in its turn. *I hope you are well:* like a stranger, formal, meaningless. *I love you.* Forbidden; the truth. The perilous truth. Surely she knew this with no need for words. *Why did you leave me?* Selfish; petulant; an implication that she should feel guilty for obeying the Shining One's command. That could not be said. *Come with me now, now, I need you . . .* Showing her with his hands, his mouth, his body just what this need had become, a thing that seemed fit to devour him unless it were satisfied . . . That, most of all, he must crush. He would terrify his friend of the heart, he would turn her away forever. He had little to offer her; if he was careful with his words, with his actions, at least he might keep her friendship, even though they must be apart. What, then, could be spoken? What was there left to say?

They came up under the walls of Banmerren. Bridei knew, now, just where the oak tree stood: his plan had been complete in every detail before he had presented it to Faolan. The Gael was not a man who ever went in unprepared. He might follow his own rules, he might go where others would fear to tread, but he calculated his risks finely. Faolan's planning was impeccable, his execution faultless: it was no wonder he commanded such a high price.

They were beneath the spot now. The bare branches of the tree could be seen above the wall, stark and strong in the cold light of the full moon. Bridei gave a little whistling sound, the call of a night bird, and waited. After a few moments an answer came, the unmistakable hooting of an owl. She was there. He whistled again, just to be sure, even as he took the rope from his shoulder and readied it to throw. Now the owl-voice was closer, as if she had moved along a branch to the top of the wall.

"What is this girl, half cat?" muttered Faolan. "Aren't you concerned she might fall and break her neck? That's quite a height."

An image of Tuala perched on the top of Eagle Scar and turning like a wind vane came bright and clear to Bridei's mind, and with it her small, precise voice reciting: *Fortrenn, Fotlaid, Fidach, Fib, Circinn, Caitt, Ce.* "She won't fall," he said. "If you want to be anxious, worry about me." He looked up again, thought that perhaps he could see her, a pale form atop the wall, a cloud of dark hair. He gestured, hoping she would understand, and, holding the rope's end in one hand, threw the coil upward.

She missed it the first time. Her hand stretched out, grasping; the rope fell back to the ground. Bridei coiled it again. Faolan was scanning the shore, the bushes, the track beyond.

"Remember," he whispered, "keep it quick. No lingering farewells."

Bridei threw again and felt the rope caught at the top. Now he could see, dimly, Tuala's small crouching figure as she hauled it up and fastened it to a sturdy branch. It hung from oak to ground, ready for a strong-armed man to make an ascent.

"Go on, then," hissed Faolan. "Keep within earshot; if we're detected, I need to be able to get you away quickly. If you hear my signal move without delay. You know how much is riding on your safety. Keep your feet flat against the wall going up . . ."

A little later, somewhat breathless, Bridei reached the top and scrambled less than gracefully to sit astride the wall. This was a narrow purchase; beyond, the wall plunged down to dark gardens and, farther off, the gray stones of a high dwelling house. No lights burned save the pale orb of the Shining One. Tuala had retreated to a branch of the oak. She regarded him with her solemn owl-eyes, her hair a soft shadow around her small face, her form as sweetly pleasing to him as on that day by the cairns, the day he had first seen that she was a woman. He gazed back at her. Able strategist, subtle courtier that he had become, he was entirely without words for this moment. If Tuala could hear the wild drumming of his heart, he thought, if she could feel the way he wanted to weep, to shout, to sing, to burst apart with feelings, then she would know the truth, and there would be no need to speak at all.

"You came," Tuala said. "I don't have long; I'm not supposed to be here."

"Nor me," Bridei said. "There's a man waiting for me, down below. Can we—?" He was perched somewhat precariously, all too aware of the long drop on either side of him. He had never possessed Tuala's instinctive sense of balance.

"We can't go in," said Tuala. "I did something wrong, and the tower room's shut up now. Come over to the tree. You'll be safer here."

Bridei eyed the gap: not so very far, save that it was dark, and the ground was a long way down. The branches of the oak seemed no more secure than the narrow stone wall.

"Don't be afraid, Bridei," Tuala said. The small, clear voice transported him back to childhood: even as a tiny girl she had possessed such certainty, such inner assurance that one could not but believe her. "Here, take my hand." She came closer, feet steady on a branch, one arm stretched out toward him.

He reached, clasped, stepped across. He looked at her; she gazed steadily back, eyes clear as moonlight, deep as a secret pool, lovely as the dew on a spring morning. He felt her touch in every part of his body. Desire coursed through him, heady and dangerous. Releasing her hand, he moved to sit awkwardly in a crook of the tree where a massive branch joined the great trunk.

"I—" he began.

"I—" Tuala spoke at the same moment.

"You first," he said, wondering if they would waste this entirely, between them; wondering if there were any right way to do it.

"I've waited so long to see you," Tuala said softly, "and now there don't seem to be any words. Not after Gateway. Not after what they made you do."

He was horrified. "You know of that?"

"I saw it. I looked in the water; I needed to see. Fola was angry, and rightly so. Bridei, that was . . . it was a terrible thing. Dark and cruel. You were very strong that night. It is no wonder the king looks weary."

"He clings to life by a thread. Nobody expected he would survive so long. Tuala?"

"Mm?"

He wished she would move closer; she sat just out of reach, leaning against a rising bough of the tree, her knees drawn up under her skirt, her arms wrapped around her. Her hair had grown; it was long enough, now, to be gathered in a ribbon once more at the nape. Soft curls escaped to frame her face. He observed the fey, winged brows; the neat, small nose; the sweet mouth. His hands seemed to know, without stirring, just how it would feel to brush that pale cheek, to linger on the delicate neck, to caress the soft curves of her with passion and reverence; his body was telling him with utter certainty what joy it would take in pleasing her . . .

"Were you going to ask me something?" Tuala said.

Bridei wrenched his mind back to the here and now. "You know, don't you? You've worked it out, what they intend for me?"

Tuala nodded. "I've known since I was little."

"You never said."

"It was best for you to grow up not knowing. To find out in your own time. It's a heavy thing to carry."

Bridei did not answer for a little. "I did not know how

heavy," he said at length, "until Gateway. I did what was required; Drust needed me, and I respect and love him as my king and as the Flamekeeper's champion on earth. But I don't know if I can do it again and again, all the long years of a kingship. I am obedient to the gods, as a true son of Fortriu must be. I long to carry our land and people forward. But . . . I think perhaps I shouldn't present myself as a candidate for kingship, Tuala. This is a rite that appalls me, repels me. I speak thus under the eye of the Shining One and hope she forgives my blunt words. If it is set down that Fortriu's king must enact this sacrifice to appease the Nameless One, then perhaps that king should not be Bridei son of Maelchon. I saw what the ritual did to Broichan, whom I always believed impervious. He was wracked with shame, shattered and old. Should any man bear that? I'm sorry. I didn't come here to burden you with this."

Tuala was looking down at her hands. "You did not want to share it with me?" she asked.

He heard the careful tone, the effort at neutrality, and felt like weeping. "It isn't fair," he said. "You are a wise woman now, called by the Shining One; you live in the daily knowledge of the goddess's love. The last thing you need is the weight of my uncertainties."

"You will find others to share them, Bridei." The voice was very small. "More acceptable others. But I will always be your friend." The words seemed to him a crushing, final blow; a death sentence. The distance between them was suddenly vast, deep, a yawning gap. She had detached herself; he heard it in her voice. The Shining One had set an unbridgeable chasm between them.

"My friend," he managed. "I hope so, indeed; but I will see nothing of you, now you have chosen the path of the goddess. She honors you in this; you will be an asset to Banmerren, I'm sure." Gods aid him, now he was sounding as prim and formal as if he addressed a distant acquaintance. His head began to throb.

"Bridei?"

"Yes?"

"You must be king. You must put yourself forward. It's

what has to be. I've seen it, and Broichan has seen it. Fola, too, I think. You have to do it."

"I don't think I can." *Not without you.*

"I know Gateway was bad; cruel; terrible. I know about the other things: the battle, Donal. Sad things; sorry things. I wish I had been there to share them. But you must go forward bravely, as you have always done. There is an answer to this, I'm certain, an answer acceptable to both gods and men. I know you will find it. Promise me, Bridei. Promise me you'll go through with this."

He opened his mouth; closed it again. He could not look at her now. Her voice had been suddenly full of the old warmth, her words vibrant and challenging. What had she meant, more acceptable others? Who could be more acceptable than Tuala herself? Surely she knew how much he loved her.

"Promise me," Tuala said again, and at that moment a whistle came from beyond the wall: Faolan alerting Bridei that it was time to go. So soon.

"I promise," he said, and looked up.

She smiled. Gods help him, how could he see that and not put his arms around her, blurting out his need like a foolish youth who knew nothing of druids' discipline? Yet how could he bear to look away? This might be the last time he would ever see her. He must not touch her again; that would be to do her a terrible injustice. He must make a new corner in his mind for her, a separate place, and leave her there pure and untouched, safe within high walls, a servant of the goddess unscathed by the dark trials, the perilous power games of his own future. To do otherwise would be utterly selfish.

"I have to go," he said, and watched the smile fade. Her eyes, in an instant, became those of a child who waits alone in the darkness, afraid to sleep.

"It's better like this," Bridei said, but his attempt to control his voice was woefully unsuccessful; his words came out in a strangled whisper.

"If that's what you want, Bridei."

"I have to go. Faolan's waiting. I—"

"Be careful climbing over; here, take my hand—"

"No, I can manage—"

Somehow, on the branch that bridged the gap, it became impossible not to touch, for all he sought to move away, to leave before he lost control completely and made a mockery of Broichan's teaching. Somehow, she was right beside him, her hand in his, and he halted, breathing hard, fighting with everything he had the flood of longing that coursed through him, stronger than logic, stronger than common sense, more powerful than the goddess's will . . . almost . . .

"Not like this," Bridei whispered. "Not this way . . ."

"Bridei."

Tuala stood on tiptoe, perfectly balanced, and reached to curve a hand around his cheek, where the swirls and sweeps of his warrior markings now stood bravely on his fair skin. He felt her thumb moving gently; he saw the look in her eyes, a look belying utterly the coolness of her earlier tone. His hand came up over hers, holding it against his face, and then, despite himself, he brought her palm to his lips. He heard her sudden exhalation, an echo of what was in his own heart.

Below them in the shadows of the garden, a light flared. Someone was walking up the path with a lantern, perhaps searching.

"Quick!" hissed Tuala. "Quickly, go! They must not find you here!"

He edged across. His hand was still in hers; his fingers seemed unable to let go. At the last moment he turned back, and she lifted her face to his, eyes bright, lovely mouth beguiling as a summer rose, skin translucent under the lamp of the Shining One. Below, he could hear footsteps approaching.

"Good-bye," he said unsteadily, and made to turn away. He could do this; he must, for her sake.

"Bridei." It was a whisper. "I didn't mean it, what I said before. I've missed you so much . . ."

He felt her hands on either side of his face; she drew him toward her. A moment later, her mouth met his, a little shy, a little awkward but oh, so sweet he thought he might die of it, save for the fire in his body that told him he was very much alive, more alive, indeed, than he had ever been before. He snatched at a supporting branch with one hand; he was in danger of forgetting where he was, so high above the earth that a single step might be sudden death. Her lips parted; the kiss deepened, arousing sensations somewhat akin to torture, a torture one would wish to last long, until it became something more, something he needed so badly he might sacrifice much to have it . . . but not her safety or her reputation. He must leave. If he were found here Tuala would lose her place at Banmerren and his own future would be in jeopardy. He drew his lips away, hearing the ragged sound of his own breathing, sensing the same in her. Her hand clutched his, tight enough to hurt.

"Next full moon," she whispered. "Good-bye, Bridei. Be safe."

"You too," he managed, and let go. She waited, crouched near the top of the wall, while he made his descent; when he was on the ground, the rope came snaking down as she released its loop from the oak. Bridei glanced up, but Tuala was already gone. He was alone with the moon, and the silent Faolan, and the thunderous beating of his own heart.

THE GOOD FOLK need not speak aloud to understand one another's minds. To the elderly wise woman, Luthana, who now scolded Tuala down from her high perch and led her indoors, the lamp wobbling indignantly in her hand, it seemed the oak was deserted save for this one disobedient student with her white face and unruly dark hair, this strange young woman who seemed determined to bend rules and stretch boundaries to their limits. But they were there: the creatures known to Tuala as Gossamer and Woodbine, she of the cobweb gown and silver hair like chains of dewdrops, he of all the rich life of the forest, twig and leaf, creeping moss and curling fern. They crouched now in a fork of the oak and spoke without the need to make a sound.

"So, the journey moves on at last. Did you see what she did; how she looked, touched, offered her lips? Our little pale creature is indeed become a woman, for all her air of remoteness. I fear she will make this too easy for Bridei."

"You think so? He cannot choose her and pursue the king-ship. That is what he believes. Will he place his duty to For-triu before the longings of his heart? How will he reconcile this?"

"He must find the way for himself. That is the test. He must prove true, not only to the men and women he will lead, but to the ancient powers as well. To the gods; this, he understands. And to us."

"That, he forgets."

"Maybe. We must remind him of it. Fortriu needs him. There is no other who can lead us forward."

"And he needs her. A conundrum. They'll never accept her. What of Broichan?"

Woodbine gave a crooked smile. "Broichan plays with them all, moving them on the board at his whim. Making them hop. The druid is not the only one who can play this game. He may find it is more complex than he ever dreamed of. I think he may find himself outplayed."

"By—?"

Woodbine turned his mud-brown eyes on the light, enig-matic ones of his friend. "We shall see," he said. "For this young man, the gods reserve a final trial of their own mak-ing. That is for later, for the end. Meanwhile, it is for us to play our part. We will lead them a dance, the two of them."

Gossamer laughed, a brief, high tinkle. "These folk frus-trate me. They can be so blind. Ah, well . . . how much does he want her, I wonder? Will he pursue her into a realm where even the Shining One dares not show her face? Will he stand strong in defiance before the one he respects and loves like a father?"

"We'll know that soon enough," Woodbine said with a shrug. "Drust is not long for this world; already they gather, knives at the ready. Foolish folk. This young man shines among them like a bright star. Still, he must face the last trial. Did she see us, do you think?"

"She knew we were watching." Gossamer tossed back her shining hair. "It curbed her words, to begin with; made her guard her eyes. But her love shone through her little effort at coolness; her pathetic attempt to convince herself that he'd be better off with some smooth-haired princess, and Tuala herself wasting away behind the walls of Banmerren. She is far surer than he."

"Of course," said Woodbine. "She's one of us."

15

W INTER MADE ITS presence known emphatically, whipping Caer Pridne with chilly winds and drenching it in persistent rain. It was not possible to ride out; only those with business of the utmost urgency ventured forth. Faolan's demeanor did not vary from its customary cool detachment, but he was growing impatient. Bridei, attuned to the subtlest alteration of a man's voice and manner, saw the Gael's frustration plainly. Faolan's plan to draw the enemy into the open and force an attack had been foiled, and by something as simple as the weather. He prowled the hallways of Caer Pridne; he could be found listening intently to the idle talk of kitchen slaves, of workers mending leaking thatch, of children playing with a ball during a brief respite in the downpour. *Making a new plan,* Bridei thought. *And meanwhile someone, somewhere, is plotting to kill me.*

Bridei fought to keep his mind on what must inevitably come soon. King Drust had hung on grimly for a full turning of the moon since Gateway, but the end was close, and now he called them, one by one, to the chamber where he spent his days wrapped in a cloak and struggling for breath despite the warm fire and curative herbs. Drust spoke to each a form of farewell: words of recognition, guidance for the future, an expression of friendship or gratitude. Sometimes it was merely acknowledgment that change was upon them, willed by the gods who ruled their lives and the life of Fortriu itself.

With this loss impending, Bridei wondered that his own thoughts rested so much on Tuala: on every move she had made, on every word she had spoken, on the unsaid things he believed he had seen in her eyes. On her touch; that above all. His mind played it over and over: his own stumbling efforts to tell her what was in his heart, his pathetic failure to express it, the words she had whispered at the end, the fact that he had allowed himself to return her kiss—ah, the memory of that, sweet on his lips—when he knew he should not tempt her to leave her sanctuary, not when there was so little to offer her beyond its walls. Did not the goddess want this rare small creature as her own? Yet Tuala had said, *Next full moon,* and he had not been able to whisper, *No, I can't, we mustn't.* He had not been able to refuse her, and he would go, Faolan or no Faolan. What would come of it, there was no telling. It would be taking a terrible risk. The election for kingship might be in progress by then, and his every move under scrutiny. Every instinct told him he should not do it. But he must; Tuala would be expecting him. He must; every corner of his body craved it. She was in his thoughts night and day, so much a part of him he wondered how he could possibly go on without her. This was like a sickness; it ate at him, following him into his fitful sleep, filling that time with troubling dreams in which he followed her tracks through the forest alone, in darkness, knowing that if he did not find her soon he would never see her again. Knowing she fled him, seeking to cross a margin to a place where he could not follow. Knowing he should not pursue her, not if he might be king; knowing that without her he was at best but half a man. He willed the visions away, but they would not obey.

He told himself it was all his fault; he should never have gone to Banmerren. He was learning now why those rules existed, the ones that kept men out of that place of the goddess. But he would not for the world have changed things. He would not for any price have missed that meeting. And he would go again. This time he would tell her straight out. He would speak the words of his heart; he would ask her to come with him. To be his wife. That was what he had got wrong. He had not put it to her; he had not given her the opportunity to choose for herself. And she was very much herself; he had understood that from the first. It had seemed to him, from her whispered words and from her kiss, that she might say yes, but he was by no means certain of it. If she said no, he must accept it and walk on without her. He did not rightly know how he would manage to do that.

There came a morning when Bridei, in his turn, was summoned. It was a long time now since Drust had ventured forth from the small chamber to which his world had dwindled as sickness overtook him, and Bridei was taken aback at the king's appearance, all jutting bones and pallid, parchment-dry skin. The room was uncomfortably hot; Queen Rhian was scarlet-faced, her brother Owain stripped to shirt and trousers and sweating. Drust shivered in a woolen cloak, a thick blanket over his knees. A dog crouched at his feet, anxiety in its loyal eyes.

"My lord." Bridei did not allow his thoughts to show on his face; he greeted his monarch with the formal bow, the courteous tone such occasions required. "You sent for me?"

"Come. Sit." Drust was conserving what strength remained in order to see each of them in turn, to say what must be said while he still had a voice.

Bridei sat. Around him, the queen and her helpers moved with the quiet efficiency of folk long accustomed to tending the sick. Linen was changed, vessels emptied, the fire made up, herbs prepared for an infusion, yet so unobtrusive were these attendants that Bridei might almost have been alone with the king. Drust's eyes were bright; a fierce will burned in his ravaged body.

"Carnach," Drust said. "Talk to him. Offer him . . . position. Trust . . . status . . ."

Bridei nodded. "The two of us must work together," he said. "I will find him. What of Tharan?"

Drust attempted a smile; it transformed his features into a death's-head, and Bridei suppressed the instinct to make a sign of ward with his hands. Black Crow hovered close today; he could feel the beating of her dark wings.

"It's Carnach's decision," the king said. "He's his own man. If Carnach won't stand, he won't stand. If he falls in beside you, Tharan . . . no choice . . . follow. Tharan knows . . . he recognizes . . . Gateway . . ."

Bridei hesitated. "My lord—"

Drust's gaze seemed to pierce through him, strong as an iron blade. "You can do it," the king said. "You must."

It became impossible for Bridei to say what he needed to say: that he did not think he could, year after year, winter after winter; that the weight of one such death was almost too much to bear, and that he doubted himself capable of repeating it and remaining sane. To say this was not only disobedient to the gods, it was weak. Before this dying man, whose spirit blazed from his red-rimmed eyes, Bridei's words fled unspoken.

"Main threat . . . south . . . Bargoit," Drust whispered, sipping from a cup of water his wife held for him. "Be sure . . . numbers . . ."

Bridei nodded. "If Carnach joins me, between us we can come close to the votes required," he said. "Aniel's working on that. Broichan, too."

"Ah, Broichan . . . did well with you, son . . . my druid . . . long service, and loyal . . . Fortriu . . . best gift . . . yourself . . ."

The king was tiring. His breathing was shallow, painful, for all the chamber's heat, the steam from pots that simmered on the hearth, the soothing scent of herbs.

"I hope I will prove worthy of your trust, my lord king." The Shining One aid him, he could never in a lifetime be the king Drust was, so strong, so obedient, so much a leader of men.

"One . . . thing," the king said in a thread of a voice. "Wife . . . choose well . . . makes all . . . difference . . ." Drust turned his too-bright eyes on Rhian, who was kneeling by the hearth, stirring something in a little pot. The softness of his gaze, the shadow in his expression, an anticipation of imminent parting, revealed starkly that this powerful monarch was, underneath the iron exterior, a mortal man and vulnerable. "Not for blood," Drust said. "Not for lineage . . . not for wealth . . . Find the one who can walk beside you . . . all . . . difference . . ."

"Yes, my lord," said Bridei, and did not say, *I know. I have found her, and I do not know if I can have her.*

"Go now," Drust said, "son of . . . Flamekeeper . . ."

"Farewell, my lord king. May the gods grant you a safe journey. I do not think Fortriu will see your like again."

"No weeping. Not . . . for me. New king . . . new path . . . brighter, better . . . flight of . . . eagle . . . Be strong, Bridei."

Bridei could not speak. He bowed, and as Drust began a storm of coughing, and both Rhian and Owain hastened to help him sit upright, to wipe the blood from his face as he choked and gasped through the spasm, Bridei slipped out of the little chamber, past the guards and away to the wall-walk, where he paced long, oblivious to the rain.

SOMEWHAT LATER IN the morning, a slight figure made its way up the steps and walked toward him, tonsured hair tousled by the wind from the sea. It seemed Brother Suibne, too, had been spending time on the wall-walks deep in thought. Bridei managed a courteous greeting. Although the Christian priest represented ideas that were abhorrent to him, teachings that had led to the division of the Priteni and the destruction of the sacred places in the south, he had been obliged to acknowledge, over the time Suibne had spent at Caer Pridne, that the fellow was clever, deep, and possessed of a wryly earthy sense of humor. Had Suibne not been who he was, they might have been friends.

Suibne settled himself alongside Bridei, folded arms on the parapet, looking out to sea. The sharp northerly wind was whipping the gray water into white-capped, churning disorder. "I'm sorry to hear the news about King Drust," the priest said quietly. "I'm told he is saying his farewells today. I've been praying for him."

"To what gods?" Bridei asked, knowing this was discourteous, but unable to hold it back.

"There is only one God, Bridei." The priest was smiling; it was by no means the first time they had discussed this topic. "A God with much to offer you, if you would turn to him. I see in your eyes that you are troubled; confused. I suspect your mind is plagued by difficult decisions to be made, quandaries to be faced, pressing questions to be addressed."

"All that shows in my eyes? You assume too much. I was called to speak with the king this morning. I am sad to see him go, that's all."

"And?"

Suibne was starting to sound a little like Broichan. Bridei found that distinctly unsettling. "True," he said, "we will face a time of change; a time of great difficulty. A leader of Drust's status is not so easily replaced. You suggest I look to the cross for answers. There is no point in attempting to convert me to your own faith. I was brought up in the love of the old gods. I wish nothing more than to see the lands of the Priteni united in the practice of the ancient rituals, in reverence and loyalty to the Shining One and to the Flamekeeper. I know you are, at heart, a good man. But I cannot approve your presence amongst us, nor your influence within Circinn. Your kind has wrought havoc among our people. You have fractured our kingdom and severely weakened our ability to defend our borders."

"Ah," said Suibne, eyes bright with interest. "But if Fortriu turned to the Christian faith, as Circinn is doing even as we speak, you would be reunited under the cross. The doctrine of Our Lord Jesus Christ is based on love, peace, and tolerance. Our holy book teaches us to love our neighbor. When men turn to the true God, they are united in love. There is then no need for armies, or for borders."

"In principle, a fine sentiment," Bridei said. "Tell me, what of the Gaels? The folk of Dalriada follow your own beliefs; a cross stands in the center of their settlement at Galany's Reach, the settlement we overran last spring. The Gaels are well known as the most savage fighters our warriors have ever encountered. They are cruel; they do not understand the meaning of mercy. How may we reconcile that with a doctrine of love?"

Suibne smiled. "Your questions reveal your background, Bridei; you have been well tutored in this, I think. Place yourself in the mind of King Gabhran of Dalriada. To a Gael, your own people seem wild, heathen, recalcitrant, and dangerous: an obstacle standing in the way of a clean conquest of the north and the establishment of the very realm you once spoke of yourself: one kingdom, one people, one faith."

"Under the rule of an invader? That would be a travesty. Such unity, if thus it can be called, would not be achieved until every man and woman of Fortriu lay slain on this good earth. Clean? It would be a victory soaked in the blood of the Priteni; a peace won by slaughter and destruction."

Suibne did not attempt to dispute this. "With the right leader," he said, "it need not be so. With an open-minded king in place here, the peace could be won by negotiation."

"Is that what Drust of Circinn told you to say? Or Bargoit?"

"Not at all. I merely point out to you that tolerance and forbearance can carry a man, or his kingdom, a long way. It requires the right leader to do it. A man of outstanding qualities."

"You speak of Drust the Boar?"

"I speak of the distant future; of a peace that could be won if men of great heart would lay down their weapons and open their spirits to God's light."

Bridei was puzzled by the expression on the cleric's face; it was almost like that Broichan wore when he sat in meditative trance before a pattern of augury or a scrying vessel. He had not thought Christians were subject to the visions of the Otherworld. "I would never turn against the gods of my people," he said quietly.

"Even the god who requires an act of murder?" Suibne asked.

"I will not speak of that. It is forbidden to do so."

"But you will think of it. It will be in your mind, season by season, year by year, from each dark enactment to the next. It will plague your conscience and darken your spirit. To adhere to this is not loyalty, Bridei. It is madness. I cannot believe a man such as yourself, a man surely destined for greatness, can truly condone such barbarism."

"Destined for greatness? The religious adviser to Drust of Circinn speaks thus of me? You jest, surely."

"I speak thus as one man to another, Bridei. In your heart, you are a man of peace. That, too, I see in your eyes. And you are young; who knows what lies in your future, and in

the future of Fortriu? Let us pray the chieftains of the Priteni
vote wisely. Much can change in the lifetime of a king."

THERE WAS NO need for Bridei to seek out Carnach. Carnach found him, later in the day, and suggested they go to a
quiet corner to talk undisturbed. Undisturbed did not mean
alone, not when each of them had a claim to kingship. They
met in the stables, where it was easy enough for a man to
pretend to be showing another fellow a horse he might want
to buy; it was amazing, the breadth of conversation that
could take place while examining a hoof or a set of teeth.
Breth stood watchful at a slight distance; Carnach's own personal guard, a lanky, bearded fellow, lounged against the
half-door, making a good show of unconcern.

"You've spoken with the king?" Carnach was direct; there
was little time for the niceties of court etiquette, and Bridei
welcomed the red-haired man's bluntness.

"This morning. You?"

Carnach nodded. "Have you a proposal for me?"

"I do. You'll wish to suggest amendments; I'm ready to
listen."

"Go on, then." And, observing Bridei's glance at the
bearded guard, "Gwrad can be trusted, as I'm certain can
your man, or you would not have brought him here. Tell me."

Bridei laid out a set of terms he had been working on for
some time with Aniel's assistance, in a knowledge of Carnach's status, his background, and the location of his ancestral lands right on the border with Circinn. Carnach would
be entrusted with overseeing border security along the considerable length of the River Thorn, which plunged through
the very center of the land, skirting the great mountain range
that divided Fortriu proper in the northwest from Circinn in
the south and east. All the chieftains of that region would answer to him, and would be bound by the king to provide men
for the defense as Carnach required them. In addition, he
would be appointed one of the king's personal advisers, a
rank that would allow a special place at court when he chose
to be there. He would play a critical part in all future deci-

sions on the conduct of action against invaders, whether they be Gaels, Angles, or something unknown. There would be further incentives: Carnach's own stronghold would be provided with whatever improvements he wished, stone outer walls, earthen barriers, anything Carnach deemed appropriate to his elevated position. This would be at the king's expense. There was also the possibility of a marriage, if Carnach wanted that. There were young women of noble blood at court; comely young women. Bridei presented all this as coolly as he could, knowing, all the time, just how great a sacrifice he was asking of his rival claimant.

"I see," said Carnach coolly. "Border defenses. You want me to do the hard work for you."

"Not for me, with me. That's what this is about, working together. The border with Circinn is vulnerable. I shrink from the possibility that we may one day face our own in battle, but the differences between us were made starkly clear to me by the arrival of Bargoit and his lackeys. Keep that margin strong and we resist not merely their grasp for power but also the insidious creep of their new faith. Keep the Thorn secure and we can in time fix our own attentions on the west. I intend to have a wide circle of advisers. Some of my choices will be disconcerting to the older and more conservative men at court. It would be a privilege to count you as foremost among my inner circle, Carnach. You have King Drust's respect, and that of many men whose opinions I rely on, Aniel and Talorgen among them."

"And Broichan?"

"Broichan was uncertain as to whether you would deal, even after Gateway. I said I was confident you would listen, at least. I recognize you are a man of good judgment. I know you love Fortriu."

"Yet I could not do it. At Gateway."

Bridei said nothing.

"Tell me," Carnach said, "what if I were to make a counteroffer? To present similar terms for you, the price of withdrawing your own claim?"

"You could present them. I would listen; it would be discourteous not to do so. But I will not withdraw my claim. I know that I must stand. The Flamekeeper requires it."

"Mm." Carnach was almost smiling. "I don't want a wife. There's a young woman back home; once I know what the outcome is here, we'll be handfasted. She's no royal daughter, but she pleases me well. Two things more: I want the services of the king's stone carver for a summer, to set my kin signs on the hillside above my home. I can wait for that on the strength of an assurance that he'll be made available to me. I imagine Garvan will be busy for a year or so."

"And the other thing?"

Carnach looked a little embarrassed. "My wife; my wife to be, that is; I'd like to be in a position to make her a special bride-gift, as she has little by way of jewels or finery of her own. Perhaps a small supply of best silver and the services of an expert craftsman? I know the design I want, spirals and dogs; she's fond of dogs. Perhaps a little something for my mother, as well."

"Most certainly," Bridei said. "As for Garvan, we'll put it to him. He can decide which task comes first. There will be work for him here, of course; that's if . . ." His voice trailed off. He had an idea about Caer Pridne, and about the future, an idea that had been forming in his mind since the night he saw Tuala and had to say good-bye with the words of his heart still mute within him. But he must not speak of this now. He was still far from being king.

"Indeed," Carnach said, misunderstanding. "We must not get too far ahead of ourselves. Well, I need a little time to consider this. I should speak with a few people, Tharan in particular. I think I can promise you an answer this evening. Your terms seem not unreasonable. You frown, Bridei. You will discover in time that I am trustworthy, and that I make my own decisions. In consulting the king's councillor I merely show appropriate prudence. A man does not give up the chance of kingship lightly."

"I'm sorry," Bridei said. "Take what time you need."

"The sand runs swiftly through the glass," said Carnach soberly. "I saw Drust this morning, as you did. If we are to reach agreement while he still lives, I think it must be before the Flamekeeper sinks below the horizon once more. Gwrad will bring you my answer before then."

So it was that, when the household of Caer Pridne gathered for supper that night, Bridei knew that the contest had narrowed to two men: himself, young, unknown, untried; and Drust son of Girom, the Christian king of Circinn, who sought to rule both realms. Barring any surprises such as a claim from the Caitt, that was how it was going to be. Carnach had accepted the terms; it had been agreed between them that this would be kept secret until the formal presentation of candidates, so that the faction from Circinn might continue to believe Fortriu's vote split and their own man a probable winner. Wredech had been persuaded of the wisdom of sticking to cattle and relative obscurity, and was out of the race.

The queen and her brother had not attended the evening meal for many days now; Drust required the constant presence of one or the other, and in between they took turns to collapse into exhausted sleep. Tonight, others too were missing: Broichan, Aniel, Tharan, Eogan, and several of the personal guards were nowhere to be seen. Bargoit was present, with Fergus and Brother Suibne. Bargoit had amazed them all at the Well of Shades; none had believed he could bring himself to witness this rite after expressing utter revulsion for what he considered a barbaric and disgusting practice, but he had been there, watching. Afterward he had said little. Bridei had his own ideas about this. Bargoit could not be banned from the Well; he was the emissary of the king of Circinn, and as such might walk freely in the secret places of the men of Fortriu. The lore said nothing about Christians. Indeed, it had never been made entirely clear whether Bargoit's stated support for the changes within the territory of Drust son of Girom equated to a personal decision to seek Christian baptism. Brother Suibne's earlier words had troubled Bridei. He wondered whether, at heart, a man of Fortriu could ever quite renounce the old gods. Of course, Bargoit was a strategist. No doubt, when the representatives from Circinn arrived in force, this councillor of Drust the Boar would regale them with a full account of what had taken place in the Well of Shades, putting heavy emphasis on the roles played by the influential and dangerous Broichan and the foster son who was nothing more than the druid's tool. Bargoit would tell in detail what he had seen: their hands outstretched, holding the girl under the water. He would make it known that he had witnessed no less than the murder of the innocent.

It was quiet in the hall. The talk was subdued; folk ate sparingly. The king's bard sat with chin in hand, staring into his ale, the harp silent in its leather bag by his side. When he awoke the strings once more, it would be to play a lament.

Bridei could see Dreseida with a little frown on her brow, staring at Gartnait. Ferada looked pale and distant, Ana ill at ease, for so many were absent from the king's table that she sat almost alone. Gartnait was talking to his father. Bridei sat between Garth and Ged of Abertornie, while Breth stood behind and acted as taster. Even Ged was subdued tonight; he worked his way through the mutton pie with hardly a word. All of them were waiting.

The platters had not long been cleared away when Broichan came to the hall. There was something in his face that rendered every tongue there silent.

"Our good king is gone," the druid said simply. "Bone Mother has drawn him beyond the veil. An act of mercy. Drink to his memory; tell tales of his great deeds; celebrate his courage. At dusk tomorrow we will conduct the funeral rites."

"And then it begins," Ged muttered. "I hope you're ready for it, Bridei. One turning of the moon, and then the assembly. You'll see Caer Pridne become a place of utter madness. May the Shining One watch over us."

"We must endeavor to keep it orderly," Bridei whispered. "For his sake. He was a fine king, worthy and strong. Gods grant him a peaceful journey."

"One thing's certain," Ged said, glaring across the hall at Bargoit. "He's best out of this."

IN ACCORDANCE WITH the king's wishes and under Broichan's impassive supervision, they built a great pyre on the shore below Caer Pridne and sent Drust the Bull on his last journey by fire and water. The rain held back just long enough. Then Broichan cast the birch rods in augury and consulted the Shining One, and declared that, in view of the season, a degree of flexibility might be allowed as to the timing of the forthcoming assembly, since the voting chieftains from Circinn might not receive news of the king's passing early enough to allow their difficult winter journey to the north within the usual span, a single turning of the moon. This time, Broichan said, they would allow an additional period of seven days. There was some muttering at that; why not keep the time short and ensure Fortriu had a better chance of being in the majority? Wiser voices, Aniel's among them, quieted the dissenters. Restricting the time for travel meant giving Circinn grounds to declare the election invalid, and opening the door on another long period of conflict. To allow an extra seven days would be both wise and expedient.

The new timing meant the candidates would be making their formal claims to kingship at Midwinter, an auspicious conjunction. Each would stand before the court and present his credentials. Should any claimant be unable to reach Caer Pridne in time for this presentation, a proxy might stand up in his place. Seven days later, the assembly proper would convene and the voting occur. At the last election there had been twelve voting chieftains from Circinn and twelve from Fortriu, including the representative from the Light Isles. It was probable, but not certain, that the numbers would be the same this time, if all those eligible to vote arrived within the allotted period. Should a casting vote be required, they would call upon the wise woman, Fola.

"That's unacceptable," Bargoit said when Broichan announced this crucial detail. He rose to his feet, brows crooked in a thunderous frown. "It gives Fortriu the advantage. If the wise woman gets a vote, so should Brother Suibne here, as Drust's religious adviser."

Brother Suibne smiled vaguely, saying nothing. His demeanor suggested a profound wish to be somewhere else.

"Besides," put in the other southern councillor, Fergus,

"everyone knows Fola's a crony of yours, Broichan. You've got her in your pocket. Her vote is your vote."

There was an ominous rumble in the hall, roughly centered around Ged of Abertornie.

Aniel spoke, his expression bland. "That is incorrect," he said. "You little know Fola if you imagine her any man's creature. I'm aware this did cause a certain difficulty at the last election. Your point, therefore, does have some validity."

"Give 'em both a vote," Ged said. "Christian and priestess. Why not?"

"In fact, that would serve no purpose. The numbers would still be tied," said Bargoit testily.

"May I speak?" Bridei rose to his feet. "You talk as if each man's vote is known already; as if our chieftains possess no flexibility at all in their opinions. Are we indeed become so fixed in our ways that we have room in our minds for neither compromise nor new ideas? If this is so, there seems no point in the formal process of presenting the candidates seven days before the voting. Why would a man need to know more than a claimant's name and origins if he votes solely on this partisan basis? Let us do our candidates the courtesy of listening to what they tell us; to what they believe they can offer us. A casting vote may not be needed at all. If it is, surely we can rely on the experience of men such as Broichan, and yourself, Bargoit, to make that decision at the time." A buzz of talk followed this, and reluctant agreement. It remained to be seen whether all would adhere to it when the time came.

Over the ensuing days Bridei worked hard, sending messengers, consulting with his advisers, making plans, and trying to accept the astonishing possibility that, in less than a season, he himself might be foremost in this realm of powerful men. Sometimes the prospect made him afraid: afraid that he might stumble and fall, failing Broichan, failing King Drust, failing the gods. But increasingly, when he prayed, he felt the Flamekeeper's warmth in his spirit and the voice of the god whispering in his ear, *Go forward, my son. Be strong.* For all this, in his heart the days stretched forward only as far as next full moon. Seeing Tuala again loomed large, making it hard to concentrate as he must on wooing certain men and placating others. The headache remained constant; he had almost forgotten how it felt to be without it.

Nonetheless, Bridei walked the steps of this dance of possibilities, knowing the very future of Fortriu and its people depended on the accuracy of his instincts and the capacity of others to traverse with speed and safety the high, bare passes and deep, dark valleys of the Glen in winter. The streams would be in spate; if snow came, some tracks would be blocked. Horses could be used only on the easier parts of the journey, such as the coastal stretch between the mouth of Serpent Lake and Caer Pridne. And time was short. It was as well Bridei had sent his messengers early. Broichan had helped with that; a divination, carried out with smoke after fasting, had predicted the day of Drust's passing with an accuracy that reflected perfectly the intent of the gods.

Bargoit must have done something similar. Perhaps the Christian, Suibne, had his own methods for seeing ahead. It was soon clear that the twelve representatives from Circinn had already traveled a good distance from their southern strongholds in anticipation of this assembly. Well before the allotted time was up they began to arrive at court, cold, weary, and full of fighting words. Drust the Boar's supporters were all too ready to argue their case loudly and at length with the northerners. Suibne began to conduct a daily religious service in the chamber allotted to Bargoit. Broichan would not show in public how deeply this offended him, but he sent a man to walk the hallway outside Bargoit's door with a vessel of water in which seven white stones lay. Thus the good influence of the Shining One might prevent the conduct of this alien rite from polluting the king's household. Sometimes Broichan himself walked by, bearing fire in an earthenware bowl, with powdered herbs of protection adding their pungent aroma to the cleansing smoke. At night the druid knelt long in his darkened chamber, praying in silence.

AT FULL MOON Bridei summoned the charm that gave him protection against the eyes of the curious, and left Caer

Pridne by the water-gate to make his way to Banmerren alone. Heavy clouds veiled the Shining One; he suspected they would wait only for him to reach the midpoint of the bay before releasing a pounding, drenching torrent on his head. He thought of Tuala, alone and exposed in her tree. He would not leave her there; if she agreed, he would bring her away with him tonight. She must not be cold, lonely, afraid. He must not leave her all by herself, without a friend. He would bring her back . . . She could stay with Gartnait's family, surely that would be acceptable . . . No, rein in those thoughts. He was getting ahead of himself, making assumptions he had no right to make. This must be Tuala's choice.

By all the gods, a man needed cat's eyes to see tonight. Thunder rumbled distantly, somewhere to the north. There was a breathlessness in the air, an anticipation of storm. His own heart held the same sense, fear and wonder mingled, a heady foreknowledge of change. Soon he would see her . . . Soon he would ask her . . . Soon he would know . . .

Bridei dodged behind the low bushes fringing the dunes, wincing as his foot slipped into a sudden hollow; he must tread more cautiously. His churning thoughts were making him careless; he was walking the earth as if he were an outsider, an intruder. Oh, for home . . . Oh, for Pitnochie, for the Glen in summertime with its soft forest canopies and fern-fringed streamlets, its rustling, secret life, its noble heights and wide, empty skies. If only he could be there again with his dear friend by him, her hand in his, her tousled head resting on his shoulder . . . the warmth of her body against him . . .

Bridei forced his mind back to the night, the path, the distant, shadowy form of the far headland where Banmerren's dark walls could barely be seen in the gloom. It had been hard to give Faolan the slip, but essential: he could not tell the Gael about tonight. A man who believed a single brief visit would be enough to resolve this could not conceive of the true complexity of it. Faolan could not know how much rode on Tuala's decision. One way or another, he would have ensured this expedition did not take place.

Bridei thought he had made a convincing pretense that this night was no different from any other. Somewhere between supper, with Garth in attendance, and bedtime, when Faolan generally assumed the role of watcher over Bridei's sleepless nights, he had managed to evade them both with a judicious use of what little magic Broichan had taught him. His ability in such arts was weak indeed beside his foster father's; the charm of concealment lasted no longer than it took him to flee into the dunes, but that was all he needed tonight. Only an utter fool would be roaming out here with such a storm brewing. A fool . . . Perhaps that was all he was. What if Tuala was not there? What if he threw his rope up and it simply fell back, time after time? Worse still, she might hear him out and then offer him a polite refusal. She had kissed him. But she was young, perhaps too young to understand what that touch had ignited in him . . .

A fork of lightning split the sky, illuminating pale shore, dunes like snowy hillocks, wind-ravaged bushes. Darkness fell again as the thunder cracked close at hand, deafening him. A moment later they erupted from cover. Bridei's heart lurched. He grabbed for his knife, whirled even as hands seized him, three men at least, one behind, one on either side. Rain hammered down, sudden and violent. His fingers slipped on the knife. The man on his back was dragging him to the ground, another was trying to stuff something into his mouth . . . Bridei slashed wildly, heard a shriek of pain, felt the knife fall as something blunt and heavy smashed across his wrist. A white light flashed; he heard shouting, perhaps his own name. An instant later there was a jarring blow to the back of his head, and the world turned to darkness.

THE CHAMBER SWAM into focus: woolen hangings softening stone walls, a lamp on a chest in the corner, someone bent over a shelf, pouring an infusion from a steaming kettle to a cup. A pungent smell arose; it was one of Luthana's brews, crammed with healing herbs and bitter to the tongue. Voices came to Tuala's ears, not close but outside somewhere. Fola's voice, held quiet. "I don't think she can stay here. Not after this. If she persists in such behavior we risk losing her anyway."

The figure by the shelf turned. It was Luthana herself, cup in hand, elderly features kindly. Memory returned; Tuala turned her face into the pillow.

"Come, child. You must try to drink. You've had a terrible chill; this will give strength to your heart and help clear your head. Come on, Tuala, I know you're awake. Sit up; let me help you . . ."

It seemed pointless to drink; pointless to try. Nothing made sense anymore. What was the Shining One doing? The illuminator of pathways had obscured the road before Tuala's feet; had snatched from her the one chance she had of making the future bright and good, as she had always believed it must be. Always, always, even in deepest despair, when the folk of Pitnochie turned against her, when she cut her hair and passed the care of Bridei into the hands of the goddess, when Broichan sent her away, Tuala recognized that a tiny, hidden part of her had still believed in that future, a future in which she walked forward by Bridei's side, a life in which her love would make him strong enough for the great task the gods had laid on him. Despite all, in her secret heart she had clung to that. Why else had the Shining One delivered her to Bridei's own doorstep and ensured that he would be the one to find her? Why else had the goddess allowed her an education such as no other girl in all Fortriu was granted? They were bound together, the two of them; bound in a sacred trust, and in a love that had grown, wondrously, from the innocent devotion, the comfortable familiarity of childhood to a deep, strong thing, a heady, tumultuous thing, the burgeoning passion between man and woman. She had felt the pull of that as she touched his hand; as her lips sought his with a hunger that surged in her like a spring tide. She had believed Bridei felt it, too, for all his restraint. His kiss had seemed to speak the words for him.

Yet he had not come back. All night she had waited, until under a pale dawn Kethra had found her wretched and soaked, still clinging to the bare branches of the oak, her teeth gritted, her eyes squeezed shut, and on her cheeks hot tears mingling with the rain. She had been too cramped to move; they'd had to send two of the more agile seniors up a ladder to get her safely to the ground. After that it was all a blur. She supposed she had slept awhile. She had no idea where she was; there were no such small, private chambers in the students' area of Banmerren. It didn't matter. Nothing mattered beyond the misery of it. Bridei hadn't come. It seemed she had been wrong. He did not love her, save in the affectionate manner of a brother and friend. He had decided to move on without her. Or Broichan had decided for him. Didn't Broichan decide everything?

"Good, child," Luthana said, tipping the cup against Tuala's lips. "All of it, now. Later we'll try some soup. Don't shake your head like that, you'll make me spill it. You must eat. We nearly lost you. Don't make a mockery of Bone Mother's decision to let you stay awhile longer. That's it, good. You can rest now. Fola will come in later; she wants to talk to you."

"H-how—?" Tuala could hardly find her voice; her body felt shaky, weak, like a garment pounded on the rocks to utter limpness. "How long—?"

Luthana's gaze was shrewd, compassionate. "You've been gravely ill, Tuala. That was a strange thing to do, indeed; I cannot understand what drives you to such wild and pointless behavior. You'd do well to seek the wisdom of the Shining One; to ask for her direction."

Tuala closed her eyes. The Shining One? Hardly. Perhaps, once, the goddess had illuminated her way, had smiled on her daughter in recognition and love. Now she had turned her bright gaze away. Who knew what she wanted? "Please," Tuala whispered, as the wise woman rose to her feet. "How long have I been here, like this?"

"Three days," Luthana said. "In a fever for most of that; you had us very worried. The worst is over now. If you make an effort to eat and apply your mind to what Fola tells you, you should be out of bed in a day or two."

"Where—?"

"You're in the wise women's quarters, Tuala. Fola thought that more appropriate. The junior girls have had enough disruption already this winter, as you'll be well aware. Here, we can keep an eye on you. Now rest awhile. You'll see Fola later."

Keep an eye on you. That translated loosely as, *stop you from doing anything like this again.* It hardly mattered now if she was some kind of prisoner. Nothing at all mattered, really. Without Bridei there seemed no point to any of it. Without his love and without the love of the Shining One, life shrank to something so small and insignificant it was hardly worth having. Perhaps the best thing was simply to curl up here in this little room, close her eyes and wish the world away. Luthana could hardly force her to eat . . .

Time passed. The two of them were there with her in the quiet chamber, as they had been in the tree, keeping up their commentary, maintaining their blend of coaxing, persuasive argument, and blunt analysis.

"It's as I expected." Gossamer's voice, light, mocking, but with a softness in it. Compassion was not in the nature of the Good Folk; still, these two had made themselves close to Tuala. If they cared nothing for her, why were they here at all? "He desires you, or did so when he came here; that was plain enough. But men's desire is short-lived. A moment of heady arousal, a few second thoughts, and by next full moon he's off pursuing more appropriate quarry. That girl Ana, for instance. No doubt Bridei saw the error of his ways and transferred his attentions to her."

Tuala held her silence; she had not the energy to protest. Where once she would have thrown these cruel words back in the forest girl's face, now she found them all too believable.

"You're sad," said Woodbine, settling himself on the bed by her feet. He was no heavier than a cat. "That isn't so surprising. You thought he would put you before the kingship. You were wrong. You thought you had a sort of haven here, a second best, at least. That was wrong, too; Fola doesn't want you anymore. You're becoming a liability, unpredictable, a danger both to your fellow students and to yourself. If you choose to stay out all night in a storm and perish from exposure to the elements, Broichan must be told, and so must Bridei. And while Bridei may have decided a king cannot wed a woman of the Good Folk, that does not mean he cares nothing at all for you. Your death would anger him greatly. It would cause a rift between himself and a certain influential druid. Fola doesn't want to be responsible for that. She doesn't want to be responsible for you, not now the task has grown so difficult."

They would send her away, Tuala thought vaguely. Where? Where could she go?

"Ah, well," Woodbine said cheerfully, "at least there's that fellow, Garvan. Didn't he say he'd have you whenever you were ready? It looks as if the time's come sooner than anyone expected. And he's at court just now, waiting to find out what commissions the new king will have for him. Eagle stones, I imagine."

Garvan; lumpish Garvan with his big hands. Herself by his side, running his household, sharing his bed, bearing his children . . . It was not to be contemplated. It was not to be numbered in the possibilities. Possibilities . . . it seemed suddenly there were none. All had shrunk to this chamber, this bed, these walls . . . this day . . .

"Look up there!" Gossamer's voice rang out like a clear chime. "Someone's been marking the wall; scratching it with a knife. Oh, and look here, another set of marks. How odd. It's as if there were a prisoner here, counting off days."

"All the days from Maiden Dance to Gateway," said Woodbine softly. "All the days of a life. It's a cozy little cell. They try to keep a girl comfortable in here. All the same, Morna must have been very lonely; lonely and frightened. Who could ever be truly prepared for such a trial? These lines, so neatly cut into the stone, must have helped her; her own little ritual, orderly and sure, in the midst of a world suddenly turned dark and unreal. How their minds must have plagued them as they watched over her, cosseted her, trained her, readied her. How their visions must have tormented their sleep, while the girl sat here alone with her candle and her little knife, carving a lonely litany of days. I wonder why they chose this place for you, Tuala? I wonder what they plan?"

"I don't really care anymore," Tuala whispered. "Nothing seems to matter."

"Exactly," said Woodbine. "Have a good sleep, now. Talk

to Fola. We'll be back. Unlike you, we have a plan; I think you'll approve of it. It's far superior to a marriage made out of desperation, and much better than staying where you'll never be truly welcome. Sweet dreams, Tuala." And they were gone; the cat, Shade, sauntering in through the doorway, bristled in sudden alarm, tail rigid. Tuala lay, wide awake now, staring up at the little marks on the wall, desperate scratchings in stone, the more pathetic for their very neatness and order. What had Morna been thinking as she made them, night after night? What had all those girls been seeing as they waited out the lonely seasons of preparation for one Gateway or another? So many young lives gone; so much of beauty and vitality lost in the well of the dark god, tossed away to feed a hunger that could never be satisfied. How could this go on? How could Bridei be a part of it? How could he live with that if she were not there to help him?

Shade jumped to the bed, landing heavily on Tuala's legs. He turned three times and settled behind her knees, pinning the blankets tightly. His presence was comforting; it reminded her of Mist. Mist in the forest, searching for martens; Mist in the kitchen, laying a fat mouse proudly at Ferat's feet. Mist on Erip's knee, warming the fitful sleep of a sick old man. Mist locked in; Mist yowling in protest as Tuala rode away from Pitnochie for the last time . . .

It came to Tuala that there was no need to listen to Fola; she knew already what the wise woman would say. Behavior unsuited to a servant of the goddess . . . disruption . . . take time to consider your future . . . She didn't even need to wait for Woodbine and Gossamer to tell her their grand plan; it didn't require much insight to guess what it was. Even without it, her mind was made up. She could not remain here in this little chamber with its sad record of wasted lives, of seasons of loneliness and despair. Banmerren would be closed to her; even if it were not, she could not remain here if Bridei was so near, and wed to another. Pitnochie would hardly welcome her; she could not live in Broichan's household. She would not have Garvan, for she could never love him, and to wed without love was a travesty. To agree to that would be fair neither to Garvan nor to herself. So, she would take the step she had never dared to take; she would trust in her own folk, those elusive creatures whose teasing, vexing presence had become more or less constant during her stay at Banmerren. It was a long way back to the Great Glen, and it was winter. Never mind that; Gossamer and Woodbine would find an answer. Tuala was going home.

"WHEN WILL HE be restored to himself?" Aniel asked. "How soon will he be ready?"

"You speak as if you cared only for the battle to be won here, and nothing for the young man himself," said Talorgen wearily, passing a cup of ale to the councillor and pouring a second for himself. They were sitting in the antechamber to Broichan's quarters; it had become a regular gathering place for certain men in recent days. "He hovers between life and death. You'd best not put such a question to Broichan."

"I heard a hint that the lad's coming out of it," said Aniel. "If I thought Bridei was dying I'd have been less blunt. Uist says he's fighting his way back, though how our druidic friends can determine that is a puzzle to me; the last time they let me in, the boy seemed deep in unconsciousness and little changed since they carried him home, save that he's considerably thinner. From time to time he stirs, they say, and it's possible to get a little broth into him, half a cup of water. He mutters nonsense; the stuff of ancient memories twisted and tangled. I suppose a druid knows how to interpret that. We must hope he returns to us with no loss of wit or understanding. The entire future of our kingdom depends on this young man."

"He could do no better for attendants. Between Broichan's herbs and Uist's incantations, along with the labor of his devoted complement of guards, one would think the lad would hardly dare not get well again. Bridei inspires great trust; one might almost call it love. There's the spark of kingship in him already. All they need to do is get him on his feet before the presentation of claimants. And keep him well until the election."

"Ah, yes," said Aniel, smiling. "The election. And aren't

there going to be some surprises then . . . Sour-faced and taciturn as that man Faolan is, I salute him for his abilities. He has the miscreant in custody, secretly; in addition, there's evidence linking the assailant firmly to Drust the Boar, or to his advisers at least. We've Uist to thank for that. His little sojourn in Circinn, coupled with his astonishing memory, fixed the man's face in his head clearly. Of course, Bargoit's folk will think of an excuse to try to discredit Uist as a witness when we make this public."

"Not difficult. Uist's known to be somewhat eccentric; some would go further and call him addled in his wits. His thoughts inhabit a different plane from those of ordinary men; the simplest interpretation of that is to call him crazy. Who but a madman would decide to walk back from Circinn alone, so close to Midwinter?"

"That doesn't matter. Folk will recognize the truth. Besides, Faolan will make his prisoner talk: how he was paid to track Bridei, to eliminate him before the candidates were presented; who was handing out purses of silver for such a deed."

"Where is this would-be assassin? He should be questioned also about the earlier attempt, when a man was poisoned at my own table."

"He's not here at Caer Pridne. Faolan has him safe."

"That Gael's a busy fellow. The others, I understand, lie buried somewhere in the dunes."

"What others?" Aniel raised his brows in mock surprise.

"Mm," Talorgen mused. "And we're certain Bargoit knows nothing of what we plan?"

"Oh, he'll be suspicious. After all, his assassins failed to report back. And he knows Bridei's still alive; that's unless he thinks our story of a bad case of the flux is designed to cover a desperate search for a new candidate. Unlikely; we'd simply put Carnach up instead. At least he'd be better than a southerner."

"I'll be happier when Bridei opens his eyes and begins to talk sense to us," Talorgen said. "In that I'm fully in agreement with you, my friend. Midwinter is almost upon us; he's lain there in apparent sleep for a long time, and that must take a toll on body and mind. We don't want him weak and incapable. We don't want to have to use a proxy; Bridei is his own best spokesman. He has a gift with words; his speeches, plain as they are, stir men's spirits. All the same, one of us must be ready to speak for him."

"Broichan will want that privilege," Aniel said.

"Broichan? That would be unwise. He has many enemies and is much feared. A more straightforward man would do better."

"Yourself?" asked Aniel wryly.

"Hardly. I'd do it only if there were no other suitable choice. Ged, perhaps?"

There was a tap at the door and Carnach came in, ducking under the lintel. He was the tallest man at Caer Pridne, dwarfing even Breth. "How is he?" the red-haired man inquired.

"Much the same. Getting better, we're told. This makes for an anxious time of waiting. We were discussing the matter of proxies."

"I'll do it," Carnach offered immediately, sitting down beside Talorgen and reaching for the ale. "That would have some impact, I think. I step up, and instead of doing what they all expect, that is, announcing my own claim and setting out my own qualities, I tell the assembled voters I'm there to present Bridei as the future king of Fortriu; Bridei who, a whisper told me, is absent only because his main rival in the race tried to have him murdered before he could so much as state his intention to claim. That would make an impression. Mind you, I'd prefer that Bridei himself be well enough to stand up and speak. We all want that. That wretched Bargoit! I long to set my hands around that fellow's neck and give a good, hard squeeze."

"You're not alone in that, believe me," said Aniel. "But we'll snuff him out with words, not deeds. In setting up this attempt at assassination, Drust the Boar has sealed his own fate. Thank the gods for Faolan."

"Somehow," Talorgen said, "that seems most inappropriate. Whatever it is we must thank for the presence of that Gael, gods are most certainly not a part of it."

UIST SAT BY Bridei's pallet, wiping his patient's brow with
a damp cloth and studying the planes and shadows of the unconscious features, where nothing at all seemed to hint at
life. Nonetheless, Bridei breathed; there seemed an eternity
between each outward sigh, each inward gasp, as if to move
from that point of balance took, each time, a tremendous
strength of will. It was the gods, perhaps, that drove his
choice to live. He had lain thus, deep in unconsciousness, for
many days. Those brief times when he seemed to struggle
toward awareness were disturbed by dark visions; what
words he had uttered had been garbled even beyond a druid's
understanding. They had been something less than honest,
Uist and Broichan, in their reports to the others, trusted
friends as they were. Even Aniel, even Talorgen did not
know how this had drained them; how close despair had
crept. Broichan's features were gaunt with exhaustion.
Garth slept now on a bench by the wall, covered with a
cloak, while Breth busied himself heating water in preparation to bathe the unconscious man. Bridei's guards would
not let the Caer Pridne servants in; none but the inner circle
might tend to this fallen leader. Beyond the door, Aniel's
bodyguard stood on watch; Talorgen's personal attendants
were stationed on the wall-walk beyond. Of Faolan there
was no sign today. He had much to occupy him. All the
same, each night the Gael returned to keep vigil by Bridei's
bedside, a silent presence among them, taking his turn with
the changing of linen, the brewing of draughts, the lifting of
the patient and the washing of his ever thinner body; remaining wakeful through the night while the others slept, all but
the two druids, dark-clad, shadow-eyed Broichan and wild
Uist of the flowing white garments and aureole of snowy
hair. These two did not seem to sleep. They rested standing
in meditation, or kneeling with open, unseeing eyes, listening for the whispering voices of the gods. In the morning
Faolan would slip away without a word.

"He will wake soon," Broichan said now, moving to look
down on his foster son. "What possessed them, I wonder?

When I trusted his security to Faolan, I did not expect the Gael to take such a risk. Setting out to draw an attack is all very well, but you don't place the man you're paid to keep safe in such a perilous position. If you hadn't happened along with staff in hand, my friend, who knows if Faolan could have felled two and captured the third so neatly?"

"A fortunate coincidence," said Uist with a cryptic smile. "Who'd have thought my mare would have carried me by that spot at precisely the right time? I did rather enjoy my small lightning bolt; my staff still quivers in memory when I set my hand on it. Even Faolan was alarmed. But not for long; the fellow is every bit as capable as Drust always told us. Bridei should keep him."

"He put Bridei at great risk, sending him out alone thus, at night, and only lightly armed. We could have lost him."

There was something in Broichan's voice that gave the old druid pause. Uist looked in the other's eyes and smiled again. "I imagine sometimes," he said quietly, "how it must be for a father of many sons, of many daughters. So many moments of terror; so many small griefs, so many anxieties. I find myself doubly glad I embraced the way of the gods and never took a wife. Not that I wasn't tempted, a long time ago. Fola was a delightful girl, so tiny and so determined. A little like that fosterling of yours, what was her name?"

"Tuala." A tight mask descended over Broichan's features, forbidding further questions. But Uist, too, was a druid.

"Didn't Fola send a messenger here some time ago, just after the attack on Bridei? What did she want? Have you passed on this news?"

"She knows my foster son is sick. Her message to me was personal."

"I see." Uist did not ask what kind of personal news had required the despatch of a rider in such inclement weather. "Of course," he went on, "you do understand that any information that might relate in any way whatever to our plan cannot be classified as personal, however private it may seem to you. If it's to do with the girl, Tuala, it may well relate to Bridei. And he is the center of our plan. Do not forget what we agreed, the five of us; do not forget our undertaking of total honesty."

"It was personal."

A tap at the door; Aniel looked in. "We've had visitors," he said. "Tharan and Eogan. Expressed their sorrow that Bridei was still laid low and told me somewhat indirectly that we had their support, since Carnach won't be in the contest. Tharan wouldn't put it in so many words, of course; Carnach has wounded his mentor's pride with this decision. Still, I read this as genuine enough."

Broichan nodded. "Good," he said. "I may detest your fellow councillor, but I do know we can rely on him to put the best interests of Fortriu before any other considerations. This wretched attempt on Bridei's life has served only to unite us against the south. We still don't have the numbers, for all that. And time grows ever shorter."

"Bridei's got that under control." To their surprise it was the bodyguard, Breth, who spoke from his place by the hearth. "He'll get his numbers."

"I hope you're correct," said Aniel drily. "Bridei's hardly in a position of control right now. I pray the gods restore him in time, and that we can trust his forward planning."

"He's to be king," said Breth simply. "Of course you can trust him."

☙

"So," DRESEIDA SAID, pacing the rush-strewn floor of the women's quarters, "the girl has fled Banmerren. Gone wild. I suppose it was inevitable that she'd do so eventually. She could never have become one of Fola's sisterhood; that was a misguided notion from the first. She'll have gone back. Couldn't help herself."

"Gone back?" echoed Ferada. "Gone where?"

"Back beyond the margin; back where she came from. Back where her kind belong. It's not helpful news for us. If the girl's gone, we can't make use of her. I'd hoped her devotion to her foster brother, and his to her, might offer an opportunity . . . How is Bridei? What's being said?"

Ferada stared at her mother in surprise. "Why would I

know any more than you do, Mother? I've only just come back from Banmerren. As far as I know, Bridei's improving, but still too sick to have visitors. That's what Ana said; she tried to go and see him and they wouldn't let her in. If you want news, why don't you ask Father?"

"Your father's as tight as a limpet on this particular topic," Dreseida said. "But I've heard enough to unsettle me. It seems you were right for once, Daughter. Against all logic, it appears the chosen candidate is not to be the obvious one after all. They really are intending to put Bridei up, that's if he recovers in time. Bridei, that mealymouthed scholar with his head in the clouds. Broichan's pawn. I can scarcely believe it! The blood runs but weakly in that boy. His father is a man of Gwynedd, a foreigner; his mother's only a distant cousin of Drust the Bull. How can such a half-breed have the strength to serve as king of Fortriu? It's all Broichan's doing. Druids carry too much power. That man should have been stopped before his influence began to corrupt others. Others who should have known better. It is regrettable. It is a great deal more than regrettable." Dreseida was twisting her hands together, pacing up and down like a caged creature.

Ferada cleared her throat nervously. "But, Mother . . . I agree that it is somewhat surprising if Carnach has agreed to support Bridei's claim rather than stand against him. But it does make sense, when you think about it. We need just one strong candidate from the north, not two or three, if we are to have the numbers to defeat Drust the Boar. Certainly, as you said, Carnach is the obvious choice. Or was. They're saying Bridei has widespread support now, and that it's growing daily. His honesty, his courage, his gift for plain speaking are much admired. And King Drust the Bull thought highly of him. That is widely known, and must count strongly in his favor."

The look her mother turned on her then made Ferada suck in her breath. She stood very still, wondering what sin she had committed this time; what punishment would be meted out.

"Very well, Ferada," said Dreseida briskly, clasping her hands before her. Ferada saw her mother's attempt to restore calm to her tight features; to will the fury from her eyes. To a stranger, it would have been entirely convincing. "A slight change of plan. We've only a matter of days before Drust the Boar arrives and all of this begins in earnest. The moment Bridei recovers sufficiently, you must create an opportunity to talk with him in private. Today, tomorrow, no later."

"But, Mother—you know how tight the guard is around him. Even more so now, with the election close and Bridei so sick."

"Stop babbling and listen to me. By all the gods, I sometimes wonder why folk think you clever. I have a job for you. Not special confidences this time, he'll be too weary for that. Just a sickbed visit, just yourself and Bridei alone together. Be sweet, be charming, be a girl, if you can stretch to that. I wish you to administer a . . . I hesitate to call it a love potion, that sounds so crude, but in effect that is exactly what it is. You'll make an opportunity, you'll see Bridei alone, and you'll slip it into his drink. Make sure his eyes are on you when he takes it."

"What?" This was so unexpected that Ferada thought she had misheard.

"Weigh it up, Ferada. Bridei or Cealtran. A healthy young man, whom you already tolerate quite well, or a pot-bellied ancient with creeping hands. I know which I'd choose."

Ferada was lost for words.

"You could be queen," her mother said softly. "Is that enough power for you, Daughter? This will be easy. I have a little ring here, a trifle of a thing, with a cunning hinged setting; a few grains of the powder can be concealed within and released into a cup of water or ale with ease, arousing no suspicion whatever. They'll let you in. Blush, smile, flutter your eyelashes. Convince the guards that you are a woman in love. Make sure it's Breth or Garth on duty and not that wretched Gael."

"But, Mother, this doesn't make sense at all. You've always disliked Bridei; you just implied that you despise him. That you think he doesn't have a will of his own. Why would you want your only daughter to wed such a man?"

"Answer me one question, Ferada," said Dreseida very softly. "What have I told you about marriage, over and over since you were an infant? What is the one reason to wed, the one basis for choosing a spouse?"

"Strategy." Ferada's tone was full of bitterness. "We marry for power. For influence."

"Good girl." Dreseida smiled, making her daughter shudder. "If, against all common sense, Bridei is to be king, then I must accept it. But only if it is my child who becomes his queen. So he is a bore, more content with his books and prayers than with the councils of the powerful. Never mind that. He's a man. He can be influenced. Even Broichan can be influenced. So, you will do as I ask. Unless, of course, you really do prefer Cealtran."

Ferada swallowed, desperately searching for words. Oddly, the feeling that was strongest in her at this moment seemed to be relief. "I . . . You know that I have no desire to wed, Mother. If I must do so, I would rather not rely on old wives' potions to snare a mate. Why can't Father just ask Broichan if he'd consider this match? It's entirely suitable. Indeed, Father has hinted more than once that he views it as desirable."

"There is no time for that." Dreseida's voice was cold. "I want it settled now. I want it certain. The moment the boy is sufficiently recovered to see his friends, you'll do this. And you'll keep quiet about it. It will reflect far better on you in the future if it's believed Bridei chose you because he admires you and thinks you suited to be queen of Fortriu. In that, your talk of old wives' potions is entirely accurate."

"In a way," Ferada said, "I am heartened by this. By your decision. I would prefer not to marry Bridei. I would prefer not to wed at all. But you've allayed my fears on one point. I thought—I was coming to think—no, I realize that was foolish. Of course you wouldn't put Gartnait up as a contender for the kingship; that would be too cruel."

Dreseida had turned away as her daughter spoke. Ferada could not see her mother's face. The voice, when it came, was under iron control. "The ring is on the table, there, by the candle stand. Take it. Use it. If you don't go through with this, Ferada, believe me, your life won't be worth living. The moment the boy is sufficiently recovered to see his friends, do it. I'm relying on you."

"Couldn't this wait until Bridei is fully recovered? Perhaps until after the election? I don't see—"

"Ferada." It was that tone again; the tone that caused ice to trickle down the spine of the listener.

"Yes, Mother?"

"You'll do this now. Within two days, if possible. Get it wrong, and what awaits you will be far worse than the elderly Cealtran, I promise you."

"Mother . . ." Ferada drew a deep, shuddering breath. "This is—it seems wrong . . ."

"Enough!" Dreseida's voice was a whiplash; Ferada cringed, despite herself. "Don't think to criticize me! Believe me, time is of the essence here. I am perhaps the only one at court who understands what is at stake. Now that Drust is gone, I am the truest of the blood: I and mine. Be glad this is all I ask of you, Ferada. And don't ever think to challenge me, for there is no doubt who would be the victor in such a contest. Now go."

"I will; but—"

"Go!"

"Yes, Mother."

IT WAS A hard and weary journey. Tuala had thought it might be quick with Woodbine and Gossamer to guide her; could not such creatures change their form at will, glide above the wintry land, dive deep in bottomless lakes, fly swift as swallows on currents above the Glen? If she were of their kind, could not she do the same and bridge the gap from Banmerren to Pitnochie as easily and lightly as she had danced across the wall from rooftop to tree, heedless of danger? Could not she be as an owl of the forest, a salmon of the river, a deer, a hare, a creature running free? It seemed not; at least, not yet.

"You've been too many seasons among human folk," Gossamer said. "We warned you long ago. It's weakened you; softened your will and diluted your magic. A little time in the realm beyond, and everything will come back to you. Meanwhile, you're going to have to walk. We'll watch over you."

But as Tuala maintained a dogged progress in the general direction of the Glen, spending her nights huddled in the shelter of outhouses or sodden haystacks, eating a moldering loaf that was all she had managed to snatch before her midnight flight from Banmerren—out through a tiny window while her keepers were at prayer, up the tree, onto the wall, then descending in the one, brief moment of proof that she was indeed more than human, for she had closed her eyes, imagined herself an owl, and jumped—she realized her companions were every bit as elusive and unpredictable now, when their help made the difference between life and death for her, as they had been in easier times. Sometimes they were there beside her, encouraging her with kind words, with songs and tales; sometimes she would wake at first light, cramped, chill, and despondent, to find herself all alone. When that happened, she trusted her senses to find the path and blessed Erip's lessons in geography and the lore of sun, moon, and stars. Such an education made it unlikely she would ever be lost.

She had thought herself beyond caring about anything, after last full moon. But certain matters worried her. It seemed to be getting colder, and from time to time snow fell, lightly still, but setting a deep chill in the bones, so that she was never quite without a longing for fire. Her boots were soaked right through; her feet were a mass of blisters. Why didn't Gossamer and Woodbine feel the cold? When they returned, slipping down beside her in the straw behind a pigpen, the best refuge she could find, she asked them this question and received a familiar answer.

"You've been too long among them. Your tides have begun to move in the pattern of theirs. When we are home, you will recover quickly. There, there is no more heat, no more cold; there is no more pain."

"But . . ." Tuala ventured, "it might not mean that. Maybe I'm cold and tired and hungry because I'm *not* one of you. Maybe I'm human, like Bridei." To speak his name was bittersweet: a charm of love and loss.

"Huh!" scoffed Woodbine, settling himself more comfortably in the straw. "Didn't you fly down from the walls of Banmerren? A human girl would have broken her neck."

"Then maybe I am half and half: the offspring of a union between your kind and the human kind."

"We'd know," Gossamer assured her. "It's rare. Think about your tales. Consider Amna of the White Shawl. She didn't even bother to keep that wretch Conn for more than a night at a time, and in the end she finished him off. His weakness disgusted her. What would such a one as she want with an infant that was half his? She certainly wouldn't deliver it to the door of a dwelling of human kind, all wrapped up warm against the winter. She loathed the man. He couldn't satisfy her. The last thing she'd concern herself with was the survival of his child."

"But you said—Woodbine said—Amna was a made-up story," Tuala protested. "And what about the owl woman? She had children. It does happen. Besides, whatever I am, my parents didn't want me. If I do belong among you, if my mother and father were indeed of the Good Folk, why didn't they keep me? No, don't vanish, answer the question! Why won't you tell me? Don't I deserve the truth if I'm to come with you? What if I walk across this margin you speak of and find that even there nobody wants me?"

"Is that what you believe?" A coldness had entered Gossamer's voice. "You wish that we leave you here to seek your future among these human folk who have treated you so unjustly, so unkindly? Where would you go?"

"I don't want that," Tuala whispered. "I only want to know who I am. And I want to get warm and dry. It seems such a long way."

"Hmm." Woodbine regarded her with his round, strange eyes. "I can't do much about the cold. Light a fire, and we'll have farm folk out to see who's wandering on their land with an eye out for a fat sheep or two. How long have we been on the road? Three days, four?"

"Four," Tuala said grimly. "And we've barely reached Serpent Lake. It's almost dark of the moon, and I think it's going to snow."

"Yes," said Woodbine. "A man on a horse could travel the distance far more quickly, of course, given a fortunate conjunction of weather and moonlight. He'd need a mount of exceptional qualities. As for our kind, we do not make our journeys idly. Each follows its own particular pathway and unfolds in its own perfect timing. We cannot transport you home in an eye blink, which is what they say druids do. But we can move more quickly now. Dark of the moon is good."

"No, it isn't," said Tuala. "It means we can't go by night, not unless we want to stumble into a bog, or fall in the lake and become fodder for the serpents."

"Dark of the moon is the right time to end our journey," said Gossamer. "Dark of the moon falls at Midwinter; it is a conjunction of great significance, almost as great as that of the night you were found on Broichan's doorstep, a vision of light and hope. Then, the Shining One revealed her true beauty in all its radiant power; this time, she hides her face from the world of men and from our own world as the season turns. Who knows what may unfold on such a night? At Caer Pridne, the candidates for kingship will stand up and declare themselves. Your friend will be among them; a certain young noblewoman will be close by, smiling on him, applauding him. And we will be in the woods above Pitnochie; we will stand by the Dark Mirror. One step, that's all it will take, and you will be forever free of these human cares. In that realm, all your questions will be answered . . ."

16

"FERADA," said Ana gently, "I think you're sewing that onto your skirt."

"Oh." Ferada looked down at her work, muttered an unladylike oath, and proceeded to unpick a line of crooked stitching, her mouth tight. The two of them were sitting by lamplight, for the winter day was dark even so early in the afternoon, heavy clouds obscuring the face of the Flamekeeper, who burned low and weakly so close to solstice time. Ana's embroidery was exquisite: a pattern of tiny flowers, cream on cream, each with a narrow border of duck-egg blue.

"What's the matter?" she asked now, observing the impatient movement of Ferada's hands as the red-haired girl jerked the thread out, almost tearing the fabric. "You're upset about something, it's obvious. You look exhausted. Are you still thinking about Gateway?"

"How can I not think about it?" Ferada's tone was grim. "After I heard, I couldn't decide if I despised Fola for letting such atrocities happen or admired her for her unflinching obedience to the gods. I still can't decide. Such a ritual could only have been devised by men. How could any right-thinking woman accept it? I can't believe the Shining One would allow it to continue, year after year. It is so wrong."

"Shh." Ana glanced about nervously, as if the gods might be just behind her, listening. The two girls were alone in this quiet chamber in the women's quarters, but at any moment others might join them for sewing. There were many women at Caer Pridne now, all waiting with their menfolk for the presentation of candidates, the assembly, the announcement of the new structures of power. Within the next ten days many futures would be decided. The cold season allowed much time for the pursuit of such crafts as embroidery, spinning, and weaving. Nonetheless, the older women showed a marked preference for the great hall, with its wide hearth, its music, and its wealth of interesting conversations. At such times of change, women were useful conveyers of information and might bring considerable influence to bear on their menfolk, provided they had sharp ears and well-honed persuasive skills. "Maybe you do think that," Ana went on, "but you shouldn't say it aloud."

"I'm beginning to wonder why not." Ferada ripped out the last of the wayward thread and bit off the frayed end. "I'm beginning to wonder if I believe in anything at all, beyond the fact that men and women are motivated by greed and the lust for power."

"Ferada!" Ana put down her work and stared at her friend in alarm. "That's a terrible thing to say. What about love? What about the wish to help others? What about the betterment of your people and your realm?"

Ferada lifted her brows. "I believed in all that once," she said. "If you still hold to such ideals I'm glad for you. I suppose it gives you hope, something you need if you're to stay trapped here as a hostage until someone decides to let you go home."

"You're very cynical," Ana said quietly. "And you don't believe your own words, deep down. There are many worthy men and women, good, unselfish ones. What about Bridei?"

Ferada's hands jerked involuntarily and she winced as the needle jabbed her finger.

"Come on," Ana said. "Out with it."

"I need to see him. Bridei. Only they won't let him have visitors."

"Mm," said Ana. "Me, too; as I told you, Aniel sent me packing. One of us needs to get in. One of us needs to tell him."

Ferada stared at her.

"About Tuala," Ana said. "About what's happened to her. He'd want to know as soon as he was well enough."

"But . . ." Ferada frowned, twisting her fingers together. "Wouldn't Broichan have told him already? Fola did send him a messenger."

Ana's gaze was grave. "Yes; I'm sure Broichan knows that Tuala ran away. As her foster father, it would be his responsibility to send searchers after her; to try to find her. But I'm not sure he'd pass the news on to Bridei. The presentation of candidates is only three days away, and Bridei's still sick, or so everyone says. He'd be very upset to know Tuala was missing; that she'd gone off all by herself in the middle of winter and that nobody had been able to find out where. Broichan will want Bridei at his best for the presentation."

"But you'd tell him anyway," Ferada said.

"Wouldn't you?"

"I don't know." Ferada's tone was quite lacking in its usual confidence. "I just know I need to see him, and I don't know how to do it."

A group of women entered the chamber, their voices low and pleasant: Queen Rhian, pale but composed, and three of her court ladies. All carried work baskets. The two girls rose to their feet and bowed their heads politely.

"Don't disturb yourselves, girls," Rhian said, settling on a bench by the small hearth fire. "We're merely seeking a quiet spot; the hall is swarming with folk, most of them talking utter nonsense, or so it seems to me. I do have some news that will interest you. Aniel tells me Bridei is much improved today; sitting up and showing an interest in warm broth, was the way he put it. I thank the gods for this. It's been long; I've never known a case of the flux to lay a healthy man low for so many days. What is it, ten, twelve? I pray Bridei improves sufficiently to speak for himself at the presentation. We've had news that the king of Circinn is only one day's travel away, and will be making his own claim in person."

Ana looked at Ferada, and Ferada looked back. The same idea had occurred to each of them. Ana gave a little nod, as if to say, *You do it.*

"My lady," Ferada ventured, "I'm certain it would aid Bridei's recovery greatly, were you to pay him a visit in person. He valued the king's good opinion above all. It would encourage him, I believe, if . . ." She allowed her voice to trail away in what seemed a sudden attack of girlish shyness. Ana suppressed a smile.

Queen Rhian's eyes were shrewd. "You ask this as a family friend?" she queried.

"And as a personal friend," Ferada said, blushing without the need for artifice. To make such a suggestion to one's queen was somewhat bolder than the niceties of court behavior allowed.

"I see," Rhian said, glancing from Ferada to Ana and back again. "And you'd be wanting to come, too, I suppose."

Ferada looked down at her hands. "I would very much welcome that. Just for a moment; I know he's been seriously ill."

"Both of you?" The queen's brows rose.

"Oh, no," Ana said hurriedly. "Ferada can do it; that is, one of us is enough. I'm happy to wait until Bridei is well enough to be among folk again."

"Mm," said Rhian. "It's almost worth trying, just to see if I can get past that formidable army of protectors they've assembled. I don't know which are the more intimidating, the bodyguards or the druids. Very well, Ferada. Perhaps tomorrow, after breakfast. I'll send for you. Will that suit?"

"Yes, my lady." Ferada did her best to look like a lovestruck girl, all downcast eyes and demurely clasped hands. The ring her mother had given her felt heavy and awkward on her finger; the green-enameled setting with its cunning hinge was tightly closed, concealing its cargo of inoffensive-looking brown powder. "Thank you."

"It's no trouble," said Rhian. "I can't understand why you don't simply ask your father; he's up there half the day as it is. Still, in affairs of the heart, perhaps fathers are not the best source of help. And maybe it takes a queen to pass through Broichan's doorway. We'll see."

"FAOLAN . . ." BRIDEI WAS saying. "Fetch Faolan . . . now . . . find him now . . ."

"Lie down," Broichan ordered. "Breth's gone to look for him. Nothing is so urgent that it can't wait while you eat and rest and take some time to come back to yourself."

"Message . . . must send . . ."

"Drink this." Broichan's voice was calm and deep. He slipped an arm behind Bridei's shoulders, lifting and supporting him. His long fingers held a cup to the sick man's lips.

Bridei took a mouthful and spat it out explosively; Broichan remained still as the liquid splashed over the blankets. "What are you doing?" Bridei gasped. "Can't . . . sleep . . . no sleep . . . Faolan . . ."

"Faolan will only add his voice to ours." Uist stood at the foot of the pallet, his light, changeable eyes assessing Bridei as he struggled to free himself from the swathing coverlets and swing his feet to the floor. "You're in no fit state to do anything but rest, especially if you've any thoughts of standing up for yourself at the presentation. Time's short; I understand how you feel, but it's in your best interest—"

"Short," said Bridei, staring at the old druid. "How short? How long . . . like this?"

"Since last full moon," Broichan said, raising the cup

again. "Drink, Bridei. Your sleep has been much troubled. You need this."

"No!" The cup went flying as Bridei's hand came up with a violence that surprised all of them. "No, I won't take it! How long, how many days? What's wrong with me?"

"Thirteen," Uist said, watching his charge closely.

"What?"

"Hush, Bridei," said Broichan. "There is still time. We have three days yet until the presentation. And if you are too weak, Carnach has agreed to stand proxy—"

"What's wrong with me?" Bridei managed to get his feet to the floor, made an attempt to rise, fell back to the bed as his knees buckled under him.

"Can you remember nothing?" Broichan moved to sit on a bench; in the outer chamber there was now a sound of men's voices.

"Not since . . . not since full moon." Bridei's voice had shrunk to a whisper. His eyes were fierce. "What . . . ?"

"You were attacked, as Faolan had predicted," Broichan said tightly. "It was an ill-conceived idea, fraught with risk. To send you out alone at night on that shore, in such weather . . . But the Gael, as we know, is not a man to adhere to the accepted rules. Nor does he run risks unless he's sure of success. You were set upon by three men. Faolan was not far behind you. One was captured, two slain. It was a lot for your keeper to take on himself; too much, I believe. Conveniently, Uist here happened along at a certain point and assisted in the capture. Still more fortunately, he recognized Faolan's prisoner from an encounter in Circinn. The fellow has talked; he was in Bargoit's employ. This attempt on your life and, we suspect, others in the past were carried out on the orders of Drust the Boar."

"You realize what this means," Uist said. "We have the evidence to discredit your rival in the contest. If you have the numbers to match his, we'll present this as the deciding argument. Faolan has achieved what the most powerful men in Fortriu couldn't do; he's virtually assured your victory."

"Which would have been less than useful had Bridei been killed in this attack," Broichan commented.

"Thirteen days," Bridei said blankly, as if he had heard none of it after that. *"Thirteen days?"*

"Indeed," Uist said, "you have lain here unconscious, or half-conscious, all that long time. You've suffered a very heavy blow to the head. We've put it about that you fell victim to the flux. That will explain your weakness when you emerge. Your guards have proven extremely effective at keeping out the—"

"Now," Bridei said, rising once more by sheer force of will, though it was necessary for him to clutch the back of a chair to remain upright. "Clothes . . . out . . . Faolan . . ."

"No." Broichan's hand on his shoulder forced Bridei back to the bed; Broichan's dark eyes bore an expression of command. "You must not be seen in this state. You must not appear in public until your mind is restored to clarity. You have whispered, wept, shouted, ranted much through this time of dark dreams. Now you must rest. Faolan will come; speak to him if you believe it essential. Thank him, for his rash action has in fact worked greatly to our advantage. Give him all the messages you will. Then take the soporific draught and sleep. I have hopes the morning will see you greatly restored."

IT WAS A matter of waiting. Waiting, while his head reeled with images and his body resisted his attempts to make it work for him; he had not the strength to hold and lift his own cup, and his legs refused to support him for more than a single step before turning to jelly. The headache had changed to something new, a dull, pounding presence that more closely resembled anger than pain. Tuala . . . Tuala there in the tree, waiting for him . . . perhaps waiting all night in the cold, in the rain . . . thirteen days, a whole thirteen days and no message . . . she would have thought . . . she must have believed . . .

"Bridei." Faolan was here at last. He'd taken a long time; it must be dark outside by now, the sun gone, another day already past, another opportunity lost. The druids were over by the hearth, talking together in low voices. The Gael stood in the doorway, a heavy cloak around his shoulders as if he had been out somewhere and but recently returned. Faolan seemed pale; his gaze was unusually intent.

"Come . . ." Bridei whispered. "Come closer . . ."

Faolan moved to the bedside; sat on a stool, his back to the druids, screening Bridei from their view. It was one of the talents that made him so useful: the ability to understand a great deal without being told. Broichan and Uist could see nothing. On the other hand, druids were known to possess an alarming acuity of hearing.

"Broichan?" Bridei asked.

"Yes?"

"I wish . . . speak Faolan . . . alone. You and Uist . . . fresh air . . . long time . . . tending sick . . ."

"Not in the least—" Broichan began, and fell abruptly silent. A moment later he was following Uist out into the antechamber, and the door closed behind them.

"Amazing," Faolan observed. "I thought nobody could tell that man what to do."

"Only another . . . druid," Bridei said. "Why . . . said it was you? Plan . . . attack? Why?"

"Ah. I should have known that would be your first question. It seemed—expedient. Would you have preferred me to tell the truth?"

"What . . . truth?"

"That you were on your way to visit a certain young lady in a forbidden place and had neglected to mention it to your guards."

"You knew?"

"I saw you the time before, don't forget: eyes full of stars, feet walking on air, all the usual symptoms. I thought it just possible you might be misguided enough to try it again, next full moon. Of course you didn't tell me; you knew I wouldn't let you go. I already had my suspicions as to the source of a likely attack."

"What are you saying, Faolan? That you told them where to find me? That it's thanks to you that I . . . that I couldn't . . ."

"That you couldn't see her? Is this so important that it

erases from your mind a certain question of the kingship of Fortriu? Surely we have not all misjudged you, Bridei?"

Bridei shook his head and instantly regretted it, for the headache sprang to new life, drumming persistently behind his temples. "Not misjudged . . . misunderstood . . . Faolan . . . ?"

"What is it?"

It seemed to Bridei, through the fog of pain and weariness, that there was a new look in the Gael's eye. Nobody could call Faolan soft; there was, however, a certain directness in his gaze now that spoke of a change in the way things were between the two of them. Bridei hoped his instincts were serving him well, illness or no. "I must send her a message," he said. "Now, straightaway. She would have waited . . . long time . . . She wouldn't have known why . . ."

Faolan gave a grim smile. "A message to Banmerren? I think not. Do you know we have barely three days until you must stand up before all of them and declare yourself? We may have eliminated these assassins, but they are not your only enemies. This place is full of powerful men, men from the south; Drust the Boar is expected at Caer Pridne tomorrow. They're all alert for opportunities to discredit anyone they think will stand against him. That means Carnach, since he's still thought by most people to be a candidate. And it means you. This is too great a risk."

Bridei attempted to seize the Gael's wrist; his hand felt as weak as a child's, his grip feeble. "I must," he said. "I promised . . ."

Faolan frowned. "Promised what?" he asked.

"That I . . . that I would be . . . responsible." The weakness flowed through his body like a tide, numbing him, slowing him, seeking to sap his will. "That I would . . . be there . . . when she . . ."

"Bridei," Faolan said softly, "I can't do anything tonight. If you had your wits about you, you'd recognize that. I'll talk to you again in the morning. I think you may have to let this go. After a night's sleep, perhaps you'll see that. To do otherwise is not just risking your own future. It's putting this girl's in jeopardy as well. Now I think you'd better get Broichan to make up that potion again, and when he gives it to you, drink it. You've been having nightmares. Loud ones."

"Did I—?"

"Most of it was too garbled for me to interpret; those druids may have made more sense of it. And yes, there was a certain name you spoke a great deal more than others."

Bridei closed his eyes. "I need her," he whispered, hating his weakness.

"Hush," said Faolan. "Wait for morning. You've been through more than you realize. We nearly lost you. Now I will go. Your keepers are no doubt waiting impatiently for readmittance."

"You said . . . heard . . . nightmares. You . . . here?"

"Night shifts seem to be part of my job," Faolan said levelly. "I've been here, yes. One night I missed, conveying my captive to a place of security. The others I've shared, not always with Broichan's good will. I think he wanted you to himself. I'd better go; this cloak's dripping."

"Put it . . . by fire. Stay . . . just a bit . . ." Bridei found he could no longer maintain a sitting position; he lay back on the pillow, frustration at his helpless state warring with a profound wish for dreamless sleep.

"Feet up," Faolan said, and tucked the blankets over him.

"Funny . . . you . . . nursemaid . . ."

"I told you," Faolan rose to remove his cloak and drape it over the bench by the fire, "it's what they pay me for: keeping fools like you alive long enough to achieve what's set out for them. I'm only doing my job."

"Not paid . . . be . . . friend . . ."

At this, Faolan fell completely silent. Through half-closed eyes, Bridei observed the Gael's face, on which a remarkable sequence of emotions passed with rapidity: surprise, sadness, something remarkably like humility, then, abruptly, the blank, hard expression with which it was Faolan's habit to mask any evidence of what he felt. He sat quiet by Bridei's bedside, staring at the wall. In time the druids returned to brew their soporific potions, and Bridei drank and slept.

THE SHINING ONE had shrunk to a sliver; it was close to solstice night and dark of the moon. It was strange how everything was changing. Tuala didn't feel hungry anymore, nor thirsty, yet it had been several days since the last crumbs of the loaf were finished. She knew that she was tired, and that there was something wrong with her feet, but she could no longer get her boots off to look at them. This did not seem to matter. Damaged as they were, her feet simply kept on walking, steady on the muddy tracks through the forest. Her hands were raw with chilblains; she wrapped them under her sodden shawl and ignored the pain. It was of no import. She was leaving this world. She was going away. Indeed, she thought perhaps she already had one foot beyond that margin; that she had strayed already partway into that secret realm. Not only could she go without eating, but she had started to see things, odd things that had never been visible in the forest above Serpent Lake before. There were creatures in the trees, looking down at her; from every fork, on every branch, something fixed strange, luminous eyes on the girl walking beneath; under each bush, within each tangle of damp undergrowth, small faces showed, wrinkle-browed, long-eared, spike-haired, sharp-nosed, all kinds, their beady eyes alive with curiosity. On every path, something scampered ahead, heard but unseen. On every climb, pattering footsteps followed. Subtle voices called, eerie in the gloom of the winter day. *Tuala! Tuala! Sister, come home!*

As they came farther down the lake and drew closer to Pitnochie, shelter grew harder to find. She was reduced to scraping out a hollow in the moldering leaf litter and dragging whatever fronds of bracken she could find over herself in a vain effort to keep out the cold. Once she reached the Dark Mirror, once she had truly crossed that margin, she would never be cold again. Crouched trembling under a massive oak, Tuala thought dimly that it would almost be worth doing it for the sole purpose of making this shivering stop.

"Not far to go now." Woodbine was seated on a stump, entirely at ease in the chill of the gathering dusk. The moon was grown so dim, the leaf man was reduced to a shadowy figure, dark on dark. Tuala wondered at that. If she were one of the Good Folk, shouldn't she be able to find her way by night as these two evidently could? "Another day or two," Woodbine announced, "and this will all be over."

"I wonder what they're up to at Caer Pridne?" said Gossamer lightly, running long fingers through her silvery hair, which held its lustrous shine even in the dark. "Haven't you been tempted to seek guidance in the water, Tuala? To see what your Bridei is doing?"

"No." This was a lie; she had indeed sought a glimpse of him, one day when her Otherworld companions were absent and a pool of rainwater had presented itself under a cloudy sky. She had crouched by the rim, awaiting the images of the goddess. She had prayed; had breathed deep; had done her best to clear her mind and open her seer's eye. The water had remained obstinately no more than itself: a pool reflecting gray clouds. Not a single image had danced across its surface, although Tuala had stayed there until her back ached and her legs were seized by cramps. The Shining One had turned her face away; she had abandoned her daughter. Now, Tuala would not look; if this window were to be closed to her forever, she would rather not know it just yet. If the scrying bowl were to reveal its secrets no more, she would never see him again. Never. "Why would I seek such visions? Haven't you told me over and over that this way is best? Bridei will be getting ready to make his claim for the kingship. Broichan will be preparing him. That's all. Didn't you say it will be at Midwinter?"

"Indeed. At solstice time the candidates step forward and declare themselves. At solstice time you step back to the realm where you belong. A satisfying balance; with your education, you'll appreciate that."

"I'm cold," Tuala muttered, wrapping her arms around herself and clenching her teeth. "It's snowing, look." And it was; between the great, bare limbs of the oak, a delicate fall of white flakes was drifting to earth.

"Two days more," Gossamer said. "It's not long. We'll see you at the Dark Mirror." With that she was gone, quick as an eyeblink. Woodbine had vanished without a word.

"Don't—" Tuala began, feebly. "Don't go—" She made

herself stop. She made herself breathe slowly; she could do this, she could go on, even if they chose to desert her at the last. She had been alone before. There was nothing new to it. She would simply set her feet forward and walk on to the end of the road.

BRIDEI INSISTED ON getting up and dressing. He forced himself to walk to the outer room; to sit at the table there and greet all those who came by to ask after him: Aniel, Talorgen, Carnach accompanied by Tharan, which was somewhat surprising. He thought he made a passable job of it. After a while Breth and Garth ushered the visitors out, then stood over Bridei while he ate a serving of porridge with honey. He felt like a cosseted child, and told them so.

"Enjoy it while it lasts," said Breth, grinning. "Now, you need your bed; a man doesn't get over such an illness in the twinkle of an eye. I'll help you back to the other room—"

Garth, by the outer doorway, cleared his throat. "More visitors coming," he said quietly. "Ladies this time."

"He's had enough—"

"No refusing these."

Queen Rhian swept in, head high, figure clad in finest wool dyed to a soft dove-gray, both becoming and well suited to mourning. Behind her came Ferada, daughter of Talorgen, in a blue gown with a silver clasp at the shoulder, her russet hair dressed high in a crown of plaits.

"Ah," said the queen, smiling. "I see you are sufficiently recovered to sit at table, Bridei. This is indeed reassuring; from what they've been saying, I expected to find you prostrate and babbling nonsense. No, don't get up; we're not here for long. Oh, I see we have forgotten our little gift, Ferada. I'm sure Bridei can spare one of his men to fetch it— Garth, there's a small pot of rather good chicken broth in my quarters; go and speak to my maid, will you, and she'll give it to you. It is of my own making. However lacking your appetite may be, Bridei, you will drink this happily. It's remarkably restorative. Go on, then, young man!" She smiled, and Garth obeyed without a word.

Rhian seated herself opposite Bridei, regarding him closely with her kindly blue eyes. Ferada stood behind, twisting her fingers together. "A little mead, do you think?" The queen glanced at Breth, who disappeared to the inner chamber; if he had thought to bar her from Broichan's quarters, he had been unable to find the words for it under such an onslaught of confident good will.

"Now tell me, Bridei," Rhian said. "Are you really getting better? This has laid you low a long time. An unusual illness for a healthy young man."

"I am much better, my lady. I hope to be in full health by Midwinter."

"Ah, yes, Midwinter . . . You have a little leeway. As long as you are restored to us by the assembly itself, that is what really matters. My husband thought highly of you, Bridei. You owe it to his memory to do your best. Don't forget that." Perhaps a tear glistened in her eye, but she was a queen; it would not be allowed to fall.

"You are gracious, my lady. It was a sad loss. I can never hope to equal him, but I will offer my best, I promise you."

"Mm-hm." The queen fell silent a moment as Breth returned with a small jug of mead and three cups, and set them on the table. "I'm sure you will, son. May the breath of the gods inspire you. It is a time of great change; daunting change. We'll all need to be strong. Now," Rhian rose to her feet as if suddenly reminded of something, "I need a word with Broichan. Is he within?" She glanced at Breth, then walked with complete confidence to the inner door, rapped sharply, and went straight in. Breth, a look of alarm on his features, hastened after her.

Ferada picked up the mead jug, pouring the pale liquid into two cups. Bridei was taken aback by the change in her. She had ever seemed a poised, confident girl, whose assurance had often made him feel awkward and ill at ease. Today she looked pale and drawn; her hands fumbled clumsily as she set the jug down and placed a cup before him. But he would not spend time on that; an opportunity had presented itself and he must seize it quickly before the others returned.

"Ferada, I need you to take a message. A message to Banmerren. Can you do it?"

She stared at him blankly; it was almost as if she didn't understand the words.

"To Tuala. It's urgent. Will you?"

She was still holding her own cup; her hands were shaking so much the mead slopped over the rim. "To Tuala . . . oh . . ."

"Just let her know what has happened. That I have been sick since the night of full moon; that I couldn't . . ." By all the gods, what ailed the girl? Surely he was not imagining her state of agitation; her face was sheet-white, the freckles standing out starkly, and her lips were pressed together in a thin line. Something was terribly wrong. He must put her at her ease. The thought of mead turned his stomach; still, if he took a sip or two, pretended nothing was amiss, perhaps she would relax and listen to him.

He reached for the mead, but somehow Ferada's hand knocked his at that moment, and the cup she had filled for him tipped over, sending a stream of liquid across the stone tabletop.

"Oh!" gasped Ferada, reaching to set the empty cup upright.

Bridei had avoided the worst of it; he moved the jug aside, out of the pool of mead. Evidently none of those in the inner chamber had heard the small commotion; the queen's voice could be heard from beyond the door, briskly cheerful. "What is it, Ferada?" Bridei asked her, observing that she had turned still paler. "What's happened? Is it Gartnait?"

"What? Why would it be Gartnait?" Her voice was shaking; she made a futile attempt to scrub the front of her skirt, where the mead had darkened the blue of the woolen cloth to storm-gray, with a tiny kerchief. "Bridei, I need to tell you something." Her voice shrank to a whisper. "It's about Tuala. She's run away."

"What?"

"Bridei, you're hurting me."

Bridei realized he was on his feet and gripping Ferada's shoulders hard; she was wincing with pain. "I'm sorry," he said, releasing her as his heart continued to drum, fast and urgent. "Run away? Where? When?"

"Soon after full moon. A few days after. Nobody knows where."

Now he was cold; colder than winter. "What do you mean, nobody knows? They must know!"

"We've had no news. One night she just disappeared. Fola sent men out looking, from the farm. They didn't find any tracks or anything. Then Ana and I came back here. I haven't heard anything more."

Bridei's head reeled; where to start, which question to ask, what to do? Thirteen days, he had been unconscious thirteen whole days, while she . . . "Why didn't they tell me? Why didn't anyone tell me?" So long; so far; he must go, now, straightaway . . .

"They probably knew how upset you'd be," Ferada said, attempting to mop the table top with the sodden kerchief. "They'll want you at your best for the presentation."

"A pox on the presentation! All this time, on her own, in winter—what are they thinking of? What's Broichan doing here, when—Pitnochie, that's where she'd have gone. Surely he could have tracked her, found her . . . If she reaches Pitnochie she'll be safe, and I can go for her . . ."

"I don't think she'd be wanting to stay there," Ferada said soberly. "She said they didn't want her; she seemed quite unhappy there when I passed through. If she'd been able to stay at Broichan's house, she'd never have chosen to go to Banmerren. Didn't you know?"

Voices within the inner chamber were approaching the door; the queen was returning.

"Tell me," Bridei hissed. "Quickly!"

"Broichan made her choose. Marry a man who had offered for her, or go to Fola. She didn't want marriage. Banmerren was the lesser evil. She never wanted to leave home. Bridei, I need to warn you—you must be careful—"

"What man?" The words came from a cold place within him, a place with no room for forgiveness.

"Garvan the stone carver. Tuala said he was a good man, but she couldn't . . . She believed the goddess had made the choice for her. Before she left Pitnochie she . . . she . . ."

"What? Be quick."

"She cut her hair and shed her blood to make a charm of protection for you. She didn't want to leave. She didn't want to go. But there's no place for her there anymore. If she's gone home, it's not to Broichan's house."

Bridei stared at her; Ferada looked back, her eyes full of shadows. "What will you do?" she asked him.

"Find her," said Bridei. "Find her before it's too late. Will you cover for me?" His cloak was here, and a pair of Garth's boots in the corner. It was a slim chance; perhaps the only one. If any of them was alerted, Breth, Garth, Faolan, Broichan—Broichan who had lied to him, Broichan who had betrayed him—he would be stopped. They thought only of the presentation, the assembly, the long plan now at last reaching fruition. They did not think of a girl out in the snow, a girl wandering alone in the depths of winter, entirely without friends. His gut twisted within him. "Tell them Faolan came for me; that we're in consultation privately and will return here by midday."

"How will you—"

Bridei did not wait to hear her words. Time was precious; time was life and death. Willing strength to his limbs, he seized the boots, threw his cloak over his shoulder and slipped through the outer door to the wall-walk. Then, summoning the charm of concealment, he headed for the stables.

IN HER PRIVATE chamber at Banmerren, Fola stood alone, a bronze bowl on the table before her. She had been long in trance. The visions in the water were gone now, but the wise woman held her stillness, searching deep within her for the voice of the goddess, a light to reveal the pathway ahead. Acceptance was slow to come, slow and painful. They had been wrong, both she and Broichan. They had let ambition, pride, and self-belief cloud their judgment. They had not heeded what the Shining One made plain from the start: that the unthinkable was indeed to be accepted, that the impossible must be embraced or all would fail and their long efforts be thwarted at the very last. It was bitter to swallow; it was a lesson in humiliation. So simple; so obvious; yet they had not seen it, the two of them, each dedicated to the gods, each living a life of celibacy, of obedience, of scholarship, and self-discipline. Each without lover or children. Fola knew it now for truth. Perhaps she had known, deep inside, the very first time she met Tuala under the oaks, tiny, intense, brimming with feelings and fighting to conceal them. As for Broichan, perhaps he could never accept it. His plan had been perfect, every factor calculated, every small detail attended to. Fifteen years of his life sacrificed to it; fifteen years given to the great cause of Fortriu's unity: the creation of the perfect king, the making of the leader who would bring this benighted realm forth into light. If Broichan would not bend, if Broichan could not accept that his edifice was built on a flawed foundation, then all would indeed be lost. If Broichan held his own judgment surer than that of the goddess, perhaps they deserved to lose.

Fola began to awaken her clay self, stirring fingers, toes, changing her breathing, blinking, stretching. At length she bowed, palms together, and moved to return the water from bowl to jug. Then she called Luthana, sought outdoor cloak, sturdy boots, a snug woolen hood against the cold and, accompanied only by the herbalist, made her way out through the gates of Banmerren and across the windswept sands to Caer Pridne.

A CHOICE. SNOWFIRE, eagerly watching, ready for him, anticipating a fine ride such as Bridei and Faolan had enjoyed across the moorland to the place of the three cairns. Snowfire was strong and willing, but he would not well endure this long race through the winter dark. Lucky, with whom Bridei had been unable to part; tall, mottled Lucky, the ugliest horse in the royal stables . . . Donal's mount was a hard worker, a stayer; age had only improved him. The men had made sure he was regularly exercised, and he was in good condition. He was not known for speed, for all his long legs. Quick, quick, choose and be gone; any moment now one of the minders would get suspicious and start a search. Take a horse, any horse, and just *go* . . . By the half-door, a white shadow moved: Uist's mare, Spindrift, that eldritch creature with her snowy, perfect coat, her silken mane, her waterfall of a tail and her odd eyes, as fluid and tricky as the wild druid's own. She looked at Bridei, shifting her feet a little as if to say, *Come on, make up your mind.* She would go swiftly, tirelessly . . . She would go as the best of ordinary horses could not go, heedless of snow and rain, moving un-scathed through woodland and marshland, maintaining her steady pace all the way to Pitnochie.

Bridei had forced himself thus far, exerting control over his uncooperative body by will alone. Nonetheless, he was greatly weakened; there was only so much the mind could do. He opened the half-door. It was necessary to clamber to a mounting block and thence to a rail in order to reach the mare's back; a clumsy performance. Bridei leaned forward, hands on Spindrift's neck, and whispered in her ear. "Take me home." He hoped she would understand. He would need all the strength he had left to remain on her back and keep breathing; he would have little capacity to guide her. He had brought nothing; no food, no water, no weapons, no supplies of any kind. No time. He must go now, before he was dis-covered, and hope this rare creature could outrun the best his keepers could muster. Somewhere in his mind there still lin-gered the election, the men and women who depended on him, the question of destiny. But those things had shrunk to an acorn, a hazelnut, crowded out by the weight of his fear, his fury, his burning need to find his dear one quickly, quickly, before he lost her forever.

"Go," he whispered, and in a whirl and a flurry, graceful as a swan in flight, the mare bore him out from Caer Pridne, making her way southwestward toward the Great Glen. A pale presence in the winter gloom, she moved with the con-fidence of a creature who goes under the protection of pow-ers older than time, and on the soft ground behind her, she left not a single mark.

IT WAS FREEZING cold out on the wall-walk beyond the women's quarters. Ferada huddled behind the steps, cloak up over her head and clutched across her chest, hiding the fine blue gown, the handsome silver clasp, the hated, heavy ring of silver and enamel. She had been here a long time, unseen by anyone. Somewhere within her belly she could feel a weight like a cold stone; she thought maybe it was fear. Fear of her mother's quick hand; fear of her mother's mad eyes. Fear of what was to come, for herself, for all of them. Her fingers ached; she had bitten every nail to the quick and had gnawed the flesh of her forefinger until it was raw and bleeding. And yet, for all that heavy sense of dread, in her heart there was something else, something good and new. After all, she had not done it. Perhaps it really had been a love potion, as Dreseida had told her. Perhaps. Ferada wanted to believe that; she wanted more than anything for that to be the truth, unlikely as it was. But she had seen the look on Dreseida's face; she knew the strength in her mother's hand, the power, the terrible anger. Why would Dreseida seek to make Bridei fall in love with Ferada? She had never wanted Broichan's foster son as her daughter's husband, and she did not want him as king. If Bridei had taken that mead, Dreseida would have made her own daughter into a murderer.

Perhaps it wasn't true. Perhaps it was just her wild imagination. Her mother was a woman of impeccable pedigree, of high intelligence. Her father was fair, just, widely admired; he was Broichan's friend. *Let it not be true,* Ferada thought. *Let it all be just a bad dream.* But she could not stop thinking of another time, the time when Donal had died in Bridei's place, in the dining hall of her own home at Raven's Well. Died by poison. Was there a servant who, out of loyalty or terror, had been prepared to kill on his mistress's orders?

It was getting late, and she could not hide here in this corner all day. Bridei would be long gone by now. And her mother would want an accounting. She would have to tell . . . She would have to tell the truth, Ferada thought grimly, rising to her feet and smoothing out her crumpled garments. From now on she was going to do precisely that, and if people didn't like it, that was just unfortunate for them. She shivered convulsively. Such bold pronouncements were all very well out here, on her own, not spoken aloud. It would be a different matter facing her mother's piercing eyes, her excoriating tongue, her punishing hand. Never mind; she would do it. But first . . . With trembling fingers, Ferada took off the ring, weighing it a moment in her palm. She knelt; between the stones by the foot of the wall there was a deep crack, with moss growing thickly on either side. Ferada slipped the ring in; heard it drop down to rest, invisible, in the chink. Then she got to her feet and went inside.

Gartnait and Dreseida were in the family's allotted chamber. Dreseida and Ferada slept in the women's quarters, along with the smaller boys, Talorgen and Gartnait in the men's. But, as a noble family and kin of the king, they had certain apartments for their exclusive use; this was their principal meeting place. Her mother and brother fell silent as Ferada came in.

"Well, well," Dreseida said softly. "You've surprised me, daughter. It seems your errand may have succeeded. I didn't think you had it in you."

Ferada's stomach clenched in dismay; she stared at Gartnait, at her mother, at Gartnait again. "What?" she said. "I don't understand—"

"The tale they're putting about is that Bridei's taken a sudden turn for the worse." Dreseida's voice was calm, but her eyes bore a gloating excitement that sickened Ferada. "At breakfast time he's sitting up and receiving visitors; before midday he's completely indisposed once more, the door barred, grim-faced guards on watch outside. I'd say we can expect an announcement soon. If our young friend's received his last visit from Bone Mother, Broichan can hardly keep it secret beyond Midwinter. They'll need a new candidate, or Drust the Boar will step in and take all."

"But—" Ferada protested; this was wrong, all wrong, it was the nightmare reborn. "It's just—"

"You were clever, daughter; remarkably clever. I heard about the queen's little visit. That provided you with the perfect cover. Rhian is so noble and upright, no taint of wrong could ever touch her. Good work, my dear."

Ferada drew a deep breath. "So it wasn't a love potion," she said, thinking fast.

Dreseida's brows rose to an extravagant height; her lips twisted. "Come now, Ferada. You didn't ever actually believe that, did you?"

Ferada looked at her brother; he was pale, his jaw tight, his hands behind his back. She knew exactly how he was feeling; as she would have done, had she carried out her mission as instructed. "He's your best friend," she whispered.

"He's in my way." Gartnait's tone was flat. "He always has been." It was as if he were repeating a lesson memorized.

"In your way for what? You'll never be king. What about Carnach, Wredech, Ana's kinsmen, any of them? Father's never even considered—"

"Hold your tongue!" Dreseida rapped out, and Ferada halted, eyes on her brother's stricken features. He must know; surely he must know how hopeless it was. What had Dreseida told him, to bend him into believing he could do this? "Your brother has been working hard. And he is my son. He will be ready."

"Mother," Ferada said, knowing what she must tell them and yet unable to bring herself to do so, "why? Why do this? Do you hate Bridei so much?"

Dreseida gave a grim smile. "Not for himself. For his mother. Anfreda took what was mine. She robbed me of my opportunity; she stole my future. Mincing little thing that she was, they were all panting after her as if she were a bitch in heat. It was disgusting. The prospect of a son of hers as ruler of Fortriu sickens me."

"Took what was yours? What do you mean? Maelchon?"

"He was ready to offer for me; he'd told me as much. I would have been a queen. He was a powerful man, a real leader. As his wife, I'd have enjoyed immense influence. Then she came dancing along, the sweet little Anfreda, and he never looked at me again."

"But you wed Father."

"So I did," Dreseida said through gritted teeth. "And I

have my son, and it is my son who will be king of Fortriu, not her son. That is the will of the gods."

There was something in her face that frightened Ferada more than any threat, any blow. "Mother," she said, "have you considered how this is for Gartnait? We have less than two days until the declarations. He's never made a formal speech in his life. You can't do this to him. It's cruel and unfair."

"I can do it," Gartnait snapped. His sister heard the desperation in his tone, for all his attempt at confidence, and her heart bled for him.

"I will speak for Gartnait at Midwinter," said Dreseida firmly. "Proxies are allowable, and I am of the royal line. I will present his claim in a way even Broichan cannot refute. All Gartnait need do is stand up at the assembly, give a prepared speech, and be present for the voting. I'm not a fool, daughter."

"No, Mother." Ferada watched her brother shuffle his feet, make to say something, think better of it, and close his mouth. She was going to have to tell them. She had sworn to tell the truth . . . All she wanted to do was run away and hide, like a frightened child.

"Mother," she made herself say. "I don't think Gartnait really wants to be king. And I don't think he will be king."

"What is this foolishness? Of course he wants—"

"Mother. I didn't give Bridei the potion. He's not dying; he's gone off to look for Tuala. She ran away from Banmerren some time ago. I gave him the news, and he left."

Dreseida's face had changed alarmingly during this speech; now it was distorted with furious disbelief. Her voice was deathly quiet. "Say that again, Ferada, and tell me it's not true. Remember, as you speak, exactly what I've told you in the past about the consequences of disobedience."

"I'm not prepared to be a murderer, not even in the best of causes. Most certainly not in a hopeless cause such as this. Gartnait's not suited for kingship, a blind woman could see that. Bridei's gone back to Pitnochie. He won't be here for the declarations. But, as you said, that need not matter. Proxies are acceptable. Maybe Father will do it."

Dreseida took a step toward her daughter. Her arm came

back in preparation for a stunning blow; Ferada held her breath and stood quite still, unflinching.

"No, Mother." Gartnait put his hands on Dreseida's arm, restraining her. "Not this way." He glanced at Ferada. "Better go. Leave this to me. And keep your mouth shut, for everyone's sake. You've done enough damage already."

Ferada paused a moment on the threshold, then, at the look in her mother's eyes, she fled.

WHEN FERADA WAS gone and the door safely closed behind her, Dreseida looked into her son's eyes and said, "Your sister has failed me. You are my son. This is your chance to prove yourself. To show them what you can be."

Gartnait swallowed, then squared his shoulders. "I'll find him. I'll do it. I'll make you all proud of me."

Dreseida nodded. "You'll need to be quick; he has the advantage of you, it seems. You must go immediately, and when you have your chance, the deed must be carried out effectively and invisibly. It must be flawless. You understand? No taint of this must cling to you."

"Yes, Mother. I am a warrior proven; don't forget that. I know what to do."

"Go, then."

"What about the presentations? I won't be—"

"Better, perhaps, if you are absent; it provides the justification for me to speak in your place. Of course, you must return in time for the assembly. Nine days; it is sufficient. With luck, you will overtake him long before he nears Pitnochie. He's been ill; that will slow him. Others, too, may pursue him. Be on your guard for them."

"Farewell, Mother. I'll do my best for you, I promise."

Dreseida sighed, and set a hand on her tall son's shoulder. "Farewell, Gartnait. Ride swift and safely. The breath of the gods be at your back."

"The Shining One watch over you until I return."

OUTSIDE THE ENTRY to Broichan's quarters stood two grim-faced guards: Gwrad, who was usually to be found in attendance on the king's cousin Carnach, and another man whose scarred face and prominent ears identified him as Tharan's man, Imbeg. They barred Fola's way, until she raised her voice sufficiently to bring Talorgen out to investigate. Soon after, in Broichan's inner chamber, the five of them were gathered once more: a secret council, now not so secret, as the change of guards must have alerted Caer Pridne to unusual happenings, at the very least.

Fola seated herself by the empty pallet, now stripped of its bedding. The four men were standing. Of them all, only Uist seemed tranquil, a white form in the shadows by the hearth. Aniel was drumming his fingers on the table; Talorgen paced; Broichan, imperturbable Broichan, was twisting a scrap of green ribbon in his long fingers as if he wished to tear it to shreds, and his face was skull-like with strain.

"How did you know?" he demanded almost before she had sat down.

"How did I know what?" Fola kept her tone calm.

"That he was missing. That he has somehow been taken, for all the assurances I had that these guards were expert; that they would allow no danger near him—"

"You cannot blame Breth and Garth," Aniel put in. "Their loyalty has been faultless. Besides, we don't know yet what has happened—"

"Our enemy has abducted him; perhaps already killed him." Broichan's voice shook. "What else could this be? How could they let it happen? Was nobody watching?"

"Broichan."

At Fola's tone, they all fell silent.

"Bridei has not been abducted. He's riding home to Pitnochie. He's gone to find Tuala."

Nobody said a word. Broichan's hands stilled; the ribbon hung between them.

"I've seen this in the water. A true vision. I have come here to warn you that another must stand up for Bridei at Midwinter. By then he will be far from Caer Pridne, on a journey of his own."

"No!" Broichan exclaimed, striding toward her and fixing

her with his dark eyes. Fola stared steadily back at him. "Impossible! Bridei is committed to this. He obeys the call of the Flamekeeper in all things. He would not—"

"He has done. He's already well on the way; Talorgen's daughter passed him the news of Tuala, and he was gone in a flash."

"What news?" asked Talorgen, frowning. "What could Ferada know?"

Fola looked at him. "That Tuala has run away," she said. "You were not told of this?"

"You're saying Bridei intends to ride all the way to Pitnochie?" Aniel queried. "He was much weakened by the injury and the illness that followed. He could barely walk, let alone undertake such a long and perilous ride in this inclement season. He'll be slow; he can be overtaken, brought back—"

"He'll be hard to track," said Fola, looking at Uist, who gazed back bright-eyed. "That's if my vision gave me a true image of the mare he was riding."

"How long has the girl been gone?" Talorgen asked. "I can understand how this would distress Bridei. Was a search mounted?"

Fola's expression was suddenly very stern. She fixed her eyes on Broichan as if he were a student who had committed an unpardonable transgression. "Tell them," she said, "since it seems this news I sent so urgently, near fourteen days ago, has traveled no farther than your own ears. Tell them how your foster daughter ran away from Banmerren alone at night. Tell them how my people searched and found not a single trace of her. Tell them where you think she went, and why. And explain to your trusted friends why it did not occur to you to pass this news to Bridei, kindly and carefully, when he came to himself, perhaps adding reassurances that you had sent out your own search parties promptly, just to soften the blow for him. Go on, Broichan. Truth is our code here; we are a council of five, bound through mutual trust to share all information pertinent to our cause. Tell them."

"The mare," Broichan said, as if he had not heard her. "You let him take Spindrift. This is your doing . . ." He had turned his fierce gaze on the white-haired druid; his voice cut like a blade. "That creature would never carry another without your consent! How can we track him in time, if it is she who bears him there? You have betrayed me—" He took a step toward Uist, raising his hands, perhaps to seize the other by the shoulders and shake him, perhaps to deliver a harsher punishment, for the fizz and crackle of an angry spell seemed to inhabit the air around him. Uist's eyes were full of deceptive, swirling movement; his fingers curled around the staff resting against the wall beside him and a silver light seemed to glow at its tip, where the egglike stone was lodged.

"Stop it, the two of you," said Fola wearily. "We don't fight like little boys. This has not only been very poorly handled; it has been wrong from the first. Tuala's place in it is critical. I did not read the signs correctly until now, when it is almost too late."

"What do you mean?" demanded Broichan. "Tuala has no part in our plans. If she is gone, it is for the best. There was no need to institute a search; no point in it. You know what she is. Those arguments, a long journey, the weather, are irrelevant for her kind. She'll have gone back to her own folk. It was inevitable, eventually. It is Bridei who must concern us; only Bridei."

"Uist," Fola said, "I suspect you have been aware of this small difficulty longer than I; otherwise your mare would not have made herself available. Perhaps my friend here will comprehend it better from another man."

"I know something of this girl's history," Uist said, setting the staff back against the wall. "Left on the doorstep at Midwinter under a full moon; found by Bridei. Raised in a druid's house; educated by sages. Sent to Banmerren for that education to be completed. I've met the girl. She's a remarkable little creature, wise, solemn, full of a natural sweetness and possessed of a beauty I have not been privileged to see since I first clapped eyes on Fola here as a comely young thing of sixteen."

Fola gave a snort.

"Get on with it," Aniel said testily. "We need Bridei back; tell us how it's to be done."

"I will fetch him." Broichan's tone was commanding. "There's no need for anyone else to be involved."

"We are a council of five," Talorgen said grimly. "Let us not forget that. Uist, finish what you were saying."

"I asked myself why the Shining One had set such an un- usual pathway before this girl. Tuala's a good child, and she loves our young man, that much is plain, for all her efforts to guard her eyes when she speaks of him."

"Loves him? Like a sister?"

"No, Aniel, not like a sister. With the passionate devotion of one who will in time be heart-friend, lover, and wife. With the dedication of one who will stand by him through all the trials and tests of kingship. And he loves her; have I not lain awake these fourteen nights in company with his dreams? Bridei needs this girl. Without her, our perfect king will fail."

"Utter nonsense!" Broichan's outrage was almost pal- pable. Ordinary men would have shrunk before his glare. His companions stared at him, their expressions ranging from concern to horrified recognition. He was fallible. The king's druid had made an error, and now, unless the right moves were effected skillfully and with speed, the long game would be lost. "She's a child of the Good Folk! She'd never be accepted as queen! Bridei would make himself a laughingstock!"

"Is he not strong enough to weather this?" Fola asked. "Do you think so little of your own creation that you would throw away the game for fear he would buckle under the dis- approval of a few narrow-minded courtiers? He's strong, Broichan, strong in himself. And so is she. Together, I be- lieve they will walk forward rich in the love of the gods, and make a powerful force for change."

"It seems rather odd, I must confess: one of *them* as the king's wife," mused Aniel. "Persuading the court that it's a sound idea will certainly be a challenge. But I trust your judgment, Fola. What must we do?"

"Let Bridei go," Fola said. "Leave him to follow his own journey; to find her and bring her back."

"Have you lost your wits entirely?" Broichan shouted, fist coming down on the table with a crash. "Bridei is sick; he's confused in his mind. We've endured many nights of dark dreams; no wonder he has acted so irrationally now. Have you forgotten what it was that laid him low in the first place? To make such a journey alone is to be wide open to attack. Besides, how will he fend for himself when he is too weak to walk more than two paces before his legs give way under him? I must go after him."

"Even you won't track him easily," Uist said. "Spindrift is only found when she wants to be. That's why she can't be confined to stables."

"Then I will go to Pitnochie and wait for him." Broichan had taken a cloak from a peg and suddenly his staff, a fine length of dark oak carven with many small signs and patterns, was in his hand. "I will travel at speed; I will not go by the paths of men. I will make the boy see sense. And I will bring him back in time for the assembly. One of you must stand up for him at Midwinter. The girl's hold over him is stronger than I believed; who knows what unpredictable paths she may lead him down if her wild influence is left unchecked? Gods, that it should come to this, at the very last! It seems your daughter has played a part in this debacle, Talorgen. You'd best bid Ferada put a curb on her tongue before she wreaks any more havoc."

Talorgen stiffened; his fists came up.

"Broichan." Fola rose to her feet and moved between them. "You must not go. Bridei will be far better served if you leave him to follow this path alone. He will return in time for the assembly; he is dedicated to the future for which you have prepared him. Don't you trust your own son?"

Nobody corrected her. After a moment Broichan said, "I trust him. It is Tuala I do not trust. I saw from the first that she was my enemy. I knew she would meddle. My error lay in letting her stay too long in my home; in letting her worm her way into his affections . . ."

"You speak like a jealous lover," Fola said bluntly. "Ask yourself why you did so; why you did not turn the infant out of your house. Was it because you loved the boy and wished to keep him happy? Or was it because, deep within you, you recognized this was the will of the Shining One?"

"While we waste time in futile argument," Broichan said

coldly, "Bridei travels alone across snow-covered fields, confused and sick. I'll have no more of this."

"You will go, regardless of our advice?"

"I will go, and ensure our long efforts are not wasted. I will go, and bring back our future king." He swept out of the chamber, plaited hair swinging about his black-clad shoulders, long cloak swirling behind him like an angry storm cloud. The others stared at one another, stunned into silence.

"On one point at least, he's right," Aniel said eventually. "Bridei's in danger of attack out there, random or planned. We should at least—"

"Faolan," said Talorgen. "He'll take charge of that, as best anyone can under the circumstances. I'll send Gwrad to fetch him. You may say, let him do it alone, Fola; but even you must agree a protector wouldn't go amiss."

"I bow to the judgment of a warrior."

"Who will stand up for him at Midwinter? Are we agreed on Carnach?"

There was a tap at the door and, to their surprise, it was Ferada who entered, with Gwrad behind her, his expression apologetic. They stared. Talorgen's daughter was known for her immaculate appearance, her elegant dress, her excellent bearing, a mirror of her mother's. Now her hair was disheveled, her face ghost-pale save for the swollen and reddened eyes. Her skirt was stained and she hugged a shawl around her shoulders with white-knuckled hands. She was shivering as if she had been long outdoors in the cold. Fola gave a hushed exclamation of dismay. Talorgen started forward in alarm.

"Ferada! What's wrong?"

"Father," Ferada said in a voice that was cracked and distorted from long weeping, "I need to speak to you in private. There's something I have to tell you."

17

T HERE HAD BEEN more snow in the night. As she came
along the lake shore, passing beneath thickly needled pines,
Tuala could hear the soft plopping sound as boughs released
the weight of it to the ground below. She did not know how
long she had been walking. She had lost count of the days.
Small drifts clutched at her boots, sucking them deep, and
her skirt was clammy around her legs. Her breath made a
cloud in the chill air; her ears ached and her nose streamed.
She was nearly there. These tall pines, this white-blanketed
slope, that stretch of dark water were familiar; the voices of
birds screaming high above, beyond the treetops, were calling her home. Home . . . some sort of home . . . no cold, no
hunger, no pain . . . no death . . . It was strange to imagine
that. Immortality: a state men yearned for, an impossible gift
to be dreamed of and never attained . . . That was what the
Good Folk had offered her. And yet, at this moment, it meant
nothing. All she wanted was a warm hearth and dry stockings, and to see him again, just once, just one more time before the end . . .

THE DRUID STOOD in the doorway, looking up the hill to the
northeast. For some time he had known that the girl was
coming; that she was on the border of his land. He himself
had traveled from Caer Pridne in several forms, first as fleet
hunting hound, then as white-pelted hare, last as snowy owl,
flying through the woods of Pitnochie and up to his own
front door, where he rendered wings into dark cloak, bird-
guise into man-form, before stepping inside and giving
Mara such a fright she dropped a bowl of onions. He had
seen no sign of Bridei, but he had passed over Tuala on the
way, pausing on a branch to watch her dogged, miserable

progress; noting that she seemed to be talking to herself, as
if the long, solitary journey had begun to addle her wits. By
now she must be almost at Pitnochie; soon the house would
be in her view. He must ensure she never reached it.
Broichan raised his arms and closed his eyes. Breathing
deeply, he summoned the words of an ancient spell of
glamour.

When it was done to his satisfaction, he went back inside
and bolted the door behind him, although it was still day. He
had done what must be done to protect his boy from the
meddling influence that sought to set his path awry. He had
fulfilled his responsibility to the gods. Nothing and nobody
must be allowed to stand in the way of this perfect king.

TUALA ROUNDED A corner and there, below her, were the
walled fields, and Fidich's cottage, and the deceptive trees
that cloaked the druid's house. Sheep huddled for shelter in
the lee of the barn. The neat brown forms of ducks were
clustered together under the bushes by the frozen pond.
Home . . . She could see the oaks where she had sat long,
waiting for Bridei to finish his lessons. She could see the
yard where he and Donal had rehearsed their intricate
dances of war. She could see the house now, Broichan's
house, where she had sat by the hearth with her two old
sages and learned of matters mysterious and enchanting, di-
verting and solemn . . . Where she had perched on a bench
by Bridei's side, long ago, and listened to a story . . . *And
there on the doorstep, what did he find . . . A baby* . . . Tuala
screwed up her eyes; she would not cry, crying was weak,
and if she was to do this, she would at least do it with
courage and dignity. The house . . . she was quite close
now . . . and it was cold; her bones seemed to have turned to
ice, and she could not stop shivering . . . *The Dark Mirror,*
they had said before they abandoned her. *We'll see you at the
Dark Mirror.* She should go on, then, up the hill and over to
the west, so she could be sure of getting there before dusk.
There would be no finding the way by night, with the moon

in darkness. She must waste no time. But . . . just beyond that door was the hearth fire of Pitnochie, shelter, warmth, dry clothes, probably hot soup and newly baked bread. That they did not want her hardly seemed to matter. Mara could always be relied upon to exercise plain common sense. There might not be a rapturous welcome, but Mara, she thought, would at least see her warm and dry before she went on her way. The thought of the fire made her tremble with weariness. Surely just a quick visit would do no harm. It needn't take long. She hesitated a moment, then turned down between the leafless oaks toward the kitchen door.

There was no sign of guards, nor any tracks of their boots in the soft snow. Across the door an iron bar had been set, a new one, on the outside. Tuala raised a feeble hand to knock, and lowered it again. She was standing in a snowdrift, up and over the doorstep where she had once lain cradled in swansdown. She stepped back; looked up. No smoke arose from the rooftop; on this coldest of days, the fires had not been lit. Glancing across the fields to Fidich's house, she saw that there, too, no haze lingered above the roof thatch; no sign of habitation moved near that small dwelling. Tuala walked around Broichan's house, peering up at the few places where window openings were set in its thick walls of stone and earth. Each was shuttered tightly; the inside would be as black as night. Lamps might be burning; but why no fire?

Only the tiny window of Bridei's old sleeping chamber was uncovered, and that was set too high for her to see in. Back at the door, she knocked, the need to rouse them suddenly urgent. This was like one of those tales, the frightening ones where the world changes while one sleeps, to become entirely empty save for the one lonely wanderer through a sudden nightmare; or those where a girl steps into another realm where time moves more slowly, and when she comes home all the familiar faces are long dead. There was an odd hush about the place, as if everything were holding its breath. She knocked again; there was no response. Perhaps her efforts had been too weak to be heard. Tuala found a heavy stick and used it to beat a loud rat-a-tat on the solid oak boards. Once, twice, three times she sent her sharp message. The sound of it echoed away under the snow-clad trees and into the silence of the woods. There was nobody home.

Tuala went over to the barn. Here, at least, there was some sign of life, the sheep pressed tight on one another for warmth, and a small bird hunting for insects in a pile of rotting wood. Perhaps the men were within, tending to horses or other stock. Pearl must still be here, and Blaze . . . But the barn, too, was shut up, the big double doors fastened and chained; peeping through a chink in the wood, Tuala could glimpse neither man nor horse, neither sheep nor dog nor chicken in the empty space inside. Her heart as cold as her shaking limbs, Tuala hugged her cloak more tightly around her and set her steps away from Pitnochie, up through the wilder reaches of the forest, where strong dark oaks were joined by silvery pale birches and thickets of spiky holly bright with winter berries. *Don't go past the hollies, Tuala* . . . Where had that come from? Was she a child again, to be held back by keepers, her every move governed by Broichan's will? Today she was a woman, and she would go on. She would leave this world where there was no longer a place for her, and journey to the realm where she had always truly belonged . . . then she would never be cold again . . . oh, but to see him, just once, just once more, a little glimpse, that was all she needed . . .

It seemed to take a long time, although Tuala judged the unseen sun to be only at its midpoint when she made her way gingerly down the narrow track into the Vale of the Fallen. Her feet slid on the muddy surface; her hands reached out for balance, clutching wildly, and she felt the stinging whip of briars against already damaged flesh. Foolishly, that brought the tears she had sworn she would not shed. She sniffed, wiping her cheeks with the back of her hand, and stumbled on to the foot of the track.

The little valley was deserted. The pool lay dark and still; the ancient rocks brooded in silence, crouched under their mossy cloaks. The swathing creeper had spread more widely since she had last visited this place, and now blanketed one of the seven druid stones with its exuberant, glossy growth.

There was no sign of Gossamer and Woodbine. There was no sign of anyone.

Tuala sank to the ground on the rim of the Dark Mirror. There was no choice but to wait, and hope they would keep their word. They had said they would meet her here and guide her across the margin. They had not said when.

Perhaps it was meant that she should keep vigil thus alone in this place of ancient truth. Had she not longed for a vision of the one she loved: a last image, so she had something to carry with her into that other world? It was unthinkable that, once passed across, she would not remember him. Now, then, now she must seek it. No matter that, last time she had tried, this gift had deserted her completely. Sit quiet, breathe deep, open the eye of the spirit. And find him. *Find him* . . .

The day passed. Tuala moved beyond cold; beyond weariness; almost beyond the world where she sat cross-legged on the rocks, staring into the chill water. In the deep, sheltered rift that housed the pool, nothing stirred. No bird hopped between the twists of vine, seeking what fodder might be found in the hungry season; no insect hovered above the dark water; no small fish, darting for cover, rippled the still surface. No image came; not a single one. There seemed nothing to do but sit, and breathe, and wait. Sit until her back became a rod of fiery pain; breathe ever more shallowly, for to gasp in this air was to fill the lungs with ice; wait, until at last they took pity and came for her. The sun was sinking lower; the shortest of days was nearing its end, and the little glen had grown shadowy and strange. Tuala's head drooped; her eyelids were closing, she could not stay awake . . .

Abrupt as the flare of a torch, color flashed across the water's surface. She blinked, lifting her head; the small effort of that set her heart pounding. She stared into the pool.

He was standing in a great hall, no doubt at Caer Pridne. His clothing was rich, a far cry from the plain, serviceable garments of his days at Pitnochie. He wore blue: a fine-spun woolen tunic and trousers, and over this a short soft cloak of dark gray, braid-edged and clasped with a silver brooch wrought in the form of an eagle in flight. His curling brown hair was plaited down his back. Ah, his eyes, so bright, so full of hope and courage, as if it were the Flamekeeper himself who looked out thus, the very bearer of Fortriu's dreams! Those eyes were bluer than the deep sea; bluer than the summer sky; as blue as the petals of a wood violet. There were folk around him and they seemed to be in a jubilant mood, perhaps offering congratulations. There was Broichan, his usually impassive features full of a pride quite undisguised; there was Talorgen, smiling, and Fox Girl looking elegant in green, and Gartnait with his mischievous small brothers. Many other folk were there, clustering about, offering Bridei their hands, speaking words Tuala could not hear, but which she knew for, *Well done, Bridei! We knew you were the one, right from the first! An auspicious day!*

She saw him turn a little to the side, reach out a hand, give a sweet smile. He saved his smiles; folk did not see them often. A moment later, there she was in the vision: Ana of the Light Isles, all rippling ash-pale hair and white silk gown, her lovely face a vision of creamy skin and rose-flushed cheeks, her grave eyes looking up at Bridei as if he were the only man in the world. He took her hand; she spoke a word or two; he answered. Tuala could see the look in his eyes. He lifted his other hand, brushing Ana's cheek with gentle fingers. His wrist was bare of adornment. The green ribbon was gone.

As the image faded, leaving Tuala empty, hollow, drained of the last scrap of anything that mattered, a voice seemed to sound from the top of the path, the rim of the vale. "Come! Higher up! Follow me!"

There was one more part to this: one last, small ritual to be enacted. With numb fingers Tuala reached into the pouch at her belt and drew out the little talisman of woven cord, the record of her oldest friendship. After long parting, the two strands had been brought together one last time to twine and cling with wondrous delicacy, as if born to be one. Full moon . . . And after that they separated once more, each going on its own journey. The cords had almost reached their natural endings, and were beginning to fray into nothing. Tuala closed her fist tightly around the little thing, gritted her teeth, then threw the cord out into the middle of the Dark

Mirror. For all its light weight, the talisman sank like a stone, making a spreading ripple.

"Come! Come up!" called the voice. There was no telling if it was Gossamer's bell-like tinkle or Woodbine's deeper tone, or something else altogether. It mingled with a stranger sound, a sorrowful, eldritch howling like the cry of a small, deserted dog. That, she had heard before in this place.

It seemed to be possible to get up, although it took a great deal longer than it should have done. Her feet obeyed her command to shuffle forward; to ascend with slow, uneven steps the steep path out of the vale. Her hands gripped whatever came their way; without the support of these thorny, tearing bushes she could not have remained upright at all. By the time she reached the top, Tuala's breath was coming in sucking, painful gasps. The light was starting to fade now, even up here. She could not go on for long.

"Come! Follow me! Higher! Higher!" Now there seemed to be a whole chorus of them out in the dimness. She could not see them. The sound led her forward, now on a new path, a way that wound steadily upward between the trees, first a muddy quagmire, then a narrow track densely packed with decaying leaf mold, last a steep scramble up slippery, moss-covered rocks. *I can't,* was there somewhere in her mind, but the voices were insistent, compelling; it was nearly time for this pain to cease . . . If she could just do this next bit, if she could just go on a little, soon none of it would matter anymore . . .

"Higher! Higher! Farther! Farther!"

Creeping, crawling, hauling herself up, hands leaving bloody smears on the stones, feet scrabbling for a purchase they could scarcely feel, Tuala fought her desperate way ever closer to the top of Eagle Scar.

"IT SEEMS ODD to say this," the creature known as Woodbine communicated to his companion in his own way, "but this strikes me as somewhat . . . cruel. I find myself almost moved to sympathy with the girl."

Gossamer laughed. "It is a test," she said. "It is necessary. What are these small human ills, an empty belly, a little scratch, a night without sleep? They are nothing."

"The child is a good child. Our blood kin. I see no need to prolong her suffering."

Gossamer shook her head; threads of bright hair danced, sending a shimmer of light across the gloomy hillside beneath the bare-limbed oaks. "This will make her think. It will make her ponder. It will ensure she never forgets whence she came, or who she really is."

"She doesn't know who she really is," Woodbine pointed out.

"No. But she will feel it. When she is old, and dreams by the hearth fire with her grandson on her knee, she will feel it deep in the bone and tell it in her tales. She will hold it in her heart."

"That's if she does not first perish from cold, loneliness, or despair."

"These folk are so weak; so flawed; so fragile. At least it is not raining."

"Could we not send her a companion?" Woodbine queried. "A small one would suffice."

"What, are you become like a man, that you turn sentimental the moment you see this girl experiencing a little inconvenience?" Gossamer's tone was full of scorn. "Are you yourself fallen victim to the pangs of love?"

"Love? Hardly. I think, all the same . . ."

"Do what you will." Gossamer shrugged. "Bridei comes; soon he will be at Pitnochie, he and the mare without peer. A clever choice; the old man walks with one foot in each world, and sees entirely true. Only this creature, Spindrift, could have brought Bridei here in time. But the young man has a companion of his own; one who wears the mask of a friend to hide the face of a traitor. So it begins . . ."

"Begins?" echoed Woodbine. "It began with a little child, and a newborn babe, and the cool gaze of the Shining One. What if he fails? What if he gets this wrong?"

Gossamer turned her wide, bright eyes on him. "We must hope that he does not," she said gravely. "Such a leader as Bridei is found but rarely among mortal men. Such a com-

panion as Tuala is beyond price. If he fails today, I think Fortriu is lost."

BRIDEI COULD FEEL his weakness in every limb; the injury
and the long time of unconsciousness had sorely sapped his
strength. That was countered by the sudden miraculous disappearance of the headache, leaving him clearer in his mind
than he had been in a long time. Then there was the mare,
Spindrift, who proved to be everything he had hoped for.
She found her way entirely unguided, pacing herself across
the changing terrain, apparently quite tireless. Her only fault
was the way she halted, sometimes, in the shelter of a rock
wall or a dense stand of pines, and toppled him from her
back so he was forced to rest awhile. She did not stand to
sleep, as Snowfire or Lucky would have done, but lay down
by him, warming his body with her own.

Bridei was impatient. It seemed to him there was no time
for rest. Tuala was long gone, perhaps already at Pitnochie
and moving on . . . moving where? The thought of that made
him shudder, for the more his mind dwelled on what Ferada
had told him and the more he thought about the way it had
all unfolded, the easier it was to believe Tuala had decided to
leave him; to step across the last margin into a place where
he could not follow her. He had failed her at full moon. She
had waited for him and he had not come. If Ferada had spoken the truth, Pitnochie, too, had rejected its small forest
daughter. And she had fled from Banmerren. Tuala had never
wanted to be a servant of the Shining One. She had
wanted . . . she had wanted what he wanted, and he had not
seen it, blind as he was to all but his own needs. He had got
it all wrong, and now, if he could not find her quickly, he
would lose her forever.

He chafed at each delay, knowing at the same time the utter necessity of rest and warmth. Without Spindrift, he could
not go on; on foot, he could not reach Tuala in time. Unless
she waited at Pitnochie . . . He did not think she would. If
the best Broichan had been able to offer her was marriage to
a stranger or a life behind stone walls, the king's druid was

unlikely to welcome her back into his house. Bridei
clenched his teeth. Broichan . . . Broichan had as good as
lied to him. To say that Banmerren was Tuala's choice was
all very well. To omit the fact that the only other choice offered to her had been to wed Garvan was a cruel concealment of the real truth. Broichan had let her run away, all
alone, and had not said a word about it. From the first, the
druid had distrusted the Shining One's Midwinter gift. This
was a betrayal pure and simple. On an instant, his foster father had become a stranger: a man who did not trust him,
and whom he could no longer trust.

Twice they had stopped to sleep. It was day now, and
Bridei judged by the position of the cloud-veiled sun that the
afternoon was well advanced. As they drew closer to Pitnochie, picking a way along the steep track by the lake
shore, Spindrift grew increasingly restless, twitching her
ears, turning her head, swishing her tail. Bridei was acutely
aware that he had no weapons with him, not even the smallest knife with which to defend himself; he had come away
with nothing. Donal would have been less than impressed
with him.

Now Bridei could hear what had alerted the mare: hoof-
beats behind them, a rider approaching. His mind sifted the
possibilities: an assassin, another in the pay of Circinn's
kingmakers. Broichan himself, seeking to track down his
disobedient foster son and force him back to court. No; if
Broichan had decided to pursue him, he would have traveled
as a druid does, by paths unknown to ordinary men. One of
his keepers, Breth or Garth. Or Faolan; this was by far the
most likely. Faolan must earn his fee, and to do so, he must
ensure his charge was at Caer Pridne for the assembly, not
off on what the Gael would doubtless see as a fool's errand.
Faolan had the strength and skill to track him thus, to be here
now, at the end. Spindrift halted, turning to face the on-
comer. Bridei summoned what reserves he had. Weapons or
no weapons, he would not go down without a fight.

The rider rounded a corner and was in full view: a freckle-
faced youth, tall, red-haired, his unprepossessing features
creased by a smile.

"Gartnait!" Bridei exclaimed; his friend was the last person he had expected.

"Caught you up at long last," Gartnait said, reining in behind him. "What a chase . . . That mare certainly keeps up a cracking pace. Bridei, you look worn out. What were you—"

"Why have you come here?" Time was passing. He wanted no companions; once at Pitnochie, he scarcely knew where the path would lead him. "Why did you follow me?"

Gartnait frowned. "That's not much of a greeting for a friend, Bridei. I was worried about you. A man doesn't leap out of his sick bed and go rushing off on some wild quest in the middle of winter without giving his friends some cause for concern, you know. Especially not if he's about to stand up and contest the kingship. What were you thinking of?"

"You must know that," Bridei said. "Ferada certainly knew all about it. The kingship can wait; I must find Tuala. And time's short. If you want to come with me, come. But this isn't just a simple matter of walking into the house and fetching her out. She won't be there; I think she may have gone to a secret place up in the woods."

"A secret place," echoed Gartnait as Bridei's mare set off once more along the track and he guided his own mount after her. "Dangerous?"

"Not in the way you mean, I expect. It's quite isolated."

"Then you'll need a friend by your side. Don't bother to thank me for half killing myself catching up with you."

"Thank you," said Bridei tightly; to talk at all seemed a waste of precious time and strength. "There was no need."

There were folk about at Pitnochie, though fewer than in the old times. A small figure could be seen outside the barn, with children and dogs at foot: Fidich leaning on his crutch, inspecting some sheep. The guards were changing shift, a fortunate accident of timing. "Keep to the trees," Bridei told Gartnait. "I've no idea what they'll do if they see me, but time's short, and I must get to the Dark Mirror without delay."

"The Dark Mirror?" queried Gartnait as they guided their

horses up under the pines, where they could not be seen from house or yard.

"The place I must go to. A haunt of the Good Folk; a narrow glen that once saw a terrible massacre unfold, men of Fortriu cut down by the Gaels. If she came back here, that's where she'll have gone."

"Why?" asked Gartnait blankly. His voice was sounding odd, unlike itself.

"She used to go there for answers when she was worried or upset or lonely. There's a dark pool; a pool in which some people can see visions . . . That is where she would go."

"Mm-hm," Gartnait said, and they rode on in silence, into the deeper places of the forest where sunlight penetrated but dimly. The foliage was damp and clinging; the ground was covered by a thick mat of decaying leaves, richly dark and releasing a pungent smell under the horses' hooves. A cold vapor crept among the trees, drifting close above their gnarled roots, sending its tendrils up to weave a chill net about their trunks. Under the canopy of twisting branches, the mist clothed the slopes so thickly Bridei could see no more than three strides ahead. At length, he slipped down from Spindrift's back and walked forward with his hand on her neck. Behind him Gartnait, too, dismounted.

"Here," Bridei said. "This is the little track into the Vale of the Fallen." There were no white stones by the path today. Never mind that; he would go on, Good Folk or no Good Folk. Perhaps she was just down there, no farther than a shouted word away . . . He did not shout. "We must leave the horses here," he told Gartnait. "This is too narrow for them. If you're coming with me, come now."

"Bridei—"

Bridei did not wait to hear what his friend wanted to tell him. Already he was slipping and sliding down the precarious path, his sleeves catching in the thorny foliage to either side, his breath coming hard. Something had possessed him, a new, dark sense of urgency, as if a voice were calling him on, a voice that was like a challenge: *Come out and do battle with us! Prove yourself! Show us what you are made of!*

He gritted his teeth and plunged on downward. *Tuala, Tuala* . . . She was the only thing that mattered. Without her he could do none of it. Why couldn't Broichan understand that? Why couldn't Faolan, why couldn't anyone? He had to find her . . . He had to stop her . . .

Bridei hissed an oath as something shot past his feet, near toppling him: a small, gray-furred fury streaking up the path from the glen of the Dark Mirror and away into the forest.

"Black Crow save us!" exclaimed Gartnait. "What was *that*?"

Her cat, Mist; Mist fleeing in utter terror, or pursuing an errand of equal urgency with his own . . . "Quick," muttered Bridei, and scrambled down the track to the water's edge.

It was instantly plain that Tuala was not here. Perhaps she had been, before, but now the place was gripped by a deep chill and shut in an impenetrable silence; the cold was enough to stop the heart and freeze the breath. Bridei paused by the dark water, on the brink. Had she stood here? There were marks on the earth, the impression of small boots, a cat's paw prints. Where was she? Where had she gone? It was almost dusk. How would he find her out here at dark of the moon?

"I'm sorry." Gartnait's voice came from just behind him, and then Gartnait's hands were around his neck and squeezing hard. Bridei staggered, his heart pounding, his breath squealing in his lungs as he fought to wrench the constricting fingers from his throat. So close, so near and now *this,* what in the name of the gods was *this* . . . Gartnait had the advantage of him, taller, stronger today for all the long ride . . . a vise around his neck . . . he couldn't breathe, everything was going dark . . . Donal, what would Donal do . . . Bridei threw his weight forward, sending them both off balance. An instant later he was toppling into the icy water of the Dark Mirror and, still clutching him in a strangling grip, Gartnait fell with him.

There was a choking, gasping, clawing struggle for survival. The water was far colder than any normal pool, even at solstice time. It froze the very blood in his veins. Gartnait, ever the stronger swimmer, was doing a good job of holding him under . . . no time, no time . . . Still Bridei fought, for all the things that mattered, for Breth's loyalty and Garth's kindness, for Faolan's strange reluctant friendship, for the hearth fire of Pitnochie and the banners that flew above the field of Galany's Reach, for the fierce strong eyes of Drust the Bull and the twisted body of a tattooed warrior . . . for Broichan's discipline and the long years of learning . . . even for that . . . for Tuala . . . above all, for Tuala . . . Gods, Gartnait was strong. He had not realized how strong . . .

"Why?" Bridei spluttered as the other's hands slackened a moment in the thrashing chaos of the struggle. "Why?"

There was no answer; only a glimpse of Gartnait's white face, Gartnait's furious, unseeing eyes, and then the grip again. "I'm sorry," said Gartnait in a gasping whisper, and forced Bridei's head back under the water.

He was drowning . . . he was dying . . . his lungs were full of a fiery pain, and his head was crowded with visions tangled and twisted . . . Somewhere down beneath the water, a dog was barking . . .

He was deep in the earth, cradled in darkness, curled on himself like a sleeping babe. Above him the roots of great oaks made their slow, searching journey through layer on layer of soil, and about their winding paths crept the lesser ways of myriad tiny creatures, beetle and slow-worm, ant and wriggling larva . . . Their little excavations, their minuscule chambers and hallways and storehouses honeycombed the earth, a whole world invisible beneath the wooded hillside, the grassy field, the heather-clad moor . . . He was buried underground . . . He was trapped . . . *Tuala* . . .

"Forget your body, trust your mind." Broichan's voice came deep and strong. "Apply your learning."

"It's all right, Bridei." Tuala's clear, small tone, making him want to weep. "You can do it."

Think, then . . . Think of Bone Mother, in whose arms he lay, within whose long patterns each of them lived his own small span, be he king of Fortriu or foundling child, great soaring eagle or least of subterranean tunnelers. She held them all; to each she granted a certain time, a certain span. A certain opportunity. When she judged it enough, the long sleep would come. For him, this was not the time. Bone Mother, in whose womb he rested now, safe and quiet, warm . . . warm at last . . . Her hands were strong, her reach wide, from the western glens to the shores by the king's fortress, from the softer hills of Circinn to the bare, rocky peaks of the northwest . . . It was all one, one and the same; her love existed in every part of it . . . the great realm of Fortriu, which needed him . . .

I will not beg to live, Bridei prayed in silence. *I will give myself into your hands. Let me find her. I am bound to go forward; bound to lead. I make no bargains. I am not so foolish that I dare to test the gods' will so. I love. I trust. Let me go forward on this journey . . .*

He felt the water around him. Creatures strange and wondrous swam on every side, glowing balls of color with attenuated limbs, fish fat and squat with bulging eyes, or long, slender, and studded with forbidding spikes. There was a being like the sea-beast of the islands, and a small white dog with the tail of a salmon. They circled him in flamboyant dance, above, below, around, dazzling his eyes and beguiling his senses. He could not see Gartnait. Whatever realm he now journeyed through, it seemed his friend had not followed. But someone else was here. On the surface above him, a girl was swimming, struggling to stay afloat, heavy gray robes dragging her down. Her small, pale feet could be seen kicking, kicking ever more feebly as cold and weariness sapped her strength. Her arms moved weakly in the water . . . she was sinking, drowning . . . A great hand came down from above, fastening around her head, pushing her under the water . . . her eyes stared . . . her dark hair drifted around her features like fronds of graceful weed . . .

No! Bridei shouted, but the water turned his voice into helpless bubbles. He thrust out with his feet, stretched up with his hands, she was there, right there, two arm's-lengths above him, he could touch her, he could save her . . . His foot was caught, he could not move . . . He looked down, his movement slow against the water's weight. Something was holding him, a strip of tangled weed, a shred of net, a length of rope . . . *Tuala!* he shouted, and the bubbles rose to burst beside her drowning face. *Tuala!*

"Use what we have taught you," came the voice of bald-headed, round-bellied Erip. "Water. Tides. Ebb and flow."

Ebb and flow . . . the Shining One . . . Bridei closed his eyes, imagined the full, round, majestic form of the goddess as he had seen her once at Midwinter, looking down on the quiet fields of Pitnochie. So lovely; so good; so wise. She would not let her daughter go thus, cruelly; she would not cut off the path so soon. *I loved her as a baby,* he said, and the bubbles bore his silent words upward to the light. *I loved her as a little girl. I loved her as my heart-friend. I love her as a woman, and I love her as your daughter.*

"Look around you . . ." Wid's dry voice, whispering in his ear. "Observe, boy, observe . . ."

Darting fish, drifting weeds, dark rocks at the bottom, soft mud . . . there, by his foot, caught around the fastening of his boot, a cord, a string, tethering him . . . this was what held him down. Bridei reached, grasped, pulled. The little cord came loose in his hand, and he kicked off for the surface, clutching it as he rose. Now, now he could reach her . . . Where was she? . . . Where had they taken her? . . . Somewhere up above, beyond the water, a dog was barking . . .

He surfaced, and felt the heat, saw the blaze of light even as his feet moved onto solid ground. The dog was here, not fish-tailed now but four-limbed, shaggy and white, standing before him as if to guard him, its voice too big for so diminutive a hound. He had seen it before, long ago in a vision, keeping faithful watch over a fallen warrior. Around them fire swirled and shimmered; great waves of heat throbbed from it. It was as if they stood in the roaring heart of the Flamekeeper himself. *Tuala.* Where had she gone? Into this mass of seething flame? Beyond place and time, on a journey he could not share? It could not be. It must not be. He was Bridei, son of Maelchon, raised in a druid's house and destined to be Fortriu's leader, and he would not let them take her. He filled his lungs with air, slowly, methodically, as Broichan had taught him to do. He looked down at the little dog, and the dog fell quiet, gazing up at him. Then, as one, they stepped forward into the fire.

It was not pain, not exactly; more a sensation of stripping away, layer by layer, skin, flesh, veins, muscle, bone . . .

mind, heart . . . all gone, all consumed in the white heat of purification, all sacrificed to the god's will . . . save the one thing left, the essence, the courage, the spirit that lay deep inside each true son of Fortriu, each true daughter, marking them forever as children of the blood . . . it was the kernel, the seed, the core that meant they would always go on. Whatever the losses, whatever the pain, this truth inside ensured they would never be defeated . . . *Fortriu*, Bridei gasped as the flame seared through him. *Fortriu* . . . and felt the beating pulse of the fire as if his chest were a war drum, and the god's blows raining on it hard and fast, sounding a furious music of challenge. *Fortriu! Fortriu!*

His mouth was open, his jaw slack. There were twigs and leaves under his face. He was cold. His clothing was soaked, and someone was pressing on his sides with cruel hands, a rhythmic squeezing that hurt, gods, how it hurt, why couldn't they stop, didn't they know he was dead already, dead three times over or maybe four . . . A gush of foul-tasting liquid welled up in his throat and spilled out of his mouth, and he choked out, "Stop it, Gartnait . . . done enough . . ."

The squeezing stopped. A pair of hands took hold of his shoulders, turning him onto his side. Then someone was trying to take off his wet clothes, the tunic, the cloak he still seemed to be wearing. Someone was saying, "Curse it, Bridei, help me a bit here, can't you? Get this off, quick now, and this . . . If there were any gods I was prepared to give credence to, I'd be thanking them now, man . . ."

The voice had a Gaelic twang to it, and was most certainly not Gartnait's. Now Bridei was propped on his elbows, staring up at a sky that held the very last dusky traces of the sun's sinking, and a small white dog was licking his face with a great deal of enthusiasm. A real dog, flesh and blood. Had he somehow set it free from its long vigil? A hundred years of waiting . . .

He attempted to sit up. A dry tunic was slipped over his head, its warm folds blissful against his chill, damp skin. A moment later, a woolen cloak dropped around his shoulders, and he hugged it close. Who would have dreamed so simple a thing could be such a wondrous gift? He turned his head.

"Don't look that way," said Faolan, who was in his shirt-sleeves. "There's a man dead."

Bridei looked; by the edge of the Dark Mirror Gartnait lay sprawled on his back, his red hair almost in the water, his eyes open on the night.

"Beyond saving," Faolan said. "Already gone by the time I fished him out. As for you, you've been even more of a fool than I thought you were. What in the name of all that's holy happened here?"

Bridei did not answer. He was staring down at the little thing still clutched in his hand, a talisman woven from two strands of strong cord, tied and twisted in an intricate pattern. "Tuala . . ." he whispered. "Where's Tuala? Did you see her? Is she here?" His eyes scoured the rocks, the banks, the overgrown path; scanned the surface of the dark water.

"Not a sign. Only our friend here, and eventually yourself, bobbing up in the middle of the pool. And the dog. It played its part in getting you out. Where's it gone now?" Faolan peered into the deepening darkness. "Never mind," he said. "The horses are not far off; we need to get you down to warmth and shelter before the last of the light goes. I don't intend to forfeit my bag of silver just because you take it into your head to go swimming at Midwinter."

"Tuala," said Bridei, his fingers working absently on the cords he held, knotting, binding, joining up the loose ends, as if such activity might help him think. "Tuala . . . I must find her . . . but where? Where have they taken her?"

"Bridei," said Faolan, his tone calm and kindly, as if he were humoring a wayward child, "Gartnait is dead. You are half drowned, and I've given you most of my own dry clothes. And it's nearly dark. We must go down to the house. Now. Horses. Come on."

From the top of the path the dog barked, its note high and urgent.

"We must get you out of this cold air, and fast. Come on, Bridei. Lean on me."

"Air," Bridei said. "Earth, water, fire . . . and air. Air is the final test. Air, wings, flight . . . the eagle . . . flying, falling . . . oh, gods . . ." He leaped to his feet and ran toward the path, and Faolan, cursing, ran after him.

~~~

"HIGHER! HIGHER!" CALLED the voices. They were all around her, shrill, unavoidable. "Come up! Come up!" It was so dark she could scarcely see the path before her. Her hands were hurting and her feet could barely carry her. But something outside her was pulling Tuala forward now, a force too strong to resist. It was time to step across. It was time to leave the bad things behind.

As a child she had scaled Eagle Scar without a thought, agile as a marten. It was different now. Her feet slipped, jarring her body; her hands were slippery with blood and could not grip the rocks; her breath rasped in her chest. Her teeth were clenched so tightly her jaw ached from it. Where were Woodbine and Gossamer? Why hadn't they come, when they had promised to help her? There was no sign of them; only the voices, singing, calling, shrieking, ringing painfully in the bones of her skull. Upward, upward: one faltering step, one feeble handhold, one shuddering breath. There was no choice; she must go on.

At last Tuala reached the rock slab at the top of the Scar, the place where two children had sat side by side on summer days, sharing a frugal meal and each other's silent company. Summer . . . those sunlit times, that simple happiness seemed now the stuff of dreams, long ago, far away, never to be reached again. Tuala slumped to the ground, her legs too weary to hold her.

"Up! Up!" screamed the voices. "Higher! Higher!"

There was nowhere else to go. Nowhere, save for the little rocky pinnacle where she had stood, as a child, turning and turning in the wind, while Bridei pretended he was not scared she would fall.

"Up! Up!"

She forced herself upright; stepped onto that topmost rock. So small; she had not remembered it was so small, or so high. Below her the Scar fell away into utter darkness.

Above, the last traces of light ebbed from a sky the color of shadow, the color of sleep, the color of Bone Mother's eyes.

"Ahhh . . ." The voices sighed as Tuala stood shivering under her damp cloak, her arms wrapped around her body. "Now . . . now is the time . . . Come . . . step over . . ."

Step over? Step where? Her fingers tightened on the fabric of the cloak; her feet shifted uneasily on the wet surface of the rock. Tuala had never been afraid of heights; indeed, had never understood what such a fear was. Now, suddenly, her head reeled and her stomach churned as she looked down into an abyss of shadows. *Step over . . .* What could they mean?

"Do it now, Tuala!" This was Gossamer's voice, light but insistent, not an invitation but an order. "You know you can. Do what you did for us at Banmerren. Shut your eyes, stretch out your arms, and fly! Fly across to us, my sister! Forget weariness! Leave pain and sorrow behind! Now, Tuala, now!"

It didn't really matter, Tuala thought vaguely. Who would care if she flew or fell? Nothing would change in the world, whether she became the owl of her imagination and soared into the night sky, crossing an invisible margin to the land beyond dreams, or tumbled down to the rocks below Eagle Scar, a sprawling, broken thing of no account. Whatever happened, Bridei would go on without her. They would tell him, and he would shed a tear or two and then forget. He would be king; his life would be too full for such small sorrows. Tuala drew a deep breath, screwed her eyes shut, opened her arms wide.

Something brushed against her ankles, soft as a feather yet insistent and real. It set her off balance. "Ah!" she gasped, teetering on the rocks. Her eyes snapped open; she fought to keep her footing. Mist sprang up without warning and as she caught the cat in her arms Tuala felt the stab of claws, sudden and sharp on her hands. This pain was somehow worse than anything, like a last blow, a final betrayal by those she had loved and trusted. Mist clung on; the claws dug deeper. Gods, it hurt . . .

"Now, Tuala!" the voices screamed. "Now, now! Fly!"

She couldn't move. Frozen here in place, with the night

wind tearing at her cloak and her feet slipping on the rocks
and the cat's claws piercing her chilblained hands, Tuala
recognized the truth. She could feel this; the pain, the sorrow, the fear of falling, the terror of the unknown. She could
feel it, and the other side of it, the hearth fire, the feasts of
oaten bread and crisp apples, the old men's wry laughter,
and Bridei . . . Bridei's smile . . . Bridei's touch . . . Bridei's
kiss . . . Tuala's grip tightened, hugging the soft, warm body
of the cat against her chest. She loved those things. The pain,
the fear, the wisdom, the joy were part of her, part of being
alive. Part of being human. Whatever she was, wherever she
had come from, surely it was in this world she belonged, not
the other.

"Come now, Tuala!" called Gossamer, and Tuala thought
she could discern, on the very margin of her vision, a
glimpse of unearthly brightness, a flash of brilliant color;
she could hear snatches of a wondrous music, a song such
as one might ache to hear again, such solace it brought to
the weary heart. She thought there was a sweet smell in the
air, like every kind of spring flower mixed into one and
borne on the balmiest breeze that ever crossed over the
meadows of the Glen. All good things lay just beyond that
margin . . . How foolish to throw it away, just because . . .
just because . . .

"Come, Tuala." Woodbine's lower tone, gentle, beguiling,
warm with promise. "One step, that's all it takes. You know
this is best for him, best for the two of you . . . Come home,
dearest child . . ."

She closed her eyes. Mist . . . Mist must be left behind
again. She set the cat down by her feet, straightened, spread
out her arms once more.

"Good, good," Woodbine murmured. "Close your eyes
and take my hand . . ."

"Tuala!"

Her heart drummed; her head reeled. Sudden tears
blinded her eyes.

"Tuala, don't leave me! I love you!"

His voice was distorted by terror, but she knew it instantly. He was here. After all, he had come for her. Tuala
turned her head, peering into the darkness. The wind

clutched at her clothing, hard and insistent. She staggered. To fall now, now that the miracle had happened, would be too cruel . . .

"Take my hand." This wasn't Woodbine but a stranger, reaching out to her, grasping both her hands, helping her down from the pinnacle onto the relative safety of the flat rock. His hands were warm and strong; Tuala clung to them, her whole body shaking. When she found her voice, it was the hiccupping, uneven tone of a terrified child.

"Bridei?" she said.

The other man stepped back, and Bridei was here, his arms tight around her, his heart thudding against her cheek, his mouth against her hair. He was breathing hard, perhaps weeping; she felt a deep shivering in him that spoke of desperation. Her own clutching embrace was as wild; the feelings that surged through her were too strong to be named, too jumbled to make sense of. All that mattered was that she was alive, and that he had come for her. She buried her face against the breast of his tunic, and felt his hands gentle in the long flow of her hair, and heard him whisper in a tone he had never used before, "Tuala . . . Tuala . . ." Hoarse and ragged as it was, it sounded like a prayer.

After a little the other man cleared his throat. "Bridei," he said, and Tuala became aware that Bridei was as cold as ice, and that the other man appeared to be wearing neither tunic nor jacket nor cloak against the piercing chill of solstice night. Oddly, there was a small dog sitting politely by Bridei's feet. "We must go," the stranger went on. "Your young lady's in as bad a state as you are. I thank my masters I'm contracted only to protect you until the assembly, for the prospect of trying to keep the two of you in order fills me with alarm. Back to the horses, *now*. We need a fire and dry clothing. Can you manage the climb down?"

It seemed to be her the fellow meant. Tuala opened her mouth to say, of course she could, but when she tried to set one foot before the other, everything swayed and turned around her, and it was only Bridei's arm that kept her from falling. Mist had headed off down the steep path already; the little white dog sat patiently, its eyes intent on Bridei. Its pale form shone in the darkness like a dim beacon.

"I will—" Bridei began, but his companion preempted him, scooping Tuala up in capable arms and moving to the track.

"You'll do nothing of the kind. I'm in charge here, at least until we're back at Caer Pridne. Get yourself safely down to the horses and leave the lady to me. You'll have time enough for each other back at the house. Go on, Bridei. You're dropping from exhaustion, for all your efforts to hide it. Nobody expects you to exhibit the strength of the Flamekeeper himself. Not yet, anyway."

"The house . . ." Tuala whispered as she was carried down the steep way. "Nobody there . . . all closed up . . ."

"There are people there now," the man said. "A fire, food, warm beds. Leave it to us, my lady. We'll see you safe."

She closed her eyes, submitting to the unimaginable luxury of not having to make all the choices alone. At the foot of the track, three horses waited. "Lucky," she murmured, smiling to see the familiar mottled coat and angular form of Donal's old friend.

"Lucky indeed," said the man who was carrying her. He lifted her up onto a white mare, a lovely creature who stood gentle and quiet as Bridei was helped to mount; as Bridei's arms came around Tuala's waist, holding her close against him, and the other fellow sprang to Lucky's back, holding the reins of the third horse. "What about . . . ?" this man now queried, glancing at Bridei.

"In the morning. Some of the men can go back up for him. We must get Tuala to shelter, she's freezing and hurt."

"Not to mention a small matter of yourself, a near-drowning, and a certain blow to the head. Come, then. Make your way carefully; it's pitch dark down there under the trees."

The creature that bore her and Bridei seemed more akin to that other realm, Tuala thought as they moved slowly onward, the world whose music and light, whose wonders and secrets she had glimpsed, just for a moment, before the power of her own world had drawn her back. Above her as she rode the voices still called, not angry or disappointed or accusatory as she might have expected, but chanting a song of recognition and farewell, a kind of salute in which nothing could be heard but her name and his, and all around them a wordless garland of melody.

· And, after all, the night was not so full of shadows that the way home could not be found. The little dog trotted ahead, quiet now. Its bobbing white form seemed to carry its own light, guiding the riders on safe ways until they reached the forest's margin and saw below them the flaming torches, the watchful guards, the thatched roof and rising smoke of Broichan's house under the oaks. There were no snowdrifts about the steps; there was no iron bar across the doorway. As they rode up to the entry, the door swung open and warm light streamed out toward them, accompanied by voices and the excited barking of Pitnochie's three hounds, which erupted from within. The little dog stood its ground, stalwart and defiant between the white horse and danger. Then, as Bridei slid down from the mare and held up his arms to Tuala, a dark figure appeared in the doorway, his form outlined by the golden light from hearth fire and welcoming lamp. Broichan watched in silence as his foster son caught Tuala up in his arms and carried her across the threshold into the house.

The warmth, the noise, the savory smells made Tuala's head dizzy; abruptly, she was aware of her exhaustion, the aches and pains all over her body, an urgent need for a drink of water. Everything moved in confusion around her; the only certainty was Bridei's arms, holding her safe as he carried her through to the hall and set her down on a bench as carefully as if she were a cargo of new-laid eggs. And Bridei's voice, giving a series of sharp orders. Of Broichan, she heard nothing at all.

"Cinioch, take Brenna over to the cottage and fetch dry clothes for Tuala, there'll be nothing small enough here. Mara, we need warm water, she's frozen through. And we need some things for Faolan here, he's given me most of what he was wearing . . ."

Looking about, Tuala saw that the house was decked for the season. Wreaths hung over the doors and windows, glossy leaves, scarlet berries; by the hearth a great Midwin-ter log stood ready for the dousing and ceremonial rekin-dling of the house fires. A rich aroma of roast meat and fruit puddings came from the kitchen; it was clear to her that there had been folk in the house and yards all day, preparing for this ritual. The empty barn, the deserted fields, the shuttered windows had been a trick, a vision sent to lead her away from Pitnochie and up to the Dark Mirror. Had Gossamer and Woodbine done this? Why would they be so cruel? Unless it had all been a trick, the coaxing, the enticement, the long, lonely journey. Perhaps it had been a test . . . a test of loyalty . . .

"Bridei," Faolan was saying, "leave this to me, will you? The one who most needs dry clothing and warm water is yourself."

"Indeed." Broichan spoke at last, his deep voice awakening Tuala's old dread. The druid despised her; he wanted her gone. Nothing had changed. She turned her head into Bridei's chest, hating her own weakness, and felt his arms tighten around her where he sat cradling her on the bench. "Whatever has passed here today, my household will provide warmth and shelter for you all," the druid said. "The women will tend to Tuala. As for you, Bridei, to undertake this journey straight from your sickbed was not the act of a rational man. You are not yourself. You must eat, drink, and rest. Leave the decisions to others, for now at least. Time enough for talk in the morning."

Bridei made no move.

"I mean it, Bridei. Let Mara take Tuala. You must rest and recover yourself."

"I am no longer a child." Bridei's voice was cool, controlled: the voice of a man, and a leader. In the chamber around him there was a sudden deep silence; her eyes tightly shut, Tuala sensed that everyone was watching him. "There is a reckoning to be made here, and it will not wait for morning. Mara! I pass Tuala into your care and Brenna's for now. Faolan, stay as close to them as decency permits. Not a hair of her head is to be harmed, not an unkind word spoken in her presence. Know, all of you, that in seven days' time I will stand up as a candidate for the kingship of Fortriu. From this moment on, Tuala is under my protection. You will treat her with courtesy, respect, and love. You should feel deepest shame that there is any need for me to tell you this." His arms loosed themselves gently; he stood, keeping one of Tuala's hands in his. She opened her eyes on a circle of faces frozen in surprise, save for Mara's; Mara was already setting a pile of folded cloths to warm by the fire, and pushing the tumble of dogs—four now—out of her way. The housekeeper glanced at the impassive form of Faolan.

"And who's he?" she demanded. "There's never been a place for Gaels in this household, and I don't see why that should change now."

"Faolan is my friend," Bridei said simply. "He takes care of my business. You can trust him. And now . . ."

Releasing Tuala's hand, he turned his sweet smile on her in reassurance. "I won't be long," he whispered. Then he walked across the room toward Broichan. It was an impressive effort; Tuala, holding her breath, could see what it cost him now to stay straight and steady. A sickbed? What sickbed? What had Faolan meant earlier about a blow to the head?

"Come," Bridei said to his foster father, and the two of them went into Broichan's private chamber. The door closed behind them.

"Tell me," Tuala asked the Gael as a flurry of activity began around them. "What's wrong with him? What happened?"

"Bath first, questions later," snapped Mara as a clatter of pots and pans from the kitchen indicated Ferat had returned to preparing the Midwinter feast. "And not only do we not have Gaels watching women undress in my hall, at such times we don't have men anywhere near at all. Off with you! Uven, take this fellow through to the sleeping quarters and find him something presentable to wear, he looks like a drowned rat. What have you all been doing, fishing for serpents in the lake? Go on, now!"

"You heard what he said." Faolan's tone was level.

"I did, and it wasn't necessary. I know what's right, I always have done. I'm insulted that the lad thinks he can't trust me."

"Things are changing," said the Gael. "You'll need to get used to it."

"Maybe they're not changing so much," Mara muttered,

glancing at the inner door. "Now off with you, all of you. No men in here until I say we're ready. Black Crow save us, Tuala, what have you done to yourself? You're as skinny as a plucked wren, and as for those boots . . . Brenna, come and help me here, will you? Send Cinioch for the clothes. Ferat! When's that hot water coming?"

Tuala glanced at the Gael, who was still standing in the center of the room, stony-faced, his arms folded. "It's all right," she told him. "You can go. I'll be safe here. And thank you. It seems you are a loyal friend to him."

Faolan nodded, saying nothing, then turned on his heel and followed Uven out of the chamber.

"There's no teaching a Gael good manners," Mara observed. "And where did *that* come from?" The little white dog had disentangled itself from the bigger hounds and now stood by Tuala's feet, looking up bright-eyed.

"Far away," Tuala said, recalling the visions of the Dark Mirror, both her own and those Bridei had recounted. "Very, very far. I think Bridei has released him from a terrible duty."

"Mm," said Mara as Ferat and his assistants appeared with a large, shallow pan and ewers of warm water. "There's a dog howls up in the woods, night after night. Folk say it's been there a hundred years." She eyed the creature dubiously.

"I don't think he'll howl any longer," said Tuala. "I think at last he's come home."

18

I WILL NOT ASK," Bridei said, "why you sent her away from Pitnochie again, nor why you thought to arrange a marriage for her while I was gone from home. I will not ask why, when you heard she had run away, you did not exert yourself to search for her. You need not explain why you failed to tell me she was lost; why you lied to me. I have never understood your reasons for distrusting Tuala so. It is clear to me in all respects that she carries the blessing of the Shining One within her; that she walks a path of light and can bring us only good. You are the king's druid. Knowledge of the gods lies deep in your heart and courses strongly in your blood. Where have I learned those ways, but through you? That you have never been able to recognize the truth about Tuala is a mystery to me. You have disappointed me, Broichan. And you have awoken misgivings in me that are disturbing. I wonder if perhaps you do not realize that I am no longer a child, but am become a man. I wonder if you do not recognize that a man who would be king must in time learn to think for himself."

"Sit down, Bridei."

To refuse would be churlish; besides, common sense told Bridei his legs would not hold him up much longer. It had been apparent, from the moment that last, terrifying race up Eagle Scar was over and he held Tuala safe in his arms, how much the success of his journey had owed to the remarkable Spindrift and, at the end, to Faolan. Bridei knew he was weak and exhausted. Nonetheless, he had been trained in self-control: trained by the best there was. What must be faced now was a contest, and he had no intention of losing it.

"Now," Broichan said, sitting opposite him at the table and pouring mead into a pair of cups, "I hope you will hear me out, for all your talk of not seeking explanations."

"I want none. There can be none that make any sense to me. She was in our care; entrusted to us by the goddess. You knew what she meant to me. You ensured, by your machinations, by your inaction, by your silences, that Tuala was almost lost forever. You caused her untold grief and pain. If you expect forgiveness, you will be disappointed. If you expect compliance, you are a fool."

Broichan sighed. "Bridei," he said, "we have seven days until the assembly. Your earlier words told me you have not forgotten that fact, although your impetuous actions suggest you have lost sight of its significance. Seven days, Bridei. It is winter. Drust the Boar will already be at Caer Pridne, coaxing, cajoling, bribing, turning men against you, gathering support for his own cause. Every day you are away from court, your opponent's influence increases. The election will not wait for us. We must get back to Caer Pridne as soon as we can. You need to be there, to be seen and heard, to work on the hearts and minds of those who can still be turned. To come here was folly. To stay here any longer than you must would be the death of our hopes. The death of Fortriu's future."

Bridei was silent a moment, regarding his hands, which were relaxed on the table before him. He did not touch the mead. "An overstatement, surely," he said. "There are other good candidates."

"That's disingenuous, Bridei. Carnach will stand up as your proxy at the presentation, not in his own name. It is my considered opinion, and that of all in my close circle, that the only other claimant will be Drust the Boar. Both of us know, all of us know that you are the Flamekeeper's chosen candidate. This has been fifteen years in the preparation; far longer in the planning. Your country needs you. Your people need you. I recognize that you do require a little time to rest, to regain your strength. One day, two, no more. Then we must ride back to court."

Bridei said nothing.

Broichan steepled his fingers; his expression did not change. "There is the question of Tuala. I understand that. I give you my personal assurance that she will be provided with shelter here for as long as it is necessary. As for her future, now is not the time to consider that. She'd far better have remained at Banmerren, where there was a place for her. Her escapade has lost us precious time. Never mind that; it can wait. After the assembly, when you are king, this can be attended to."

"I don't intend to let her out of my sight," Bridei said.

"She cannot travel to court with us." Broichan's tone was blunt. "She will not be accepted there in any capacity whatever. One glance, and it's apparent she bears the blood of the Good Folk. What would the voters from Circinn think of that? Even our own view her with distrust. Why else do you imagine she had to leave Pitnochie?"

"I think," Bridei spoke slowly, weighing each word, "that

such distrust arises only if it is allowed to do so. Your people love and respect you. A word or two from you would have been all that was needed to set such misgivings at rest. Instead, you sent her away. You robbed her of the only home she had ever known. Your assurances are worthless to me. I will not return to Caer Pridne without Tuala."

There was a little silence.

"I'm sorry, Bridei. I understand the childhood bond between you. I see the qualities in Tuala that seem admirable: wit, subtlety, loyalty, and a physical charm that might indeed set a young man to forgetting what is correct in the choice of a . . . mate." Broichan spoke this last word with evident distaste. "Let me be blunt with you. I do not know what role you see for the girl at court. I realize it is not that of a sister. Perhaps an arrangement could be made. She would be housed, not at Caer Pridne itself, openly, but—"

"Enough." Bridei held his voice level, for all the fury that had seized him. "Evidently I did not make myself sufficiently clear. I intend that Tuala and I should marry. I will have no other. This is not a matter for debate. My choice is made."

"Oh, Bridei." Broichan's words came out on a sigh. "You are still young. The future stretches out before you, full of possibilities. This simply isn't one of them, son. A king of Fortriu doesn't marry a daughter of the Good Folk. Such an action would lay you open to lifelong ridicule. It would fetter you, cripple you. Her influence would render your course perilously unpredictable. We cannot allow this."

"We?" Bridei breathed slowly, keeping his hands still, holding his expression calm.

"Your advisers. Although he never speaks directly about it, Talorgen has long hoped an alliance might be made between you and his own daughter. She's entirely suitable: clever, well-presented, not ill-looking, and of the royal blood of Fortriu. And she's the sister of your best friend."

"I respect and admire Ferada; I always have done. I do not intend to marry her." A vision of Gartnait, drowned face gazing blindly up at the night sky, came to Bridei's mind, and he shivered despite himself.

THE DARK MIRROR § 537

"Aniel," Broichan went on, "suggested the royal hostage, Ana. Very beautiful, and apparently a model of kindness and courtesy. She would be an excellent choice. There are others. Bridei, I understand a young man is subject to strong urges, to the bodily passions the Flamekeeper awakens. There is no doubt in my mind that it is time you took a wife."

"But not Tuala."

"Most certainly not Tuala. That you could ever have considered such an option possible makes a mockery of your education."

"I see. Does not a decision to overlook her make a still greater mockery of the Shining One's trust? It was the goddess who gave Tuala into my care on another Midwinter, long ago. Would you dismiss that so lightly?"

There was a pause. "Tuala can be provided for, as I said." Broichan's fingers toyed with a mead cup. "You do not need to wed the girl to fulfill a promise of responsibility."

"I think I do. It is my belief the Shining One brought her to Pitnochie for just this reason: so that, if I become king of Fortriu, I will have a perfect companion by my side, one who will strengthen me for the tests and trials that must attend such a path. The goddess sent Tuala as my heart-friend so that, in this great work, I will not falter or fail. I love her, and she loves me. Is that too simple for a druid to comprehend?"

"Bridei," said Broichan, "you are extremely weary and still quite weak, and I suspect you haven't eaten since you rode away from Caer Pridne. Believe me, this is best left until morning. Or better, until after the assembly itself. Such decisions should not be made in haste. If you will not leave Tuala here, then she can be conveyed back to Banmerren until the kingship is decided. It's vital that you concentrate all your energies on the election. We can afford no distractions. Let this go for now. Fola will keep the girl safe until we have time to work things out—"

"No," Bridei said. "It cannot wait. Tuala nearly died tonight because of your failure to comprehend this; because she believed herself all alone in this world. I was witness to your own dark time at Gateway. I saw then what a toll your chosen path takes on you. I know how hard it is. Tell me, has your life been bent so strongly on discipline and loyalty that you never learned what love is?"

"This is not love," Broichan said, his tone suddenly hard as iron, "but a young man's delusion. You will not wed Tuala. As king, you cannot."

Bridei looked straight into his foster father's dark, impenetrable eyes. "Then it seems I will not be king," he said quietly.

The eyes changed. It was evident that Broichan, in his wildest dreams, had never anticipated this. "What are you saying, Bridei?"

"Tuala will be my wife. I will not be swayed from that decision, for I know I cannot go on without her. It seems you are presenting me with a choice: Tuala or the kingship. I will not give her up, Broichan. And if I decide the cost of fulfilling this fifteen-year dream of yours is simply too high for me, then you must find another man to be your puppet. Without her, I cannot do it."

"Don't be ridiculous! Of course you can do it!" The druid was on his feet, his face white as chalk.

"Let me rephrase that," said Bridei. "Without her, I will not put myself forward as a candidate. I hope that is sufficiently clear for you. I am a man, Broichan. I've grown up, and I make my own decisions. I have never lost sight of the destiny for which you prepared me. I do not let it go lightly, believe me. But I mean what I say, every word. If you refuse to sanction our marriage, Tuala and I will walk away and make our own life elsewhere, beyond the reach of narrow-minded power brokers. There is nothing you can do or say that will change my mind."

"I don't believe this—"

"Consider only what you have done to Tuala. In your misguided actions you sowed the seed of this. My perfect obedience lasts only until I see the cracks appear on the faces of those I believed beyond reproach. I cannot forgive what you have done to her. I cannot forgive your lies. But I do not make this choice in order to punish you. I want to contest the kingship, Broichan. I've worked hard for it. I believe it is the will of the gods; I am confident that I am the best man for it. And I know that, if I am elected king, I cannot survive it without her. It is for that reason alone that I will walk away if you and your allies do not support my choice. Now I will do as you suggest: seek dry clothes, food, and rest. And the Midwinter ritual is still to be enacted. This is a season of awakening, a time of the birth of new light, the stretching out of the days until the Flamekeeper reaches his radiant zenith once more. An auspicious night. As you said, a little time can be taken for this decision. Your decision, that is. Mine is already made."

"What are you asking?" Broichan's tone was constrained.

"For your support in all things. That you not only approve my choice, but show her friendship and courtesy, and ensure others at court do the same. That you speak no ill of her; that you enact no ill against her. That no word of your true attitude on this matter ever becomes known outside the confines of this chamber."

"And if I refuse, you really would—"

"I would walk away from Pitnochie, and from Fortriu, with Tuala by my side. You would never see me again."

"You really mean it."

Bridei rose to his feet. "If I become king, I intend to have a number of advisers," he said, "yourself among them. What has occurred here does not diminish my gratitude for the years you have devoted to my upbringing, for the wisdom you have shared with me, for the opportunities you have provided for me. It has, however, ensured that I will never be prepared to trust you again. A king should listen to his advisers and then make his own decisions." He inclined his head politely, walked to the door, and left the room. Behind him, there was utter silence.

THE MIDWINTER RITUAL lacked something of its usual vitality. Broichan spoke the prayers as if his mind were in another place entirely. They doused the fire only briefly: it was important to keep the hall warm, with three of those present suffering the ill effects of long exposure to the winter chill. At the point in the ceremony where question and answer must be spoken, Broichan looked at Bridei, and Bridei, calm and quiet, performed the part long perfected under the druid's exacting tuition. At the end, when all stood in a circle to speak the words of blessing, Tuala took her place by Bridei's side, her hand in his. Faolan looked on unsmiling from a corner of the room.

Then there was the feast, a very fine one, but neither Bridei nor Tuala could eat much. A little soup, a bite of bread seemed more than sufficient, and the ale and mead set before them went untouched. They spoke little; they sat side by side on the bench where once, as children, they had huddled in the evenings telling stories of magic and mystery. Tonight a new tale was unfolding for the two of them, a tale with enough of wonder and promise in it to last a lifetime. They had eyes for nothing but each other.

The Midwinter log burned brightly. Before the hearth Mist dozed, curled in a ball, and close by her the white dog lay sleeping on its side, straight-legged, its head resting on Bridei's foot, its ears twitching every now and then. Perhaps, in its dreams, it still kept guard in the lonely vale where once, long ago, a beloved warrior had fallen to a Dalriadan axe.

The household retired to bed. There was a place for Tuala in Mara's quarters and one for Bridei in his old chamber, but neither seemed prepared to move, and nobody was giving any orders. At length, when Mara had bolted the door and quenched all but a single lamp, then taken herself off with a pointed glance over her shoulder, Broichan arose and went in silence to his chamber.

There was a big chair near the fire, carven oak with a wide back to it. Bridei had moved to settle himself in this, with Tuala on his knee. Her head was on his shoulder, her small body curved against his. A warm blanket covered the two of them. Beneath this, it was possible for hands to move, to stroke, to create a sequence of delicious surprises. Bridei's cheeks were somewhat flushed; Tuala's eyes were bright. It was as well, perhaps, that each was far too weary to wish for more than this delicate exploration of their newfound closeness. On a bench by the far wall Faolan lay supine under a cloak. It seemed unlikely that he slept. Even here, he would not leave Bridei unguarded.

"I have something to ask you," Bridei whispered. "Only I don't think I can; if you say no, not only will you break my heart, but you'll make me look extremely foolish in front of the whole household."

"I won't say no, Bridei." Her hand moved gently against the skin of his chest under the fresh shirt he had been given.

Bridei swallowed. "I wanted to ask you before . . . I was going to ask you . . . Will you be my wife, Tuala?" His heart was beating fast; it was astonishing, after all they had been through, how much this terrified him.

"Yes, Bridei." Her voice was small, sweet, and precise; it had not changed so very much since she was a child.

He bent his head and kissed her; her kiss was unmistakably that of a woman. After some time he drew his lips away. "You understand what it will mean?" he asked her. "If I am successful at the election, then you will become queen of Fortriu. That life is very different. Lonely. Testing."

"I know that. Bridei, what about Broichan? What did he say to you? Has he agreed to this?"

"Not yet. He will agree; he has no other option. I told him I would withdraw my candidacy if he refused to approve our marriage."

"Oh."

"He must capitulate. He knows it's possible for me to win this. I should have the numbers as long as Fokel of Galany reaches Caer Pridne in time. Should the vote be tied, the evidence Faolan has of Drust's attempt on my life can be made public. That should seal it."

"Attempt on your life? This is the head wound your Faolan spoke of?"

"At full moon. I was set upon as I made my way to Banmerren. I'm sorry . . . I'm so sorry I couldn't let you know . . ."

Her hand reached up, stroked his hair gently, touched the skull where the wound was still evident. "I don't know how I could have thought . . ." she murmured. "They showed me visions: you and Ana, you and Ferada . . . I shouldn't have believed them . . ."

"Them? Who?"

Tuala smiled. "I have a long story to tell you, Bridei. A long and strange one. I think perhaps I was set a kind of test."

He nodded, his fingers twining themselves in the silky dark strands of her hair. "My tale, too, is difficult to believe. It seems the gods have tested the two of us. Gartnait was here. He came after me. And Gartnait is dead."

"Dead? What happened?"

"The true account is one I can give only to you. Faolan and I know it, nobody else. I must find a different tale for Talorgen."

Tuala was staring at him now; whatever she saw in his face, it rendered her silent.

"He came after me, all the way from Caer Pridne. I had Uist's mare; Gartnait must have pushed himself and his horse to breaking point. He caught me just before I reached Pitnochie; said he had come to bear me company, to help. We rode up to the Dark Mirror in search of you. Then . . ."

"Then what, Bridei?" She held his hand between hers.

"Then he set his hands around my throat and tried to strangle me. It was as if a madness came over him. All he could say was that he was sorry. The only way I had any chance of breaking his hold was to force him into the water."

"Into the Dark Mirror?" Tuala breathed.

"It was . . . a journey. A trial. When I came to myself once more it was to find Faolan squeezing the water from my lungs and Gartnait lying drowned on the bank. Faolan had fished the two of us out. The dog was there, the dog from the Dark Mirror, only now it was real. There was no time to think, not then. We came straight up to fetch you. As to why Gartnait would act thus, that remains a mystery."

"What will you tell Talorgen?"

Bridei glanced at the bench where Faolan lay. "That there was an accident; that Gartnait tried to save me and was drowned. In death, at least, let him have his father's good opinion."

"Ferada will be sad."

"Yes. For all their squabbling, she and Gartnait were close. She helped me. But for her, I could not have got away from Caer Pridne."

"Do you think Talorgen and Fola and the others would support you even if you intended to wed a girl who was not . . . suitable?"

"You are entirely suitable," Bridei told her. "It's just a matter of showing them. And yes, I believe the others will fall in behind me, for all Broichan's influence. If they do not, then I am not as strong a candidate as I should be. As for the chieftains of Fortriu, it is I who have worked to sway them this past season more than anyone. They will support me. By morning, if not before, my foster father will have accepted that his argument is no argument."

"He fears my influence on you," Tuala observed. "That it will be greater than his own. There was a time when we were almost allies, he and I. But he will never trust me, no matter how often I prove myself. I am not part of his plan."

"His plan is ended," Bridei said. "This path is ours now, yours and mine."

"He loves you. You should not lose sight of that."

"Not for what I am. Only for what I can do for him; for Fortriu."

"You're wrong. You are like a son to him."

"I think not."

There was a little silence. The white dog sighed and shifted. Tuala held Bridei's hand against her cheek, touched it with her lips.

"Bridei?"

"Mm?"

"When will we be married?"

"Ah." He sat up a little; wrapped the blanket more closely around her shoulders. "I wanted to talk to you about that."

"You're sounding anxious, dear one. Tell me."

"It's just that . . . well, there is a great wish in me that our wedding night should be . . . perfect."

"I expect it will be," Tuala said.

"Not if it must be here, where there has been such unhappiness for you, here where Broichan's influence is so strong.

And not at Caer Pridne. I wish to make changes. Not just for us, but for the kingship. It is connected with . . ."

"With Gateway?"

He nodded. "If this goes as I hope it will, in seven days I may well be king. The first change I intend to make is to establish my court away from Caer Pridne. I will build a new fortress; make a new center for the affairs of Fortriu. That, I believe, will be a powerful symbol of better times to come. I have a place in mind, one Ged of Abertornie described to me, situated near the mouth of Serpent Lake. There is a high hill, with the remains of an ancient fortification of stone and fired wood. The rise is crowned with great trees and has a fine expanse of open ground at the top. From that vantage point it is possible to see not only the ocean, but also the waters of the lake and the hills of the Great Glen. I do not think you should live where you cannot see the forest."

"Nor you where you cannot see the eagle's flight across the great wild places," Tuala said softly. "There are some who will not like your plan. The fortress of Caer Pridne has been the seat of Fortriu's kings for many years."

"It is a time of change," Bridei said. "If we are not prepared to open our minds to that, we are doomed."

"How long will it take to build your new fortress?"

"I don't know, Tuala. A summer, maybe two."

"Oh. That is a long time."

He sighed, his hand moving beneath the blanket to cup the small swell of her breast. Her answering sigh made him wonder if he was in fact being unbelievably foolish. "Yes, dear one, it is long. And I have to tell you of a promise I made . . . a vow to the Flamekeeper . . ."

"Bridei, you're blushing."

He glanced quickly at Faolan; the Gael's eyes were shut, and a faint snoring could be heard. "That I would . . . that I would not . . . until my formal handfasting," he said under his breath. "To be celibate until then. I'm sorry, it was . . ."

"Oh. I see. Two summers, you said?"

"Perhaps the builders could work quickly."

"Let us hope they can. Bridei, where will I stay until then? I don't want to be here at Pitnochie, not without you. And I will not go back to Banmerren."

"I could not countenance either. Vow of abstinence or not, I want you near me. We can at least look, and speak, and touch . . ."

"Mm. It will be a further test, I think. Bridei, I want to be the best help to you that I can be. But if I am at court and we are not yet married, I think it might be easy for folk to gossip. My presence will be a burden to you, as Broichan always believed—"

"I have a solution to that. I think it will please you."

"You have a solution to everything."

"Not quite. I'm doing my best. It is as much as any man can do, be he druid or warrior, servant or king."

"WAIT A MOMENT, Tuala." Ana reached to make a small adjustment to the way Tuala's hair spilled over the braided band to curl becomingly down around her ears. The band was dyed a deep blue and matched the soft skirt and tunic Tuala wore, plain and elegant above kidskin slippers. It was the first time she had been without the salve and bandages; she had told them firmly that she was not going to attend the election of a king with her feet trussed up in strips of linen. The blisters were healing. Warmth and kindness had gone a long way to mending the other hurts.

"Ready, girls? We must go in now." Rhian of Powys stood watching them, regal in her dove-gray gown, a smile hovering on her lips. "You look very well, the two of you. Back straight, chin up, Tuala. We'll stand on either side of you. Look folk directly in the eye. You're a queen in waiting; nothing can touch you."

"Thank you, my lady. For everything." Bridei's plan had worked out miraculously well so far. Drust's widow had expressed delight at his request that she remain at court, retaining her old apartments, and act as chaperone and mentor to his betrothed until the time of their handfasting. Bridei's intuition had been sound. Rhian was less than keen to return to her kin in Powys, having forged strong bonds during her years in Fortriu. Her brother, too, was happy to remain at Caer Pridne. Tuala suspected both had played a far more influential role in the former king's decisions than anyone had given them credit for. Their gentle, unobtrusive demeanor was somewhat deceptive; in the quiet of the women's quarters, Rhian debated political strategy over her embroidery with a depth that was a challenge even for a girl reared by scholars. Frustrating as the time of waiting might be, it would certainly not be boring. Besides, Tuala recognized the advantages to be gained from a period under the supervision and protection of the royal widow. Rhian could teach her how to walk, how to dress, whom to look in the eye and whom to be wary of. Tuala could learn the subtle games of court; she could learn how to look after both herself and Bridei. Such education was priceless, and to have it at the hands of this kindly, fair-minded woman was a rare gift. Besides, Rhian's protection and influence should go a long way to silencing those who might whisper that one of the Good Folk was not a suitable wife for a king. Ana, too, would play her part in this. Thus far, nobody had spoken out. Thus far, Tuala had remained principally in the queen's private apartments. Tonight was the first real test.

"Ready?"

"Yes, my lady."

They walked out into a hall packed with men and women. Many lamps burned; the tables had been set by the walls tonight and an open space left before the dais. Taking her place between Rhian and Ana, Tuala scanned the faces for those she knew. There was Ferada, looking pinched and exhausted but holding her head high; her auburn hair was perfectly groomed, her green gown pleated and pinned just so. She had one small brother on either side. Tonight, the irrepressible Bedo and Uric stood solemn and silent, and Bedo was holding his sister's hand. Talorgen stood behind them. The chieftain of Raven's Well had aged ten years since his eldest son's heroic death, followed by the strangely abrupt departure of his wife to a distant and unspecified part of the country. The whispers were that Dreseida was so overwhelmed by grief that she had lost her mind. They said she would not be coming back. Those who knew the truth, Tuala among them, kept it to themselves. It was Talorgen who had sent his wife away. For what she had done, and for what she had almost done, Dreseida had been banished from home and family, from land and kin forever. Poor Ferada. She had always longed to make something of her life beyond the restrictions of a strategic marriage. Her future had narrowed now; she must travel back to Raven's Well and take her mother's place in running Talorgen's household and raising his sons.

There was Fola with a group of wise women, Kethra among them. They nodded and smiled at Tuala, and she returned the greeting with a certain wonder. This still felt unreal, especially when Bridei was not nearby.

There was Uist in his floating white robes, and beside him another old man . . . Tuala suppressed a cry of joy; it was all she could manage to stand still, to stop herself from running across the hall to throw her arms around the white-bearded, hawk-nosed ancient who stood next to the wild druid. "Wid," she breathed, and felt herself grinning in a most unladylike manner. Her old friend bowed his head courteously in her direction, then winked.

"This pleases you?" Rhian murmured.

"Oh, yes! Wid taught me everything I know. Well, at least half of it. I'm so happy to see him."

"He'll be at court indefinitely, so I'm told. Bridei requested his presence. Your betrothed is solicitous for your well-being; he wishes you to be surrounded by friends. He's very good to you, Tuala."

"I know."

"Look," Ana whispered, "there's Drust the Boar, all got up in the red of Circinn. And here come the others. Bridei looks nervous."

"Yes. That's the way it always is with him; he'll be terrified of doing something wrong, even though he knows he can speak and act perfectly. It's just the way he is."

"That man's staring at you. Over there, look. Garvan the stone carver."

Tuala looked; caught Garvan's eye. He smiled and turned away. There was a sadness in his plain features that was disconcerting. Surely he had not actually imagined she would come around to marrying him? Surely he had not really intended to wait indefinitely until she made up her mind one way or the other? Men were indeed strange creatures. Even Bridei, whom she knew better than he knew himself, had surprised her with his vow to the Flamekeeper. Two whole years. It was indeed a long time. Of course, if another man became king, there would be no need for such a delay. Tuala thought that unlikely. How could the gods not let Bridei be chosen?

The candidates walked to the center of the hall, Drust the Boar resplendent in scarlet-dyed wool, Bridei in the same shade of blue that Tuala wore, his cloak pinned with the silver eagle. Drust of Circinn was a big man, burly and dark. With his corpulent figure and small eyes, he seemed well suited to his title. Beside him Bridei seemed slight and young, although he was the taller. Each man was flanked by his supporters, Bridei with Broichan and Aniel, Drust accompanied by the councillors Bargoit and Fergus and the unprepossessing figure of Brother Suibne.

At a sign from Tharan, who was standing on the dais at the end of the hall, the crowd fell silent. "Let the voting chieftains stand forward," the councillor said.

From the ranks of those present a number of men stepped out. There were not many whom Tuala recognized; Talorgen was one, and Ged of Abertornie in his rainbow garb; and Morleo of Longwater. Bridei had introduced her to these two; Ged had made much of her beauty and her diminutive size, and expressed an intention to slip her in his pocket and take her home with him on the sly. She had liked him. Morleo had been courteous and formal, as if she were already a queen.

"Very well," Tharan said. "Is this all? Can we proceed?"

"It is not quite all," Aniel said levelly. "As we all know, parties from the west are on their way here, and expected this very night. Were it not for the formal decree of a seven-day span from presentations to assembly, we would request a further delay so they can be present. In addition, it is still possible a representative from the Light Isles may come. The weather—"

"Get on with it." Bargoit seemed to have dispensed with diplomacy. "How are we doing this? Do the priest and the wise woman get a vote?"

"They will be allowed to participate," Tharan said. "It can make no difference to the final result." Fola stood up and moved forward to the group of chieftains. She was dwarfed by them, their bright raiment, their silver clasps and gold torcs making her as small and unobtrusive as a rock dove; nonetheless, there was a power in her upright stance, her beak of a nose and her penetrating eyes that ensured a circle of untenanted space was left around her.

"We have heard the claims of the two candidates when they were presented at Midwinter," Tharan went on gravely, "those of Drust son of Girom in person, and those of Bridei son of Maelchon by a proxy, Carnach of the house of Fortrenn. We give each now an opportunity to speak again. Briefly. If these latecomers arrive before the final vote is taken, they may participate. If not, I'm afraid they have missed their opportunity. Let us hear first from the more senior candidate, Drust."

The Boar of Circinn spoke well; he had been king of that southern realm for many years and was accustomed to addressing his people. He spoke of his maturity and experience; of how, if the last election had been conducted fairly, he would already be king in both Circinn and Fortriu, since the accession of Drust the Bull had been based on a faulty voting system. Tuala felt Rhian tense alongside her and saw the tight set of the older woman's lips. She touched Rhian on the arm. "A lie," she said under her breath. "It will set folk against him. A cheap trick. Ignore it, my lady."

Rhian glanced at her, lips curving in a rueful smile. "So young, and already so wise," she said.

Tuala watched Bridei as he waited his turn. He was very pale, and his jaw was clenched tight. His hands were relaxed by his sides. That was something he had trained himself to do, that and the breathing. Beside him, Broichan looked every bit as nervous. Others seemed more confident. Bridei was surrounded by his supporters now: red-haired Carnach, somber Aniel, Talorgen, Ged, and Morleo. Faolan, too, was close by, adopting the not-quite-present look of the experienced bodyguard, his eyes not on Bridei himself but on corners, shadows, subtle glances and sudden movements. The others, Breth and Garth, were stationed strategically behind and to either side of Tuala and her companions. Bridei was leaving nothing to chance.

Drust's speech came to an end, Tharan making it clear by gestures that *brief* must be taken to mean precisely that. There had been something in it about the Christian faith and how embracing it would unite all Fortriu and change it for the better. An alarming number of the voting chieftains had applauded this with enthusiasm. Tuala bit her lip. Was it possible that Bridei had got it wrong, after so much care in the planning? By her own count, if the representatives from the west did not arrive soon, he would not have his twelve. It had been expected that Ana's cousin in the Light Isles would send a kinsman to vote on behalf of his people. He had failed to do so. Tuala wondered what would happen to Ana if this lost Bridei the crown.

"Bridei, speak now," said Tharan.

Bridei glanced across; his eyes met Tuala's, blue as a summer sky, bright with courage, and he smiled. She gave a little nod; she knew the message of her heart was written on her face. *I love you. You can do this.*

"I am Bridei, son of Maelchon." The young voice was clear and strong. "My father is king of Gwynedd. My mother is Lady Anfreda, kinswoman to our late great king, Drust son of Wdrost, known as the Bull. I am young. I offer a full life of service to our beloved land of Fortriu. I am a man grown; I fought by the side of our chieftains in the battle of Galany's Reach, and proved myself on that field, and in the restoration of Fortriu's wounded pride by the claiming of the Mage Stone. I was raised by the king's druid, Broichan, and I am scholar as well as warrior. I love the ancient gods of Fortriu, whose bones are the land we walk on; whose sweet breath is the air that gives us life. I will lead my people in their paths for all the years of my kingship. I will serve you with the best I can give, and with the inspiration of the Flamekeeper, the wisdom of the Shining One, and the deep certainty of Bone Mother to guide me. I offer you my youth, my blood, my courage, and my energy. I will lead you forward into a new future, one in which Fortriu's borders will be made safe once more and its people united. This I swear to you by all that is good."

It seemed to Tuala a light shone from his face as he spoke; she did not know if others could see it, but the utter silence that followed his speech suggested it was so. She reached up to wipe her eyes.

"Very well," Tharan said after a little. "Let the voting commence. Drust son of Girom, take your place to the left. Bridei son of Maelchon, to the right. All men save the voting chieftains, leave the area before the dais."

The right to vote was restricted to a certain number of chieftains from the seven houses of the Priteni, which were named for the seven sons of the original ancestor, Pridne. The voters represented the oldest families and the greatest landholdings within each house or tribe. Some houses had one vote, some two or three. On Bridei's side of the hall stood Talorgen, Ged, and Morleo; Carnach and Wredech also, for each was eligible to cast a vote provided he did not stand for election himself. Fola stood by Talorgen's side. Other men had stepped up. Uist and Wid had retreated. It was generally considered that druids had enough influence already, without needing a vote as well.

There were twelve men on Drust's side, as all had predicted; twelve chieftains and Brother Suibne, who stood quietly, his cross in his hands. In fact, now that Tuala looked properly, she could see the priest had not moved to the left, but had his sandaled feet one on either side of what might be considered the midline of the hall. More men had moved to the right; on Bridei's side the count now numbered eleven.

"Ahem." Above the suppressed buzz of excited voices, Tharan cleared his throat loudly. "Do you understand the conduct of this proceeding, Brother Suibne? You must move to right or left to indicate your intention." The councillor's voice had acquired an edge; he might once have opposed Bridei, but there was not a single man of northern Fortriu who would have wished the Christian Drust on the throne, with the poisonous Bargoit whispering in his ear.

"I need time for reflection." Suibne's voice was quiet; nonetheless, Tuala noted the firm tone, the direct look. "A man must consider these speeches at least briefly before being expected to make up his mind. A moment or two, I pray you."

Tuala saw Fola's lips quirk with amusement and a kind of recognition. Others were less patient; an angry muttering arose from the Circinn camp. Their minds had been made up long ago. To leave a decision until the final speeches were delivered was ridiculous. They had known before they traveled to Caer Pridne which way their votes would go; they had expected the priest to be of the same mind.

At the back of the hall, the doors swung open; newcomers had arrived. There was a hubbub of voices.

"We will allow you a little time," Tharan said. He did a commendable job of keeping his tone calm and his expression impartial as he glanced across the crowd to the doorway. "A few moments for reflection. As a Gael you are, I suppose, unfamiliar with such formalities."

"As a thinking man," Suibne said, "I prefer to make my decisions only after weighing up all the arguments. I thank you for your consideration."

Bargoit moved forward, seized the priest by the arm, and began to hiss furiously in his ear.

"Step back, Bargoit." Tharan's voice was coldly authoritative now. "Only voting men and women are to be in this area. I imagine the fellow can think for himself. One would hope so."

"Voting men, is it?" A powerful voice came from the back of the hall; the crowd parted as a figure came striding through, clad in the dark riding clothes, the boots and fur cloak of a winter journey. His face and body wore a network of tattoos, the complex record of many battles; his eyes were dark and fierce, his jaw grim. Tuala saw Bridei's expression change, lighten. "That includes myself: Fokel son of Duchil, chieftain of Galany's Reach."

"Galany's Reach is lost!" Bargoit spat out, eyes furious. "How can you be chieftain of a territory that lies once more in the hands of the Gaels?" He whirled to face Tharan, pointing an accusatory finger. "He should not be allowed to vote! It's a gross breach of the rules! This election is a sham!"

"Incorrect." It was Broichan's voice, deep and steady. "The law allows his vote; Fokel is chieftain in exile. It was proven last summer that those lands are within our grasp.

This young man you see before you, our new king in the making, has seen to it that the symbol of Galany's freedom was restored to Fortriu intact. That was an act great in spirit and vision; an act surely blessed by the Flamekeeper himself. Fokel will be chieftain there once more ere long. To deny him a vote is tantamount to saying our people have no future in the west. It is the statement of a traitor."

"Enough," Tharan said firmly. "Fokel, you may vote, of course. I have to say that your timing leaves something to be desired."

Fokel was already standing beside Talorgen on the right side of the hall. Tuala counted again. Without the Christian priest, who remained alone in the center, there were now twelve on Drust's side and twelve on Bridei's, including Fola. The hall had become very crowded; it seemed Fokel's entire band of fighters had accompanied him on this trip to Caer Pridne, and now every corner was occupied by some wild-looking fellow all spiraled and cross-hatched skin, twists of long hair, and ferocious eyes. They were well armed; iron hung all about them. The eyes of the court ladies reflected a mixture of admiration and apprehension.

"Well, Brother Suibne?"

"I need a little longer."

"We can't wait all night. It's a simple enough decision but, most unfortunately, it seems to rest with yourself. Make your choice, please."

"There might be a wee something I forgot to mention," Fokel said casually. "Do I have it right that at least one chieftain from each of the seven houses ought to vote? Yes?"

"That is correct," Tharan said. "Since no representative from the Light Isles has made the effort to be present, they forfeit their right this time."

"But there's another house not represented here," said Fokel, scratching his chin.

"Another—oh, you mean the north?" Tharan's brows rose. "The Caitt haven't voted for years. They've never held to our law. There's no requirement . . . Besides, if they don't come, they can't vote."

"They've come this time," Fokel said.

Another man stepped forward from the shadows, an im-

mensely tall man with black hair to his waist and a face like
a granite slab, entirely covered with intricate markings that
made the warrior tattoos of Fortriu look like the scribbling
of children. The fellow wore a long, hooded cloak made of
many small skins sewn together. Tuala shivered, thinking of
Mist, who now drowsed before the fire in Rhian's quarters.
The man's garment was fringed with what appeared to be
cats' tails. Around his neck was an ornament of small bones
threaded on knotted leather. His eyes were dangerous; his
fists were huge. The axe on his back, figured all across the
blade with signs of moon and stars, gleamed like polished
silver in the lamplight.

"I am Umbrig of the Caitt." The voice rang out like a war
trumpet, the language an accented, guttural variant of the
Priteni tongue. Umbrig folded his arms, and broad silver
rings wrought in twists and plaits revealed themselves beneath the cloak, encircling heavily muscled limbs. "I cast
my vote for the man who honors the old powers. Had I
known this court would give credence to a claimant whose
beliefs mock the wisdom of the ancient gods, I would have
come by less peaceable paths to lend my support to this
young warrior. I see in his eyes that he is stalwart in his faith
and strong in his intentions. The vote of the Caitt goes to
Bridei son of Maelchon."

"Set up by druids," muttered Bargoit. "Planned, plotted,
and unfair in every respect—"

On the dais, Drust the Boar was beginning to look very
uncomfortable. His broad face was almost as red as his tunic. Were the voting to be tied, a certain matter of a botched
assassination attempt would likely be aired in public for the
first time. He knew they knew. He would be well aware of
how things might unfold here, and the probable consequences for his own reputation. Tuala glanced at Bridei. He
appeared calm, although he had grown still paler.

"By my count, the present state of affairs gives thirteen
votes to Bridei son of Maelchon and twelve to Drust," Tharan announced in a commendably steady voice. "And there
is but one vote yet to be cast; yours, Brother Suibne. Unless
there are to be any more surprises?" He glanced about the
hall. "No? Come then, Brother, let us end this."

"By all means." The Christian folded his hands before him; his face was serene. "I have considered the speeches, and what I know of this divided realm. I have thought about the nature of the two candidates, so different in faith and belief, in age and demeanor, in convictions and priorities—"

"Brother," said Aniel testily, "there is no requirement for voters to make a speech. Please give us your decision."

"I cannot do so," Suibne said quietly. "As a man of God, I think it inappropriate that mine should be the decisive vote in this secular contest. As a Gael, I think it still less fitting. I have no option but to abstain." The little man stepped back into the crowd, which had erupted in a chorus of raucous protests and jubilant cheering.

"Enough! Enough!" Tharan's voice could scarcely be heard. It was Broichan who stepped to the dais, raising both hands and holding them high until the hubbub died down. His eyes were blazing.

"I declare Bridei son of Maelchon the victor, by thirteen votes to twelve," said Tharan solemnly. "And I decree that our new king will be crowned here at Caer Pridne within one turning of the moon. Under the gaze of the gods, I salute Fortriu's new ruler. Bridei, do you wish to speak?"

Tuala pressed her lips together; this was no time to shed tears. She wished that Bridei would look at his foster father. One glance at Broichan's face, and he would never again say the druid did not know what love was. But Bridei was looking out over the crowd, giving a nod, a smile to each of those who had supported him, pacing his breathing so he could speak calmly and strongly over the thundering beat of his heart, the swarming distraction of a mind too full of thoughts. She knew him all too well.

"I will speak only briefly; this is a time for celebration, for feasting and music, for hope and good fellowship. Our great work together, yours and mine, begins in the morning. You know what is in my heart; I thank you, and pledge to serve you. I have only two things to say now. Firstly, I wish to express my respect to a worthy opponent, Drust son of Girom, and to wish him well. I hope for a future of cooperation and understanding, so we can work together despite our differences. Only thus can we free our land from the scourge of invaders. Drust has been king a long time in the south. I can only learn from his experience."

This was greeted by a deathly silence. Bridei seemed unperturbed; his plans were long, and Tuala knew he did not expect instant acceptance of change. This had needed to be said, for Drust's expression was thunderous and Bargoit looked like a snake about to strike. It was a difficult situation. Circinn's own had turned against them. By doing so, Brother Suibne had saved them the embarrassment of having their attempt on Bridei's life exposed. Tuala wondered if the priest had known about that. Either way, she would not want to be in his shoes tonight.

"I wish also to present to you my future wife, the dear companion of my childhood: Tuala of Pitnochie." Bridei looked across at her, eyes shining, cheeks a little flushed. Tuala held her back straight; put her chin up as Rhian had shown her how to do. Bridei reached out a hand.

"Go, child," Rhian whispered. "Go with the goddess's blessing."

"You look lovely, Tuala," said Ana. "Walk slowly, and smile."

But she did not smile. It seemed too solemn a moment. She simply fixed her eyes on his and crossed the hall as if floating on air. He took her hand; she stood beside him, feeling the tremor in his body, knowing his immense courage and his deep vulnerability. She stood straight and strong, gazing out at the lords and ladies, the warriors and chieftains, the druids and wise women of the king's court. She inclined her head briefly. Then she caught Wid's eye and the smile came despite her.

A ripple of sound ran around the hall, whispering, murmuring, with an unmistakable tone of shock. This was it, Tuala thought; this was the start of it. The gossip, the distrust, the rejection; she would have to be strong. Certain voices could be heard now, and she thought she could detect the words *wild creature* and *Wife? Surely not!* and *one of them.* Bridei did not seem to hear them.

"I wish to extend a welcome to Tuala on behalf of all at Caer Pridne." This was a deep voice, commanding in its resonance. Broichan had stepped forward, features under iron control, and raised a hand for quiet. "As some of you may know, Tuala grew up in my own household. She is a young woman of exceptional qualities, and in every way fitted to be your future queen. I trust you will make her welcome here at court, where she will stay under the guidance of Queen Rhian until the time of the handfasting. This is a season of great change for all of us, a time of challenge and of opportunity. We must be open to that; we must learn from it." If the king's druid spoke these words with gritted teeth, he concealed his reluctance expertly. The unspoken message was clear. Speak out against the king's betrothed because of her difference, and you risked a druid's wrath.

The hall was suddenly quiet. Then Fokel of Galany stepped forward. "By the Flamekeeper's manhood, you surely know how to pick 'em, Bridei," he declared, a grin creasing his dark features. "Your young lady got any sisters?" Laughter erupted, closely followed by a clatter of dishes as servants began to carry in the goblets and jugs, the platters and knives required for the feast. Men clustered around the dais; all at once, everyone wanted to talk to Bridei.

"It's all right," Tuala murmured. "They want to be heard. Do what you must."

"Stay by me," he whispered, holding her hand tightly. "I need you."

"I'll be here," Tuala said. "I'll always be here."

"TALES WITHIN TALES," said Woodbine to Gossamer. "Dreams within dreams. Pattern on pattern and path beyond path. For such short-lived folk, the human kind seem determined to make things as complicated as possible for themselves. It is fortunate for us and for our endeavor that Bridei walks under the gods' protection, and can see more clearly than his kind is wont to do."

"And that we have ensured he has Tuala by his side."

"Indeed. So, it seems our task is complete. I feel a certain dejection, for all the triumph of tonight. The small lives of these folk are, in their own way, absorbing."

"Oh, there's still plenty here to keep you entertained," Gossamer said with a ripple of laughter. "Our work may be over with the young king and queen of Fortriu, but there are many paths, many possibilities. I look down on Caer Pridne tonight and I observe a man who can hear no more than a single note from the bard's harp before he must take himself from the hall. That sweet music is poison to his ears. I see a young woman whose path has been cruelly cut short before her, and I wonder if she will spend a life teetering there on the brink, or leap into the unknown. I see a craftsman whose hands create magic, a magic that can never match the dreams that course through his mind. I see a druid standing alone, pondering questions of love and duty; confronting his own humanity. This is not over yet, my friend. Even Bridei and Tuala, strong as they are, will need us again."

"Ah, Tuala . . . a rare creature. I find myself almost wishing she had come to us . . ."

"What, and cut Bridei adrift? Don't be foolish. Forget Tuala; fix your eye on another. What of that royal hostage, a delectable creature with long tresses like spun gold and skin fresh and sweet as a ripe fruit? Young . . . good . . . innocent . . . What havoc could we not wreak through her? These men could be set dancing, dancing until they begged to stop . . ."

"Come," Woodbine said. "We linger where we have no cause. I will not play yet awhile with the men and women of Bridei's court. My heart is heavy; there is no desire in me for such tricks and meddling."

"Not yet," said Gossamer. "It matters little. They are human, after all. They will make their own complications; dance to their own tunes; play out the moves of their own games. Come! Follow me!"

And with a whisper of cobweb, the flash of a bright wing, and a glitter of silvery hair, they were gone. Standing alone on the wall-walk outside the great hall, Faolan shivered, glancing skyward. Something had passed; he had not seen it, but he had felt its presence. Had the Gael been a man who gave any credence to gods, he might have uttered a prayer, made a sign of ward, or touched fingers to a hidden talisman. But Faolan relied only on himself. It was much easier that way. Through the open doors, the sound of the harp pursued him out into the darkness, making his fingers itch. He stared into the night.

"Faolan?"

It was Bridei, alone now, coming along the walk on quiet feet, the little dog at his heels.

"You almost surprised me," Faolan said. "I must be losing my touch."

"I wanted to speak with you alone."

"Best be quick, then. Tonight everyone wants a piece of you."

"I will take what time is needed; this is important. I wondered if you had given any consideration to the future."

Faolan said nothing for a little. When it came, the answer was diffident. "A man with any good sense can hardly fail to do so."

"And have you reached a conclusion?"

"Not yet."

Bridei leaned his forearms on the parapet. It was a clear night; the stars made bright points of light in a sky where the Shining One hung sleeping, a silver sickle. "You know I would like you to stay," he said quietly. "Not as bodyguard; I had in mind a different role for you, one that would offer you new challenges, new opportunities."

"You are dissatisfied with the work I have done?" Faolan was persistently looking away.

"You must know that is not the reason," Bridei said. "You've more than earned whatever they were paying you. It seems to me your talents are somewhat wasted on the simple job of keeping me safe."

"Simple! You've already put me through ten times more than Drust ever did in the years I served him. But it's true, I am able to perform a variety of other roles and have done so regularly. Translator, assassin, spy. Which did you have in mind?"

"I suppose," Bridei said, "it is possible you may be called upon to do any or all of them in due course. But I was thinking more of a position as adviser, councillor, companion. If you would consider it."

Faolan did not answer for some time. They stood side by

side looking at the stars, while the white dog sat at Bridei's feet, watchful in the night.

"You said something when you were sick. About not being paid to be a friend. It seems to me a friend is what you are looking for. Someone to take the place of Gartnait, or of the fellow you had before, the one who was poisoned. They say the two of you were close."

Bridei said nothing, simply waited.

"I don't think I'm the man for such a job, Bridei. A simple task that tests my skills, with an appropriate payment at the end of it, that I'll undertake gladly. I don't have it in me to offer more."

"I see. You disappoint me, Faolan. I think you deny your own nature."

"You were raised by a druid. You look for complications where there are none. I wish to keep the path straightforward, that's all."

"I'm sorry. I will miss you greatly."

There was another silence, of a different quality this time.

"Are you saying this is the only position you have to offer?" Faolan's tone was painfully careful; it made Bridei want to weep. "You do not intend to retain me as a personal protector for yourself and your betrothed?"

"I had anticipated that you would accept the other offer. I had no alternative ready."

"I see."

"You would consider that? The continuing burden of ensuring our safety, with a simple payment in food and lodgings and a little silver?"

"I don't know about *little*," Faolan said on a rush of outward breath. "I command a high price."

"I'll meet it," said Bridei.

"Then we have an agreement." Faolan extended a hand; Bridei grasped it. "I wish to stay. I did not think I would need to tell you so."

"Guard duty. Long days, sleepless nights, constant anxiety."

"It's what I do. It's what suits me. I will undertake, also, those additional duties that took me periodically to the lands of Dalriada when I worked for Drust the Bull. You cannot afford to dispense with a source of good intelligence."

"No," agreed Bridei, "nor a good friend. You will discover, in time, what that means. Come, let's go in and face them again. I don't like to leave Tuala alone for too long. This is all new to her."

Faolan grimaced. "Like you, she seems to learn with startling speed. You'll be a formidable pair, you and she."

"I hope so," said Bridei. "A kingdom depends on it."

AUTHOR'S NOTE

HISTORY, CONJECTURE, AND IMAGINATION

The Bridei Chronicles are a blend of known history, informed guesswork, and imagination. The Picts were a mysterious people, all the more fascinating for the lack of contemporary records of their culture. What we know of them comes chiefly from Roman references and from clerics such as Adomnan, who recorded the story of St. Columba's mission to the north of Britain. The Picts were a dominant force in this region for centuries until the Gaels established themselves in what became known as Scotland. At that point the highly developed culture of the Picts quickly disappeared, leaving its footprint behind in the form of the carved symbol stones that bear the cryptic designs also shown on Pictish jewelry: the crescent and V-rod, the double-disc and Z-rod, the mirror and comb, the sea-beast. Historians still dispute their meaning. The remnants of Pictish fortresses can still be found in places such as Burghead and Craig Phadraig, which appear in these novels as Caer Pridne and White Hill.

In writing the story of Bridei, son of Maelchon, who ruled the Picts from 554 A.D., I made a number of choices. My tale is based on known history: Bridei, his mentor, Broichan, the main political players, and the situations of the books are all real. However, as we have so little information about Pictish society and as so much of it is debatable, I relied on informed guesswork for much of the detail of the story. My treatment of matrilineal succession and of the election of kings is in this category. It is not historical fact, although it is based on existing evidence as to the Pictish tradition.

I have avoided using place names derived from either Gaelic or Norse (such as, for instance, Loch Linnhe or Burghead) as both these cultures stamped their influence on the region after Bridei's time. The Pictish language was in the same group as Welsh and Breton, but little of it survived. The names I have given to familiar Scottish locations are a blend of English descriptive names (Oak Ridge, Serpent Lake) and invented names derived from Pictish/Brythonic components (Caer Pridne, Banmerren). Where it suits the history I have used the actual names (the Great Glen, Five Sisters, Dunadd).

The Pictish religion as depicted in these books is my own invention, based on other pagan faiths of the time and on the Picts' evident love and respect for nature (the symbol stones feature animals of many kinds, and it is likely these formed part of Pictish ritual practice). We do know there were druids or mages among them: Broichan appears in Adomnan's *Life of St. Columba* as one of these. The well at Caer Pridne (Burghead Well) is a real place and can still be visited.

The Good Folk are the ancient fairy folk of Scotland, who appear in many traditional tales. Hearth magic was commonly used to placate these tricky visitors.

The geography of the Bridei Chronicles is that of the Scottish Highlands, and most places in the books will be recognizable to those familiar with the region. However, I have taken some liberties with distances and locations for the purpose of better storytelling.

A MORE DETAILED version of these notes can be found on the author's Web site at www.julietmarillier.com under the Bridei Chronicles. The page includes a bibliography for readers who wish to find out more about the Picts and their culture.

Turn the page for a preview of

JULIET MARILLIER'S

THE WELL OF SHADES

(0-765-30997-1)

Available May 2007 in Hardcover

IT WAS TIME, Tuala had decided, to broach a particularly delicate subject with the king's druid. She had avoided it up till now, lacking the courage to confront the man she had feared since childhood, when he had bent all his considerable will on ensuring she and his foster son did not form too strong a bond. As a child of the Good Folk, Tuala was an unlikely wife for a king of Fortriu. If Broichan had had his way, Bridei would have wed a far more suitable girl, someone like Ana of the Light Isles, for instance. Tuala and Bridei, between them, had won that battle and in time Broichan had become almost a friend to her. He had saved Derelei's life when fever nearly took him. Tuala had helped Broichan battle his own long illness. She had agreed to let him tutor her gifted son. Now, with a second child expected and Bridei away seeing to a matter at Abertornie, it was time to confront Broichan with an event in his past. She did not expect him to welcome it.

For a long time Tuala had struggled with the mystery of her identity in silence. She might never have acted on what little she had discovered if she had not observed her son's talent developing in all its confident precocity. She had seen Broichan watching Derelei; seen the watchful love in the druid's eyes. If what she believed was true, the two of them should know it, Broichan now, her son when he grew older.

There were some painful truths, Tuala thought, whose importance was such that they must be exposed to the light.

She willed herself calm as she made her way to the druid's private chamber. Even now her heart thumped and her palms grew clammy at the prospect of raising such a matter with her old adversary. What if she was wrong? This was conjecture, after all, based on her own interpretation of a vision in the scrying bowl. One of her very first lessons at Banmerren, the school for wise women, had been how deceptive such images could be and how easily misinterpreted. The gods used them to tease and to test, and the seer walked a narrow path between giving good counsel or ill.

Tuala used her skill rarely; there were those who would seize any opportunity to point out the strangeness of her origins, seeking thus to weaken the foundations of her husband's kingship. For a while she had not used her craft at all. She had come to it again after a vision of hers helped save Bridei's life at the time of the great battle for Dalriada. She had known then that the risk was worth it. Today she planned to scry again.

She knocked. Broichan opened the door, showing no sign of surprise when he saw who it was.

"I need to speak to you in private," Tuala said. "If you will."

"Of course, Tuala. Come in."

She thought perhaps she had interrupted him in prayer, for two candles burned on a shelf and before them a thin mat was laid on the stone floor, a small concession to his illness. The chamber was orderly. Shelves were neatly packed with the accoutrements of his calling; an oak table held a jug of water and a single cup. From the rafters hung plaits of garlic and bundles of healing herbs. His scrying mirror was nowhere to be seen.

"Please sit. You wish to discuss Derelei's progress? His welfare?"

"Not today. I see that he is doing well, though he does get very tired. I have a difficult matter to set before you, Broichan. You may have some idea what it is; I've heard Fola refer to it once or twice, obliquely."

Broichan waited, a tall figure, dark-robed. His hair was

more gray than black now and fell in a multitude of small plaits across his shoulders. In the candlelight, the moon-disc, a circle of pale bone he wore on a cord around his neck in tribute to the Shining One, gleamed softly. His deep-set eyes gave nothing away.

"It would be easier for me to show you this in the water of a scrying vessel," Tuala told him. "I feel a certain reluctance to put it straight into words; I'm afraid it will offend you."

"If you wish." His voice was at its most constrained. Tuala suspected he knew what was coming. "You are confident you can summon what you need and reveal it in one form to the two of us? That's a prodigiously difficult task, Tuala."

Not for me. "If the Shining One wishes us to see this, we will see it. Have you a bowl we can use?"

He fetched a vessel without further comment, uncovered it, and poured water from a ewer. "You prefer this to the mirror," he said. It was not a question.

Tuala nodded, not speaking. Already the water called her, too powerful to resist. She stood, and Broichan, opposite, reached over to take her hands. They faced one another across the bowl. Tuala felt his hands, strong and bony, relax in hers as he looked down. He was expert in the seer's art, as in all branches of magic. He knew without the need for telling that, in order to grant Tuala control over the vision, he must submit his formidable will to hers. And indeed, for all his long years of training and discipline, it was she, the child of the Good Folk, who had the greater facility in this branch of the craft. Perhaps it was not so surprising that some folk distrusted her.

The water rippled, shimmered, and was still. The vision came: the same Tuala had seen once before. That first time neither Broichan nor the wise woman Fola, both of whom had been in attendance, had discerned it. Now she felt Broichan start. His hands gripped tightly for a moment, then relaxed again as he forced his body to obey his will.

In the water, a younger Broichan, clad in a white robe, walked a forest path in springtime. Another figure shadowed him, a slight, lovely woman whose fey eyes and milk-pale skin marked her out as one of the Good Folk, that diverse band of Otherworld people who inhabited the woodlands of the Great Glen and beyond. This person was one of Tuala's own kind, akin to the two beings who had shown themselves to her in her childhood, interfering in her life and Bridei's, tempting her with promises to reveal her true identity and always holding that knowledge back. She knew only that she'd been a foundling, an abandoned infant. If she had parents, they had never come forward to claim her, not in all the nineteen years since they had left her on Broichan's doorstep.

In the water, the white-clad druid looked around; he had sensed he was not alone. A voice seemed to speak, though in the candlelit chamber where Broichan and Tuala stood all was silent. *Come, my son. Come and honor me.* And, when the younger Broichan hesitated, suddenly very still on the sunlit path amid the dappled greens and golds of the spring-time forest, *Come, faithful one. I require this of you.*

Tuala did not doubt that the goddess spoke. The fey woman was only a messenger. Perhaps, for this one day, she was an avatar: the earthly embodiment of the Shining One, whose own presence was ever veiled in the daylight. The white-clad druid saw the woman. His face paled and his jaw tightened. Obedient he might be, but this was plainly difficult for him. The woman smiled. She was beguiling, her lips full and rosy, her slender figure shapely and enticing beneath the sheer fabric of her floating gown. She reached out a hand toward the druid.

Go, my son. The voice again, not that of this charming creature but a deep, strong one that made every tree in the wildwood shiver. *I call you to my service. Do you hesitate?*

The druid took the proffered hand in his. Tuala could feel his reluctance and, along with it, the coursing pull of physical desire in his body. It was customary for his kind to perform a solitary three-day vigil to mark the festival of Balance, when day and night were equal and spring stirred even in the north. If the Shining One required of a believer, at such a time, a devotion expressed with the body rather than the mind, how could a faithful man hold back? If such an act felt wanton, abhorrent, lacking in self-control, he must still perform it, for at the heart of spiritual practice was the love of god and goddess, Flamekeeper and Shining One, and perfect obedience to their will. Indeed, he must exercise mind and body to perform it in a spirit of good faith, for to practice a rite reluctantly was to cause the goddess most bitter offense.

The woman stepped closer. Her free hand slipped down to touch the front of the white robe, between the druid's legs; if he was shy, she most certainly was not. Caught as she was in the vision, Tuala found herself sufficiently aware of the here and now to hope profoundly that the goddess would draw a veil over what was to come. She had called this up to illustrate her theory to Broichan, not to embarrass and shame him.

The water swirled; the image broke up into brief glimpses, snatches of sight: here a white hand on the plane of thigh or back or chest; here a sensuous mouth, lips parted, tongue moving to lap and lick, to taste and tease; here muscular buttocks clenching and unclenching; here long fingers stroking, playing, clearly not fettered by lack of experience. They were in a grove. They lay on the druid's white robe, which was spread in a grassy hollow. The woman's gown hung from a willow branch, its gauzy fabric as insubstantial as cobweb. Their bodies moved, at first slowly, with sensuous delight in every moment of their concourse, then more quickly as urgency overtook them, until their hearts surely shared the same desperate drumbeat. It was the oldest dance of all, beautiful, powerful, over all too quickly, leaving forest woman and druid lying together on the grass-stained linen, bodies sheened with sweat, chests rising and falling fast as the pounding heartbeat slowed and the fierce breath calmed. A cloud darkened the sun; a shadow passed over the little grove. The vision dissipated and was gone.

Broichan drew his hands away from Tuala's. There was a silence as each returned slowly to the shadowy chamber. A practiced seer allowed such a vision to release its hold gradually. To hasten the process led to dizziness, nausea, and distress. Tuala blinked, moving her fingers, stretching her arms. Broichan reached for the dark cloth that had lain on a shelf beside the scrying bowl and draped it over to conceal the water. When he spoke his voice was tight with constraint and decidedly chilly.

"I cannot imagine why you would wish to view such images in my company," he said. "This was unseemly. Distasteful. I had thought us almost friends, Tuala. I had come to believe we trusted one another; to think my first assessment of you, long ago, was incorrect. I believed you dangerous: to me, to Bridei, to all you touched. This makes me suspect I was right."

Tuala felt his words like a blow. For a moment she could not speak. Then she reminded herself that she was Queen of Fortriu and that, as Derelei's mother and Bridei's wife, she had power over the king's druid whether he liked it or not. It didn't help much; she was amazed at how her heart shrank before his repudiation.

"Please go now," Broichan said, walking to the door and holding it open.

"If that is your preference, of course. I'll ask you a question first."

He waited, eyes cold and remote.

"I don't imagine such events occur often. Very likely, a man experiences them only once in his life, and therefore may have an excellent recall of when they happened. I must tell you that when I saw this before, the vision was far briefer; I did not expect such . . . I did not call this up to shame you, Broichan. The goddess showed far more than I anticipated."

"Please leave now, Tuala."

"It was springtime, wasn't it, at the feast of Balance? Was that the spring of the year I came to Pitnochie? Was the winter after those events the one when unknown hands delivered me to your doorstep as a newborn babe?"

"I will not discuss this." His voice was hard as iron. "I will answer no questions."

"There's no need to answer them," said Tuala, walking past him and out into the passageway. "All I request is that you give them consideration. The idea must have occurred to you. Or is the possibility that I might be your daughter so painful to contemplate that you have closed your mind to it and thrown away the key?"

He shut the door in her face. Tuala stood outside, working on her breathing, willing back tears, slowing the painful thudding of her heart. She had known Broichan a long time. Part of her had anticipated this rejection, this refusal to acknowledge any error. And yet, the wave of sorrow that swept through her was so profound that for long moments it paralyzed her there on his doorstep. Her father. Her own father. How wonderful it would have been if he had offered a little, a wary trust, a tentative recognition of that bond. She realized that, in her heart, she had hoped for more: an embrace; words of affection; perhaps a guarded apology. That had been foolish. Even if he had been prepared to acknowledge the possibility of blood kinship, the closest Broichan ever came to an expression of feelings was a wintry smile or approving nod of the head. Only with Bridei, his foster son, had he ever come close to revealing what was in his heart. And with Derelei because, after all, Derelei was Bridei's son.

She had wanted to ask, *Does it mean nothing to you that this would make you Derelei's blood kin? That the infant mage whose rare talents you nurture with all your skill might be your own grandson? Do you not long to acknowledge him?* How could she say those things when she herself stood in the way? The thought of her as a daughter was abhorrent to him. That had been in his affronted eyes; it had been in the tight distaste of his tone. He would never tell the truth about this. He would never accept it. Apart from his deep distrust of her, which had existed since the moment he first set eyes on her as a tiny babe, to acknowledge her as his daughter was to admit shutting his own kin out for all the years of her growing up. He had provided her with food and shelter. At the same time, he had made no secret of his hostility toward her. To admit the truth was to recognize the greatest error of his life: an unforgivable insult to the Shining One. And is not a druid's whole existence bent to the goddess's service? Dashing the tears from her cheeks, Tuala forced herself to walk away. Maybe her own father did not want her, but she was still queen of Fortriu, and there were things to do.

TOR

Award-winning authors
Compelling stories

Please join us at the website
below for more information
about this author and other great
Tor selections, and to sign up for
our monthly newsletter!